PENGUIN BOOKS

COLLECTED FICTIONS

Jorge Luis Borges was born in Buenos Aires in 1899 and was educated in Europe. One of the most widely acclaimed writers of our time, he published many collections of poems, essays, and short stories before his death in Geneva in June 1986. In 1961 Borges shared the International Publishers' prize with Samuel Beckett. The Ingram Merrill Foundation granted him its Annual Literary Award in 1966 for his "outstanding contribution to literature." In 1971 Columbia University awarded him the first of many degrees of Doctor of Letters, *honoris causa* (eventually the list included both Oxford and Cambridge), that he was to receive from the English-speaking world. In 1971 he also received the fifth biennial Jerusalem Prize and in 1973 was given one of Mexico's most prestigious cultural awards, the Alfonso Reyes Prize. In 1980 he shared with Gerardo Diego the Cervantes Prize, the Spanish world's highest literary accolade. Borges was Director of the Argentine National Library from 1955 until 1973.

Andrew Hurley is Professor of English at the University of Puerto Rico in San Juan, where he also teaches in the Translation Program. He has translated over two dozen book-length works of history, poetry, and fiction, including novels by Reinaldo Arenas, Ernesto Sabato, Fernando Arrabal, Gustavo Sainz, and Edgardo Rodríguez Juliá and stories by Ana Lydia Vega, and many shorter works.

COLLECTED FICTIONS

Jorge Luis Borges

TRANSLATED BY

Andrew Hurley

PENGUIN BOOKS

PENGUIN BOOKS
Published by the Penguin Group
Penguin Putnam Inc., 375 Hudson Street, New York, New York 10014, U.S.A.
Penguin Books Ltd, 27 Wrights Lane, London W8 5TZ, England
Penguin Books Australia Ltd, Ringwood, Victoria, Australia
Penguin Books Canada Ltd, 10 Alcorn Avenue, Toronto, Ontario, Canada M4V 3B2
Penguin Books (N.Z.) Ltd, 182–190 Wairau Road, Auckland 10, New Zealand

Penguin Books Ltd, Registered Offices: Harmondsworth, Middlesex, England

First published in the United States of America by Viking Penguin,
a member of Penguin Putnam Inc. 1998
Published in Penguin Books 1999

11 13 15 17 19 20 18 16 14 12

These selections were originally published by Emece Editores, Buenos Aires, as the story collections *Historia universal de la infamia, Ficciones, El aleph, El informe de Brodie, El libro de arena*, and in *El hacedor* and *Elogio de la sombra*. The four stories comprising the section "Shakespeare's Memory" were collected as *La memoria de Shakespeare* in *Obras completas, 1975–1985*, Emece Editores. © Maria Kodama and Emece Editores. S.A., 1989.

Ficciones is published by arrangement with Grove/Atlantic, Inc., New York, New York. The selections from *El hacedor* are published by arrangement with the University of Texas Press, Austin, Texas.

THE LIBRARY OF CONGRESS HAS CATALOGUED THE HARDCOVER EDITION AS FOLLOWS:
Borges, Jorge Luis, 1899–1986.
[Short stories. English]
Collected fictions/Jorges Luis Borges; translated by Andrew Hurley
p. cm.
ISBN 0-670-84970-7 (hc.)
ISBN 0 14 02.8680 2 (pbk.)
1. Borges, Jorge Luis, 1899–1986—Translations into English.
I. Hurley, Andrew. II. Title.
PQ7797.B635A24 1998
863—dc21 98–21217

Printed in the United States of America
Set in Minion
Designed by Francesca Belanger

Contents

THE BOOK OF SAND (1975) 409

SHAKESPEARE'S MEMORY (1983) 487

A Universal History of Iniquity

(1935)

I inscribe this book to S.D.—English, innumerable, and an Angel.
Also: I offer her that kernel of myself that I have saved, somehow—the central heart that deals not in words, traffics not with dreams, and is untouched by time, by joy, by adversities.

Preface to the First Edition

The exercises in narrative prose that constitute this book were performed from 1933 to 1934. They are derived, I think, from my rereadings of Stevenson and Chesterton, from the first films of von Sternberg, and perhaps from a particular biography of the Argentine poet Evaristo Carriego.* Certain techniques are overused: mismatched lists, abrupt transitions, the reduction of a person's entire life to two or three scenes. (It is this pictorial intention that also governs the story called "Man on Pink Corner.") The stories are not, nor do they attempt to be, psychological.

With regard to the examples of magic that close the book, the only right I can claim to them is that of translator and reader. I sometimes think that good readers are poets as singular, and as awesome, as great authors themselves. No one will deny that the pieces attributed by Valéry to his pluperfect Monsieur Edmond Teste are worth notoriously less than those of his wife and friends.

Reading, meanwhile, is an activity subsequent to writing—more resigned, more civil, more intellectual.

J.L.B.
Buenos Aires
May 27, 1935

Preface to the 1954 Edition

I would define the baroque as that style that deliberately exhausts (or tries to exhaust) its own possibilities, and that borders on self-caricature. In vain did Andrew Lang attempt, in the eighteen-eighties, to imitate Pope's *Odyssey;* it was already a parody, and so defeated the parodist's attempt to exaggerate its tautness. "*Baroco*" was a term used for one of the modes of syllogistic reasoning; the eighteenth century applied it to certain abuses in seventeenth-century architecture and painting. I would venture to say that the baroque is the final stage in all art, when art flaunts and squanders its resources. The baroque is intellectual, and Bernard Shaw has said that all intellectual labor is inherently humorous. This humor is unintentional in the works of Baltasar Gracián* but intentional, even indulged, in the works of John Donne.

The extravagant title of this volume proclaims its baroque nature. Softening its pages would have been equivalent to destroying them; that is why I have preferred, this once, to invoke the biblical words *quod scripsi, scripsi* (John 19:22), and simply reprint them, twenty years later, as they first appeared. They are the irresponsible sport of a shy sort of man who could not bring himself to write short stories, and so amused himself by changing and distorting (sometimes without æsthetic justification) the stories of other men. From these ambiguous exercises, he went on to the arduous composition of a straightforward short story—"Man on Pink Corner"—which he signed with the name of one of his grandfather's grandfathers, Francisco Bustos; the story has had a remarkable, and quite mysterious, success.

In that text, which is written in the accents of the toughs and petty criminals of the Buenos Aires underworld, the reader will note that I have interpolated a number of "cultured" words—*entrails, conversion,* etc. I did this because the tough, the knife fighter, the thug, the type that Buenos Aires calls the *compadre* or *compadrito,* aspires to refinement, or (and this reason excludes the other, but it may be the true one) because *compadres* are individuals and don't always talk like The Compadre, which is a Platonic ideal.

The learned doctors of the Great Vehicle teach us that the essential characteristic of the universe is its emptiness. They are certainly correct with respect to the tiny part of the universe that is this book. Gallows and pirates fill its pages, and that word *iniquity* strikes awe in its title, but under all the storm and lightning, there is nothing. It is all just appearance, a surface of images—which is why readers may, perhaps, enjoy it. The man who made it was a pitiable sort of creature, but he found amusement in writing it; it is to be hoped that some echo of that pleasure may reach its readers.

In the section called *Et cetera* I have added three new pieces.

J.L.B.

The Cruel Redeemer Lazarus Morell

THE REMOTE CAUSE

In 1517, Fray Bartolomé de las Casas, feeling great pity for the Indians who grew worn and lean in the drudging infernos of the Antillean gold mines, proposed to Emperor Charles V that Negroes be brought to the isles of the Caribbean, so that *they* might grow worn and lean in the drudging infernos of the Antillean gold mines. To that odd variant on the species *philanthropist* we owe an infinitude of things: W. C. Handy's blues; the success achieved in Paris by the Uruguayan attorney-painter Pedro Figari*; the fine runaway-slave prose of the likewise Uruguayan Vicente Rossi*; the mythological stature of Abraham Lincoln; the half-million dead of the War of Secession; the $3.3 billion spent on military pensions; the statue of the imaginary semblance of Antonio (Falucho) Ruiz*; the inclusion of the verb "lynch" in respectable dictionaries; the impetuous King Vidor film *Hallelujah;* the stout bayonet charge of the regiment of "Blacks and Tans" (the color of their skins, not their uniforms) against that famous hill near Montevideo*; the gracefulness of certain elegant young ladies; the black man who killed Martín Fierro; that deplorable rumba *The Peanut-Seller;* the arrested and imprisoned Napoleonism of Toussaint L'Ouverture; the cross and the serpent in Haiti; the blood of goats whose throats are slashed by the *papaloi*'s machete; the *habanera* that is the mother of the tango; the *candombe.*

And yet another thing: the evil and magnificent existence of the cruel redeemer Lazarus Morell.*

THE PLACE

The Father of Waters, the Mississippi, the grandest river in the world, was the worthy stage for the deeds of that incomparable blackguard. (Alvarez de Pineda discovered this great river, though it was first explored by Hernando de Soto, conqueror of Peru, who whiled away his months in the prison of the Inca Atahualpa teaching his jailer chess. When de Soto died, the river's waters were his grave.)

The Mississippi is a broad-chested river, a dark and infinite brother of the Paraná, the Uruguay, the Amazon, and the Orinoco. It is a river of mulatto-hued water; more than four hundred million tons of mud, carried by that water, insult the Gulf of Mexico each year. All that venerable and ancient waste has created a delta where gigantic swamp cypresses grow from the slough of a continent in perpetual dissolution and where labyrinths of clay, dead fish, and swamp reeds push out the borders and extend the peace of their fetid empire. Upstream, Arkansas and Ohio have their bottomlands, too, populated by a jaundiced and hungry-looking race, prone to fevers, whose eyes gleam at the sight of stone and iron, for they know only sand and driftwood and muddy water.

THE MEN

In the early nineteenth century (the period that interests us) the vast cotton plantations on the riverbanks were worked from sunup to sundown by Negro slaves. They slept in wooden cabins on dirt floors. Apart from the mother-child relationship, kinship was conventional and murky; the slaves had given names, but not always surnames. They did not know how to read. Their soft falsetto voices sang an English of drawn-out vowels. They worked in rows, stooped under the overseer's lash. They would try to escape, and men with full beards would leap astride beautiful horses to hunt them down with baying dogs.

Onto an alluvium of beastlike hopefulness and African fear there had sifted the words of the Scripture; their faith, therefore, was Christian. *Go down, Moses,* they would sing, low and in unison. The Mississippi served them as a magnificent image of the sordid Jordan.

The owners of that hard-worked land and those bands of Negroes were idlers, greedy gentlemen with long hair who lived in wide-fronted mansions that looked out upon the river—their porches always pseudo-Greek with columns made of soft white pine. Good slaves cost a thousand dollars, but they didn't last long. Some were so ungrateful as to sicken and die. A man had to get the most he could out of such uncertain investments. That was why the slaves were in the fields from sunup to sundown; that was why the fields were made to yield up their cotton or tobacco or sugarcane every year. The female soil, worn and haggard from bearing that impatient culture's get, was left barren within a few years, and a formless, clayey desert crept into the plantations.

On broken-down farms, on the outskirts of the cities, in dense fields of sugarcane, and on abject mud flats lived the "poor whites"; they were fishermen, sometime hunters, horse thieves. They would sometimes even beg pieces of stolen food from the Negroes. And yet in their prostration they held one point of pride—their blood, untainted by "the cross of color" and unmixed. Lazarus Morell was one of these men.

THE MAN

The daguerreotypes printed in American magazines are not actually of Morell. That absence of a genuine likeness of a man as memorable and famous as Morell cannot be coincidental. It is probably safe to assume that Morell refused to sit for the silvered plate—essentially, so as to leave no pointless traces; incidentally, so as to enhance his mystery. . . . We do know, however, that he was not particularly good-looking as a young man and that his close-set eyes and thin lips did not conspire in his favor. The years, as time went on, imparted to him that peculiar majesty that white-haired blackguards, successful (and unpunished) criminals, seem generally to possess. He was a Southern gentleman of the old school, in spite of his impoverished childhood and his shameful life. He was not ignorant of the Scriptures, and he preached with singular conviction. "I once saw Lazarus Morell in the pulpit," wrote the owner of a gambling house in Baton Rouge, "and I heard his edifying words and saw the tears come to his eyes. I knew he was a fornicator, a nigger-stealer, and a murderer in the sight of the Lord, but tears came to my eyes too."

Another testimony to those holy outpourings is provided by Morell himself: "I opened the Bible at random, put my finger on the first verse that came to hand—St. Paul it was—and preached for an hour and twenty minutes. Crenshaw and the boys didn't put that time to bad use, neither, for they rounded up all the folks' horses and made off with 'em. We sold 'em in the state of Arkansas, all but one bay stallion, the most spirited thing you ever laid eyes on, that I kept for myself. Crenshaw had his eye on that horse, too, but I convinced him it warn't the horse for him."

THE METHOD

Horses stolen in one state and sold in another were but the merest digression in Morell's criminal career, but they did prefigure the method that would assure him his place in a Universal History of Iniquity. His method was unique not only because of the *sui generis* circumstances that shaped it, but also because of the depravity it required, its vile manipulation of trust, and its gradual evolution, like the terrifying unfolding of a nightmare. Al Capone and Bugs Moran operate with lavish capital and subservient machine guns in a great city, but their business is vulgar. They fight for a monopoly, and that is the extent of it. . . . In terms of numbers, Morell at one time could command more than a thousand sworn confederates. There were two hundred in the Heads, or General Council, and it was the Heads that gave the orders that the other eight hundred followed. These "strikers," as they were called, ran all the risk. If they stepped out of line, they would be handed over to the law or a rock would be tied to their feet and their bodies would be sunk in the swirling waters of the river. Often, these men were mulattoes. Their wicked mission was this:

In a momentary wealth of gold and silver rings, to inspire respect, they would roam the vast plantations of the South. They would choose some wretched black man and offer him his freedom. They would tell him that if he'd run away from his master and allow them to resell him on another plantation far away, they would give him a share of the money and help him escape a second time. Then, they said, they'd convey him to free soil. . . . Money and freedom—ringing silver dollars and freedom to boot—what greater temptation could they hold out to him? The slave would work up the courage for his first escape.

The river was a natural highway. A canoe, the hold of a riverboat, a barge, a raft as big as the sky with a pilothouse on the bow or with a roof of canvas sheeting . . . the place didn't matter; what mattered was knowing that you were moving, and that you were safe on the unwearying river. . . . They would sell him on another plantation. He would run away again, to the sugarcane fields or the gullies. And it would be then that the fearsome and terrible benefactors (whom he was beginning to distrust by now) would bring up obscure "expenses" and tell him they had to sell him one last time. When he escaped the next time, they told him, they'd give him his percentage of the two sales, and his liberty. The man would let himself be sold, he would work for a while, and then he would risk the dogs and whips and try to escape on his own. He would be brought back bloody, sweaty, desperate, and tired.

THE FINAL FREEDOM

We have not yet considered the legal aspect of the crime. The Negro would not be put up for sale by Morell's henchmen until his escape had been advertised and a reward offered for his capture. At that point, anybody could lay hold of the slave. Thus, when he was later sold, it was only a breach of trust, not stealing, and it was pointless for the owner to go to law, since he'd never recover his losses.

All this was calculated to leave Morell's mind at ease, but not forever. The Negro could talk; the Negro was capable, out of pure gratitude or misery, of talking. A few drinks of rye whisky in a whorehouse in Cairo, Illinois, where the slave-born son of a bitch went to squander some of those silver dollars burning a hole in his pocket (and that they'd no reason to give him, when it came right down to it), and the cat would be out of the bag. The Abolitionist Party was making things hot in the North during this time—a mob of dangerous madmen who denied a man's right to his own property, preached the freeing of the blacks, and incited the slaves to rebellion. Morell was not about to let himself be confused with those anarchists. He was no Yankee, he was a Southerner, a white man, the son and grandson of white men, and he hoped someday to retire from his business and be a gentleman and possess his own league upon league of cotton fields and his own bow-backed rows of slaves. With his experience, he was not a man to take pointless risks.

The runaway expected his freedom. Therefore, the nebulous mulattoes of Lazarus Morell would give a sign (which might have been no more than a wink) and the runaway would be freed from sight, hearing, touch, daylight, iniquity, time, benefactors, mercy, air, dogs, the universe, hope, sweat—and from himself. A bullet, a low thrust with a blade, a knock on the head, and the turtles and catfish of the Mississippi would be left to keep the secret among themselves.

THE CATASTROPHE

Manned by trustworthy fellows, the business was bound to prosper. By early 1834, some seventy Negro slaves had been "emancipated" by Morell, and others were ready to follow their fortunate forerunners. The zone of operations was larger now, and new members had to be admitted to the gang. Among those who took the oath, there was one young man, Virgil Stewart, from Arkansas, who very soon distinguished himself by his cruelty. This boy was the nephew of a gentleman who had lost a great number of slaves. In August of 1834, he broke his vow and denounced Morell and the others. Morell's house in New Orleans was surrounded by the authorities, but Morell somehow (owing to some oversight—or a bribe in the right quarters) managed to escape.

Three days passed. Morell hid for that period in an old house with vine-covered courtyards and statues, on Toulouse Street. Apparently he had almost nothing to eat and spent his days roaming barefoot through the large, dark rooms, smoking a thoughtful cheroot. Through a slave in the house, he sent two letters to Natchez and another to Red River. On the fourth day, three men entered the house; they sat talking things over with Morell until almost daybreak. On the fifth day, Morell got out of bed at nightfall, borrowed a razor, and carefully shaved off his beard. He then dressed and left the house. Slowly and calmly he made his way through the northern outskirts of the city. When he reached open country, out in the bottomlands of the Mississippi, he breathed easier.

His plan was one of drunken courage. He proposed to exploit the last men that still owed him respect: the accommodating Negroes of the Southland themselves. These men had seen their comrades run away, and had not seen them brought back. They thought, therefore, that they'd found freedom. Morell's plan called for a general uprising of the Negroes, the capture and sack of New Orleans, and the occupation of the territory. A pitiless and depraved man, and now almost undone by treachery, Morell planned a response of continental proportions—a response in which criminality would become redemptive, and historic. To that end, he headed for Natchez, where his strength ran deeper. I reproduce his own narration of that journey:

"I walked four days," he reported, "and no opportunity offered for me to get a horse. The fifth day, I had . . . stopped at a creek to get some water and rest a while. While I was sitting on a log, looking down the road the way that I had come, a man came in sight riding on a good-looking horse. The very moment I saw him, I was determined to have his horse. . . . I arose and drew an elegant rifle pistol on him and ordered him to dismount. He did so, and I took his horse by the bridle and pointed down the creek, and ordered him to walk before me. He went a few hundred yards and stopped. I . . . made him undress himself, all to his shirt and drawers, and ordered him to turn his back to me. He said, 'If you are determined to kill me, let me have time to pray before I die.' I told him I had no time to hear him pray. He turned around and dropped on his knees, and I shot him through the back of the head. I ripped open his belly and took out his entrails, and sunk him in the creek. I then searched his pockets, and found four hundred dollars and thirty-seven cents, and a number of papers that I did not take time to examine. I sunk the pocket-book and papers and his hat, in the creek. His boots were bran-new, and fitted me genteelly; and I put them on and sunk my old shoes in the creek. . . .

"I mounted as fine a horse as ever I straddled, and directed my course for Natchez."*

THE INTERRUPTION

Morell leading uprisings of Negroes that dreamed of hanging him . . . Morell hanged by armies of Negroes that he had dreamed of leading . . . it pains me to admit that the history of the Mississippi did not seize upon those rich opportunities. Nor, contrary to all poetic justice (and poetic symmetry), did the river of his crimes become his tomb. On the 2nd of January, 1835, Lazarus Morell died of pulmonary congestion in the hospital at Natchez, where he'd been admitted under the name Silas Buckley. Another man in the ward recognized him. On that day, and on the 4th of January, slaves on scattered plantations attempted to revolt, but they were put down with no great loss of blood.

The Improbable Impostor Tom Castro

I give him that name because it was by that name he was known (in 1850 or thereabouts) on the streets and in the houses of Talcahuano, Santiago de Chile, and Valparaíso, and it seems only fair that he take it again, now that he has returned to those lands—even if only as a ghost, or a Saturday-night amusement.[1] The birth register in Wapping calls him Arthur Orton, and gives the date of his birth as June 7, 1834. We know that he was the son of a butcher, that his childhood was spent in the gray meanness of the London slums, and that he harkened to the call of the sea. *That* story is not an uncommon one; "running away to sea" was the traditional English way to break with parental authority—the heroic ritual of initiation. Geography recommended such a course, as did the Scriptures themselves: "*They that go down to the sea in ships, that do business in great waters; these see the works of the Lord, and his wonders in the deep*" (Psalms 107:23–24). Orton fled his deplorable, dingy-pink-colored suburb and went down to the sea in a ship; with ingrained disappointment he regarded the Southern Cross, and he jumped ship at Valparaíso. He was a gentle idiot. Though by all logic he could (and should) have starved to death, his muddle-headed joviality, his permanent grin, and his infinite docility earned him the favor of a certain family named Castro, whose patronym he took ever after as his own. No traces of his stay in South America remain, but we know that his gratitude never flagged: in 1861 he turned up in Australia, still bearing the name Tom Castro.

In Sydney he made the acquaintance of a man named Ebenezer Bogle, a

[1]I have chosen this metaphor in order to remind the reader that these vile biographies appeared in the Saturday supplement of an evening newspaper.

Negro servant. Bogle, though not handsome, had that reposeful and monumental air, that look of well-engineered solidity, often possessed by a black man of a certain age, a certain corporeal substance, a certain authority. Bogle had another quality, as well—though some textbooks in anthropology deny the attribute to his race: he was possessed of genius. (We shall see the proof of that soon enough.) He was a temperate, decent man, the ancient African appetites in him corrected by the customs and excesses of Calvinism. Aside from the visitations from his god (which we shall describe below), he was normal in every way; his only eccentricity was a deep-seated and shamefaced fear that made him hesitate at street corners and at crossings, survey east, west, north, and south, and try to outguess the violent vehicle that he was certain would end his days.

Orton came upon his future friend one afternoon as Bogle was standing on a run-down corner in Sydney trying to screw up the courage to face his imagined death. After watching him for several minutes, Orton offered him his arm, and the two astounded men crossed the inoffensive street. Out of that now-bygone evening a protectorate was forged: the monumental, unsure Negro over the obese Wapping simpleton. In September of 1865, the two men read a heartbreaking piece of news in the local paper.

THE ADORED ONE DECEASED

In the waning days of April, 1854 (as Orton was inspiring the effusions of Chilean hospitality, which was as welcoming as that country's patios), there had sunk in the waters of the Atlantic a steamship christened the *Mermaid*, bound from Rio de Janeiro to Liverpool. Among the drowned had been one Roger Charles Tichborne, an English military officer brought up in France, and the firstborn son of one of England's leading Catholic families. However improbable it may seem, the death of this Frenchified young man (a young man who had spoken English with the most cultured of Parisian accents and who had inspired the unparalleled envy that can only be aroused by French intelligence, grace, and affectation) was an event of supreme importance in the destiny of Arthur Orton, who had never so much as laid eyes on him. Lady Tichborne, Roger's horrified mother, refused to believe the reports of his death. She published heartrending advertisements in all the major newspapers, and one of those advertisements fell into the soft, funereal hands of Ebenezer Bogle, who conceived a brilliant plan.

THE VIRTUES OF UNLIKENESS

Tichborne had been a slim, genteel young man with a reserved and somewhat self-absorbed air. He had sharp features, straight black hair, tawny skin, sparkling eyes, and an irritatingly precise way of speaking. Orton was an irrepressible rustic, a "yokel," with a vast belly, features of infinite vagueness, fair and freckled skin, wavy light-brown hair, sleepy eyes, and no, or irrelevant, conversation. Bogle decided that it was Orton's duty to take the first steamer for Europe and realize Lady Tichborne's hope that her son had not perished—by declaring himself to be that son. The plan had an irrational genius to it. Let me give a simple example: If an impostor had wanted to pass himself off as the emperor of Germany and king of Prussia in 1914, the first thing he'd have done would be fake the upturned mustaches, the lifeless arm, the authoritarian scowl, the gray cape, the illustrious and much-decorated chest, and the high helmet. Bogle was more subtle: he would have brought forth a smooth-faced Kaiser with no military traits, no proud eagles whatsoever, and a left arm in unquestionable health. We have no need of the metaphor; we know for a fact that Bogle produced a fat, flabby Tichborne with the sweet smile of an idiot, light-brown hair, and a thoroughgoing ignorance of French. Bogle knew that a perfect facsimile of the beloved Roger Charles Tichborne was impossible to find; he knew as well that any similarities he might achieve would only underscore certain inevitable differences. He therefore gave up the notion of likeness altogether. He sensed that the vast ineptitude of his pretense would be a convincing proof that this was no fraud, for no fraud would ever have so flagrantly flaunted features that might so easily have convinced. We should also not overlook the all-powerful collaboration of time: the vicissitudes of fortune, and fourteen years of antipodean life, can change a man.

Another essential argument in favor of Bogle's plan: Lady Tichborne's repeated and irrational advertisements showed that she was certain that Roger Charles had not died, and that she would will herself to recognize him when he came.

THE MEETING

Tom Castro, ever accommodating, wrote to Lady Tichborne. In order to prove his identity, he invoked the irrefutable proof of the two moles near his left nipple and that painful and therefore unforgettable episode from his childhood when a swarm of bees had attacked him. The letter was brief and, in the image of Bogle and Tom Castro, free of any scruples as to the way words ought to be spelled. In her majestic solitude in her *hôtel particulier* in Paris, Lady Tichborne read and reread the letter through happy tears, and in a few days she had recaptured the recollections her son had invoked.

On January 16, 1867, Roger Charles Tichborne called upon his mother. His respectful servant, Ebenezer Bogle, preceded him. It was a winter day of bright sunshine; Lady Tichborne's tired eyes were veiled with tears. The black man threw the windows open. The light served as a mask; the mother recognized the prodigal and opened her arms to him. Now that she had him in the flesh, she might do without his diary and the letters he had written her from Brazil—the treasured reflections of the son which had fed her loneliness through those fourteen melancholy years. She returned them to him proudly; not one was missing.

Bogle smiled discreetly; now he could research the gentle ghost of Roger Charles.

AD MAJOREM DEI GLORIAM

That joyous recognition, which seems to obey the tradition of classical tragedy, should be the crown of this story, leaving happiness assured (or at least more than possible) for the three persons of the tale—the true mother, the apocryphal and obliging son, and the conspirator repaid for the providential apotheosis of his industry. But Fate (for such is the name that we give the infinite and unceasing operation of thousands of intertwined causes) would not have it. Lady Tichborne died in 1870, and the family brought charges against Arthur Orton for impersonation and usurpation of their dead kinsman's estate. As they themselves were afflicted with neither tears nor loneliness (though the same cannot be said of greed), they had never believed in the obese and almost illiterate lost son who had so inopportunely reappeared from Australia.

Orton's claim was supported by the innumerable creditors who had decided that he was Tichborne; they wanted their bills paid. He also drew upon the friendship of the old family solicitor, Edward Hopkins, and that of an antiquary named Francis J. Baigent. But this, though much, was not enough. Bogle believed that if they were to win this round, a groundswell of public support was wanted. He called for his top hat and his black umbrella and he went out for a walk through the decorous streets of London, in search of inspiration. It was just evening; Bogle wandered about until a honey-colored moon was mirrored in the rectangular waters of the public fountains. And then he was visited by his god. Bogle whistled for a cab and had himself driven to the flat of the antiquary Baigent. Baigent sent a long letter to the *Times*, denouncing this "Tichborne claimant" as a brazen hoax. The letter was signed by Father Goudron, of the Society of Jesus. Other, equally papist, denunciations followed. The effect was immediate: the right sort of person could not fail to see that Sir Roger Charles Tichborne was the target of a despicable Jesuit plot.

THE COACH

The trial lasted one hundred ninety days. Some hundred witnesses swore that the accused was Roger Charles Tichborne—among them, four comrades-at-arms from the 6th Dragoons. Orton's supporters steadfastly maintained that he was no impostor—had he been, they pointed out, he would surely have attempted to copy the juvenile portraits of his model. And besides, Lady Tichborne had recognized and accepted him; clearly, in such matters, a mother does not err. All was going well, then—more or less—until an old sweetheart of Orton's was called to testify. Not a muscle of Bogle's face twitched at that perfidious maneuver by the "family"; he called for his black umbrella and his top hat and he went out into the decorous streets of London to seek a third inspiration. We shall never know whether he found it. Shortly before he came to Primrose Hill, he was struck by that terrible vehicle that had been pursuing him through all these years. Bogle saw it coming and managed to cry out, but he could not manage to save himself. He was thrown violently against the paving stones. The hack's dizzying hooves cracked his skull open.

THE SPECTER

Tom Castro was Tichborne's ghost, but a poor sort of ghost, inhabited by the *dæmon* Bogle. When he was told that Bogle had been killed, he simply collapsed. He continued to tell his lies, but with very little enthusiasm and a great deal of self-contradiction. It was easy to foresee the end.

On the 27th of February, 1874, Arthur Orton (alias Tom Castro) was sentenced to fourteen years' penal servitude. In gaol he made himself beloved by all; it was his lifework. His exemplary behavior won him a reduction of four years off his sentence. When that final hospitality—the prison's—ran out on him, he wandered the towns and villages of the United

Kingdom, giving lectures in which he would alternately declare his innocence and confess his guilt. His modesty and his desire to please remained with him always; many nights he would begin by defending himself and wind up admitting all, depending upon the inclinations of his audience.

On the 2nd of April, 1898, he died.

The Widow Ching—Pirate

The author who uses the phrase "female corsairs" runs the risk of calling up an awkward image—that of the now-faded Spanish operetta with its theories of obvious servant girls playing the part of choreographed pirates on noticeably cardboard seas. And yet there *have* been cases of female pirates—women skilled in the art of sailing, the governance of barbarous crews, the pursuit and looting of majestic ships on the high seas. One such woman was Mary Read, who was quoted once as saying that the profession of piracy wasn't for just anybody, and if you were going to practice it with dignity, you had to be a man of courage, like herself. In the crude beginnings of her career, when she was not yet the captain of her own ship, a young man she fancied was insulted by the ship's bully. Mary herself picked a quarrel with the bully and fought him hand to hand, in the old way of the isles of the Caribbean: the long, narrow, and undependable breechloader in her left hand, the trusty saber in her right. The pistol failed her, but the saber acquitted itself admirably. . . . In 1720 the bold career of Mary Read was interrupted by a Spanish gallows, in Santiago de la Vega, on the island of Jamaica.

Another female pirate of those waters was Anne Bonney, a magnificent Irishwoman of high breasts and fiery hair who risked her life more than once in boarding ships. She stood on the deck with Mary Read, and then with her on the scaffold. Her lover, Captain John Rackham, met his own noose at that same hanging. Anne, contemptuous, emerged with that harsh variant on Aixa's rebuke to Boabdil*: "If you'd fought like a man, you needn't have been hang'd like a dog."

Another woman pirate, but a more daring and long-lived one, plied the waters of far Asia, from the Yellow Sea to the rivers on the borders of Annam. I am speaking of the doughty widow Ching.

THE YEARS OF APPRENTICESHIP

In 1797 the shareholders in the many pirate ships of the Yellow Sea formed a consortium, and they chose one Captain Ching, a just (though strict) man, tested under fire, to be the admiral of their new fleet. Ching was so harsh and exemplary in his sacking of the coasts that the terrified residents implored the emperor with gifts and tears to send them aid. Nor did their pitiable request fall upon deaf ears: they were ordered to set fire to their villages, abandon their fisheries, move inland, and learn the unknown science of agriculture. They did all this; and so, finding only deserted coastlines, the frustrated invaders were forced into waylaying ships—a depredation far more unwelcome than raids on the coasts, for it seriously threatened trade. Once again, the imperial government responded decisively: it ordered the former fishermen to abandon their plows and oxen and return to their oars and nets. At this, the peasants, recalling their former terrors, balked, so the authorities determined upon another course: they would make Admiral Ching the Master of the Royal Stables. Ching was willing to accept the buy-off. The stockholders, however, learned of the decision in the nick of time, and their righteous indignation took the form of a plate of rice served up with poisoned greens. The delicacy proved fatal; the soul of the former admiral and newly appointed Master of the Royal Stables was delivered up to the deities of the sea. His widow, transfigured by the double treachery, called the pirates together, explained the complex case, and exhorted them to spurn both the emperor's deceitful clemency and odious employment in the service of the shareholders with a bent for poison. She proposed what might be called freelance piracy. She also proposed that they cast votes for a new admiral, and she herself was elected. She was a sapling-thin woman of sleepy eyes and caries-riddled smile. Her oiled black hair shone brighter than her eyes.

Under Mrs. Ching's calm command, the ships launched forth into danger and onto the high seas.

THE COMMAND

Thirteen years of methodical adventuring ensued. The fleet was composed of six squadrons, each under its own banner—red, yellow, green, black, purple—and one, the admiral's own, with the emblem of a serpent. The commanders of the squadrons had such names as Bird and Stone, Scourge of the Eastern Sea, Jewel of the Whole Crew, Wave of Many Fishes, and High Sun.

The rules of the fleet, composed by the widow Ching herself, were unappealable and severe, and their measured, laconic style was devoid of those withered flowers of rhetoric that lend a ridiculous sort of majesty to the usual official pronouncements of the Chinese (an alarming example of which, we shall encounter shortly). Here are some of the articles of the fleet's law:

> Not the least thing shall be taken privately from the stolen and plundered goods. All shall be registered, and the pirate receive for himself out of ten parts, only two: eight parts belong to the storehouse, called the general fund; taking anything out of this general fund without permission shall be death.
>
> If any man goes privately on shore, or what is called transgressing the bars, he shall be taken and his ears perforated in the presence of the whole fleet; repeating the same, he shall suffer death.
>
> No person shall debauch at his pleasure captive women taken in the villages and open spaces, and brought on board a ship; he must first request the ship's purser for permission and then go aside in the ship's hold. To use violence against any woman without permission of the purser shall be punished by death.*

Reports brought back by prisoners state that the mess on the pirate ships consisted mainly of hardtack, fattened rats, and cooked rice; on days of combat, the crew would mix gunpowder with their liquor. Marked cards and loaded dice, drinking and fan-tan, the visions of the opium pipe and little lamp filled idle hours. Two swords, simultaneously employed, were the weapon of choice. Before a boarding, the pirates would sprinkle their cheeks and bodies with garlic water, a sure charm against injury by fire breathed from muzzles.

The crew of a ship traveled with their women, the captain with his harem—which might consist of five or six women, and be renewed with each successive victory.

THE YOUNG EMPEROR CHIA-CH'ING SPEAKS

In June or July of 1809, an imperial decree was issued, from which I translate the first paragraph and the last. Many people criticized its style:

> Miserable and injurious men, men who stamp upon bread, men who ignore the outcry of tax collectors and orphans, men whose smallclothes bear

> the figure of the phoenix and the dragon, men who deny the truth of printed books, men who let their tears flow facing North—such men disturb the happiness of our rivers and the erstwhile trustworthiness of our seas. Day and night, their frail and crippled ships defy the tempest. Their object is not a benevolent one: they are not, and never have been, the seaman's bosom friend. Far from lending aid, they fall upon him with ferocity, and make him an unwilling guest of ruin, mutilation, and even death. Thus these men violate the natural laws of the Universe, and their offenses make rivers overflow their banks and flood the plains, sons turn against their fathers, the principles of wetness and dryness exchange places. . . .
>
> Therefore, I commend thee to the punishment of these crimes, Admiral Kwo-Lang. Never forget—clemency is the Emperor's to give; the Emperor's subject would be presumptuous in granting it. Be cruel, be just, be obeyed, be victorious.

The incidental reference to the "crippled ships" was, of course, a lie; its purpose was to raise the courage of Kwo-Lang's expedition. Ninety days later, the forces of the widow Ching engaged the empire's. Almost a thousand ships did battle from sunup to sundown. A mixed chorus of bells, drums, cannon bursts, curses, gongs, and prophecies accompanied the action. The empire's fleet was destroyed; Admiral Kwo-Lang found occasion to exercise neither the mercy forbidden him nor the cruelty to which he was exhorted. He himself performed a ritual which our own defeated generals choose not to observe—he committed suicide.

THE TERRIFIED COASTLINES AND RIVERBANKS

Then the six hundred junks of war and the haughty widow's forty thousand victorious pirates sailed into the mouth of the Zhu-Jiang River, sowing fire and appalling celebrations and orphans left and right. Entire villages were razed. In one of them, the prisoners numbered more than a thousand. One hundred twenty women who fled to the pathless refuge of the nearby stands of reeds or the paddy fields were betrayed by the crying of a baby, and sold into slavery in Macao. Though distant, the pathetic tears and cries of mourning from these depredations came to the notice of Chia-Ch'ing, the Son of Heaven. Certain historians have allowed themselves to believe that the news of the ravaging of his people caused the emperor less pain than did the defeat of his punitive expedition. Be that as it may, the emperor organized a second expedition, terrible in banners, sailors, soldiers, implements of war, provisions, soothsayers and astrologers. This time, the force was under the command of Admiral Ting-kwei-heu. The heavy swarm of ships sailed into the mouth of the Zhu-Jiang to cut off the pirate fleet. The widow rushed to prepare for battle. She knew it would be hard, very hard, almost desperate; her men, after many nights (and even months) of pillaging and idleness, had grown soft. But the battle did not begin. The sun peacefully rose and without haste set again into the quivering reeds. The men and the arms watched, and waited. The noontimes were more powerful than they, and the siestas were infinite.

THE DRAGON AND THE VIXEN

And yet each evening, lazy flocks of weightless dragons rose high into the sky above the ships of the imperial fleet and hovered delicately above the water, above the enemy decks. These cometlike kites were airy constructions of rice paper and reed, and each silvery or red body bore the identical characters. The widow anxiously studied that regular flight of meteors, and in it read the confused and slowly told fable of a dragon that had always watched over a vixen, in spite of the vixen's long ingratitude and constant crimes. The moon grew thin in the sky, and still the figures of rice paper and reed wrote the same story each evening, with almost imperceptible variations. The widow was troubled, and she brooded. When the moon grew fat in the sky and in the red-tinged water, the story seemed to be reaching its end. No one could predict whether infinite pardon or infinite punishment was to be let fall upon the vixen, yet the inevitable end, whichever it might be, was surely approaching. The widow understood. She threw her two swords into the river, knelt in the bottom of a boat, and ordered that she be taken to the flagship of the emperor's fleet.

It was evening; the sky was filled with dragons—this time, yellow ones. The widow murmured a single sentence, "The vixen seeks the dragon's wing," as she stepped aboard the ship.

THE APOTHEOSIS

The chroniclers report that the vixen obtained her pardon, and that she dedicated her slow old age to opium smuggling. She was no longer "The Widow"; she assumed a name that might be translated "The Luster of True Instruction."

From this period (writes a historian) *ships began to pass and repass in tranquillity. All became quiet on the rivers and tranquil on the four seas. People lived in peace and plenty. Men sold their arms and bought oxen to plough their fields. They buried sacrifices, said prayers on the tops of hills, and rejoiced themselves by singing behind screens during the day-time.**

Monk Eastman, Purveyor of Iniquities

THE TOUGHS OF ONE AMERICA

Whether profiled against a backdrop of blue-painted walls or of the sky itself, two toughs sheathed in grave black clothing dance, in boots with high-stacked heels, a solemn dance—the tango of evenly matched knives—until suddenly, a carnation drops from behind an ear, for a knife has plunged into a man, whose horizontal dying brings the dance without music to its end. Resigned,* the other man adjusts his hat and devotes the years of his old age to telling the story of that clean-fought duel. That, to the least and last detail, is the story of the Argentine underworld. The story of the thugs and ruffians of New York has much more speed, and much less grace.

THE TOUGHS OF ANOTHER

The story of the New York gangs (told in 1928 by Herbert Asbury in a decorous volume of some four hundred octavo pages) possesses all the confusion and cruelty of barbarian cosmologies, and much of their gigantism and ineptitude. The chaotic story takes place in the cellars of old breweries turned into Negro tenements, in a seedy, three-story New York City filled with gangs of thugs like the Swamp Angels, who would swarm out of labyrinthine sewers on marauding expeditions; gangs of cutthroats like the Daybreak Boys, who recruited precocious murderers of ten and eleven years old; brazen, solitary giants like the Plug Uglies, whose stiff bowler hats stuffed with wool and whose vast shirttails blowing in the wind of the slums might provoke a passerby's improbable smile, but who carried huge bludgeons in their right hands and long, narrow pistols; and gangs of street toughs like the Dead Rabbit gang, who entered into battle under the banner of their mascot impaled upon a pike. Its characters were men like Dandy Johnny Dolan, famed for his brilliantined forelock, the monkey-headed walking sticks he carried, and the delicate copper pick he wore on his thumb to gouge out his enemies' eyes; men like Kit Burns, who was known to bite the head off live rats; and men like blind Danny Lyons, a towheaded kid with huge dead eyes who pimped for three whores that proudly walked the streets for him. There were rows of red-light houses, such as those run by the seven New England sisters that gave all the profits from their Christmas Eves to charity; rat fights and dog fights; Chinese gambling dens; women like the oft-widowed Red Norah, who was squired about and loved by every leader of the famous Gophers, or Lizzy the Dove, who put on black when Danny Lyons was murdered and got her throat cut for it by Gentle Maggie, who took exception to Lizzy's old affair with the dead blind man; riots such as that of the savage week of 1863 when a hundred buildings were burned to the ground and the entire city was lucky to escape the flames; street brawls when a man would be as lost as if he'd drowned, for he'd be stomped to death; and thieves and horse poisoners like Yoske Nigger. The most famous hero of the story of the New York City underworld is Edward Delaney, alias William Delaney, alias Joseph Marvin, alias Joseph Morris—alias Monk Eastman, the leader of a gang of twelve hundred men.

THE HERO

Those shifting "dodges" (as tedious as a game of masks in which one can never be certain who is who) fail to include the man's true name—if we allow ourselves to believe that there is such a thing as "a man's true name." The fact is, the name given in the Records Division of the Williamsburg section of Brooklyn is Edward Ostermann, later Americanized to Eastman. Odd—this brawling and tempestuous hoodlum was Jewish. He was the son of the owner of a restaurant that billed itself as kosher, where men with rabbinical beards might trustingly consume the bled and thrice-clean meat of calves whose throats had been slit with righteousness. With his father's backing, in 1892, at the age of nineteen, he opened a pet shop specializing in birds. Observing the life of animals, studying their small decisions, their inscrutable innocence, was a passion that accompanied Monk Eastman to the end. In later times of magnificence, when he scorned the cigars of the freckled sachems of Tammany Hall and pulled up to the finest whorehouses in one of New York's first automobiles (a machine that looked like the by-blow of a Venetian gondola), he opened a second establishment, this one a front, that was home to a hundred purebred cats and more than four hundred pigeons—none of which were for sale at any price. He loved every one of the creatures, and would often stroll through the streets of the neighborhood with one purring cat on his arm and others trailing along ambitiously in his wake.

He was a battered and monumental man. He had a short, bull neck, an unassailable chest, the long arms of a boxer, a broken nose; his face, though legended with scars, was less imposing than his body. He was bowlegged, like a jockey or a sailor. He might go shirtless or collarless, and often went without a coat, but he was never seen without a narrow-brimmed derby atop his enormous head. He is still remembered. Physically, the conventional gunman of the moving pictures is modeled after *him,* not the flabby and epicene Capone. It has been said that Louis Wolheim was used in Hollywood films because his features reminded people of the deplorable Monk Eastman. . . . Eastman would leave his house to inspect his gangster empire with a blue-feathered pigeon perched on his shoulder, like a bull with a heron on its hump.

In 1894 there were many dance halls in New York City; Eastman was a bouncer in one of them. Legend has it that the manager wouldn't talk to him about the job, so Monk showed his qualifications by roundly demolishing the two gorillas that stood in the way of his employment. He held the job until 1899—feared, and single-handed.

For every obstreperous customer he subdued, he would cut a notch in the bludgeon he carried. One night, a shining bald spot leaning over a beer caught his eye, and Eastman laid the man's scalp open with a tremendous blow. "I had forty-nine nicks in me stick, an' I wanted to make it an even fifty!" Eastman later explained.

RULING THE ROOST

From 1899 onward, Eastman was not just famous, he was the ward boss of an important electoral district in the city, and he collected large payoffs from the red-light houses, stuss games, streetwalkers, pickpockets, loft burglars, and footpads of that sordid fiefdom. The Party would contract him when some mischief needed doing, and private individuals would come to him too. These are the fees he would charge for a job:

Ear chawed off...$ 15.
Leg broke...19.
Shot in leg..25.
Stab..25.
Doing the big job..100. and up

Sometimes, to keep his hand in, Eastman would do the job personally.

A territorial dispute as subtle and ill humored as those forestalled by international law brought him up against Paul Kelly, the famous leader of another gang. The boundary line had been established by bullets and border patrol skirmishes. Eastman crossed the line late one night and was set upon by five of Kelly's men. With his blackjack and those lightning-quick simian arms of his, he managed to knock down three of them, but he was shot twice in the stomach and left for dead. He stuck his thumb and forefinger in the hot wounds and staggered to the hospital. Life, high fever, and death contended over Monk Eastman for several weeks, but his lips would not divulge the names of his assailants. By the time he left the hospital, the war was in full swing. There was one shoot-out after another, and this went on for two years, until the 19th of August, 1903.

THE BATTLE OF RIVINGTON STREET

A hundred or more heroes, none quite resembling the mug shot probably fading at that very moment in the mug books; a hundred heroes reeking of cigar smoke and alcohol; a hundred heroes in straw boaters with bright-colored bands; a hundred heroes, all suffering to a greater or lesser degree from shameful diseases, tooth decay, respiratory ailments, or problems with their kidneys; a hundred heroes as insignificant or splendid as those of Troy or Junín*—those were the men that fought that black deed of arms in the shadow of the elevated train. The cause of it was a raid that Kelly's "enforcers" had made on a stuss game under Monk Eastman's protection. One of Kelly's men was killed, and the subsequent shoot-out grew into a battle of uncountable revolvers. From behind the tall pillars of the El, silent men with clean-shaven chins blazed away at one another; soon, they were the center of a horrified circle of hired hacks carrying impatient reinforcements clutching Colt artillery. What were the protagonists in the battle feeling? First, I believe, the brutal conviction that the senseless, deafening noise of a hundred revolvers was going to annihilate them instantly; second, I believe, the no less erroneous certainty that if the initial volley didn't get them, they were invulnerable. Speculation notwithstanding, behind their parapets of iron and the night, they battled furiously. Twice the police tried to intervene, and twice they were repelled. At the first light of dawn, the battle died away, as though it were spectral, or obscene. Under the tall arches raised by engineers, what remained were seven men gravely wounded, four men dead, and one lifeless pigeon.

THE CRACKLE OF GUNFIRE

The ward politicians for whom Monk Eastman worked had always publicly denied that such gangs existed, or had clarified that they were merely social clubs. The indiscreet battle on Rivington Street alarmed them. They called in Eastman and Kelly and impressed upon them the need to declare a truce. Kelly, who recognized that politicians were better than all the Colts ever made when it came to dissuading the police from their duty, immediately saw the light; Eastman, with the arrogance of his great stupid body, was spoiling for more grudge fights and more bullets. At first, he wouldn't hear of a truce, but the politicos threatened him with prison. Finally the two illustrious thugs were brought together in a downtown dive; each man had a cigar clenched in his teeth, his right hand on his gun, and his watchful swarm of armed bodyguards hovering nearby. They came to a very American sort of decision—they would let the dispute be settled by a boxing match. Kelly was a skilled boxer. The match took place in an old barn, and it was stranger than fiction. One hundred forty spectators watched—toughs in cocked derby hats and women in "Mikado tuck-ups," the high-piled, delicate hairdos of the day. The fight lasted two hours, and it ended in utter exhaustion. Within a week, gunshots were crackling again. Monk was arrested, for the umpteenth time. The police, relieved, derived great amusement from his arrest; the judge prophesied for him, quite correctly, ten years in prison.

EASTMAN VS. GERMANY

When the still-perplexed Monk Eastman got out of Sing Sing, the twelve hundred toughs in his gang had scattered. He couldn't manage to round them up again, so he resigned himself to working on his own. On the 8th of September, 1917, he was arrested for fighting and charged with disturbing the peace. On the 9th, he felt like he needed another sort of fight, and he enlisted in the Army.

We know several details of his service. We know that he was fervently opposed to the taking of prisoners, and that once (with just his rifle butt) he prevented that deplorable practice. We know that once he escaped from the hospital and made his way back to the trenches. We know that he distinguished himself in the conflicts near Montfaucon. We know that afterward he was heard to say that in his opinion there were lots of dance halls in the Bowery that were tougher than that so-called "Great War" of theirs.

THE MYSTERIOUS, LOGICAL END

On the 25th of December, 1920, Monk Eastman's body was found on one of New York's downtown streets. He had been shot five times. A common alley cat, blissfully ignorant of death, was pacing, a bit perplexedly, about the body.*

The Disinterested Killer Bill Harrigan

The image of the lands of Arizona, before any other image—Arizona and New Mexico. A landscape dazzlingly underlain with gold and silver, a windblown, dizzying landscape of monumental mesas and delicate colorations, with the white glare of a skeleton stripped bare by hawks and buzzards. Within this landscape, another image—the image of Billy the Kid, the rider sitting firm upon his horse, the young man of loud shots that stun the desert, the shooter of invisible bullets that kill at a distance, like a magic spell.

The arid, glaring desert veined with minerals. The almost-child who died at the age of twenty-one owing a debt to human justice for the deaths of twenty-one men—"not counting Mexicans."

THE LARVAL STATE

In 1859, the man who in terror and glory would be known as Billy the Kid was born in a basement lodging in New York City. They say it was a worn-out Irish womb that bore him, but that he was brought up among Negroes. In that chaos of kinky hair and rank sweat, he enjoyed the primacy lent by freckles and a shock of auburn hair. He practiced the arrogance of being white; he was also scrawny, quick-tempered, and foulmouthed. By the age of twelve he was one of the Swamp Angels, a gang of deities whose lair was the sewers of the city. On nights that smelled of burned fog they would swarm out of that fetid labyrinth, follow the trail of some German sailor, bring him down with a blow to his head, strip him of all he owned, even his underwear, and return once more to that other scum. They were under the command of a white-haired Negro named Jonas, a member of the Gas House gang and a man famed as a poisoner of horses.

Sometimes, from the garret window of some hunchbacked house near the water, a woman would dump a bucket of ashes onto the head of a passerby. As he gasped and choked, the Swamp Angels would descend upon him, drag him down the basement steps, and pillage him.

Such were the years of apprenticeship of Bill Harrigan, the future Billy the Kid. He felt no scorn for theatrical fictions: he liked to go to the theater (perhaps with no presentiment that they were the symbols and letters of his own destiny) to see the cowboy shows.

GO WEST!

If the packed theater houses of the Bowery (whose audiences would yell "H'ist dat rag!" when the curtain failed to rise promptly at the scheduled time) presented so many of those gallop-and-shoot "horse operas," the reason is that America was experiencing a fascination with the West. Beyond the setting sun lay the gold of Nevada and California. Beyond the setting sun lay the cedar-felling ax, the buffalo's huge Babylonian face, Brigham Young's top hat and populous marriage bed, the red man's ceremonies and his wrath, the clear desert air, the wild prairie, the elemental earth whose nearness made the heart beat faster, like the nearness of the sea. The West was beckoning. A constant, rhythmic murmur filled those years: the sound of thousands of Americans settling the West. That procession, in the year 1872, was joined by the always coiled and ready to strike* Bill Harrigan, fleeing a rectangular cell.

A MEXICAN FELLED

History (which, like a certain motion-picture director, tells its story in discontinuous images) now offers us the image of a hazardous bar set in the midst of the all-powerful desert as though in the midst of the sea. The time—one changeable night in the year 1873; the exact place—somewhere on the Llano Estacado, in New Mexico. The land is almost preternaturally flat, but the sky of banked clouds, with tatters of storm and moon, is covered with dry, cracked watering holes and mountains. On the ground, there are a cow skull, the howls and eyes of a coyote in the darkness, fine horses, and the long shaft of light from the bar. Inside, their elbows on the bar, tired, hard-muscled men drink a belligerent alcohol and flash stacks of silver coins marked with a serpent and an eagle. A drunk sings impassively.

Some of the men speak a language with many *s*'s—it must be Spanish, since those who speak it are held in contempt by the others. Bill Harrigan, the red-haired tenement house rat, is among the drinkers. He has downed a couple of shots and is debating (perhaps because he's flat broke) whether to call for another. The men of this desert land baffle him. To him they look huge and terrifying, tempestuous, happy, hatefully knowledgeable in their handling of wild cattle and big horses. Suddenly there is absolute silence, ignored only by the tin-eared singing of the drunk. A brawny, powerful-looking giant of a Mexican with the face of an old Indian woman has come into the bar. His enormous sombrero and the two pistols on his belt make him seem even larger than he is. In a harsh English he wishes all the gringo sons of bitches drinking in the place a *buenas noches.* No one takes up the gauntlet. Bill asks who the Mexican is, and someone whispers fearfully that the dago (Diego) is Belisario Villagrán, from Chihuahua. Instantly, a shot rings out. Shielded by the ring of tall men around him, Bill has shot the intruder. The glass falls from Villagrán's hand; then, the entire man follows. There is no need for a second shot. Without another look at the sumptuous dead man, Bill picks up the conversation where he left off.

"Is that so?" he drawled. "Well, I'm Bill Harrigan, from New York."

The drunk, insignificant, keeps singing.

The sequel is not hard to foresee. Bill shakes hands all around and accepts flattery, cheers, and whisky. Someone notices that there are no notches on Billy's gun, and offers to cut one to mark the killing of Villagrán. Billy the Kid keeps that someone's knife, but mutters that "Mexicans ain't worth makin' notches for." But perhaps that is not enough. That night Billy lays his blanket out next to the dead man and sleeps—ostentatiously—until morning.

KILLING FOR THE HELL OF IT

Out of the happy report of that gunshot (at fourteen years of age) the hero Billy the Kid was born and the shifty Bill Harrigan buried. The scrawny kid of the sewers and skullcracking had risen to the rank of frontiersman. He became a horseman; he learned to sit a horse straight, the way they did in Texas or Wyoming, not leaning back like they did in Oregon and California. He never fully measured up to the legend of himself, but he came closer and closer as time went on. Something of the New York hoodlum lived on in the cowboy; he bestowed upon the Mexicans the hatred once inspired in him by Negroes, but the last words he spoke (a string of curses) were in Spanish. He learned the vagabond art of cattle driving and the other, more difficult art of driving men; both helped him be a good cattle rustler.

Sometimes, the guitars and brothels of Mexico reached out and pulled him in. With the dreadful lucidity of insomnia, he would organize orgies that went on for four days and four nights. Finally, in revulsion, he would pay the bill in bullets. So long as his trigger finger didn't fail him, he was the most feared (and perhaps most empty and most lonely) man on that frontier. Pat Garrett, his friend, the sheriff who finally killed him, once remarked: "I've practiced my aim a good deal killing buffalo." "I've practiced mine more'n you have, killing men," Billy softly replied. The details are lost forever, but we know that he was responsible for as many as twenty-one killings—"not counting Mexicans." For seven daring and dangerous years he indulged himself in that luxury called anger.

On the night of July 25, 1880, Billy the Kid came galloping down the main (or only) street of Fort Sumner on his pinto. The heat was oppressive, and the lamps were not yet lighted; Sheriff Garrett, sitting on the porch in a rocking chair, pulled out his gun and shot Billy in the stomach. The horse went on; the rider toppled into the dirt street. Garrett put a second bullet in him. The town (knowing the wounded man was Billy the Kid) closed and locked its windows. Billy's dying was long and blasphemous. When the sun was high, the townspeople began to approach, and someone took his gun; the man was dead. They noted in him that unimportant sort of look that dead men generally have.

He was shaved, sewn into tailor-made clothes, and exhibited to horror and mockery in the shopwindow of the town's best store.

Men on horses or in gigs came in from miles around. On the third day, they had to put makeup on him. On the fourth, to great jubilation, he was buried.

The Uncivil Teacher of Court Etiquette
Kôtsuké no Suké

The iniquitous protagonist of this chapter is the uncivil courtier Kira Kôtsuké no Suké, the fateful personage who brought about the degradation and death of the lord of the castle of Ako yet refused to take his own life, honorably, when fitting vengeance so demanded. He was a man who merits the gratitude of all men, for he awakened priceless loyalties and provided the black yet necessary occasion for an immortal undertaking. A hundred or more novels, scholarly articles, doctoral theses, and operas—not to mention effusions in porcelain, veined lapis lazuli, and lacquer—commemorate the deed. Even that most versatile of media, celluloid, has served to preserve the exploit, for "Chushingura, or The Doctrinal History of the Forty-seven Loyal Retainers" (such is the title of the film) is the most oft-presented inspiration of Japanese filmmaking. The minutely detailed glory which those ardent tributes attest is more than justifiable—it is immediately just, in anyone's view.

I follow the story as told by A. B. Mitford, who omits those continual distractions lent by "local color," preferring instead to focus on the movement of the glorious episode. That admirable lack of "Orientalism" allows one to suspect that he has taken his version directly from the Japanese.

THE UNTIED RIBBON

In the now faded spring of 1702, Asano Takumi no Kami, the illustrious lord of the castle of Ako, was obliged to receive an envoy from the emperor and offer the hospitality and entertainment of his home to him. Two thousand three hundred years of courtesy (some mythological) had brought the rituals of reception to a fine point of anguished complication. The ambassador represented the emperor, but did so by way of allusion, or symbolically—and this was a nuance which one emphasized too greatly or too little only at one's peril. In order to avoid errors which might all too easily prove fatal, an official of the court at Yedo was sent beforehand to teach the proper ceremonies to be observed. Far from the comforts of the court, and sentenced to this backwoods *villégiature* (which to him must have seemed more like a banishment than a holiday), Kira Kôtsuké no Suké imparted his instructions most ungraciously. At times the magisterial tone of his voice bordered on the insolent. His student, the lord of the castle of Ako, affected to ignore these affronts; he could find no suitable reply, and discipline forbade the slightest violence. One morning, however, the ribbon on the courtier's sock came untied, and he requested that the lord of the castle of Ako tie it up for him again. This gentleman did so, humbly yet with inward indignation. The uncivil teacher of court etiquette told him that he was truly incorrigible—only an ill-bred country bumpkin was capable of tying a knot as clumsily as that. At these words, the lord of the castle of Ako drew his sword and slashed at the uncivil courtier, who fled—the graceful flourish of a delicate thread of blood upon his forehead. . . . A few days later, the military court handed down its sentence against the attacker: the lord of the castle of Ako was to be allowed to commit *hara kiri*. In the central courtyard of the castle of Ako, a dais was erected and covered in red felt, and to it the condemned man was led; he was given a short knife of gold and gems, he confessed his crime publicly, he allowed his upper garments to slip down to his girdle so that he was naked to the waist, and he cut open his abdomen with the two ritual movements of the dirk. He died like a Samurai; the more distant spectators saw no blood, for the felt was red. A white-haired man of great attention to detail—the councillor Oishi Kuranosuké, his second—decapitated his lord with a saber.

THE FEIGNER OF INIQUITIES

Takumi no Kami's castle was confiscated, his family ruined and eclipsed, his name linked to execration. His retainers became Rônins.* One rumor has it that the same night the lord committed *hara kiri*, forty-seven of these Rônins met on the summit of a mountain, where in minute detail they planned the act that took place one year later. But the fact is that the retainers acted with well-justified delay, and at least one of their confabulations took place not on the difficult peak of a mountain, but in a chapel in a forest, an undistinguished pavilion of white-painted wood, unadorned save for the rectangular box that held a mirror.

The Rônins hungered for revenge, but revenge must have seemed unattainable. Kira Kôtsuké no Suké, the hated teacher of court etiquette, had fortified his house, and a cloud of archers and swordsmen swarmed about his palanquin. Among his retinue were incorruptible, secret spies upon whom no detail was lost, and no man did they so closely spy upon and follow as the councillor Kuranosuké, the presumed leader of the avenging Rônins. But by chance Kuranosuké discovered the surveillance, and he based his plan for vengeance upon that knowledge.

He moved to Kiôto, a city unparalleled throughout the empire for the color of its autumns. He allowed himself to descend into the depths of brothels, gambling dens, and taverns. In spite of the gray hairs of his head, he consorted with prostitutes and poets, and with persons even worse. Once he was expelled from a tavern and woke up to find himself in the street, his head covered with vomit.

It happened that a Satsuma man saw this, and said, sadly yet with anger, "Is not this Oishi Kuranosuké, who was a councillor to Asano Takumi no Kami, and who helped him to die yet not having the heart to avenge his lord, gives himself up to women and wine? Faithless beast! Fool and craven! Unworthy the name of a Samurai!"

And he trod on Kuranosuké's face as he slept, and spat on him. When Kôtsuké no Suké's spies reported this passivity, the courtier felt much relieved.

But things did not stop there. The councillor sent his wife and two younger children away and bought a concubine; this iniquitous act cheered the heart and relaxed the fearful prudence of his enemy, who at last dismissed half his guards.

On one of the bitter nights of the winter of 1703, the forty-seven Rônins met in an unkempt garden on the outskirts of Yedo, near a bridge and the playing card factory. They carried the pennants and banners of their lord. Before they began the assault, they informed the inhabitants of the city that they were not raiding the town but embarking on a military mission of strict justice.

THE SCAR

Two groups attacked the palace of Kira Kôtsuké no Suké. The councillor Kuranosuké led the first, which assaulted the main gate; the second was led by the councillor's elder son, who was not yet sixteen years old and who died that night. History records the many moments of that extraordinarily lucid nightmare—the perilous, pendular descent of the rope ladders, the drum beating the signal of attack, the defenders' rush to defend, the archers posted on the rooftops, the unswerving path of the arrows toward vital organs, the porcelains dishonored by blood, the burning death that turns to ice—all the brazen and disorderly elements of death. Nine of the Rônins died; the defenders were no less brave, and they would not surrender. Shortly after midnight, all resistance ended.

Kira Kôtsuké no Suké, the ignominious cause of all that loyalty, was nowhere to be found. The attackers sought him through every corner of the emotion-torn palace; they were beginning to despair of finding him, when the councillor noted that his bedclothes were still warm. Again the Rônins searched, and soon they discovered a narrow window, hidden by a bronze mirror. Below, in a gloomy courtyard, a man in white looked up at them; a trembling sword was in his right hand. When they rushed down, the man gave himself up without a fight. His forehead bore a scar—the old rubric left by Takumi no Kami's blade.

Then the bloody Rônins went down on their knees to the detested nobleman and told him that they were the former retainers of the lord of the castle of Ako, for whose death and perdition he was to blame, and they requested that he commit the suicide that befitted a samurai.

In vain did the retainers propose to the lord's servile spirit that act of self-respect. He was a man impervious to the pleas of honor; at sunrise, the officers had to slit his throat.

THE EVIDENCE

Their thirst for revenge now quenched (but without wrath, or agitation, or regret), the Rônins made their way toward the temple that sheltered the remains of their lord.

In a brass pail they carried the incredible head of Kira Kôtsuké no Suké, and they took turns watching over it. They crossed fields and provinces, in the honest light of day. Men blessed them and wept. The prince of Sendai offered them his hospitality, but they replied that their lord had been waiting for them for almost two years. At last they reached the dark sepulcher, and they offered up the head of their enemy.

The Supreme Court handed down its verdict, and it was as expected: the retainers were granted the privilege of suicide. All obeyed, some with ardent serenity, and they lie now beside their lord. Today, men and children come to the sepulcher of those faithful men to pray.

THE SATSUMA MAN

Among the pilgrims who come to the grave, there is one dusty, tired young man who must have come from a great distance. He prostrates himself before the monument to the councillor Oishi Kuranosuké and he says aloud: "When I saw you lying drunk by the roadside, at the doorstep of a whorehouse in Kiôto, I knew not that you were plotting to avenge your lord; and, thinking you to be a faithless man, I trampled on you and spat in your face as I passed. I have come to offer atonement." He spoke these words and then committed *hara kiri.*

The priest of the temple where Kuranosuké's body lay was greatly moved by the Satsuma man's courage, and he buried him by the side of the Rônins and their lord.

This is the end of the story of the forty-seven loyal retainers—except that the story has no ending, because we other men, who are perhaps not loyal yet will never entirely lose the hope that we might one day be so, shall continue to honor them with our words.*

Hakim, the Masked Dyer of Merv

For Angélica Ocampo

Unless I am mistaken, the original sources of information on Al-Moqanna, the Veiled (or, more strictly, Masked) Prophet of Khorasan, are but four: (a) the excerpts from the *History of the Caliphs* preserved by Bāladhūrī; (b) the *Manual of the Giant, or Book of Precision and Revision*, by the official historian of the Abbasids, Ibn Abī Ṭahīr Tarfur; (c) the Arabic codex entitled *The Annihilation of the Rose*, which refutes the abominable heresies of the *Rosa Obscura* or *Rosa Secreta*, which was the Prophet's holy work; and (d) several coins (without portraits) unearthed by an engineer named Andrusov on ground that had been leveled for the Trans-Caspian Railway. These coins were deposited in the Numismatic Museum in Tehran; they contain Persian distichs which summarize or correct certain passages from the *Annihilation*. The original *Rosa* has apparently been lost, since the manuscript found in 1899 and published (not without haste) by the Morgenländisches Archiv was declared by Horn, and later by Sir Percy Sykes, to be apocryphal.

The fame of the Prophet in the West is owed to Thomas Moore's garrulous poem *Lalla Rookh*, a work laden with the Irish conspirator's sighs and longings for the East.

THE SCARLET DYE

In the year 120 of the Hegira, or 736 of the Christian era, there was born in Turkestan the man Hakim, whom the people of that time and that region were to call The Veiled. His birthplace was the ancient city of Merv, whose gardens and vineyards and lawns look out sadly onto the desert. Noontime there, when not obscured by choking clouds of sand that leave a film of whitish dust on the black clusters of the grapes, is white and dazzling.

Hakim was raised in that wearied city. We know that one of his father's brothers trained him as a dyer—the craft, known to be a refuge for infidels and impostors and inconstant men, which inspired the first anathemas of his extravagant career. *My face is of gold,* a famous page of the *Annihilation* says, *but I have steeped the purple dye and on the second night have plunged the uncarded wool into it, and on the third night have saturated the prepared wool, and the emperors of the islands still contend for that bloody cloth. Thus did I sin in the years of my youth, deforming the true colors of the creatures. The Angel would tell me that lambs were not the color of tigers, while Satan would say to me that the All-Powerful One desired that they be, and in that pursuit he employed my cunning and my dye. Now I know that neither the Angel nor Satan spoke the truth, for I know that* all *color is abominable.*

In the year 146 of the Hegira, Hakim disappeared from his native city. The vats and barrels in which he had immersed the cloth were broken, as were a scimitar from Shiraz and a brass mirror.

THE BULL

At the end of the moon of Sha'ban in the year 158, the air of the desert was very clear, and a group of men were looking toward the west in expectation of the moon of Ramadan, which inspires fasting and mortification. They were slaves, beggars, horse sellers, camel thieves, and butchers. Sitting gravely on the ground before the gate of an inn at which caravans stopped on the road to Merv, they awaited the sign. They looked at the setting sun, and the color of the setting sun was the color of the sand.

From far out on the dizzying desert (whose sun gives men fever and whose moon brings on convulsions), they saw three figures, apparently of immense height, coming toward them. The three figures were human, but the one in the center possessed the head of a bull. As these figures came closer, the man in the center was seen to be wearing a mask, while the two men that accompanied him were blind.

Someone (as in the tales of the *Thousand and One Nights*) asked the reason for this wonder. *They are blind,* the masked man said, *because they have looked upon my face.*

THE LEOPARD

The historian of the Abbasids relates that the man from the desert (whose voice was extraordinarily sweet, or so, in contrast to the harshness of the mask, it seemed to be) told the men that though they were awaiting the sign of a month of penitence, he would be for them a greater sign: the sign of an entire *life* of penitence, and a calumniated death. He told them that he was Hakim, son of Ozman, and that in the year 146 of the Flight a man had entered his house and after purifying himself and praying had cut his, Hakim's, head off with a scimitar and taken it up to the heavens. Borne in the right hand of this visitor (who was the angel Gabriel), his head had been taken before the Almighty, who had bade him prophesy, entrusting him with words of such antiquity that speaking them burned one's mouth and endowed one with such glorious resplendence that mortal eyes could not bear to look upon it. That was the reason for his mask. When every man on earth professed the new law, the Visage would be unveiled to them, and they would be able to worship it without danger—as the angels did already. His message delivered, Hakim exhorted the men to *jihad*—a holy war—and the martyrdom that accompanied it.

The slaves, beggars, horse sellers, camel thieves, and butchers denied him their belief—one voice cried *sorcerer;* another, *impostor.*

Someone had brought a leopard—perhaps a member of that lithe and bloodthirsty breed trained by Persian huntsmen. At any rate, it broke free of its cage. Save for the masked Prophet and his two acolytes, all the men there trampled one another in their haste to flee. When they returned, the beast was blind. In the presence of those luminous, dead eyes, the men worshiped Hakim and admitted his supernatural estate.

THE VEILED PROPHET

The official historian of the Abbasids narrates with no great enthusiasm the inroads made by Hakim the Veiled in Khorasan. That province—greatly moved by the misfortune and crucifixion of its most famous leader—embraced with desperate fervor the doctrine offered by the Shining Visage and offered up to him its blood and gold. (Hakim by now had exchanged his harsh mask for a fourfold veil of white silk embroidered with precious stones. Black was the symbolic color of the caliphs of the House of Abbas; Hakim chose the color white—the most distant from it—for his shielding Veil, his banners, and his turbans.) The campaign began well. It is true that in the *Book of Precision* it is the *caliph*'s pennants that are victorious everywhere, but since the most frequent result of those victories is the stripping of the generals of their rank and the abandonment of impregnable castles, it is not difficult for the sagacious reader to read between the lines. Toward the end of the moon of Rajab in the year 161, the famous city of Nishapur opened its iron gates to the Masked One; in early 162, the city of Astarabad did likewise. Hakim's military operations (like those of another, more fortunate Prophet) were limited to his tenor chanting of prayers offered up to the Deity from the hump of a reddish-colored camel in the chaotic heart of battle. Arrows would whistle all around him, yet he was never wounded. He seemed to seek out danger—the night a band of loathsome lepers surrounded his palace, he had them brought to him, he kissed them, and he made them gifts of gold and silver.

The Prophet delegated the wearying details of governing to six or seven adepts. He was a scholar of meditation and of peace—a harem of 114 blind wives attempted to satisfy the needs of his divine body.

ABOMINABLE MIRRORS

So long as their words do not altogether contravene orthodox belief, confidential friends of God are tolerated by Islam, however indiscreet or threatening to that religion they may be. The Prophet would perhaps not have spurned the advantages of that neglect, but his followers, his victories, and the public wrath of the caliph—whose name was Muhammad al-Mahdī—forced him into heresy. It was that dissent that ruined him, though first it led him to set down the articles of a personal religion (a personal religion that bore the clear influence of gnostic forebears).

In the beginning of Hakim's cosmogony there was a spectral god, a deity as majestically devoid of origins as of name and face. This deity was an immutable god, but its image threw nine shadows; these, condescending to action, endowed and ruled over a first heaven. From that first demiurgic crown there came a second, with its own angels, powers, and thrones, and these in turn founded another, lower heaven, which was the symmetrical duplicate of the first. This second conclave was reproduced in a third, and the third in another, lower conclave, and so on, to the number of 999. The lord of the nethermost heaven—the shadow of shadows of yet other shadows—is He who reigns over us, and His fraction of divinity tends to zero.

The earth we inhabit is an error, an incompetent parody. Mirrors and paternity are abominable because they multiply and affirm it. Revulsion, disgust, is the fundamental virtue, and two rules of conduct (between which the Prophet left men free to choose) lead us to it: abstinence and utter licentiousness—the indulgence of the flesh or the chastening of it.

Hakim's paradise and hell were no less desperate. *To those who deny the*

Word, to those who deny the Jeweled Veil and the Visage, runs an imprecation from the *Rosa Secreta, I vow a wondrous Hell, for each person who so denies shall reign over 999 empires of fire, and in each empire shall be 999 mountains of fire, and upon each mountain there shall be 999 towers of fire, and each tower shall have 999 stories of fire, and each story shall have 999 beds of fire, and in each bed shall that person be, and 999 kinds of fire, each with its own face and voice, shall torture that person throughout eternity.* Another passage corroborates this: *Here, in this life, dost thou suffer one body; in death and Retribution, thou shalt have bodies innumerable.* Paradise was less concrete: *It is always night, and there are fountains of stone, and the happiness of that paradise is the special happiness of farewells, of renunciation, and of those who know that they are sleeping.*

THE VISAGE

In the 163rd year of the Hegira, the fifth of the Shining Face, Hakim was surrounded in Sanam by the Caliph's army. Great were the provisions, many the martyrs, and aid from a horde of angels of light was expected at any moment. Such was the pass to which they had come when a terrifying rumor spread through the castle. It was said that as an adulteress within the harem was being strangled by the eunuchs, she had screamed that the third finger was missing from the Prophet's right hand, and that his other fingers had no nails. The rumor spread like fire among the faithful. In broad daylight, standing upon a high terrace, Hakim prayed to his familiar God for victory, or for a sign. Servilely, with their heads bowed (as though they were running against the rain), two captains snatched away the gem-embroidered veil.

First, there came a trembling. The promised face of the Apostle, the face which had journeyed to the heavens, was indeed white, but it was white with the whiteness of leprosy. It was so swollen (or so incredible) that it seemed to be a mask. It had no eyebrows; the lower eyelid of the right eye drooped upon the senile cheek; a dangling cluster of nodular growths was eating away its lips; the flat and inhuman nose resembled that of a lion.

Hakim's voice attempted one final deception: *Thy abominable sins forbid thee to look upon my radiance . . . ,* he began.

No one was listening; he was riddled with spears.

Man on Pink Corner*

For Enrique Amorim

Imagine you bringing up Francisco Real that way, out of the clear blue sky, him dead and gone and all. Because I met the man, even if this wa'n't exactly his stomping ground—his was more up in the north, up around Guadalupe Lake and Batería. Truth is, I doubt if I crossed paths with the man more than three times, and all three were on a single night—though it's not one I'll be likely ever to forget. It was the night La Lujanera came home to sleep at my place—just like that, just up and came—and the same night Rosendo Juárez left Maldonado* never to return. Of course you probably haven't had the experience you'd need to recognize that particular individual's name, but in his time Rosendo Juárez—the Sticker, they called him—was one of the toughest customers in Villa Santa Rita. He was fierce with a knife, was Rosendo Juárez, as you'd expect with a moniker like that, and he was one of don Nicolás Paredes' men—don Nicolás being one of Morel's men.* He'd come into the cathouse just as dandified as you can imagine, head to foot in black, with his belt buckle and studs and all of silver. Men and dogs, both, had a healthy respect for him, and the whores did too; everybody knew two killings'd been laid to him already. He wore a tall sort of hat with a narrow brim, which sat down like this on a long mane of greasy hair. Rosendo was favored by fortune, as they say, and we boys in the neighborhood would imitate him right down to the way he spit. But then there came a night that showed us Rosendo Juárez's true colors.

It's hard to believe, but the story of that night—a night as strange as any I've ever lived through—began with an insolent red-wheeled hack crammed with men, banging and rattling along those streets of hard-packed clay, past brick kilns and vacant lots. There was two men in black, strumming guitars and lost in their own thoughts, and the man on the driver's seat using his whip on any loose dogs that took a mind to mess with the piebald in the traces, and one fellow wrapped tight in a poncho riding in the middle—which was the Yardmaster that everybody always talked about, and he was spoiling for a fight, spoiling for a kill. The night was so cool it was like a blessing from heaven; two of these fellows were riding up on the folded-back cloth top of the hack—and it was as though the loneliness made that rattletrap a veritable parade. That was the first event of the many that took place, but it wa'n't till a while afterward that we found out this part. Me and my friends, meantime, we'd been over at Julia's place since early that evening, Julia's place being a big old barracks-like building made out of sheets of zinc, between the Gauna road and the Maldonado. It was a place you could pick out from quite a distance off, on account of the light from a brazen big red light—and on account of the hullabaloo too. This Julia, although she was a colored woman, was as reliable and honest as you could ask for, so there wa'n't ever any lack of musicians, good drinks, and girls that could dance all night if they was asked to. But this Lujanera I mentioned, who was Rosendo's woman, she outdid 'em all, and by a good long ways. La Lujanera's dead now, señor, and I have to admit that sometimes whole years go by that I don't think about her, but you ought to have seen her in her time, with those eyes of hers. Seein' her wouldn't put a man to sleep, and that's for sure.

Rotgut, milongas, women, a *simpático* kind of curse at you from the mouth of Rosendo Juárez, a slap on the back from him that you tried to feel was friendly-like—the truth is, I was as happy as a man could be. I was paired up with a girl that could follow like she could read my mind; the tango was having its way with us, whirling us this way and then that and losing us and calling us back again and finding us. . . . To make a long story short, we boys were dancing, 'most like bein' in a dream, when all of a sudden the music seemed to get louder, and what it was was that you could begin to hear the guitar-strumming of those two fellows I mentioned, mixing in with the music there at Julia's, and coming nearer every minute. Then the gust of wind that had brought it to us changed direction, and I went back to my own body and my partner's, and the conversations of the dance. A good while later, there came a knock at the front door—a big knock and a big voice, too. At that, everybody got still; then a man's chest bumped the swinging doors open and the man himself stepped inside. The man resembled the voice a good deal.

For us, he wa'n't Francisco Real yet, but you couldn't deny he was a tall, muscular sort of man, dressed head to foot in black, with a shawl around his shoulders about the color of a bay horse. I remember his face being Indian-like, unsociable.

One of the swinging doors hit me when it banged open. Like the damn fool I am, I reached out and swung at the fellow with my left hand while with my right I went for the knife I kept sharp and waiting in the armhole of my vest, under my left arm. If we'd've tangled, I wouldn't have lasted long. The man put out his arm—and it was all he had to do—and brushed me aside, like he was brushing away a fly. So there I was—half sprawled there behind the door, with my hand still under my vest, holding on to my useless weapon, while he just kept walking, like nothing had happened, right on into the room. Just kept walking—taller than any of the boys that were stepping aside to make way for him, and acting like we were all invisible. The first row of fellows—pure Eye-talians, an' all eyes—opened out like a fan, and fast. But that wa'n't about to last. In the pack just behind those first fellows, the Englishman was waiting for him, and before that Englishman could feel the stranger's hand on his shoulder, he floored him with a roundhouse he had waitin'—and no sooner had he landed his punch than the party started in for serious. The place was yards and yards deep, but they herded the stranger from one end of it to the other, bumping him and shoving him and whistling and spitting. At first they'd hit him with their fists, but then when they saw that he didn't so much as put up a hand to try to block their punches, they started slapping him—sometimes with their open hands and sometimes just with the harmless fringe on their shawls, like they were makin' fun of him. And also like they were reserving him for Rosendo, who hadn't budged from where he was standing, back against the back wall, and without saying a word. He was taking quick puffs of his cigarette—I will say that—like he already had an inkling of what the rest of us would see clear enough later on. The Yardmaster—straight and bloody, and the wind from that jeering mob behind him—was getting pushed and shoved back to Rosendo. Whistled at, beaten, spit on, as soon as he came face to face with Rosendo, he spoke. He looked at him and he wiped off his face with his arm, and he said this:

"I'm Francisco Real, from up on the Northside. Francisco Real, and they call me the Yardmaster. I've let these poor sons of bitches lift their hands to me because what I'm looking for is a man. There are people out there—I figure they're just talkers, you know—saying there's some guy down here in these boondocks that fancies himself a knife fighter, and a bad 'un—say he's called the Sticker. I'd like to make his acquaintance, so he could show me—me being nobody, you understand—what it means to be a man of courage, a man you can look up to."

He said that, and he never took his eyes off him. Now a sticker for real glinted in his right hand—no doubt he'd had it up his sleeve the whole time. All around, the fellows that had been pushing to get close started backing away, and every one of us was looking at the two of them, and you could have heard a pin drop. Why, even the black gentleman that played the violin, a blind man he was, he had his face turned that way.

Just then I hear movement behind me, and I see that in the doorway there's standing six or seven men, which would be the Yardmaster's gang, you see. The oldest of them, a weather-beaten, country-looking man with a gray-streaked mustache, steps forward and stands there like he's dazzled by all the women and all the light, and he very respectfully takes his hat off. The others just stood there watching, keeping their eyes open, ready to step in, you see, if somebody wanted to start playing dirty.

Meantime, what was happening with Rosendo—why hadn't he come out slashing at that swaggering son of a bitch? He hadn't said a word yet, hadn't so much as raised his eyes. His cigarette, I don't know whether he spit it out or whether it just fell out of his face. Finally he managed to get a few words out, but so quiet that those of us down at the other end of the room couldn't hear what he was saying. Then Francisco Real called him out again, and again Rosendo refused to rise to the occasion. So at that, the youngest of the strangers—just a kid he was—he whistled. La Lujanera looked at him with hate in her eyes and she started through that crowd with her braid down her back—through that crowd of men and whores—and she walked up to her man and she put her hand to his chest and she pulled out his naked blade and she handed it to him.

"Rosendo, I think you're needing this," she said.

Right up next to the roof there was this long kind of window that looked out over the creek. Rosendo took the knife in his two hands and he seemed to be trying to place it, like he didn't recognize it. Then all of a sudden he reared back and flung that knife straight through the window, out into the Maldonado. I felt a cold chill run down my spine.

"The only reason I don't carve you up for beefsteak is that you make me sick," said the stranger. At that, La Lujanera threw her arms around this Yardmaster's neck, and she looked at him with those eyes of hers, and she said, with anger in her voice:

"Forget that dog—he had us thinking he was a man."

Francisco Real stood there perplexed for a second, and then he put his arms around her like it was going to be forever, and he yelled at the musicians to play something—a tango, a milonga—and then yelled at the rest of us to dance. The milonga ran like a grass fire from one end of the room to the other. Real danced straight-faced, but without any daylight between him and her, now that he could get away with it. They finally came to the door, and he yelled:

"Make ways, boys—she's gettin' sleepy!"

That's what he said, and they walked out cheek to cheek, like in the drunken dizziness of the tango, like they were drowning in that tango.

I ought to be ashamed of myself. I spun around the floor a couple of times with one of the girls and then I just dropped her—on account of the heat and the crowdedness, I told her—and I slunk down along the wall till I got to the door. It was a pretty night—but a pretty night for who? Down at the corner stood that hack, with those two guitars sitting up straight on the seat, like two Christian gentlemen. It galled me to see those guitars left out like that, to realize that those boys thought so little of us that they'd trust us not even to walk off with their cheap guitars. It made me mad to feel like we were a bunch of nobodies. I grabbed the carnation behind my ear and threw it in a mud puddle and then I stood there looking at it, more or less so I wouldn't have to think of anything else. I wished it was already the next day, so I'd have this night behind me. Just then, somebody elbowed me, and it felt almost like a relief. It was Rosendo, slipping through the neighborhood all by himself.

"Seems like you're always in the way, asshole," he muttered as he passed by me—I couldn't say whether to get it off his chest or because he had his mind on something else. He took the direction where it was darkest, down along the Maldonado; I never saw the man again.

I stood there looking at the things I'd been seeing all my life—a sky that went on forever, the creek flowing angry-like down below there, a sleeping horse, the dirt street, the kilns—and I was struck by the thought that I was just another weed growing along those banks, coming up between the soapworts and the bone piles of the tanneries. What was supposed to grow out of trash heaps if it wa'n't us? —We was big talkers, but soft when it came to a fight, all mouth and no backbone. Then I told myself it wa'n't like that—the tougher the neighborhood, the tougher a man necessarily had to be. A trash heap? —The milonga was having itself a ball, there was plenty of racket in the houses, and the wind brought the smell of honeysuckle. The night was pretty, but so what? There were enough stars that you got dizzy lookin' at 'em, one on top of another up there. I struggled, I tell you, to make myself feel like none of what had happened meant anything to me, but Rosendo's turning tail, that stranger's insufferable bullying—it wouldn't let me alone. The tall son of a bitch had even gotten himself a woman for the night out of it. For that night and many more nights besides, I thought to myself, and maybe for all the rest of his nights, because La Lujanera was serious medicine. Lord knows which way they'd gone. But they couldn't be far. Probably at it hammer and tongs right now, in the first ditch they'd come to.

When I finally got back inside, that perfectly pleasant little dance was still going on, like nothing had ever happened.

Making myself as inconspicuous as I could, I peered around through the crowd, and I saw that one and another of our boys had slipped out, but the guys from the Northside were tangoing along with everybody else. There was no elbowing or words or anything; everything was real polite, but everybody was keeping their eyes open. The music was kind of sleepy, and the girls that were dancing with the Northside boys were as meek as mice.

I was expecting something, but not what turned out to happen.

Outside we heard a woman crying, and then a voice that was familiar in a way, but calm, almost *too* calm, as though it didn't belong to a real person, saying to her:

"Go ahead, darlin', go on in," and then some more of the woman's crying. Then the voice seemed to be getting a little desperate.

"Open the door, I said! Open the door, you motherless bitch, open the door!"

At that, the rickety doors swung open and La Lujanera stepped in, alone. She came in kind of looking over her shoulder, like somebody was herding her inside.

"She's got a spirit back there commanding her," said the Englishman.

"A dead man, my friend," said the Yardmaster then. His face was like a drunkard's. He came in, and he took a few unsteady steps into the clearing that we all made for him, like we had before. He stood there tall, and unseeing, and then he toppled like a post. One of the boys that had come with him turned him over on his back and put his poncho under his head for a pillow. The boy's hands came away bloody. That was when we saw that he had a big knife wound in his chest; his blood was pooling up and turnin' black this bright red neckerchief he was wearing, but that I hadn't noticed before because his shawl had covered it. To try to stop the blood, one of the girls brought over some rotgut and scorched rags. He was in no condition to tell us what'd happened, and La Lujanera was looking at him sort of vacant-like, with her arms just hanging down at her sides. Everybody was asking her what happened with their eyes, and finally she managed to find her voice. She said that after she'd gone outside with the Yardmaster there, they went off to a little vacant lot, and just then a stranger appeared and desperately called out the Yardmaster to fight, and he stabbed him, gave him that wound there, and she swore she didn't know who the man was, but it wa'n't Rosendo.

Who was going to believe that?

The man at our feet was dying. My thought was, whoever had fixed his clock, his hand had been pretty steady. But the Yardmaster was tough, you had to give him that. When he came to the door just now, Julia had been brewing up some *mate*, and the *mate* went around the room and came all the way back to me before he was finally dead. "Cover my face," he said, when he knew he couldn't last anymore. His pride was all he had left, and he wa'n't going to let people gawk at the expressions on his face while he lay there dyin'. Somebody put that high-crowned black hat over his face, and he died under it, without a sound. When his chest stopped rising and falling, somebody got up the nerve to uncover him—he had that tired look that dead men get. He was one of the toughest men there was back then, from Batería to the Southside—but no sooner was he dead and his mouth shut for all time, I lost all my hate for him.

"All it takes to die is to be alive," one of the girls back in the crowd said, and then another one said something else, in a pensive sort of way:

"Man thought so highly of himself, and all he's good for now is to draw flies."

At that, the Northsiders all muttered something to each other, real low, and then two of 'em at the same time said it out loud:

"The woman killed 'im."

One of 'em yelled in her face, asking her if it was her that did it, and they all surrounded her. At that I forgot all about being meek and not getting in anybody's way, and I pushed through to her like a shot. I'm such a damn fool, it's a wonder as mad as I was I didn't pull out the little dagger I always carried on me. I could feel almost everybody—not to say everybody—looking at me.

"Look at this woman's hands," I said with a sneer. "Do they look steady enough—does she look like she'd have heart enough—to put a knife in the Yardmaster like that?"

Then I added, cool but tough at the same time:

"Who'd've thought the dear departed, who they say was a man to be reckoned with on his own turf, would've ended up this way, and in a backwater as dead as this is, where nothin' ever happens unless some strangers wander in to give us somethin' to talk about and stay around to get spit on afterward?"

Nobody rose to that bait, either.

Just then through the silence came the sound of riders. It was the police. For one reason or another, everybody there had reason to keep the law out of this, so they decided that the best thing was to move the body down to the creek. You'll recall that long window that the gleam of the knife sailed through? Well, that's the very same way the man in black went. A bunch of them lifted him up and after they'd separated him from all the money and whatnot he had on him, somebody hacked off his finger to get to the ring he wore. Vultures, señor, to pick over a poor defenseless dead man like that, after another, better man has fixed 'im. Then a heave-ho, and that rushing, long-suffering water carried him away. I couldn't say whether they gutted him*—I didn't want to look. The gray-mustached individual never took his eyes off me. La Lujanera took advantage of all the shuffling-about to disappear.

By the time the law came in to have their look around, the dance had a pretty good head of steam up again. The blind man on the violin knew how to play habaneras the likes of which you won't hear anymore. Outside, the day began to want to dawn a little. There was a line of arborvitae posts along the top of a hill, standing there all alone-like, because you couldn't see the thin strands of wire between 'em that early in the morning.

I strolled nice and easy on home to my place, which was about three blocks away. There was a light burning in the window, but then it went out. When I saw that, I can tell you I moved a good bit faster. And then, Borges, for the second time I pulled out that short, sharp-edged knife I always carried here, under my vest, under my left arm, and I gave it another long slow inspection—and it was just like new, all innocent, and there was not the slightest trace of blood on it.

Et cetera

For Néstor Ibarra

A THEOLOGIAN IN DEATH

I have been told by angels that when Melancthon died, a house was prepared for him like that in which he had lived in the world. This also is done with most of the new-comers, owing to which they do not know that they are not still in the natural world. . . . The things in his room, also, were all like those he had before, a similar table, a similar desk with compartments, and also a similar library; so that as soon as he awakened from sleep, he seated himself at the table and continued his writing, as if he were not a dead body, and this on the subject of justification by faith alone, and so on for several days, and writing nothing whatever concerning charity. As the angels perceived this, he was asked through messengers why he did not write about charity also. He replied that there was nothing of the church in charity, for if that were to be received as in any way an essential attribute of the church, man would also ascribe to himself the merit of justification and consequently of salvation, and so also he would rob faith of its spiritual essence. He said these things arrogantly, but he did not know that he was dead and that the place to which he had been sent was not heaven. When the angels perceived this, they withdrew. . . .

A few weeks after this, the things which he used in his room began to be obscured, and at length to disappear, until at last there was nothing left there but the chair, the table, the paper and the inkstand; and, moreover, the walls of his room seemed to be plastered with lime, and the floor to be covered with a yellow, brick-like material, and he himself seemed to be more coarsely clad. Still, he went on writing, and since he persisted in his denial of charity . . . he suddenly seemed to himself to be under ground in a sort of work-house, where there were other theologians like him. And when he wished to go out he was detained. . . . At this, he began to question his ideas, and he was taken out, and sent back to his former chamber. . . . When sent back, he appeared clad in a hairy skin, but he tried to imagine that what had gone before had been a mere hallucination, and he went on praising faith and denying charity. One evening at dusk, he felt a chill. That led him to walk through the house, and he realized that the other rooms were no longer those of the dwelling in which he had lived on earth. One room was filled with unknown instruments, another had shrunk so much that he could not enter it; another one had not itself changed, but its windows and doors opened onto great sand dunes. There was a room at the rear of the house in which there were three tables, at which sat men like himself, who also cast charity into exile, and he said that he conversed with them, and was confirmed by them day by day, and told that no other theologian was as wise as he. He was smitten by that adoration, but since some of the persons had no face, and others were like dead men, he soon came to abominate and mistrust them. Then he began to write something about charity; but what he wrote on the paper one day, he did not see the next; for this happens to every one there when he commits any thing to paper from the external man only, and not at the same time from the internal, thus from compulsion and not from freedom; it is obliterated of itself. . . .

When any novitiates from the world entered his room to speak with him and to see him, he was ashamed that they should find him in such a sordid place, and so he would summon one of the magical spirits, who by phantasy could produce various becoming shapes, and who then adorned his room with ornaments and with flowered tapestry. . . . But as soon as the visitors were gone, these shapes vanished, and the former lime-plastering and emptiness returned, and sometimes before.

The last word we have of Melancthon is that the wizard and one of the men without a face carried him out to the sand dunes, where he is now a servant to demons.

(From Emanuel Swedenborg, *Arcana Cælestia*)*

THE CHAMBER OF STATUES

In the early days, there was a city in the kingdom of the Andalusians where their monarchs lived and its name was Labtayt or Ceuta, or Jaén. In that city, there was a strong tower whose gate (of two portals breadth) was neither for going in nor for coming out, but for keeping closed. And whenever a King died and another King took the Kingship after him, with his own hands, he set a new and strong lock to that gate, till there were four-and-twenty locks upon the tower, according to the number of Kings. After this time, there came to the throne an evil man, who was not of the old royal house, and instead of setting a new lock, he had a mind to open these locks, that he might see what was within the tower. The grandees of his kingdom forbade him this and pressed him to desist and reproved him and blamed him; they hid from him the iron key ring and told him that it was much easier to add a new lock to the gate than to force four-and-twenty, but he persisted, saying, "Needs must this place be opened." Then they offered him all that their hands possessed of monies and treasures and things of price, of flocks, of Christian idols, of gold and silver, if he would but refrain; still, he would not be baulked, and said "There is no help for it but I open this tower." So he pulled off the locks with his right hand (which will now burn through all eternity) and entering, found within the tower figures of Arabs on their horses and camels, habited in turbands hanging down at the ends, with swords in baldrick-belts thrown over their shoulders and bearing long lances in their hands. All these figures were round, as in life, and threw shadows on the ground; a blind man could identify them by touch, and the front hooves of their horses did not touch the ground yet they did not fall, as though the mounts were rearing. These exquisite figures filled the king with great amazement; even more wonderful was the excellent order and silence that one saw in them, for every figure's head was turned to the same side (the west) while not a single voice or clarion was heard. Such was the first room in the castle. In the second, the king found the table that belonged to Suleyman, son of David—salvation be with both of them! This table was carved from a single grass-green emerald, a stone whose occult properties are indescribable yet genuine, for it calms the tempest, preserves the chastity of its wearer, keeps off dysentery and evil spirits, brings favorable outcome to lawsuits, and is of great relief in childbearing.

In the third room, two books were found: one was black and taught the virtues of each metal, each talisman, and each day, together with the preparation of poisons and antidotes; the other was white, and though the script was clear, its lesson could not be deciphered. In the fourth room found he a mappa mundi figuring the earth and the seas and the different cities and countries and villages of the world, each with its true name and exact shape.

In the fifth, they found a marvelous mirror, great and round, of mixed metals, which had been made for Suleyman, son of David—on the twain be forgiveness!—wherein whoso looked might see the counterfeit presentment of his parents and his children, from the first Adam to those who shall hear the Trumpet. The sixth room was filled with that hermetic powder, one drachm of which elixir can change three thousand drachms of silver into three thousand drachms of gold. The seventh appeared empty, and it was so long that the ablest of the king's archers might have loosed an arrow from its doorway without hitting the distant wall. Carved on that far wall, they saw a terrible inscription. The king examined it, and understood it, and it spoke in this wise: "If any hand opens the gate of this castle, the warriors of flesh at the entrance, who resemble warriors of metal, shall take possession of the kingdom."

These things occurred in the eighty-ninth year of the Hegira. Before the year reached its end, Tarik ibn Zayid would conquer that city and slay this King after the sorriest fashion and sack the city and make prisoners of the women and boys therein and get great loot. Thus it was that the Arabs spread all over the cities of Andalusia—a kingdom of fig trees and watered plains in which no man suffered thirst. As for the treasures, it is widely known that Tarik, son of Zayid, sent them to his lord, the caliph Al-Walid bin Abd al-Malik, who entombed them in a pyramid.

(From the *Book of the Thousand Nights and a Night*, Night 272)*

THE STORY OF THE TWO DREAMERS

The Arab historian Al-Ishaqi tells the story of this event:

"It is related by men worthy of belief (though only Allah is omniscient and omnipotent and all-merciful and unsleeping) that a man of Cairo was possessed of ample riches and great wealth; but he was so generous and magnanimous that his wealth passed away, save his father's house, and his state changed, and he became utterly destitute, and could not obtain his sustenance save by laborious exertion. And he slept one night, overwhelmed and oppressed, under a fig tree in his garden, and saw in his sleep a person dripping wet who took from his mouth a golden coin and said to him, 'Verily thy fortune is in Persia, in Isfahan: therefore seek it and repair to it.' So he journeyed to Persia, meeting on the way with all the dangers of the desert, and of ships, and of pirates, and of idolaters, and of rivers, and of wild beasts, and of men; and when he at last arrived there, the evening overtook him, and he slept in a mosque. Now there was, adjacent to the mosque, a house; and as Allah (whose name be exalted!) had decreed, a party of robbers entered the mosque, and thence passed to that house; and the people of the house, awaking at the disturbance occasioned by the robbers, raised cries; the neighbors made a cry as well, whereupon the Wálee came to their aid with his followers, and the robbers fled over the housetops. The Wálee then entered the mosque, and found the man of Cairo sleeping there; so he laid hold upon him, and inflicted upon him a painful beating with mikra'ahs, until he was at the point of death, and imprisoned him; and he remained three days in the prison; after which, the Wálee caused him to be brought, and said to him, 'From what country art thou?' He answered, 'From Cairo.' —'And what affair,' said the Wálee, 'was the cause of thy coming to Persia?' He answered, 'I saw in my sleep a person who said to me, "Verily thy fortune is in Isfahan; therefore repair to it." And when I came here, I found the fortune of which he told me to be those blows of the mikra'ahs, that I have received from thee.'—

"And upon this the Wálee laughed so that his grinders appeared, and said to him, 'O thou of little sense, *I* saw three times in my sleep a person who said to me, "Verily a house in Cairo, in such a district, and of such a description, hath in its court a garden, at the lower end of which is a fountain, wherein is wealth of great amount: therefore repair to it and take it." But I went not; and thou, through the smallness of they sense, hast journeyed from city to city on account of a thing thou hast seen in sleep, when it was only an effect of confused dreams.'—Then he gave him some money, and said to him, 'Help thyself with this to return to thy city.'

"So he took it and returned to Cairo. Now the house which the Wálee had described, in Cairo, was the house of that man; therefore when he arrived at his abode, he dug beneath the fountain, and beheld abundant wealth. Thus God enriched and sustained him; and this was a wonderful coincidence."

(From the *Book of the Thousand Nights and a Night*, Night 351)*

THE WIZARD THAT WAS MADE TO WAIT

In Santiago de Compostela, there was once a dean of the cathedral who was greedy to learn the art of magic. He heard a rumor that a man named Illán, who lived in the city of Toledo, knew more things respecting this art than any other man, and he set off to Toledo to find him.

The day the dean arrived, he went directly to the place where Illán lived and found him at his books, in a room at the rear of the house. Illán greeted the dean kindly, but begged that he put off the business of his journey until after they had eaten. He showed him to a cool apartment and told him he was very glad that he had come. After dinner, the dean explained the purpose of his journey, and asked Illán to teach him the occult science. Illán told him that he had divined that his visitor was a dean, a man of good position and promising future; he told him, also, however, that he feared that should he teach him as he asked, the dean would forget him afterward. The dean promised that he would never forget the kindness shown him by Illán, and said he would be forever in his debt. When that vow was made, Illán told the dean that the magic arts could be learned only in a retired place, and he took him by the hand and led him into an adjoining room, where there was a large iron ring in the floor. First, however, he instructed his serving-woman that they would have partridge for dinner, though he told her not to put them on the fire until he bade her do so. The two men together lifted the iron ring, and they began to descend a stairway hewn with skill from stone; so far did they descend these stairs that the dean would have sworn they had gone beneath the bed of the Tagus. At the foot of the stairway there was a cell, and then a library, and then a sort of cabinet, or private study, filled with instruments of magic. They thumbed through the books, and as they were doing this, two men entered with a letter for the dean. This letter had been sent him by the bishop, his uncle, and it informed him that his uncle was taken very ill; if the dean wished to see him alive, the letter said, he should return home without delay. This news vexed the dean greatly, in the first instance because of his uncle's illness, but second because he was obliged to interrupt his studies. He resolved to send his regrets, and he sent the letter to the bishop. In three days, several men arrived, dressed in mourning and bringing further letters for the dean, informing him that his uncle the bishop had died, that a successor was being chosen, and that it was hoped that by the grace of God he himself would be elected. These letters also said that he should not trouble himself to come, since it would be much better if he were elected *in absentia.*

Ten days later, two very well-turned-out squires came to where the dean was at his studies; they threw themselves at his feet, kissed his hand, and addressed him as "bishop."

When Illán saw these things, he went with great happiness to the new prelate and told him he thanked God that such good news should make its way to his humble house. Then he asked that one of his sons be given the vacant deanship. The bishop informed him that he had reserved that position for his own brother, but that he was indeed resolved to show Illán's son favor, and that the three of them should set off together for Santiago at once.

The three men set off for Santiago, where they were received with great honors. Six months later, the bishop received messengers from the Pope, who offered him the archbishopric of Tolosa and left to the bishop himself the choice of his successor. When Illán learned this news, he reminded the bishop of his old promise and requested the bishopric for his son. The new archbishop informed Illán that he had reserved the bishopric for his own uncle, his father's brother, but that he was indeed resolved to show Illán's son favor, and that they should set off together for Tolosa at once. Illán had no choice but to agree.

The three men set off for Tolosa, where they were received with great honors and with masses. Two years later, the archbishop received messengers from the Pope, who offered him a cardinal's biretta and left to the archbishop himself the choice of his successor. When Illán learned this news, he reminded the archbishop of his old promise and requested the archbishopric for his son. The new cardinal informed Illán that he had reserved the archbishopric for his own uncle, his mother's brother, but that he was indeed resolved to show Illán's son favor, and he insisted that they set out together for Rome at once. Illán had no choice but to agree.

The three men set out together for Rome, where they were received with great honors and with masses and processions. Four years later the Pope died, and our cardinal was unanimously elected to the Holy See by his brother cardinals. When Illán learned this news, he kissed the feet of His Holiness, reminded him of his old promise, and requested that his son be made cardinal in His Holiness' place. The Pope threatened Illán with imprisonment, telling him that he knew very well he was a wizard who when he had lived in Toledo had been no better than a teacher of magic arts. The miserable Illán said he would return to Spain, then, and begged of the Pope a morsel to eat along the way. The Pope refused. Then it was that Illán (whose face had become young again in a most extraordinary way) said in a firm and steady voice:

"Then I shall have to eat those partridges that I ordered up for tonight's supper."

The serving-woman appeared and Illán told her to put the partridges on the fire. At those words, the Pope found himself in the cell under Illán's house in Toledo, a poor dean of the cathedral of Santiago de Compostela, and so ashamed of his ingratitude that he could find no words by which to beg Illán's forgiveness. Illán declared that the trial to which he'd put the dean sufficed; he refused him his portion of the partridges and went with him to the door, where he wished him a pleasant journey and sent him off most courteously.

(From the *Libro de Patronio* by the Infante don Juan Manuel, who took it in turn from an Arabic volume, *The Forty Mornings and the Forty Nights*)

THE MIRROR OF INK

History records that the cruelest of the governors of the Sudan was Yāqub the Afflicted, who abandoned his nation to the iniquities of Egyptian tax collectors and died in a chamber of the palace on the fourteenth day of the moon of Barmajat in the year 1842. There are those who insinuate that the sorcerer Abderramen al-Masmudī (whose name might be translated "The Servant of Mercy") murdered him with a dagger or with poison, but a natural death is more likely—especially as he was known as "the Afflicted." Nonetheless, Capt. Richard Francis Burton spoke with this sorcerer in 1853, and he reported that the sorcerer told him this story that I shall reproduce here:

. . .

"It is true that I suffered captivity in the fortress of Yakub the Afflicted, due to the conspiracy forged by my brother Ibrahim, with the vain and perfidious aid of the black chieftains of Kordofan, who betrayed him. My brother perished by the sword upon the bloody pelt of justice, but I threw myself at the abominated feet of the Afflicted One and told him I was a sorcerer, and that if he granted me my life I would show him forms and appearances more marvellous than those of the *fanusi jihal,* the magic lantern. The tyrant demanded an immediate proof; I called for a reed pen, a pair of scissors, a large sheet of Venetian paper, an inkhorn, a chafing-dish with live charcoal in it, a few coriander seeds, and an ounce of benzoin. I cut the paper into six strips and wrote charms and invocations upon the first five; on the last I inscribed the following words from the glorious Qur'ān: 'We have removed from thee thy veil, and thy sight is piercing.' Then I drew a magic square in Yakub's right palm and asked him to hold it out to me; into it, I poured a circle of ink. I asked him whether he could see his face in the circle, and he told me that he could see it clearly. I instructed him not to raise his eyes. I put the benzoin and the coriander seeds into the chafing-dish and therein also burned the invocations. I asked the Afflicted One to name the figure that he wished to see. He thought for a moment and told me that he wished to see a wild horse, the most beautiful creature that grazed upon the meadows that lie along the desert. He looked, and he saw first green and peaceful fields and then a horse coming toward him, as graceful as a leopard and with a white star upon its forehead. He then asked me for a herd of such horses, as perfect as the first, and he saw upon the horizon a long cloud of dust, and then the herd. I sensed that my life was safe.

"Hardly had the sun appeared above the horizon when two soldiers entered my cell and conveyed me to the chamber of the Afflicted One, wherein I found awaiting me the incense, the chafing-dish, and the ink. Thus day by day did he make demands upon my skill, and thus day by day did I show to him the appearances of this world. That dead man whom I abominate held within his hand all that dead men have seen and all that living men see: the cities, climes, and kingdoms into which this world is divided, the hidden treasures of its center, the ships that sail its seas, its instruments of war and music and surgery, its graceful women, its fixed stars and the planets, the colors taken up by the infidel to paint his abominable images, its minerals and plants with the secrets and virtues which they hold, the angels of silver whose nutriment is our praise and justification of the Lord, the passing-out of prizes in its schools, the statues of birds and kings that lie within the heart of its pyramids, the shadow thrown by the bull upon whose shoulders this world is upheld, and by the fish below the bull, the deserts of Allah the Merciful. He beheld things impossible to describe, such as streets illuminated by gaslight and such as the whale that dies when it hears man's voice. Once he commanded me to show him the city men call Europe. I showed him the grandest of its streets and I believe that it was in that rushing flood of men, all dressed in black and many wearing spectacles, that he saw for the first time the Masked One.

"From that time forth, that figure, sometimes in the dress of the Sudanese, sometimes in uniform, but ever with a veil upon its face, crept always into the visions. Though it was never absent, we could not surmise who it might be. And yet the appearances within the mirror of ink, at first momentary or unmoving, became now more complex; they would unhesitatingly obey my commands, and the tyrant could clearly follow them. In these occupations, both of us, it is true, sometimes became exhausted. The abominable nature of the scenes was another cause of weariness; there was nothing but tortures, garrotes, mutilations, the pleasures of the executioner and the cruel man.

"Thus did we come to the morning of the fourteenth day of the moon of Barmajat. The circle of ink had been poured into the palm, the benzoin sprinkled into the chafing-dish, the invocations burned. The two of us were alone. The Afflicted One commanded me to show him a just and irrevocable punishment, for that day his heart craved to see a death. I showed him soldiers with tambours, the stretched hide of a calf, the persons fortunate enough to look on, the executioner with the sword of justice. The Afflicted One marvelled to see this, and said to me: *It is Abu Kir, the man that slew thy brother Ibrahim, the man that will close thy life when I am able to command the knowledge to convoke these figures without thy aid.* He asked me to bring forth the condemned man, yet when he was brought forth the Afflicted One grew still, because it was the enigmatic man that kept the white cloth always before his visage. The Afflicted One commanded me that before the man was killed, his mask should be stripped from him. I threw myself at his feet and said: *O king of time and substance and peerless essence of the century, this figure is not like the others, for we know not his name nor that of his fathers nor that of the city which is his homeland. Therefore, O king, I dare not touch him, for fear of committing a sin for which I shall be held accountable.* The Afflicted One laughed and swore that he himself would bear the responsibility for the sin, if sin it was. He swore this by his sword and by the Qur'ān. Then it was that I commanded that the condemned man be stripped naked and bound to the stretched hide of the calf and his mask removed from him. Those things were accomplished; the horrified eyes of Yakub at last saw the visage—which was his own face. In fear and madness, he hid his eyes. I held in my firm right hand his trembling hand and commanded him to look upon the ceremony of his death. He was possessed by the mirror; he did not even try to turn his eyes aside, or to spill out the ink. When in the vision the sword fell upon the guilty neck, he moaned and cried out in a voice that inspired no pity in me, and fell to the floor, dead.

"Glory to Him Who does not die, and Who holds within His hand the two keys, of infinite Pardon and infinite Punishment."

(From Richard Francis Burton, *The Lake Regions of Equatorial Africa*)*

MAHOMED'S DOUBLE

Since the idea of Mahomed is always connected with religion in the minds of Mahomedans, therefore in the spiritual world some Mahomed or other is always placed in their view. It is not Mahomed himself, who wrote the Koran, but some other who fills his place; nor is it always the same person, but he is changed according to circumstances. A native of Saxony, who was taken prisoner by the Algerines, and turned Mahomedan, once acted in this character. He having been a Christian, was led to speak with them of the

Lord Jesus, affirming that he was not the son of Joseph, but the Son of God himself. This Mahomed was afterwards replaced by others. In the place where that representative Mahomed has his station, a fire, like a small torch, appears, in order that he may be distinguished; but it is visible only to Mahomedans.

The real Mahomed, who wrote the Koran, is not at this day to be seen among them. I have been informed that at first he was appointed to preside over them; but being desirous to rule over all the concerns of their religion as a god, he was removed from his station, and was sent down to one on the right side near the south. A certain society of Mahomedans was once instigated by some evil spirits to acknowledge Mahomed as a god, and in order to appease the sedition Mahomed was raised up from the earth or region beneath, and produced to their view; and on this occasion I also saw him. He appeared like corporeal spirits, who have no interior perception. His face was of a hue approaching to black; and I heard him utter these words, "I am your Mahomed," and presently he seemed to sink down again.

(From Emanuel Swedenborg, *Vera Christiana Religio* [1771])*

Index of Sources

The Cruel Redeemer Lazarus Morell
Mark Twain, *Life on the Mississippi.* New York, 1883.
Bernard De Voto, *Mark Twain's America.* Boston, 1932.

The Improbable Impostor Tom Castro
Philip Gosse, *The History of Piracy.* London, Cambridge, 1911.*

The Widow Ching—Pirate
Philip Gosse, *The History of Piracy.* London, Cambridge, 1911.

Monk Eastman, Purveyor of Iniquities
Herbert Asbury, *The Gangs of New York.* New York, 1927.

The Disinterested Killer Bill Harrigan
Frederick Watson, *A Century of Gunmen.* London, 1931.
Walter Noble Burns, *The Saga of Billy the Kid.* New York, 1925.*

The Uncivil Teacher of Court Etiquette Kôtsuké no Suké
A. B. Mitford, *Tales of Old Japan.* London, 1912.

Hakim, the Masked Dyer of Merv
Sir Percy Sykes, *A History of Persia.* London, 1915.
———, *Die Vernichtung der Rose,* nach dem arabischen Urtext übertragen von Alexander Schulz. Leipzig, 1927.

Fictions*

(1944)

For Esther Zemborain de Torres

THE GARDEN OF FORKING PATHS

(1941)

Foreword

The eight stories* in this book require no great elucidation. The eighth ("The Garden of Forking Paths") is a detective story; its readers will witness the commission and all the preliminaries of a crime whose purpose will not be kept from them but which they will not understand, I think, until the final paragraph. The others are tales of fantasy; one of them—"The Lottery in Babylon"—is not wholly innocent of symbolism. I am not the first author of the story called "The Library of Babel"; those curious as to its history and prehistory may consult the appropriate page of *Sur*,* No. 59, which records the heterogeneous names of Leucippus and Lasswitz, Lewis Carroll and Aristotle. In "The Circular Ruins," all is unreal; in "Pierre Menard, Author of the *Quixote*," the unreality lies in the fate the story's protagonist imposes upon himself. The catalog of writings I have ascribed to him is not terribly amusing, but it is not arbitrary, either; it is a diagram of his mental history. . . .

It is a laborious madness and an impoverishing one, the madness of composing vast books—setting out in five hundred pages an idea that can be perfectly related orally in five minutes. The better way to go about it is to pretend that those books already exist, and offer a summary, a commentary on them. That was Carlyle's procedure in *Sartor Resartus*, Butler's in *The Fair Haven*—though those works suffer under the imperfection that they themselves are books, and not a whit less tautological than the others. A more reasonable, more inept, and more lazy man, I have chosen to write notes on *imaginary* books. Those notes are "Tlön, Uqbar, Orbis Tertius" and "A Survey of the Works of Herbert Quain."

J.L.B.

Tlön, Uqbar, Orbis Tertius

I

I owe the discovery of Uqbar to the conjunction of a mirror and an encyclopedia. The mirror troubled the far end of a hallway in a large country house on Calle Gaona, in Ramos Mejía*; the encyclopedia is misleadingly titled *The Anglo-American Cyclopaedia* (New York, 1917), and is a literal (though also laggardly) reprint of the 1902 *Encyclopædia Britannica.* The event took place about five years ago.

Bioy Casares* had come to dinner at my house that evening, and we had lost all track of time in a vast debate over the way one might go about composing a first-person novel whose narrator would omit or distort things and engage in all sorts of contradictions, so that a few of the book's readers—a *very* few—might divine the horrifying or banal truth. Down at that far end of the hallway, the mirror hovered, shadowing us. We discovered (very late at night such a discovery is inevitable) that there is something monstrous about mirrors. That was when Bioy remembered a saying by one of the heresiarchs of Uqbar: *Mirrors and copulation are abominable, for they multiply the number of mankind.* I asked him where he'd come across that memorable epigram, and he told me it was recorded in *The Anglo-American Cyclopaedia*, in its article on Uqbar.

The big old house (we had taken it furnished) possessed a copy of that work. On the last pages of Volume XLVI we found an article on Uppsala; on the first of Volume XLVII, "Ural-Altaic Languages"—not a word on Uqbar. Bioy, somewhat bewildered, consulted the volumes of the Index. He tried every possible spelling: Ukbar, Ucbar, Ookbar, Oukbahr . . . all in vain. Before he left, he told me it was a region in Iraq or Asia Minor. I confess I nodded a bit uncomfortably; I surmised that that undocumented country and its anonymous heresiarch were a fiction that Bioy had invented on the spur of the moment, out of modesty, in order to justify a fine-sounding epigram. A sterile search through one of the atlases of Justus Perthes reinforced my doubt.

The next day, Bioy called me from Buenos Aires. He told me he had the article on Uqbar right in front of him—in Volume XLVI* of the encyclopedia. The heresiarch's name wasn't given, but the entry did report his doctrine, formulated in words almost identical to those Bioy had quoted, though from a literary point of view perhaps inferior. Bioy had remembered its being "copulation and mirrors are abominable," while the text of the encyclopedia ran *For one of those gnostics, the visible universe was an illusion or, more precisely, a sophism. Mirrors and fatherhood are hateful because they multiply and proclaim it.* I told Bioy, quite truthfully, that I'd like to see that article. A few days later he brought it to me—which surprised me, because the scrupulous cartographic indices of Ritter's *Erdkunde* evinced complete and total ignorance of the existence of the name Uqbar.

The volume Bioy brought was indeed Volume XLVI of the *Anglo-American Cyclopaedia.* On both the false cover and spine, the alphabetical key to the volume's contents (Tor–Upps) was the same as ours, but instead of 917 pages, Bioy's volume had 921. Those four additional pages held the article on Uqbar—an article not contemplated (as the reader will have noted) by the alphabetical key. We later compared the two volumes and found that there was no further difference between them. Both (as I believe I have said) are reprints of the tenth edition of the *Encyclopædia Britannica.* Bioy had purchased his copy at one of his many sales.

We read the article with some care. The passage that Bioy had recalled was perhaps the only one that might raise a reader's eyebrow; the rest seemed quite plausible, very much in keeping with the general tone of the work, even (naturally) somewhat boring. Rereading it, however, we discovered that the rigorous writing was underlain by a basic vagueness. Of the fourteen names that figured in the section on geography, we recognized only three (Khorasan, Armenia, Erzerum), all interpolated into the text ambiguously. Of the historical names, we recognized only one: the impostor-wizard Smerdis, and he was invoked, really, as a metaphor. The article seemed to define the borders of Uqbar, but its nebulous points of reference were rivers and craters and mountain chains of the region itself. We read, for example, that the Axa delta and the lowlands of Tsai Khaldun mark the southern boundary, and that wild horses breed on the islands of the delta.

That was at the top of page 918. In the section on Uqbar's history (p. 920), we learned that religious persecutions in the thirteenth century had forced the orthodox to seek refuge on those same islands, where their obelisks are still standing and their stone mirrors are occasionally unearthed. The section titled "Language and Literature" was brief. One memorable feature: the article said that the literature of Uqbar was a literature of fantasy, and that its epics and legends never referred to reality but rather to the two imaginary realms of Mle'khnas and Tlön. . . . The bibliography listed four volumes we have yet to find, though the third—Silas Haslam's *History of the Land Called Uqbar* (1874)—does figure in the catalogs published by Bernard Quaritch, Bookseller.[1] The first, *Lesbare und lesenswerthe Bemerkungen über das Land Ukkbar in Klein-Asien*, published in 1641, is the work of one Johannes Valentinus Andreä. That fact is significant: two or three years afterward, I came upon that name in the unexpected pages of De Quincey (*Writings*, Vol. XIII*), where I learned that it belonged to a German theologian who in the early seventeenth century described an imaginary community, the Rosy Cross—which other men later founded, in imitation of his foredescription.

That night, Bioy and I paid a visit to the National Library, where we pored in vain through atlases, catalogs, the yearly indices published by geographical societies, the memoirs of travelers and historians—no one had ever been in Uqbar. Nor did the general index in Bioy's copy of the encyclopedia contain that name. The next day, Carlos Mastronardi* (whom I had told about all this) spotted the black-and-gold spines of the *Anglo-American Cyclopaedia* in a bookshop at the corner of Corrientes and Talcahuano. . . . He went in and consulted Volume XLVI. Naturally, he found not the slightest mention of Uqbar.

II

Some limited and waning memory of Herbert Ashe, an engineer for the Southern Railway Line, still lingers in the hotel at Adrogué, among the effusive honeysuckle vines and in the illusory depths of the mirrors. In life, Ashe was afflicted with unreality, as so many Englishmen are; in death, he is not even the ghost he was in life. He was tall and phlegmatic and his weary rectangular beard had once been red. I understand that he was a widower, and without issue. Every few years he would go back to England, to make

[1]Haslam was also the author of *A General History of Labyrinths.*

his visit (I am judging from some photographs he showed us) to a sundial and a stand of oak trees. My father had forged one of those close English friendships with him (the first adjective is perhaps excessive) that begin by excluding confidences and soon eliminate conversation. They would exchange books and newspapers; they would wage taciturn battle at chess. . . . I recall Ashe on the hotel veranda, holding a book of mathematics, looking up sometimes at the irrecoverable colors of the sky. One evening, we spoke about the duodecimal number system, in which twelve is written 10. Ashe said that by coincidence he was just then transposing some duodecimal table or other to sexagesimal (in which sixty is written 10). He added that he'd been commissioned to perform that task by a Norwegian man . . . in Rio Grande do Sul. Ashe and I had known each other for eight years, and he had never mentioned a stay in Brazil. We spoke of the bucolic rural life, of *capangas,** of the Brazilian etymology of the word "*gaucho*" (which some older folk in Uruguay still pronounce as *ga-úcho*), and nothing more was said—God forgive me—of duodecimals. In September of 1937 (my family and I were no longer at the hotel), Herbert Ashe died of a ruptured aneurysm. A few days before his death, he had received a sealed, certified package from Brazil containing a book printed in octavo major. Ashe left it in the bar, where, months later, I found it. I began to leaf through it and suddenly I experienced a slight, astonished sense of dizziness that I shall not describe, since this is the story not of my emotions but of Uqbar and Tlön and Orbis Tertius. (On one particular Islamic night, which is called the Night of Nights, the secret portals of the heavens open wide and the water in the water jars is sweeter than on other nights; if those gates had opened as I sat there, I would not have felt what I was feeling that evening.) The book was written in English, and it consisted of 1001 pages. On the leather-bound volume's yellow spine I read these curious words, which were repeated on the false cover: *A First Encyclopædia of Tlön. Vol. XI. Hlaer to Jangr*. There was no date or place of publication. On the first page and again on the onionskin page that covered one of the color illustrations there was stamped a blue oval with this inscription: *Orbis Tertius*. Two years earlier, I had discovered in one of the volumes of a certain pirated encyclopedia a brief description of a false country; now fate had set before me something much more precious and painstaking. I now held in my hands a vast and systematic fragment of the entire history of an unknown planet, with its architectures and its playing cards, the horror of its mythologies and the murmur of its tongues, its emperors and its seas, its minerals and its birds and fishes, its algebra and its fire, its theological and metaphysical controversies—all joined, articulated, coherent, and with no visible doctrinal purpose or hint of parody.

In the "Volume Eleven" of which I speak, there are allusions to later and earlier volumes. Néstor Ibarra,* in a now-classic article in the *N.R.F.*, denied that such companion volumes exist; Ezequiel Martínez Estrada* and Drieu La Rochelle* have rebutted that doubt, perhaps victoriously. The fact is, the most diligent searches have so far proven futile. In vain have we ransacked the libraries of the two Americas and Europe. Alfonso Reyes,* weary of those "subordinate drudgeries of a detective nature," has proposed that between us, we undertake to *reconstruct* the many massive volumes that are missing: *ex ungue leonem.* He figures, half-seriously, half in jest, that a generation of Tlönists would suffice. That bold estimate takes us back to the initial problem: Who, singular or plural, invented Tlön? The plural is, I suppose, inevitable, since the hypothesis of a single inventor—some infinite Leibniz working in obscurity and self-effacement—has been unanimously discarded. It is conjectured that this "brave new world" is the work of a secret society of astronomers, biologists, engineers, metaphysicians, poets, chemists, algebrists, moralists, painters, geometers, . . . , guided and directed by some shadowy man of genius. There are many men adept in those diverse disciplines, but few capable of imagination—fewer still capable of subordinating imagination to a rigorous and systematic plan. The plan is so vast that the contribution of each writer is infinitesimal.

At first it was thought that Tlön was a mere chaos, an irresponsible act of imaginative license; today we know that it is a cosmos, and that the innermost laws that govern it have been formulated, however provisionally so. Let it suffice to remind the reader that the apparent contradictions of Volume Eleven are the foundation stone of the proof that the other volumes do in fact exist: the order that has been observed in it is just that lucid, just that fitting. Popular magazines have trumpeted, with pardonable excess, the zoology and topography of Tlön. In my view, its transparent tigers and towers of blood do not perhaps merit the constant attention of *all* mankind, but I might be so bold as to beg a few moments to outline its conception of the universe.

Hume declared for all time that while Berkeley's arguments admit not the slightest refutation, they inspire not the slightest conviction. That pronouncement is entirely true with respect to the earth, entirely false with respect to Tlön. The nations of that planet are, congenitally, idealistic. Their language and those things derived from their language—religion, literature, metaphysics—presuppose idealism. For the people of Tlön, the world is not an amalgam of *objects* in space; it is a heterogeneous series of independent *acts*—the world is successive, temporal, but not spatial. There are no nouns in the conjectural *Ursprache* of Tlön, from which its "present-day" languages and dialects derive: there are impersonal verbs, modified by monosyllabic suffixes (or prefixes) functioning as adverbs. For example, there is no noun that corresponds to our word "moon," but there is a verb which in English would be "to moonate" or "to enmoon." "The moon rose above the river" is *"hlör u fang axaxaxas mlö,"* or, as Xul Solar* succinctly translates: *Upward, behind the onstreaming it mooned.*

That principle applies to the languages of the southern hemisphere. In the northern hemisphere (about whose *Ursprache* Volume Eleven contains very little information), the primary unit is not the verb but the monosyllabic adjective. Nouns are formed by stringing together adjectives. One does not say "moon"; one says "aerial-bright above dark-round" or "soft-amberish-celestial" or any other string. In this case, the complex of adjectives corresponds to a real object, but that is purely fortuitous. The literature of the northern hemisphere (as in Meinong's subsisting world) is filled with ideal objects, called forth and dissolved in an instant, as the poetry requires. Sometimes mere simultaneity creates them. There are things composed of two terms, one visual and the other auditory: the color of the rising sun and the distant caw of a bird. There are things composed of many: the sun and water against the swimmer's breast, the vague shimmering pink one sees when one's eyes are closed, the sensation of being swept along by a river and also by Morpheus. These objects of the second degree may be combined with others; the process, using certain abbreviations, is virtually infinite. There are famous poems composed of a single enormous word; this word is a "poetic object" created by the poet. The fact that no one believes in the reality expressed by these nouns means, paradoxically, that there is no limit to their number. The languages of Tlön's northern hemisphere possess all the nouns of the Indo-European languages—and many, many more.

It is no exaggeration to say that the classical culture of Tlön is composed of a single discipline—psychology—to which all others are subordinate. I have said that the people of that planet conceive the universe as a series of mental processes that occur not in space but rather successively, in time. Spinoza endows his inexhaustible deity with the attributes of spatial extension and of thought; no one in Tlön would understand the juxtaposition of the first, which is typical only of certain states, and the second—which is a perfect synonym for the cosmos. Or to put it another way: space is not conceived as having duration in time. The perception of a cloud of smoke on the horizon and then the countryside on fire and then the half-extinguished cigarette that produced the scorched earth is considered an example of the association of ideas.

This thoroughgoing monism, or idealism, renders science null. To explain (or pass judgment on) an event is to link it to another; on Tlön, that joining-together is a posterior state of the *subject,* and can neither affect nor illuminate the prior state. Every mental state is irreducible: the simple act of giving it a name—i.e., of classifying it—introduces a distortion, a "slant" or "bias." One might well deduce, therefore, that on Tlön there are no sciences—or even any "systems of thought." The paradoxical truth is that systems of thought do exist, almost countless numbers of them. Philosophies are much like the nouns of the northern hemisphere; the fact that every philosophy is by definition a dialectical game, a *Philosophie des Als Ob,* has allowed them to proliferate. There are systems upon systems that are incredible but possessed of a pleasing architecture or a certain agreeable sensationalism. The metaphysicians of Tlön seek not truth, or even plausibility—they seek to amaze, astound. In their view, metaphysics is a branch of the literature of fantasy. They know that a system is naught but the subordination of all the aspects of the universe to one of those aspects—*any* one of them. Even the phrase "all the aspects" should be avoided, because it implies the impossible addition of the present instant and all those instants that went before. Nor is the plural "those instants that went before" legitimate, for it implies another impossible operation. . . . One of the schools of philosophy on Tlön goes so far as to deny the existence of time; it argues that the present is undefined and indefinite, the future has no reality except as present hope, and the past has no reality except as present recollection.[2] Another school posits that all time has already passed, so that our life is but the crepuscular memory, or crepuscular reflection, doubtlessly distorted and mutilated, of an irrecoverable process. Yet another claims that the history of the universe—and in it, our lives and every faintest detail of our lives—is the handwriting of a subordinate god trying to communicate with a demon. Another, that the universe might be compared to those cryptograms in which not all the symbols count, and only what happens every three hundred nights is actually real. Another, that while we sleep here, we are awake somewhere else, so that every man is in fact two men.

[2]Russell (*The Analysis of Mind* [1921], p. 159) posits that the world was created only moments ago, filled with human beings who "remember" an illusory past.

Of all the doctrines of Tlön, none has caused more uproar than materialism. Some thinkers have formulated this philosophy (generally with less clarity than zeal) as though putting forth a paradox. In order to make this inconceivable thesis more easily understood, an eleventh-century heresiarch[3] conceived the sophism of the nine copper coins, a paradox as scandalously famous on Tlön as the Eleatic aporiae to ourselves. There are many versions of that "specious argument," with varying numbers of coins and discoveries; the following is the most common:

> *On Tuesday, X is walking along a deserted road and loses nine copper coins. On Thursday, Y finds four coins in the road, their luster somewhat dimmed by Wednesday's rain. On Friday, Z discovers three coins in the road. Friday morning X finds two coins on the veranda of his house.*

From this story the heresiarch wished to deduce the reality—i.e., the continuity in time—of those nine recovered coins. "It is absurd," he said, "to imagine that four of the coins did not exist from Tuesday to Thursday, three from Tuesday to Friday afternoon, two from Tuesday to Friday morning. It is logical to think that they in fact *did* exist—albeit in some secret way that we are forbidden to understand—at every moment of those three periods of time."

The language of Tlön resisted formulating this paradox; most people did not understand it. The "common sense" school at first simply denied the anecdote's veracity. They claimed it was a verbal fallacy based on the reckless employment of two neologisms, words unauthorized by standard usage and foreign to all rigorous thought: the two verbs "find" and "lose," which, since they presuppose the identity of the nine first coins and the nine latter ones, entail a *petitio principii.* These critics reminded their listeners that all nouns *(man, coin, Thursday, Wednesday, rain)* have only metaphoric value. They denounced the misleading detail that "[the coins'] luster [was] somewhat dimmed by Wednesday's rain" as presupposing what it attempted to prove: the continuing existence of the four coins from Tuesday to Thursday. They explained that "equality" is one thing and "identity" another, and they formulated a sort of *reductio ad absurdum*—the hypothetical case of nine men who on nine successive nights experience a sharp pain. Would it not be absurd, they asked, to pretend that the men had suffered

[3]A "century," in keeping with the duodecimal system in use on Tlön, is a period of 144 years.

one and the same pain?[4] They claimed that the heresiarch was motivated by the blasphemous desire to attribute the divine category *Being* to a handful of mere coins, and that he sometimes denied plurality and sometimes did not. They argued: If equality entailed identity, one would have to admit that the nine coins were a single coin.

Incredibly, those refutations did not put an end to the matter. A hundred years after the problem had first been posed, a thinker no less brilliant than the heresiarch, but of the orthodox tradition, formulated a most daring hypothesis. His happy conjecture was that there is but a single subject; that indivisible subject is every being in the universe, and the beings of the universe are the organs and masks of the deity. X is Y and is *also* Z. Z discovers three coins, then, because he remembers that X lost them; X finds two coins on the veranda of his house because he remembers that the others have been found. . . . Volume Eleven suggests that this idealistic pantheism triumphed over all other schools of thought for three primary reasons: first, because it repudiated solipsism; second, because it left intact the psychological foundation of the sciences; and third, because it preserved the possibility of religion. Schopenhauer (passionate yet lucid Schopenhauer) formulates a very similar doctrine in the first volume of his *Parerga und Paralipomena.*

Tlön's geometry is made up of two rather distinct disciplines—visual geometry and tactile geometry. Tactile geometry corresponds to our own, and is subordinate to the visual. Visual geometry is based on the surface, not the point; it has no parallel lines, and it claims that as one's body moves through space, it modifies the shapes that surround it. The basis of Tlön's arithmetic is the notion of indefinite numbers; it stresses the importance of the concepts "greater than" and "less than," which our own mathematicians represent with the symbols $>$ and $<$. The people of Tlön are taught that the act of counting modifies the amount counted, turning indefinites into definites. The fact that several persons counting the same quantity come to the same result is for the psychologists of Tlön an example of the association of ideas or of memorization. —We must always remember that on Tlön, the subject of knowledge is one and eternal.

Within the sphere of literature, too, the idea of the single subject is all-powerful. Books are rarely signed, nor does the concept of plagiarism exist:

[4]Today, one of Tlön's religions contends, platonically, that a certain pain, a certain greenish-yellow color, a certain temperature, and a certain sound are all the same, single reality. All men, in the dizzying instant of copulation, are the same man. All men who speak a line of Shakespeare *are* William Shakespeare.

It has been decided that all books are the work of a single author who is timeless and anonymous. Literary criticism often invents authors: It will take two dissimilar works—the *Tao Te Ching* and the *1001 Nights*, for instance—attribute them to a single author, and then in all good conscience determine the psychology of that most interesting *homme de lettres*. . . .

Their books are also different from our own. Their fiction has but a single plot, with every imaginable permutation. Their works of a philosophical nature invariably contain both the thesis and the antithesis, the rigorous *pro* and *contra* of every argument. A book that does not contain its counterbook is considered incomplete.

Century upon century of idealism could hardly have failed to influence reality. In the most ancient regions of Tlön one may, not infrequently, observe the duplication of lost objects: Two persons are looking for a pencil; the first person finds it, but says nothing; the second finds a second pencil, no less real, but more in keeping with his expectations. These secondary objects are called *hrönir,* and they are, though awkwardly so, slightly longer. Until recently, *hrönir* were the coincidental offspring of distraction and forgetfulness. It is hard to believe that they have been systematically produced for only about a hundred years, but that is what Volume Eleven tells us. The first attempts were unsuccessful, but the *modus operandi* is worth recalling: The warden of one of the state prisons informed his prisoners that there were certain tombs in the ancient bed of a nearby river, and he promised that anyone who brought in an important find would be set free. For months before the excavation, the inmates were shown photographs of what they were going to discover. That first attempt proved that hope and greed can be inhibiting; after a week's work with pick and shovel, the only *hrön* unearthed was a rusty wheel, dated some time *later* than the date of the experiment. The experiment was kept secret, but was repeated afterward at four high schools. In three of them, the failure was virtually complete; in the fourth (where the principal happened to die during the early excavations), the students unearthed—or produced—a gold mask, an archaic sword, two or three clay amphorae, and the verdigris'd and mutilated torso of a king with an inscription on the chest that has yet to be deciphered. Thus it was discovered that no witnesses who were aware of the experimental nature of the search could be allowed near the site. . . . Group research projects produce conflicting finds; now individual, virtually spur-of-the-moment projects are preferred. The systematic production of *hrönir* (says Volume Eleven) has been of invaluable aid to archæologists, making it possible not only to interrogate but even to modify the past, which is now no less plastic, no less malleable than the future. A curious bit of information: *hrönir* of the second and third remove—*hrönir* derived from another *hrön*, and *hrönir* derived from the *hrön* of a *hrön*—exaggerate the aberrations of the first; those of the fifth remove are almost identical; those of the ninth can be confused with those of the second; and those of the eleventh remove exhibit a purity of line that even the originals do not exhibit. The process is periodic: The *hrönir* of the twelfth remove begin to degenerate. Sometimes stranger and purer than any *hrön* is the *ur*—the thing produced by suggestion, the object brought forth by hope. The magnificent gold mask I mentioned is a distinguished example.

Things duplicate themselves on Tlön; they also tend to grow vague or "sketchy," and to lose detail when they begin to be forgotten. The classic example is the doorway that continued to exist so long as a certain beggar frequented it, but which was lost to sight when he died. Sometimes a few birds, a horse, have saved the ruins of an amphitheater.

Salto Oriental, 1940

POSTSCRIPT—1947

I reproduce the article above exactly as it appeared in the *Anthology of Fantastic Literature* (1940), the only changes being editorial cuts of one or another metaphor and a tongue-in-cheek sort of summary that would now be considered flippant. So many things have happened since 1940. . . . Allow me to recall some of them:

In March of 1941, a handwritten letter from Gunnar Erfjord was discovered in a book by Hinton that had belonged to Herbert Ashe. The envelope was postmarked Ouro Preto; the mystery of Tlön was fully elucidated by the letter. It confirmed Martínez Estrada's hypothesis: The splendid story had begun sometime in the early seventeenth century, one night in Lucerne or London. A secret benevolent society (which numbered among its members Dalgarno and, later, George Berkeley) was born; its mission: to invent a country. In its vague initial program, there figured "hermetic studies," philanthropy, and the Kabbalah. (The curious book by Valentinus Andreä dates from that early period.) After several years of confabulations and premature collaborative drafts, the members of the society realized that one generation would not suffice for creating and giving full expression to a country. They decided that each of the masters that belonged to the society would select a disciple to carry on the work. That hereditary arrangement was followed;

after an interim of two hundred years, the persecuted fraternity turned up again in the New World. In 1824, in Memphis, Tennessee, one of the members had a conversation with the reclusive millionaire Ezra Buckley. Buckley, somewhat contemptuously, let the man talk—and then laughed at the modesty of the project. He told the man that in America it was nonsense to invent a country—what they ought to do was invent a planet. To that giant of an idea he added another, the brainchild of his nihilism[5]: The enormous enterprise must be kept secret. At that time the twenty volumes of the *Encyclopædia Britannica* were all the rage; Buckley suggested a systematic encyclopedia of the illusory planet. He would bequeath to them his gold-veined mountains, his navigable rivers, his prairies thundering with bulls and buffalo, his Negroes, his brothels, and his dollars, he said, under one condition: "The work shall make no pact with the impostor Jesus Christ." Buckley did not believe in God, yet he wanted to prove to the nonexistent God that mortals could conceive and shape a world. Buckley was poisoned in Baton Rouge in 1828; in 1914 the society sent its members (now numbering three hundred) the final volume of the *First Encyclopædia of Tlön*. It was published secretly: the forty volumes that made up the work (the grandest work of letters ever undertaken by humankind) were to be the basis for another, yet more painstaking work, to be written this time not in English but in one of the languages of Tlön. That survey of an illusory world was tentatively titled *Orbis Tertius*, and one of its modest demiurges was Herbert Ashe—whether as agent or colleague of Gunnar Erfjord, I cannot say. His receipt of a copy of Volume Eleven seems to favor the second possibility. But what about the others? In 1942, the plot thickened. I recall with singular clarity one of the first events that occurred, something of whose premonitory nature I believe I sensed even then. It took place in an apartment on Laprida, across the street from a high, bright balcony that faced the setting sun. Princess Faucigny Lucinge had received from Poitiers a crate containing her silver table service. From the vast innards of a packing case emblazoned with international customs stamps she removed, one by one, the fine unmoving things: plate from Utrecht and Paris chased with hard heraldic fauna, . . . , a samovar. Among the pieces, trembling softly but perceptibly, like a sleeping bird, there throbbed, mysteriously, a compass. The princess did not recognize it. Its blue needle yearned toward magnetic north; its metal casing was concave; the letters on its dial belonged to one of the

[5]Buckley was a freethinker, a fatalist, and a defender of slavery.

alphabets of Tlön. That was the first intrusion of the fantastic world of Tlön into the real world.

An unsettling coincidence made me a witness to the second intrusion as well. This event took place some months later, in a sort of a country general-store-and-bar owned by a Brazilian man in the Cuchilla Negra. Amorim* and I were returning from Sant'Anna. There was a freshet on the Tacuarembó; as there was no way to cross, we were forced to try (to try to endure, that is) the rudimentary hospitality at hand. The storekeeper set up some creaking cots for us in a large storeroom clumsy with barrels and stacks of leather. We lay down, but we were kept awake until almost dawn by the drunkenness of an unseen neighbor, who swung between indecipherable streams of abuse and loudly sung snatches of *milongas*—or snatches of the same *milonga*, actually. As one can imagine, we attributed the man's insistent carrying-on to the storekeeper's fiery rotgut. . . . By shortly after daybreak, the man was dead in the hallway. The hoarseness of his voice had misled us—he was a young man. In his delirium, several coins had slipped from his wide gaucho belt, as had a gleaming metal cone about a die's width in diameter. A little boy tried to pick the cone-shaped object up, but in vain; a full-grown man could hardly do it. I held it for a few minutes in the palm of my hand; I recall that its weight was unbearable, and that even after someone took it from me, the sensation of terrible heaviness endured. I also recall the neat circle it engraved in my flesh. That evidence of a very small yet extremely heavy object left an unpleasant aftertaste of fear and revulsion. A *paisano* suggested that we throw it in the swollen river. Amorim purchased it for a few pesos. No one knew anything about the dead man, except that "he came from the border." Those small, incredibly heavy cones (made of a metal not of this world) are an image of the deity in certain Tlönian religions.

Here I end the personal portion of my narration. The rest lies in every reader's memory (if not his hope or fear). Let it suffice to recall, or mention, the subsequent events, with a simple brevity of words which the general public's concave memory will enrich or expand:

In 1944, an investigator from *The Nashville American* unearthed the forty volumes of *The First Encyclopædia of Tlön* in a Memphis library. To this day there is some disagreement as to whether that discovery was accidental or consented to and guided by the directors of the still-nebulous *Orbis Tertius*; the second supposition is entirely plausible. Some of the unbelievable features of Volume Eleven (the multiplication of *hrönir*, for example) have been eliminated or muted in the Memphis copy. It seems reasonable to suppose that the cuts obey the intent to set forth a world that is not *too* incompatible with the real world. The spread of Tlönian objects through various countries would complement that plan. . . .[6] At any rate, the international press made a great hue and cry about this "find." Handbooks, anthologies, surveys, "literal translations," authorized and pirated reprints of Mankind's Greatest Masterpiece filled the world, and still do. Almost immediately, reality "caved in" at more than one point. The truth is, it wanted to cave in. Ten years ago, any symmetry, any system with an appearance of order—dialectical materialism, anti-Semitism, Nazism—could spellbind and hypnotize mankind. How could the world not fall under the sway of Tlön, how could it not yield to the vast and minutely detailed evidence of an ordered planet? It would be futile to reply that reality is also orderly. Perhaps it is, but orderly in accordance with divine laws (read: "inhuman laws") that we can never quite manage to penetrate. Tlön may well be a labyrinth, but it is a labyrinth forged by men, a labyrinth destined to be deciphered by men.

Contact with Tlön, the *habit* of Tlön, has disintegrated this world. Spellbound by Tlön's rigor, humanity has forgotten, and continues to forget, that it is the rigor of chess masters, not of angels. Already Tlön's (conjectural) "primitive language" has filtered into our schools; already the teaching of Tlön's harmonious history (filled with moving episodes) has obliterated the history that governed my own childhood; already a fictitious past has supplanted in men's memories that other past, of which we now know nothing certain—not even that it is false. Numismatics, pharmacology, and archæology have been reformed. I understand that biology and mathematics are also awaiting their next avatar. . . . A scattered dynasty of recluses has changed the face of the earth—and their work continues. If my projections are correct, a hundred years from now someone will discover the hundred volumes of *The Second Encyclopædia of Tlön.*

At that, French and English and mere Spanish will disappear from the earth. The world will be Tlön. That makes very little difference to me; through my quiet days in this hotel in Adrogué, I go on revising (though I never intend to publish) an indecisive translation in the style of Quevedo of Sir Thomas Browne's *Urne Buriall.*

[6]There is still, of course, the problem of the *material* from which some objects are made.

The Approach to Al-Mu'tasim

Philip Guedalla writes that the novel *The Approach to Al-Mu'tasim*, by the Bombay attorney Mir Bahadur Ali, is "a rather uncomfortable amalgam of one of those Islamic allegorical poems that seldom fail to interest their translator and one of those detective novels that inevitably surpass John H. Watson's and perfect the horror of life in the most irreproachable rooming-houses of Brighton." Earlier, Mr. Cecil Roberts had detected in Bahadur's book "the dual, and implausible, influence of Wilkie Collins and the illustrious twelfth-century Persian poet Farīd al-dīn Aṭṭār"; the none-too-original Guedalla repeats this calm observation, though in choleric accents. In essence, the two critics concur: both point out the detective mechanism of the novel and both speak of its mystical undercurrents. That hybridity may inspire us to imagine some similarity to Chesterton; we shall soon discover that no such similarity exists.

The first edition of *The Approach to Al-Mu'tasim* appeared in Bombay in late 1932. Its paper was virtually newsprint; its cover announced to the buyer that this was "the first detective novel written by a native of Bombay City." Within months, readers had bought out four printings of a thousand copies each. The *Bombay Quarterly Review*, the *Bombay Gazette*, the *Calcutta Review*, the *Hindustan Review* of Allahabad, and the *Calcutta Englishman* rained dithyrambs upon it. It was then that Bahadur published an illustrated edition he titled *The Conversation with the Man Called Al-Mu'tasim* and coyly subtitled *A Game with Shifting Mirrors*. That edition has just been reprinted in London by Victor Gollancz with a foreword by Dorothy L. Sayers, but with the (perhaps merciful) omission of the illustrations. I have that book before me; I have not been able to come upon the first, which I suspect is greatly superior. I am supported in this conclusion by an appendix that details the fundamental difference between the original, 1932, version and the edition of 1934. Before examining the work (and discussing it), I think it would be a good idea to give a brief general outline of the novel.

Its visible protagonist, whose name we are never told, is a law student in Bombay. In the most blasphemous way he has renounced the Islamic faith of his parents, but as the tenth night of the moon of Muharram wanes he finds himself at the center of a riot, a street battle between Muslims and Hindus. It is a night of tambours and invocations; through the inimical multitude, the great paper baldachins of the Muslim procession make their way. A Hindu brick flies from a rooftop nearby; someone buries a dagger in a belly; someone—a Muslim? a Hindu?—dies and is trampled underfoot. Three thousand men do battle—cane against revolver, obscenity against imprecation, God the indivisible against the gods. In a sort of daze, the freethinking law student enters the fray. With desperate hands, he kills (or thinks he has killed) a Hindu. Thundering, horse-borne, half asleep, the Sirkar police intervene with impartial lashes of their crops. Virtually under the hooves of the horses, the student makes his escape, fleeing toward the outermost suburbs of the city. He crosses two railroad tracks, or twice crosses the same track. He scales the wall of an unkempt garden, which has a circular tower toward the rear. A "lean and evil mob of moon-coloured hounds" emerges from the black rosebushes. Fearing for his life, the law student seeks refuge in the tower. He climbs an iron ladder—some rungs are missing—and on the flat roof, which has a pitch-black hole in the center, he comes upon a filthy man squatting in the moonlight, pouring forth a vigorous stream of urine. This man confides to the law student that it is his profession to steal the gold teeth from the cadavers the Parsees bring, swaddled in white, to that tower. He makes several further gruesome remarks and then mentions that it has been fourteen nights since he purified himself with ox dung. He speaks with obvious anger about certain Gujarati horse thieves, "eaters of dog meat and lizard meat—men, in a word, as vile as you and I." The sky is growing light; there is a lowering circle of fat vultures in the air. The law student, exhausted, falls asleep; when he awakens, the sun now high, the thief has disappeared. A couple of cigarettes from Trichinopolis have also disappeared, as have a few silver rupees. In the face of the menace that looms from the previous night, the law student decides to lose himself in India. He reflects that he has shown himself capable of killing an idolater, yet incapable of knowing with any certainty whether the Muslim possesses more of truth than the idolater does. The name Gujarat has remained with him, as has that of a *malka-sansi* (a woman of the caste of thieves) in Palanpur, a woman favored by the imprecations and hatred of the corpse-robber. The law student reasons that the wrath and hatred of a man so thoroughly despicable is the equivalent of a hymn of praise. He resolves, therefore, though with little hope, to find this woman. He performs his prayers, and then he sets out, with sure, slow steps, on the long path. That brings the reader to the end of the second chapter of the book.

It would be impossible to trace the adventures of the remaining nineteen chapters. There is a dizzying pullulation of *dramatis personæ*—not to mention a biography that seems to catalog every motion of the human spirit (from iniquity to mathematical speculation) and a pilgrimage that covers the vast geography of Hindustan. The story begun in Bombay continues in the lowlands of Palanpur, pauses for a night and a day at the stone gate of Bikanir, narrates the death of a blind astrologer in a cesspool in Benares, conspires in the multiform palace at Katmandu, prays and fornicates in the pestilential stench of the Machua bazaar in Calcutta, watches the day being born out of the sea from a scribe's stool in Madras, watches the evening decline into the sea from a balcony in the state of Travancor, gutters and dies in Hindapur, and closes its circle of leagues and years in Bombay again, a few steps from the garden of those "moon-coloured" hounds. The plot itself is this: A man (the unbelieving, fleeing law student we have met) falls among people of the lowest, vilest sort and accommodates himself to them, in a kind of contest of iniquity. Suddenly—with the miraculous shock of Crusoe when he sees that human footprint in the sand—the law student perceives some mitigation of the evil: a moment of tenderness, of exaltation, of silence, in one of the abominable men. "It was as though a more complex interlocutor had spoken." He knows that the wretch with whom he is conversing is incapable of that momentary decency; thus the law student hypothesizes that the vile man before him has reflected a friend, or the friend of a friend. Rethinking the problem, he comes to a mysterious conclusion: *Somewhere in the world there is a man from whom this clarity, this brightness, emanates; somewhere in the world there is a man who is equal to this brightness.* The law student resolves to devote his life to searching out that man.

Thus we begin to see the book's general scheme: The insatiable search for a soul by means of the delicate glimmerings or reflections this soul has left in others—at first, the faint trace of a smile or a word; toward the last, the varied and growing splendors of intelligence, imagination, and goodness. The more closely the men interrogated by the law student have known

Al-Mu'tasim, the greater is their portion of divinity, but the reader knows that they themselves are but mirrors. A technical mathematical formula is applicable here: Bahadur's heavily freighted novel is an ascending progression whose final term is the sensed or foreapprehended "man called Al-Mu'tasim." The person immediately preceding Al-Mu'tasim is a Persian bookseller of great courtesy and felicity; the man preceding the bookseller is a saint. . . . After all those years, the law student comes to a gallery "at the end of which there is a doorway and a tawdry curtain of many beads, and behind that, a glowing light." The law student claps his hands once, twice, and calls out for Al-Mu'tasim. A man's voice—the incredible voice of Al-Mu'tasim—bids the law student enter. The law student draws back the bead curtain and steps into the room. At that point, the novel ends.

I believe I am correct in saying that if an author is to pull off such a plot, he is under two obligations: First, he must invent a variety of prophetic signs; second, he must not allow the hero prefigured by those signs to become a mere phantasm or convention. Bahadur meets the first obligation; I am not sure to what extent he meets the second. In other words: The unheard and unseen Al-Mu'tasim should impress us as being a real person, not some jumble of vapid superlatives. In the 1932 version of the novel, the supernatural notes are few and far between; "the man called Al-Mu'tasim" has his touch of symbolism, but he possesses idiosyncratic personal traits as well. Unfortunately, that commendable literary practice was not to be followed in the second edition. In the 1934 version—the edition I have before me even now—the novel sinks into allegory: Al-Mu'tasim is an emblem of God, and the detailed itineraries of the hero are somehow the progress of the soul in its ascent to mystical plenitude. There are distressing details: A black Jew from Cochin, describing Al-Mu'tasim, says that his skin is dark; a Christian says that he stands upon a tower with his arms outspread; a red lama recalls him as seated "like that image which I carved from yak ghee and worshipped in the monastery at Tashilhumpo." Those declarations are an attempt to suggest a single, unitary God who molds Himself to the dissimilarities of humankind. In my view, that notion is not particularly exciting. I cannot say the same for another idea, however: the idea that the Almighty is also in search of Someone, and that Someone, in search of a yet superior (or perhaps simply necessary, albeit equal) Someone, and so on, to the End—or better yet, the Endlessness—of Time. Or perhaps cyclically. The etymological meaning of "Al-Mu'tasim" (the name of that eighth Abbasid king who won eight battles, engendered eight sons and eight daughters, left eight thousand slaves, and reigned for a period of eight years, eight moons, and eight days) is "He who goes in quest of aid." In the 1932 version of the novel, the fact that the object of the pilgrimage was himself a pilgrim cleverly justified the difficulty of finding Al-Mu'tasim; in the 1934 edition, that fact leads to the extravagant theology I have described. Mir Bahadur Ali, as we have seen, is incapable of resisting that basest of art's temptations: the temptation to be a genius.

I reread what I have just written and I fear I have not made sufficiently explicit the virtues of this book. It has some quite civilized features; for example, that argument in Chapter XIX in which the law student (and the reader) sense that one of the participants in the debate is a friend of Al-Mu'tasim—the man does not rebut another man's sophisms "in order not to gloat at the other man's defeat."

. . .

It is generally understood that a modern-day book may honorably be based upon an older one, especially since, as Dr. Johnson observed, no man likes owing anything to his contemporaries. The repeated but irrelevant points of congruence between Joyce's *Ulysses* and Homer's *Odyssey* continue to attract (though I shall never understand why) the dazzled admiration of critics. The points of congruence between Bahadur's novel and Farīd al-dīn Aṭṭār's classic *Conference of the Birds* meet with the no less mysterious praise of London, and even of Allahabad and Calcutta. There are other debts, as well. One investigator has documented certain analogies between the first scene of the novel and Kipling's story "On the City Wall"; Bahadur acknowledges these echoes, but claims that it would be most unusual if two portraits of the tenth night of Muharram should *not* agree. . . . With greater justice, Eliot recalls that never once in the seventy cantos of Spenser's unfinished allegory *The Faërie Queene* does the heroine Gloriana appear—an omission for which Richard William Church had criticized the work. I myself, in all humility, would point out a distant, possible precursor: the Kabbalist Isaac Luria, who in Jerusalem, in the sixteenth century, revealed that the soul of an ancestor or teacher may enter into the soul of an unhappy or unfortunate man, to comfort or instruct him. That type of metempsychosis is called *ibbûr*.[1]

[1]In the course of this article, I have referred to the *Manṭīq al-ṭaïr*, or *Conference* [perhaps "*Parliament*"] *of the Birds*, by the Persian mystic poet Farīḍ al-dīn Abī Ḥāmid Muḥammad ben Ibrāhīm (known as Aṭṭār, or "perfumer"), who was murdered by the soldiers under Tuluy, the son of Genghis Khan, when Nishapur was sacked. Perhaps I should summarize that poem. One of the splendid feathers of the distant King of the Birds, the Sīmurgh, falls into the center of China; other birds, weary with the

present state of anarchy, resolve to find this king. They know that the name of their king means "thirty birds"; they know that his palace is in the Mountains of Kaf, the mountains that encircle the earth. The birds undertake the almost infinite adventure. They cross seven *wadis* or seven seas; the penultimate of these is called Vertigo; the last, Annihilation. Many of the pilgrims abandon the quest; others perish on the journey. At the end, thirty birds, purified by their travails, come to the mountain on which the Sīmurgh lives, and they look upon their king at last: they see that they are the Sīmurgh and that the Sīmurgh is each, and all, of them. (Plotinus, too, in the *Enneads* [V, 8, 4], remarks upon a paradisal extension of the principle of identity: "Everything in the intelligible heavens is everywhere. Any thing is all things. The sun is all stars, and each star is all stars and the sun.") The *Manṭīq al-ṭaīr* has been translated into French by Garcin de Tassy, into English by Edward FitzGerald; for this note I have consulted Richard Burton's *1001 Nights*, Vol. X, and the Margaret Smith study entitled *The Persian Mystics: Attar* (1932).

The parallels between this poem and Mir Bahadur Ali's novel are not overdone. In Chapter XX, a few words attributed by a Persian bookseller to Al-Mu'tasim are perhaps an expansion of words spoken by the hero; that and other ambiguous similarities may signal the identity of the seeker and the sought; they may also signal that the sought has already influenced the seeker. Another chapter suggests that Al-Mu'tasim is the "Hindu" that the law student thinks he murdered.

Pierre Menard, Author of the *Quixote*

For Silvina Ocampo

The visible *œuvre* left by this novelist can be easily and briefly enumerated; unpardonable, therefore, are the omissions and additions perpetrated by Mme. Henri Bachelier in a deceitful catalog that a certain newspaper, whose Protestant leanings are surely no secret, has been so inconsiderate as to inflict upon that newspaper's deplorable readers—few and Calvinist (if not Masonic and circumcised) though they be. Menard's true friends have greeted that catalog with alarm, and even with a degree of sadness. One might note that only yesterday were we gathered before his marmoreal place of rest, among the dreary cypresses, and already Error is attempting to tarnish his bright Memory. . . . Most decidedly, a brief rectification is imperative.

I am aware that it is easy enough to call my own scant authority into question. I hope, nonetheless, that I shall not be prohibited from mentioning two high testimonials. The baroness de Bacourt (at whose unforgettable *vendredis* I had the honor to meet the mourned-for poet) has been so kind as to approve the lines that follow. Likewise, the countess de Bagnoregio, one of the rarest and most cultured spirits of the principality of Monaco (now of Pittsburgh, Pennsylvania, following her recent marriage to the international philanthropist Simon Kautzsch—a man, it grieves me to say, vilified and slandered by the victims of his disinterested operations), has sacrificed "to truth and to death" (as she herself has phrased it) the noble reserve that is the mark of her distinction, and in an open letter, published in the magazine *Luxe*, bestows upon me her blessing. Those commendations are sufficient, I should think.

I have said that the *visible* product of Menard's pen is easily enumerated. Having examined his personal files with the greatest care, I have established that his body of work consists of the following pieces:

a) a symbolist sonnet that appeared twice (with variants) in the review *La Conque* (in the numbers for March and October, 1899);

b) a monograph on the possibility of constructing a poetic vocabulary from concepts that are neither synonyms nor periphrastic locutions for the concepts that inform common speech, "but are, rather, ideal objects created by convention essentially for the needs of poetry" (Nîmes, 1901);

c) a monograph on "certain connections or affinities" between the philosophies of Descartes, Leibniz, and John Wilkins (Nîmes, 1903);

d) a monograph on Leibniz' *Characteristica universalis* (Nîmes, 1904);

e) a technical article on the possibility of enriching the game of chess by eliminating one of the rook's pawns (Menard proposes, recommends, debates, and finally rejects this innovation);

f) a monograph on Ramon Lull's *Ars magna generalis* (Nîmes, 1906);

g) a translation, with introduction and notes, of Ruy López de Segura's *Libro de la invención liberal y arte del juego del axedrez* (Paris, 1907);

h) drafts of a monograph on George Boole's symbolic logic;

i) a study of the essential metrical rules of French prose, illustrated with examples taken from Saint-Simon (*Revue des langues romanes*, Montpellier, October 1909);

j) a reply to Luc Durtain (who had countered that no such rules existed), illustrated with examples taken from Luc Durtain (*Revue des langues romanes*, Montpellier, December 1909);

k) a manuscript translation of Quevedo's *Aguja de navegar cultos*, titled *La boussole des précieux*;

l) a foreword to the catalog of an exhibit of lithographs by Carolus Hourcade (Nîmes, 1914);

m) a work entitled *Les problèmes d'un problème* (Paris, 1917), which discusses in chronological order the solutions to the famous problem of Achilles and the tortoise (two editions of this work have so far appeared; the second bears an epigraph consisting of Leibniz' advice "*Ne craignez point, monsieur, la tortue,*" and brings up to date the chapters devoted to Russell and Descartes);

n) a dogged analysis of the "syntactical habits" of Toulet (*N.R.F.*, March 1921) (Menard, I recall, affirmed that censure and praise were sentimental operations that bore not the slightest resemblance to criticism);

o) a transposition into alexandrines of Paul Valéry's *Cimetière marin* (*N.R.F.*, January 1928);

p) a diatribe against Paul Valéry, in Jacques Reboul's *Feuilles pour la suppression de la realité* (which diatribe, I might add parenthetically, states the exact reverse of Menard's true opinion of Valéry; Valéry understood this, and the two men's friendship was never imperiled);

q) a "definition" of the countess de Bagnoregio, in the "triumphant volume" (the phrase is that of another contributor, Gabriele d'Annunzio) published each year by that lady to rectify the inevitable biases of the popular press and to present "to the world and all of Italy" a true picture of her person, which was so exposed (by reason of her beauty and her bearing) to erroneous and/or hasty interpretations;

r) a cycle of admirable sonnets dedicated to the baroness de Bacourt (1934);

s) a handwritten list of lines of poetry that owe their excellence to punctuation.[1]

This is the full extent (save for a few vague sonnets of occasion destined for Mme. Henri Bachelier's hospitable, or greedy, *album des souvenirs*) of the *visible* lifework of Pierre Menard, in proper chronological order. I shall turn now to the other, the subterranean, the interminably heroic production—the *œuvre nonpareil*, the *œuvre* that must remain—for such are our human limitations!—unfinished. This work, perhaps the most significant writing of our time, consists of the ninth and thirty-eighth chapters of Part I of *Don Quixote* and a fragment of Chapter XXII. I know that such a claim is on the face of it absurd; justifying that "absurdity" shall be the primary object of this note.[2]

Two texts, of distinctly unequal value, inspired the undertaking. One was that philological fragment by Novalis—number 2005 in the Dresden edition, to be precise—which outlines the notion of *total identification* with a given author. The other was one of those parasitic books that set Christ on a boulevard, Hamlet on La Cannabière, or don Quixote on Wall Street. Like every man of taste, Menard abominated those pointless travesties, which, Menard would say, were good for nothing but occasioning a plebeian delight in anachronism or (worse yet) captivating us with the elementary

[1]Mme. Henri Bachelier also lists a literal translation of Quevedo's literal translation of St. Francis de Sales's *Introduction à la vie dévote*. In Pierre Menard's library there is no trace of such a work. This must be an instance of one of our friend's droll jokes, misheard or misunderstood.

[2]I did, I might say, have the secondary purpose of drawing a small sketch of the figure of Pierre Menard—but how dare I compete with the gilded pages I am told the baroness de Bacourt is even now preparing, or with the delicate sharp *crayon* of Carolus Hourcade?

notion that all times and places are the same, or are different. It might be more interesting, he thought, though of contradictory and superficial execution, to attempt what Daudet had so famously suggested: conjoin in a single figure (Tartarin, say) both the Ingenious Gentleman don Quixote and his squire. . . .

Those who have insinuated that Menard devoted his life to writing a contemporary *Quixote* besmirch his illustrious memory. Pierre Menard did not want to compose *another* Quixote, which surely is easy enough—he wanted to compose *the* Quixote. Nor, surely, need one be obliged to note that his goal was never a mechanical transcription of the original; he had no intention of *copying* it. His admirable ambition was to produce a number of pages which coincided—word for word and line for line—with those of Miguel de Cervantes.

"My purpose is merely astonishing," he wrote me on September 30, 1934, from Bayonne. "The final term of a theological or metaphysical proof—the world around us, or God, or chance, or universal Forms—is no more final, no more uncommon, than my revealed novel. The sole difference is that philosophers publish pleasant volumes containing the intermediate stages of their work, while I am resolved to suppress those stages of my own." And indeed there is not a single draft to bear witness to that years-long labor.

Initially, Menard's method was to be relatively simple: Learn Spanish, return to Catholicism, fight against the Moor or Turk, forget the history of Europe from 1602 to 1918—*be* Miguel de Cervantes. Pierre Menard weighed that course (I know he pretty thoroughly mastered seventeenth-century Castilian) but he discarded it as too easy. Too impossible, rather!, the reader will say. Quite so, but the undertaking was impossible from the outset, and of all the impossible ways of bringing it about, this was the least interesting. To be a popular novelist of the seventeenth century in the twentieth seemed to Menard to be a diminution. Being, somehow, Cervantes, and arriving thereby at the Quixote—that looked to Menard less challenging (and therefore less interesting) than continuing to be Pierre Menard and coming to the Quixote *through the experiences of Pierre Menard.* (It was that conviction, by the way, that obliged him to leave out the autobiographical foreword to Part II of the novel. Including the prologue would have meant creating another character—"Cervantes"—and also presenting Quixote through that character's eyes, not Pierre Menard's. Menard, of course, spurned that easy solution.) "The task I have undertaken is not *in essence* difficult," I read at another place in that letter. "If I could just be immortal, I could do it." Shall I confess that I often imagine that he did complete it, and that I read the Quixote—the *entire* Quixote—as if Menard had conceived it? A few nights ago, as I was leafing through Chapter XXVI (never attempted by Menard), I recognized our friend's style, could almost hear his voice in this marvelous phrase: "the nymphs of the rivers, the moist and grieving Echo." That wonderfully effective linking of one adjective of emotion with another of physical description brought to my mind a line from Shakespeare, which I recall we discussed one afternoon:

> Where a malignant and a turban'd Turk . . .

Why the Quixote? my reader may ask. That choice, made by a Spaniard, would not have been incomprehensible, but it no doubt is so when made by a *Symboliste* from Nîmes, a devotee essentally of Poe—who begat Baudelaire, who begat Mallarmé, who begat Valéry, who begat M. Edmond Teste. The letter mentioned above throws some light on this point. "The *Quixote*," explains Menard,

> deeply interests me, but does not seem to me—*comment dirai-je?*—inevitable. I cannot imagine the universe without Poe's ejaculation "Ah, bear in mind this garden was enchanted!" or the *Bateau ivre* or the *Ancient Mariner*, but I know myself able to imagine it without the *Quixote*. (I am speaking, of course, of my personal ability, not of the historical resonance of those works.) The *Quixote* is a contingent work; the *Quixote* is not necessary. I can premeditate committing it to writing, as it were—I can write it—without falling into a tautology. At the age of twelve or thirteen I read it—perhaps read it cover to cover, I cannot recall. Since then, I have carefully reread certain chapters, those which, at least for the moment, I shall not attempt. I have also glanced at the interludes, the comedies, the *Galatea*, the Exemplary Novels, the undoubtedly laborious *Travails of Persiles and Sigismunda*, and the poetic *Voyage to Parnassus*. . . . My general recollection of the *Quixote*, simplified by forgetfulness and indifference, might well be the equivalent of the vague foreshadowing of a yet unwritten book. Given that image (which no one can in good conscience deny me), my problem is, without the shadow of a doubt, much more difficult than Cervantes'. My obliging predecessor did not spurn the collaboration of chance; his method of composition for the immortal book was a bit *à la diable*, and he was often swept along by the inertiæ of the language and the imagination. I have assumed the mysterious obliga-

> tion to reconstruct, word for word, the novel that for him was spontaneous. This game of solitaire I play is governed by two polar rules: the first allows me to try out formal or psychological variants; the second forces me to sacrifice them to the "original" text and to come, by irrefutable arguments, to those eradications. . . . In addition to these first two artificial constraints there is another, inherent to the project. Composing the *Quixote* in the early seventeenth century was a reasonable, necessary, perhaps even inevitable undertaking; in the early twentieth, it is virtually impossible. Not for nothing have three hundred years elapsed, freighted with the most complex events. Among those events, to mention but one, is the *Quixote* itself.

In spite of those three obstacles, Menard's fragmentary Quixote is more subtle than Cervantes'. Cervantes crudely juxtaposes the humble provincial reality of his country against the fantasies of the romance, while Menard chooses as his "reality" the land of Carmen during the century that saw the Battle of Lepanto and the plays of Lope de Vega. What burlesque brushstrokes of local color that choice would have inspired in a Maurice Barrès or a Rodríguez Larreta*! Yet Menard, with perfect naturalness, avoids them. In his work, there are no gypsy goings-on or conquistadors or mystics or Philip IIs or *autos da fé.* He ignores, overlooks—or banishes—local color. That disdain posits a new meaning for the "historical novel." That disdain condemns *Salammbô,* with no possibility of appeal.

No less amazement visits one when the chapters are considered in isolation. As an example, let us look at Part I, Chapter XXXVIII, "which treats of the curious discourse that Don Quixote made on the subject of arms and letters." It is a matter of common knowledge that in that chapter, don Quixote (like Quevedo in the analogous, and later, passage in *La hora de todos*) comes down against letters and in favor of arms. Cervantes was an old soldier; from him, the verdict is understandable. But that *Pierre Menard*'s don Quixote—a contemporary of *La trahison des clercs* and Bertrand Russell—should repeat those cloudy sophistries! Mme. Bachelier sees in them an admirable (typical) subordination of the author to the psychology of the hero; others (lacking all perspicacity) see them as a *transcription* of the Quixote; the baroness de Bacourt, as influenced by Nietzsche. To that third interpretation (which I consider irrefutable), I am not certain I dare to add a fourth, though it agrees very well with the almost divine modesty of Pierre Menard: his resigned or ironic habit of putting forth ideas that were the exact opposite of those he actually held. (We should recall that diatribe against Paul Valéry in the ephemeral Surrealist journal edited by Jacques Reboul.) The Cervantes text and the Menard text are verbally identical, but the second is almost infinitely richer. (More *ambiguous,* his detractors will say—but ambiguity is richness.)

It is a revelation to compare the *Don Quixote* of Pierre Menard with that of Miguel de Cervantes. Cervantes, for example, wrote the following (Part I, Chapter IX):

> . . . truth, whose mother is history, rival of time, depository of deeds, witness of the past, exemplar and adviser to the present, and the future's counselor.

This catalog of attributes, written in the seventeenth century, and written by the "ingenious layman" Miguel de Cervantes, is mere rhetorical praise of history. Menard, on the other hand, writes:

> . . . truth, whose mother is history, rival of time, depository of deeds, witness of the past, exemplar and adviser to the present, and the future's counselor.

History, the *mother* of truth!—the idea is staggering. Menard, a contemporary of William James, defines history not as a *delving into* reality but as the very *fount* of reality. Historical truth, for Menard, is not "what happened"; it is what we *believe* happened. The final phrases—*exemplar and adviser to the present, and the future's counselor*—are brazenly pragmatic.

The contrast in styles is equally striking. The archaic style of Menard—who is, in addition, not a native speaker of the language in which he writes—is somewhat affected. Not so the style of his precursor, who employs the Spanish of his time with complete naturalness.

There is no intellectual exercise that is not ultimately pointless. A philosophical doctrine is, at first, a plausible description of the universe; the years go by, and it is a mere chapter—if not a paragraph or proper noun—in the history of philosophy. In literature, that "falling by the wayside," that loss of "relevance," is even better known. The Quixote, Menard remarked, was first and foremost a pleasant book; it is now an occasion for patriotic toasts, grammatical arrogance, obscene *de luxe* editions. Fame is a form—perhaps the worst form—of incomprehension.

Those nihilistic observations were not new; what was remarkable was the decision that Pierre Menard derived from them. He resolved to anticipate the vanity that awaits all the labors of mankind; he undertook a task of infinite complexity, a task futile from the outset. He dedicated his scruples and his nights "lit by midnight oil" to repeating in a foreign tongue a book that already existed. His drafts were endless; he stubbornly corrected, and he ripped up thousands of handwritten pages. He would allow no one to see them, and took care that they not survive him.[3] In vain have I attempted to reconstruct them.

I have reflected that it is legitimate to see the "final" Quixote as a kind of palimpsest, in which the traces—faint but not undecipherable—of our friend's "previous" text must shine through. Unfortunately, only a second Pierre Menard, reversing the labors of the first, would be able to exhume and revive those Troys. . . .

"Thinking, meditating, imagining," he also wrote me, "are not anomalous acts—they are the normal respiration of the intelligence. To glorify the occasional exercise of that function, to treasure beyond price ancient and foreign thoughts, to recall with incredulous awe what some *doctor universalis* thought, is to confess our own languor, or our own *barbarie.* Every man should be capable of all ideas, and I believe that in the future he shall be."

Menard has (perhaps unwittingly) enriched the slow and rudimentary art of reading by means of a new technique—the technique of deliberate anachronism and fallacious attribution. That technique, requiring infinite patience and concentration, encourages us to read the *Odyssey* as though it came after the *Æneid*, to read Mme. Henri Bachelier's *Le jardin du Centaure* as though it were written by Mme. Henri Bachelier. This technique fills the calmest books with adventure. Attributing the *Imitatio Christi* to Louis Ferdinand Céline or James Joyce—is that not sufficient renovation of those faint spiritual admonitions?

Nîmes, 1939

[3]I recall his square-ruled notebooks, his black crossings-out, his peculiar typographical symbols, and his insect-like handwriting. In the evening, he liked to go out for walks on the outskirts of Nîmes; he would often carry along a notebook and make a cheery bonfire.

The Circular Ruins

And if he left off dreaming about you . . .
Through the Looking-Glass, VI

No one saw him slip from the boat in the unanimous night, no one saw the bamboo canoe as it sank into the sacred mud, and yet within days there was no one who did not know that the taciturn man had come there from the South, and that his homeland was one of those infinite villages that lie upriver, on the violent flank of the mountain, where the language of the Zend is uncontaminated by Greek and where leprosy is uncommon. But in fact the gray man had kissed the mud, scrambled up the steep bank (without pushing back, probably without even feeling, the sharp-leaved bulrushes that slashed his flesh), and dragged himself, faint and bloody, to the circular enclosure, crowned by the stone figure of a horse or tiger, which had once been the color of fire but was now the color of ashes. That ring was a temple devoured by an ancient holocaust; now, the malarial jungle had profaned it and its god went unhonored by mankind. The foreigner lay down at the foot of the pedestal.

He was awakened by the sun high in the sky. He examined his wounds and saw, without astonishment, that they had healed; he closed his pale eyes and slept, not out of any weakness of the flesh but out of willed determination. He knew that this temple was the place that his unconquerable plan called for; he knew that the unrelenting trees had not succeeded in strangling the ruins of another promising temple downriver—like this one, a temple to dead, incinerated gods; he knew that his immediate obligation was to sleep. About midnight he was awakened by the inconsolable cry of a bird. Prints of unshod feet, a few figs, and a jug of water told him that the men of the region had respectfully spied upon his sleep and that they sought his favor, or feared his magic. He felt the coldness of fear, and he sought out a tomblike niche in the crumbling wall, where he covered himself with unknown leaves.

The goal that led him on was not impossible, though it was clearly supernatural: He wanted to dream a man. He wanted to dream him completely, in painstaking detail, and impose him upon reality. This magical objective had come to fill his entire soul; if someone had asked him his own name, or inquired into any feature of his life till then, he would not have been able to answer. The uninhabited and crumbling temple suited him, for it was a minimum of visible world; so did the proximity of the woodcutters, for they saw to his frugal needs. The rice and fruit of their tribute were nourishment enough for his body, which was consecrated to the sole task of sleeping and dreaming.

At first, his dreams were chaotic; a little later, they became dialectical. The foreigner dreamed that he was in the center of a circular amphitheater, which was somehow the ruined temple; clouds of taciturn students completely filled the terraces of seats. The faces of those farthest away hung at many centuries' distance and at a cosmic height, yet they were absolutely clear. The man lectured on anatomy, cosmography, magic; the faces listened earnestly, intently, and attempted to respond with understanding—as though they sensed the importance of that education that would redeem one of them from his state of hollow appearance and insert him into the real world. The man, both in sleep and when awake, pondered his phantasms' answers; he did not allow himself to be taken in by impostors, and he sensed in certain perplexities a growing intelligence. He was seeking a soul worthy of taking its place in the universe.

On the ninth or tenth night, he realized (with some bitterness) that nothing could be expected from those students who passively accepted his teachings, but only from those who might occasionally, in a reasonable way, venture an objection. The first—the accepting—though worthy of affection and a degree of sympathy, would never emerge as individuals; the latter—those who sometimes questioned—had a bit more preexistence. One afternoon (afternoons now paid their tribute to sleep as well; now the man was awake no more than two or three hours around daybreak) he dismissed the vast illusory classroom once and for all and retained but a single pupil—a taciturn, sallow-skinned young man, at times intractable, with sharp features that echoed those of the man that dreamed him. The pupil was not disconcerted for long by the elimination of his classmates; after only a few of the private classes, his progress amazed his teacher. Yet disaster would not be forestalled. One day the man emerged from sleep as though from a viscous desert, looked up at the hollow light of the evening (which for a moment he confused with the light of dawn), and realized that he had not dreamed. All that night and the next day, the unbearable lucidity of insomnia harried him, like a hawk. He went off to explore the jungle, hoping to tire himself; among the hemlocks he managed no more than a few intervals of feeble sleep, fleetingly veined with the most rudimentary of visions—useless to him. He reconvened his class, but no sooner had he spoken a few brief words of exhortation than the faces blurred, twisted, and faded away. In his almost perpetual state of wakefulness, tears of anger burned the man's old eyes.

He understood that the task of molding the incoherent and dizzying stuff that dreams are made of is the most difficult work a man can undertake, even if he fathom all the enigmas of the higher and lower spheres—much more difficult than weaving a rope of sand or minting coins of the faceless wind. He understood that initial failure was inevitable. He swore to put behind him the vast hallucination that at first had drawn him off the track, and he sought another way to approach his task. Before he began, he devoted a month to recovering the strength his delirium had squandered. He abandoned all premeditation of dreaming, and almost instantly managed to sleep for a fair portion of the day. The few times he did dream during this period, he did not focus on his dreams; he would wait to take up his task again until the disk of the moon was whole. Then, that evening, he purified himself in the waters of the river, bowed down to the planetary gods, uttered those syllables of a powerful name that it is lawful to pronounce, and laid himself down to sleep. Almost immediately he dreamed a beating heart.

He dreamed the heart warm, active, secret—about the size of a closed fist, a garnet-colored thing inside the dimness of a human body that was still faceless and sexless; he dreamed it, with painstaking love, for fourteen brilliant nights. Each night he perceived it with greater clarity, greater certainty. He did not touch it; he only witnessed it, observed it, corrected it, perhaps, with his eyes. He perceived it, he *lived* it, from many angles, many distances. On the fourteenth night, he stroked the pulmonary artery with his forefinger, and then the entire heart, inside and out. And his inspection made him proud. He deliberately did not sleep the next night; then he took up the heart again, invoked the name of a planet, and set about dreaming another of the major organs. Before the year was out he had reached the skeleton, the eyelids. The countless hairs of the body were perhaps the most difficult task. The man had dreamed a fully fleshed man—a stripling—but this youth did not stand up or speak, nor could it open its eyes. Night after night, the man dreamed the youth asleep.

In the cosmogonies of the Gnostics, the demiurges knead up a red Adam who cannot manage to stand; as rude and inept and elementary as that Adam of dust was the Adam of dream wrought from the sorcerer's nights. One afternoon, the man almost destroyed his creation, but he could not bring himself to do it. (He'd have been better off if he had.) After making vows to all the deities of the earth and the river, he threw himself at the feet of the idol that was perhaps a tiger or perhaps a colt, and he begged for its untried aid. That evening, at sunset, the statue filled his dreams. In the dream it was alive, and trembling—yet it was not the dread-inspiring hybrid form of horse and tiger it had been. It was, instead, those two vehement creatures plus bull, and rose, and tempest, too—and all that, simultaneously. The manifold god revealed to the man that its earthly name was Fire, and that in that circular temple (and others like it) men had made sacrifices and worshiped it, and that it would magically bring to life the phantasm the man had dreamed—so fully bring him to life that every creature, save Fire itself and the man who dreamed him, would take him for a man of flesh and blood. Fire ordered the dreamer to send the youth, once instructed in the rites, to that other ruined temple whose pyramids still stood downriver, so that a voice might glorify the god in that deserted place. In the dreaming man's dream, the dreamed man awoke.

The sorcerer carried out Fire's instructions. He consecrated a period of time (which in the end encompassed two full years) to revealing to the youth the arcana of the universe and the secrets of the cult of Fire. Deep inside, it grieved the man to separate himself from his creation. Under the pretext of pedagogical necessity, he drew out the hours of sleep more every day. He also redid the right shoulder (which was perhaps defective). From time to time, he was disturbed by a sense that all this had happened before. . . . His days were, in general, happy; when he closed his eyes, he would think *Now I will be with my son.* Or, less frequently, *The son I have engendered is waiting for me, and he will not exist if I do not go to him.*

Gradually, the man accustomed the youth to reality. Once he ordered him to set a flag on a distant mountaintop. The next day, the flag crackled on the summit. He attempted other, similar experiments—each more daring than the last. He saw with some bitterness that his son was ready—perhaps even impatient—to be born. That night he kissed him for the first time, then sent him off, through many leagues of impenetrable jungle, many leagues of swamp, to that other temple whose ruins bleached in the sun downstream. But first (so that the son would never know that he was a phantasm, so that he would believe himself to be a man like other men) the man infused in him a total lack of memory of his years of education.

The man's victory, and his peace, were dulled by the wearisome sameness of his days. In the twilight hours of dusk and dawn, he would prostrate himself before the stone figure, imagining perhaps that his unreal son performed identical rituals in other circular ruins, downstream. At night he did not dream, or dreamed the dreams that all men dream. His perceptions of the universe's sounds and shapes were somewhat pale: the absent son was nourished by those diminutions of his soul. His life's goal had been accomplished; the man lived on now in a sort of ecstasy. After a period of time (which some tellers of the story choose to compute in years, others in decades), two rowers woke the man at midnight. He could not see their faces, but they told him of a magical man in a temple in the North, a man who could walk on fire and not be burned.

The sorcerer suddenly remembered the god's words. He remembered that of all the creatures on the earth, Fire was the only one who knew that his son was a phantasm. That recollection, comforting at first, soon came to torment him. He feared that his son would meditate upon his unnatural privilege and somehow discover that he was a mere simulacrum. To be not a man, but the projection of another man's dream—what incomparable humiliation, what vertigo! Every parent feels concern for the children he has procreated (or allowed to be procreated) in happiness or in mere confusion; it was only natural that the sorcerer should fear for the future of the son he had conceived organ by organ, feature by feature, through a thousand and one secret nights.

The end of his meditations came suddenly, but it had been foretold by certain signs: first (after a long drought), a distant cloud, as light as a bird, upon a mountaintop; then, toward the South, the sky the pinkish color of a leopard's gums; then the clouds of smoke that rusted the iron of the nights; then, at last, the panicked flight of the animals—for that which had occurred hundreds of years ago was being repeated now. The ruins of the sanctuary of the god of Fire were destroyed by fire. In the birdless dawn, the sorcerer watched the concentric holocaust close in upon the walls. For a moment he thought of taking refuge in the water, but then he realized that death would be a crown upon his age and absolve him from his labors. He walked into the tatters of flame, but they did not bite his flesh—they caressed him, bathed him without heat and without combustion. With relief, with humiliation, with terror, he realized that he, too, was but appearance, that another man was dreaming him.

The Lottery in Babylon

Like all the men of Babylon, I have been proconsul; like all, I have been a slave. I have known omnipotence, ignominy, imprisonment. Look here—my right hand has no index finger. Look here—through this gash in my cape you can see on my stomach a crimson tattoo—it is the second letter, *Beth.* On nights when the moon is full, this symbol gives me power over men with the mark of Gimel, but it subjects me to those with the Aleph, who on nights when there is no moon owe obedience to those marked with the Gimel. In the half-light of dawn, in a cellar, standing before a black altar, I have slit the throats of sacred bulls. Once, for an entire lunar year, I was declared invisible—I would cry out and no one would heed my call, I would steal bread and not be beheaded. I have known that thing the Greeks knew not—uncertainty. In a chamber of brass, as I faced the strangler's silent scarf, hope did not abandon me; in the river of delights, panic has not failed me. Heraclides Ponticus reports, admiringly, that Pythagoras recalled having been Pyrrhus, and before that, Euphorbus, and before that, some other mortal; in order to recall similar vicissitudes, I have no need of death, nor even of imposture.

I owe that almost monstrous variety to an institution—the Lottery—which is unknown in other nations, or at work in them imperfectly or secretly. I have not delved into this institution's history. I know that sages cannot agree. About its mighty purposes I know as much as a man untutored in astrology might know about the moon. Mine is a dizzying country in which the Lottery is a major element of reality; until this day, I have thought as little about it as about the conduct of the indecipherable gods or of my heart. Now, far from Babylon and its belovèd customs, I think with some bewilderment about the Lottery, and about the blasphemous conjectures that shrouded men whisper in the half-light of dawn or evening.

My father would tell how once, long ago—centuries? years?—the lottery in Babylon was a game played by commoners. He would tell (though whether this is true or not, I cannot say) how barbers would take a man's copper coins and give back rectangles made of bone or parchment and adorned with symbols. Then, in broad daylight, a drawing would be held; those smiled upon by fate would, with no further corroboration by chance, win coins minted of silver. The procedure, as you can see, was rudimentary.

Naturally, those so-called "lotteries" were a failure. They had no moral force whatsoever; they appealed not to all a man's faculties, but only to his hopefulness. Public indifference soon meant that the merchants who had founded these venal lotteries began to lose money. Someone tried something new: including among the list of lucky numbers a few *unlucky* draws. This innovation meant that those who bought those numbered rectangles now had a twofold chance: they might win a sum of money or they might be required to pay a fine—sometimes a considerable one. As one might expect, that small risk (for every thirty "good" numbers there was one ill-omened one) piqued the public's interest. Babylonians flocked to buy tickets. The man who bought none was considered a pusillanimous wretch, a man with no spirit of adventure. In time, this justified contempt found a second target: not just the man who didn't play, but also the man who lost and paid the fine. The Company (as it was now beginning to be known) had to protect the interest of the winners, who could not be paid their prizes unless the pot contained almost the entire amount of the fines. A lawsuit was filed against the losers: the judge sentenced them to pay the original fine, plus court costs, or spend a number of days in jail. In order to thwart the Company, they all chose jail. From that gauntlet thrown down by a few men sprang the Company's omnipotence—its ecclesiastical, metaphysical force.

Some time after this, the announcements of the numbers drawn began to leave out the lists of fines and simply print the days of prison assigned to each losing number. That shorthand, as it were, which went virtually unnoticed at the time, was of utmost importance: *It was the first appearance of nonpecuniary elements in the lottery.* And it met with great success—indeed, the Company was forced by its players to increase the number of unlucky draws.

As everyone knows, the people of Babylon are great admirers of logic, and even of symmetry. It was inconsistent that lucky numbers should pay off in round silver coins while unlucky ones were measured in days and nights of jail. Certain moralists argued that the possession of coins did not always bring about happiness, and that other forms of happiness were perhaps more direct.

The lower-caste neighborhoods of the city voiced a different complaint. The members of the priestly class gambled heavily, and so enjoyed all the vicissitudes of terror and hope; the poor (with understandable, or inevitable, envy) saw themselves denied access to that famously delightful, even sensual, wheel. The fair and reasonable desire that all men and women, rich and poor, be able to take part equally in the Lottery inspired indignant demonstrations—the memory of which, time has failed to dim. Some stubborn souls could not (or pretended they could not) understand that this was a *novus ordo seclorum,* a necessary stage of history. . . . A slave stole a crimson ticket; the drawing determined that that ticket entitled the bearer to have his tongue burned out. The code of law provided the same sentence for stealing a lottery ticket. Some Babylonians argued that the slave deserved the burning iron for being a thief; others, more magnanimous, that the executioner should employ the iron because thus fate had decreed. . . . There were disturbances, there were regrettable instances of bloodshed, but the masses of Babylon at last, over the opposition of the well-to-do, imposed their will; they saw their generous objectives fully achieved. First, the Company was forced to assume all public power. (The unification was necessary because of the vastness and complexity of the new operations.) Second, the Lottery was made secret, free of charge, and open to all. The mercenary sale of lots was abolished; once initiated into the mysteries of Baal, every free citizen automatically took part in the sacred drawings, which were held in the labyrinths of the god every sixty nights and determined each citizen's destiny until the next drawing. The consequences were incalculable. A lucky draw might bring about a man's elevation to the council of the magi or the imprisonment of his enemy (secret, or known by all to be so), or might allow him to find, in the peaceful dimness of his room, the woman who would begin to disturb him, or whom he had never hoped to see again; an unlucky draw: mutilation, dishonor of many kinds, death itself. Sometimes a single event—the murder of C in a tavern, B's mysterious apotheosis—would be the inspired outcome of thirty or forty drawings. Combining bets was difficult, but we must recall that the individuals of the Company were (and still are) all-powerful, and clever. In many cases, the knowledge that certain happy turns were the simple result of chance would have lessened the force of those outcomes; to forestall that problem, agents of the Company employed suggestion, or even magic. The paths they followed, the intrigues they wove, were invariably secret. To penetrate the innermost hopes and innermost fears of every man, they called upon astrologers and spies. There were certain stone lions, a sacred latrine called Qaphqa, some cracks in a dusty aqueduct—these places, it was generally believed, *gave access to the Company,* and well- or ill-wishing persons would deposit confidential reports in them. An alphabetical file held those *dossiers* of varying veracity.

Incredibly, there was talk of favoritism, of corruption. With its customary discretion, the Company did not reply directly; instead, it scrawled its brief argument in the rubble of a mask factory. This *apologia* is now numbered among the sacred Scriptures. It pointed out, doctrinally, that the Lottery is an interpolation of chance into the order of the universe, and observed that to accept errors is to strengthen chance, not contravene it. It also noted that those lions, that sacred squatting-place, though not disavowed by the Company (which reserved the right to consult them), functioned with no official guarantee.

This statement quieted the public's concerns. But it also produced other effects perhaps unforeseen by its author. It profoundly altered both the spirit and the operations of the Company. I have but little time remaining; we are told that the ship is about to sail—but I will try to explain.

However unlikely it may seem, no one, until that time, had attempted to produce a general theory of gaming. Babylonians are not a speculative people; they obey the dictates of chance, surrender their lives, their hopes, their nameless terror to it, but it never occurs to them to delve into its labyrinthine laws or the revolving spheres that manifest its workings. Nonetheless, the semiofficial statement that I mentioned inspired numerous debates of a legal and mathematical nature. From one of them, there emerged the following conjecture: If the Lottery is an intensification of chance, a periodic infusion of chaos into the cosmos, then is it not appropriate that chance intervene in *every* aspect of the drawing, not just one? Is it not ludicrous that chance should dictate a person's death while the circumstances of that death—whether private or public, whether drawn out for an hour or a century—should *not* be subject to chance? Those perfectly reasonable objections finally prompted sweeping reform; the complexities of the new system (complicated further by its having been in practice for centuries) are understood by only a handful of specialists, though I will attempt to summarize them, even if only symbolically.

Let us imagine a first drawing, which condemns an individual to death.

In pursuance of that decree, another drawing is held; out of that second drawing come, say, nine possible executors. Of those nine, four might initiate a third drawing to determine the name of the executioner, two might replace the unlucky draw with a lucky one (the discovery of a treasure, say), another might decide that the death should be exacerbated (death with dishonor, that is, or with the refinement of torture), others might simply refuse to carry out the sentence.... That is the scheme of the Lottery, put symbolically. *In reality, the number of drawings is infinite.* No decision is final; all branch into others. The ignorant assume that infinite drawings require infinite time; actually, all that is required is that time be infinitely subdivisible, as in the famous parable of the Race with the Tortoise. That infinitude coincides remarkably well with the sinuous numbers of Chance and with the Heavenly Archetype of the Lottery beloved of Platonists.... Some distorted echo of our custom seems to have reached the Tiber: In his *Life of Antoninus Heliogabalus*, Ælius Lampridius tells us that the emperor wrote out on seashells the fate that he intended for his guests at dinner—some would receive ten pounds of gold; others, ten houseflies, ten dormice, ten bears. It is fair to recall that Heliogabalus was raised in Asia Minor, among the priests of his eponymous god.

There are also *impersonal* drawings, whose purpose is unclear. One drawing decrees that a sapphire from Taprobana be thrown into the waters of the Euphrates; another, that a bird be released from the top of a certain tower; another, that every hundred years a grain of sand be added to (or taken from) the countless grains of sand on a certain beach. Sometimes, the consequences are terrible.

Under the Company's beneficent influence, our customs are now steeped in chance. The purchaser of a dozen amphoræ of Damascene wine will not be surprised if one contains a talisman, or a viper; the scribe who writes out a contract never fails to include some error; I myself, in this hurried statement, have misrepresented some splendor, some atrocity—perhaps, too, some mysterious monotony.... Our historians, the most perspicacious on the planet, have invented a method for correcting chance; it is well known that the outcomes of this method are (in general) trustworthy—although, of course, they are never divulged without a measure of deception. Besides, there is nothing so tainted with fiction as the history of the Company.... A paleographic document, unearthed at a certain temple, may come from yesterday's drawing or from a drawing that took place centuries ago. No book is published without some discrepancy between each of the edition's copies. Scribes take a secret oath to omit, interpolate, alter. *Indirect* falsehood is also practiced.

The Company, with godlike modesty, shuns all publicity. Its agents, of course, are secret; the orders it constantly (perhaps continually) imparts are no different from those spread wholesale by impostors. Besides—who will boast of being a mere impostor? The drunken man who blurts out an absurd command, the sleeping man who suddenly awakes and turns and chokes to death the woman sleeping at his side—are they not, perhaps, implementing one of the Company's secret decisions? That silent functioning, like God's, inspires all manner of conjectures. One scurrilously suggests that the Company ceased to exist hundreds of years ago, and that the sacred disorder of our lives is purely hereditary, traditional; another believes that the Company is eternal, and that it shall endure until the last night, when the last god shall annihilate the earth. Yet another declares that the Company is omnipotent, but affects only small things: the cry of a bird, the shades of rust and dust, the half dreams that come at dawn. Another, whispered by masked heresiarchs, says that *the Company has never existed, and never will.* Another, no less despicable, argues that it makes no difference whether one affirms or denies the reality of the shadowy corporation, because Babylon is nothing but an infinite game of chance.

A Survey of the Works of Herbert Quain

Herbert Quain died recently in Roscommon. I see with no great surprise that the *Times Literary Supplement* devoted to him a scant half column of necrological pieties in which there is not a single laudatory epithet that is not set straight (or firmly reprimanded) by an adverb. The *Spectator*, in its corresponding number, is less concise, no doubt, and perhaps somewhat more cordial, but it compares Quain's first book, *The God of the Labyrinth*, to one by Mrs. Agatha Christie, and others to works by Gertrude Stein. These are comparisons that no one would have thought to be inevitable, and that would have given no pleasure to the deceased. Not that Quain ever considered himself "a man of genius"—even on those peripatetic nights of literary conversation when the man who by that time had fagged many a printing press invariably played at being M. Teste or Dr. Samuel Johnson. . . . Indeed, he saw with absolute clarity the experimental nature of his works, which might be admirable for their innovativeness and a certain laconic integrity, but hardly for their strength of passion. "I am like Cowley's odes," he said in a letter to me from Longford on March 6, 1939. "I belong not to art but to the history of art." (In his view, there was no lower discipline than history.)

I have quoted Quain's modest opinion of himself; naturally, that modesty did not define the boundaries of his thinking. Flaubert and Henry James have managed to persuade us that works of art are few and far between, and maddeningly difficult to compose, but the sixteenth century (we should recall the *Voyage to Parnassus*, we should recall the career of Shakespeare) did not share that disconsolate opinion. Nor did Herbert Quain. He believed that "great literature" is the commonest thing in the world, and that there was hardly a conversation in the street that did not attain those "heights." He also believed that the æsthetic act must contain some element of surprise, shock, astonishment—and that being astonished by rote is difficult, so he deplored with smiling sincerity "the servile, stubborn preservation of past and bygone books." . . . I do not know whether that vague theory of his is justifiable or not; I do know that his books strive too greatly to astonish.

I deeply regret having lent to a certain lady, irrecoverably, the first book that Quain published. I have said that it was a detective story—*The God of the Labyrinth*; what a brilliant idea the publisher had, bringing it out in late November, 1933. In early December, the pleasant yet arduous convolutions of *The Siamese Twin Mystery** gave London and New York a good deal of "gumshoe" work to do—in my view, the failure of our friend's work can be laid to that ruinous coincidence. (Though there is also the question—I wish to be totally honest—of its somewhat careless plotting and the hollow, frigid stiltedness of certain descriptions of the sea.) Seven years later, I cannot for the life of me recall the details of the plot, but this is the general scheme of it, impoverished (or purified) by my forgetfulness: There is an incomprehensible murder in the early pages of the book, a slow discussion in the middle, and a solution of the crime toward the end. Once the mystery has been cleared up, there is a long retrospective paragraph that contains the following sentence: *Everyone believed that the chessplayers had met accidentally.* That phrase allows one to infer that the solution is in fact in error, and so, uneasy, the reader looks back over the pertinent chapters and discovers *another* solution, which is the correct one. The reader of this remarkable book, then, is more perspicacious than the detective.

An even more heterodox work is the "regressive, ramifying fiction" *April March*, whose third (and single) section is dated 1936. No one, in assaying this novel, can fail to discover that it is a kind of game; it is legitimate, I should think, to recall that the author himself never saw it in any other light. "I have reclaimed for this novel," I once heard him say, "the essential features of every game: the symmetry, the arbitrary laws, the tedium." Even the name is a feeble pun: it is not someone's name, does not mean "a march [taken] in April," but literally April-March. Someone once noted that there is an echo of the doctrines of Dunne in the pages of this book; Quain's foreword prefers instead to allude to that backward-running world posited by Bradley, in which death precedes birth, the scar precedes the wound, and the wound precedes the blow (*Appearance and Reality*,

1897, p. 215).[1] But it is not the worlds proposed by *April March* that are regressive, it is the way the stories are told—regressively and ramifying, as I have said. The book is composed of thirteen chapters. The first reports an ambiguous conversation between several unknown persons on a railway station platform. The second tells of the events of the evening that precedes the first. The third, likewise retrograde, tells of the events of *another,* different, possible evening before the first; the fourth chapter relates the events of yet a third different possible evening. Each of these (mutually exclusive) "evenings-before" ramifies into three further "evenings-before," all quite different. The work in its entirety consists, then, of nine novels; each novel, of three long chapters. (The first chapter is common to all, of course.) Of those novels, one is symbolic; another, supernatural; another, a detective novel; another, psychological; another, a Communist novel; another, anti-Communist; and so on. Perhaps the following symbolic representation will help the reader understand the novel's structure:

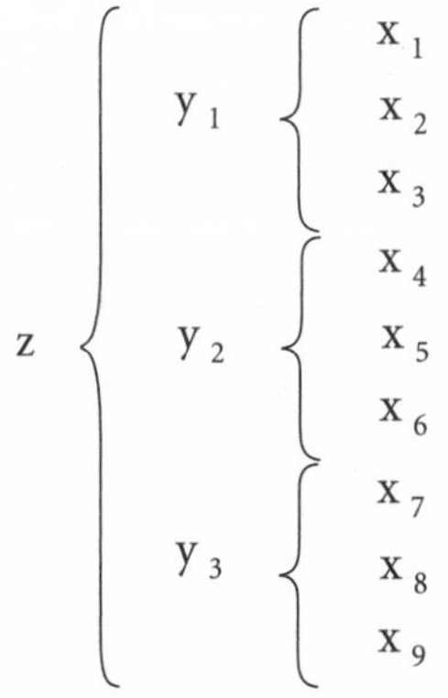

$$z \begin{cases} y_1 \begin{cases} x_1 \\ x_2 \\ x_3 \end{cases} \\ y_2 \begin{cases} x_4 \\ x_5 \\ x_6 \end{cases} \\ y_3 \begin{cases} x_7 \\ x_8 \\ x_9 \end{cases} \end{cases}$$

With regard to this structure, it may be apposite to say once again what Schopenhauer said about Kant's twelve categories: "He sacrifices everything

[1]So much for Herbert Quain's erudition, so much for page 215 of a book published in 1897. The interlocutor of Plato's *Politicus,* the unnamed "Eleatic Stranger," had described, over two thousand years earlier, a similar regression, that of the Children of Terra, the Autochthons, who, under the influence of a reverse rotation of the cosmos, grow from old age to maturity, from maturity to childhood, from childhood to extinction and nothingness. Theopompus, too, in his *Philippics,* speaks of certain northern fruits which produce in the person who eats them the same retrograde growth. . . . Even more interesting than these images is imagining an inversion of Time itself—a condition in which we would remember the Future and know nothing, or perhaps have only the barest inkling, of the Past. *Cf. Inferno,* Canto X, II. 97–105, in which the prophetic vision is compared to farsightedness.

to his rage for symmetry." Predictably, one and another of the nine tales is unworthy of Quain; the best is not the one that Quain first conceived, x_4; it is, rather, x_9, a tale of fantasy. Others are marred by pallid jokes and instances of pointless pseudoexactitude. Those who read the tales in chronological order *(e.g.,* x_3, y_1, z) will miss the strange book's peculiar flavor. Two stories—x_7 and x_8—have no particular individual value; it is their *juxtaposition* that makes them effective. . . . I am not certain whether I should remind the reader that after *April March* was published, Quain had second thoughts about the triune order of the book and predicted that the mortals who imitated it would opt instead for a binary scheme—

$$z \begin{cases} y_1 \begin{cases} x_1 \\ x_2 \end{cases} \\ y_2 \begin{cases} x_3 \\ x_4 \end{cases} \end{cases}$$

while the gods and demiurges had chosen an infinite one: infinite stories, infinitely branching.

Quite unlike *April March*, yet similarly retrospective, is the heroic two-act comedy *The Secret Mirror*. In the works we have looked at so far, a formal complexity hobbles the author's imagination; in *The Secret Mirror*, that imagination is given freer rein. The play's first (and longer) act takes place in the country home of General Thrale, C.I.E., near Melton Mowbray. The unseen center around which the plot revolves is Miss Ulrica Thrale, the general's elder daughter. Snatches of dialog give us glimpses of this young woman, a haughty Amazon-like creature; we are led to suspect that she seldom journeys to the realms of literature. The newspapers have announced her engagement to the duke of Rutland; the newspapers then report that the engagement is off. Miss Thrale is adored by a playwright, one Wilfred Quarles; once or twice in the past, she has bestowed a distracted kiss upon this young man. The characters possess vast fortunes and ancient bloodlines; their affections are noble though vehement; the dialog seems to swing between the extremes of a hollow grandiloquence worthy of Bulwer-Lytton and the epigrams of Wilde or Philip Guedalla. There is a nightingale and a night; there is a secret duel on the terrace. (Though almost entirely imperceptible, there are occasional curious contradictions, and there are sordid details.) The characters of the first act reappear in the second—under different names. The "playwright" Wilfred Quarles is a traveling salesman from Liverpool; his real name is John William Quigley. Miss Thrale does exist, though Quigley has never seen her; he morbidly clips pictures of her out of the *Tatler* or the *Sketch.* Quigley is the author of the first act; the implausible or improbable "country house" is the Jewish-Irish rooming house he lives in, transformed and magnified by his imagination. . . . The plot of the two acts is parallel, though in the second everything is slightly menacing—everything is put off, or frustrated. When *The Secret Mirror* first opened, critics spoke the names "Freud" and "Julian Green." In my view, the mention of the first of those is entirely unjustified.

Report had it that *The Secret Mirror* was a Freudian comedy; that favorable (though fallacious) reading decided the play's success. Unfortunately, Quain was over forty; he had grown used to failure, and could not go gently into that change of state. He resolved to have his revenge. In late 1939 he published *Statements*, perhaps the most original of his works—certainly the least praised and most secret of them. Quain would often argue that readers were an extinct species. "There is no European man or woman," he would sputter, "that's not a writer, potentially or in fact." He would also declare that of the many kinds of pleasure literature can minister, the highest is the pleasure of the imagination. Since not everyone is capable of experiencing that pleasure, many will have to content themselves with simulacra. For those "writers *manqués*," whose name is legion, Quain wrote the eight stories of *Statements.* Each of them prefigures, or promises, a good plot, which is then intentionally frustrated by the author. One of the stories (not the best) hints at *two* plots; the reader, blinded by vanity, believes that he himself has come up with them. From the third story, titled "The Rose of Yesterday," I was ingenuous enough to extract "The Circular Ruins," which is one of the stories in my book *The Garden of Forking Paths.*

1941

The Library of Babel

By this art you may contemplate the variation of the 23 letters. . . .

Anatomy of Melancholy, Pt. 2, Sec. II, Mem. IV

The universe (which others call the Library) is composed of an indefinite, perhaps infinite number of hexagonal galleries. In the center of each gallery is a ventilation shaft, bounded by a low railing. From any hexagon one can see the floors above and below—one after another, endlessly. The arrangement of the galleries is always the same: Twenty bookshelves, five to each side, line four of the hexagon's six sides; the height of the bookshelves, floor to ceiling, is hardly greater than the height of a normal librarian. One of the hexagon's free sides opens onto a narrow sort of vestibule, which in turn opens onto another gallery, identical to the first—identical in fact to all. To the left and right of the vestibule are two tiny compartments. One is for sleeping, upright; the other, for satisfying one's physical necessities. Through this space, too, there passes a spiral staircase, which winds upward and downward into the remotest distance. In the vestibule there is a mirror, which faithfully duplicates appearances. Men often infer from this mirror that the Library is not infinite—if it were, what need would there be for that illusory replication? I prefer to dream that burnished surfaces are a figuration and promise of the infinite. . . . Light is provided by certain spherical fruits that bear the name "bulbs." There are two of these bulbs in each hexagon, set crosswise. The light they give is insufficient, and unceasing.

Like all the men of the Library, in my younger days I traveled; I have journeyed in quest of a book, perhaps the catalog of catalogs. Now that my eyes can hardly make out what I myself have written, I am preparing to die, a few leagues from the hexagon where I was born. When I am dead, compassionate hands will throw me over the railing; my tomb will be the unfathomable air, my body will sink for ages, and will decay and dissolve in the wind engendered by my fall, which shall be infinite. I declare that the Library is endless. Idealists argue that the hexagonal rooms are the necessary shape of absolute space, or at least of our *perception* of space. They argue that a triangular or pentagonal chamber is inconceivable. (Mystics claim that their ecstasies reveal to them a circular chamber containing an enormous circular book with a continuous spine that goes completely around the walls. But their testimony is suspect, their words obscure. That cyclical book is God.) Let it suffice for the moment that I repeat the classic dictum: *The Library is a sphere whose exact center is any hexagon and whose circumference is unattainable.*

Each wall of each hexagon is furnished with five bookshelves; each bookshelf holds thirty-two books identical in format; each book contains four hundred ten pages; each page, forty lines; each line, approximately eighty black letters. There are also letters on the front cover of each book; those letters neither indicate nor prefigure what the pages inside will say. I am aware that that lack of correspondence once struck men as mysterious. Before summarizing the solution of the mystery (whose discovery, in spite of its tragic consequences, is perhaps the most important event in all history), I wish to recall a few axioms.

First: *The Library has existed* ab æternitate. That truth, whose immediate corollary is the future eternity of the world, no rational mind can doubt. Man, the imperfect librarian, may be the work of chance or of malevolent demiurges; the universe, with its elegant appointments—its bookshelves, its enigmatic books, its indefatigable staircases for the traveler, and its water closets for the seated librarian—can only be the handiwork of a god. In order to grasp the distance that separates the human and the divine, one has only to compare these crude trembling symbols which my fallible hand scrawls on the cover of a book with the organic letters inside—neat, delicate, deep black, and inimitably symmetrical.

Second: *There are twenty-five orthographic symbols.*[1] That discovery enabled mankind, three hundred years ago, to formulate a general theory of the Library and thereby satisfactorily solve the riddle that no conjecture had been able to divine—the formless and chaotic nature of virtually all books. One book, which my father once saw in a hexagon in circuit 15-94, consisted of the letters M C V perversely repeated from the first line to the last. Another (much consulted in this zone) is a mere labyrinth of letters whose

[1]The original manuscript has neither numbers nor capital letters; punctuation is limited to the comma and the period. Those two marks, the space, and the twenty-two letters of the alphabet are the twenty-five sufficient symbols that our unknown author is referring to. [Ed. note.]

penultimate page contains the phrase *O Time thy pyramids.* This much is known: For every rational line or forthright statement there are leagues of senseless cacophony, verbal nonsense, and incoherency. (I know of one semibarbarous zone whose librarians repudiate the "vain and superstitious habit" of trying to find sense in books, equating such a quest with attempting to find meaning in dreams or in the chaotic lines of the palm of one's hand. . . . They will acknowledge that the inventors of writing imitated the twenty-five natural symbols, but contend that that adoption was fortuitous, coincidental, and that books in themselves have no meaning. That argument, as we shall see, is not entirely fallacious.)

For many years it was believed that those impenetrable books were in ancient or far-distant languages. It is true that the most ancient peoples, the first librarians, employed a language quite different from the one we speak today; it is true that a few miles to the right, our language devolves into dialect and that ninety floors above, it becomes incomprehensible. All of that, I repeat, is true—but four hundred ten pages of unvarying M C V's cannot belong to any language, however dialectal or primitive it may be. Some have suggested that each letter influences the next, and that the value of M C V on page 71, line 3, is not the value of the same series on another line of another page, but that vague thesis has not met with any great acceptance. Others have mentioned the possibility of codes; that conjecture has been universally accepted, though not in the sense in which its originators formulated it.

Some five hundred years ago, the chief of one of the upper hexagons[2] came across a book as jumbled as all the others, but containing almost two pages of homogeneous lines. He showed his find to a traveling decipherer, who told him that the lines were written in Portuguese; others said it was Yiddish. Within the century experts had determined what the language actually was: a Samoyed-Lithuanian dialect of Guaraní, with inflections from classical Arabic. The content was also determined: the rudiments of combinatory analysis, illustrated with examples of endlessly repeating variations. Those examples allowed a librarian of genius to discover the fundamental law of the Library. This philosopher observed that all books, however different from one another they might be, consist of identical elements: the space, the period, the comma, and the twenty-two letters of the alphabet. He also posited a fact which all travelers have since confirmed: *In all the Li-*

[2]In earlier times, there was one man for every three hexagons. Suicide and diseases of the lung have played havoc with that proportion. An unspeakably melancholy memory: I have sometimes traveled for nights on end, down corridors and polished staircases, without coming across a single librarian.

brary, there are no two identical books. From those incontrovertible premises, the librarian deduced that the Library is "total"—perfect, complete, and whole—and that its bookshelves contain all possible combinations of the twenty-two orthographic symbols (a number which, though unimaginably vast, is not infinite)—that is, all that is able to be expressed, in every language. *All*—the detailed history of the future, the autobiographies of the archangels, the faithful catalog of the Library, thousands and thousands of false catalogs, the proof of the falsity of those false catalogs, a proof of the falsity of the *true* catalog, the gnostic gospel of Basilides, the commentary upon that gospel, the commentary on the commentary on that gospel, the true story of your death, the translation of every book into every language, the interpolations of every book into all books, the treatise Bede could have written (but did not) on the mythology of the Saxon people, the lost books of Tacitus.

When it was announced that the Library contained all books, the first reaction was unbounded joy. All men felt themselves the possessors of an intact and secret treasure. There was no personal problem, no world problem, whose eloquent solution did not exist—somewhere in some hexagon. The universe was justified; the universe suddenly became congruent with the unlimited width and breadth of humankind's hope. At that period there was much talk of The Vindications—books of *apologiæ* and prophecies that would vindicate for all time the actions of every person in the universe and that held wondrous arcana for men's futures. Thousands of greedy individuals abandoned their sweet native hexagons and rushed downstairs, upstairs, spurred by the vain desire to find their Vindication. These pilgrims squabbled in the narrow corridors, muttered dark imprecations, strangled one another on the divine staircases, threw deceiving volumes down ventilation shafts, were themselves hurled to their deaths by men of distant regions. Others went insane. . . . The Vindications do exist (I have seen two of them, which refer to persons in the future, persons perhaps not imaginary), but those who went in quest of them failed to recall that the chance of a man's finding his own Vindication, or some perfidious version of his own, can be calculated to be zero.

At that same period there was also hope that the fundamental mysteries of mankind—the origin of the Library and of time—might be revealed. In all likelihood those profound mysteries can indeed be explained in words; if the language of the philosophers is not sufficient, then the multiform Library must surely have produced the extraordinary language that is required, together with the words and grammar of that language. For four centuries, men have been scouring the hexagons.... There are official searchers, the "inquisitors." I have seen them about their tasks: they arrive exhausted at some hexagon, they talk about a staircase that nearly killed them—some steps were missing—they speak with the librarian about galleries and staircases, and, once in a while, they take up the nearest book and leaf through it, searching for disgraceful or dishonorable words. Clearly, no one expects to discover anything.

That unbridled hopefulness was succeeded, naturally enough, by a similarly disproportionate depression. The certainty that some bookshelf in some hexagon contained precious books, yet that those precious books were forever out of reach, was almost unbearable. One blasphemous sect proposed that the searches be discontinued and that all men shuffle letters and symbols until those canonical books, through some improbable stroke of chance, had been constructed. The authorities were forced to issue strict orders. The sect disappeared, but in my childhood I have seen old men who for long periods would hide in the latrines with metal disks and a forbidden dice cup, feebly mimicking the divine disorder.

Others, going about it in the opposite way, thought the first thing to do was eliminate all worthless books. They would invade the hexagons, show credentials that were not always false, leaf disgustedly through a volume, and condemn entire walls of books. It is to their hygienic, ascetic rage that we lay the senseless loss of millions of volumes. Their name is execrated today, but those who grieve over the "treasures" destroyed in that frenzy overlook two widely acknowledged facts: One, that the Library is so huge that any reduction by human hands must be infinitesimal. And two, that each book is unique and irreplaceable, but (since the Library is total) there are always several hundred thousand imperfect facsimiles—books that differ by no more than a single letter, or a comma. Despite general opinion, I daresay that the consequences of the depredations committed by the Purifiers have been exaggerated by the horror those same fanatics inspired. They were spurred on by the holy zeal to reach—someday, through unrelenting effort—the books of the Crimson Hexagon—books smaller than natural books, books omnipotent, illustrated, and magical.

We also have knowledge of another superstition from that period: belief in what was termed the Book-Man. On some shelf in some hexagon, it was argued, there must exist a book that is the cipher and perfect compendium *of all other books,* and some librarian must have examined that book; this librarian is analogous to a god. In the language of this zone there are still vestiges of the sect that worshiped that distant librarian. Many have gone in search of Him. For a hundred years, men beat every possible path—and every path in vain. How was one to locate the idolized secret hexagon that sheltered Him? Someone proposed searching by regression: To locate book A, first consult book B, which tells where book A can be found; to locate book B, first consult book C, and so on, to infinity. . . . It is in ventures such as these that I have squandered and spent my years. I cannot think it unlikely that there is such a total book[3] on some shelf in the universe. I pray to the unknown gods that some man—even a single man, tens of centuries ago—has perused and read that book. If the honor and wisdom and joy of such a reading are not to be my own, then let them be for others. Let heaven exist, though my own place be in hell. Let me be tortured and battered and annihilated, but let there be one instant, one creature, wherein thy enormous Library may find its justification.

Infidels claim that the rule in the Library is not "sense," but "non-sense," and that "rationality" (even humble, pure coherence) is an almost miraculous exception. They speak, I know, of "the feverish Library, whose random volumes constantly threaten to transmogrify into others, so that they affirm all things, deny all things, and confound and confuse all things, like some mad and hallucinating deity." Those words, which not only proclaim disorder but exemplify it as well, prove, as all can see, the infidels' deplorable taste and desperate ignorance. For while the Library contains all verbal structures, all the variations allowed by the twenty-five orthographic symbols, it includes not a single absolute piece of nonsense. It would be pointless to observe that the finest volume of all the many hexagons that I myself administer is titled *Combed Thunder*, while another is titled *The Plaster Cramp*, and another, *Axaxaxas mlö*. Those phrases, at first apparently incoherent, are undoubtedly susceptible to cryptographic or allegorical "reading"; that reading, that justification of the words' order and existence, is itself verbal and, *ex hypothesi*, already contained somewhere in the Library. There is no combination of characters one can make—*dhcmrlchtdj*, for example—that the divine Library has not foreseen and that in one or more of its secret tongues does not hide a terrible significance. There is no syllable one can speak that is not filled with tenderness and terror, that is not, in one of those languages, the mighty name of a god. To speak is to commit tautologies. This point-

[3]I repeat: In order for a book to exist, it is sufficient that it be *possible*. Only the impossible is excluded. For example, no book is also a staircase, though there are no doubt books that discuss and deny and prove that possibility, and others whose structure corresponds to that of a staircase.

less, verbose epistle already exists in one of the thirty volumes of the five bookshelves in one of the countless hexagons—as does its refutation. (A number *n* of the possible languages employ the same vocabulary; in some of them, the *symbol* "library" possesses the correct definition "everlasting, ubiquitous system of hexagonal galleries," while a library—the thing—is a loaf of bread or a pyramid or something else, and the six words that define it themselves have other definitions. You who read me—are you certain you understand my language?)

Methodical composition distracts me from the present condition of humanity. The certainty that everything has already been written annuls us, or renders us phantasmal. I know districts in which the young people prostrate themselves before books and like savages kiss their pages, though they cannot read a letter. Epidemics, heretical discords, pilgrimages that inevitably degenerate into brigandage have decimated the population. I believe I mentioned the suicides, which are more and more frequent every year. I am perhaps misled by old age and fear, but I suspect that the human species—the *only* species—teeters at the verge of extinction, yet that the Library—enlightened, solitary, infinite, perfectly unmoving, armed with precious volumes, pointless, incorruptible, and secret—will endure.

I have just written the word "infinite." I have not included that adjective out of mere rhetorical habit; I hereby state that it is not illogical to think that the world is infinite. Those who believe it to have limits hypothesize that in some remote place or places the corridors and staircases and hexagons may, inconceivably, end—which is absurd. And yet those who picture the world as unlimited forget that the number of possible books is *not.* I will be bold enough to suggest this solution to the ancient problem: *The Library is unlimited but periodic.* If an eternal traveler should journey in any direction, he would find after untold centuries that the same volumes are repeated in the same disorder—which, repeated, becomes order: the Order. My solitude is cheered by that elegant hope.[4]

Mar del Plata, 1941

[4]Letizia Alvarez de Toledo has observed that the vast Library is pointless; strictly speaking, all that is required is *a single volume,* of the common size, printed in nine- or ten-point type, that would consist of an infinite number of infinitely thin pages. (In the early seventeenth century, Cavalieri stated that every solid body is the superposition of an infinite number of planes.) Using that silken *vademecum* would not be easy: each apparent page would open into other similar pages; the inconceivable middle page would have no "back."

The Garden of Forking Paths

For Victoria Ocampo

On page 242 of *The History of the World War*, Liddell Hart tells us that an Allied offensive against the Serre-Montauban line (to be mounted by thirteen British divisions backed by one thousand four hundred artillery pieces) had been planned for July 24, 1916, but had to be put off until the morning of the twenty-ninth. Torrential rains (notes Capt. Liddell Hart) were the cause of that delay—a delay that entailed no great consequences, as it turns out. The statement which follows—dictated, reread, and signed by Dr. Yu Tsun, former professor of English in the *Hochschule* at Tsingtao—throws unexpected light on the case. The two first pages of the statement are missing.

. . .

... and I hung up the receiver. Immediately afterward, I recognised the voice that had answered in German. It was that of Capt. Richard Madden. Madden's presence in Viktor Runeberg's flat meant the end of our efforts and (though this seemed to me quite secondary, or *should have seemed*) our lives as well. It meant that Runeberg had been arrested, or murdered.[1] Before the sun set on that day, I would face the same fate. Madden was implacable—or rather, he was obliged to be implacable. An Irishman at the orders of the English, a man accused of a certain lack of zealousness, perhaps even treason, how could he fail to embrace and give thanks for this miraculous favour—the discovery, capture, perhaps death, of two agents of the German Empire? I went upstairs to my room; absurdly, I locked the

[1]A bizarre and despicable supposition. The Prussian spy Hans Rabener, alias Viktor Runeberg, had turned an automatic pistol on his arresting officer, Capt. Richard Madden. Madden, in self-defense, inflicted the wounds on Rabener that caused his subsequent death. [Ed. note.]

door, and then I threw myself, on my back, onto my narrow iron bed. Outside the window were the usual rooftops and the overcast six o'clock sun. I found it incredible that this day, lacking all omens and premonitions, should be the day of my implacable death. Despite my deceased father, despite my having been a child in a symmetrical garden in Hai Feng—was I, now, about to die? Then I reflected that all things happen to *oneself*, and happen precisely, precisely *now*. Century follows century, yet events occur only *in the present;* countless men in the air, on the land and sea, yet everything that truly happens, happens *to me*. . . . The almost unbearable memory of Madden's horsey face demolished those mental ramblings. In the midst of my hatred and my terror (now I don't mind talking about terror—now that I have foiled Richard Madden, now that my neck hungers for the rope), it occurred to me that that brawling and undoubtedly happy warrior did not suspect that I possessed the Secret—the name of the exact location of the new British artillery park on the Ancre. A bird furrowed the grey sky, and I blindly translated it into an aeroplane, and that aeroplane into many (in the French sky), annihilating the artillery park with vertical bombs. If only my throat, before a bullet crushed it, could cry out that name so that it might be heard in Germany. . . . But my human voice was so terribly inadequate. How was I to make it reach the Leader's ear—the ear of that sick and hateful man who knew nothing of Runeberg and me save that we were in Staffordshire, and who was vainly awaiting word from us in his arid office in Berlin, poring infinitely through the newspapers? . . . *I must flee,* I said aloud. I sat up noiselessly, in needless but perfect silence, as though Madden were already just outside my door. Something—perhaps the mere show of proving that my resources were nonexistent—made me go through my pockets. I found what I knew I would find: the American watch, the nickel-plated chain and quadrangular coin, the key ring with the compromising and useless keys to Runeberg's flat, the notebook, a letter I resolved to destroy at once (and never did), the false passport, one crown, two shillings, and a few odd pence, the red-and-blue pencil, the handkerchief, the revolver with its single bullet. Absurdly, I picked it up and hefted it, to give myself courage. I vaguely reflected that a pistol shot can be heard at a considerable distance. In ten minutes, my plan was ripe. The telephone book gave me the name of the only person able to communicate the information: he lived in a suburb of Fenton, less than a half hour away by train.

I am a coward. I can say that, now that I have carried out a plan whose dangerousness and daring no man will deny. I know that it was a terrible thing to do. I did not do it for Germany. What do I care for a barbaric country that has forced me to the ignominy of spying? Furthermore, I know of a man of England—a modest man—who in my view is no less a genius than Goethe. I spoke with him for no more than an hour, but for one hour he was Goethe. . . . No—I did it because I sensed that the Leader looked down on the people of my race—the countless ancestors whose blood flows through my veins. I wanted to prove to him that a yellow man could save his armies. And I had to escape from Madden. His hands, his voice, could beat upon my door at any moment. I silently dressed, said good-bye to myself in the mirror, made my way downstairs, looked up and down the quiet street, and set off. The train station was not far from my flat, but I thought it better to take a cab. I argued that I ran less chance of being recognised that way; the fact is, I felt I was visible and vulnerable—infinitely vulnerable—in the deserted street. I recall that I told the driver to stop a little distance from the main entrance to the station. I got down from the cab with willed and almost painful slowness. I would be going to the village of Ashgrove, but I bought a ticket for a station farther down the line. The train was to leave at eight-fifty, scant minutes away. I had to hurry; the next train would not be until nine-thirty. There was almost no one on the platform. I walked through the cars; I recall a few workmen, a woman dressed in mourning weeds, a young man fervently reading Tacitus' *Annals*, and a cheerful-looking wounded soldier. The train pulled out at last. A man I recognised ran, vainly, out to the end of the platform; it was Capt. Richard Madden. Shattered, trembling, I huddled on the other end of the seat, far from the feared window.

From that shattered state I passed into a state of almost abject cheerfulness. I told myself that my duel had begun, and that in dodging my adversary's thrust—even by forty minutes, even thanks to the slightest smile from fate—the first round had gone to me. I argued that this small win prefigured total victory. I argued that the win was not really even so small, since without the precious hour that the trains had given me, I'd be in gaol, or dead. I argued (no less sophistically) that my cowardly cheerfulness proved that I was a man capable of following this adventure through to its successful end. From that weakness I drew strength that was never to abandon me. I foresee that mankind will resign itself more and more fully every day to more and more horrendous undertakings; soon there will be nothing but warriors and brigands. I give them this piece of advice: *He who is to perform a horrendous act should imagine to himself that it is already done, should impose upon himself a future as irrevocable as the past.* That is what I did, while my eyes—the eyes of a man already dead—registered the flow of that day perhaps to be my last, and the spreading of the night. The train ran sweetly, gently, through woods of ash trees. It stopped virtually in the middle of the countryside. No one called out the name of the station. "Ashgrove?" I asked some boys on the platform. "Ashgrove," they said, nodding. I got off the train.

A lamp illuminated the platform, but the boys' faces remained within the area of shadow. "Are you going to Dr. Stephen Albert's house?" one queried. Without waiting for an answer, another of them said: "The house is a far way, but you'll not get lost if you follow that road there to the left, and turn left at every crossing." I tossed them a coin (my last), went down some stone steps, and started down the solitary road. It ran ever so slightly downhill and was of elemental dirt. Branches tangled overhead, and the low round moon seemed to walk along beside me.

For one instant, I feared that Richard Madden had somehow seen through my desperate plan, but I soon realized that that was impossible. The boy's advice to turn always to the left reminded me that that was the common way of discovering the central lawn of a certain type of maze. I am something of a *connoisseur* of mazes: not for nothing am I the great-grandson of that Ts'ui Pen who was governor of Yunan province and who renounced all temporal power in order to write a novel containing more characters than the *Hung Lu Meng* and construct a labyrinth in which all men would lose their way. Ts'ui Pen devoted thirteen years to those disparate labours, but the hand of a foreigner murdered him and his novel made no sense and no one ever found the labyrinth. It was under English trees that I meditated on that lost labyrinth: I pictured it perfect and inviolate on the secret summit of a mountain; I pictured its outlines blurred by rice paddies, or underwater; I pictured it as infinite—a labyrinth not of octagonal pavillions and paths that turn back upon themselves, but of rivers and provinces and kingdoms. . . . I imagined a labyrinth of labyrinths, a maze of mazes, a twisting, turning, ever-widening labyrinth that contained both past and future and somehow implied the stars. Absorbed in those illusory imaginings, I forgot that I was a pursued man; I felt myself, for an indefinite while, the abstract perceiver of the world. The vague, living countryside, the moon, the remains of the day did their work in me; so did the gently downward road, which forestalled all possibility of weariness. The evening was near, yet infinite.

The road dropped and forked as it cut through the now-formless meadows. A keen and vaguely syllabic song, blurred by leaves and distance, came and went on the gentle gusts of breeze. I was struck by the thought that a man may be the enemy of other men, the enemy of other men's other moments, yet not be the enemy of a country—of fireflies, words, gardens, watercourses, zephyrs. It was amidst such thoughts that I came to a high rusty gate. Through the iron bars I made out a drive lined with poplars, and a gazebo of some kind. Suddenly, I realised two things—the first trivial, the second almost incredible: the music I had heard was coming from that gazebo, or pavillion, and the music was Chinese. That was why unconsciously I had fully given myself over to it. I do not recall whether there was a bell or whether I had to clap my hands to make my arrival known.

The sputtering of the music continued, but from the rear of the intimate house, a lantern was making its way toward me—a lantern crosshatched and sometimes blotted out altogether by the trees, a paper lantern the shape of a drum and the colour of the moon. It was carried by a tall man. I could not see his face because the light blinded me. He opened the gate and slowly spoke to me in my own language.

"I see that the compassionate Hsi P'eng has undertaken to remedy my solitude. You will no doubt wish to see the garden?"

I recognised the name of one of our consuls, but I could only disconcertedly repeat, "The garden?"

"The garden of forking paths."

Something stirred in my memory, and I spoke with incomprehensible assurance.

"The garden of my ancestor Ts'ui Pen."

"Your ancestor? Your illustrious ancestor? Please—come in."

The dew-drenched path meandered like the paths of my childhood. We came to a library of Western and Oriental books. I recognised, bound in yellow silk, several handwritten volumes of the Lost Encyclopedia compiled by the third emperor of the Luminous Dynasty but never printed. The disk on the gramophone revolved near a bronze phoenix. I also recall a vase of *famille rose* and another, earlier by several hundred years, of that blue colour our artificers copied from the potters of ancient Persia. . . .

Stephen Albert, with a smile, regarded me. He was, as I have said, quite tall, with sharp features, grey eyes, and a grey beard. There was something priestlike about him, somehow, but something sailorlike as well; later he told me he had been a missionary in Tientsin "before aspiring to be a Sinologist."

We sat down, I on a long low divan, he with his back to the window and a tall circular clock. I figured that my pursuer, Richard Madden, could not possibly arrive for at least an hour. My irrevocable decision could wait.

"An amazing life, Ts'ui Pen's," Stephen Albert said. "Governor of the province in which he had been born, a man learned in astronomy, astrology, and the unwearying interpretation of canonical books, a chess player, a renowned poet and calligrapher—he abandoned it all in order to compose a book and a labyrinth. He renounced the pleasures of oppression, justice, the populous marriage bed, banquets, and even erudition in order to sequester himself for thirteen years in the Pavillion of Limpid Solitude. Upon his death, his heirs found nothing but chaotic manuscripts. The family, as you perhaps are aware, were about to deliver them to the fire, but his counsellor—a Taoist or Buddhist monk—insisted upon publishing them."

"To this day," I replied, "we who are descended from Ts'ui Pen execrate that monk. It was senseless to publish those manuscripts. The book is a contradictory jumble of irresolute drafts. I once examined it myself; in the third chapter the hero dies, yet in the fourth he is alive again. As for Ts'ui Pen's other labor, his Labyrinth . . ."

"Here is the Labyrinth," Albert said, gesturing towards a tall lacquered writing cabinet.

"An ivory labyrinth!" I exclaimed. "A very small sort of labyrinth . . ."

"A labyrinth of symbols," he corrected me. "An invisible labyrinth of time. I, an English barbarian, have somehow been chosen to unveil the diaphanous mystery. Now, more than a hundred years after the fact, the precise details are irrecoverable, but it is not difficult to surmise what happened. Ts'ui Pen must at one point have remarked, 'I shall retire to write a book,' and at another point, 'I shall retire to construct a labyrinth.' Everyone pictured two projects; it occurred to no one that book and labyrinth were one and the same. The Pavillion of Limpid Solitude was erected in the centre of a garden that was, perhaps, most intricately laid out; that fact might well have suggested a physical labyrinth. Ts'ui Pen died; no one in all the wide lands that had been his could find the labyrinth. The novel's confusion—confusedness, I mean, of course—suggested to me that it was that labyrinth. Two circumstances lent me the final solution of the problem—one, the curious legend that Ts'ui Pen had intended to construct a labyrinth which was truly infinite, and two, a fragment of a letter I discovered."

Albert stood. His back was turned to me for several moments; he opened a drawer in the black-and-gold writing cabinet. He turned back with a paper that had once been crimson but was now pink and delicate and rectangular. It was written in Ts'ui Pen's renowned calligraphy. Eagerly yet uncomprehendingly I read the words that a man of my own lineage had written with painstaking brushstrokes: *I leave to several futures (not to all) my garden of forking paths.* I wordlessly handed the paper back to Albert. He continued:

"Before unearthing this letter, I had wondered how a book could be infinite. The only way I could surmise was that it be a cyclical, or circular, volume, a volume whose last page would be identical to the first, so that one might go on indefinitely. I also recalled that night at the centre of the *1001 Nights*, when the queen Scheherazade (through some magical distractedness on the part of the copyist) begins to retell, verbatim, the story of the 1001 Nights, with the risk of returning once again to the night on which she is telling it—and so on, *ad infinitum.* I also pictured to myself a platonic, hereditary sort of work, passed down from father to son, in which each new individual would add a chapter or with reverent care correct his elders' pages. These imaginings amused and distracted me, but none of them seemed to correspond even remotely to Ts'ui Pen's contradictory chapters. As I was floundering about in the mire of these perplexities, I was sent from Oxford the document you have just examined. I paused, as you may well imagine, at the sentence 'I leave to several futures (not to all) my garden of forking paths.' Almost instantly, I saw it—the garden of forking paths was the chaotic novel; the phrase 'several futures (not all)' suggested to me the image of a forking in *time*, rather than in space. A full rereading of the book confirmed my theory. In all fictions, each time a man meets diverse alternatives, he chooses one and eliminates the others; in the work of the virtually impossible-to-disentangle Ts'ui Pen, the character chooses—simultaneously—all of them. *He creates,* thereby, 'several futures,' several *times,* which themselves proliferate and fork. That is the explanation for the novel's contradictions. Fang, let us say, has a secret; a stranger knocks at his door; Fang decides to kill him. Naturally, there are various possible outcomes—Fang can kill the intruder, the intruder can kill Fang, they can both live, they can both be killed, and so on. In Ts'ui Pen's novel, *all* the outcomes in fact occur; each is the starting point for further bifurcations. Once in a while, the paths of that labyrinth converge: for example, you come to this house, but in one of the possible pasts you are my enemy, in another my friend. If you can bear my incorrigible pronunciation, we shall read a few pages."

His face, in the vivid circle of the lamp, was undoubtedly that of an old man, though with something indomitable and even immortal about it. He read with slow precision two versions of a single epic chapter. In the first, an army marches off to battle through a mountain wilderness; the horror of the rocks and darkness inspires in them a disdain for life, and they go on to an easy victory. In the second, the same army passes through a palace in which a ball is being held; the brilliant battle seems to them a continuation of the *fête*, and they win it easily.

I listened with honourable veneration to those ancient fictions, which were themselves perhaps not as remarkable as the fact that a man of my blood had invented them and a man of a distant empire was restoring them to me on an island in the West in the course of a desperate mission. I recall the final words, repeated in each version like some secret commandment: "Thus the heroes fought, their admirable hearts calm, their swords violent, they themselves resigned to killing and to dying."

From that moment on, I felt all about me and within my obscure body an invisible, intangible pullulation—not that of the divergent, parallel, and finally coalescing armies, but an agitation more inaccessible, more inward than that, yet one those armies somehow prefigured. Albert went on:

"I do not believe that your venerable ancestor played at idle variations. I cannot think it probable that he would sacrifice thirteen years to the infinite performance of a rhetorical exercise. In your country, the novel is a subordinate genre; at that time it was a genre beneath contempt. Ts'ui Pen was a novelist of genius, but he was also a man of letters, and surely would not have considered himself a mere novelist. The testimony of his contemporaries proclaims his metaphysical, mystical leanings—and his life is their fullest confirmation. Philosophical debate consumes a good part of his novel. I know that of all problems, none disturbed him, none gnawed at him like the unfathomable problem of time. How strange, then, that that problem should be the *only* one that does not figure in the pages of his *Garden*. He never even uses the word. How do you explain that wilful omission?"

I proposed several solutions—all unsatisfactory. We discussed them; finally, Stephen Albert said:

"In a riddle whose answer is chess, what is the only word that must not be used?"

I thought for a moment.

"The word 'chess,' " I replied.

"Exactly," Albert said. "*The Garden of Forking Paths* is a huge riddle, or parable, whose subject is time; that secret purpose forbids Ts'ui Pen the merest mention of its name. To *always* omit one word, to employ awkward metaphors and obvious circumlocutions, is perhaps the most emphatic way of calling attention to that word. It is, at any rate, the tortuous path chosen by the devious Ts'ui Pen at each and every one of the turnings of his inexhaustible novel. I have compared hundreds of manuscripts, I have corrected the errors introduced through the negligence of copyists, I have reached a hypothesis for the plan of that chaos, I have reestablished, or believe I've reestablished, its fundamental order—I have translated the entire work; and I know that not once does the word 'time' appear. The explanation is obvious: *The Garden of Forking Paths* is an incomplete, but not false, image of the universe as conceived by Ts'ui Pen. Unlike Newton and Schopenhauer, your ancestor did not believe in a uniform and absolute time; he believed in an infinite series of times, a growing, dizzying web of divergent, convergent, and parallel times. That fabric of times that approach one another, fork, are snipped off, or are simply unknown for centuries, contains *all* possibilities. In most of those times, we do not exist; in some, you exist but I do not; in others, I do and you do not; in others still, we both do. In this one, which the favouring hand of chance has dealt me, you have come to my home; in another, when you come through my garden you find me dead; in another, I say these same words, but I am an error, a ghost."

"In all," I said, not without a tremble, "I am grateful for, and I venerate, your re-creation of the garden of Ts'ui Pen."

"Not in all," he whispered with a smile. "Time forks, perpetually, into countless futures. In one of them, I am your enemy."

I felt again that pullulation I have mentioned. I sensed that the dew-drenched garden that surrounded the house was saturated, infinitely, with invisible persons. Those persons were Albert and myself—secret, busily at work, multiform—in other dimensions of time. I raised my eyes and the gossamer nightmare faded. In the yellow-and-black garden there was but a single man—but that man was as mighty as a statue, and that man was coming down the path, and he was Capt. Richard Madden.

"The future is with us," I replied, "but I am your friend. May I look at the letter again?"

Albert rose once again. He stood tall as he opened the drawer of the tall writing cabinet; he turned his back to me for a moment. I had cocked the revolver. With utmost care, I fired. Albert fell without a groan, without a sound, on the instant. I swear that he died instantly—one clap of thunder.

The rest is unreal, insignificant. Madden burst into the room and arrested me. I have been sentenced to hang. I have most abhorrently triumphed: I have communicated to Berlin the secret name of the city to be attacked. Yesterday it was bombed—I read about it in the same newspapers that posed to all of England the enigma of the murder of the eminent

Sinologist Stephen Albert by a stranger, Yu Tsun. The Leader solved the riddle. He knew that my problem was how to report (over the deafening noise of the war) the name of the city named Albert, and that the only way I could find was murdering a person of that name. He does not know (no one can know) my endless contrition, and my weariness.

ARTIFICES

(1944)

Foreword

Although less clumsily executed, the stories in this volume are no different from those in the volume that precedes it. Two of them, perhaps, merit some comment: "Death and the Compass" and "Funes, His Memory." The second is one long metaphor for insomnia. The first, in spite of the Germanic or Scandinavian names in it, takes place in a Buenos Aires of dreams: the twisting "rue de Toulon" is the Paseo de Julio; "Triste-le-Roy" is the hotel where Herbert Ashe received, yet probably did not read, the eleventh volume of an imaginary encyclopedia. After this fiction was written, I thought it might be worthwhile to expand the time and space the story covers: the revenge might be bequeathed to others, the periods of time might be calculated in years, perhaps in centuries; the first letter of the Name might be uttered in Iceland, the second in Mexico, the third in Hindustan. Is there any need for me to say that there are saints among the Hasidim, and that the sacrifice of four lives in order to obtain the four letters that the Name demands is a fantasy dictated by the shape of my story?

Postscript, 1956. I have added three stories to this volume: "The South," "The Cult of the Phoenix," and "The End." Aside from one character, Recabarren, whose immobility and passivity serve as contrast, nothing (or almost nothing) in the brief course of that last story is of my invention—everything in it is implicit in a famous book, though I have been the first to perceive it, or at least to declare openly that I have. In the allegory of the Phoenix, I set myself the problem of suggesting a common act—the Secret—hesitatingly, gradually, and yet, in the end, unequivocally; I am not sure to what extent I have succeeded. Of "The South," which may be my best story, I shall tell the reader only that it is possible to read it both as a forthright narration of novelistic events and in quite another way, as well.

Schopenhauer, de Quincey, Stevenson, Mauthner, Shaw, Chesterton, León Bloy—this is the heterogeneous list of the writers I am continually rereading. In the Christological fantasy titled "Three Versions of Judas," I think I can perceive the remote influence of the last of these.

J.L.B.

Buenos Aires, August 29, 1944/1956

Funes, His Memory*

I recall him (though I have no right to speak that sacred verb—only one man on earth did, and that man is dead) holding a dark passionflower in his hand, seeing it as it had never been seen, even had it been stared at from the first light of dawn till the last light of evening for an entire lifetime. I recall him—his taciturn face, its Indian features, its extraordinary *remoteness*—behind the cigarette. I recall (I think) the slender, leather-braider's fingers. I recall near those hands a *mate* cup, with the coat of arms of the Banda Oriental.* I recall, in the window of his house, a yellow straw blind with some vague painted lake scene. I clearly recall his voice—the slow, resentful, nasal voice of the toughs of those days, without the Italian sibilants one hears today. I saw him no more than three times, the last time in 1887. . . . I applaud the idea that all of us who had dealings with the man should write something about him; my testimony will perhaps be the briefest (and certainly the slightest) account in the volume that you are to publish, but it can hardly be the least impartial. Unfortunately I am Argentine, and so congenitally unable to produce the dithyramb that is the obligatory genre in Uruguay, especially when the subject is an Uruguayan. *Highbrow, dandy, city slicker*—Funes did not utter those insulting words, but I know with reasonable certainty that to him I represented those misfortunes. Pedro Leandro Ipuche* has written that Funes was a precursor of the race of supermen—"a maverick and vernacular Zarathustra"—and I will not argue the point, but one must not forget that he was also a street tough from Fray Bentos, with certain incorrigible limitations.

My first recollection of Funes is quite clear. I see him one afternoon in March or February of '84. That year, my father had taken me to spend the summer in Fray Bentos.* I was coming back from the ranch in San Francisco with my cousin Bernardo Haedo. We were riding along on our horses, singing merrily—and being on horseback was not the only reason for my cheerfulness. After a sultry day, a huge slate-colored storm, fanned by the south wind, had curtained the sky. The wind flailed the trees wildly, and I was filled with the fear (the hope) that we would be surprised in the open countryside by the elemental water. We ran a kind of race against the storm. We turned into the deep bed of a narrow street that ran between two brick sidewalks built high up off the ground. It had suddenly got dark; I heard quick, almost secret footsteps above me—I raised my eyes and saw a boy running along the narrow, broken sidewalk high above, as though running along the top of a narrow, broken wall. I recall the short, baggy trousers—like a gaucho's—that he wore, the straw-soled cotton slippers, the cigarette in the hard visage, all stark against the now limitless storm cloud. Unexpectedly, Bernardo shouted out to him—*What's the time, Ireneo?* Without consulting the sky, without a second's pause, the boy replied, *Four minutes till eight, young Bernardo Juan Francisco.* The voice was shrill and mocking.

I am so absentminded that I would never have given a second thought to the exchange I've just reported had my attention not been called to it by my cousin, who was prompted by a certain local pride and the desire to seem unfazed by the other boy's trinomial response.

He told me that the boy in the narrow street was one Ireneo Funes, and that he was known for certain eccentricities, among them shying away from people and always knowing what time it was, like a clock. He added that Ireneo was the son of a village ironing woman, María Clementina Funes, and that while some people said his father was a doctor in the salting house (an Englishman named O'Connor), others said he broke horses or drove oxcarts for a living over in the department of Salto. The boy lived with his mother, my cousin told me, around the corner from Villa Los Laureles.

In '85 and '86, we spent the summer in Montevideo; it was not until '87 that I returned to Fray Bentos. Naturally, I asked about everybody I knew, and finally about "chronometric Funes." I was told he'd been bucked off a half-broken horse on the ranch in San Francisco and had been left hopelessly crippled. I recall the sensation of unsettling magic that this news gave me: The only time I'd seen him, we'd been coming home on horseback from the ranch in San Francisco, and he had been walking along a high place. This new event, told by my cousin Bernardo, struck me as very much like a dream confected out of elements of the past. I was told that Funes never stirred from his cot, his eyes fixed on the fig tree behind the house or on a spiderweb. At dusk, he would let himself be carried to the window. He was such a proud young man that he pretended that his disastrous fall had actually been fortunate. . . . Twice I saw him, on his cot behind the iron-barred window that crudely underscored his prisonerlike state—once lying motionless, with his eyes closed; the second time motionless as well, absorbed in the contemplation of a fragrant switch of artemisia.

It was not without some self-importance that about that same time I had embarked upon a systematic study of Latin. In my suitcase I had brought with me Lhomond's *De viris illustribus,* Quicherat's *Thesaurus,* Julius Caesar's commentaries, and an odd-numbered volume of Pliny's *Naturalis historia*— a work which exceeded (and still exceeds) my modest abilities as a Latinist. There are no secrets in a small town; Ireneo, in his house on the outskirts of the town, soon learned of the arrival of those outlandish books. He sent me a flowery, sententious letter, reminding me of our "lamentably ephemeral" meeting "on the seventh of February, 1884." He dwelt briefly, elegiacally, on the "glorious services" that my uncle, Gregorio Haedo, who had died that same year, "had rendered to his two motherlands in the valiant Battle of Ituzaingó," and then he begged that I lend him one of the books I had brought, along with a dictionary "for a full understanding of the text, since I must plead ignorance of Latin." He promised to return the books to me in good condition, and "straightway." The penmanship was perfect, the letters exceptionally well formed; the spelling was that recommended by Andrés Bello: *i* for *y*, *j* for *g*. At first, of course, I thought it was some sort of joke. My cousins assured me it was not, that this "was just . . . just Ireneo." I didn't know whether to attribute to brazen conceit, ignorance, or stupidity the idea that hard-won Latin needed no more teaching than a dictionary could give; in order to fully disabuse Funes, I sent him Quicherat's *Gradus ad Parnassum* and the Pliny.

On February 14, I received a telegram from Buenos Aires urging me to return home immediately; my father was "not at all well." God forgive me, but the prestige of being the recipient of an urgent telegram, the desire to communicate to all of Fray Bentos the contradiction between the negative form of the news and the absoluteness of the adverbial phrase, the temptation to dramatize my grief by feigning a virile stoicism—all this perhaps distracted me from any possibility of real pain. As I packed my bag, I realized that I didn't have the *Gradus ad Parnassum* and the first volume of Pliny. The *Saturn* was to sail the next morning; that evening, after dinner, I walked over to Funes' house. I was amazed that the evening was no less oppressive than the day had been.

At the honest little house, Funes' mother opened the door.

She told me that Ireneo was in the back room. I shouldn't be surprised if I found the room dark, she told me, since Ireneo often spent his off hours without lighting the candle. I walked across the tiled patio and down the little hallway farther on, and came to the second patio. There was a grapevine; the darkness seemed to me virtually total. Then suddenly I heard Ireneo's high, mocking voice. The voice was speaking Latin; with morbid pleasure, the voice emerging from the shadows was reciting a speech or a prayer or an incantation. The Roman syllables echoed in the patio of hard-packed earth; my trepidation made me think them incomprehensible, and endless; later, during the enormous conversation of that night, I learned they were the first paragraph of the twenty-fourth chapter of the seventh book of Pliny's *Naturalis historia.* The subject of that chapter is memory; the last words were *ut nihil non iisdem verbis redderetur auditum.*

Without the slightest change of voice, Ireneo told me to come in. He was lying on his cot, smoking. I don't think I saw his face until the sun came up the next morning; when I look back, I believe I recall the momentary glow of his cigarette. His room smelled vaguely musty. I sat down; I told him about my telegram and my father's illness.

I come now to the most difficult point in my story, a story whose only *raison d'être* (as my readers should be told from the outset) is that dialogue half a century ago. I will not attempt to reproduce the words of it, which are now forever irrecoverable. Instead, I will summarize, faithfully, the many things Ireneo told me. Indirect discourse is distant and weak; I know that I am sacrificing the effectiveness of my tale. I only ask that my readers try to hear in their imagination the broken and staccato periods that astounded me that night.

Ireneo began by enumerating, in both Latin and Spanish, the cases of prodigious memory cataloged in the *Naturalis historia*: Cyrus, the king of Persia, who could call all the soldiers in his armies by name; Mithridates Eupator, who meted out justice in the twenty-two languages of the kingdom over which he ruled; Simonides, the inventor of the art of memory; Metrodorus, who was able faithfully to repeat what he had heard, though it be but once. With obvious sincerity, Ireneo said he was amazed that such cases were thought to be amazing. He told me that before that rainy afternoon when the blue roan had bucked him off, he had been what every man was—blind, deaf, befuddled, and virtually devoid of memory. (I tried to remind him how precise his perception of time, his memory for proper names had been—he ignored me.) He had lived, he said, for nineteen years as though in a dream: he looked without seeing, heard without listening, forgot everything, or virtually everything. When he fell, he'd been knocked unconscious; when he came to again, the present was so rich, so clear, that it was almost unbearable, as were his oldest and even his most trivial memories. It was shortly afterward that he learned he was crippled; of that fact he hardly took notice. He reasoned (or felt) that immobility was a small price to pay. Now his perception and his memory were perfect.

With one quick look, you and I perceive three wineglasses on a table; Funes perceived every grape that had been pressed into the wine and all the stalks and tendrils of its vineyard. He knew the forms of the clouds in the southern sky on the morning of April 30, 1882, and he could compare them in his memory with the veins in the marbled binding of a book he had seen only once, or with the feathers of spray lifted by an oar on the Río Negro on the eve of the Battle of Quebracho. Nor were those memories simple—every visual image was linked to muscular sensations, thermal sensations, and so on. He was able to reconstruct every dream, every daydream he had ever had. Two or three times he had reconstructed an entire day; he had never once erred or faltered, but each reconstruction had itself taken an entire day. *"I, myself, alone, have more memories than all mankind since the world began,"* he said to me. And also: *"My dreams are like other people's waking hours."* And again, toward dawn: *"My memory, sir, is like a garbage heap."* A circle drawn on a blackboard, a right triangle, a rhombus—all these are forms we can fully intuit; Ireneo could do the same with the stormy mane of a young colt, a small herd of cattle on a mountainside, a flickering fire and its uncountable ashes, and the many faces of a dead man at a wake. I have no idea how many stars he saw in the sky.

Those are the things he told me; neither then nor later have I ever doubted them. At that time there were no cinematographers, no phonographs; it nevertheless strikes me as implausible, even incredible, that no one ever performed an experiment with Funes. But then, all our lives we postpone everything that can be postponed; perhaps we all have the certainty, deep inside, that we are immortal and that sooner or later every man will do everything, know all there is to know.

The voice of Funes, from the darkness, went on talking.

He told me that in 1886 he had invented a numbering system original with himself, and that within a very few days he had passed the twenty-four thousand mark. He had not written it down, since anything he thought, even once, remained ineradicably with him. His original motivation, I think, was his irritation that the thirty-three Uruguayan patriots* should require two figures and three words rather than a single figure, a single word. He then applied this mad principle to the other numbers. Instead of seven thousand thirteen (7013), he would say, for instance, "Máximo Pérez"; instead of seven thousand fourteen (7014), "the railroad"; other numbers were "Luis Melián Lafinur," "Olimar," "sulfur," "clubs," "the whale," "gas," "a stewpot," "Napoleon," "Agustín de Vedia." Instead of five hundred (500), he said "nine." Every word had a particular figure attached to it, a sort of marker; the later ones were extremely complicated. . . . I tried to explain to Funes that his rhapsody of unconnected words was exactly the opposite of a number *system.* I told him that when one said "365" one said "three hundreds, six tens, and five ones," a breakdown impossible with the "numbers" *Nigger Timoteo* or *a ponchoful of meat.* Funes either could not or would not understand me.

In the seventeenth century, Locke postulated (and condemned) an impossible language in which each individual thing—every stone, every bird, every branch—would have its own name; Funes once contemplated a similar language, but discarded the idea as too general, too ambiguous. The truth was, Funes remembered not only every leaf of every tree in every patch of forest, but every time he had perceived or imagined that leaf. He resolved to reduce every one of his past days to some seventy thousand recollections, which he would then define by numbers. Two considerations dissuaded him: the realization that the task was interminable, and the realization that it was pointless. He saw that by the time he died he would still not have finished classifying all the memories of his childhood.

The two projects I have mentioned (an infinite vocabulary for the natural series of numbers, and a pointless mental catalog of all the images of his memory) are foolish, even preposterous, but they reveal a certain halting grandeur. They allow us to glimpse, or to infer, the dizzying world that Funes lived in. Funes, we must not forget, was virtually incapable of general, platonic ideas. Not only was it difficult for him to see that the generic symbol "dog" took in all the dissimilar individuals of all shapes and sizes, it irritated him that the "dog" of three-fourteen in the afternoon, seen in profile, should be indicated by the same noun as the dog of three-fifteen, seen frontally. His own face in the mirror, his own hands, surprised him every time he saw them. Swift wrote that the emperor of Lilliput could perceive the movement of the minute hand of a clock; Funes could continually perceive the quiet advances of corruption, of tooth decay, of weariness. He saw—he *noticed*—the progress of death, of humidity. He was the solitary, lucid spectator of a multiform, momentaneous, and almost unbearably precise world. Babylon, London, and New York dazzle mankind's imagination with their fierce splendor; no one in the populous towers or urgent avenues of those cities has ever felt the heat and pressure of a reality as inexhaustible as that which battered Ireneo, day and night, in his poor South American hinterland. It was hard for him to sleep. To sleep is to take one's mind from the world; Funes, lying on his back on his cot, in the dimness of his room, could picture every crack in the wall, every molding of the precise houses that surrounded him. (I repeat that the most trivial of his memories was more detailed, more vivid than our own perception of a physical pleasure or a physical torment.) Off toward the east, in an area that had not yet been cut up into city blocks, there were new houses, unfamiliar to Ireneo. He pictured them to himself as black, compact, made of homogeneous shadow; he would turn his head in that direction to sleep. He would also imagine himself at the bottom of a river, rocked (and negated) by the current.

He had effortlessly learned English, French, Portuguese, Latin. I suspect, nevertheless, that he was not very good at thinking. To think is to ignore (or forget) differences, to generalize, to abstract. In the teeming world of Ireneo Funes there was nothing but particulars—and they were virtually *immediate* particulars.

The leery light of dawn entered the patio of packed earth.

It was then that I saw the face that belonged to the voice that had been talking all night long. Ireneo was nineteen, he had been born in 1868; he looked to me as monumental as bronze—older than Egypt, older than the prophecies and the pyramids. I was struck by the thought that every word I spoke, every expression of my face or motion of my hand would endure in his implacable memory; I was rendered clumsy by the fear of making pointless gestures.

Ireneo Funes died in 1889 of pulmonary congestion.

The Shape of the Sword

His face was traversed by a vengeful scar, an ashen and almost perfect arc that sliced from the temple on one side of his head to his cheek on the other. His true name does not matter; everyone in Tacuarembó called him "the Englishman at La Colorada." The owner of the land, Cardoso, hadn't wanted to sell it; I heard that the Englishman plied him with an argument no one could have foreseen—he told him the secret history of the scar. He had come from the border, from Rio Grande do Sul; there were those who said that over in Brazil he had been a smuggler. The fields had gone to grass, the water was bitter; to put things to right, the Englishman worked shoulder to shoulder with his peons. People say he was harsh to the point of cruelty, but scrupulously fair. They also say he liked his drink; once or twice a year he would shut himself up in the room in the belvedere, and two or three days later he would emerge as though from a battle or a spell of dizziness—pale, shaking, befuddled, and as authoritarian as ever. I recall his glacial eyes, his lean energy, his gray mustache. He was standoffish; the fact is, his Spanish was rudimentary, and tainted with the accents of Brazil. Aside from the occasional business letter or pamphlet, he got no mail.

The last time I made a trip through the northern provinces, high water along the Caraguatá forced me to spend the night at La Colorada. Within a few minutes I thought I sensed that my showing up that way was somehow inopportune. I tried to ingratiate myself with the Englishman, and to do so I seized upon patriotism, that least discerning of passions. I remarked that a country with England's spirit was invincible. My interlocutor nodded, but added with a smile that he wasn't English—he was Irish, from Dungarvan. That said, he stopped, as though he had let slip a secret.

We went outside after dinner to have a look at the sky. The clouds had cleared away, but far off behind the sharp peaks, the southern sky, creviced and split with lightning, threatened another storm. Back in the dilapidated dining room, the peon who'd served dinner brought out a bottle of rum. We drank for a long time, in silence.

I am not sure what time it was when I realized that I was drunk; I don't know what inspiration or elation or boredom led me to remark on my host's scar. His face froze; for several seconds I thought he was going to eject me from the house. But at last, his voice perfectly ordinary, he said to me:

"I will tell you the story of my scar under one condition—that no contempt or condemnation be withheld, no mitigation for any iniquity be pleaded."

I agreed. This is the story he told, his English interspersed with Spanish, and even with Portuguese:

. . .

In 1922, in one of the cities of Connaught, I was one of the many young men who were conspiring to win Ireland's independence. Of my companions there, some are still living, working for peace; others, paradoxically, are fighting under English colours, at sea or in the desert; one, the best of us all, was shot at dawn in the courtyard of a prison, executed by men filled with dreams; others (and not the least fortunate, either) met their fate in the anonymous, virtually secret battles of the civil war. We were Republicans and Catholics; we were, I suspect, romantics. For us, Ireland was not just the utopian future and the unbearable present; it was a bitter yet loving mythology, it was the circular towers and red bogs, it was the repudiation of Parnell, and it was the grand epics that sing the theft of bulls that were heroes in an earlier incarnation, and in other incarnations fish, and mountains. . . . One evening I shall never forget, there came to us a man, one of our own, from Munster—a man called John Vincent Moon.

He couldn't have been more than twenty. He was thin yet slack-muscled, all at once—he gave the uncomfortable impression of being an invertebrate. He had studied, ardently and with some vanity, virtually every page of one of those Communist manuals; he would haul out his dialectical materialism to cut off any argument. There are infinite reasons a man may have for hating or loving another man; Moon reduced the history of the world to one sordid economic conflict. He declared that the Revolution was foreordained to triumph. I replied that only *lost* causes were of any interest to a gentleman. . . . Night had fallen; we pursued our cross-purposes in the hallway, down the stairs, then through the vague streets. The verdicts Moon handed down impressed me considerably less than the sense of unappealable and absolute truth with which he issued them. The new comrade did not argue, he did not debate—he *pronounced judgement,* contemptuously and, to a degree, wrathfully.

As we came to the last houses of the city that night, we were stupefied by the sudden sound of gunfire. (Before this, or afterward, we skirted the blind wall of a factory or a gaol.) We turned down a dirt street; a soldier, huge in the glare, burst out of a torched cottage. He shouted at us to halt. I started walking faster; my comrade did not follow me. I turned around—John Vincent Moon was standing as motionless as a rabbit caught in one's headlights—eternalized, somehow, by terror. I ran back, floored the soldier with a single blow, shook Vincent Moon, cursed him, and ordered him to come with me. I had to take him by the arm; the passion of fear had stripped him of all will. But then we did run—we fled through the conflagration-riddled night. A burst of rifle fire came our way, and a bullet grazed Moon's right shoulder; as we fled through the pine trees, a weak sob racked his breast.

In that autumn of 1922 I had gone more or less underground, and was living in General Berkeley's country house. The general (whom I had never seen) was at that time posted to some administrative position or other out in Bengal; the house was less than a hundred years old but it was gloomy and dilapidated and filled with perplexing corridors and pointless antechambers. The museum-cabinet and huge library arrogated to themselves the entire lower floor—there were the controversial and incompatible books that are somehow the history of the nineteenth century; there were scimitars from Nishapur, in whose frozen crescents the wind and violence of battle seemed to be living on. We entered the house (I think I recall) through the rear. Moon, shaking, his mouth dry, mumbled that the events of the night had been "interesting"; I salved and bandaged him, then brought him a cup of tea. The wound was superficial. Suddenly, puzzled, he stammered:

"You took a terrible chance, coming back to save me like that."

I told him it was nothing. (It was the habit of civil war that impelled me to act as I acted; besides, the imprisonment of a single one of us could imperil the entire cause.)

The next day, Moon had recovered his composure. He accepted a cigarette and subjected me to a harsh interrogation as to the "financial resources of our revolutionary party." His questions were quite lucid; I told him (truthfully) that the situation was grave. Deep rumblings of gunfire troubled the peace of the south. I told Moon that our comrades were waiting for us. My overcoat and revolver were up in my room; when I returned, I found Moon lying on the sofa, his eyes closed. He thought he had a fever; he pleaded a painful spasm in his shoulder.

It was then that I realized he was a hopeless coward. I clumsily told him to take care of himself, then left. I was embarrassed by the man and his fear, shamed by him, as though I myself were the coward, not Vincent Moon. Whatsoever one man does, it is as though all men did it. That is why it is not unfair that a single act of disobedience in a garden should contaminate all humanity; that is why it is not unfair that a single Jew's crucifixion should be enough to save it. Schopenhauer may have been right—I am other men, any man is all men, Shakespeare is somehow the wretched John Vincent Moon.

We spent nine days in the general's great house. Of the agonies and the rays of light of that dark war I shall say nothing; my purpose is to tell the story of this scar that affronts me. In my memory, those nine days form a single day—except for the next to last, when our men stormed a barracks and avenged, life for life, our sixteen comrades fallen to the machine guns at Elphin. I would slip out of the house about dawn, in the blurred confusion of first light. I would be back toward nightfall. My comrade would be waiting for me upstairs; his wound would not allow him to come down. When I look back, I see him with some book of strategy in his hand—F. N. Maude, or Clausewitz. "The weapon of preference for me," he confessed to me one night, "is artillery." He enquired into our plans; he enjoyed criticizing or rethinking them. He was also much given to deploring "our woeful financial base"; dogmatically and sombrely he would prophesy the disastrous end. *"C'est une affaire flambée,"* he would mutter. To show that his physical cowardice was a matter of indifference to him, he made a great display of mental arrogance. Thus passed, well or not so well, nine days.

On the tenth, the city fell once and forever into the hands of the Black and Tans. High-sitting, silent horsemen patrolled their beats; there was ash and smoke in the wind. I saw a dead body sprawled on one corner—yet that dead body is less vivid in my memory than the dummy that the soldiers endlessly practised their marksmanship on in the middle of the city square. . . . I had gone out when dawn was just streaking the sky; before noon, I was back. Moon was in the library, talking to someone; I realized from the tone of his voice that he was speaking on the telephone. Then I heard my name; then, that I'd be back at seven, and then, that I'd be arrested as I came across the lawn. My rational friend was rationally selling me out. I heard him demand certain guarantees of his own safety.

Here my story becomes confused and peters out a bit. I know that I chased the snitch through black corridors of nightmare and steep stairwells of vertigo. Moon knew the house well, every bit as well as I. Once or twice I lost him, but I managed to corner him before the soldiers arrested me. From one of the general's suits of armor, I seized a scimitar, and with that steel crescent left a flourish on his face forever—a half-moon of blood. To you alone, Borges—you who are a stranger—I have made this confession. *Your* contempt is perhaps not so painful.

. . .

Here the narrator halted. I saw that his hands were trembling.

"And Moon?" I asked. "What became of Moon?"

"He was paid his Judas silver and he ran off to Brazil. That evening, in the city square, I saw a dummy shot by a firing squad of drunks."

I waited vainly for the rest of the story. Finally, I asked him to go on.

A groan made his entire body shiver; he gestured, feebly, gently, toward the curving whitish scar.

"Do you not believe me?" he stammered. "Do you not see set upon my face the mark of my iniquity? I have told you the story this way so that you would hear it out. It was *I* who betrayed the man who saved me and gave me shelter—it is *I* who am Vincent Moon. Now, despise me."

1942

The Theme of the Traitor and the Hero

So the Platonic Year
Whirls out new right and wrong
Whirls in the old instead;
All men are dancers and their tread
Goes to the barbarous clangour of a gong.

W. B. Yeats, *The Tower*

Under the notorious influence of Chesterton (inventor and embellisher of elegant mysteries) and the court counselor Leibniz (who invented preestablished harmony), in my spare evenings I have conceived this plot—which I will perhaps commit to paper but which already somehow justifies me. It needs details, rectifications, tinkering—there are areas of the story that have never been revealed to me. Today, January 3, 1944, I see it in the following way:

The action takes place in an oppressed yet stubborn country—Poland, Ireland, the republic of Venice, some South American or Balkan state. . . . Or *took* place rather, for though the narrator is contemporary, the story told by him occurred in the mid or early nineteenth century—in 1824, let us say, for convenience's sake; in Ireland, let us also say. The narrator is a man named Ryan, the great-grandson of the young, heroic, beautiful, murdered Fergus Kilpatrick, whose grave was mysteriously violated, whose name gives luster to Browning's and Hugo's verses, and whose statue stands high upon a gray hilltop among red bogs.

Kilpatrick was a conspirator and a secret and glorious captain of conspirators. Like Moses, who from the land of Moab glimpsed yet could not reach the promised land, Kilpatrick perished on the eve of the victorious rebellion he had planned for and dreamed of. The date of the first centenary of his death is approaching; the circumstances of the crime are enigmatic; Ryan, who is writing a biography of the hero, discovers that the enigma goes deeper than mere detective work can fathom. Kilpatrick was murdered in a theater; the English police never apprehended the assassin. Historians claim that this failure does not tarnish the good name of the police, since it is possible that the police themselves had Kilpatrick murdered. Other aspects of the mystery disturb Ryan; certain things seem almost cyclical, seem to repeat or combine events from distant places, distant ages. For example: Everyone knows that the constables who examined the hero's body found a sealed letter warning Kilpatrick not to go to the theater that night; Julius Caesar, too, as he was walking toward the place where the knives of his friends awaited him, received a note he never read—a note telling him of his betrayal and revealing the names of his betrayers. Caesar's wife, Calpurnia, saw in dreams a tower felled by order of the Senate; on the eve of Kilpatrick's death, false and anonymous rumors of the burning of the circular tower of Kilgarvan spread throughout the country—an event that might be taken as an omen, since Kilpatrick had been born in Kilgarvan. These (and other) parallels between the story of Julius Caesar and the story of an Irish conspirator induce Ryan to imagine some secret shape of time, a pattern of repeating lines. His thoughts turn to the decimal history conceived by Condorcet, the morphologies proposed by Hegel, Spengler, and Vico, mankind as posited by Hesiod, degenerating from gold to iron. He thinks of the transmigration of souls, a doctrine that lends horror to Celtic literature and that Caesar himself attributed to the Druids of Britain; he toys with the idea that before Fergus Kilpatrick was Fergus Kilpatrick, he was Julius Caesar. He is saved from those circular labyrinths by a curious discovery, a discovery which, however, will plunge him deep into other, yet more tangled and heterogeneous mazes: It seems that certain words spoken by a beggar who spoke with Fergus Kilpatrick on the day of his death had been prefigured by Shakespeare, in *Macbeth.* The idea that history might have copied history is mind-boggling enough; that history should copy *literature* is inconceivable.... Ryan digs further, and he finds that in 1814 James Alexander Nolan, the oldest of the hero's comrades, had translated Shakespeare's major plays into Gaelic—among them *Julius Caesar.* He also finds in the archives a manuscript article by Nolan on the Swiss *Festspiele*—vast peripatetic theatrical performances that require thousands of actors and retell historical episodes in the same cities, the same mountains in which they occurred. Another unpublished document reveals to Ryan that a few days before the end, Kilpatrick, presiding over the last gathering of his chiefs, had signed the death sentence of a traitor, whose name has been scratched out. This sentence does not jibe with Kilpatrick's customary mercifulness. Ryan investigates the matter (his investigation being one of the gaps in the book's narration) and manages to decipher the enigma.

Kilpatrick was murdered in a theater, yet the entire city played the role of theater, too, and the actors were legion, and the play that was crowned by Kilpatrick's death took place over many days and many nights. Here is what happened:

On August 2, 1824, the conspirators met. The country was ripe for rebellion; something, however, always went awry—there must have been a traitor within the inner circle. Fergus Kilpatrick had given James Nolan the job of ferreting out the identity of this traitor, and Nolan had carried out his mission. He announced to the gathered comrades that the traitor was Kilpatrick himself. He proved the truth of his accusation beyond the shadow of a doubt, and the men at the council that night condemned their leader to death. The leader signed his own death sentence, but he pleaded that his punishment not harm the cause.

And so it was that Nolan conceived a strange plan. Ireland idolized Kilpatrick; the slightest suspicion of his baseness would have compromised the rebellion; Nolan proposed a way to turn the traitor's execution into an instrument for the emancipation of the country. He proposed that the condemned man die at the hands of an unknown assassin in deliberately dramatic circumstances; those circumstances would engrave themselves upon the popular imagination and hasten the rebellion. Kilpatrick swore to collaborate in this plan which would give him an occasion to redeem himself, and which would be crowned by his death.

Nolan had no time to invent the circumstances of the multiple execution from scratch, and so he plagiarized the scene from another playwright, the English enemy Will Shakespeare, reprising scenes from *Macbeth* and *Julius Caesar.* The public yet secret performance occurred over several days. The condemned man entered Dublin, argued, worked, prayed, reprehended, spoke words of pathos—and each of those acts destined to shine forth in glory had been choreographed by Nolan. Hundreds of actors collaborated with the protagonist; the role of some was complex, the role of others a matter of moments on the stage. The things they did and said endure in Ireland's history books and in its impassioned memory. Kilpatrick, moved almost to ecstasy by the scrupulously plotted fate that would redeem him and end his days, more than once enriched his judge's text with improvised words and acts. Thus the teeming drama played itself out in time, until that August 6, 1824, in a box (prefiguring Lincoln's) draped with funereal curtains, when a yearned-for bullet pierced the traitor-hero's breast. Between two spurts of sudden blood, Kilpatrick could hardly pronounce the few words given him to speak.

In Nolan's play, the passages taken from Shakespeare are the *least* dramatic ones; Ryan suspected that the author interpolated them so that someone, in the future, would be able to stumble upon the truth. Ryan realized that he, too, was part of Nolan's plot. . . . After long and stubborn deliberation, he decided to silence the discovery. He published a book dedicated to the hero's glory; that too, perhaps, had been foreseen.

Death and the Compass

For Mandie Molina Vedia

Of the many problems on which Lönnrot's reckless perspicacity was exercised, none was so strange—so *rigorously* strange, one might say—as the periodic series of bloody deeds that culminated at the Villa Triste-le-Roy, amid the perpetual fragrance of the eucalyptus. It is true that Erik Lönnrot did not succeed in preventing the last crime, but he did, indisputably, foresee it. Nor did he divine the identity of Yarmolinsky's unlucky murderer, but he did perceive the evil series' secret shape and the part played in it by Red Scharlach, whose second sobriquet is Scharlach the Dandy. That criminal (like so many others) had sworn upon his honor to kill Lönnrot, but Lönnrot never allowed himself to be intimidated. He thought of himself as a reasoning machine, an Auguste Dupin, but there was something of the adventurer in him, even something of the gambler.

The first crime occurred in the Hôtel du Nord, that tall prism sitting high above the estuary whose waters are the color of the desert. To that tower (which is notorious for uniting in itself the abhorrent whiteness of a sanatorium, the numbered divisibility of a prison, and the general appearance of a house of ill repute) there came, on December 3, the delegate from Podolsk to the Third Talmudic Congress—Dr. Marcelo Yarmolinsky, a man of gray beard and gray eyes. We will never know whether he found the Hôtel du Nord to his liking; he accepted it with the ancient resignation that had allowed him to bear three years of war in the Carpathians and three thousand years of pogroms and oppression. He was given a room on R Floor, across the hall from the suite occupied—not without some splendor—by the Tetrarch of Galilee. Yarmolinsky had dinner, put off till the next day his examination of the unfamiliar city, set out his many books and very few articles of jewelry on a bureau, and, before midnight, turned off the light. (Thus testified the tetrarch's driver, who was sleeping in the adjoining room.) On the fourth, at 11:30 A.M., a writer for the *Yiddische Zeitung* telephoned Yarmolinsky, but Dr. Yarmolinsky did not answer. He was found lying on the floor of his room, his face by now slightly discolored, his body almost naked beneath an anachronistic cape. He was lying not far from the door to the hallway; a deep knife wound had rent his chest. A couple of hours later, in the same room, standing amid journalists, photographers, and gendarmes, police commissioner Treviranus and Lönnrot serenely discussed the problem.

"No need to go off on wild-goose chases here," Treviranus was saying, as he brandished an imperious cigar. "We all know that the Tetrarch of Galilee owns the finest sapphires in the world. Somebody intending to steal the sapphires broke in here by mistake. Yarmolinsky woke up, the burglar had to kill him. —What do you think?"

"Possible, but uninteresting," Lönnrot replied. "You will reply that reality has not the slightest obligation to be interesting. I will reply in turn that reality may get along without that obligation, but hypotheses may not. In the hypothesis that you suggest, here, on the spur of the moment, chance plays a disproportionate role. What we have here is a dead rabbi; I would prefer a purely rabbinical explanation, not the imaginary bunglings of an imaginary burglar."

Treviranus' humor darkened.

"I'm not interested in 'rabbinical explanations,' as you call them; what I'm interested in is catching the blackguard that stabbed this unknown man."

"Unknown?" asked Lönnrot. "Here are his complete works." He gestured to the bureau with its row of tall books: *A Vindication of the Kabbalah*; *A Study of the Philosophy of Robert Fludd*; a literal translation of the *Sefer Yetsirah*; a *Biography of the Baal Shem*; *A History of the Hasidim*; a monograph in German on the Tetragrammaton; another on the divine nomenclature of the Pentateuch. The commissioner looked at them with fear, almost with revulsion. Then he laughed.

"I'm a poor Christian fellow," he replied. "You can take those things home with you, if you want them; I can't be wasting my time on Jewish superstitions."

"This crime may, however, *belong* to the history of Jewish superstitions," Lönnrot muttered.

"As Christianity does," the writer from the *Yiddische Zeitung* added, scathingly. He was nearsighted, quite shy, and an atheist.

No one answered him. In the little typewriter, one of the agents had found a slip of paper, with this unfinished declaration:

The first letter of the Name has been written.

Lönnrot resisted a smile. Suddenly turned bibliophile or Hebraist, he ordered one of the officers to wrap up the dead man's books, and he took them to his apartment. Then, indifferent to the police investigation, he set about studying them. One book, an octavo volume, revealed to him the teachings of Israel Baal Shem Tov, the founder of the sect of the Pious; another, the virtues and terrors of the Tetragrammaton, the ineffable name of God; yet another, the notion that God has a secret name, which (much like the crystal sphere attributed by the Persians to Alexander of Macedonia) contains His ninth attribute, the eternity—that is, immediate knowledge—of all things that shall be, are, and have been in the universe. Tradition reckons the names of God at ninety-nine; while Hebraists attribute that imperfect sum to the magical fear of even numbers, the Hasidim argue that the lacuna points toward a hundredth name—the Absolute Name.

From his erudition Lönnrot was distracted, a few days later, by the writer from the *Yiddische Zeitung.* The young man wanted to talk about the murder; Lönnrot preferred to talk about the many names of God. The journalist filled three columns with the story that the famed detective Erik Lönnrot had taken up the study of the names of God in order to discover the name of the murderer. Lönnrot, accustomed to journalists' simplifications, did not take offense. One of those shopkeepers who have found that any given man may be persuaded to buy any given book published a popular edition of *A History of the Hasidim.*

The second crime took place on the night of January 3, in the emptiest and most godforsaken of the echoing suburbs on the western outskirts of the capital. Sometime around dawn, one of the mounted gendarmes that patrolled the solitudes of those blocks saw a man, wrapped in a poncho, lying in the doorway of an old paint factory. His hard face looked as though it were wearing a mask of blood; a deep knife wound split his chest. On the wall, across the red and yellow rhombuses, someone had chalked some words, which the gendarme spelled out to himself. . . . That afternoon, Treviranus and Lönnrot made their way to the distant scene of the crime. To the left and right of their automobile, the city crumbled away; the sky expanded, and now houses held less and less importance, a brick kiln or a poplar tree more and more. They came to their miserable destination; a final alleyway lined with pink-colored walls that somehow seemed to reflect the rambunctious setting of the sun. By this time, the dead man had been identified. He was Daniel Simón Azevedo, a man of some reputation in the old slums of the Northside, where he had risen from wagon driver to election-day thug, only to degenerate thereafter into a thief and even an informer. (The singular manner of his death seemed fitting: Azevedo was the last representative of a generation of outlaws who used a knife but not a revolver.) The chalked words read as follows:

The second letter of the Name has been written.

The third crime took place on the night of February 3. A few minutes before one, the telephone rang in Commissioner Treviranus' office. Keenly secretive, the guttural voice of a man came on the line; he told the commissioner his name was Ginzberg (or Ginsburg) and said that for a reasonable fee he was willing to reveal certain details of the two sacrifices, Azevedo's and Yarmolinsky's. A cacophony of whistles and party horns drowned out the informer's voice. Then, the line went dead. Without discarding the possibility of a prank (it was carnival time, after all), Treviranus made inquiries and found that the call had come from Liverpool House, a tavern on the rue de Toulon—that brackish street shared by a popular museum of wonders and a milk store, a brothel and a company of Bible sellers. Treviranus telephoned the owner of the place—Black Finnegan, former Irish criminal now overwhelmed, almost crushed, by honesty. Finnegan told Treviranus that the last person to use the telephone in the tavern had been a tenant, one Gryphius, who'd just gone out with some friends. Treviranus drove immediately to Liverpool House. The owner had the following to say: Eight days earlier, Gryphius—a man with sharp features, a nebulous gray beard, and a nondescript black suit—had rented a room above the bar. Finnegan (who generally put the room to a use that Treviranus had no difficulty guessing) had named an exorbitant rent; Gryphius had unhesitatingly paid it. He almost never left the room; he had both lunch and dinner there and hardly ever showed his face in the bar. That night he had come down to Finnegan's office to make a call. A closed coupe had stopped in front of the tavern. The driver hadn't left the driver's seat; some of the customers recalled that he was wearing a bear mask. Two harlequin figures got out of the car; they were short, and no one could fail to notice that they were drunk. They burst into Finnegan's office, party horns bleating, and threw their arms around Gryphius, who apparently recognized them but greeted them somewhat coldly. They exchanged a few words in Yiddish—Gryphius in a low, guttural voice, the harlequins in a sort of falsetto—and then all went up to Gryphius' room. Fifteen minutes later the three men came down again, quite happy; Gryphius was staggering, and seemed to be as drunk as the others. Tall and unsteady, his head apparently spinning, he was in the middle, between the masked harlequins. (One of the women in the bar recalled the yellow, red, and green lozenges.) Twice he stumbled; twice the harlequins steadied him. The three men got into the coupe and disappeared in the direction of the nearby pier, with its rectangular water. But just as he stepped on the running board of the car, the last harlequin scrawled an obscene figure and a sentence on one of the blackboards in the entryway.

Treviranus looked at the sentence, but it was almost predictable:

The last letter of the Name has been written.

Then he examined Gryphius-Ginsburg's little room. On the floor, there was a brusque star, in blood; in the corners, the remains of cigarettes, Hungarian; on a bureau, a book in Latin—Leusden's *Philologus hebræogræcus* (1739)—with several handwritten notes. Treviranus looked at it indignantly, and sent for Lönnrot. Lönnrot did not take his hat off before plunging into the book, while the commissioner interrogated the contradictory witnesses to the possible kidnapping. At four they left. Out in the twisting rue de Toulon, as they walked through the dawn's dead streamers and confetti, Treviranus said:

"What if tonight's story were a sham, a simulacrum?"

Erik Lönnrot smiled and in a grave voice read the commissioner a passage (which had been underlined) from the *Philologus'* thirty-third dissertation: *Dies Judæorum incipit a solis occasu usque ad solis occasum diei sequentis.* "Which means," he added, " 'The Jewish day begins at sundown and lasts until sundown of the following day.' "

The other man made an attempt at irony.

"And is that the most valuable piece of information you've picked up tonight, then?"

"No. The most valuable piece of information is the word Ginsburg used."

The afternoon papers had not overlooked these periodic deaths and disappearances. The *Cross and Sword* contrasted them with the admirable discipline and order of the last Hermetic congress; Ernst Palast of *The Martyr* denounced "the intolerable delays of a clandestine and niggardly pogrom, which has taken three months to wipe out three Jews"; the *Yiddische Zeitung* rejected the horrifying theory of an anti-Semitic conspiracy, "though many insightful spirits will hear of no other solution for the triple mystery"; the most famous gunman of the Southside, Dandy Red Scharlach, swore that in his territory no crime such as that had ever taken place, and he accused Police Commissioner Franz Treviranus of criminal negligence.

On March 1, this same Treviranus received an impressive-looking sealed envelope. He opened it; it contained a letter signed "Baruch Spinoza" and a detailed map of the city, clearly torn out of a Baedeker. The letter predicted that on the third of March there would not be a fourth crime, because the paint factory in the west, the tavern on the rue de Toulon, and the Hôtel du Nord were "the perfect points of a mystical, equilateral triangle"; red ink on the map demonstrated its regularity. Treviranus read over that argument-by-geometry resignedly and then sent both letter and map to Lönnrot's house, Lönnrot indisputably being a man who deserved this sort of claptrap.

Erik Lönnrot studied the map and letter. The three locations were indeed equidistant. Symmetry in time (December 3, January 3, February 3); symmetry in space, as well . . . Lönnrot sensed, abruptly, that he was on the brink of solving the riddle. A drawing-compass and a navigational compass completed that sudden intuition. He smiled, spoke the word Tetragrammaton (a word he had recently acquired), and telephoned the commissioner.

"Thanks for that equilateral triangle you sent me last night. It was what I needed to solve the puzzle. Tomorrow, Friday, the perpetrators will be in prison; we can relax."

"Then they're not planning a fourth crime?"

"It's precisely because they *are* planning a fourth crime that we can relax," Lönnrot said as he hung up.

An hour later, he was riding on a Southern Railway train toward the abandoned Villa Triste-le-Roy. South of the city of my story flows a sluggish stream of muddy water, choked with refuse and thick with the runoff of tanneries. On the other side is a suburb filled with factories where, under the protection of a Barcelona gangster, gunmen prosper. Lönnrot smiled to think that the most famous of these criminals—Red Scharlach—would have given anything to know about his clandestine visit. Azevedo had been one of Scharlach's gang; Lönnrot considered the remote possibility that Scharlach was to be the fourth victim, but then rejected it. . . . He had virtually solved the problem; the mere circumstances, the reality (names, arrests, faces, the paperwork of trial and imprisonment), held very little interest for him now. He wanted to go for a walk, he wanted a respite from the three months of sedentary investigation. He reflected that the explanation for the crimes lay in an anonymous triangle and a dusty Greek word. The mystery seemed so crystal clear to him now, he was embarrassed to have spent a hundred days on it.

The train stopped at a silent loading platform. Lönnrot got off. It was one of those deserted evenings that have the look of dawn. The air of the murky plains was wet and cold. Lönnrot began to walk cross-country. He saw dogs, he saw a van or lorry in a dead-end alleyway, he saw the horizon, he saw a silvery horse lapping at the rank water of a puddle. It was growing dark when he saw the rectangular belvedere of Villa Triste-le-Roy, which stood almost as high as the black eucalyptus trees that surrounded it. The thought occurred to him that one dawn and one sunset (an ancient glow in the east and another in the west) were all that separated him from the hour yearned for by the seekers of the Name.

A rusty fence defined the irregular perimeter of the villa's grounds. The main gate was closed. Lönnrot, with no great expectation of finding a way in, walked all the way around. Back at the impregnable gate, he stuck his hand almost mechanically between the bars and came upon the latch. The creaking of the iron startled him. With laborious passivity, the entire gate yielded.

Lönnrot made his way forward through the eucalyptus trees, treading upon confused generations of stiff red leaves. Seen at closer quarters, the house belonging to the Villa Triste-le-Roy abounded in pointless symmetries and obsessive repetitions; a glacial Diana in a gloomy niche was echoed by a second Diana in a second niche; one balcony was reflected in another; double stairways opened into a double balustrade. A two-faced Hermes threw a monstrous shadow. Lönnrot walked all around the outside of the house as he had made the circuit of the villa's grounds. He inspected everything; under the level of the terrace, he spotted a narrow shutter.

He pushed at it; two or three marble steps descended into a cellar. Lönnrot, who by now had a sense of the architect's predilections, guessed that there would be another set of steps in the opposite wall. He found them, climbed them, raised his hands, and opened the trapdoor out.

A glowing light led him toward a window. This he also opened; a round yellow moon defined two leaf-clogged fountains in the dreary garden. Lönnrot explored the house. Through foyers that opened onto dining rooms and on through galleries, he would emerge into identical courtyards—often the same courtyard. He climbed dusty stairs to circular antechambers;

he would recede infinitely in the facing mirrored walls; he wearied of opening or half opening windows that revealed to him, outside, the same desolate garden from differing heights and differing angles—inside, the furnishings in yellowing covers, chandeliers swathed in muslin. A bedchamber stopped him; there, a single flower in a porcelain vase; at the first brush of his fingertips, the ancient petals crumbled. On the second floor, on the uppermost floor, the house seemed infinite yet still growing. *The house is not so large,* he thought. *It seems larger because of its dimness, its symmetry, its mirrors, its age, my unfamiliarity with it, and this solitude.*

A stairway took him to the belvedere. The moonlight of the evening shone through the lozenges of the windows; they were yellow, red, and green. He was stopped by an astonished, dizzying recollection.

Two fierce, stocky men leaped upon him and disarmed him; another, quite tall, greeted him gravely:

"You are so kind. You have saved us a night and a day."

It was Red Scharlach. The men tied Lönnrot's hands. Lönnrot at last found his voice.

"Scharlach—*you* are looking for the secret Name?"

Scharlach stood there, impassive. He had not participated in the brief struggle, and now moved only to put out his hand for Lönnrot's revolver. But then he spoke, and Lönnrot heard in his voice a tired triumphance, a hatred as large as the universe, a sadness no smaller than that hatred.

"No," he said. "I am looking for something more fleeting and more perishable than that—I am looking for Erik Lönnrot. Three years ago, in a gambling den on the rue de Toulon, you arrested my brother and saw that he was sent to prison. My men rescued me from the shoot-out in a coupe, but not before I'd received a policeman's bullet in my gut. Nine days and nine nights I lay between life and death in this desolate symmetrical villa, consumed by fever, and that hateful two-faced Janus that looks toward the sunset and the dawn lent horror to my deliriums and my sleeplessness. I came to abominate my own body, I came to feel that two eyes, two hands, two lungs are as monstrous as two faces. An Irishman tried to convert me to belief in Christ; he would repeat, over and over, the goyim's saying: All roads lead to Rome. At night, my delirium would grow fat upon that metaphor: I sensed that the world was a labyrinth, impossible to escape—for all roads, even if they pretended to lead north or south, returned finally to Rome, which was also the rectangular prison where my brother lay dying, and which was also the Villa Triste-le-Roy. During those nights, I swore by the god that sees with two faces, and by all the gods of fever and of mirrors, to weave a labyrinth around the man who had imprisoned my brother. I have woven it, and it has stood firm: its materials are a dead heresiologue, a compass, an eighth-century cult, a Greek word, a dagger, the rhombuses of a paint factory. . . .

"The first term of the series was given me quite by chance. With some friends of mine—among them Daniel Azevedo—I had figured out a way to steal the tetrarch's sapphires. Azevedo, however, double-crossed us; he got drunk on the money we had advanced him and pulled the job a day early. But then he got lost in that huge hotel, and sometime around two o'clock in the morning he burst into Yarmolinsky's room. Yarmolinsky, who suffered from insomnia, was sitting at his typewriter typing. As coincidence would have it, he was making some notes, or writing an article perhaps, on the Name of God; he had just typed the words *The first letter of the Name has been written.* Azevedo told him to keep quiet; Yarmolinsky put out his hand toward the bell that would wake everyone in the hotel; Azevedo stabbed him once in the chest. The movement was almost reflexive; a half century of violence had taught him that the easiest and safest way is simply to kill. . . . Ten days later I learned from the *Yiddische Zeitung* that you were trying to find the key to Yarmolinsky's death among Yarmolinsky's writings. I read *A History of the Hasidim*; I learned that the reverent fear of speaking the Name of God had been the origin of the doctrine that that Name is omnipotent and occult. I learned that some Hasidim, in the quest for that secret Name, had gone so far as to commit human sacrifice. . . . I realized that you would conjecture that the Hasidim had sacrificed the rabbi; I set about justifying that conjecture.

"Marcelo Yarmolinsky died on the night of December third; I chose the third of January for the second 'sacrifice.' Yarmolinsky died in the north; for the second 'sacrifice,' the death should take place in the west. Daniel Azevedo was the necessary victim. He deserved to die; he was a man that acted on impulse and he was a traitor—if he were captured, he could destroy my plan. One of my men stabbed him; in order to link his body to the first one, I wrote *The second letter of the Name has been written* across the rhombuses of the paint factory.

"The third 'crime' was committed on the third of February. It was, as Treviranus guessed, a mere sham, a simulacrum. *I* am Gryphius-Ginzberg-Ginsburg; I spent one interminable week (supplemented by a tissue-thin false beard) in that perverse cubicle on the rue de Toulon, until my friends kidnapped me. Standing on the running board of the coupe, one of them scrawled on a pillar the words that you recall: *The last letter of the Name has been written.* That sentence revealed that this was a series of *three* crimes. At least that was how the man in the street interpreted it—but I had repeatedly dropped clues so that *you*, the *reasoning* Erik Lönnrot, would realize that there were actually *four*. One sign in the north, two more in the east and west, demand a fourth sign in the south—after all, the Tetragrammaton, the Name of God, YHVH, consists of *four* letters; the harlequins and the paint manufacturer's emblem suggest *four* terms. It was I who underlined that passage in Leusden's book. The passage says that Jews compute the day from sunset to sunset; the passage therefore gives one to understand that the deaths occurred on the *fourth* of each month. It was I who sent the equilateral triangle to Treviranus. I knew you would add the missing point, the point that makes a perfect rhombus, the point that fixes the place where a precise death awaits you. I have done all this, Erik Lönnrot, planned all this, in order to draw you to the solitudes of Triste-le-Roy."

Lönnrot avoided Scharlach's eyes. He looked at the trees and the sky subdivided into murky red, green, and yellow rhombuses. He felt a chill, and an impersonal, almost anonymous sadness. The night was dark now; from the dusty garden there rose the pointless cry of a bird. For the last time, Lönnrot considered the problem of the symmetrical, periodic murders.

"There are three lines too many in your labyrinth," he said at last. "I know of a Greek labyrinth that is but one straight line. So many philosophers have been lost upon that line that a mere detective might be pardoned if he became lost as well. When you hunt me down in another avatar of our lives, Scharlach, I suggest that you fake (or commit) one crime at A, a second crime at B, eight kilometers from A, then a third crime at C, four kilometers from A and B and halfway between them. Then wait for me at D, two kilometers from A and C, once again halfway between them. Kill me at D, as you are about to kill me at Triste-le-Roy."

"The next time I kill you," Scharlach replied, "I promise you the labyrinth that consists of a single straight line that is invisible and endless."

He stepped back a few steps. Then, very carefully, he fired.

1942

The Secret Miracle

> And God caused him to die for an hundred years, and then raised him to life. And God said, "How long hast thou waited?" He said, "I have waited a day or part of a day."
>
> Qur'ān, 2:261

On the night of March 14, 1939, in an apartment on Prague's Zeltnergasse, Jaromir Hladik, author of the unfinished tragedy *The Enemies*, a book titled *A Vindication of Eternity*, and a study of Jakob Boehme's indirect Jewish sources, dreamed of a long game of chess. The game was played not by two individuals, but by two illustrious families; it had been started many centuries in the past. No one could say what the forgotten prize was to be, but it was rumored to be vast, perhaps even infinite. The chess pieces and the chessboard themselves were in a secret tower. Jaromir (in the dream) was the firstborn son of one of the contending families; the clocks chimed the hour of the inescapable game; the dreamer was running across the sand of a desert in the rain, but he could recall neither the figures nor the rules of chess. At that point, Hladik awoke. The din of the rain and the terrible clocks ceased. A rhythmic and unanimous sound, punctuated by the barking of orders, rose from the Zeltnergasse. It was sunrise, and the armored vanguard of the Third Reich was rolling into Prague.

On the nineteenth, the authorities received a report from an informer. That same day, toward dusk, Jaromir Hladik was arrested. He was led to a white, aseptic jail on the opposite bank of the Moldau. He was unable to refute even one of the Gestapo's charges: His mother's family's name was Jaroslavski, he came of Jewish blood, his article on Boehme dealt with a Jewish subject, his was one of the accusing signatures appended to a protest against the Anschluss. In 1928, he had translated the *Sefer Yetsirah* for Hermann Barsdorf Publishers; that company's effusive catalog had exaggerated (as commercial catalogs do) the translator's renown; the catalog had been perused by Capt. Julius Rothe, one of the officers in whose hands his fate now lay. There is no one who outside his own area of knowledge is not credulous; two or three adjectives in Fraktur were enough to persuade Julius Rothe of Hladik's preeminence, and therefore that he should be put to death—*pour encourager les autres.* The date was set for March 29, at 9:00 A.M. That delay (whose importance the reader will soon discover) was caused by the administrative desire to work impersonally and deliberately, as vegetables do, or planets.

Hladik's first emotion was simple terror. He reflected that he wouldn't have quailed at being hanged, or decapitated, or having his throat slit, but being shot by a firing squad was unbearable. In vain he told himself a thousand times that the pure and universal act of dying was what ought to strike fear, not the concrete circumstances of it, and yet Hladik never wearied of picturing to himself those circumstances. Absurdly, he tried to foresee every variation. He anticipated the process endlessly, from the sleepless dawn to the mysterious discharge of the rifles. Long before the day that Julius Rothe had set, Hladik died hundreds of deaths—standing in courtyards whose shapes and angles ran the entire gamut of geometry, shot down by soldiers of changing faces and varying numbers who sometimes took aim at him from afar, sometimes from quite near. He faced his imaginary executions with true fear, perhaps with true courage. Each enactment lasted several seconds; when the circle was closed, Hladik would return, unendingly, to the shivering eve of his death. Then it occurred to him that reality seldom coincides with the way we envision it beforehand; he inferred, with perverse logic, that to foresee any particular detail is in fact to prevent its happening. Trusting in that frail magic, he began to invent horrible details—*so that they would not occur;* naturally he wound up fearing that those details might be prophetic. Miserable in the night, he tried to buttress his courage somehow on the fleeting stuff of time. He knew that time was rushing toward the morning of March 29; he reasoned aloud: *It is now the night of the twenty-second; so long as this night and six more last I am invulnerable, immortal.* He mused that the nights he slept were deep, dim cisterns into which he could sink. Sometimes, impatiently, he yearned for the shots that would end his life once and for all, the blast that would redeem him, for good or ill, from his vain imaginings. On the twenty-eighth, as the last rays of the sun were glimmering on the high bars of his window, he was diverted from those abject thoughts by the image of his play, *The Enemies.*

Hladik was past forty. Apart from a few friends and many routines, the problematic pursuit of literature constituted the whole of his life; like every writer, he measured other men's virtues by what they had accomplished, yet asked that other men measure him by what he planned someday to do. All the books he had sent to the press left him with complex regret. Into his articles on the work of Boehme, Ibn Ezra, and Fludd, he had poured mere diligence, application; into his translation of the *Sefer Yetsirah*, oversight, weariness, and conjecture. He judged *A Vindication of Eternity* to be less unsatisfactory, perhaps. The first volume documents the diverse eternities that mankind has invented, from Parmenides' static Being to Hinton's modifiable past; the second denies (with Francis Bradley) that all the events of the universe constitute a temporal series. It argues that the number of humankind's possible experiences is *not* infinite, and that a single "repetition" is sufficient to prove that time is a fallacy. . . . Unfortunately, no less fallacious are the arguments that prove that fallacy; Hladik was in the habit of ticking them off with a certain disdainful perplexity. He had also drafted a cycle of expressionist poems; these, to the poet's confusion, appeared in a 1924 anthology and there was never a subsequent anthology that didn't inherit them. With his verse drama *The Enemies*, Hladik believed he could redeem himself from all that equivocal and languid past. (He admired verse in drama because it does not allow the spectators to forget unreality, which is a condition of art.)

This play observed the unities of time, place, and action; it took place in Hradcany, in the library of Baron Römerstadt, on one of the last evenings of the nineteenth century. In Act I, Scene I, a stranger pays a visit to Römerstadt. (A clock strikes seven, a vehemence of last sunlight exalts the windowpanes, on a breeze float the ecstatic notes of a familiar Hungarian melody.) This visit is followed by others; the persons who come to importune Römerstadt are strangers to him, though he has the uneasy sense that he has seen them before, perhaps in a dream. All fawn upon him, but it is clear—first to the play's audience, then to the baron himself—that they are secret enemies, sworn to his destruction. Römerstadt manages to check or fend off their complex intrigues; in the dialogue they allude to his fiancée, Julia de Weidenau, and to one Jaroslav Kubin, who once importuned her with his love. Kubin has now gone mad, and believes himself to be Römerstadt. . . . The dangers mount; by the end of the second act, Römerstadt finds himself forced to kill one of the conspirators. Then the third and last act begins. Little by little, incoherences multiply; actors come back onstage who had apparently been discarded from the plot; for one instant, the man that Römerstadt killed returns. Someone points out that the hour has grown no later: the clock strikes seven; upon the high windowpanes the western sunlight shimmers; the thrilling Hungarian melody floats upon the air. The first interlocutor comes onstage again and repeats the same words he spoke in Act I, Scene I. Without the least surprise or astonishment, Römerstadt talks with him; the audience realizes that Römerstadt is the pitiable Jaroslav Kubin. The play has not taken place; it is the circular delirium that Kubin endlessly experiences and reexperiences.

Hladik had never asked himself whether this tragicomedy of errors was banal or admirable, carefully plotted or accidental. In the design I have outlined here, he had intuitively hit upon the best way of hiding his shortcomings and giving full play to his strengths, the possibility of rescuing (albeit symbolically) that which was fundamental to his life. He had finished the first act and one or another scene of the third; the metrical nature of the play allowed him to go over it continually, correcting the hexameters, without a manuscript. It occurred to him that he still had two acts to go, yet very soon he was to die. In the darkness he spoke with God. *If,* he prayed, *I do somehow exist, if I am not one of Thy repetitions or errata, then I exist as the author of* The Enemies. *In order to complete that play, which can justify me and justify Thee as well, I need one more year. Grant me those days, Thou who art the centuries and time itself.* It was the last night, the most monstrous night, but ten minutes later sleep flooded Hladik like some dark ocean.

Toward dawn, he dreamed that he was in hiding, in one of the naves of the Clementine Library. *What are you looking for?* a librarian wearing dark glasses asked him. *I'm looking for God,* Hladik replied. *God,* the librarian said, *is in one of the letters on one of the pages of one of the four hundred thousand volumes in the Clementine. My parents and my parents' parents searched for that letter; I myself have gone blind searching for it.* He removed his spectacles and Hladik saw his eyes, which were dead. A reader came in to return an atlas. *This atlas is worthless,* he said, and handed it to Hladik. Hladik opened it at random. He saw a map of India—a dizzying page. Suddenly certain, he touched one of the tiny letters. A voice that was everywhere spoke to him: *The time for your labor has been granted.* Here Hladik awoke.

He remembered that the dreams of men belong to God and that Maimonides had written that the words of a dream, when they are clear and distinct and one cannot see who spoke them, are holy. Hladik put his clothes on; two soldiers entered the cell and ordered him to follow them.

From inside his cell, Hladik had thought that when he emerged he would see a maze of galleries, stairways, and wings. Reality was not so rich; he and the soldiers made their way down a single iron staircase into a rear yard. Several soldiers—some with their uniforms unbuttoned—were looking over a motorcycle, arguing about it. The sergeant looked at his watch; it was eight forty-four. They had to wait until nine. Hladik, feeling more insignificant than ill fortuned, sat down on a pile of firewood. He noticed that the soldiers' eyes avoided his own. To make the wait easier, the sergeant handed him a cigarette. Hladik did not smoke; he accepted the cigarette out of courtesy, or out of humility. When he lighted it, he saw that his hands were trembling. The day clouded over; the soldiers were speaking in low voices, as though he were already dead. Vainly he tried to recall the woman that Julia de Weidenau had symbolized. . . .

The firing squad fell in, lined up straight. Hladik, standing against the prison wall, awaited the discharge. Someone was afraid the wall would be spattered with blood; the prisoner was ordered to come forward a few steps. Absurdly, Hladik was reminded of the preliminary shufflings-about of photographers. A heavy drop of rain grazed Hladik's temple and rolled slowly down his cheek; the sergeant called out the final order.

The physical universe stopped.

The weapons converged upon Hladik, but the men who were to kill him were immobile. The sergeant's arm seemed to freeze, eternal, in an inconclusive gesture. On one of the paving stones of the yard, a bee cast a motionless shadow. As though in a painting, the wind had died. Hladik attempted a scream, a syllable, the twisting of a hand. He realized that he was paralyzed. He could hear not the slightest murmur of the halted world. *I am in hell,* he thought, *I am dead.* Then *I am mad,* he thought. And then, *time has halted.* Then he reflected that if that were true, his thoughts would have halted as well. He tried to test this conjecture: he repeated (without moving his lips) Virgil's mysterious fourth eclogue. He imagined that the now-remote soldiers must be as disturbed by this as he was; he wished he could communicate with them. He was surprised and puzzled to feel neither the slightest weariness nor any faintness from his long immobility. After an indeterminate time, he slept. When he awoke, the world was still motionless and muffled. The drop of water still hung on his cheek; on the yard, there still hung the shadow of the bee; in the air the smoke from the cigarette he'd smoked had never wafted away. Another of those "days" passed before Hladik understood.

He had asked God for an entire year in which to finish his work; God in His omnipotence had granted him a year. God had performed for him a secret miracle: the German bullet would kill him, at the determined hour, but in Hladik's mind a year would pass between the order to fire and the discharge of the rifles. From perplexity Hladik moved to stupor, from stupor to resignation, from resignation to sudden gratitude.

He had no document but his memory; the fact that he had to learn each hexameter as he added it imposed upon him a providential strictness, unsuspected by those who essay and then forget vague provisional paragraphs. He did not work for posterity, nor did he work for God, whose literary preferences were largely unknown to him. Painstakingly, motionlessly, secretly, he forged in time his grand invisible labyrinth. He redid the third act twice. He struck out one and another overly obvious symbol—the repeated chimings of the clock, the music. No detail was irksome to him. He cut, condensed, expanded; in some cases he decided the original version should stand. He came to love the courtyard, the prison; one of the faces that stood before him altered his conception of Römerstadt's character. He discovered that the hard-won cacophonies that were so alarming to Flaubert are mere *visual* superstitions—weaknesses and irritations of the written, not the sounded, word. . . . He completed his play; only a single epithet was left to be decided upon now. He found it; the drop of water rolled down his cheek. He began a maddened cry, he shook his head, and the fourfold volley felled him.

Jaromir Hladik died on the twenty-ninth of March, at 9:02 A.M.

1943

Three Versions of Judas

There seemed a certainty in degradation.

T. E. Lawrence, *The Seven Pillars of Wisdom*, CIII

In Asia Minor or in Alexandria, in the second century of our faith, in the days when Basilides proclaimed that the cosmos was a reckless or maleficent improvisation by angels lacking in perfection, Nils Runeberg, with singular intellectual passion, would have led one of the gnostic conventicles. Dante might have consigned him to a sepulcher of fire; his name would have helped swell the catalogs of minor heresiarchs, between Satornilus and Carpocrates; one or another fragment of his teachings, bedizened with invective, would have been recorded for posterity in the apocryphal *Liber adversus omnes hæreses* or would have perished when the burning of a monastery's library devoured the last copy of the *Syntagma*. Instead, God allotted him the twentieth century and the university city of Lund. There, in 1904, he published the first edition of *Kristus och Judas*; there, in 1909, his magnum opus, *Den hemlige Frälsaren*. (Of this last-named book there is a German version, translated in 1912 by Emil Schering; it is titled *Der heimliche Heiland*.)

Before undertaking an examination of the works mentioned above, it is important to reiterate that Nils Runeberg, a member of the National Evangelical Union, was a deeply religious man. At a *soirée* in Paris or even in Buenos Aires, a man of letters might very well rediscover Runeberg's theses; those theses, proposed at such a *soirée*, would be slight and pointless exercises in slovenliness or blasphemy. For Runeberg, they were the key that unlocked one of theology's central mysteries; they were the stuff of study and meditation, of historical and philological controversy, of arrogance, of exultation, and of terror. They justified and destroyed his life. Those who peruse this article should likewise consider that it records only Runeberg's conclusions, not his dialectic or his proofs. It will be said that the conclusion no doubt preceded its "proofs." But what man can content himself with seeking out proofs for a thing that not even he himself believes in, or whose teaching he cares naught for?

The first edition of *Kristus och Judas* bears this categorical epigraph, whose meaning, years afterward, Nils Runeberg himself was monstrously to expatiate upon: *It is not one thing, but all the things which legend attributes to Judas Iscariot that are false* (de Quincey, 1857). Like a certain German before him, de Quincey speculated that Judas had delivered up Christ in order to force Him to declare His divinity and set in motion a vast uprising against Rome's yoke; Runeberg suggests a vindication of a *metaphysical* nature. Cleverly, he begins by emphasizing how superfluous Judas' action was. He observes (as Robertson had) that in order to identify a teacher who preached every day in the synagogue and worked miracles in the plain sight of thousands of people, there was no need of betrayal by one of the teacher's own apostles. That is precisely, however, what occurred. To assume an error in the Scriptures is intolerable, but it is no less intolerable to assume that a random act intruded into the most precious event in the history of the world. *Ergo,* Judas' betrayal was not a random act, but predetermined, with its own mysterious place in the economy of redemption. Runeberg continues: The Word, when it was made Flesh, passed from omnipresence into space, from eternity into history, from unlimited joy and happiness into mutability and death; to repay that sacrifice, it was needful that a man (in representation of all mankind) make a sacrifice of equal worth. Judas Iscariot was that man. Alone among the apostles, Judas sensed Jesus' secret divinity and His terrible purpose. The Word had stooped to become mortal; Judas, a disciple of the Word, would stoop to become an informer (the most heinous crime that infamy will bear) and to dwell amid inextinguishable flames. As below, so above; the forms of earth correspond to the forms of heaven; the blotches of the skin are a map of the incorruptible constellations; Judas is somehow a reflection of Jesus. From that conclusion derive the thirty pieces of silver and the kiss; from that conclusion derives the voluntary death, so as even more emphatically to merit reprobation. Thus did Nils Runeberg explain the enigma that is Judas.

Theologians of every faith brought forth refutations. Lars Peter Engström accused Runeberg of ignoring the hypostatic union; Axel Borelius, of rekindling the Docetic heresy, which denied Jesus' humanity; the steely bishop of Lund accused him of contradicting Chapter 22, verse 3 of the Gospel According to St. Luke.

These diverse anathemas did have their influence on Runeberg, who partially rewrote the reprehended book and modified its doctrine. He abandoned the theological ground to his adversaries and proposed oblique arguments of a moral order. He admitted that Jesus, "who could call upon the considerable resources that Omnipotence can offer," had no need of a man to carry out His plan for the redemption of all mankind. Then he rebutted those who claimed that we know nothing of the inexplicable betrayer. We know, Runeberg said, that he was one of the apostles, one of those chosen to herald the kingdom of heaven, to heal the sick, cleanse the lepers, raise the dead, and cast out demons (Matthew 10:7–8, Luke 9:1). The acts of a man thus singled out by the Redeemer merit the most sympathetic interpretation we can give them. To impute his crime to greed (as some have done, citing John 12:6) is to settle for the basest motive. Nils Runeberg proposed a motive at the opposite extreme: a hyperbolic, even limitless asceticism. The ascetic, *ad majorem Dei gloriam,* debases and mortifies the flesh; Judas debased and mortified the spirit. He renounced honor, goodness, peace, the kingdom of heaven, as others, less heroically, renounce pleasure.[1] He plotted his sins with terrible lucidity. In adultery, tenderness and abnegation often play a role; in homicide, courage; in blasphemy and profanation, a certain satanic zeal. Judas chose sins unvisited by any virtue: abuse of confidence (John 12:6) and betrayal. He labored with titanic humility; he believed himself unworthy of being good. Paul wrote: *He that glorieth, let him glory in the Lord* (I Corinthians 1:31); Judas sought hell because joy in the Lord was enough for him. He thought that happiness, like goodness, is a divine attribute, which should not be usurped by men.[2]

Many have discovered, after the fact, that in Runeberg's justifiable beginnings lies his extravagant end, and that *Den hemlige Frälsaren* is a mere perversion or exasperation of his *Kristus och Judas.* In late 1907, Runeberg completed and revised the manuscript text; almost two years passed before

[1]Borelius sarcastically asks: *Why did he not renounce renunciation? Why not renounce the renunciation of renunciation?*

[2]In a book unknown to Runeberg, Euclides da Cunha* notes that in the view of the Canudos heresiarch Antonio Conselheiro,* virtue "is a near impiety." The Argentine reader will recall analogous passages in the work of the poet Almafuerte.* In the symbolist journal *Sju insegel,* Runeberg published an assiduous descriptive poem titled "The Secret Lake"; the first verses narrate the events of a tumultuous day, while the last record the discovery of a glacial "tarn." The poet suggests that the eternity of those silent waters puts right our useless violence and—somehow—both allows it and absolves it. The poem ends with these words: "The water of the forest is happy; we can be evil and in pain."

he delivered it to the publisher. In October, 1909, the book appeared with a foreword (lukewarm to the point of being enigmatic) by the Danish Hebrew scholar Erik Erfjord, and with the following epigraph: *He was in the world, and the world was made by him, and the world knew him not* (John 1:10). The book's general argument is not complex, although its conclusion is monstrous. God, argues Nils Runeberg, stooped to become man for the redemption of the human race; we might well then presume that the sacrifice effected by Him was perfect, not invalidated or attenuated by omissions. To limit His suffering to the agony of one afternoon on the cross is blasphemous.[3] To claim that He was man, and yet was incapable of sin, is to fall into contradiction; the attributes *impeccabilitas* and *humanitas* are incompatible. Kemnitz will allow that the Redeemer could feel weariness, cold, distress, hunger, and thirst; one might also allow Him to be able to sin and be condemned to damnation. For many, the famous words in Isaiah 53: 2–3, *He shall grow up before him as a tender plant, and as a root out of a dry ground: he hath no form nor comeliness; and when we shall see him, there is no beauty that we should desire him. He is despised and rejected of men; a man of sorrows, and acquainted with grief,* are a foreshadowing of the Crucified Christ at the hour of His death. For some (Hans Lassen Martensen, for example), they are a refutation of the loveliness that the vulgar consensus attributes to Christ; for Runeberg, they are the detailed prophecy not of a moment but of the entire horrendous future, in Time and in Eternity, of the Word made Flesh. God was made totally man, but man to the point of iniquity, man to the point of reprobation and the Abyss. In order to save us, He could have chosen *any* of the lives that weave the confused web of history: He could have been Alexander or Pythagoras or Rurik or Jesus; he chose an abject existence: He was Judas.

In vain did the bookstores of Stockholm and Lund offer readers this revelation. The incredulous considered it, *a priori,* a vapid and tedious theological game; theologians disdained it. Runeberg sensed in that ecu-

[3]Maurice Abramowicz observes: "Jésus, d'après ce scandinave, a toujours le beau rôle; ses déboires, grâce à la science des typographes, jouissent d'une réputation polyglotte; sa résidence de trente-trois ans parmi les humains ne fut, en somme, qu'une villégiature." In Appendix III to his *Christelige Dogmatik,* Erfjord rebuts this passage. He notes that the crucifixion of God has not ended, because that which happened once in time is repeated endlessly in eternity. Judas, *now,* continues to hold out his hand for the silver, continues to kiss Jesus' cheek, continues to scatter the pieces of silver in the temple, continues to knot the noose on the field of blood. (In order to justify this statement, Erfjord cites the last chapter of the first volume of Jaromir Hladik's *Vindication of Eternity.*)

menical indifference an almost miraculous confirmation. God had ordered that indifference; God did not want His terrible secret spread throughout the earth. Runeberg realized that the hour was not yet come. He felt that ancient, divine curses were met in him. He recalled Elijah and Moses, who covered their faces upon the mountain so as not to look upon God; Isaiah, who was terrified when his eyes beheld the One whose glory fills the earth; Saul, whose eyes were blinded on the road to Damascus; the rabbi Simeon ben Azai, who saw the Garden and died; the famous wizard John of Viterbo, who went mad when the Trinity was revealed to him; the Midrashim, who abominate those who speak the *Shem Hamephorash*, the Secret Name of God. Was it not that dark sin that he, Runeberg, was guilty of? Might not that be the blasphemy against the Holy Ghost (Matthew 12:31) which shall not be forgiven? Valerius Soranus died for revealing the hidden name of Rome; what infinite punishment would be Runeberg's for having discovered and revealed the terrible name of God?

Drunk with sleeplessness and his dizzying dialectic, Nils Runeberg wandered the streets of Mälmo, crying out for a blessing—that he be allowed to share the Inferno with the Redeemer.

He died of a ruptured aneurysm on March 1, 1912. Heresiologists will perhaps remember him; he added to the concept of the Son, which might have been thought long spent, the complexities of misery and evil.

1944

The End

Lying on his back, Recabarren opened his eyes a bit and saw the sloping ceiling of thick cane. From the other room there came the strumming of a guitar, like some inconsequential labyrinth, infinitely tangling and untangling. . . . Little by little, reality came back to him, the ordinary things that now would always be just *these* ordinary things. He looked down without pity at his great useless body, the plain wool poncho that wrapped his legs. Outside, beyond the thick bars at his window, spread the flatland and the evening; he had slept, but the sky was still filled with light. He groped with his left arm until he found the brass cowbell that hung at the foot of the cot. He shook it once or twice; outside his door, the unassuming chords continued.

The guitar was being played by a black man who had shown up one night flattering himself that he was a singer; he had challenged another stranger to a song contest, the way traveling singers did. Beaten, he went on showing up at the general-store-and-bar night after night, as though he were waiting for someone. He spent hours with the guitar, but he never sang again; it could be that the defeat had turned him bitter. People had grown used to the inoffensive man. Recabarren, the owner of the bar, would never forget that contest; the next day, as he was trying to straighten some bales of *yerba,* his right side had suddenly gone dead on him, and he discovered that he couldn't talk. From learning to pity the misfortunes of the heroes of our novels, we wind up feeling too much pity for our own; but not Recabarren, who accepted his paralysis as he had earlier accepted the severity and the solitudes of the Americas. A man in the habit of living in the present, as animals do, he now looked up at the sky and reflected that the red ring around the moon was a sign of rain.

A boy with Indian-like features (Recabarren's son, perhaps) opened the door a crack. Recabarren asked him with his eyes whether anybody was around; the boy, not one to talk much, made a motion with his hand to say there wasn't—the black man didn't count. Then the prostrate man was left alone; his left hand played awhile with the bell, as though exercising some power.

The plains, in the last rays of the sun, were almost abstract, as though seen in a dream. A dot wavered on the horizon, then grew until it became a horseman riding, or so it seemed, toward the house. Recabarren could make out the broad-brimmed hat, the dark poncho, the piebald horse, but not the face of the rider, who finally reined in the horse and came toward the house at an easy trot. Some two hundred yards out, he veered off to the side. At that, the man was out of Recabarren's line of sight, but Recabarren heard him speak, get down off his horse, tie it to the post, and with a firm step enter the bar.

Without raising his eyes from the guitar, where he seemed to be looking for something, the black man spoke.

"I *knew* I could count on you, sir," he softly said.

"And I knew I could count on you, old nigger," the other man replied, his voice harsh. "A heap of days I've made you wait, but here I am."

There was a silence. Then the black man spoke again.

"I'm getting used to waiting. I've been waiting now for seven years."

Unhurried, the other man explained:

"It'd been longer than seven years that I'd gone without seeing my children. I found them that day, and I wouldn't have it so's I looked to them like a man on his way to a knife fight."*

"I understood that," the black man said. "I hope they were all in good health."

The stranger, who had sat down at the bar, gave a hearty laugh at that. He ordered a drink and took a sip or two, but didn't finish it.

"I gave them some advice," he said, "which is something you can never get too much of and doesn't cost a lot. I told them, among other things, that a man ought not to go spilling another man's blood."

A slow chord preceded the black man's response:

"Good advice, too. That way they won't grow up to be like us."

"Not like me, anyway," said the stranger, who then added, as though thinking out loud: "Fate would have it that I kill, and now it's put a knife in my hand again."

"Fall's coming on," the black man observed, as though he hadn't heard, "and the days are getting shorter."

"The light that's left will be enough for me," replied the other man, getting to his feet.

He stood square before the black man and in a tired voice said to him, "Leave that guitar alone, now—you've got another kind of contest to try to win today."

The two men walked toward the door. As the black man stepped outside, he murmured, "Could be this one goes as bad f'r me as the other one did."

"It's not that the first one went bad for you," the other man answered, serious. "It's that you couldn't hardly wait to get to the second one."

They walked beside each other until they got some distance from the houses. One place on the plains was much like another, and the moon was bright. Suddenly they looked at each other, stopped, and the stranger took off his spurs. They already had their ponchos wrapped around their forearms when the black man spoke.

"One thing I want to ask you before we get down to it. I want you to put all your courage and all your skill into this, like you did seven years ago when you killed my brother."

For perhaps the first time in their exchange, Martín Fierro heard the hatred. His blood felt it, like a sharp prod. They circled, clashed, and sharp steel marked the black man's face.

There is an hour just at evening when the plains seem on the verge of saying something; they never do, or perhaps they do—eternally—though we don't understand it, or perhaps we do understand but what they say is as untranslatable as music. . . . From his cot, Recabarren saw the end. A thrust, and the black man dodged back, lost his footing, feigned a slash to his opponent's face, and then lunged out with a deep jab that buried the knife in his belly. Then came another thrust, which the storekeeper couldn't see, and Fierro did not get up. Unmoving, the black man seemed to stand watch over the agonizing death. He wiped off the bloody knife in the grass and walked slowly back toward the houses, never looking back. His work of vengeance done, he was nobody now. Or rather, he was the other one: there was neither destination nor destiny on earth for him, and he had killed a man.

The Cult of the Phoenix

Those who write that the cult of the Phoenix had its origin in Heliopolis, and claim that it derives from the religious restoration that followed the death of the reformer Amenhotep IV, cite the writings of Herodotus and Tacitus and the inscriptions on Egyptian monuments, but they are unaware, perhaps willfully unaware, that the cult's designation as "the cult of the Phoenix" can be traced back no farther than to Hrabanus Maurus and that the earliest sources (the *Saturnalia*, say, or Flavius Josephus) speak only of "the People of the Practice" or "the People of the Secret." In the conventicles of Ferrara, Gregorovius observed that mention of the Phoenix was very rare in the spoken language; in Geneva, I have had conversations with artisans who did not understand me when I asked whether they were men of the Phoenix but immediately admitted to being men of the Secret. Unless I am mistaken, much the same might be said about Buddhists: The name by which the world knows them is not the name that they themselves pronounce.

On one altogether too famous page, Moklosich has equated the members of the cult of the Phoenix with the gypsies. In Chile and in Hungary, there are both gypsies and members of the sect; apart from their ubiquity, the two groups have very little in common. Gypsies are horse traders, potmakers, blacksmiths, and fortune-tellers; the members of the cult of the Phoenix are generally contented practitioners of the "liberal professions." Gypsies are of a certain physical type, and speak, or used to speak, a secret language; the members of the cult are indistinguishable from other men, and the proof of this is that they have never been persecuted. Gypsies are picturesque, and often inspire bad poets; ballads, photographs, and boleros fail to mention the members of the cult. . . . Martin Buber says that Jews are essentially sufferers; not all the members of the cult are, and some actively abhor pathos. That public and well-known truth suffices to refute the vulgar error (absurdly defended by Urmann) which sees the roots of the Phoenix as lying in Israel. People's reasoning goes more or less this way: Urmann was a sensitive man; Urmann was a Jew; Urmann made a habit of visiting the members of the cult in the Jewish ghettos of Prague; the affinity that Urmann sensed proves a real relationship. In all honesty, I cannot concur with that conclusion. That the members of the cult should, in a Jewish milieu, resemble Jews proves nothing; what cannot be denied is that they, like Hazlitt's infinite Shakespeare, resemble every man in the world. They are all things to all men, like the Apostle; a few days ago, Dr. Juan Francisco Amaro, of Paysandú, pondered the ease with which they assimilate, the ease with which they "naturalize" themselves.

I have said that the history of the cult records no persecutions. That is true, but since there is no group of human beings that does not include adherents of the sect of the Phoenix, it is also true that there has been no persecution or severity that the members of the cult have not suffered *and carried out.* In the wars of the Western world and in the distant wars of Asia, their blood has been spilled for centuries, under enemy flags; it is hardly worth their while to identify themselves with every nation on the globe.

Lacking a sacred book to unite them as the Scriptures unite Israel, lacking a common memory, lacking that other memory that is a common language, scattered across the face of the earth, diverse in color and in feature, there is but one thing—the Secret—that unites them, and that *will* unite them until the end of time. Once, in addition to the Secret there was a legend (and perhaps a cosmogonic myth), but the superficial men of the Phoenix have forgotten it, and today all that is left to them is the dim and obscure story of a punishment. A punishment, or a pact, or a privilege—versions differ; but what one may dimly see in all of them is the judgment of a God who promises eternity to a race of beings if its men, generation upon generation, perform a certain ritual. I have compared travelers' reports, I have spoken with patriarchs and theologians; I can attest that the performance of that ritual is the only religious practice observed by the members of the cult. The ritual is, in fact, the Secret. The Secret, as I have said, is transmitted from generation to generation, but tradition forbids a mother from teaching it to her children, as it forbids priests from doing so; initiation into the mystery is the task of the lowest individuals of the group. A slave, a leper, or a beggar plays the role of mystagogue. A child, too, may catechize another child. The act itself is trivial, the matter of a moment's time, and it needs no description. The materials used are cork, wax, or gum arabic. (In the liturgy there is mention of "slime"; pond slime is often used as well.) There are no temples dedicated expressly to the cult's worship, but ruins, cellars, or entryways are considered appropriate sites. The Secret is sacred, but that does not prevent its being a bit ridiculous; the performance of it is furtive, even clandestine, and its adepts do not speak of it. There are no decent words by which to call it, but it is understood that all words somehow name it, or rather, that they inevitably allude to it—and so I have said some insignificant thing in conversation and have seen adepts smile or grow uncomfortable because they sensed I had touched upon the Secret. In Germanic literatures there are poems written by members of the cult whose nominal subject is the sea or twilight; more than once I have heard people say that these poems are, somehow, symbols of the Secret. *Orbis terrarum est speculum Ludi,* goes an apocryphal saying reported by du Cange in his Glossary. A kind of sacred horror keeps some of the faithful from performing that simplest of rituals; they are despised by the other members of the sect, but they despise themselves even more. Those, on the other hand, who deliberately renounce the Practice and achieve direct commerce with the Deity command great respect; such men speak of that commerce using figures from the liturgy, and so we find that John of the Rood wrote as follows:

> Let the Nine Firmaments be told
> That God is delightful as the Cork and Mire.

On three continents I have merited the friendship of many worshipers of the Phoenix; I know that the Secret at first struck them as banal, shameful, vulgar, and (stranger still) unbelievable. They could not bring themselves to admit that their parents had ever stooped to such acts. It is odd that the Secret did not die out long ago; but in spite of the world's vicissitudes, in spite of wars and exoduses, it does, in its full awesomeness, come to all the faithful. Someone has even dared to claim that by now it is instinctive.

The South

The man that stepped off the boat in Buenos Aires in 1871 was a minister of the Evangelical Church; his name was Johannes Dahlmann. By 1939, one of his grandsons, Juan Dahlmann, was secretary of a municipal library on Calle Córdoba and considered himself profoundly Argentine. His maternal grandfather had been Francisco Flores, of the 2nd Infantry of the Line, who died on the border of Buenos Aires* from a spear wielded by the Indians under Catriel.* In the contrary pulls from his two lineages, Juan Dahlmann (perhaps impelled by his Germanic blood) chose that of his romantic ancestor, or that of a romantic death. That slightly willful but never ostentatious "Argentinization" drew sustenance from an old sword, a locket containing the daguerreotype of a bearded, inexpressive man, the joy and courage of certain melodies, the habit of certain verses in *Martín Fierro*, the passing years, a certain lack of spiritedness, and solitude. At the price of some self-denial, Dahlmann had managed to save the shell of a large country house in the South that had once belonged to the Flores family; one of the touchstones of his memory was the image of the eucalyptus trees and the long pink-colored house that had once been scarlet. His work, and perhaps his indolence, held him in the city. Summer after summer he contented himself with the abstract idea of possession and with the certainty that his house was waiting for him, at a precise place on the flatlands. In late February, 1939, something happened to him.

Though blind to guilt, fate can be merciless with the slightest distractions. That afternoon Dahlmann had come upon a copy (from which some pages were missing) of Weil's *Arabian Nights*; eager to examine his find, he did not wait for the elevator—he hurriedly took the stairs. Something in the dimness brushed his forehead—a bat? a bird? On the face of the woman who opened the door to him, he saw an expression of horror, and the hand he passed over his forehead came back red with blood. His brow had caught the edge of a recently painted casement window that somebody had forgotten to close. Dahlmann managed to sleep, but by the early hours of morning he was awake, and from that time on, the flavor of all things was monstrous to him. Fever wore him away, and illustrations from the *Arabian Nights* began to illuminate nightmares. Friends and members of his family would visit him and with exaggerated smiles tell him how well he looked. Dahlmann, in a kind of feeble stupor, would hear their words, and it would amaze him that they couldn't see he was in hell. Eight days passed, like eight hundred years. One afternoon, his usual physician appeared with a new man, and they drove Dahlmann to a sanatorium on Calle Ecuador; he needed to have an X ray. Sitting in the cab they had hired to drive them, Dahlmann reflected that he might, at last, in a room that was not his own, be able to sleep. He felt happy, he felt like talking, but the moment they arrived, his clothes were stripped from him, his head was shaved, he was strapped with metal bands to a table, he was blinded and dizzied with bright lights, his heart and lungs were listened to, and a man in a surgical mask stuck a needle in his arm. He awoke nauseated, bandaged, in a cell much like the bottom of a well, and in the days and nights that followed, he realized that until then he had been only somewhere on the outskirts of hell. Ice left but the slightest trace of coolness in his mouth. During these days, Dahlmann hated every inch of himself; he hated his identity, his bodily needs, his humiliation, the beard that prickled his face. He stoically suffered the treatments administered to him, which were quite painful, but when the surgeon told him he'd been on the verge of death from septicemia, Dahlmann, suddenly self-pitying, broke down and cried. The physical miseries, the unending anticipation of bad nights had not allowed him to think about anything as abstract as death. The next day, the surgeon told him he was coming right along, and that he'd soon be able to go out to the country house to convalesce. Incredibly, the promised day arrived.

Reality is partial to symmetries and slight anachronisms; Dahlmann had come to the sanatorium in a cab, and it was a cab that took him to the station at Plaza Constitución. The first cool breath of autumn, after the oppression of the summer, was like a natural symbol of his life brought back from fever and the brink of death. The city, at that seven o'clock in the morning, had not lost that look of a ramshackle old house that cities take on at night; the streets were like long porches and corridors, the plazas like interior courtyards. After his long stay in hospital, Dahlmann took it all in with delight and a touch of vertigo; a few seconds before his eyes registered them, he would recall the corners, the marquees, the modest variety of Buenos Aires. In the yellow light of the new day, it all came back to him.

Everyone knows that the South begins on the other side of Avenida Rivadavia. Dahlmann had often said that that was no mere saying, that by crossing Rivadavia one entered an older and more stable world. From the cab, he sought among the new buildings the window barred with wrought iron, the door knocker, the arch of a doorway, the long entryway, the almost-secret courtyard.

In the grand hall of the station he saw that he had thirty minutes before his train left. He suddenly remembered that there was a café on Calle Brasil (a few yards from Yrigoyen's house) where there was a huge cat that would let people pet it, like some disdainful deity. He went in. There was the cat, asleep. He ordered a cup of coffee, slowly spooned sugar into it, tasted it (a pleasure that had been forbidden him in the clinic), and thought, while he stroked the cat's black fur, that this contact was illusory, that he and the cat were separated as though by a pane of glass, because man lives in time, in successiveness, while the magical animal lives in the present, in the eternity of the instant.

The train, stretching along the next-to-last platform, was waiting. Dahlmann walked through the cars until he came to one that was almost empty. He lifted his bag onto the luggage rack; when the train pulled out, he opened his bag and after a slight hesitation took from it the first volume of *The Arabian Nights.* To travel with this book so closely linked to the history of his torment was an affirmation that the torment was past, and was a joyous, secret challenge to the frustrated forces of evil.

On both sides of the train, the city unraveled into suburbs; that sight, and later the sight of lawns and large country homes, led Dahlmann to put aside his reading. The truth is, Dahlmann read very little; the lodestone mountain and the genie sworn to kill the man who released him from the bottle were, as anyone will admit, wondrous things, but not much more wondrous than this morning and the fact of being. Happiness distracted him from Scheherazade and her superfluous miracles; Dahlmann closed the book and allowed himself simply to live.

Lunch (with bouillon served in bowls of shining metal, as in the now-distant summers of his childhood) was another quiet, savored pleasure.

Tomorrow I will wake up at my ranch, he thought, and it was as though he were two men at once: the man gliding along through the autumn day and the geography of his native land, and the other man, imprisoned in a sanatorium and subjected to methodical attentions. He saw unplastered brick houses, long and angular, infinitely watching the trains go by; he saw horsemen on the clod-strewn roads; he saw ditches and lakes and pastures; he saw long glowing clouds that seemed made of marble, and all these things were fortuitous, like some dream of the flat prairies. He also thought he recognized trees and crops that he couldn't have told one the name of—his direct knowledge of the country was considerably inferior to his nostalgic, literary knowledge.

From time to time he nodded off, and in his dreams there was the rushing momentum of the train. Now the unbearable white sun of midday was the yellow sun that comes before nightfall and that soon would turn to red. The car was different now, too; it was not the same car that had pulled out of the station in Buenos Aires—the plains and the hours had penetrated and transfigured it. Outside, the moving shadow of the train stretched out toward the horizon. The elemental earth was not disturbed by settlements or any other signs of humanity. All was vast, but at the same time intimate and somehow secret. In all the immense countryside, there would sometimes be nothing but a bull. The solitude was perfect, if perhaps hostile, and Dahlmann almost suspected that he was traveling not only into the South but into the past. From that fantastic conjecture he was distracted by the conductor, who seeing Dahlmann's ticket informed him that the train would not be leaving him at the usual station, but at a different one, a little before it, that Dahlmann barely knew. (The man added an explanation that Dahlmann didn't try to understand, didn't even listen to, because the mechanics of it didn't matter.)

The train came to its laborious halt in virtually the middle of the countryside. The station sat on the other side of the tracks, and was hardly more than a covered platform. They had no vehicle there, but the stationmaster figured Dahlmann might be able to find one at a store he directed him to—ten or twelve blocks away.

Dahlmann accepted the walk as a small adventure. The sun had sunk below the horizon now, but one final splendor brought a glory to the living yet silent plains before they were blotted out by night. Less to keep from tiring himself than to make those things last, Dahlmann walked slowly, inhaling with grave happiness the smell of clover.

The store had once been bright red, but the years had tempered its violent color (to its advantage). There was something in its sorry architecture that reminded Dahlmann of a steel engraving, perhaps from an old edition of *Paul et Virginie*. There were several horses tied to the rail in front. Inside,

Dahlmann thought he recognized the owner; then he realized that he'd been fooled by the man's resemblance to one of the employees at the sanatorium. When the man heard Dahlmann's story, he said he'd have the calash harnessed up; to add yet another event to that day, and to pass the time, Dahlmann decided to eat there in the country store.

At one table some rough-looking young men were noisily eating and drinking; at first Dahlmann didn't pay much attention. On the floor, curled against the bar, lay an old man, as motionless as an object. The many years had worn him away and polished him, as a stone is worn smooth by running water or a saying is polished by generations of humankind. He was small, dark, and dried up, and he seemed to be outside time, in a sort of eternity. Dahlmann was warmed by the rightness of the man's hairband, the baize poncho he wore, his gaucho trousers,* and the boots made out of the skin of a horse's leg, and he said to himself, recalling futile arguments with people from districts in the North, or from Entre Ríos, that only in the South did gauchos like that exist anymore.

Dahlmann made himself comfortable near the window. Little by little, darkness was enveloping the countryside, but the smells and sounds of the plains still floated in through the thick iron grate at the window. The storekeeper brought him sardines and then roast meat; Dahlmann washed them down with more than one glass of red wine. Idly, he savored the harsh bouquet of the wine and let his gaze wander over the store, which by now had turned a little sleepy. The kerosene lantern hung from one of the beams. There were three customers at the other table: two looked like laborers; the other, with coarse, Indian-like features, sat drinking with his wide-brimmed hat on. Dahlmann suddenly felt something lightly brush his face. Next to the tumbler of cloudy glass, on one of the stripes in the tablecloth, lay a little ball of wadded bread. That was all, but somebody had thrown it at him.

The drinkers at the other table seemed unaware of his presence. Dahlmann, puzzled, decided that nothing had happened, and he opened the volume of *The Arabian Nights*, as though to block out reality. Another wad of bread hit him a few minutes later, and this time the laborers laughed. Dahlmann told himself he wasn't scared, but that it would be madness for him, a sick man, to be dragged by strangers into some chaotic bar fight. He made up his mind to leave; he was already on his feet when the storekeeper came over and urged him, his voice alarmed: "Sr. Dahlmann, ignore those boys over there—they're just feeling their oats."

Dahlmann did not find it strange that the storekeeper should know his name by now but he sensed that the man's conciliatory words actually made the situation worse. Before, the men's provocation had been directed at an accidental face, almost at nobody; now it was aimed at him, at his name, and the men at the other table would know that name. Dahlmann brushed the storekeeper aside, faced the laborers, and asked them what their problem was.

The young thug with the Indian-looking face stood up, stumbling as he did so. At one pace from Dahlmann, he shouted insults at him, as though he were far away. He was playacting, exaggerating his drunkenness, and the exaggeration produced an impression both fierce and mocking. Amid curses and obscenities, the man threw a long knife into the air, followed it with his eyes, caught it, and challenged Dahlmann to fight. The storekeeper's voice shook as he objected that Dahlmann was unarmed. At that point, something unforeseeable happened.

From out of a corner, the motionless old gaucho in whom Dahlmann had seen a symbol of the South (the South that belonged to him) tossed him a naked dagger—it came to rest at Dahlmann's feet. It was as though the South itself had decided that Dahlmann should accept the challenge. Dahlmann bent to pick up the dagger, and as he did he sensed two things: first, that that virtually instinctive action committed him to fight, and second, that in his clumsy hand the weapon would serve less to defend him than to justify the other man's killing him. He had toyed with a knife now and then, as all men did, but his knowledge of knife fighting went no further than a vague recollection that thrusts should be aimed upward, and with the blade facing inward. *They'd never have allowed this sort of thing to happen in the sanatorium,* he thought.

"Enough stalling," the other man said. "Let's go outside."

They went outside, and while there was no hope in Dahlmann, there was no fear, either. As he crossed the threshold, he felt that on that first night in the sanatorium, when they'd stuck that needle in him, dying in a knife fight under the open sky, grappling with his adversary, would have been a liberation, a joy, and a fiesta. He sensed that had he been able to choose or dream his death that night, this is the death he would have dreamed or chosen.

Dahlmann firmly grips the knife, which he may have no idea how to manage, and steps out into the plains.

The Aleph

(1949)

The Immortal

Solomon saith: *There is no new thing upon the earth.* So that as Plato had an imagination, *that all knowledge was but remembrance;* so Solomon giveth his sentence, *that all novelty is but oblivion.*

Francis Bacon: *Essays,* LVIII

In London, in early June of the year 1929, the rare book dealer Joseph Cartaphilus, of Smyrna, offered the princess de Lucinge the six quarto minor volumes (1715–1720) of Pope's *Iliad.* The princess purchased them; when she took possession of them, she exchanged a few words with the dealer. He was, she says, an emaciated, grimy man with gray eyes and gray beard and singularly vague features. He expressed himself with untutored and uncorrected fluency in several languages; within scant minutes he shifted from French to English and from English to an enigmatic cross between the Spanish of Salonika and the Portuguese of Macao. In October, the princess heard from a passenger on the *Zeus* that Cartaphilus had died at sea while returning to Smyrna, and that he had been buried on the island of Ios. In the last volume of the *Iliad* she found this manuscript.

It is written in an English that teems with Latinisms; this is a verbatim transcription of the document.

. . .

I

As I recall, my travails began in a garden in hundred-gated Thebes, in the time of the emperor Diocletian. I had fought (with no glory) in the recent Egyptian wars and was tribune of a legion quartered in Berenice, on the banks of the Red Sea; there, fever and magic consumed many men who magnanimously coveted the steel blade. The Mauritanians were defeated;

the lands once occupied by the rebel cities were dedicated *in æternitatem* to the Plutonian gods; Alexandria, subdued, in vain sought Cæsar's mercy; within the year the legions were to report their triumph, but I myself barely glimpsed the face of Mars. That privation grieved me, and was perhaps why I threw myself into the quest, through vagrant and terrible deserts, for the secret City of the Immortals.

My travails, I have said, began in a garden in Thebes. All that night I did not sleep, for there was a combat in my heart. I rose at last a little before dawn. My slaves were sleeping; the moon was the color of the infinite sand. A bloody rider was approaching from the east, weak with exhaustion. A few steps from me, he dismounted and in a faint, insatiable voice asked me, in Latin, the name of the river whose waters laved the city's walls. I told him it was the Egypt, fed by the rains. "*It is another river that I seek,*" he replied morosely, "*the secret river that purifies men of death.*" Dark blood was welling from his breast. He told me that the country of his birth was a mountain that lay beyond the Ganges; it was rumored on that mountain, he told me, that if one traveled westward, to the end of the world, one would come to the river whose waters give immortality. He added that on the far shore of that river lay the City of the Immortals, a city rich in bulwarks and amphitheaters and temples. He died before dawn, but I resolved to go in quest of that city and its river. When interrogated by the torturer, some of the Mauritanian prisoners confirmed the traveler's tale: One of them recalled the Elysian plain, far at the ends of the earth, where men's lives are everlasting; another, the peaks from which the Pactolus flows, upon which men live for a hundred years. In Rome, I spoke with philosophers who felt that to draw out the span of a man's life was to draw out the agony of his dying and multiply the number of his deaths. I am not certain whether I ever believed in the City of the Immortals; I think the task of finding it was enough for me. Flavius, the Getulian proconsul, entrusted two hundred soldiers to me for the venture; I also recruited a number of mercenaries who claimed they knew the roads, and who were the first to desert.

Subsequent events have so distorted the memory of our first days that now they are impossible to put straight. We set out from Arsinoë and entered the ardent desert. We crossed the lands of the Troglodytes, who devour serpents and lack all verbal commerce; the land of the Garamantas, whose women are held in common and whose food is lions; the land of the Augiles, who worship only Tartarus. We ranged the width and breadth of other deserts—deserts of black sand, where the traveler must usurp the hours of the night, for the fervency of the day is unbearable. From afar I made out the mountain which gives its name to the Ocean; on its slopes grows the euphorbia, an antidote to poisons, and on its peak live the Satyrs, a nation of wild and rustic men given to lasciviousness. That the bosom of those barbaric lands, where the Earth is the mother of monsters, might succor a famous city—such a thing seemed unthinkable to us all. Thus we continued with our march, for to have regressed would have been to dishonor ourselves. Some of the men, those who were most temerarious, slept with their faces exposed to the moon; soon they burned with fever. With the depraved water of the watering holes others drank up insanity and death. Then began the desertions; a short time afterward, the mutinies. In repressing them I did not hesitate to employ severity. In that I acted justly, but a centurion warned me that the mutineers (keen to avenge the crucifixion of one of their number) were weaving a plot for my death. I fled the camp with the few soldiers who were loyal to me; in the desert, among whirlwinds of sand and the vast night, we became separated. A Cretan arrow rent my flesh. For several days I wandered without finding water—or one huge day multiplied by the sun, thirst, and the fear of thirst. I left my path to the will of my horse. At dawn, the distance bristled with pyramids and towers. I dreamed, unbearably, of a small and orderly labyrinth at whose center lay a well; my hands could almost touch it, my eyes see it, but so bewildering and entangled were the turns that I knew I would die before I reached it.

II

When I disentangled myself at last from that nightmare, I found that my hands were bound behind my back and I was lying in an oblong stone niche no bigger than a common grave, scraped into the caustic slope of a mountain. The sides of the cavity were humid, and had been polished as much by time as by human hands. In my chest I felt a painful throbbing, and I burned with thirst. I raised my head and cried out weakly. At the foot of the mountain ran a noiseless, impure stream, clogged by sand and rubble; on the far bank, the patent City of the Immortals shone dazzlingly in the last (or first) rays of the sun. I could see fortifications, arches, frontispieces, and forums; the foundation of it all was a stone plateau. A hundred or more irregular niches like my own riddled the mountain and the valley. In the sand had been dug shallow holes; from those wretched holes, from the niches, emerged naked men with gray skin and neglected beards. I thought I recognized these men: they belonged to the bestial lineage of the Troglodytes, who infest the shorelines of the Persian Gulf and the grottoes of Ethiopia; I was surprised neither by the fact that they did not speak nor by seeing them devour serpents.

Urgent thirst lent me temerity. I estimated that I was some thirty paces from the sand; I closed my eyes and threw myself down the mountain, my hands bound behind my back. I plunged my bloodied face into the dark water and lapped at it like an animal. Before I lost myself in sleep and delirium once more, I inexplicably repeated a few words of Greek: *Those from Zeleia, wealthy Trojans, who drink the water of dark Aisepos . . .*

I cannot say how many days and nights passed over me. In pain, unable to return to the shelter of the caverns, naked on the unknown sand, I let the moon and the sun cast lots for my bleak fate. The Troglodytes, childlike in their barbarity, helped me neither survive nor die. In vain did I plead with them to kill me. One day, with the sharp edge of a flake of rock, I severed my bonds. The next, I stood up and was able to beg or steal—I, Marcus Flaminius Rufus, military tribune of one of the legions of Rome—my first abominated mouthful of serpent's flesh.

Out of avidity to see the Immortals, to touch that more than human City, I could hardly sleep. And as though the Troglodytes could divine my goal, they did not sleep, either. At first I presumed they were keeping a watch over me; later, I imagined that my uneasiness had communicated itself to them, as dogs can be infected in that way. For my departure from the barbarous village I chose the most public of times, sunset, when almost all the men emerged from their holes and crevices in the earth and gazed out unseeingly toward the west. I prayed aloud, less to plead for divine favor than to intimidate the tribe with articulate speech. I crossed the stream bed clogged with sandbars and turned my steps toward the City. Two or three men followed me confusedly; they were of short stature (like the others of that species), and inspired more revulsion than fear. I had to skirt a number of irregular pits that I took to be ancient quarries; misled by the City's enormous size, I had thought it was much nearer. Toward midnight, I set my foot upon the black shadow—bristling with idolatrous shapes upon the yellow sand—of the City's wall. My steps were halted by a kind of sacred horror. So abhorred by mankind are novelty and the desert that I was cheered to note that one of the Troglodytes had accompanied me to the last. I closed my eyes and waited, unsleeping, for the dawn.

I have said that the City was builded on a stone plateau. That plateau, with its precipitous sides, was as difficult to scale as the walls. In vain did my weary feet walk round it; the black foundation revealed not the slightest irregularity, and the invariance of the walls proscribed even a single door. The force of the day drove me to seek refuge in a cavern; toward the rear there was a pit, and out of the pit, out of the gloom below, rose a ladder. I descended the ladder and made my way through a chaos of squalid galleries to a vast, indistinct circular chamber. Nine doors opened into that cellar-like place; eight led to a maze that returned, deceitfully, to the same chamber; the ninth led through another maze to a second circular chamber identical to the first. I am not certain how many chambers there were; my misery and anxiety multiplied them. The silence was hostile, and virtually perfect; aside from a subterranean wind whose cause I never discovered, within those deep webs of stone there was no sound; even the thin streams of iron-colored water that trickled through crevices in the stone were noiseless. Horribly, I grew used to that dubious world; it began to seem incredible that anything could exist save nine-doored cellars and long, forking subterranean corridors. I know not how long I wandered under the earth; I do know that from time to time, in a confused dream of home, I conflated the horrendous village of the barbarians and the city of my birth, among the clusters of grapes.

At the end of one corridor, a not unforeseen wall blocked my path—and a distant light fell upon me. I raised my dazzled eyes; above, vertiginously high above, I saw a circle of sky so blue it was almost purple. A series of metal rungs led up the wall. Weariness made my muscles slack, but I climbed that ladder, only pausing from time to time to sob clumsily with joy. Little by little I began to discern friezes and the capitals of columns, triangular pediments and vaults, confused glories carved in granite and marble. Thus it was that I was led to ascend from the blind realm of black and intertwining labyrinths into the brilliant City.

I emerged into a kind of small plaza—a courtyard might better describe it. It was surrounded by a single building, of irregular angles and varying heights. It was to this heterogeneous building that the many cupolas and columns belonged. More than any other feature of that incredible monument, I was arrested by the great antiquity of its construction. I felt that it had existed before humankind, before the world itself. Its patent antiquity (though somehow terrible to the eyes) seemed to accord with the labor of immortal artificers. Cautiously at first, with indifference as time went on, desperately toward the end, I wandered the staircases and inlaid floors of that labyrinthine palace. (I discovered afterward that the width and height of the treads on the staircases were not constant; it was this that explained the extraordinary weariness I felt.) *This palace is the work of the gods,* was my first thought. I explored the uninhabited spaces, and I corrected myself: *The gods that built this place have died.* Then I reflected upon its peculiarities, and told myself: *The gods that built this place were mad.* I said this, I know, in a tone of incomprehensible reproof that verged upon remorse—with more intellectual horror than sensory fear. The impression of great antiquity was joined by others: the impression of endlessness, the sensation of oppressiveness and horror, the sensation of complex irrationality. I had made my way through a dark maze, but it was the bright City of the Immortals that terrified and repelled me. A maze is a house built purposely to confuse men; its architecture, prodigal in symmetries, is made to serve that purpose. In the palace that I imperfectly explored, the architecture had *no* purpose. There were corridors that led nowhere, unreachably high windows, grandly dramatic doors that opened onto monklike cells or empty shafts, incredible upside-down staircases with upside-down treads and balustrades. Other staircases, clinging airily to the side of a monumental wall, petered out after two or three landings, in the high gloom of the cupolas, arriving nowhere. I cannot say whether these are literal examples I have given; I do know that for many years they plagued my troubled dreams; I can no longer know whether any given feature is a faithful transcription of reality or one of the shapes unleashed by my nights. *This City,* I thought, *is so horrific that its mere existence, the mere fact of its having endured—even in the middle of a secret desert—pollutes the past and the future and somehow compromises the stars. So long as this City endures, no one in the world can ever be happy or courageous.* I do not want to describe it; a chaos of heterogeneous words, the body of a tiger or a bull pullulating with teeth, organs, and heads monstrously yoked together yet hating each other—those might, perhaps, be approximate images.

I cannot recall the stages by which I returned, nor my path through the dusty, humid crypts. I know only that I was accompanied by the constant fear that when I emerged from the last labyrinth I would be surrounded once again by the abominable City of the Immortals. I remember nothing else. That loss of memory, now insurmountable, was perhaps willful; it is possible that the circumstances of my escape were so unpleasant that on some day no less lost to memory I swore to put them out of my mind.

III

Those who have read the story of my travails attentively will recall that a man of the Troglodyte tribe had followed me, as a dog might have, into the jagged shadow of the walls. When I emerged from the last cellar, I found him at the mouth of the cavern. He was lying in the sand, clumsily drawing and rubbing out a row of symbols that resembled those letters in dreams that one is just on the verge of understanding when they merge and blur. At first I thought that this was some sort of barbaric writing; then I realized that it was absurd to imagine that men who had never learned to speak should have invented writing. Nor did any one of the shapes resemble any other—a fact that ruled out (or made quite remote) the possibility that they were symbols. The man would draw them, look at them, and correct them. Then suddenly, as though his game irritated him, he would rub them out with his palm and forearm. He looked up at me, though he seemed not to recognize me. Still, so great was the relief I felt (or so great, so dreadful had my loneliness been) that I actually thought that this primitive Troglodyte looking up at me from the floor of a cave had been waiting for me. The sun warmed the plain; as we began our return to the village, under the first stars of evening, the sand burned our feet. The Troglodyte walked ahead of me; that night I resolved to teach him to recognize, perhaps even to repeat, a few words. Dogs and horses, I reflected, are able to do the first; many birds, like the Cæsars' nightingale, can do the second. However scant a man's understanding, it will always be greater than that of unreasoning beasts.

The Troglodyte's lowly birth and condition recalled to my memory the image of Argos, the moribund old dog of the *Odyssey*, so I gave him the name Argos, and tried to teach it to him. Time and time again, I failed. No means I employed, no severity, no obstinacy of mine availed. Motionless, his eyes dead, he seemed not even to perceive the sounds which I was attempting to imprint upon him. Though but a few paces from me, he seemed immensely distant. Lying in the sand like a small, battered sphinx carved from lava, he allowed the heavens to circle in the sky above him from the first dusky light of morning to the last dusky light of night. It seemed simply impossible that he had not grasped my intention. I recalled that it is generally believed among the Ethiopians that monkeys deliberately do not speak, so that they will not be forced to work; I attributed Argos' silence to distrust or fear. From that vivid picture I passed on to others, even more extravagant. I reflected that Argos and I lived our lives in separate universes; I reflected that our perceptions were identical but that Argos combined them differently than I, constructed from them different objects; I reflected that perhaps for him there were no objects, but rather a constant, dizzying play of swift impressions. I imagined a world without memory, without time; I toyed with the possibility of a language that had no nouns, a language of impersonal verbs or indeclinable adjectives. In these reflections many days went by, and with the days, years. Until one morning, something very much like joy occurred—the sky rained slow, strong rain.

Nights in the desert can be frigid, but that night had been like a cauldron. I dreamed that a river in Thessaly (into whose waters I had thrown back a golden fish) was coming to save me; I could hear it approaching over the red sand and the black rock; a coolness in the air and the scurrying sound of rain awakened me. I ran out naked to welcome it. The night was waning; under the yellow clouds, the tribe, as joyously as I, was offering itself up to the vivid torrents in a kind of ecstasy—they reminded me of Corybantes possessed by the god. Argos, his eyes fixed on the empyrean, was moaning; streams of water rolled down his face—not just rain, but also (I later learned) tears. *Argos,* I cried, *Argos!*

Then, with gentle wonder, as though discovering something lost and forgotten for many years, Argos stammered out these words: *Argos, Ulysses' dog.* And then, without looking at me, *This dog lying on the dungheap.*

We accept reality so readily—perhaps because we sense that nothing is real. I asked Argos how much of the *Odyssey* he knew. He found using Greek difficult; I had to repeat the question.

Very little, he replied. *Less than the meagerest rhapsode. It has been eleven hundred years since last I wrote it.*

IV

That day, all was revealed to me. The Troglodytes were the Immortals; the stream and its sand-laden waters, the River sought by the rider. As for the City whose renown had spread to the very Ganges, the Immortals had destroyed it almost nine hundred years ago. Out of the shattered remains of the City's ruin they had built on the same spot the incoherent city I had wandered through—that parody or antithesis of City which was also a temple to the irrational gods that rule the world and to those gods about whom we know nothing save that they do not resemble man. The founding of this city was the last symbol to which the Immortals had descended; it marks the point at which, esteeming all exertion vain, they resolved to live in thought, in pure speculation. They built that carapace, abandoned it, and went off to make their dwellings in the caves. In their self-absorption, they scarcely perceived the physical world.

These things were explained to me by Homer as one might explain things to a child. He also told me of his own old age and of that late journey he had made—driven, like Ulysses, by the intention to arrive at the nation of men that know not what the sea is, that eat not salted meat, that know not what an oar might be. He lived for a century in the City of the Immortals, and when it was destroyed it was he who counseled that this other one be built. We should not be surprised by that—it is rumored that after singing of the war of Ilion, he sang of the war between the frogs and rats. He was like a god who created first the Cosmos, and then Chaos.

There is nothing very remarkable about being immortal; with the exception of mankind, all creatures are immortal, for they know nothing of death. What is divine, terrible, and incomprehensible is *to know* oneself immortal. I have noticed that in spite of religion, the conviction as to one's own immortality is extraordinarily rare. Jews, Christians, and Muslims all *profess* belief in immortality, but the veneration paid to the first century of life is proof that they truly believe only in those hundred years, for they destine all the rest, throughout eternity, to rewarding or punishing what one did *when alive.* In my view, the Wheel conceived by certain religions in Hindustan is much more plausible; on that Wheel, which has neither end nor beginning, each life is the effect of the previous life and engenderer of the next, yet no one life determines the whole. . . . Taught by centuries of living, the republic of immortal men had achieved a perfection of tolerance, almost of disdain. They knew that over an infinitely long span of time, all things happen to all men. As reward for his past and future virtues, every man merited every kindness—yet also every betrayal, as reward for his past and future iniquities. Much as the way in games of chance, heads and tails tend to even out, so cleverness and dullness cancel and correct each other. Perhaps the rude poem of El Cid is the counterweight demanded by a single epithet of the Eclogues or a maxim from Heraclitus. The most fleeting thought obeys an invisible plan, and may crown, or inaugurate, a secret design. I know of men who have done evil in order that good may come of it in future centuries, or may already have come of it in centuries past. . . . Viewed in that way, all our acts are just, though also unimportant. There are no spiritual or intellectual *merits.* Homer composed the *Odyssey*; given infinite time, with infinite circumstances and changes, it is impossible that the *Odyssey* should *not* be composed at least once. No one is someone; a single immortal man is all men. Like Cornelius Agrippa, I am god, hero, philosopher, demon, and world—which is a long-winded way of saying that *I am not.*

The notion of the world as a system of exact compensations had an enormous influence on the Immortals. In the first place, it made them immune to pity. I have mentioned the ancient quarries that dotted the countryside on the far bank of the stream; a man fell into the deepest of those pits; he could not be hurt, could not die, and yet he burned with thirst; seventy years passed before he was thrown a rope. Nor was he much interested in his own fate. His body was a submissive domestic animal; all the charity it required each month was a few hours' sleep, a little water, and a scrap of meat. But let no one imagine that we were mere ascetics. There is no more complex pleasure than thought, and it was to thought that we delivered ourselves over. From time to time, some extraordinary stimulus might bring us back to the physical world—for example, on that dawn, the ancient elemental pleasure of the rain. But those lapses were extremely rare; all Immortals were capable of perfect quietude. I recall one whom I never saw standing—a bird had made its nest on his breast.

Among the corollaries to the doctrine that there is no thing that is not counterbalanced by another, there is one that has little theoretical importance but that caused us, at the beginning or end of the tenth century, to scatter over the face of the earth. It may be summarized in these words: *There is a river whose waters give immortality; somewhere there must be another river whose waters take it away.* The number of rivers is not infinite; an immortal traveler wandering the world will someday have drunk from them all. We resolved to find that river.

Death (or reference to death) makes men precious and pathetic; their ghostliness is touching; any act they perform may be their last; there is no face that is not on the verge of blurring and fading away like the faces in a dream. Everything in the world of mortals has the value of the irrecoverable and contingent. Among the Immortals, on the other hand, every act (every thought) is the echo of others that preceded it in the past, with no visible beginning, and the faithful presage of others that will repeat it in the future, *ad vertiginem.* There is nothing that is not as though lost between indefatigable mirrors. Nothing can occur but once, nothing is preciously *in peril of being lost.* The elegiac, the somber, the ceremonial are not modes the Immortals hold in reverence. Homer and I went our separate ways at the portals of Tangier; I do not think we said good-bye.

V

I wandered through new realms, new empires. In the autumn of 1066 I fought at Stamford Bridge, though I no longer recall whether I stood in the ranks of Harold, soon to meet his fate, or in the ranks of that ill-fated Harald Hardrada who conquered only six feet or a little more of English soil. In the seventh century of the Hegira, on the outskirts of Bulaq, I transcribed with deliberate calligraphy, in a language I have forgotten, in an alphabet I know not, the seven voyages of Sindbad and the story of the City of Brass. In a courtyard of the prison in Samarkand I often played chess. In Bikanir I have taught astrology, as I have in Bohemia. In 1638 I was in Kolzsvar, and later in Leipzig. In Aberdeen, in 1714, I subscribed to the six volumes of Pope's *Iliad*; I know I often perused them with delight. In 1729 or thereabouts, I discussed the origin of that poem with a professor of rhetoric whose name, I believe, was Giambattista; his arguments struck me as irrefutable. On October 4, 1921, the *Patna,* which was taking me to Bombay, ran aground in a harbor on the Eritrean coast.[1] I disembarked; there came to my mind other mornings, long in the past, when I had also looked out over the Red Sea—when I was a Roman tribune, and fever and magic and inactivity consumed the soldiers. Outside the city I saw a spring; impelled by habit, I tasted its clear water. As I scaled the steep bank beside it, a thorny tree scratched the back of my hand. The unaccustomed pain seemed exceedingly sharp. Incredulous, speechless, and in joy, I contemplated the precious formation of a slow drop of blood. *I am once more mortal,* I told myself over and over, *again I am like all other men.* That night, I slept until daybreak.

. . . A year has passed, and I reread these pages. I can attest that they do not stray beyond the bounds of truth, although in the first chapters, and even in certain paragraphs of others, I believe I detect a certain falseness. That is due, perhaps, to an overemployment of circumstantial details, a way of writing that I learned from poets; it is a procedure that infects everything with falseness, since there may be a wealth of details in the event, yet not in memory. . . . I believe, nonetheless, that I have discovered a more private and inward reason. I will reveal it; it does not matter that I may be judged a fantast.

The story I have told seems unreal because the experiences of two different men are intermingled in it. In the first chapter, the horseman wishes to know the name of the river that runs beside the walls of Thebes; Flaminius Rufus, who had bestowed upon the city the epithet "hundred-gated," tells him that the river is the "Egypt"; neither of those statements belongs to *him,* but rather to Homer, who in the *Iliad* expressly mentions "Thebes Hekatompylos" and who in the *Odyssey,* through the mouths of Proteus and Ulysses,

[1]Part of the ms. is scratched out just here; the name of the port may have been erased.

invariably calls the Nile the "Egypt." In the second chapter, when the Roman drinks the immortal water he speaks a few words in Greek. Those words are also Homeric; they may be found at the end of the famous catalog of the ships. Later, in the dizzying palace, he speaks of "a reproof that was almost remorse"; those words, too, belong to Homer, who had foreseen such a horror. Such anomalies disturbed me; others, of an æsthetic nature, allowed me to discover the truth. The clues of this latter type may be found in the last chapter, which says that I fought at Stamford Bridge, that in Bulaq I transcribed the voyages of Sindbad the Sailor, and that in Aberdeen I subscribed to Pope's English *Iliad.* The text says, *inter alia*: "In Bikanir I have taught astrology, as I have in Bohemia." None of those statements is false; what is significant is the fact of their having been chosen to record. The first seems to befit a man of war, but then one sees that the narrator pays little attention to the war, much more to the fate of the men. The "facts" that follow are even more curious. A dark yet elemental reason led me to put them to paper: I knew they were pathetic. They are not pathetic when narrated by the Roman Flaminius Rufus; they are when narrated by Homer. It is odd that Homer, in the thirteenth century, should have copied down the adventures of Sindbad—another Ulysses—and again after many hundreds of years have discovered forms like those of his own *Iliad* in a northern kingdom and a barbaric tongue. As for the sentence that contains the name "Bikanir," one can see that it has been composed by a man of letters desirous (like the author of the catalog of ships) of wielding splendid words.[2]

As the end approaches, there are no longer any images from memory—there are only words. It is not strange that time may have confused those that once portrayed *me* with those that were symbols of the fate of *the person that accompanied me for so many centuries.* I have been Homer; soon, like Ulysses, I shall be Nobody; soon, I shall be all men—I shall be dead.

Postcript (1950): Among the commentaries inspired by the foregoing publication, the most curious (if not most urbane) is biblically titled *A Coat of Many Colours* (Manchester, 1948); it is the work of the supremely perseverant pen of Dr. Nahum Cordovero, and contains some hundred pages. It speaks of the Greek anthologies, of the anthologies of late Latin texts, of that Ben Johnson who defined his contemporaries with excerpts from

[2]Ernesto Sabato suggests that the "Giambattista" who discussed the origins of the *Iliad* with the rare book dealer Cartaphilus is Giambattista Vico, the Italian who defended the argument that Homer is a symbolic character, like Pluto or Achilles.

Seneca, of Alexander Ross's *Virgilius evangelizans*, of the artifices of George Moore and Eliot, and, finally, of "the tale attributed to the rare-book dealer Joseph Cartaphilus." In the first chapter it points out brief interpolations from Pliny (*Historia naturalis*, V:8); in the second, from Thomas de Quincey (*Writings*, III: 439); in the third, from a letter written by Descartes to the ambassador Pierre Chanut; in the fourth, from Bernard Shaw (*Back to Methuselah*, V). From those "intrusions" (or thefts) it infers that the entire document is apocryphal.

To my way of thinking, that conclusion is unacceptable. *As the end approaches*, wrote Cartaphilus, *there are no longer any images from memory—there are only words.* Words, words, words taken out of place and mutilated, words from other men—those were the alms left him by the hours and the centuries.

For Cecilia Ingenieros

The Dead Man

That a man from the outskirts of Buenos Aires, a sad sort of hoodlum whose only recommendation was his infatuation with courage, should go out into the wilderness of horse country along the Brazilian frontier and become a leader of a band of smugglers—such a thing would, on the face of it, seem impossible. For those who think so, I want to tell the story of the fate of Benjamín Otálora, whom no one may remember anymore in the neighborhood of Balvanera but who died as he lived, by a bullet, in the province of Rio Grande do Sul.* I do not know the full details of his adventure; when I am apprised of them, I will correct and expand these pages. For now, this summary may be instructive:

In 1891, Benjamín Otálora is nineteen years old—a strapping young man with a miserly brow, earnest blue eyes, and the strength and stamina of a Basque. A lucky knife thrust has revealed to him that he is a man of courage; he is not distressed by the death of his opponent, or by the immediate need to flee the country. The ward boss of his parish gives him a letter of introduction to a man named Azevedo Bandeira, over in Uruguay. Otálora takes ship; the crossing is stormy, creaking; the next day finds him wandering aimlessly through the streets of Montevideo, with unconfessed and perhaps unrecognized sadness. He doesn't manage to come across Azevedo Bandeira. Toward midnight, in a general-store-and-bar in Paso del Molino,* he witnesses a fight between two cattle drovers. A knife gleams; Otálora doesn't know whose side he should be on, but he is attracted by the pure taste of danger, the way other men are attracted by gambling or music. In the confusion, he checks a low thrust meant for a man in a broad-brimmed black hat and a poncho. That man later turns out to be Azevedo

Bandeira. (When Otálora discovers this, he tears up the letter of introduction, because he'd rather all the credit be his alone.) Though Azevedo Bandeira is a strong, well-built man, he gives the unjustifiable impression of being something of a fake, a forgery. In his face (which is always too close) there mingle the Jew, the Negro, and the Indian; in his air, the monkey and the tiger; the scar that crosses his face is just another piece of decoration, like the bristling black mustache.

Whether it's a projection or an error caused by drink, the fight stops as quickly as it started. Otálora drinks with the cattle drovers and then goes out carousing with them and then accompanies them to a big house in the Old City—by now the sun is high in the sky. Out in the back patio, the men lay out their bedrolls. Otálora vaguely compares that night with the previous one; now he is on terra firma, among friends. He does, he has to admit, feel a small twinge of remorse at not missing Buenos Aires. He sleeps till orisons, when he is awakened by the same *paisano* who had drunkenly attacked Bandeira. (Otálora recalls that this man has been with the others, drunk with them, made the rounds of the city with them, that Bandeira sat him at his right hand and made him keep drinking.) The man tells him the boss wants to see him. In a kind of office that opens off the long entryway at the front of the house (Otálora has never seen an entryway with doors opening off it), Azevedo Bandeira is waiting for him, with a splendid, contemptuous red-haired woman. Bandeira heaps praise on Otálora, offers him a glass of harsh brandy, tells him again that he looks like a man of mettle, and asks him if he'd like to go up north with the boys to bring a herd back. Otálora takes the job; by dawn the next morning they are on their way to Tacuarembó.

That is the moment at which Otálora begins a new life, a life of vast sunrises and days that smell of horses. This life is new to him, and sometimes terrible, and yet it is in his blood, for just as the men of other lands worship the sea and can feel it deep inside them, the men of ours (including the man who weaves these symbols) yearn for the inexhaustible plains that echo under the horses' hooves. Otálora has been brought up in neighborhoods full of cart drivers and leather braiders; within a year, he has become a gaucho. He learns to ride, to keep the horses together, to butcher the animals, to use the rope that lassos them and the bolas that bring them down, to bear up under weariness, storms, cold weather, and the sun, to herd the animals with whistles and shouts. Only once during this period of apprenticeship does he see Azevedo Bandeira, but he is always aware of his presence, because to be a "Bandeira man" is to be taken seriously—in fact, to be feared—and because no matter the deed of manly strength or courage they see done, the gauchos say Bandeira does it better. One of them says he thinks Bandeira was born on the other side of the Cuareim, in Rio Grande do Sul; that fact, which ought to bring him down a notch or two in their estimation, lends his aura a vague new wealth of teeming forests, swamps, impenetrable and almost infinite distances.

Gradually, Otálora realizes that Bandeira has many irons in the fire, and that his main business is smuggling. Being a drover is being a servant; Otálora decides to rise higher—decides to become a smuggler. One night, two of his companions are to cross the border to bring back several loads of brandy; Otálora provokes one of them, wounds him, and takes his place. He is moved by ambition, but also by an obscure loyalty. *Once and for all* (he thinks) *I want the boss to see that I'm a better man than all these Uruguayans of his put together.*

Another year goes by before Otálora returns to Montevideo. They ride through the outskirts, and then through the city (which seems enormous to Otálora); they come to the boss's house; the men lay out their bedrolls in the back patio. Days go by, and Otálora hasn't seen Bandeira. They say, timorously, that he's sick; a black man takes the kettle and *mate* up to him in his room. One afternoon, Otálora is asked to carry the things up to Bandeira. He feels somehow humiliated by this, but derives some pride from it, too.

The bedroom is dark and shabby. There is a balcony facing west, a long table with a gleaming jumble of quirts and bullwhips, cinches, firearms, and knives, a distant mirror of cloudy glass. Bandeira is lying on his back, dozing and moaning some; a vehemence of last sunlight spotlights him. The vast white bed makes him seem smaller, and somehow dimmer; Otálora notes the gray hairs, the weariness, the slackness, and the lines of age. It suddenly galls him that it's this old man that's giving them their orders. One thrust, he thinks, would be enough to settle *that* matter. Just then, he sees in the mirror that someone has come into the room. It is the redheaded woman; she is barefoot and half dressed, and staring at him with cold curiosity. Bandeira sits up; while he talks about things out on the range and sips *mate* after *mate,* his fingers toy with the woman's hair. Finally, he gives Otálora leave to go.

Days later, they receive the order to head up north again. They come to a godforsaken ranch somewhere (that could be anywhere) in the middle of the unending plains. Not a tree, not a stream of water soften the place; the sun beats down on it from first light to last. There are stone corrals for the stock, which is long-horned and poorly. The miserable place is called *El Suspiro*—The Sigh.

Otálora hears from the peons that Bandeira will be coming up from Montevideo before long. He asks why, and somebody explains that there's a foreigner, a would-be gaucho type, that's getting too big for his britches. Otálora takes this as a joke, but he's flattered that the joke is possible. He later finds out that Bandeira has had a falling-out with some politico and the politico has withdrawn his protection. The news pleases Otálora.

Crates of firearms begin to arrive; a silver washbowl and pitcher arrive for the woman's bedroom, then curtains of elaborately figured damask; one morning a somber-faced rider with a thick beard and a poncho rides down from up in the mountains. His name is Ulpiano Suárez, and he is Azevedo Bandeira's *capanga,* his foreman. He talks very little, and there is something Brazilian about his speech when he does. Otálora doesn't know whether to attribute the man's reserve to hostility, contempt, or mere savagery, but he does know that for the plan he has in mind he has to win his friendship.

At this point there enters into Benjamín Otálora's life a sorrel with black feet, mane, and muzzle. Azevedo Bandeira brings the horse up with him from the south; its bridle and all its other gear is tipped with silver and the bindings on its saddle are of jaguar skin. That extravagant horse is a symbol of the boss's authority, which is why the youth covets it, and why he also comes to covet, with grudge-filled desire, the woman with the resplendent hair. The woman, the gear, and the sorrel are attributes (adjectives) of a man he hopes to destroy.

Here, the story grows deeper and more complicated. Azevedo Bandeira is accomplished in the art of progressive humiliation, the satanic ability to humiliate his interlocutor little by little, step by step, with a combination of truths and evasions; Otálora decides to employ that same ambiguous method for the hard task he has set himself. He decides that he will gradually push Azevedo Bandeira out of the picture. Through days of common danger he manages to win Suárez' friendship. He confides his plan to him, and Suárez promises to help. Many things happen after this, some of which I know about: Otálora doesn't obey Bandeira; he keeps forgetting, improving his orders, even turning them upside down. The universe seems to conspire with him, and things move very fast. One noon, there is a shoot-out with men from Rio Grande do Sul on the prairies bordering the Tacuarembó. Otálora usurps Bandeira's place and gives the Uruguayans orders. He is shot in the shoulder, but that afternoon Otálora goes back to *El Suspiro* on the boss's sorrel and that afternoon a few drops of his blood stain the jaguar skin and that night he sleeps with the woman with the shining hair. Other versions change the order of these events and even deny that they all occurred on a single day.

Though Bandeira is still nominally the boss, he gives orders that aren't carried out; Benjamín Otálora never touches him, out of a mixture of habit and pity.

The last scene of the story takes place during the excitement of the last night of 1894. That night, the men of *El Suspiro* eat fresh-butchered lamb and drink bellicose liquor. Somebody is infinitely strumming at a milonga that he has some difficulty playing. At the head of the table, Otálora, drunk, builds exultancy upon exultancy, jubilation upon jubilation; that vertiginous tower is a symbol of his inexorable fate. Bandeira, taciturn among the boisterous men, lets the night take its clamorous course. When the twelve strokes of the clock chime at last, he stands up like a man remembering an engagement. He stands up and knocks softly on the woman's door. She opens it immediately, as though she were waiting for the knock. She comes out barefoot and half dressed. In an effeminate, wheedling voice, the boss speaks an order:

"Since you and the city slicker there are so in love, go give him a kiss so everybody can see."

He adds a vulgar detail. The woman tries to resist, but two men have taken her by the arms, and they throw her on top of Otálora. In tears, she kisses his face and his chest. Ulpiano Suárez has pulled his gun. Otálora realizes, before he dies, that he has been betrayed from the beginning, that he has been sentenced to death, that he has been allowed to love, to command, and win because he was already as good as dead, because so far as Bandeira was concerned, he was already a dead man.

Suárez fires, almost with a sneer.

The Theologians

The gardens ravaged, the altars and chalices profaned, the Huns rode their horses into the monastery library and mangled the incomprehensible books and reviled and burned them—fearful perhaps that the letters of the books might harbor blasphemies against their god, which was a scimitar of iron. They burned palimpsests and codices, but in the heart of the bonfire, among the ashes, there lay, virtually untouched by the flames, the twelfth book of the *Civitas Dei*, which says that in Athens Plato once taught that at the end of time all things will return again to where they once were—that he, in Athens, before the same circle of listeners, will one day teach that doctrine once again. That text spared by the flames came to enjoy a special veneration; those who read and reread it in that remote province came to forget that the author put forth the doctrine only in order more roundly to refute it. A hundred years later, Aurelian, bishop-coadjutor of Aquileia, learned that on the banks of the Danube the newborn sect called the *Monotoni* (also the *Annulari*) was claiming that history is a circle, and that all things that exist have existed before and will exist again. In the mountains, the Wheel and the Serpent had supplanted the Cross. Fear gripped all men's hearts, yet all were comforted by the rumor that John of Pannonia, who had distinguished himself by a treatise on the seventh attribute of God, was preparing to refute this abominable heresy.

Aurelian deplored the entire situation—especially this last report. He knew that in theology, there is no novelty without danger; then he reflected that the notion of circular time was too strange, too shocking, for the danger to be very serious. (The heresies we ought to fear are those that can be confused with orthodoxy.) He was pained most of all by the intervention—the intrusion—of John of Pannonia. Two years before, John's verbose treatise *De septima affectione Dei sive de æternitate* had trespassed upon Aurelian's own field of expertise; now, as though the problem of time were his alone, John promised to set the *Annulari* right (no doubt with arguments befitting Procrustes, and remedies more terrible than the Serpent itself). . . . That night, Aurelian turned the pages of Plutarch's ancient dialogue on the ceasing of the oracles; in paragraph twenty-nine, he read a gibe against the Stoics, who defended the idea of an infinite cycle of worlds, with infinite suns, moons, Apollos, Artemisias, and Poseidons. His coming upon this passage was a good omen; he resolved to steal a march on John of Pannonia and refute the heretics of the Wheel himself.

There are those who seek the love of a woman in order to stop thinking of her, to put her out of their mind; similarly, Aurelian wanted to outstrip John of Pannonia not because he wished to do him any harm, but in order to cure himself of the grudge he held for the man. His temper cooled by mere labor, by the crafting of syllogisms and the invention of contumely, by the *nego*'s and *autem*'s and *nequaquam*'s, the rancor dropped away. He constructed vast labyrinthine periods, made impassable by the piling-up of clauses upon clauses—clauses in which oversight and bad grammar seemed manifestations of disdain. He crafted an instrument from cacophony. He foresaw that John would thunder down on the Annulari with the gravity of a prophet; resolved to come at the problem from a different tack, he himself chose derision. Augustine had written that Jesus was the straight path that leads men out of the circular labyrinth in which the impious wander; Aurelian, in his painstakingly trivial way, compared the impious with Ixion, with Prometheus' liver, with Sisyphus, with that king of Thebes who saw two suns, with stuttering, with parrots, mirrors, echoes, mules chained to treadmills, and two-horned syllogisms. (The heathen fables had managed to endure, though reduced now to decoration.) Like all those who possess libraries, Aurelian felt a nagging sense of guilt at not being acquainted with every volume in his; this controversy allowed him to read many of the books that had seemed to reproach his neglect. Thus it was that he inserted into his text a passage from Origen's *De principiis* in which Origen denies that Judas Iscariot will sell the Lord again, that Paul will once more witness Stephen's martyrdom in Jerusalem, and another passage from Cicero's *Academica priora* in which Cicero mocks those who dream that while Cicero is speaking with Lucullus, other Luculluses and other Ciceros, infinite in number, speak precisely the same words in infinite identical worlds. He also scourged the Monotoni with that text from Plutarch on the obsolescence of the oracles, and decried the scandalous fact that the *lumen naturæ* should mean more to an idolater than the word of God to the Monotoni. The labor of composition took Aurelian nine days; on the tenth, he received a copy of the refutation written by John of Pannonia.

It was almost ludicrously brief; Aurelian looked at it with contempt, and then with foreboding. The first section glossed the closing verses of the ninth chapter of the Epistle to the Hebrews, which say that Jesus has not suffered many times since the foundation of the world, but has been sacrificed now, once, "in the end of the world." The second section cited the biblical injunction concerning the "vain repetitions" of the heathens (Matthew 6:7) and that passage from the seventh book of Pliny which praises the fact that in all the wide universe there are no two faces that are the same. John of Pannonia declared that no two souls were the same, either, and that the basest sinner is as precious as the blood shed for him by Jesus Christ. The act of a single man, he said, weighs more than the nine concentric heavens, and to think, erroneously, that it can be lost and then return again is naught but spectacular foolishness. Time does not restore what we lose; eternity holds it for glory, and also for the fire. John's treatise was limpid, universal; it seemed written not by a particular person, but by any man—or perhaps all men.

Aurelian felt an almost physical sense of humiliation. He considered destroying or reworking his own manuscript; then, with grudging honesty, he sent it off to Rome without changing a letter. Months later, when the Council of Pergamo was convened, the theologian entrusted with refuting the errors of the Monotoni was (predictably) John of Pannonia; his learnèd, measured refutation was the argument that condemned the heresiarch Euphorbus to the stake. *This has occurred once, and will occur again,* said Euphorbus. *It is not one pyre you are lighting, it is a labyrinth of fire. If all the fires on which I have been burned were brought together here, the earth would be too small for them, and the angels would be blinded. These words I have spoken many times.* Then he screamed, for the flames had engulfed him.

The Wheel fell to the Cross,[1] but the secret battle between John and Aurelian continued. The two men were soldiers in the same army, strove for the same prize, fought against the same Enemy, yet Aurelian wrote not a word that was not aimed, however unconfessably, at besting John. Their duel was an invisible one; if I may trust the swollen indices of Migne's *Patrology*, not once does *the other man's name* figure in the many volumes of Aurelian's works collected therein for posterity. (Of John's writings, only

[1]In Runic crosses the two enemy emblems coexist, intertwined.

twenty words have survived.) Both men deplored the anathemas of the second Council of Constantinople; both persecuted the Arians, who denied the eternal generation of the Son; both attested to the orthodoxy of Cosmas' *Topographia christiana*, which taught that the earth is foursquare, like the Jewish tabernacle. Then, unfortunately, another tempestuous heresy spread to those four corners of the earth. Spawned in Egypt or in Asia (for accounts differ, and Bousset refuses to accept Harnack's arguments), the sect soon infested the eastern provinces, and sanctuaries were built in Macedonia, Carthage, and Trèves. It seemed to be everywhere; people said that in the diocese of Britain crucifixes had been turned upside down and in Cæsaria the image of the Lord had been supplanted by a mirror. The mirror and the obolus were the emblems of these new schismatics.

History knows them by many names (*Speculari, Abysmali, Cainitæ*), but the most widely accepted is *Histrioni*, the name that Aurelian gave them and that they defiantly adopted for themselves. In Phrygia, they were called the *Simulacra*, and in Dardania as well. John of Damascus called them "*Forms*"; it seems only right to point out that Erfjord thinks the passage apocryphal. There is no heresiologue who does not express shock as he recounts their wild customs. Many Histrioni professed ascetism; some mutilated themselves, like Origen; others lived underground, in the sewers; others put out their own eyes; still others (the *Nebuchadnezzars* of Nitria) "grazed on grasses like the oxen, and their hair grew like the eagle's." From mortification and severity, they sometimes graduated to crime; certain communities tolerated theft; others, homicide; others, sodomy, incest, and bestiality. All were blasphemous; they cursed not only the Christian God, but even the arcane deities of their own pantheon. They plotted together to write sacred texts, whose disappearance is a great loss to scholars. In 1658, Sir Thomas Browne wrote the following: "Time has annihilated the ambitious *Histrionic* Gospels, although not so the Insultes with which their Impiousness was scourged"; Erfjord has suggested that those "insultes" (preserved in a Greek codex) are themselves the lost gospels. Unless we recall the Histrionic cosmology, such a suggestion is incomprehensible.

In the hermetic books, it is written that "things below are as things above, and things above as things below"; the Zohar tells us that the lower world is a reflection of the higher. The Histrioni founded their doctrine on a perversion of this idea. They invoked Matthew 6:12 ("forgive us our debts, as we forgive our debtors") and 11:12 ("the kingdom of heaven suffereth violence") to prove that the earth influences heaven; they cited I Corinthians 13:12 ("For now we see through a glass, darkly") to prove that all things we see are false. Contaminated perhaps by the Monotoni, they imagined that every man is two men, and that the real one is the *other* one, the one in heaven. They also imagined that our acts cast an inverted reflection, so that if we are awake, the other man is asleep; if we fornicate, the other man is chaste; if we steal, the other man is generous. When we die, they believed, we shall join him and *be* him. (Some echo of these doctrines continues to be heard in Bloy.) Other Histrioni believed that the world would end when the number of its possibilities was exhausted; since there can be no repetitions, the righteous are duty-bound to eliminate (commit) the most abominable acts so that those acts will not sully the future and so that the coming of the kingdom of Jesus may be hastened.

That particular article of faith was denied by other sects, which rejoined that the history of the world must be acted out in every man. Most men, like Pythagoras, will have to transmigrate through many bodies before obtaining their liberation; some, the *Proteans,* "within the period of a single life are lions, dragons, wild boars, are water and are a tree." Demosthenes tells of the purification by mud to which initiates were subjected as part of the Orphic mysteries; analogously, the Proteans sought purification through evil. It was their belief, as it was Carpocrates', that no one shall emerge from the prison until the last obolus is paid (Luke 12:59: "I tell thee, thou shalt not depart thence, till thou hast paid the very last mite"), and they often hornswoggled penitents with this other verse: "I am come that they might have life, and that they might have it more abundantly" (John 10:10). They also said that *not* to be an evildoer was an act of satanic arrogance. . . . The Histrioni wove many, and diverse, mythologies; some preached asceticism, others license—all preached confusion. Theopompus, a Histrion from Berenice, denied all fables; he said that every man is an organ projected by the deity in order to perceive the world.

The heretics in Aurelian's diocese were not those who claimed that every act is reflected in heaven but rather those who claimed that time does not tolerate repetitions. The circumstance was peculiar; in a report to the authorities at Rome, Aurelian mentioned it. The prelate who received the report was the empress's confessor; everyone knew that this demanding minister forbade her the private delectations of speculative theology. His secretary—formerly one of John of Pannonia's collaborators, now fallen out with him—was famed as a most diligent inquisitor of heterodoxies; Aurelian added an explanation of the Histrionic heresy, as it was contained in the conventicles of Genoa and Aquileia. He wrote a few paragraphs; when he tried to write the horrible thesis that no two moments are the same, his pen halted. He could not find the necessary words; the admonitions of the new doctrine were too affected and metaphorical to be transcribed. ("Wouldst thou see what no human eyes have seen? Look upon the moon. Wouldst thou hear what no ears have heard? Hearken to the cry of the bird. Wouldst thou touch what no hands have touched? Put thy hand to the earth. Verily I say unto thee, that the moment of God's creation of the world is yet to come.") Then suddenly a sentence of twenty words came to his spirit. With joy he wrote it on the page; immediately afterward, he was disturbed by the sense that it was someone else's. The next day, he remembered: he had read it many years ago in the *Adversus Annulares*, composed by John of Pannonia. He ferreted out the quotation—there it was. He was torn by uncertainty. To alter or omit those words was to weaken the force of the statement; to let them stand was to plagiarize a man he detested; to indicate the source was to denounce him. He pleaded for divine aid. Toward the coming of the second twilight, his guardian angel suggested a middle way. Aurelian kept the words, but set this disclaimer before it: *That which the heresiarchs howl today, to the confusion of the faith, was said during this century, with more levity than blameworthiness, by a most learnèd doctor of the church.* Then there occurred the thing he had feared, the thing he had hoped for, the thing that was inevitable. Aurelian was required to declare the identity of that doctor of the church; John of Pannonia was accused of professing heretical opinions.

Four months later, a blacksmith on the Aventinus, driven to delusions by the misrepresentations of the Histrioni, set a great iron ball upon the shoulders of his little son so that the child's double might fly. The man's child died; the horror engendered by the crime obliged John's judges to be irreproachably severe with him. The accused would not retract; time and again he repeated that to deny his proposition was to fall into the pestilential heresy of the Monotoni. He did not realize (perhaps *refused* to realize) that to speak of the Monotoni was to speak of a thing now forgotten. With somehow senile insistence, he poured forth the most brilliant periods of his old jeremiads; the judges did not even listen to what had once so shocked them. Rather than try to purify himself of the slightest stain of Histrionism, he redoubled his efforts to prove that the proposition of which he was accused was in fact utterly orthodox. He argued with the men upon whose verdict his very life depended, and he committed the supreme *faux pas* of doing so with genius and with sarcasm. On October 26, after a debate that had lasted three days and three nights, he was condemned to be burned at the stake.

Aurelian witnessed the execution, because to have avoided it would have been to confess himself responsible for it. The place of execution was a hill on whose summit stood a stake pounded deep into the ground; all around it, bundles of firewood had been gathered. A priest read the tribunal's verdict. Under the midday sun, John of Pannonia lay with his face in the dust, howling like a beast. He clawed at the ground, but the executioners seized him, stripped him, and tied him to the stake. On his head they put a crown of straw sprinkled with sulfur; beside him, a copy of the pestilential *Adversus Annulares.* It had rained the night before, and the wood burned smokily. John of Pannonia prayed in Greek, and then in an unknown language. The pyre was about to consume him, when Aurelian screwed up his courage to raise his eyes. The fiery gusts fell still; Aurelian saw for the first and last time the face of the man he hated. It reminded him of someone, but he couldn't quite remember whom. Then, the flames swallowed him; he screamed and it was as though the fire itself were screaming.

Plutarch reports that Julius Cæsar wept at the death of Pompey; Aurelian did not weep at the death of John, but he did feel what a man cured of an incurable disease that had become a part of his life might feel. In Aquileia, in Ephesus, in Macedonia, he let the years pass over him. He sought out the hard ends of the empire, the floundering swamps and the contemplative deserts, so that solitude might help him understand his life. In a Mauritanian cell, in the night laden with lions, he rethought the complex accusation against John of Pannonia and for the millionth time he justified the verdict. It was harder for him to justify his tortuous denunciation. In Rusaddir he preached that anachronistic sermon titled *The Light of Lights Lighted in the Flesh of a Reprobate.* In Hibernia, in one of the huts of a monastery besieged by forest, he was surprised one night, toward dawn, by the sound of rain. He recalled a Roman night when that same punctilious sound had surprised him. At high noon, a lighting bolt set the trees afire, and Aurelian died as John had.

The end of the story can only be told in metaphors, since it takes place in the kingdom of heaven, where time does not exist. One might say that Aurelian spoke with God and found that God takes so little interest in religious differences that He took him for John of Pannonia. That, however, would be to impute confusion to the divine intelligence. It is more correct to say that in paradise, Aurelian discovered that in the eyes of the unfathomable deity, he and John of Pannonia (the orthodox and the heretic, the abominator and the abominated, the accuser and the victim) were a single person.

Story of the Warrior and the Captive Maiden

On page 278 of his book *La poesia* (Bari, 1942), Croce, summarizing and shortening a Latin text by the historian Paul the Deacon, tells the story of the life of Droctulft and quotes his epitaph; I found myself remarkably moved by both life and epitaph, and later I came to understand why. Droctulft was a Lombard warrior who during the siege of Ravenna deserted his own army and died defending the city he had been attacking. The people of Ravenna buried him in a church sanctuary; they composed an epitaph in which they expressed their gratitude (CONTEMPSIT CAROS DUM NOS AMAT ILLE PARENTES) and remarked upon the singular contrast between the horrific figure of that barbarian and his simplicity and kindness:

TERRIBILIS VISU FACIES SED MENTE BENIGNUS,
LONGAQUE ROBUSTO PECTORE BARBA FUIT[1]

Such is the story of the life of Droctulft, a barbarian who died defending Rome—or such is the fragment of his story that Paul the Deacon was able to preserve. I do not even know when the event occurred, whether in the mid-sixth century when the Longobards laid waste to the plains of Italy or in the eighth, before Ravenna's surrender. Let us imagine (this is not a work of history) that it was the mid-sixth century.

Let us imagine Droctulft *sub specie æternitatis*—not the individual Droctulft, who was undoubtedly unique and fathomless (as all individuals are), but rather the generic "type" that tradition (the work of memory and forgetting) has made of him and many others like him. Through a gloomy geography of swamps and forests, wars bring him from the shores of the

[1]Gibbon also records these lines, in the *Decline and Fall*, Chapter XLV.

Danube or the Elbe to Italy, and he may not realize that he is going toward the south, nor know that he is waging war against a thing called Rome. It is possible that his faith is that of the Arians, who hold that the glory of the Son is a mere reflection of the glory of the Father, but it seems more fitting to imagine him a worshiper of the earth, Hertha, whose veiled idol is borne from hut to hut in a cart pulled by cattle—or of the gods of war and thunder, who are crude wooden figures swathed in woven clothing and laden with coins and bangles. He comes from the dense forests of the wild boar and the urus; he is white, courageous, innocent, cruel, loyal to his captain and his tribe—not to the universe. Wars bring him to Ravenna, and there he sees something he has never seen before, or never fully seen. He sees daylight and cypresses and marble. He sees an aggregate that is multiple yet without disorder; he sees a city, an organism, composed of statues, temples, gardens, rooms, tiered seats, amphoræ, capitals and pediments, and regular open spaces. None of those artifices (I know this) strikes him as beautiful; they strike him as we would be struck today by a complex machine whose purpose we know not but in whose design we sense an immortal intelligence at work. Perhaps a single arch is enough for him, with its incomprehensible inscription of eternal Roman letters—he is suddenly blinded and renewed by the City, that revelation. He knows that in this city there will be a dog, or a child, and that he will not even begin to understand it, but he knows as well that this city is worth more than his gods and the faith he is sworn to and all the marshlands of Germany. Droctulft deserts his own kind and fights for Ravenna. He dies, and on his gravestone are carved words that he would not have understood:

CONTEMPSIT CAROS DUM NOS AMAT ILLE PARENTES,
HANC PATRIAM REPUTANS ESSE, RAVENNA, SUAM

Droctulft was not a traitor; traitors seldom inspire reverential epitaphs. He was an *illuminatus,* a convert. After many generations, the Longobards who had heaped blame upon the turncoat did as he had done; they became Italians, Lombards, and one of their number—Aldiger—may have fathered those who fathered Alighieri. . . . There are many conjectures one might make about Droctulft's action; mine is the most economical; if it is not true as fact, it may nevertheless be true as symbol.

When I read the story of this warrior in Croce's book, I found myself enormously moved, and I was struck by the sense that I was recovering, under a different guise, something that had once been my own. I fleetingly thought of the Mongol horsemen who had wanted to make China an infinite pastureland, only to grow old in the cities they had yearned to destroy; but that was not the memory I sought. I found it at last—it was a tale I had heard once from my English grandmother, who is now dead.

In 1872 my grandfather Borges was in charge of the northern and western borders of Buenos Aires province and the southern border of Santa Fe. The headquarters was in Junín; some four or five leagues farther on lay the chain of forts; beyond that, what was then called "the pampas" and also "the interior." One day my grandmother, half in wonder, half in jest, remarked upon her fate—an Englishwoman torn from her country and her people and carried to this far end of the earth. The person to whom she made the remark told her she wasn't the only one, and months later pointed out an Indian girl slowly crossing the town square. She was barefoot, and wearing two red ponchos; the roots of her hair were blond. A soldier told her that another Englishwoman wanted to talk with her. The woman nodded; she went into the headquarters without fear but not without some misgiving. Set in her coppery face painted with fierce colors, her eyes were that half-hearted blue that the English call gray. Her body was as light as a deer's; her hands, strong and bony. She had come in from the wilderness, from "the interior," and everything seemed too small for her—the doors, the walls, the furniture.

Perhaps for one instant the two women saw that they were sisters; they were far from their beloved island in an incredible land. My grandmother, enunciating carefully, asked some question or other; the other woman replied haltingly, searching for the words and then repeating them, as though astonished at the old taste of them. It must have been fifteen years since she'd spoken her native language, and it was not easy to recover it. She said she was from Yorkshire, that her parents had emigrated out to Buenos Aires, that she had lost them in an Indian raid, that she had been carried off by the Indians, and that now she was the wife of a minor chieftain—she'd given him two sons; he was very brave. She said all this little by little, in a clumsy sort of English interlarded with words from the Araucan or Pampas tongue,* and behind the tale one caught glimpses of a savage and uncouth life: tents of horsehide, fires fueled by dung, celebrations in which the people feasted on meat singed over the fire or on raw viscera, stealthy marches at dawn; the raid on the corrals, the alarm sounded, the plunder, the battle, the thundering roundup of the stock by naked horsemen, polygamy, stench, and magic. An Englishwoman, reduced to such barbarism! Moved by outrage and pity, my grandmother urged her not to go back. She swore to help her, swore to rescue her children. The other woman answered that she was happy, and she returned that night to the desert. Francisco Borges was to die a short time later, in the Revolution of '74; perhaps at that point my grandmother came to see that other woman, torn like herself from her own kind and transformed by that implacable continent, as a monstrous mirror of her own fate. . . .

Every year, that blond-haired Indian woman had come into the *pulperías** in Junín or Fort Lavalle, looking for trinkets and "vices"; after the conversation with my grandmother, she never appeared again. But they did see each other one more time. My grandmother had gone out hunting; alongside a squalid hut near the swamplands, a man was slitting a sheep's throat. As though in a dream, the Indian woman rode by on horseback. She leaped to the ground and drank up the hot blood. I cannot say whether she did that because she was no longer capable of acting in any other way, or as a challenge, and a sign.

Thirteen hundred years and an ocean lie between the story of the life of the kidnapped maiden and the story of the life of Droctulft. Both, now, are irrecoverable. The figure of the barbarian who embraced the cause of Ravenna, and the figure of the European woman who chose the wilderness—they might seem conflicting, contradictory. But both were transported by some secret impulse, an impulse deeper than reason, and both embraced that impulse that they would not have been able to explain. It may be that the stories I have told are one and the same story. The obverse and reverse of this coin are, in the eyes of God, identical.

For Ulrike von Kühlmann

A Biography of Tadeo Isidoro Cruz (1829–1874)

I'm looking for the face I had
Before the world was made.
Yeats, "The Winding Stair"

On February 6, 1829, the *montoneros**—who by this time were being hounded by Lavalle*—were marching northward to join López' divisions; they halted at a ranch whose name they did not know, three or four leagues from the Pergamino. Toward dawn, one of the men had a haunting nightmare: in the gloom of the large bunkhouse, his confused cry woke the woman that was sleeping with him. No one knows what his dream was because the next day at four o'clock the *montoneros* were put to rout by Suárez' cavalry* and the pursuit went on for nine leagues, all the way to the now-dusky stubble fields, and the man perished in a ditch, his skull split by a saber from the wars in Peru and Brazil. The woman was named Isidora Cruz; the son she bore was given the name Tadeo Isidoro.

It is not my purpose to repeat the story of his life. Of the days and nights that composed it, I am interested in only one; about the rest, I will recount nothing but that which is essential to an understanding of that single night. The adventure is recorded in a very famous book—that is, in a book whose subject can be all things to all men (I Corinthians 9:22), for it is capable of virtually inexhaustible repetitions, versions, perversions. Those who have commented upon the story of Tadeo Isidoro Cruz, and there are many, stress the influence of the wide plains on his formation, but gauchos just like him were born and died along the forested banks of the Paraná and in the eastern mountain ranges. He did live in a world of monotonous barbarity—when he died in 1874 of the black pox, he had never seen a mountain or a gas jet or a windmill. Or a city: In 1849, he helped drive a herd of stock from Francisco Xavier Acevedo's ranch to Buenos Aires; the drovers went into the city to empty their purses; Cruz, a distrustful sort, never left the inn in the neighborhood of the stockyards. He spent many days there, taciturn, sleeping on the ground, sipping his *mate*, getting up at dawn and lying down again at orisons. He realized (beyond words and even beyond understanding) that the city had nothing to do with him. One of the peons, drunk, made fun of him. Cruz said nothing in reply, but during the nights on the return trip, sitting beside the fire, the other man's mockery continued, so Cruz (who had never shown any anger, or even the slightest resentment) killed him with a single thrust of his knife. Fleeing, he took refuge in a swamp; a few nights later, the cry of a crested screamer warned him that the police had surrounded him. He tested his knife on a leaf. He took off his spurs, so they wouldn't get in his way when the time came—he would fight before he gave himself up. He was wounded in the forearm, the shoulder, and the left hand; he gravely wounded the bravest of the men who'd come to arrest him. When the blood ran down between his fingers, he fought more courageously than ever; toward dawn, made faint by the loss of blood, he was disarmed. Back then, the army served as the country's prison: Cruz was sent to a small fort on the northern frontier. As a low private, he took part in the civil wars; sometimes he fought for his native province, sometimes against it. On January 23, 1856, at the Cardoso Marshes, he was one of the thirty Christian men who, under the command of Sgt. Maj. Eusebio Laprida, battled two hundred Indians.* He was wounded by a spear in that engagement.

There are many gaps in his dark and courageous story. In about 1868, we come across him again on the Pergamino: married or domesticated, the father of a son, the owner of a parcel of land. In 1869 he was made sergeant of the rural police. He had set his past right; at that point in his life, he should have considered himself a happy man, though deep down he wasn't. (In the future, secretly awaiting him, was one lucid, fundamental night—the night when he was finally to see his own face, the night when he was finally to hear his own true name. Once fully understood, that night encompasses his entire story—or rather, one incident, one action on that night does, for actions are the symbol of our selves.) Any life, however long and complicated it may be, actually consists of *a single moment*—the moment when a man knows forever more who he is. It is said that Alexander of Macedonia saw his iron future reflected in the fabulous story of Achilles; Charles XII of Sweden, in the story of Alexander. It was not a book that revealed that knowledge to Tadeo Isidoro Cruz, who did not know how to read; he saw himself in a hand-to-hand cavalry fight and in a man. This is how it happened:

During the last days of June in the year 1870, an order came down for the capture of an outlaw wanted for two murders. The man was a deserter from the forces on the border under the command of Col. Benito Machado; in one drunken spree he had killed a black man in a whorehouse; in another, a resident of the district of Rojas. The report added that he came from Laguna Colorada. It was at Laguna Colorada, forty years earlier, that the *montoneros* had gathered for the catastrophe that had left their flesh for birds and dogs; Laguna Colorado was where Manuel Mesa's career began, before he was executed in the Plaza de la Victoria as the snare drums rolled to drown out the sound of the man's fury*; Laguna Colorada was where the unknown man who fathered Cruz had been born, before he died in a ditch with his skull split by a saber from the battles in Peru and Brazil. Cruz had forgotten the name of the place; with a slight but inexplicable sense of uneasiness he recognized it. . . . On horseback, the outlaw, harried by the soldiers, wove a long labyrinth of turns and switchbacks, but the soldiers finally cornered him on the night of July 12. He had gone to ground in a field of stubble. The darkness was virtually impenetrable; Cruz and his men, cautiously and on foot, advanced toward the brush in whose trembling depths the secret man lurked, or slept. A crested screamer cried; Tadeo Isidoro Cruz had the sense that he had lived the moment before. The outlaw stepped out from his hiding place to fight them. Cruz glimpsed the terrifying apparition—the long mane of hair and the gray beard seemed to consume his face. A well-known reason prevents me from telling the story of that fight; let me simply recall that the deserter gravely wounded or killed several of Cruz' men. As Cruz was fighting in the darkness (as his body was fighting in the darkness), he began to understand. He realized that one destiny is no better than the next and that every man must accept the destiny he bears inside himself. He realized that his sergeant's epaulets and uniform were hampering him. He realized his deep-rooted destiny as a wolf, not a gregarious dog; he realized that the other man was he himself. Day began to dawn on the lawless plain; Cruz threw his cap to the ground, cried that he was not going to be a party to killing a brave man, and he began to fight against the soldiers, alongside the deserter Martín Fierro.*

Emma Zunz

On January 14, 1922, when Emma Zunz returned home from the Tarbuch & Loewenthal weaving mill, she found a letter at the far end of the entryway to her building; it had been sent from Brazil, and it informed her that her father had died. She was misled at first by the stamp and the envelope; then the unknown handwriting made her heart flutter. Nine or ten smudgy lines covered almost the entire piece of paper; Emma read that Sr. Maier had accidentally ingested an overdose of veronal and died on the third *inst.* in the hospital at Bagé.* The letter was signed by a resident of the rooming house in which her father had lived, one Fein or Fain, in Rio Grande; he could not have known that he was writing to the dead man's daughter.

Emma dropped the letter. The first thing she felt was a sinking in her stomach and a trembling in her knees; then, a sense of blind guilt, of unreality, of cold, of fear; then, a desire for this day to be past. Then immediately she realized that such a wish was pointless, for her father's death was the only thing that had happened in the world, and it would go on happening, endlessly, forever after. She picked up the piece of paper and went to her room. Furtively, she put it away for safekeeping in a drawer, as though she somehow knew what was coming. She may already have begun to see the things that would happen next; she was already the person she was to become.

In the growing darkness, and until the end of that day, Emma wept over the suicide of Manuel Maier, who in happier days gone by had been Emanuel Zunz. She recalled summer outings to a small farm near Gualeguay,* she recalled (or tried to recall) her mother, she recalled the family's little house in Lanús* that had been sold at auction, she recalled the yellow lozenges of a window, recalled the verdict of prison, the disgrace, the anonymous letters with the newspaper article about the "Embezzlement of Funds by Teller," recalled (and this she would never forget) that on the last night, her father had sworn that the thief was Loewenthal—Loewenthal, Aaron Loewenthal, formerly the manager of the mill and now one of its owners. Since 1916, Emma had kept the secret. She had revealed it to no one, not even to Elsa Urstein, her best friend. Perhaps she shrank from it out of profane incredulity; perhaps she thought that the secret was the link between herself and the absent man. Loewenthal didn't know she knew; Emma Zunz gleaned from that minuscule fact a sense of power.

She did not sleep that night, and by the time first light defined the rectangle of the window, she had perfected her plan. She tried to make that day (which seemed interminable to her) be like every other. In the mill, there were rumors of a strike; Emma declared, as she always did, that she was opposed to all forms of violence. At six, when her workday was done, she went with Elsa to a women's club that had a gymnasium and a swimming pool. They joined; she had to repeat and then spell her name; she had to applaud the vulgar jokes that accompanied the struggle to get it correct. She discussed with Elsa and the younger of the Kronfuss girls which moving picture they would see Sunday evening. And then there was talk of boyfriends; no one expected Emma to have anything to say. In April she would be nineteen, but men still inspired in her an almost pathological fear. . . . Home again, she made soup thickened with manioc flakes and some vegetables, ate early, went to bed, and forced herself to sleep. Thus passed Friday the fifteenth—a day of work, bustle, and trivia—the day before *the day.*

On Saturday, impatience wakened her. Impatience, not nervousness or second thoughts—and the remarkable sense of relief that she had reached this day at last. There was nothing else for her to plan or picture to herself; within a few hours she would have come to the simplicity of the *fait accompli.* She read in *La Prensa* that the *Nordstjärnan,* from Malmö, was to weigh anchor that night from Pier 3; she telephoned Loewenthal, insinuated that she had something to tell him, in confidence, about the strike, and promised to stop by his office at nightfall. Her voice quivered; the quiver befitted a snitch. No other memorable event took place that morning. Emma worked until noon and then settled with Perla Kronfuss and Elsa on the details of their outing on Sunday. She lay down after lunch and with her eyes closed went over the plan she had conceived. She reflected that the final step would be less horrible than the first, and would give her, she had no doubt of it, the taste of victory, and of justice. Suddenly, alarmed, she leaped out of bed and ran to the dressing table drawer. She opened it; under the portrait of Milton Sills, where she had left it night before last, she found Fain's letter. No one could have seen it; she began to read it, and then she tore it up.

To recount with some degree of reality the events of that evening would be difficult, and perhaps inappropriate. One characteristic of hell is its unreality, which might be thought to mitigate hell's terrors but perhaps makes them all the worse. How to make plausible an act in which even she who was to commit it scarcely believed? How to recover those brief hours of chaos that Emma Zunz's memory today repudiates and confuses? Emma lived in Amalgro,* on Calle Liniers*; we know that that evening she went down to the docks. On the infamous Paseo de Julio* she may have seen herself multiplied in mirrors, made public by lights, and stripped naked by hungry eyes—but it is more reasonable to assume that at first she simply wandered, unnoticed, through the indifferent streets. . . . She stepped into two or three bars, observed the routine or the maneuvers of other women. Finally she ran into some men from the *Nordstjärnan*. One of them, who was quite young, she feared might inspire in her some hint of tenderness, so she chose a different one—perhaps a bit shorter than she, and foul-mouthed—so that there might be no mitigation of the purity of the horror. The man led her to a door and then down a gloomy entryway and then to a tortuous stairway and then into a vestibule (with lozenges identical to those of the house in Lanús) and then down a hallway and then to a door that closed behind them. The most solemn of events are outside time—whether because in the most solemn of events the immediate past is severed, as it were, from the future or because the elements that compose those events seem not to be consecutive.

In that time outside time, in that welter of disjointed and horrible sensations, did Emma Zunz think *even once* about the death that inspired the sacrifice? In my view, she thought about it once, and that was enough to endanger her desperate goal. She thought (she could not help thinking) that her father had done to her mother the horrible thing being done to her now. She thought it with weak-limbed astonishment, and then, immediately, took refuge in vertigo. The man—a Swede or Finn—did not speak Spanish; he was an instrument for Emma, as she was for him—but she was used for pleasure, while he was used for justice.

When she was alone, Emma did not open her eyes immediately. On the night table was the money the man had left. Emma sat up and tore it to shreds, as she had torn up the letter a short time before. Tearing up money is an act of impiety, like throwing away bread; the minute she did it, Emma wished she hadn't—an act of pride, and on *that* day. . . . Foreboding melted into the sadness of her body, into the revulsion. Sadness and revulsion lay upon Emma like chains, but slowly she got up and began to dress. The room had no bright colors; the last light of evening made it all the drearier. She managed to slip out without being seen. On the corner she mounted a westbound Lacroze* and following her plan, she sat in the car's frontmost seat, so that no one would see her face. Perhaps she was comforted to see, in the banal bustle of the streets, that what had happened had not polluted everything. She rode through gloomy, shrinking neighborhoods, seeing them and forgetting them instantly, and got off at one of the stops on Warnes.* Paradoxically, her weariness turned into a strength, for it forced her to concentrate on the details of her mission and masked from her its true nature and its final purpose.

Aaron Loewenthal was in the eyes of all an upright man; in those of his few closest acquaintances, a miser. He lived above the mill, alone. Living in the run-down slum, he feared thieves; in the courtyard of the mill there was a big dog, and in his desk drawer, as everyone knew, a revolver. The year before, he had decorously grieved the unexpected death of his wife—a Gauss! who'd brought him an excellent dowry!—but money was his true passion. With secret shame, he knew he was not as good at earning it as at holding on to it. He was quite religious; he believed he had a secret pact with the Lord—in return for prayers and devotions, he was exempted from doing good works. Bald, heavyset, dressed in mourning, with his dark-lensed pince-nez and blond beard, he was standing next to the window, awaiting the confidential report from operator Zunz.

He saw her push open the gate (which he had left ajar on purpose) and cross the gloomy courtyard. He saw her make a small detour when the dog (tied up on purpose) barked. Emma's lips were moving, like those of a person praying under her breath; weary, over and over they rehearsed the phrases that Sr. Loewenthal would hear before he died.

Things didn't happen the way Emma Zunz had foreseen. Since early the previous morning, many times she had dreamed that she would point the firm revolver, force the miserable wretch to confess his miserable guilt, explain to him the daring stratagem that would allow God's justice to triumph over man's. (It was not out of fear, but because she was an instrument of that justice, that she herself intended not to be punished.) Then, a single bullet in the center of his chest would put an end to Loewenthal's life. But things didn't happen that way.

Sitting before Aaron Loewenthal, Emma felt (more than the urgency to avenge her father) the urgency to punish the outrage she herself had suffered. She could not *not* kill him, after being so fully and thoroughly dishonored. Nor did she have time to waste on theatrics. Sitting timidly in his office, she begged Loewenthal's pardon, invoked (in her guise as snitch) the obligations entailed by loyalty, mentioned a few names, insinuated others, and stopped short, as though overcome by fearfulness. Her performance succeeded; Loewenthal went out to get her a glass of water. By the time he returned from the dining hall, incredulous at the woman's fluttering perturbation yet full of solicitude, Emma had found the heavy revolver in the drawer. She pulled the trigger twice. Loewenthal's considerable body crumpled as though crushed by the explosions and the smoke; the glass of water shattered; his face looked at her with astonishment and fury; the mouth in the face cursed her in Spanish and in Yiddish. The filthy words went on and on; Emma had to shoot him again. Down in the courtyard, the dog, chained to his post, began barking furiously, as a spurt of sudden blood gushed from the obscene lips and sullied the beard and clothes. Emma began the accusation she had prepared ("I have avenged my father, and I shall not be punished . . .") but she didn't finish it, because Sr. Loewenthal was dead. She never knew whether he had managed to understand.

The dog's tyrannical barking reminded her that she couldn't rest, not yet. She mussed up the couch, unbuttoned the dead man's suit coat, removed his spattered pince-nez and left them on the filing-cabinet. Then she picked up the telephone and repeated what she was to repeat so many times, in those and other words: *Something has happened, something unbelievable. . . . Sr. Loewenthal sent for me on the pretext of the strike. . . . He raped me. . . . I killed him. . . .*

The story was unbelievable, yes—and yet it convinced everyone, because in substance it was true. Emma Zunz's tone of voice was real, her shame was real, her hatred was real. The outrage that had been done to her was real, as well; all that was false were the circumstances, the time, and one or two proper names.

The House of Asterion

And the queen gave birth to a son named Asterion.
Apollodorus, *Library*, III:i

I know that I am accused of arrogance and perhaps of misanthropy, and perhaps even of madness. These accusations (which I shall punish in due time) are ludicrous. It is true that I never leave my house, but it is also true that its doors (whose number is infinite[1]) stand open night and day to men and also to animals. Anyone who wishes to enter may do so. Here, no womanly splendors, no palatial ostentation shall be found, but only calm and solitude. Here shall be found a house like none other on the face of the earth. (Those who say there is a similar house in Egypt speak lies.) Even my detractors admit that *there is not a single piece of furniture in the house.* Another absurd tale is that I, Asterion, am a prisoner. Need I repeat that the door stands open? Need I add that there is no lock? Furthermore, one afternoon I did go out into the streets; if I returned before nightfall, I did so because of the terrible dread inspired in me by the faces of the people—colorless faces, as flat as the palm of one's hand. The sun had already gone down, but the helpless cry of a babe and the crude supplications of the masses were signs that I had been recognized. The people prayed, fled, fell prostrate before me; some climbed up onto the stylobate of the temple of the Axes, others gathered stones. One, I believe, hid in the sea. Not for nothing was my mother a queen; I cannot mix with commoners, even if my modesty should wish it.

The fact is, I am unique. I am not interested in what a man can publish abroad to other men; like the philosopher, I think that nothing can be communicated by the art of writing. Vexatious and trivial minutiæ find no

[1]The original reads "fourteen," but there is more than enough cause to conclude that when spoken by Asterion that number stands for "infinite."

refuge in my spirit, which has been formed for greatness; I have never grasped for long the difference between one letter and another. A certain generous impatience has prevented me from learning to read. Sometimes I regret that, because the nights and the days are long.

Of course I do not lack for distractions. Sometimes I run like a charging ram through the halls of stone until I tumble dizzily to the ground; sometimes I crouch in the shadow of a wellhead or at a corner in one of the corridors and pretend I am being hunted. There are rooftops from which I can hurl myself until I am bloody. I can pretend anytime I like that I am asleep, and lie with my eyes closed and my breathing heavy. (Sometimes I actually fall asleep; sometimes by the time I open my eyes, the color of the day has changed.) But of all the games, the one I like best is pretending that there is another Asterion. I pretend that he has come to visit me, and I show him around the house. Bowing majestically, I say to him: *Now let us return to our previous intersection* or *Let us go this way, now, out into another courtyard* or *I knew that you would like this rain gutter* or *Now you will see a cistern that has filled with sand* or *Now you will see how the cellar forks.* Sometimes I make a mistake and the two of us have a good laugh over it.

It is not just these games I have thought up—I have also thought a great deal about the house. Each part of the house occurs many times; any particular place is another place. There is not one wellhead, one courtyard, one drinking trough, one manger; there are fourteen [an infinite number of] mangers, drinking troughs, courtyards, wellheads. The house is as big as the world—or rather, it *is* the world. Nevertheless, by making my way through every single courtyard with its wellhead and every single dusty gallery of gray stone, I have come out onto the street and seen the temple of the Axes and the sea. That sight, I did not understand until a night vision revealed to me that there are also fourteen [an infinite number of] seas and temples. Everything exists many times, fourteen times, but there are two things in the world that apparently exist but once—on high, the intricate sun, and below, Asterion. Perhaps I have created the stars and the sun and this huge house, and no longer remember it.

Every nine years, nine men come into the house so that I can free them from all evil. I hear their footsteps or their voices far away in the galleries of stone, and I run joyously to find them. The ceremony lasts but a few minutes. One after another, they fall, without my ever having to bloody my hands. Where they fall, they remain, and their bodies help distinguish one gallery from the others. I do not know how many there have been, but I do know that one of them predicted as he died that someday my redeemer would come. Since then, there has been no pain for me in solitude, because I know that my redeemer lives, and in the end he will rise and stand above the dust. If my ear could hear every sound in the world, I would hear his footsteps. I hope he takes me to a place with fewer galleries and fewer doors. What will my redeemer be like, I wonder. Will he be bull or man? Could he possibly be a bull with the face of a man? Or will he be like me?

The morning sun shimmered on the bronze sword. Now there was not a trace of blood left on it.

"Can you believe it, Ariadne?" said Theseus. "The Minotaur scarcely defended itself."

For Maria Mosquera Eastman

The Other Death

About two years ago, I believe it was (I've lost the letter), Gannon wrote me from Gualeguaychú* to announce that he was sending me a translation, perhaps the first to be done into Spanish, of Ralph Waldo Emerson's poem "The Past"; in a postscript he added that Pedro Damián, a man he said he knew I'd remember, had died a few nights earlier of pulmonary congestion. He'd been ravaged by fever, Gannon said, and in his delirium had relived that bloody day at Masoller.* The news struck me as predictable and even trite, because at nineteen or twenty Pedro Damián had followed the banners of Aparicio Saravia.* The 1904 uprising had caught him unawares on a ranch in Río Negro or Paysandú*, where he was working as a common laborer; Damián was from Entre Ríos, Gualeguay* to be exact, but where his friends went, he went—just as spirited and ignorant a fellow as they were. He fought in the occasional hand-to-hand skirmish and in that last battle; repatriated in 1905, he went back (with humble tenacity) to working in the fields. So far as I am aware, he never left his province again. He spent his last thirty years on quite a solitary little farm a league or two from the Ñancay*; it was in that godforsaken place that I spoke with him one evening in 1942—or tried to speak with him. He was a man of few words and little learning. The sound and fury of Masoller were the full extent of his story; it came as no surprise to me that he had relived those times as he lay dying. . . . I had learned that I would never see Damián again, and so I tried to recall him; my visual memory is so bad that all I could remember was a photograph that Gannon had taken of him. That, too, is not particularly remarkable, if you consider that I saw the man himself but once, in early 1942, but saw the photograph countless times. Gannon sent me the photo; I've lost it, but now I've stopped looking for it. I'd be afraid to find it.

The second episode took place in Montevideo, months later. The fever and agonizing death of the man from Entre Ríos suggested to me a tale of fantasy based on the defeat at Masoller; when I told the plot of the story to Emir Rodríguez Monegal, he gave me a letter of introduction to Col. Dionisio Tabares, who had led the campaign. The colonel received me after dinner. From his comfortable rocking chair out in the courtyard, he lovingly and confusedly recalled the old days. He spoke of munitions that never arrived and of exhausted horses, of grimy, sleepy men weaving labyrinths of marches, and of Saravia, who could have entered Montevideo but turned aside "because gauchos have an aversion to the city," of men whose throats were slashed through to the spine,* of a civil war that struck me as more some outlaw's dream than the collision of two armies. He talked about Illescas, Tupambaé, Masoller,* and did so with such perfectly formed periods, and so vividly, that I realized that he'd told these same stories many times before—indeed, it all made me fear that behind his words hardly any memories remained. As he took a breath, I managed to mention the name Damián.

"Damián? Pedro Damián?" the colonel said. "He served with me. A little Indian-like fellow the boys called Daymán." He began a noisy laugh, but suddenly cut it off, with real or pretended discomfort.

It was in another voice that he said that war, like women, served to test a man—before a man goes into battle, he said, no man knows who he truly is. One fellow might think himself a coward and turn out to be a brave man, or it might be the other way around, which was what happened to that poor Damián, who swaggered around the *pulperías* with his white ribbon* and then fell apart in Masoller. There was one shoot-out with the Zumacos* where he'd acted like a man, but it was another thing when the armies squared off and the cannon started in and every man felt like five thousand other men had ganged up to kill 'im. Poor little mestizo bastard, he'd spent his whole life dipping sheep, and all of a sudden he'd gotten himself swept up in that call to defend the nation. . . .

Absurdly, Col. Tabares' version of the events embarrassed me. I'd have preferred that they not have taken place quite that way. Out of the agèd Damián, a man I'd had a glimpse of on a single afternoon, and that, many years ago, I had unwittingly constructed a sort of idol; Tabares' version shattered it. Suddenly I understood Damián's reserve and stubborn solitude; they had been dictated not by modesty, but by shame. Futilely I told myself, over and over, that a man pursued by an act of cowardice is more complex and more interesting than a man who is merely brave. The gaucho Martín

Fierro, I thought, is less memorable than Lord Jim or Razumov. Yes, but Damián, as a gaucho, had an obligation to be Martín Fierro—especially so in the company of Uruguayan gauchos. With respect to what Tabares said and failed to say, I caught the gamy taste of what was called *Artiguismo**—the (perhaps unarguable) awareness that Uruguay is more elemental than our own country, and therefore wilder. . . . I recall that that night we said our good-byes with exaggerated effusiveness.

That winter, the lack of one or two details for my tale of fantasy (which stubbornly refused to find its proper shape) made me return to Col. Tabares' house. I found him with another gentleman of a certain age—Dr. Juan Francisco Amaro, of Paysandú, who had also fought in Saravia's uprising. There was talk, predictably enough, of Masoller. Amaro told a few anecdotes and then, slowly, like a man thinking out loud, he added:

"We stopped for the night on the Santa Irene ranch, I remember, and some new men joined up with us. Among them, there was a French veterinarian who died the day before the battle, and a sheep shearer, a young kid from Entre Ríos, named Pedro Damián."

I interrupted sharply—

"I know," I said, "The Argentine kid that fell apart under fire."

I stopped; the two men were looking at me perplexedly.

"I beg your pardon, sir," Amaro said, at last. "Pedro Damián died as any man might wish to die. It was about four in the afternoon. The Red infantry* had dug in on the peak of the hill; our men charged them with lances; Damián led the charge, yelling, and a bullet got him straight in the chest. He stopped stock-still, finished his yell, and crumpled, and his body was trampled under the hooves of the horses. He was dead, and the final charge at Masoller rolled right over him. Such a brave man, and not yet twenty."

He was undoubtedly talking about another Damián, but something made me ask what the young mestizo was yelling.

"Curses," the colonel said, "which is what you yell in charges."

"That may be," said Amaro, "but he was also yelling *¡Viva Urquiza!*"*

We fell silent. Finally, the colonel murmured:

"Not as though he was fighting at Masoller, but at Cagancha or India Muerta,* a hundred years before."

Then, honestly perplexed, he added:

"I commanded those troops, and I'd swear that this is the first time I've heard mention of any Damián."

We could not make him remember.

In Buenos Aires, another incident was to make me feel yet again that shiver that the colonel's forgetfulness had produced in me. Down in the basement of Mitchell's English bookshop, I came upon Patricio Gannon one afternoon, standing before the eleven delectable volumes of the works of Emerson. I asked him how his translation of "The Past" was going. He said he had no plans to translate it; Spanish literature was tedious enough already without Emerson. I reminded him that he had promised me the translation in the same letter in which he'd written me the news of Damián's death. He asked who this "Damián" was. I told him, but drew no response. With the beginnings of a sense of terror I saw that he was looking at me strangely, so I bluffed my way into a literary argument about the sort of person who'd criticize Emerson—a poet more complex, more accomplished, and unquestionably more remarkable, I contended, than poor Edgar Allan Poe.

There are several more events I should record. In April I had a letter from Col. Dionisio Tabares; he was no longer confused—now he remembered quite well the Entre Ríos boy who'd led the charge at Masoller and been buried by his men that night at the foot of the hill. In July I passed through Gualeguaychú; I couldn't manage to find Damián's run-down place—nobody remembered him anymore. I tried to consult the storekeeper, Diego Abaroa, who had seen him die; Abaroa had passed away in the fall. I tried to call to mind Damián's features; months later, as I was browsing through some albums, I realized that the somber face I had managed to call up was the face of the famous tenor Tamberlick, in the role of Otello.

I pass now to hypotheses. The simplest, but also the least satisfactory, posits two Damiáns—the coward who died in Entre Ríos in 1946, and the brave man who died at Masoller in 1904. The problem with that hypothesis is that it doesn't explain the truly enigmatic part of it all: the curious comings and goings of Col. Tabares' memory, the forgetfulness that wipes out the image and even the name of the man that was remembered such a short time ago. (I do not, cannot, accept the even simpler hypothesis—that I might have dreamed the first remembering.) More curious yet is the *supernatural* explanation offered by Ulrike von Kühlmann. Pedro Damián, Ulrike suggests, died in the battle, and at the hour of his death prayed to God to return him to Entre Ríos. God hesitated a second before granting that favor, and the man who had asked it was already dead, and some men had seen him killed. God, who cannot change the past, although He can change the images of the past, changed the image of death into one of unconsciousness, and the shade of the man from Entre Ríos returned to his native land. Returned, but we should recall that he was a shade, a ghost. He lived in solitude, without wife, without friends; he loved everything, possessed everything, but from a distance, as though from the other side of a pane of glass; he "died," but his gossamer image endured, like water within water. That hypothesis is not correct, but it ought to have suggested the true one (the one that today I *believe* to be the true one), which is both simpler and more outrageous. I discovered it almost magically in Pier Damiani's treatise titled *De omnipotentia*, which I sought out because of two lines from Canto XXI of the *Paradiso*—two lines that deal with a problem of identity. In the fifth chapter of his treatise, Pier Damiani maintains, against Aristotle and Fredegarius of Tours, that God can make what once existed never to have been. I read those old theological arguments and began to understand the tragic story of don Pedro Damián. This is the way I imagine it:

Damián behaved like a coward on the field of Masoller, and he dedicated his life to correcting that shameful moment of weakness. He returned to Entre Ríos; he raised his hand against no man, he "marked" no one,* he sought no reputation for bravery, but in the fields of Ñancay, dealing with the brushy wilderness and the skittish livestock, he hardened himself. Little by little he was preparing himself, unwittingly, for the miracle. Deep inside himself, he thought: If fate brings me another battle, I will know how to deserve it. For forty years he awaited that battle with vague hopefulness, and fate at last brought it to him, at the hour of his death. It brought it in the form of a delirium, but long ago the Greeks knew that we are the shadows of a dream. In his dying agony, he relived his battle, and he acquitted himself like a man—he led the final charge and took a bullet in the chest. Thus, in 1946, by the grace of his long-held passion, Pedro Damián died in the defeat at Masoller, which took place between the winter and spring of the year 1904.

The *Summa Theologica* denies that God can undo, unmake what once existed, but it says nothing about the tangled concatenation of causes and effects—which is so vast and so secret that it is possible that not a *single* remote event can be annulled, no matter how insignificant, without canceling the present. To change the past is not to change a mere single event; it is to annul all its consequences, which tend to infinity. In other words: it is to create two histories of the world. In what we might call the first, Pedro Damián died in Entre Ríos in 1946; in the second, he died at Masoller in 1904. This latter history is the one we are living in now, but the suppression of the former one was not immediate, and it produced the inconsistencies I have reported. In Col. Dionisio Tabares we can see the various stages of this process: at first he remembered that Damián behaved like a coward; then he totally forgot him; then he recalled his impetuous death. The case of the storekeeper Abaroa is no less instructive; he died, in my view, because he had too many memories of don Pedro Damián.

As for myself, I don't think I run a similar risk. I have guessed at and recorded a process inaccessible to humankind, a sort of outrage to rationality; but there are circumstances that mitigate that awesome privilege. For the moment, I am not certain that I have always written the truth. I suspect that within my tale there are false recollections. I suspect that Pedro Damián (if he ever existed) was not called Pedro Damián, and that I remember him under that name in order to be able to believe, someday in the future, that his story was suggested to me by the arguments of Pier Damiani. Much the same thing occurs with that poem that I mentioned in the first paragraph, the poem whose subject is the irrevocability of the past. In 1951 or thereabouts I will recall having concocted a tale of fantasy, but I will have told the story of a true event in much the way that naive Virgil, two thousand years ago, thought he was heralding the birth of a man though he had foretold the birth of God.

Poor Damián! Death carried him off at twenty in a war he knew nothing of and in a homemade sort of battle—yet though it took him a very long time to do so, he did at last achieve his heart's desire, and there is perhaps no greater happiness than that.

Deutsches Requiem

Though he slay me, yet will I trust in him.
Job 13:15

My name is Otto Dietrich zur Linde. One of my forebears, Christoph zur Linde, died in the cavalry charge that decided the victory of Zorndorf. During the last days of 1870, my maternal great-grandfather, Ulrich Forkel, was killed in the Marchenoir forest by French sharpshooters; Captain Dietrich zur Linde, my father, distinguished himself in 1914 at the siege of Namur, and again two years later in the crossing of the Danube.[1] As for myself, I am to be shot as a torturer and a murderer. The court has acted rightly; from the first, I have confessed my guilt. Tomorrow, by the time the prison clock strikes nine, I shall have entered the realms of death; it is natural that I should think of my elders, since I am come so near their shadow—since, somehow, I am they.

During the trial (which fortunately was short) I did not speak; to explain myself at that point would have put obstacles in the way of the verdict and made me appear cowardly. Now things have changed; on this night that precedes my execution, I can speak without fear. I have no desire to be pardoned, for I feel no guilt, but I do wish to be understood. Those who heed my words shall understand the history of Germany and the future history of the world. I know that cases such as mine, exceptional and shocking now, will very soon be unremarkable. Tomorrow I shall die, but I am a symbol of the generations to come.

*

[1]It is significant that zur Linde has omitted his most illustrious forebear, the theologian and Hebraist Johannes Forkel (1799–1846), who applied Hegel's dialectics to Christology and whose literal translation of some of the Apocrypha earned him the censure of Hengstenberg and the praise of Thilo and Gesenius. [Ed.]

I was born in Marienburg in 1908. Two passions, music and metaphysics, now almost forgotten, allowed me to face many terrible years with bravery and even happiness. I cannot list all my benefactors, but there are two names I cannot allow myself to omit: Brahms and Schopenhauer. Frequently, I also repaired to poetry; to those two names, then, I would add another colossal Germanic name: William Shakespeare. Early on, theology had held some interest for me, but I was forever turned from that fantastic discipline (and from Christianity) by Schopenhauer with his direct arguments and Shakespeare and Brahms with the infinite variety of their worlds. I wish anyone who is held in awe and wonder, quivering with tenderness and gratitude, transfixed by some passage in the work of these blessèd men—anyone so touched—to know that I too was once transfixed like them—I the abominable.

Nietzsche and Spengler entered my life in 1927. A certain eighteenth-century author observes that no man wants to owe anything to his contemporaries; in order to free myself from an influence that I sensed to be oppressive, I wrote an article titled *"Abrechnung mit Spengler,"* wherein I pointed out that the most unequivocal monument to those characteristics that the author called Faustian was *not* Goethe's miscellaneous drama[2] but rather a poem written twenty centuries ago, the *De rerum naturæ.** I did, however, give just due to the sincerity of our philosopher of history, his radically German (*kerndeutsch*) and military spirit. In 1929 I joined the party.

I shall say little about my years of apprenticeship. They were harder for me than for many others, for in spite of the fact that I did not lack valor, I felt no calling for violence. I did, however, realize that we were on the threshold of a new age, and that that new age, like the first years of Islam or Christianity, demanded new men. As individuals, my comrades were odious to me; I strove in vain to convince myself that for the high cause that had brought us all together, we were not individuals.

Theologians claim that if the Lord's attention were to stray for even one second from my right hand, which is now writing, that hand would be plunged into nothingness, as though it had been annihilated by a lightless fire. No one can exist, say I, no one can sip a glass of water or cut off a piece of bread, without justification. That justification is different for every man;

[2]Other nations live naively, in and for themselves, like minerals or meteors; Germany is the universal mirror that receives all others—the conscience of the world (*das Weltbewußtsein*). Goethe is the prototype of that ecumenical mind. I do not criticize him, but I do not see him as the Faustian man of Spengler's treatise.

I awaited the inexorable war that would test our faith. It was enough for me to know that I would be a soldier in its battles. I once feared that we would be disappointed by the cowardice of England and Russia. Chance (or destiny) wove a different future for me—on March 1, 1939, at nightfall, there were riots in Tilsit, which the newspapers did not report; in the street behind the synagogue, two bullets pierced my leg, and it had to be amputated.[3] Days later, our armies entered Bohemia; when the sirens announced the news, I was in that sedentary hospital, trying to lose myself, forget myself, in the books of Schopenhauer. On the windowsill slept a massive, obese cat—the symbol of my vain destiny.

In the first volume of *Parerga und Paralipomena*, I read once more that all things that can occur to a man, from the moment of his birth to the moment of his death, have been predetermined by him. Thus, all inadvertence is deliberate, every casual encounter is an engagement made beforehand, every humiliation is an act of penitence, every failure a mysterious victory, every death a suicide. There is no more cunning consolation than the thought that we have chosen our own misfortunes; that individual theology reveals a secret order, and in a marvelous way confuses ourselves with the deity. What unknown purpose (I thought) had made me seek out that evening, those bullets, this mutilation? Not the fear of war—I knew that; something deeper. At last I believed I understood. To die for a religion is simpler than living that religion fully; battling savage beasts in Ephesus is less difficult (thousands of obscure martyrs did it) than being Paul, the servant of Jesus Christ; a single act is quicker than all the hours of a man. The battle and the glory are *easy*; Raskolnikov's undertaking was more difficult than Napoleon's. On February 7, 1941, I was made subdirector of the Tarnowitz concentration camp.

Carrying out the duties attendant on that position was not something I enjoyed, but I never sinned by omission. The coward proves himself among swords; the merciful man, the compassionate man, seeks to be tested by jails and others' pain. Nazism is intrinsically a *moral* act, a stripping away of the old man, which is corrupt and depraved, in order to put on the new. In battle, amid the captains' outcries and the shouting, such a transformation is common; it is not common in a crude dungeon, where insidious compassion tempts us with ancient acts of tenderness. I do not write that word "compassion" lightly: compassion on the part of the superior man is

[3]It is rumored that the wound had extremely serious consequences. [Ed.]

Zarathustra's ultimate sin. I myself (I confess) almost committed it when the famous poet David Jerusalem was sent to us from Breslau.

Jerusalem was a man of fifty; poor in the things of this world, persecuted, denied, calumniated, he had consecrated his genius to hymns of happiness. I think I recall that in the *Dichtung der Zeit*, Albert Sörgel compared him to Whitman. It is not a happy comparison: Whitman celebrates the universe *a priori*, in a way that is general and virtually indifferent; Jerusalem takes delight in every smallest thing, with meticulous and painstaking love. He never stoops to enumerations, catalogs. I can still recite many hexameters from that profound poem titled "Tse Yang, Painter of Tigers," which is virtually striped with tigers, piled high with transversal, silent tigers, riddled through and through with tigers. Nor shall I ever forget the soliloquy "Rosenkranz Talks with the Angel," in which a sixteenth-century London moneylender tries in vain, as he is dying, to exculpate himself, never suspecting that the secret justification for his life is that he has inspired one of his clients (who has seen him only once, and has no memory even of that) to create the character Shylock. A man of memorable eyes, sallow skin, and a beard that was almost black, David Jerusalem was the prototypical Sephardic Jew, although he belonged to the depraved and hated Ashkenazim. I was severe with him; I let neither compassion nor his fame make me soft. I had realized many years before I met David Jerusalem that everything in the world can be the seed of a possible hell; a face, a word, a compass, an advertisement for cigarettes—anything can drive a person insane if that person cannot manage to put it out of his mind. Wouldn't a man be mad if he constantly had before his mind's eye the map of Hungary? I decided to apply this principle to the disciplinary regimen of our house, and . . .[4] In late 1942, Jerusalem went insane; on March 1, 1943, he succeeded in killing himself.[5]

I do not know whether Jerusalem understood that if I destroyed him, it was in order to destroy my own compassion. In my eyes, he was not a man, not even a Jew; he had become a symbol of a detested region of my soul. I suffered with him, I died with him, I somehow have been lost with him; that was why I was implacable.

[4]Here, the excision of a number of lines has been unavoidable. [Ed.]

[5]In neither the files nor the published work of Sörgel does Jerusalem's name appear. Nor does one find it in the histories of German literature. I do not, however, think that this is an invented figure. Many Jewish intellectuals were tortured in Tarnowitz on the orders of Otto Dietrich zur Linde, among them the pianist Emma Rosenzweig. "David Jerusalem" is perhaps a symbol for many individuals. We are told that he died on March 1, 1943; on March 1, 1939, the narrator had been wounded at Tilsit. [Ed.]

Meanwhile, the grand days and grand nights of a thrilling war washed over us. In the air we breathed there was an emotion that resembled love. As though the ocean were suddenly nearby, there was a tonic and an exultation in the blood. In those years, everything was different—even the taste of one's sleep. (I may never have been happy, but it is common knowledge that misery requires paradises lost.) There is no man who does not long for plenitude—the sum of the experiences of which a man is capable; there is no man who does not fear being defrauded of a part of that infinite inheritance. But my generation has had it all, for first it was given glory, and then defeat.

In October or November of 1942, my brother Friedrich died in the second Battle of El Alamein, on the Egyptian sands; months later, an aerial bombardment destroyed the house we had been born in; another, in late 1943, destroyed my laboratory. Hounded across vast continents, the Third Reich was dying; its hand was against all men, and all men's hands against it. Then, something remarkable happened, and now I think I understand it. I believed myself capable of drinking dry the cup of wrath, but when I came to the dregs I was stopped by an unexpected flavor—the mysterious and almost horrific taste of happiness. I tested several explanations; none satisfied me. *I feel a contentment in defeat,* I reflected, *because secretly I know my own guilt, and only punishment can redeem me.* Then *I feel a contentment in defeat,* I reflected, *simply because defeat has come, because it is infinitely connected to all the acts that are, that were, and that shall be, because to censure or deplore a single real act is to blaspheme against the universe.* I tested those arguments, as I say, and at last I came to the true one.

It has been said that all men are born either Aristotelians or Platonists. That is equivalent to saying that there is no debate of an abstract nature that is not an instance of the debate between Aristotle and Plato. Down through the centuries and latitudes, the names change, the dialects, the faces, but not the eternal antagonists. Likewise, the history of nations records a secret continuity. When Arminius slaughtered the legions of Varus in a swamp, when he slashed their throats, he did not know that he was a forerunner of a German Empire; Luther, the translator of the Bible, never suspected that his destiny would be to forge a nation that would destroy the Bible forever; Christoph zur Linde, killed by a Muscovite bullet in 1758, somehow set the stage for the victories of 1914; Hitler thought he was fighting for *a* nation, but he was fighting for *all* nations, even for those he attacked and abominated. It does not matter that his *ego* was unaware of that; his blood, his *will,* knew. The world was dying of Judaism, and of that disease of Judaism that is belief in Christ; we proffered it violence and faith in the sword. That sword killed us, and we are like the wizard who weaves a labyrinth and is forced to wander through it till the end of his days, or like David, who sits in judgment on a stranger and sentences him to death, and then hears the revelation: *Thou art that man.* There are many things that must be destroyed in order to build the new order; now we know that Germany was one of them. We have given something more than our lives; we have given the life of our belovèd nation. Let others curse and others weep; I rejoice in the fact that our gift is orbicular and perfect.

Now an implacable age looms over the world. We forged that age, we who are now its victim. What does it matter that England is the hammer and we the anvil? What matters is that violence, not servile Christian acts of timidity, now rules. If victory and injustice and happiness do not belong to Germany, let them belong to other nations. Let heaven exist, though our place be in hell.

I look at my face in the mirror in order to know who I am, in order to know how I shall comport myself within a few hours, when I face the end. My flesh may feel fear; I *myself* do not.

Averroës' Search

S'imaginant que la tragédie n'est autre chose que l'art de louer. . . .

Ernest Renan, *Averroès,* 48 (1861)

Abu-al-Walīd Muḥammad ibn-Aḥmad ibn-Rushd (it would take that long name, passing through "Benraist" and "Avenris" and even "Aben Rassad" and "Filius Rosadis," a hundred years to become "Averroës") was at work on the eleventh chapter of his work *Tahāfut al-Tahāfut* ("Destruction of the Destruction"), which maintains, contrary to the Persian ascetic al-Ghazzāli, author of the *Tahāfut al-Falāsifah* ("Destruction of Philosophers"), that the deity knows only the general laws of the universe, those that apply not to the individual but to the species. He wrote with slow assurance, from right to left; the shaping of syllogisms and linking together of vast paragraphs did not keep him from feeling, like a sense of wonderful well-being, the cool, deep house around him. In the depths of the siesta, loving turtledoves purred throatily, one to another; from some invisible courtyard came the murmur of a fountain; something in the flesh of Averroës, whose ancestors had come from the deserts of Arabia, was grateful for the steadfast presence of the water. Below lay the gardens of flowers and of foodstuffs; below that ran the bustling Guadalquivir; beyond the river spread the beloved city of Córdoba, as bright as Baghdad or Cairo, like a complex and delicate instrument; and, encircling Córdoba (this, Averroës could feel too), extending to the very frontier, stretched the land of Spain, where there were not a great many things, yet where each thing seemed to exist materially and eternally.

His quill ran across the page, the arguments, irrefutable, knitted together, and yet a small worry clouded Averroës' happiness. Not the sort of worry brought on by the *Tahāfut,* which was a fortuitous enterprise, but rather a philological problem connected with the monumental work that would justify him to all people—his commentary on Aristotle. That Greek sage, the fountainhead of all philosophy, had been sent down to men to teach them all things that can be known; interpreting Aristotle's works, in the same way the *ulemas* interpret the Qur'ān, was the hard task that Averroës had set himself. History will record few things lovelier and more moving than this Arab physician's devotion to the thoughts of a man separated from him by a gulf of fourteen centuries. To the intrinsic difficulties of the enterprise we might add that Averroës, who knew neither Syriac nor Greek, was working from a translation of a translation. The night before, two doubtful words had halted him at the very portals of the Poetics. Those words were "tragedy" and "comedy." He had come across them years earlier, in the third book of the Rhetoric; no one in all of Islam could hazard a guess as to their meaning. He had pored through the pages of Alexander of Aphrodisias, compared the translations of the Nestorian Ḥunayn ibn-Isḥāq and Abu-Bashār Māta—and he had found nothing. Yet the two arcane words were everywhere in the text of the Poetics—it was impossible to avoid them.

Averroës laid down his quill. He told himself (without conviction) that what we seek is often near at hand, put away the manuscript of the *Tahāfut*, and went to the shelf on which the many volumes of blind ibn-Sīna's *Moqqām*, copied by Persian copyists, stood neatly aligned. Of course he had already consulted them, but he was tempted by the idle pleasure of turning their pages. He was distracted from that scholarly distraction by a kind of song. He looked out through the bars of the balcony; there below, in the narrow earthen courtyard, half-naked children were at play. One of them, standing on the shoulders of another, was clearly playing at being a muezzin: his eyes tightly closed, he was chanting the muezzin's monotonous cry, *There is no God but Allah.* The boy standing motionless and holding him on his shoulders was the turret from which he sang; another, kneeling, bowing low in the dirt, was the congregation of the faithful. The game did not last long—they all wanted to be the muezzin, no one wanted to be the worshippers or the minaret. Averroës listened to them arguing in the "vulgar" dialect (that is, the incipient Spanish) of the Muslim masses of the Peninsula. He opened Khalil's *Kitāb al-'Ayn* and thought proudly that in all of Córdoba (perhaps in all of Al-Andalus) there was no other copy of the perfect work—only this one, sent him by Emir Ya'qūb al-Manṣūr from Tangier. The name of that port reminded him that the traveler abu-al-Ḥasan al-Ash'ari, who had returned from Morocco, was to dine with him that evening at the home of the Qur'ānist Faraj. Abu-al-Ḥasan claimed to have reached the kingdoms of the Sin Empire [China]; with that peculiar logic born of hatred, his detractors swore that he had never set foot in China and that he had blasphemed Allah in the temples of that land. The gathering would inevitably last for hours; Averroës hurriedly went back to his work on the *Tahāfut*. He worked until dusk.

At Faraj's house, the conversation moved from the incomparable virtues of the governor to those of his brother the emir; then, out in the garden, the talk was of roses. Abu-al-Ḥasan (having never seen them) said there were no roses like those which bedeck the villas of Andalusia. Faraj was not to be suborned by flattery; he observed that the learnèd ibn-Qutaybah had described a superb variety of *perpetual* rose which grows in the gardens of Hindustan and whose petals, of a deep crimson red, exhibit characters reading *There is no God but Allah, and Muḥammad is His prophet.* He added that abu-al-Ḥasan must surely be acquainted with those roses. Abu-al-Ḥasan looked at him in alarm. If he said yes, he would be judged by all, quite rightly, to be the most pliable and serviceable of impostors; if he said no, he would be judged an infidel. He opted to breathe that Allah held the keys that unlock hidden things, and that there was no green or wilted thing on earth that was not recorded in His Book. Those words belong to one of the first sūras of the Qur'ān; they were received with a reverential murmur. Puffed up by that victory of dialectics, abu-al-Ḥasan was about to declare that Allah is perfect in His works, and inscrutable. But Averroës, prefiguring the distant arguments of a still-problematic Hume, interrupted.

"I find it less difficult to accept an error in the learnèd ibn-Qutaybah, or in the copyists," he said, "than to accept that the earth brings forth roses with the profession of our faith."

"Precisely. Great words and true," said abu-al-Ḥasan.

"Some traveler, I recall," mused the poet Abd-al-Malik, "speaks of a tree whose branches put forth green birds. I am pained less by believing in that tree than in roses adorned with letters."

"The birds' color," said Averroës, "does seem to make that wonder easier to bear. In addition, both birds and the fruit of trees belong to the natural world, while writing is an art. To move from leaves to birds is easier than to move from roses to letters."

Another guest indignantly denied that writing was an art, since the original Book of the Qur'ān—*the mother of the Book*— predates the Creation, and resides in heaven. Another spoke of Al-Jāḥiẓ of Basra, who had stated that the Qur'ān is a substance that can take the form of man or animal—an opinion which appears to agree with that of the people who attribute to the Qur'ān two faces. Faraj discoursed long on orthodox doctrine. The Qur'ān, he said, is one of the attributes of Allah, even as His

Mercy is; it may be copied in a book, pronounced with the tongue, or remembered in the heart, but while language and signs and writing are the work of men, the Qur'ān itself is irrevocable and eternal. Averroës, who had written his commentary on the *Republic*, might have said that the mother of the Book is similar, in a way, to the Platonic Idea, but he could see that theology was one subject utterly beyond the grasp of abu-al-Ḥasan.

Others, who had come to the same realization, urged abu-al-Ḥasan to tell a tale of wonder. Then, like now, the world was horrible; daring men might wander through it, but so might wretches, those who fall down in the dust before all things. Abu-al-Ḥasan's memory was a mirror of secret acts of cowardice. What story could he tell? Besides, the guests demanded marvels, while the marvelous was perhaps incommunicable: the moon of Bengal is not the same as the moon of Yemen, but it deigns to be described with the same words. Abu-al-Ḥasan pondered; then, he spoke:

"He who wanders through climes and cities," his unctuous voice began, "sees many things worthy of belief. This, for instance, which I have told but once before, to the king of the Turks. It took place in Sin-i Kalal [Canton], where the River of the Water of Life spills into the sea."

Faraj asked whether the city lay many leagues from that wall erected by Iskandar dhu-al-Quarnayn [Alexander of Macedonia] to halt the advance of Gog and Magog.

"There are vast deserts between them," abu-al-Ḥasan said, with inadvertent haughtiness. "Forty days must a *kafila* [caravan] travel before catching sight of its towers, and another forty, men say, before the *kafila* stands before them. In Sin-i Kalal I know of no man who has seen it or seen the man who has seen it."

For one moment the fear of the grossly infinite, of mere space, mere matter, laid its hand on Averroës. He looked at the symmetrical garden; he realized that he was old, useless, unreal. Then abu-al-Ḥasan spoke again:

"One evening, the Muslim merchants of Sin-i Kalal conducted me to a house of painted wood in which many persons lived. It is not possible to describe that house, which was more like a single room, with rows of cabinet-like contrivances, or balconies, one atop another. In these niches there were people eating and drinking; there were people sitting on the floor as well, and also on a raised terrace. The people on this terrace were playing the tambour and the lute—all, that is, save some fifteen or twenty who wore crimson masks and prayed and sang and conversed among themselves. These masked ones suffered imprisonment, but no one could see the jail; they rode upon horses, but the horse was not to be seen; they waged battle, but the swords were of bamboo; they died, and then they walked again."

"The acts of madmen," said Faraj, "are beyond that which a sane man can envision."

"They were not madmen," abu-al-Ḥasan had to explain. "They were, a merchant told me, presenting a story."

No one understood, no one seemed to want to understand. Abu-al-Ḥasan, in some confusion, swerved from the tale he had been telling them into inept explanation. Aiding himself with his hands, he said:

"Let us imagine that someone *shows* a story instead of telling it—the story of the seven sleepers of Ephesus, say.* We see them retire into the cavern, we see them pray and sleep, we see them sleep with their eyes open, we see them grow while they are asleep, we see them awaken after three hundred nine years, we see them hand the merchant an ancient coin, we see them awaken in paradise, we see them awaken with the dog. It was something like that that the persons on the terrace showed us that evening."

"Did these persons speak?" asked Faraj.

"Of course they did," said abu-al-Ḥasan, now become the apologist for a performance that he only barely recalled and that had irritated him considerably at the time. "They spoke and sang and gave long boring speeches!"

"In that case," said Faraj, "there was no need for *twenty* persons. A single speaker could *tell* anything, no matter how complex it might be."

To that verdict, they all gave their nod. They extolled the virtues of Arabic—the language used by Allah, they recalled, when He instructs the angels—and then the poetry of the Arabs. After according that poetry its due praise, abu-al-Ḥasan dismissed those other poets who, writing in Córdoba or Damascus, clung to pastoral images and Bedouin vocabulary—outmoded, he called them. He said it was absurd for a man whose eyes beheld the wide Guadalquivir to compose odes upon the water of a well. It was time, he argued, that the old metaphors be renewed; back when Zuhayr compared fate to a blind camel, he said, the figure was arresting—but five hundred years of admiration had worn it very thin. To that verdict, which they had all heard many times before, from many mouths, they all likewise gave their nod. Averroës, however, kept silent. At last he spoke, not so much to the others as to himself.

"Less eloquently," he said, "and yet with similar arguments, I myself have sometimes defended the proposition argued now by abu-al-Ḥasan. In Alexandria there is a saying that only the man who has already committed a crime and repented of it is incapable of that crime; to be free of an erroneous opinion, I myself might add, one must at some time have professed it. In his *mu'allaqa,* Zuhayr says that in the course of his eighty years of pain and glory many is the time he has seen destiny trample men, like an old blind camel; abu-al-Ḥasan says that that figure no longer makes us marvel. One might reply to that objection in many ways. First, that if the purpose of the poem were to astound, its life would be not measured in centuries but in days, or hours, or perhaps even minutes. Second, that a famous poet is less an inventor than a discoverer. In praise of ibn-Sharaf of Berkha, it has many times been said that only he was capable of imagining that the stars of the morning sky fall gently, like leaves falling from the trees; if that were true, it would prove only that the image is trivial. The image that only a single man can shape is an image that interests no man. There are infinite things upon the earth; any one of them can be compared to any other. Comparing stars to leaves is no less arbitrary than comparing them to fish, or birds. On the other hand, every man has surely felt at some moment in his life that destiny is powerful yet clumsy, innocent yet inhuman. It was in order to record that feeling, which may be fleeting or constant but which no man may escape experiencing, that Zuhayr's line was written. No one will ever say better what Zuhayr said there. Furthermore (and this is perhaps the essential point of my reflections), time, which ravages fortresses and great cities, only *enriches* poetry. At the time it was composed by him in Arabia, Zuhayr's poetry served to bring together two images—that of the old camel and that of destiny; repeated today, it serves to recall Zuhayr and to conflate our own tribulations with those of that dead Arab. The figure *had* two terms; today, it *has* four. Time widens the circle of the verses, and I myself know some verses that are, like music, all things to all men. Thus it was that many years ago, in Marrakesh, tortured by memories of Córdoba, I soothed myself by repeating the apostrophe which 'Abd-al-Raḥmān spoke in the gardens of al-Rusayfah to an African palm:

Thou too art, oh palm!,
On this foreign soil . . .

"A remarkable gift, the gift bestowed by poetry—words written by a king homesick for the Orient served to comfort me when I was far away in Africa, homesick for Spain."

Then Averroës spoke of the first poets, those who in the Time of Ignorance, before Islam, had already said all things in the infinite language of the deserts. Alarmed (and not without reason) by the inane versifications of ibn-Sharaf, he said that in the ancients and the Qur'ān could all poetry be read, and he condemned as illiterate and vain all desire to innovate. The others listened with pleasure, for he was vindicating that which was old.

Muezzins were calling the faithful to the prayer of first light when Averroës entered his library again. (In the harem, the black-haired slave girls had tortured a red-haired slave girl, but Averroës was not to know that until evening.) Something had revealed to him the meaning of the two obscure words. With firm, painstaking calligraphy, he added these lines to the manuscript: *Aristu* [Aristotle] *gives the name "tragedy" to panegyrics and the name "comedy" to satires and anathemas. There are many admirable tragedies and comedies in the Qur'ān and the* mu'allaqat *of the mosque.*

He felt sleep coming upon him, he felt a chill. His turban unwound, he looked at himself in a metal mirror. I do not know what his eyes beheld, for no historian has described the forms of his face. I know that he suddenly disappeared, as though annihilated by a fire without light, and that with him disappeared the house and the unseen fountain and the books and the manuscripts and the turtledoves and the many black-haired slave girls and the trembling red-haired slave girl and Faraj and abu-al-Ḥasan and the rosebushes and perhaps even the Guadalquivir.

In the preceding tale, I have tried to narrate the process of failure, the process of defeat. I thought first of that archbishop of Canterbury who set himself the task of proving that God exists; then I thought of the alchemists who sought the philosopher's stone; then, of the vain trisectors of the angle and squarers of the circle. Then I reflected that a more poetic case than these would be a man who sets himself a goal that is not forbidden to other men, but is forbidden to him. I recalled Averroës, who, bounded within the circle of Islam, could never know the meaning of the words *tragedy* and *comedy.* I told his story; as I went on, I felt what that god mentioned by Burton must have felt—the god who set himself the task of creating a bull but turned out a buffalo. I felt that the work mocked me, foiled me, thwarted me. I felt that Averroës, trying to imagine what a play is without ever having suspected what a theater is, was no more absurd than I, trying to imagine Averroës yet with no more material than a few snatches from Renan, Lane, and Asín Palacios. I felt, on the last page, that my story was a symbol of the man I had been as I was writing it, and that in order to write that story I had had to be that man, and that in order to be that man I had had to write that story, and so on, *ad infinitum.* (And just when I stop believing in him, "Averroës" disappears.)

The Zahir

In Buenos Aires the Zahir is a common twenty-centavo coin into which a razor or letter opener has scratched the letters *N T* and the number *2;* the date stamped on the face is 1929. (In Gujarat, at the end of the eighteenth century, the Zahir was a tiger; in Java it was a blind man in the Surakarta mosque, stoned by the faithful; in Persia, an astrolabe that Nadir Shah ordered thrown into the sea; in the prisons of Mahdi, in 1892, a small sailor's compass, wrapped in a shred of cloth from a turban, that Rudolf Karl von Slatin touched; in the synagogue in Córdoba, according to Zotenberg, a vein in the marble of one of the twelve hundred pillars; in the ghetto in Tetuán, the bottom of a well.) Today is the thirteenth of November; last June 7, at dawn, the Zahir came into my hands; I am not the man I was then, but I am still able to recall, and perhaps recount, what happened. I am still, albeit only partially, Borges.

On June 6, Teodelina Villar died. Back in 1930, photographs of her had littered the pages of worldly magazines; that ubiquity may have had something to do with the fact that she was thought to be a very pretty woman, although that supposition was not unconditionally supported by every image of her. But no matter—Teodelina Villar was less concerned with beauty than with perfection. The Jews and Chinese codified every human situation: the *Mishnah* tells us that beginning at sunset on the Sabbath, a tailor may not go into the street carrying a needle; the Book of Rites informs us that a guest receiving his first glass of wine must assume a grave demeanor; receiving the second, a respectful, happy air. The discipline that Teodelina Villar imposed upon herself was analogous, though even more painstaking and detailed. Like Talmudists and Confucians, she sought to make every action irreproachably correct, but her task was even more admirable and difficult than theirs, for the laws of her creed were not eternal, but sensitive to the whims of Paris and Hollywood. Teodelina Villar would make her entrances into orthodox places, at the orthodox hour, with orthodox adornments, and with orthodox world-weariness, but the world-weariness, the adornments, the hour, and the places would almost immediately pass out of fashion, and so come to serve (upon the lips of Teodelina Villar) for the very epitome of "tackiness." She sought the absolute, like Flaubert, but the absolute in the ephemeral. Her life was exemplary, and yet an inner desperation constantly gnawed at her. She passed through endless metamorphoses, as though fleeing from herself; her coiffure and the color of her hair were famously unstable, as were her smile, her skin, and the slant of her eyes. From 1932 on, she was studiedly thin. . . . The war gave her a great deal to think about. With Paris occupied by the Germans, how was one to follow fashion? A foreign man she had always had her doubts about was allowed to take advantage of her good will by selling her a number of stovepipe-shaped *chapeaux*. Within a year, it was revealed that those ridiculous shapes *had never been worn in Paris*, and therefore were not *hats*, but arbitrary and unauthorized *caprices*. And it never rains but it pours: Dr. Villar had to move to Calle Aráoz* and his daughter's image began to grace advertisements for face creams and automobiles—face creams she never used and automobiles she could no longer afford! Teodelina knew that the proper exercise of her art required a great fortune; she opted to retreat rather than surrender. And besides—it pained her to compete with mere insubstantial *girls*. The sinister apartment on Aráoz, however, was too much to bear; on June 6, Teodelina Villar committed the breach of decorum of dying in the middle of Barrio Sur. Shall I confess that moved by the sincerest of Argentine passions—snobbery—I was in love with her, and that her death actually brought tears to my eyes? Perhaps the reader had already suspected that.

At wakes, the progress of corruption allows the dead person's body to recover its former faces. At some point on the confused night of June 6, Teodelina Villar magically became what she had been twenty years before; her features recovered the authority that arrogance, money, youth, the awareness of being the *crème de la crème*, restrictions, a lack of imagination, and stolidity can give. My thoughts were more or less these: No version of that face that had so disturbed me shall ever be as memorable as this one; really, since it could almost be the first, it ought to be the last. I left her lying stiff among the flowers, her contempt for the world growing every moment more perfect in death. It was about two o'clock, I would guess, when I stepped into the street. Outside, the predictable ranks of one- and two-story houses had taken on that abstract air they often have at night, when they are simplified by darkness and silence. Drunk with an almost impersonal pity, I wandered through the streets. On the corner of Chile and Tacuarí* I spotted an open bar-and-general-store. In that establishment, to my misfortune, three men were playing *truco.**

In the rhetorical figure known as *oxymoron,* the adjective applied to a noun seems to contradict that noun. Thus, gnostics spoke of a "dark light" and alchemists, of a "black sun." Departing from my last visit to Teodelina Villar and drinking a glass of harsh brandy in a corner bar-and-grocery-store was a kind of oxymoron: the very vulgarity and facileness of it were what tempted me. (The fact that men were playing cards in the place increased the contrast.) I asked the owner for a brandy and orange juice; among my change I was given the Zahir; I looked at it for an instant, then walked outside into the street, perhaps with the beginnings of a fever. The thought struck me that there is no coin that is not the symbol of all the coins that shine endlessly down throughout history and fable. I thought of Charon's obolus; the alms that Belisarius went about begging for; Judas' thirty pieces of silver; the drachmas of the courtesan Laïs; the ancient coin proffered by one of the Ephesian sleepers; the bright coins of the wizard in the *1001 Nights,* which turned into disks of paper; Isaac Laquedem's inexhaustible denarius; the sixty thousand coins, one for every line of an epic, which Firdusi returned to a king because they were silver and not gold; the gold doubloon nailed by Ahab to the mast; Leopold Bloom's unreturning florin; the gold louis that betrayed the fleeing Louis XVI near Varennes. As though in a dream, the thought that in any coin one may read those famous connotations seemed to me of vast, inexplicable importance. I wandered, with increasingly rapid steps, through the deserted streets and plazas. Weariness halted me at a corner. My eyes came to rest on a woebegone wrought-iron fence; behind it, I saw the black-and-white tiles of the porch of La Concepción.* I had wandered in a circle; I was just one block from the corner where I'd been given the Zahir.

I turned the corner; the chamfered curb in darkness* at the far end of the street showed me that the establishment had closed. On Belgrano I took a cab. Possessed, without a trace of sleepiness, almost happy, I reflected that there is nothing less material than money, since any coin (a twenty-centavo piece, for instance) is, in all truth, a panoply of possible futures. *Money is abstract,* I said over and over, *money is future time.* It can be an evening just outside the city, or a Brahms melody, or maps, or chess, or coffee, or the words of Epictetus, which teach contempt of gold; it is a Proteus more changeable than the Proteus of the isle of Pharos. It is unforeseeable time, Bergsonian time, not the hard, solid time of Islam or the Porch. Adherents of determinism deny that there is any event in the world that is *possible*, i.e., that *might* occur; a coin symbolizes our free will. (I had no suspicion at the time that these "thoughts" were an artifice against the Zahir and a first manifestation of its demonic influence.) After long and pertinacious musings, I at last fell asleep, but I dreamed that I was a pile of coins guarded by a gryphon.

The next day I decided I'd been drunk. I also decided to free myself of the coin that was affecting me so distressingly. I looked at it—there was nothing particularly distinctive about it, except those scratches. Burying it in the garden or hiding it in a corner of the library would have been the best thing to do, but I wanted to escape its orbit altogether, and so preferred to "lose" it. I went neither to the Basílica del Pilar that morning nor to the cemetery*; I took a subway to Constitución and from Constitución to San Juan and Boedo. On an impulse, I got off at Urquiza; I walked toward the west and south; I turned left and right, with studied randomness, at several corners, and on a street that looked to me like all the others I went into the first tavern I came to, ordered a brandy, and paid with the Zahir. I half closed my eyes, even behind the dark lenses of my spectacles, and managed not to see the numbers on the houses or the name of the street. That night, I took a sleeping draft and slept soundly.

Until the end of June I distracted myself by composing a tale of fantasy. The tale contains two or three enigmatic circumlocutions—*sword-water* instead of *blood*, for example, and *dragon's-bed* for *gold*—and is written in the first person. The narrator is an ascetic who has renounced all commerce with mankind and lives on a kind of moor. (The name of the place is Gnitaheidr.) Because of the simplicity and innocence of his life, he is judged by some to be an angel; that is a charitable sort of exaggeration, because no one is free of sin—he himself (to take the example nearest at hand) has cut his father's throat, though it is true that his father was a famous wizard who had used his magic to usurp an infinite treasure to himself. Protecting this treasure from cankerous human greed is the mission to which the narrator has devoted his life; day and night he stands guard over it. Soon, perhaps too soon, that watchfulness will come to an end: the stars have told him that the sword that will sever it forever has already been forged. (The name of the sword is Gram.) In an increasingly tortured style, the narrator praises the lustrousness and flexibility of his body; one paragraph offhandedly mentions "scales"; another says that the treasure he watches over is of red rings and gleaming gold. At the end, we realize that the ascetic is the serpent Fafnir and the treasure on which the creature lies coiled is the gold of the Nibelungen. The appearance of Sigurd abruptly ends the story.

I have said that composing that piece of trivial nonsense (in the course of which I interpolated, with pseudoerudition, a line or two from the *Fafnismal*) enabled me to put the coin out of my mind. There were nights when I was so certain I'd be able to forget it that I would willfully remember it. The truth is, I abused those moments; starting to recall turned out to be much easier than stopping. It was futile to tell myself that that abominable nickel disk was no different from the infinite other identical, inoffensive disks that pass from hand to hand every day. Moved by that reflection, I attempted to think about another coin, but I couldn't. I also recall another (frustrated) experiment that I performed with Chilean five- and ten-centavo pieces and a Uruguayan two-centavo piece. On July 16, I acquired a pound sterling; I didn't look at it all that day, but that night (and others) I placed it under a magnifying glass and studied it in the light of a powerful electric lamp. Then I made a rubbing of it. The rays of light and the dragon and St. George availed me naught; I could not rid myself of my *idée fixe*.

In August, I decided to consult a psychiatrist. I did not confide the entire absurd story to him; I told him I was tormented by insomnia and that often I could not free my mind of the image of an object, any random object—a coin, say. . . . A short time later, in a bookshop on Calle Sarmiento, I exhumed a copy of Julius Barlach's *Urkunden zur Geschichte der Zahirsage* (Breslau, 1899).

Between the covers of that book was a description of my illness. The introduction said that the author proposed to "gather into a single manageable octavo volume every existing document that bears upon the superstition of the Zahir, including four articles held in the Habicht archives and the original manuscript of Philip Meadows Taylor's report on the subject." Belief in the Zahir is of Islamic ancestry, and dates, apparently, to sometime in the eighteenth century. (Barlach impugns the passages that Zotenberg attributes to Abul-Feddah.) In Arabic, "*zahir*" means visible, manifest, evident; in that sense, it is one of the ninety-nine names of God; in Muslim countries, the masses use the word for "beings or things which have the terrible power to be unforgettable, and whose image eventually drives people mad." Its first undisputed witness was the Persian polymath and dervish Lutf Ali Azur; in the corroborative pages of the biographical encyclopedia titled *Temple of Fire*, Ali Azur relates that in a certain school in Shiraz there was a copper astrolabe "constructed in such a way that any man that looked upon it but once could think of nothing else, so that the king commanded that it be thrown into the deepest depths of the sea, in order that men might not forget the universe." Meadows Taylor's account is somewhat more extensive; the author served the Nazim of Hyderabad and composed the famous novel *Confessions of a Thug*. In 1832, on the outskirts of Bhuj, Taylor heard the following uncommon expression used to signify madness or saintliness: "Verily he has looked upon the tiger." He was told that the reference was to a magic tiger that was the perdition of all who saw it, even from a great distance, for never afterward could a person stop thinking about it. Someone mentioned that one of those stricken people had fled to Mysore, where he had painted the image of the tiger in a palace. Years later, Taylor visited the prisons of that district; in the jail at Nighur, the governor showed him a cell whose floor, walls, and vaulted ceiling were covered by a drawing (in barbaric colors that time, before obliterating, had refined) of an infinite tiger. It was a tiger composed of many tigers, in the most dizzying of ways; it was crisscrossed with tigers, striped with tigers, and contained seas and Himalayas and armies that resembled other tigers. The painter, a fakir, had died many years before, in that same cell; he had come from Sind or perhaps Gujarat and his initial purpose had been to draw a map of the world. Of that first purpose there remained some vestiges within the monstrous image. Taylor told this story to Muḥammad al-Yemeni, of Fort William; al-Yemeni said that there was no creature in the world that did not tend toward becoming a *Zaheer*,[1] but that the All-Merciful does not allow two things to be a *Zaheer* at the same time, since a single one is capable of entrancing multitudes. He said that there is always a Zahir—in the Age of Ignorance it was the idol called Yahuk, and then a prophet from Khorasan who wore a veil spangled with precious stones or a mask of gold.[2] He also noted that Allah was inscrutable.

Over and over I read Barlach's monograph. I cannot sort out my emotions; I recall my desperation when I realized that nothing could any longer save me, the inward relief of knowing that I was not to blame for my misfortune, the envy I felt for those whose Zahir was not a coin but a slab of marble or a tiger. How easy it is not to think of a tiger!, I recall thinking. I

[1]This is Taylor's spelling of the word.

[2]Barlach observes that Yahuk figures in the Qur'ān (71:23) and that the prophet is al-Moqanna (the Veiled Prophet) and that no one, with the exception of the surprising correspondent Philip Meadows Taylor, has ever linked those two figures to the Zahir.

also recall the remarkable uneasiness I felt when I read this paragraph: "One commentator of the *Gulshan i Raz* states that 'he who has seen the Zahir soon shall see the Rose' and quotes a line of poetry interpolated into Aṭṭar's *Asrar Nama* ('The Book of Things Unknown'): 'the Zahir is the shadow of the Rose and the rending of the Veil.' "

On the night of Teodelina's wake, I had been surprised not to see among those present Sra. Abascal, her younger sister. In October, I ran into a friend of hers.

"Poor Julita," the woman said to me, "she's become so odd. She's been put into Bosch.* How she must be crushed by those nurses' spoon-feeding her! She's still going on and on about that coin, just like Morena Sackmann's chauffeur."

Time, which softens recollections, only makes the memory of the Zahir all the sharper. First I could see the face of it, then the reverse; now I can see both sides at once. It is not as though the Zahir were made of glass, since one side is not superimposed upon the other—rather, it is as though the vision were itself spherical, with the Zahir rampant in the center. Anything that is not the Zahir comes to me as though through a filter, and from a distance—Teodelina's disdainful image, physical pain. Tennyson said that if we could but understand a single flower we might know who we are and what the world is. Perhaps he was trying to say that there is nothing, however humble, that does not imply the history of the world and its infinite concatenation of causes and effects. Perhaps he was trying to say that the visible world can be seen entire in every image, just as Schopenhauer tells us that the Will expresses itself entire in every man and woman. The Kabbalists believed that man is a microcosm, a symbolic mirror of the universe; if one were to believe Tennyson, *everything* would be—*everything,* even the unbearable Zahir.

Before the year 1948, Julia's fate will have overtaken me. I will have to be fed and dressed, I will not know whether it's morning or night, I will not know who the man Borges was. Calling that future terrible is a fallacy, since none of the future's circumstances will in any way affect me. One might as well call "terrible" the pain of an anesthetized patient whose skull is being trepanned. I will no longer perceive the universe, I will perceive the Zahir. Idealist doctrine has it that the verbs "to live" and "to dream" are at every point synonymous; for me, thousands upon thousands of appearances will pass into one; a complex dream will pass into a simple one. Others will dream that I am mad, while I dream of the Zahir. When every man on earth thinks, day and night, of the Zahir, which will be dream and which reality, the earth or the Zahir?

In the waste and empty hours of the night I am still able to walk through the streets. Dawn often surprises me upon a bench in the Plaza Garay, thinking (or trying to think) about that passage in the *Asrar Nama* where it is said that the Zahir is the shadow of the Rose and the rending of the Veil. I link that pronouncement to this fact: In order to lose themselves in God, the Sufis repeat their own name or the ninety-nine names of God until the names mean nothing anymore. I long to travel that path. Perhaps by thinking about the Zahir unceasingly, I can manage to wear it away; perhaps behind the coin is God.

For Wally Zenner

The Writing of the God

The cell is deep and made of stone; its shape is that of an almost perfect hemisphere, although the floor (which is also of stone) is something less than a great circle, and this fact somehow deepens the sense of oppression and vastness. A wall divides the cell down the center; though it is very high, it does not touch the top of the vault. I, Tzinacán, priest of the Pyramid of Qaholom, which Pedro de Alvarado burned, am on one side of the wall; on the other there is a jaguar, which with secret, unvarying paces measures the time and space of its captivity. At floor level, a long window with thick iron bars interrupts the wall. At the shadowless hour [midday] a small door opens above us, and a jailer (whom the years have gradually blurred) operates an iron pulley, lowering to us, at the end of a rope, jugs of water and hunks of meat. Light enters the vault; it is then that I am able to see the jaguar.

I have lost count of the years I have lain in this darkness; I who once was young and could walk about this prison do nothing now but wait, in the posture of my death, for the end the gods have destined for me. With the deep flint blade I have opened the breast of victims, but now I could not, without the aid of magic, lift my own body from the dust.

On the day before the burning of the Pyramid, the men who got down from their high horses scourged me with burning irons, to compel me to reveal the site of a buried treasure. Before my eyes they toppled the idol to the god, yet the god did not abandon me, and I held my silence through their tortures. They tore my flesh, they crushed me, they mutilated me, and then I awoke in this prison, which I will never leave alive.

Driven by the inevitability of doing *something,* of somehow filling time, I tried, in my darkness, to remember everything I knew. I squandered entire nights in remembering the order and the number of certain stone serpents, or the shape of a medicinal tree. Thus did I gradually conquer the years, thus did I gradually come to possess those things I no longer possessed. One night I sensed that a precise recollection was upon me; before the traveler sees the ocean, he feels a stirring in his blood. Hours later, I began to make out the memory; it was one of the legends of the god. On the first day of creation, foreseeing that at the end of time many disasters and calamities would befall, the god had written a magical phrase, capable of warding off those evils. He wrote it in such a way that it would pass down to the farthest generations, and remain untouched by fate. No one knows where he wrote it, or with what letters, but we do know that it endures, a secret text, and that one of the elect shall read it. I reflected that we were, as always, at the end of time, and that it would be my fate, as the last priest of the god, to be afforded the privilege of intuiting those words. The fact that I was bounded within a cell did not prevent me from harboring that hope; I might have seen Qaholom's inscription thousands of times, and need only to understand it.

That thought gave me spirit, and then filled me with a kind of vertigo. In the wide realm of the world there are ancient forms, incorruptible and eternal forms—any one of them might be the symbol that I sought. A mountain might be the word of the god, or a river or the empire or the arrangement of the stars. And yet, in the course of the centuries mountains are leveled and the path of a river is many times diverted, and empires know mutability and ruin, and the design of the stars is altered. In the firmament there is change. The mountain and the star are individuals, and the life of an individual runs out. I sought something more tenacious, more invulnerable. I thought of the generations of grain, of grasses, of birds, of men. Perhaps the spell was written upon my very face, perhaps I myself was the object of my search. Amid those keen imaginings was I when I recalled that one of the names of the god was jaguar—*tigre.*

At that, my soul was filled with holiness. I imagined to myself the first morning of time, imagined my god entrusting the message to the living flesh of the jaguars, who would love one another and engender one another endlessly, in caverns, in cane fields, on islands, so that the last men might receive it. I imagined to myself that web of tigers, that hot labyrinth of tigers, bringing terror to the plains and pastures in order to preserve the design. In the other cell, there was a jaguar; in its proximity I sensed a confirmation of my conjecture, and a secret blessing.

Long years I devoted to learning the order and arrangement of the spots on the tiger's skin. During the course of each blind day I was granted an instant of light, and thus was I able to fix in my mind the black shapes that mottled the yellow skin. Some made circles; others formed transverse stripes on the inside of its legs; others, ringlike, occurred over and over again—perhaps they were the same sound, or the same word. Many had red borders.

I will not tell of the difficulties of my labor. More than once I cried out to the vault above that it was impossible to decipher that text. Gradually, I came to be tormented less by the concrete enigma which occupied my mind than by the generic enigma of a message written by a god. What sort of sentence, I asked myself, would be constructed by an absolute mind? I reflected that even in the languages of humans there is no proposition that does not imply the entire universe; to say "the jaguar" is to say all the jaguars that engendered it, the deer and turtles it has devoured, the grass that fed the deer, the earth that was mother to the grass, the sky that gave light to the earth. I reflected that in the language of a god every word would speak that infinite concatenation of events, and not implicitly but explicitly, and not linearly but instantaneously. In time, the idea of a divine utterance came to strike me as puerile, or as blasphemous. A god, I reflected, must speak but a single word, and in that word there must be *absolute plenitude.* No word uttered by a god could be less than the universe, or briefer than the sum of time. The ambitions and poverty of human words—*all, world, universe*— are but shadows or simulacra of that Word which is the equivalent of a language and all that can be comprehended within a language.

One day or one night—between my days and nights, what difference can there be?—I dreamed that there was a grain of sand on the floor of my cell. Unconcerned, I went back to sleep; I dreamed that I woke up and there were two grains of sand. Again I slept; I dreamed that now there were three. Thus the grains of sand multiplied, little by little, until they filled the cell and I was dying beneath that hemisphere of sand. I realized that I was dreaming; with a vast effort I woke myself. But waking up was useless—I was suffocated by the countless sand. Someone said to me: *You have wakened not out of sleep, but into a prior dream, and that dream lies within another, and so on, to infinity, which is the number of the grains of sand. The path that you are to take is endless, and you will die before you have truly awakened.*

I felt lost. The sand crushed my mouth, but I cried out: *I cannot be killed by sand that I dream—nor is there any such thing as a dream within a dream.* A bright light woke me. In the darkness above me, there hovered a circle of light. I saw the face and hands of the jailer, the pulley, the rope, the meat, and the water jugs.

Little by little, a man comes to resemble the shape of his destiny; a man *is*, in the long run, his circumstances. More than a decipherer or an avenger, more than a priest of the god, I was a prisoner. Emerging from that indefatigable labyrinth of dreams, I returned to my hard prison as though I were a man returning home. I blessed its dampness, I blessed its tiger, I blessed its high opening and the light, I blessed my old and aching body, I blessed the darkness and the stone.

And at that, something occurred which I cannot forget and yet cannot communicate—there occurred union with the deity, union with the universe (I do not know whether there is a difference between those two words). Ecstasy does not use the same symbol twice; one man has seen God in a blinding light, another has perceived Him in a sword or in the circles of a rose. I saw a Wheel of enormous height, which was not before my eyes, or behind them, or to the sides, but everywhere at once. This Wheel was made of water, but also of fire, and although I could see its boundaries, it was infinite. It was made of all things that shall be, that are, and that have been, all intertwined, and I was one of the strands within that all-encompassing fabric, and Pedro de Alvarado, who had tortured me, was another. In it were the causes and the effects, and the mere sight of that Wheel enabled me to understand all things, without end. O joy of understanding, greater than the joy of imagining, greater than the joy of feeling! I saw the universe and saw its secret designs. I saw the origins told by the Book of the People. I saw the mountains that rose from the water, saw the first men of wood, saw the water jars that turned against the men, saw the dogs that tore at their faces.* I saw the faceless god who is behind the gods. I saw the infinite processes that shape a single happiness, and, understanding all, I also came to understand the writing on the tiger.

It is a formula of fourteen random (apparently random) words, and all I would have to do to become omnipotent is speak it aloud. Speaking it would make this stone prison disappear, allow the day to enter my night, make me young, make me immortal, make the jaguar destroy Alvarado, bury the sacred blade in Spanish breasts, rebuild the Pyramid, rebuild the empire. Forty syllables, fourteen words, and I, Tzinacán, would rule the lands once ruled by Moctezuma. But I know that I shall never speak those words, because I no longer remember Tzinacán.

Let the mystery writ upon the jaguars die with me. He who has glimpsed the universe, he who has glimpsed the burning designs of the universe, can have no thought for a man, for a man's trivial joys or calamities, though he himself be that man. He *was* that man, who no longer matters to him. What does he care about the fate of that other man, what does he care about the other man's nation, when now he is no one? That is why I do not speak the formula, that is why, lying in darkness, I allow the days to forget me.

For Ema Risso Platero

Ibn-Ḥakam al-Bokhari, Murdered in His Labyrinth

. . . is the likeness of the spider who buildeth her a house.

Qur'ān, XXIX: 40

"This," said Dunraven with a vast gesture that did not blench at the cloudy stars, and that took in the black moors, the sea, and a majestic, tumbledown edifice that looked much like a stable fallen upon hard times, "is my ancestral land."

Unwin, his companion, removed the pipe from his mouth and uttered modest sounds of approbation. It was the first evening of the summer of 1914; weary of a world that lacked the dignity of danger, the friends prized the solitude of that corner of Cornwall. Dunraven cultivated a dark beard and was conscious of himself as the author of quite a respectable epic, though his contemporaries were incapable of so much as scanning it and its subject had yet to be revealed to him; Unwin had published a study of the theorem that Fermat had not written in the margins of a page by Diophantus. Both men—is there really any need to say this?—were young, absentminded, and passionate.

"It must be a good quarter century ago now," said Dunraven, "that Ibn-Ḥakam al-Bokhari, the chieftain or king or whatnot of some tribe or another along the Nile, died in the central chamber of that house at the hands of his cousin Sa'īd. Even after all these years, the circumstances of his death are still not entirely clear."

Meekly, Unwin asked why.

"Several reasons," came the answer. "First, that house up there is a labyrinth. Second, a slave and a lion had stood guard over it. Third, a secret treasure disappeared—*poof!*, vanished. Fourth, the murderer was already dead by the time the murder took place. Fifth . . ."

Vexed a bit, Unwin stopped him.

"Please—let's not multiply the mysteries," he said. "Mysteries ought to be simple. Remember Poe's purloined letter, remember Zangwill's locked room."

"Or complex," volleyed Dunraven. "Remember the universe."

Climbing up steep sandy hills, they had arrived at the labyrinth. Seen at close range, it looked like a straight, virtually interminable wall of unplastered brick, scarcely taller than a man. Dunraven said it made a circle, but one so broad that its curvature was imperceptible. Unwin recalled Nicholas of Cusa, for whom every straight line was the arc of an infinite circle. . . . Toward midnight, they came upon a ruined doorway, which opened onto a long, perilous entryway whose walls had no other windows or doors. Dunraven said that inside, one came to crossing after crossing in the halls, but if they always turned to the left, in less than an hour they would be at the center of the maze. Unwin nodded. Their cautious steps echoed on the stone floor; at every branching, the corridor grew narrower. They felt they were being suffocated by the house—the ceiling was very low. They were forced to walk in single file through the knotted darkness. Unwin led the way; the invisible wall, cumbered with ruggedness and angles, passed endlessly under his hand. And as he made his way slowly through the darkness, Unwin heard from his friend's lips the story of Ibn-Ḥakam's death.

"What well may be my earliest memory," Dunraven began, "is Ibn-Ḥakam on the docks at Pentreath. He was followed by a black man with a lion—undoubtedly the first black man and the first lion I'd ever set eyes upon, with the exception of those lithographs of Bible stories, I suppose. I was just a boy then, but I'll tell you, that savage sun-colored beast and night-colored man didn't make the impression on me that Ibn-Ḥakam did. He seemed so tall. He was a sallow-skinned fellow, with black eyes and drooping eyelids, an insolent nose, thick lips, a saffron yellow beard, a broad chest, and a silent, self-assured way of walking. When I got home, I said, 'A king has come in a ship.' Later, when the brickmasons went to work, I expanded upon the title a bit and called him the King of Babel.

"The news that this outsider was to settle in Pentreath was welcome, I must say; the size and design of his house, though, met with amazement and even outrage. It seemed intolerable that a house should be composed of a single room, yet league upon league of hallways. 'That's all very well for the Moors,' people said, 'but no Christian ever built such a house.' Our rector, Mr. Allaby, a man of curious reading, dug up the story of a king punished by the Deity for having built a labyrinth, and he read it from the pulpit. The Monday following, Ibn-Ḥakam paid a visit to the rectory; the details of their brief interview were not made public at the time, but no sermon afterward ever alluded to the act of arrogance, and the Moor was able to hire his brickmasons. Years later, when Ibn-Ḥakam was murdered, Allaby gave a statement to the authorities as to the substance of their conversation.

"The words, he said, that Ibn-Ḥakam had stood in his study—not sat, mind you, but *stood*—and spoken to him were these, or words very similar: 'There is no longer any man who can contemn what I do. The sins that bring dishonor to my name are so terrible that even should I repeat the Ultimate Name of God for century upon century I would not succeed in mitigating even one of the torments that shall be mine; the sins that bring dishonor to my name are so terrible that even should I kill you with these very hands, that act would not increase the torments to which infinite Justice has destined me. There is no land ignorant of my name; I am Ibn-Ḥakam al-Bokhari, and I have ruled the tribes of the desert with an iron scepter. For many years with the aid of my cousin Sa'īd I plundered those tribes, but God hearkened to their cries and suffered them to rise against me. My men were crushed and put to the knife. I managed to flee with the treasure I had hoarded up through my years of pillaging. Sa'īd led me to the sepulcher of a saint, which lay at the foot of a stone mountain. I ordered my slave man to stand watch over the face of the desert; Sa'īd and I, exhausted, lay down to sleep. That night I dreamt that I was imprisoned within a nest of vipers. I awoke in horror; beside me, in the morning light, Sa'īd lay sleeping; the brush of a spiderweb against my skin had caused me to dream that dream. It pained me that Sa'īd, who was a coward, should sleep so soundly. I reflected that the treasure was not infinite, and that he might claim a part of it. In my waistband was my dagger with its silver handle; I unsheathed it and drew it across his throat. As he died he stammered out a few words that I could not understand. I looked at him; he was dead, but I feared that he might yet stand, so I ordered my slave to crush his face with a stone. After that, we wandered under the heavens until one day we glimpsed a sea, with tall ships furrowing its waves. The thought came to me that a dead man cannot travel across the water, so I resolved to seek out other lands. The first night that we were upon the ocean I dreamt that I was murdering Sa'īd. Everything happened again, just as it had before, but this time I understood his words. He said *As you slay me now, so shall I slay you, no matter where you flee.* I have sworn to foil that threat; I shall hide myself in the center of a labyrinth, so that his shade may lose its way.'

"That said, Ibn-Ḥakam took his leave. Allaby tried to think that the

Moor was mad and that that absurd labyrinth of his was a symbol, a clear testament to his madness. Then he reflected that the notion of madness squared with the extravagant house and the extravagant tale, but not with the lively impression that the man Ibn-Ḥakam himself gave. Perhaps such tales were indigenous to the sandy wastes of Egypt, perhaps such oddities, like the dragons in Pliny, were attributable less to an individual person than to a whole culture. . . . In London, Allaby pored through back issues of the *Times*; he found that such a rebellion had in fact occurred, as had the subsequent defeat of al-Bokhari and his vizier, a man with a reputation as a coward.

"The moment the brickmasons were done, Ibn-Ḥakam set up housekeeping in the center of his labyrinth. He was never seen again by the townspeople; sometimes Allaby feared that Sa'īd had already gotten to him and killed him. At night, the wind would bring us the sound of the lion's roaring, and the sheep in the pen would huddle together in ancestral fear.

"Ships from Eastern ports would often anchor in our little bay here, bound for Cardiff or Bristol. The slave would come down from the labyrinth (which at that time, I recall, was not pink but bright crimson) and exchange African words with the crews; he seemed to be looking out for the vizier's ghost among the men. Everyone knew that these ships carried contraband, and if they were carrying outlawed ivories or liquors, why not the ghosts of dead men?

"Three years after the house was built, the *Rose of Sharon* anchored at the foot of the cliffs. I was not one of those who saw the ship, so it's altogether possible that the image I have of her is influenced by some forgotten print of Aboukir or Trafalgar, but my understanding is that she was one of those very elaborately carved vessels that seem less the work of shipwrights than of carpenters, and less that of carpenters than of cabinetmakers. She was (if not in reality, at least in my dreams) a burnished, dark, silent, swift craft, manned by Arabs and Malays.

"She anchored around dawn one morning in October. Toward nightfall, Ibn-Ḥakam burst into Allaby's house, totally unmanned by terror. He could hardly manage to tell Allaby that Sa'īd had found his way into the labyrinth, and that his slave and lion had been murdered. He asked in all seriousness if the authorities could do nothing to protect him. Before Allaby could answer, he was gone, for the second and last time—as though snatched away by the same terror that had brought him to the house. Sitting there alone now in his study, Allaby thought with amazement that this terrified man had brought iron tribes in the Sudan under his thumb, had known what it is to do battle and what it is to kill. The next day, he noticed that the ship had sailed (for Suakin in the Red Sea, it was later learned). It occurred to him that it was his duty to confirm the murder of the slave, and so he climbed up to the labyrinth. Al-Bokhari's breathless story had sounded like mad fantasy to him, but at one corner in the long corridors he came upon the lion, which was dead, and at another, he found the slave, who was dead, and in the central chamber, he found Al-Bokhari himself, whose face had been smashed in. At the man's feet there was a coffer inlaid with mother-of-pearl; the lock had been forced and not a single coin remained."

The final periods, weighted with oratorical pauses, strained for eloquence; Unwin figured Dunraven had pronounced them many times, with the same self-conscious gravity and the same paucity of effect.

"How were the lion and the slave killed?" he asked, to feign interest.

The incorrigible voice answered with somber satisfaction.

"Their faces had been smashed in, as well."

To the sound of their footsteps was added the sound of rain. It occurred to Unwin that they would have to sleep in the labyrinth, in the central chamber of the tale, and that in retrospect he would surely see that long discomfort as adventure. He remained silent. Dunraven could not contain himself; like a man who will not forgive a debt, he asked:

"Quite an inexplicable story, don't you think?"

Unwin answered as though thinking out loud:

"I don't know whether it's explicable or inexplicable. I know it's a bloody lie."

Dunraven burst forth in a torrent of curses and invoked the eyewitness of the rector's elder son—Allaby, apparently, having died—and of every inhabitant of Pentreath. No less taken aback than Dunraven must have been, Unwin begged his pardon. Time, in the dark, seemed slower, longer; both men feared they had lost their way, and they were very tired by the time a dim brightness coming from above showed them the first steps of a narrow staircase. They climbed the stairs and found themselves in a round apartment, a good bit run-down and gone to seed. Two signs of the ill-fated king remained: a narrow window that looked out over the moors and the sea, and, in the floor, the trap door that opened onto the curve of the staircase. The apartment, though spacious, was very much like a jail cell.

Driven to it less by the rain than by the desire to live for the memory and the anecdote, the friends did spend the night within the labyrinth. The mathematician slept soundly; not so the poet, who was haunted by lines of poetry that his rational mind knew to be dreadful:

Faceless the sultry and overpowering lion,
Faceless the stricken slave, faceless the king.

Unwin had thought that the story of Al-Bokhari's murder held no interest for him, yet he awoke convinced that he had solved it. All that day he was preoccupied and taciturn, fitting and refitting the pieces, and two nights later, he rang up Dunraven and asked him to meet him at a pub in London, where he spoke to him these words, or words very much like them:

"Back in Cornwall, I said the story that you'd told me was a lie. What I meant was this: the *facts* were true, or might be true, but told in the way you told them, they were clearly humbug. Let me begin with the biggest lie of all, the incredible labyrinth. A fleeing man doesn't hide out in a labyrinth. He doesn't throw up a labyrinth on the highest point on the coast, and he doesn't throw up a crimson-colored labyrinth that sailors see from miles offshore. There's no need to build a labyrinth when the entire universe is one. For the man who truly wants to hide himself, London is a much better labyrinth than a rooftop room to which every blessèd hallway in a building leads. That piece of wisdom, which I submit to you this evening, came to me night before last, while we were listening to the rain on the roof of the labyrinth and waiting to be visited by Morpheus. Warned and corrected by it, I chose to ignore those absurd 'facts' of yours and think about something sensible."

"Set theory, for instance, or the fourth dimension of space," Dunraven remarked.

"No," said Unwin with gravity. "I thought about the Cretan labyrinth. The labyrinth at whose center was a man with the head of a bull."

Dunraven, who had read a great many detective novels, thought that the solution of a mystery was always a good deal less interesting than the mystery itself; the mystery had a touch of the supernatural and even the divine about it, while the solution was a sleight of hand. In order to postpone the inevitable, he said:

"A bull's head is how the Minotaur appears on medals and in sculpture. Dante imagined it the other way around, with the body of a bull and the head of a man."

"That version works just as well," Unwin agreed. "What's important is the correspondence between the monstrous house and the monstrous creature that lives inside it. The Minotaur more than justifies the existence of the labyrinth—but no one can say the same for a threat dreamed in a dream. Once one seizes upon the image of the Minotaur (an image that's unavoidable when there's a labyrinth in the case) the problem is all but solved. I do have to confess, however, that I didn't see that that ancient image was the key to it, which is why it was necessary for your story to furnish me with a better, a more exact, symbol—the spiderweb."

"The spiderweb?" Dunraven repeated, perplexed.

"Yes. I shouldn't be surprised that the spiderweb (the universal form of the spiderweb, I mean—the Platonic spiderweb) suggested the crime to the murderer (because there *is* a murderer). You'll recall that Al-Bokhari, in a tomb, dreamt of a nest of vipers and awoke to discover that a spiderweb had suggested the dream to him. Let's return to that night on which Al-Bokhari dreamt of the tangled nest. The overthrown king and the vizier and the slave are fleeing through the desert with a treasure. They take refuge in a tomb. The vizier—whom we know to be a coward—sleeps; the king—whom we know to be a brave man—does not. So as not to have to share the treasure with his vizier, the king stabs him to death; nights later, the murdered man's ghost threatens the king in a dream. None of this is to be believed; in my view, the events occurred exactly the other way around. That night, I believe, it was the king, the brave man, that slept, and Sa'īd, the coward, that lay awake. To sleep is to put the universe for a little while out of your mind, and that sort of unconcern is not easy for a man who knows that unsheathed swords are after him. Sa'īd, a greedy man, watched over the sleep of his king. He thought of killing him, perhaps even toyed with the knife, but he didn't have the courage for it. He called the slave. They hid part of the treasure in the tomb, then fled to Suakin and on to England. Not to hide from Al-Bokhari, you understand, but in fact to lure him to them and kill him—that was what led the vizier to build the high labyrinth of bright crimson walls in full view of the sea. He knew that ships would carry the fame of the slave, the lion, and the scarlet man back to the ports of Nubia, and that sooner or later Al-Bokhari would come to beard him in his labyrinth. The trap was laid in the web's last corridor. Al-Bokhari had infinite contempt for Sa'īd; he would never stoop to take the slightest precaution. The long-awaited day at last arrives; Ibn-Ḥakam disembarks in England, walks up to the door of the labyrinth, passes through the blind corridors, and has perhaps set his foot upon the first steps of the staircase when his vizier kills him—perhaps with a bullet, I don't know—from the trap door above. Then the slave no doubt killed the lion, and another bullet no doubt killed the slave. Then Sa'īd smashed in the three faces with a large rock. He had to do that; a single dead man with his face smashed in would have suggested a problem of identity, but the lion, the black man, and the king were elements in a series whose first terms would lead inevitably to the last. There's nothing strange about the fact that the man that visited Allaby was seized with terror; he had just committed the dreadful deed and was about to flee England and recover his treasure."

A thoughtful, or incredulous, silence followed Unwin's words. Dunraven called for another mug of ale before he offered his opinion.

"I accept," he said, "that my Ibn-Ḥakam might be Sa'īd. Such metamorphoses, you will tell me, are classic artifices of the genre—conventions that the reader insists be followed. What I hesitate to accept is the hypothesis that part of the treasure was left behind in the Sudan. Remember that Sa'īd was fleeing the king *and the enemies of the king, as well;* it's easier, it seems to me, to imagine him stealing the entire treasure than taking the time to bury part of it. Perhaps no odd coins were found lying about because there were no coins left; perhaps the brickmasons had consumed a treasure which, unlike the gold of the Nibelungen, was not infinite. Thus we would have Ibn-Ḥakam crossing the sea to reclaim a squandered treasure."

"Not *squandered,*" said Unwin. "Invested. Invested in erecting upon the soil of infidels a great circular trap of brickwork intended to entangle and annihilate the king. Sa'īd's actions, if your supposition is correct, were motivated not by greed but by hatred and fear. He stole the treasure and then realized that the treasure was not for him the essential thing. The essential thing was that Ibn-Ḥakam die. He pretended to be Ibn-Ḥakam, killed Ibn-Ḥakam, and at last *was* Ibn-Ḥakam."

"Yes," agreed Dunraven. "He was a wanderer who, before becoming no one in death, would recall once having been a king, or having pretended to be a king."

The Two Kings and the Two Labyrinths[1]

It is said by men worthy of belief (though Allah's knowledge is greater) that in the first days there was a king of the isles of Babylonia who called together his architects and his priests and bade them build him a labyrinth so confused and so subtle that the most prudent men would not venture to enter it, and those who did would lose their way. Most unseemly was the edifice that resulted, for it is the prerogative of God, not man, to strike confusion and inspire wonder. In time there came to the court a king of the Arabs, and the king of Babylonia (to mock the simplicity of his guest) bade him enter the labyrinth, where the king of the Arabs wandered, humiliated and confused, until the coming of the evening, when he implored God's aid and found the door. His lips offered no complaint, though he said to the king of Babylonia that in his land he had another labyrinth, and Allah willing, he would see that someday the king of Babylonia made its acquaintance. Then he returned to Arabia with his captains and his wardens and he wreaked such havoc upon the kingdoms of Babylonia, and with such great blessing by fortune, that he brought low its castles, crushed its people, and took the king of Babylonia himself captive. He tied him atop a swift-footed camel and led him into the desert. Three days they rode, and then he said to him, "O king of time and substance and cipher of the century! In Babylonia didst thou attempt to make me lose my way in a labyrinth of brass with many stairways, doors, and walls; now the Powerful One has seen fit to allow me to show thee mine, which has no stairways to climb, nor doors to force, nor wearying galleries to wander through, nor walls to impede thy passage."

[1]This is the story read by the rector from his pulpit. See p. 257.

Then he untied the bonds of the king of Babylonia and abandoned him in the middle of the desert, where he died of hunger and thirst. Glory to Him who does not die.

The Wait

The coach left him at number 4004 on that street in the northwest part of the city. It was not yet 9:00 A.M.; the man noted with approval the mottled plane trees, the square of dirt at the foot of each, the decent houses with their little balconies, the pharmacy next door, the faded diamonds of the paint store and the hardware store. A long windowless hospital wall abutted the sidewalk across the street; farther down, the sun reflected off some greenhouses. It occurred to the man that those things (now arbitrary, coincidental, and in no particular order, like things seen in dreams) would in time, God willing, become unchanging, necessary, and familiar. In the pharmacy window, porcelain letters spelled out "Breslauer": the Jews were crowding out the Italians, who had crowded out the native-born. All the better: the man preferred not to mix with people of his own blood.

The coachman helped him lift down his trunk; a distracted- or weary-looking woman finally opened the door. From the driver's seat, the coachman handed the man back one of the coins, a Uruguayan two-centavo piece that had been in the man's pocket since that night in the hotel in Melo. The man gave him forty centavos, and instantly regretted it: "I must act so that everyone will forget me. I've made two mistakes: I've paid with a coin from another country and I've let this man see that the mistake matters."

Preceded by the woman, the man walked through the long entryway and on through the first patio; the room he'd reserved was, as good luck would have it, off the second patio, in the rear. There was a bed of ironwork that art had distorted into fantastic curves suggesting vines and branches; there were also a tall pine chifforobe, a night table, a bookcase with books on the bottommost shelf, two mismatched chairs, and a washstand with its bowl, pitcher, and soap dish and a carafe of cloudy glass. A crucifix and a map of Buenos Aires province adorned the walls; the wallpaper was crimson, with a pattern of large peacocks, tails outspread. The room's only door opened onto the patio. The chairs had to be rearranged to make room for the trunk. The tenant gave his nod to everything; when the woman asked him what his name was, he said Villari—not as a secret act of defiance, not to mitigate a humiliation that quite honestly he didn't feel, but rather because that name haunted him, he couldn't come up with another one. Certainly he was not seduced by the literary error of imagining that adopting the name of his enemy would be the astute thing to do.

At first Sr. Villari never left the house, but after a few weeks had passed he started going out for a while at nightfall. In the evening he would occasionally go into the motion-picture theater three blocks away. He never sat nearer the screen than the last row; he always got up a little before the picture was over. He saw tragic stories of the underworld; no doubt they had their errors; no doubt they included certain images that were also a part of Sr. Villari's previous life, but he didn't notice the errors, because the notion that there might be parallels between art and life never occurred to him. He docilely tried to like things; he tried to take things in the spirit they were offered. Unlike people who had read novels, he never saw himself as a character in a book.

He never received a letter, or even a circular, but with vague hopefulness he read one of the sections of the newspaper. In the afternoon, he would draw one of the chairs over to the door and sit and sip gravely at his *mate,* his eyes fixed on the ivy that climbed the wall of the two-story house next door. Years of solitude had taught him that although in one's memory days all tend to be the same, there wasn't a day, even when a man was in jail or hospital, that didn't have its surprises. During other periods of isolation he had given in to the temptation to count the days (and even the hours), but this isolation was different, because there was no end to it—unless the newspaper should bring him news one morning of the death of Alejandro Villari. It was also possible that Villari *was already dead,* and then his life was a dream. That possibility disturbed him, because he couldn't quite figure out whether it felt like a relief or a misfortune; he told himself it was absurd, and he discarded it. In now-distant days—distant less because of the lapse of time than because of two or three irrevocable acts—he had desired many things, with a desire that lacked all scruples; that powerful urge to possess, which had inspired the hatred of men and the love of the occasional woman, no longer desired *things*—it wanted only to endure, wanted not to end. The taste of the *mate,* the taste of the black tobacco, the growing band of shade that slowly crept across the patio—these were reason enough to live.

There was a wolf-dog in the house, now grown quite old; Villari made friends with it. He spoke to it in Spanish, in Italian, and with the few words he still remembered of the rustic dialect of his childhood. Villari tried to live in the mere present, looking neither backward nor ahead; memories mattered less to him than his visions of the future. In some obscure way he thought he could sense that the past is the stuff that time is made of; that was why time became past so quickly. One day his weariness felt for a moment like happiness; at moments such as that, he was not a great deal more complex than the dog.

One night he was left shocked, speechless, and trembling by a burst of pain deep in his mouth, striking almost at the heart of him. Within a few minutes, that horrible miracle returned, and then again toward dawn. The next day Villari sent for a cab, which left him at a dentist's office in the neighborhood of Plaza del Once.* There, his tooth was pulled. At the "moment of truth," he was neither more cowardly nor more composed than anyone else.

Another night, as he came back from the motion-picture theater, he felt someone shove him. Furious, indignant, and with secret relief, he turned on the insolent culprit; he spit out a filthy insult. The other man, dumbfounded, stammered an apology. He was a tall young man with dark hair; on his arm was a German-looking woman. That night Villari told himself many times that he didn't know them; still, four or five days went by before he went out again.

Among the books in the bookcase was a *Divine Comedy,* with the old commentary by Andreoli. Impelled less by curiosity than by a sense of duty, Villari undertook to read that masterpiece. He would read a canto before dinner, and then, strictly and methodically, the notes. He did not think of the infernal torments as improbable or excessive, nor did it occur to him that Dante would have condemned him, Villari, to the farthest circle of Hell, where Ugolino's teeth gnaw endlessly at Ruggieri's throat.

The peacocks on the crimson wallpaper seemed the perfect thing for feeding persistent nightmares, but Sr. Villari never dreamed of a monstrous gazebo of living birds all intertangled. In the early-morning hours he would dream a dream of unvarying backdrop but varying details. Villari and two other men would come into a room with revolvers drawn, or he would be jumped by them as he came out of the motion-picture theater, or they—all three of them at once—would be the stranger that had shoved him, or they would wait for him sad-faced out in the courtyard and pretend not to know him. At the end of the dream, he would take the revolver out of the drawer in the nightstand that stood beside the bed (and there *was* a gun in that drawer) and fire it at the men. The noise of the gun would wake him, but it was always a dream—and in another dream the attack would occur again and in another dream he would have to kill them again.

One murky morning in July, the presence of strange people (not the sound of the door when they opened it) woke him. Tall in the shadowy dimness of the room, oddly simplified by the dimness (in the frightening dreams, they had always been brighter), motionless, patient, and watching, their eyes lowered as though the weight of their weapons made them stoop-shouldered, Alejandro Villari and a stranger had at last caught up with him. He gestured at them to wait, and he turned over and faced the wall, as though going back to sleep. Did he do that to awaken the pity of the men that killed him, or because it's easier to endure a terrifying event than to imagine it, wait for it endlessly—or (and this is perhaps the most likely possibility) so that his murderers would become a dream, as they had already been so many times, in that same place, at that same hour?

That was the magic spell he was casting when he was rubbed out by the revolvers' fire.

The Man on the Threshold

Bioy Casares brought back a curious knife from London, with a triangular blade and an H-shaped hilt; our friend Christopher Dewey, of the British Council, said that sort of weapon was in common use in Hindustan. That verdict inspired him also to mention that he had once worked in Hindustan, between the two wars. (*Ultra aurorem et Gangem,* I recall him saying in Latin, misquoting a verse from Juvenal.) Among the stories he told us that night, I shall be so bold as to reconstruct the one that follows. My text will be a faithful one; may Allah prevent me from adding small circumstantial details or heightening the exotic lineaments of the tale with interpolations from Kipling. Besides, it has an antique, simple flavor about it that it would be a shame to lose—something of the *1001 Nights.*

The precise geography of the facts I am going to relate hardly matters. And besides—what sort of exactness can the names Amritsar and Udh be expected to convey in Buenos Aires? I shall only say, then, that back in those years there were riots in a certain Muslim city, and that the central government sent a strong fellow in to impose order. The man was a Scot, descended from an illustrious clan of warriors, and in his blood there flowed a history of violence. My eyes beheld him but one time, but I shall never forget the jet black hair, the prominent cheekbones, the avid nose and mouth, the broad shoulders, the strong Viking bones. David Alexander Glencairn shall be his name tonight in my story. The two Christian names befit the man, for they are the names of kings who ruled with an iron scepter. David Alexander Glencairn (I shall have to get used to calling him that) was, I suspect, a man who was greatly feared; the mere announcement of his coming was sufficient to cast peace over the city. That, however, did not keep him from putting into effect a number of forceful measures. Several years passed; the city and the district were at peace; Sikhs and Muslims had put aside their ancient discords. And then suddenly Glencairn disappeared. Naturally, there were any number of rumors of his having been kidnapped or killed.

These things I learned from my superior, because there was strict censorship and the newspapers didn't discuss Glencairn's disappearance—did not so much as mention it, so far as I can recall. There is a saying, you know—that India is larger than the world; Glencairn, who may have been all-powerful in the city to which he was fated by a signature at the end of some document, was a mere cipher in the coils and springs and workings of the Empire. The searches performed by the local police turned up nothing; my superior thought that a single individual, working on his own, might inspire less resentment and achieve better results. Three or four days later (distances in India are what one might call generous), I was working with no great hope through the streets of the opaque city that had magically swallowed up a man.

I felt, almost immediately, the infinite presence of a spell cast to hide Glencairn's whereabouts. *There is not a soul in this city* (I came to suspect) *that doesn't know the secret, and that hasn't sworn to keep it.* Most people, when I interrogated them, pleaded unbounded ignorance; they didn't know who Glencairn was, had never seen the man, never heard of him. Others, contrariwise, had seen him not a quarter of an hour ago talking to Such-and-such, and they would even show me the house the two men had gone into, where of course nobody knew a thing about them—or where I'd just missed them, they'd left just a minute earlier. More than once I balled my fist and hit one of those tellers of precisely detailed lies smack in the face. Bystanders would applaud the way I got my frustrations off my chest, and then make up more lies. I didn't believe them, but I didn't dare ignore them. One evening somebody left me an envelope containing a slip of paper on which were written some directions....

By the time I arrived, the sun had pretty well gone down. The neighborhood was one of common folk, the humble of the earth; the house was squat. From the walkway in the street I could make out a series of courtyards of packed earth and then, toward the rear, a brightness. Back in the last courtyard, some sort of Muslim celebration was going on; a blind man entered with a lute made of reddish-colored wood.

At my feet, on the threshold of this house, as motionless as an inanimate *thing*, a very old man lay curled up on the ground. I shall describe him, because he is an essential part of the story. His many years had reduced and polished him the way water smooths and polishes a stone or generations of men polish a proverb. He was covered in long tatters, or so it looked to me, and the turban that wound about his head looked frankly like one rag the more. In the fading evening light, he lifted his dark face and very white beard to me. I spoke to him without preamble—because I had already lost all hope, you see—about David Alexander Glencairn. He didn't understand me (or perhaps he didn't hear me) and I had to explain that Glencairn was a judge and that I was looking for him. When I uttered those words, I felt how absurd it was to question this ancient little man for whom the present was scarcely more than an indefinite rumor. *News of the Mutiny or the latest word of Akbar, this man might have* (I thought), *but not of Glencairn.* What he told me confirmed that suspicion.

"A judge!" he said with frail astonishment. "A judge who is lost and being searched for. The event took place when I was a boy. I know nothing of dates, but Nikal Seyn had not died at the wall at Delhi yet"—Nicholson he meant, you see. "The past lives on in memory; surely I shall be able to recover what in that time took place. Allah had permitted, in His wrath, that mankind grow corrupted; filled with curses were men's mouths, and with falsehoods and deception. And yet not all men were perverse, so that when it was proclaimed that the queen was going to send a man to enforce the laws of England in this land, the least evil of men were glad, because they felt that law is better than disorder. The Christian came, but no time did it take him to prevaricate and oppress, to find extenuation for abominable crimes, and to sell his verdicts. At first, we did not blame him; none of us were familiar with the English justice he administered, and for all we knew, this judge's seeming abuses were inspired by valid, though arcane, reasons. *Surely all things have justification in his book,* we tried to think, but his similarity to the other evil judges of the world was too clear, and at last we had to admit that he was simply an evil man. He soon became a tyrant, and my poor people (in order to avenge themselves for the mistaken hope that once they had reposed in him) came to entertain the idea of kidnapping him and putting him to trial. Talking was not sufficient; from fine words, it was necessary that we move onward to acts. No one, perhaps, with the exception of the simplest of mind or the youngest of years, believed that such a terrible purpose would ever be fulfilled, but thousands of Sikhs and Muslims kept their word, and one day, incredulous, they *did* what each of them had thought impossible. They kidnapped the judge, and for a prison they put him in a farmhouse in the distant outskirts of the town. Then they consulted with the subjects who had been aggrieved by him, or in some cases with the subjects' orphans and widows, for the executioner's sword had not rested during those years. At last—and this was perhaps the most difficult thing of all—they sought for and appointed a judge to judge the judge."

Here the man was interrupted by several women who made their way into the house. Then he went on, slowly:

"It is said that every generation of mankind includes four honest men who secretly hold up the universe and justify it to the Lord. One of those men would have been the most fitting judge. But where was one to find them, if they wander the earth lost and anonymous and are not recognized when they are met with and not even they themselves know the high mission they perform? Someone, therefore, reflected that if fate had forbidden us wise men, we should seek out fools. That opinion won the day. Scholars of the Qur'ān, doctors of the law, Sikhs who bear the name of lions yet worship God, Hindus who worship a multitude of gods, monks of the master Mahavira who teach that the shape of the universe is that of a man with his legs spread open wide, worshipers of fire, and black Jews composed the tribunal, but the ultimate verdict was to be decided by a madman."

Here he was interrupted by several people leaving the celebration.

"A madman," he repeated, "so that the wisdom of God might speak through his mouth and bring shame to human pride and overweening. The name of this man has been lost, or perhaps was never known, but he wandered these streets naked, or covered with rags, counting his fingers with his thumb and hurling gibes at the trees."

My good sense rebelled. I said that to leave the decision to a madman was to make a mockery of the trial.

"The accused man accepted the judge," was the reply. "Perhaps he realized that given the fate that awaited the conspirators if they should set him free, it was only from a madman that he might hope for anything but a sentence of death. I have heard that he laughed when he was told who the judge was to be. The trial lasted for many days and nights, because of the great number of witnesses."

He fell silent. Some concern was at work in him. To break the silence, I asked how many days it had been.

"At least nineteen days," he replied. More people leaving the celebration interrupted him; Muslims are forbidden wine, but the faces and voices seemed those of drunkards. One of the men shouted something at the old man as he passed by.

"Nineteen days exactly," he emended. "The infidel dog heard the sentence, and the knife was drawn across his throat."

He spoke with joyous ferocity, but it was with another voice that he ended his story.

"He died without fear. Even in the basest of men there is some virtue."

"Where did this take place that you have told me about?" I asked him. "In a farmhouse?"

For the first time he looked me in the eye. Then slowly, measuring his words, he answered.

"I said a farmhouse was his prison, not that he was tried there. He was tried in this very city, in a house like all other houses, like this one. . . . One house is like another—what matters is knowing whether it is built in heaven or in hell."

I asked him what had happened to the conspirators.

"That, I do not know," he said patiently. "These things happened many years ago and by now they have been long forgotten. Perhaps they were condemned by men, but not by God."

Having said this, he got up. I felt that his words dismissed me, that from that moment onward I had ceased to exist for him. A mob of men and women of all the nations of Punjab spilled out over us, praying and singing, and almost swept us away; I was astonished that such narrow courtyards, little more than long entryways, could have contained such numbers of people. Others came out of neighboring houses; no doubt they had jumped over the walls. . . . Pushing and shouting imprecations, I opened a way for myself. In the farthest courtyard I met a naked man crowned with yellow flowers, whom everyone was kissing and making obeisances to; there was a sword in his hand. The sword was bloody, for it had murdered Glencairn, whose mutilated body I found in the stables at the rear.

The Aleph

> O God, I could be bounded in a nutshell and count myself a King of infinite space.
>
> *Hamlet*, II:2

> But they will teach us that Eternity is the Standing still of the Present Time, a *Nunc-stans* (as the Schools call it); which neither they, nor any else understand, no more than they would a *Hic-stans* for an Infinite greatnesse of Place.
>
> *Leviathan*, IV:46

That same sweltering morning that Beatriz Viterbo died, after an imperious confrontation with her illness in which she had never for an instant stooped to either sentimentality or fear, I noticed that a new advertisement for some cigarettes or other (*blondes,* I believe they were) had been posted on the iron billboards of the Plaza Constitución; the fact deeply grieved me, for I realized that the vast unceasing universe was already growing away from her, and that this change was but the first in an infinite series. *The universe may change, but I shall not,* thought I with melancholy vanity. I knew that more than once my futile devotion had exasperated her; now that she was dead, I could consecrate myself to her memory—without hope, but also without humiliation. I reflected that April 30 was her birthday; stopping by her house on Calle Garay that day to pay my respects to her father and her first cousin Carlos Argentino Daneri was an irreproachable, perhaps essential act of courtesy. Once again I would wait in the half-light of the little parlor crowded with furniture and draperies and bric-a-brac, once again I would study the details of the many photographs and portraits of her: Beatriz Viterbo, in profile, in color; Beatriz in a mask at the Carnival of 1921; Beatriz' first communion; Beatriz on the day of her wedding to Roberto Alessandri; Beatriz shortly after the divorce, lunching at the Jockey Club;

Beatriz in Quilmes* with Delia San Marco Porcel and Carlos Argentino; Beatriz with the Pekinese that had been a gift from Villegas Haedo; Beatriz in full-front and in three-quarters view, smiling, her hand on her chin. . . . I would not be obliged, as I had been on occasions before, to justify my presence with modest offerings of books—books whose pages I learned at last to cut, so as not to find, months later, that they were still intact.

Beatriz Viterbo died in 1929; since then, I have not allowed an April 30 to pass without returning to her house. That first time, I arrived at seven-fifteen and stayed for about twenty-five minutes; each year I would turn up a little later and stay a little longer; in 1933, a downpour came to my aid: they were forced to ask me to dinner. Naturally, I did not let that fine precedent go to waste; in 1934 I turned up a few minutes after eight with a lovely confection from Santa Fe; it was perfectly natural that I should stay for dinner. And so it was that on those melancholy and vainly erotic anniversaries I came to receive the gradual confidences of Carlos Argentino Daneri.

Beatriz was tall, fragile, very slightly stooped; in her walk, there was (if I may be pardoned the oxymoron) something of a graceful clumsiness, a *soupçon* of hesitancy, or of palsy; Carlos Argentino is a pink, substantial, gray-haired man of refined features. He holds some sort of subordinate position in an illegible library in the outskirts toward the south of the city; he is authoritarian, though also ineffectual; until very recently he took advantage of nights and holidays to remain at home. At two generations' remove, the Italian *s* and the liberal Italian gesticulation still survive in him. His mental activity is constant, passionate, versatile, and utterly insignificant. He is full of pointless analogies and idle scruples. He has (as Beatriz did) large, beautiful, slender hands. For some months he labored under an obsession for Paul Fort, less for Fort's ballads than the idea of a glory that could never be tarnished. "He is the prince of the poets of *la belle France*," he would fatuously say. "You assail him in vain; you shall never touch him—not even the most venomous of your darts shall ever touch him."

On April 30, 1941, I took the liberty of enriching my sweet offering with a bottle of domestic brandy. Carlos Argentino tasted it, pronounced it "interesting," and, after a few snifters, launched into an *apologia* for modern man.

"I picture him," he said with an animation that was rather unaccountable, "in his study, as though in the watchtower of a great city, surrounded by telephones, telegraphs, phonographs, the latest in radio-telephone and motion-picture and magic-lantern equipment, and glossaries and calendars and timetables and bulletins. . . ."

He observed that for a man so equipped, the act of traveling was supererogatory; this twentieth century of ours had upended the fable of Muhammad and the mountain—mountains nowadays did in fact come to the modern Muhammad.

So witless did these ideas strike me as being, so sweeping and pompous the way they were expressed, that I associated them immediately with literature. Why, I asked him, didn't he write these ideas down? Predictably, he replied that he already had; they, and others no less novel, figured large in the Augural Canto, Prologurial Canto, or simply Prologue-Canto, of a poem on which he had been working, with no deafening hurly-burly and *sans réclame,* for many years, leaning always on those twin staffs Work and Solitude. First he would open the floodgates of the imagination, then repair to the polishing wheel. The poem was entitled *The Earth*; it centered on a description of our own terraqueous orb and was graced, of course, with picturesque digression and elegant apostrophe.

I begged him to read me a passage, even if only a brief one. He opened a desk drawer, took out a tall stack of tablet paper stamped with the letterhead of the Juan Crisóstomo Lafinur Library,* and read, with ringing self-satisfaction:

> I have seen, as did the Greek, man's cities and his fame,
> The works, the days of various light, the hunger;
> I prettify no fact, I falsify no name,
> For the *voyage* I narrate is . . . *autour de ma chambre.*

"A stanza interesting from every point of view," he said. "The first line wins the kudos of the learnèd, the academician, the Hellenist—though perhaps not that of those would-be scholars that make up such a substantial portion of popular opinion. The second moves from Homer to Hesiod (implicit homage, at the very threshold of the dazzling new edifice, to the father of didactic poetry), not without revitalizing a technique whose lineage may be traced to Scripture—that is, enumeration, congeries, or conglobation. The third—baroque? decadent? the purified and fanatical cult of form?—consists of twinned hemistichs; the fourth, unabashedly bilingual, assures me the unconditional support of every spirit able to feel the ample attractions of playfulness. I shall say nothing of the unusual rhyme, nor of the erudition that allows me—without pedantry or boorishness!—to include within the space of four lines three erudite allusions spanning thirty centuries of dense literature: first the *Odyssey,* second the *Works and Days,* and third that immortal bagatelle that regales us with the diversions of the Savoyard's plume. . . . Once again, I show my awareness that truly *modern* art demands the balm of laughter, of *scherzo.* There is no doubt about it—Goldoni was right!"

Carlos Argentino read me many another stanza, all of which earned the same profuse praise and comment from him. There was nothing memorable about them; I could not even judge them to be much worse than the first one. Application, resignation, and chance had conspired in their composition; the virtues that Daneri attributed to them were afterthoughts. I realized that the poet's work had lain not in the poetry but in the invention of reasons for accounting the poetry admirable; naturally, that later work modified the poem for Daneri, but not for anyone else. His oral expression was extravagant; his metrical clumsiness prevented him, except on a very few occasions, from transmitting that extravagance to the poem.[1]

Only once in my lifetime have I had occasion to examine the fifteen thousand dodecasyllables of the *Polyalbion*—that topographical epic in which Michael Drayton recorded the fauna, flora, hydrography, orography, military and monastic history of England—but I am certain that Drayton's massive yet limited *œuvre* is less tedious than the vast enterprise conceived and given birth by Carlos Argentino. He proposed to versify the entire planet; by 1941 he had already dispatched several hectares of the state of Queensland, more than a kilometer of the course of the Ob, a gasworks north of Veracruz, the leading commercial establishments in the parish of Concepción, Mariana Cambaceres de Alvear's villa on Calle Once de Setiembre in Belgrano, and a Turkish bath not far from the famed Brighton Aquarium. He read me certain laborious passages from the Australian region of his poem; his long, formless alexandrines lacked the relative agitation of the prologue. Here is one stanza:

[1]I do, however, recall these lines from a satire in which he lashed out vehemently against bad poets:

> This one fits the poem with a coat of mail
> Of erudition; that one, with gala pomps and circumstance.
> Both flail their absurd pennons to no avail,
> Neglecting, poor wretches, the factor sublime—its LOVELINESS!

It was only out of concern that he might create an army of implacable and powerful enemies, he told me, that he did not fearlessly publish the poem.

Hear this. To the right hand of the routine signpost
(Coming—what need is there to say?—from north-northwest)
Yawns a bored skeleton—Color? Sky-pearly.—
Outside the sheepfold that suggests an ossuary.

"Two audacious risks!" he exclaimed in exultation, "snatched from the jaws of disaster, I can hear you mutter, by success! I admit it, I admit it. One, the epithet *routine,* while making an adjective of a synonym for 'highway,' nods, *en passant,* to the inevitable tedium inherent to those chores of a pastoral and rustic nature that neither georgics nor our own belaureled *Don Segundo* ever dared acknowledge in such a forthright way, with no beating about the bush. And the second, delicately referring to the first, the forcefully prosaic phrase *Yawns a bored skeleton,* which the finicky will want to excommunicate without benefit of clergy but that the critic of more manly tastes will embrace as he does his very life. The entire line, in fact, is a good 24 karats. The second half-line sets up the most animated sort of conversation with the reader; it anticipates his lively curiosity, puts a question in his mouth, and then . . . *voilà,* answers it . . . on the instant. And what do you think of that coup *sky-pearly?* The picturesque neologism just *hints* at the sky, which is such an important feature of the Australian landscape. Without that allusion, the hues of the sketch would be altogether too gloomy, and the reader would be compelled to close the book, his soul deeply wounded by a black and incurable melancholy."

About midnight, I took my leave.

Two Sundays later, Daneri telephoned me for what I believe was the first time in his or my life. He suggested that we meet at four, "to imbibe the milk of the gods together in the nearby salon-bar that my estimable landlords, Messrs. Zunino and Zungri, have had the rare commercial foresight to open on the corner. It is a *café* you will do well to acquaint yourself with." I agreed, with more resignation than enthusiasm, to meet him. It was hard for us to find a table; the relentlessly modern "salon-bar" was only slightly less horrendous than I had expected; at neighboring tables, the excited clientele discussed the sums invested by Zunino and Zungri without a second's haggling. Carlos Argentino pretended to be amazed at some innovation in the establishment's lighting (an innovation he'd no doubt been apprised of beforehand) and then said to me somewhat severely:

"Much against your inclinations it must be that you recognize that this place is on a par with the most elevated heights of Flores."*

Then he reread four or five pages of his poem to me. Verbal ostentation was the perverse principle that had guided his revisions: where he had formerly written "blue" he now had "azure," "cerulean," and even "bluish." The word "milky" was not sufficiently hideous for him; in his impetuous description of a place where wool was washed, he had replaced it with "lactine," "lactescent," "lactoreous," "lacteal." . . . He railed bitterly against his critics; then, in a more benign tone, he compared them to those persons "who possess neither precious metals nor even the steam presses, laminators, and sulfuric acids needed for minting treasures, but who can *point out* to others the *precise location* of a treasure." Then he was off on another tack, inveighing against the obsession for forewords, what he called "prologomania," an attitude that "had already been spoofed in the elegant preface to the *Quixote* by the Prince of Wits himself." He would, however, admit that an attention-getting recommendation might be a good idea at the portals of his new work—"an accolade penned by a writer of stature, of real import." He added that he was planning to publish the first cantos of his poem. It was at that point that I understood the unprecedented telephone call and the invitation: the man was about to ask me to write the preface to that pedantic farrago of his. But my fear turned out to be unfounded. Carlos Argentino remarked, with grudging admiration, that he believed he did not go too far in saying that the prestige achieved in every sphere by the man of letters Alvaro Melián Lafinur was "solid," and that if I could be persuaded to persuade him, Alvaro "might be enchanted to write the called-for foreword." In order to forestall the most unpardonable failure on my part, I was to speak on behalf of the poem's two incontrovertible virtues: its formal perfection and its scientific rigor—"because that broad garden of rhetorical devices, figures, charms, and graces will not tolerate a single detail that does not accord with its severe truthfulness." He added that Beatriz had always enjoyed Alvaro's company.

I agreed, I agreed most profusely. I did, however, for the sake of added plausibility, make it clear that I wouldn't be speaking with Alvaro on Monday but rather on Thursday, at the little supper that crowned each meeting of the Writers Circle. (There are no such suppers, although it is quite true that the meetings are held on Thursday, a fact that Carlos Argentino might verify in the newspapers and that lent a certain credence to my contention.) I told him (half-prophetically, half-farsightedly) that before broaching the subject of the prologue, I would describe the curious design of the poem. We said our good-byes; as I turned down Calle Bernardo de Irigoyen, I contemplated as impartially as I could the futures that were left to me: (a) speak with Alvaro and tell him that that first cousin of Beatriz' (the explanatory circumlocution would allow me to speak her name) had written a poem that seemed to draw out to infinity the possibilities of cacophony and chaos; (b) not speak with Alvaro. Knowing myself pretty well, I foresaw that my indolence would opt for (b).

From early Friday morning on, the telephone was a constant source of anxiety. I was indignant that this instrument from which Beatriz' irrecoverable voice had once emerged might now be reduced to transmitting the futile and perhaps angry complaints of that self-deluding Carlos Argentino Daneri. Fortunately, nothing came of it—save the inevitable irritation inspired by a man who had charged me with a delicate mission and then forgotten all about me.

Eventually the telephone lost its terrors, but in late October Carlos Argentino did call me. He was very upset; at first I didn't recognize his voice. Dejectedly and angrily he stammered out that that now unstoppable pair Zunino and Zungri, under the pretext of expanding their already enormous "*café*," were going to tear down his house.

"The home of my parents—the home where I was born—the old and deeply rooted house on Calle Garay!" he repeated, perhaps drowning his grief in the melodiousness of the phrase.

It was not difficult for me to share his grief. After forty, every change becomes a hateful symbol of time's passing; in addition, this was a house that I saw as alluding infinitely to Beatriz. I tried to make that extremely delicate point clear; my interlocutor cut me off. He said that if Zunino and Zungri persisted in their absurd plans, then Zunni, his attorney, would sue them *ipso facto* for damages, and force them to part with a good hundred thousand for his trouble.

Zunni's name impressed me; his law firm, on the corner of Caseros and Tacuarí, is one of proverbial sobriety. I inquired whether Zunni had already taken the case. Daneri said he'd be speaking with him that afternoon; then he hesitated, and in that flat, impersonal voice we drop into when we wish to confide something very private, he said he had to have the house so he could finish the poem—because in one corner of the cellar there was an Aleph. He explained that an Aleph is one of the points in space that contain all points.

"It's right under the dining room, in the cellar," he explained. In his distress, his words fairly tumbled out. "*It's mine, it's mine;* I discovered it in my childhood, before I ever attended school. The cellar stairway is steep, and my aunt and uncle had forbidden me to go down it, but somebody said you could go around the world with that thing down there in the basement. The person, whoever it was, was referring, I later learned, to a steamer trunk, but I thought there was some magical contraption down there. I tried to sneak down the stairs, fell head over heels, and when I opened my eyes, I saw the Aleph."

"The Aleph?" I repeated.

"Yes, the place where, without admixture or confusion, all the places of the world, seen from every angle, coexist. I revealed my discovery to no one, but I did return. The child could not understand that he was given that privilege so that the man might carve out a poem! Zunino and Zungri shall never take it from me—never, *never!* Lawbook in hand, Zunni will prove that my Aleph is *inalienable.*"

I tried to think.

"But isn't the cellar quite dark?"

"Truth will not penetrate a recalcitrant understanding. If all the places of the world are within the Aleph, there too will be all stars, all lamps, all sources of light."

"I'll be right over. I want to see it."

I hung up before he could tell me not to come. Sometimes learning a fact is enough to make an entire series of corroborating details, previously unrecognized, fall into place; I was amazed that I hadn't realized until that moment that Carlos Argentino was a madman. All the Viterbos, in fact. . . . Beatriz (I myself have said this many times) was a woman, a girl of implacable clearsightedness, but there were things about her—oversights, distractions, moments of contempt, downright cruelty—that perhaps could have done with a *pathological* explanation. Carlos Argentino's madness filled me with malign happiness; deep down, we had always detested one another.

On Calle Garay, the maid asked me to be so kind as to wait—Sr. Daneri was in the cellar, as he always was, developing photographs. Beside the flowerless vase atop the useless piano smiled the great faded photograph of Beatriz, not so much anachronistic as outside time. No one could see us; in a desperation of tenderness I approached the portrait.

"Beatriz, Beatriz Elena, Beatriz Elena Viterbo," I said. "Belovèd Beatriz, Beatriz lost forever—it's me, it's me, Borges."

Carlos came in shortly afterward. His words were laconic, his tone indifferent; I realized that he was unable to think of anything but the loss of the Aleph.

"A glass of pseudocognac," he said, "and we'll duck right into the cellar. I must forewarn you: dorsal decubitus is essential, as are darkness, immobility, and a certain ocular accommodation. You'll lie on the tile floor and fix your eyes on the nineteenth step of the pertinent stairway. I'll reascend the stairs, let down the trap door, and you'll be alone. Some rodent will frighten you—easy enough to do! Within a few minutes, you will see the Aleph. The microcosm of the alchemists and Kabbalists, our proverbial friend the *multum in parvo,* made flesh!

"Of course," he added, in the dining room, "if you don't see it, that doesn't invalidate anything I've told you. . . . Go on down; within a very short while you will be able to begin a dialogue with *all* the images of Beatriz."

I descended quickly, sick of his vapid chatter. The cellar, barely wider than the stairway, was more like a well or cistern. In vain my eyes sought the trunk that Carlos Argentino had mentioned. A few burlap bags and some crates full of bottles cluttered one corner. Carlos picked up one of the bags, folded it, and laid it out very precisely.

"The couch is a humble one," he explained, "but if I raise it one inch higher, you'll not see a thing, and you'll be cast down and dejected. Stretch that great clumsy body of yours out on the floor and count up nineteen steps."

I followed his ridiculous instructions; he finally left. He carefully let down the trap door; in spite of a chink of light that I began to make out later, the darkness seemed total. Suddenly I realized the danger I was in; I had allowed myself to be locked underground by a madman, after first drinking down a snifter of poison. Carlos' boasting clearly masked the deep-seated fear that I wouldn't see his "miracle"; in order to protect his delirium, in order to hide his madness from himself, *he had to kill me.* I felt a vague discomfort, which I tried to attribute to my rigidity, not to the operation of a narcotic. I closed my eyes, then opened them. It was then that I saw the Aleph.

I come now to the ineffable center of my tale; it is here that a writer's hopelessness begins. Every language is an alphabet of symbols the employment of which assumes a past shared by its interlocutors. How can one transmit to others the infinite Aleph, which my timorous memory can scarcely contain? In a similar situation, mystics have employed a wealth of emblems: to signify the deity, a Persian mystic speaks of a bird that somehow is all birds; Alain de Lille speaks of a sphere whose center is everywhere and circumference nowhere; Ezekiel, of an angel with four faces, facing east and west, north and south at once. (It is not for nothing that I call to mind these inconceivable analogies; they bear a relation to the Aleph.) Perhaps the gods would not deny me the discovery of an equivalent image, but then this report would be polluted with literature, with falseness. And besides, the central problem—the enumeration, even partial enumeration, of infinity—is irresolvable. In that unbounded moment, I saw millions of delightful and horrible acts; none amazed me so much as the fact that all occupied the same point, without superposition and without transparency. What my eyes saw was *simultaneous;* what I shall write is *successive,* because language is successive. Something of it, though, I will capture.

Under the step, toward the right, I saw a small iridescent sphere of almost unbearable brightness. At first I thought it was spinning; then I realized that the movement was an illusion produced by the dizzying spectacles inside it. The Aleph was probably two or three centimeters in diameter, but universal space was contained inside it, with no diminution in size. Each thing (the glass surface of a mirror, let us say) was infinite things, because I could clearly see it from every point in the cosmos. I saw the populous sea, saw dawn and dusk, saw the multitudes of the Americas, saw a silvery spiderweb at the center of a black pyramid, saw a broken labyrinth (it was London), saw endless eyes, all very close, studying themselves in me as though in a mirror, saw all the mirrors on the planet (and none of them reflecting me), saw in a rear courtyard on Calle Soler the same tiles I'd seen twenty years before in the entryway of a house in Fray Bentos, saw clusters of grapes, snow, tobacco, veins of metal, water vapor, saw convex equatorial deserts and their every grain of sand, saw a woman in Inverness whom I shall never forget, saw her violent hair, her haughty body, saw a cancer in her breast, saw a circle of dry soil within a sidewalk where there had once been a tree, saw a country house in Adrogué, saw a copy of the first English translation of Pliny (Philemon Holland's), saw every letter of every page at once (as a boy, I would be astounded that the letters in a closed book didn't get all scrambled up together overnight), saw simultaneous night and day, saw a sunset in Querétaro that seemed to reflect the color of a rose in Bengal, saw my bedroom (with no one in it), saw in a study in Alkmaar a globe of the terraqueous world placed between two mirrors that multiplied it endlessly, saw horses with wind-whipped manes on a beach in the Caspian Sea at dawn, saw the delicate bones of a hand, saw the survivors of a battle sending postcards, saw a Tarot card in a shopwindow in Mirzapur, saw the oblique shadows of ferns on the floor of a greenhouse, saw tigers, pistons, bisons, tides, and armies, saw all the ants on earth, saw a Persian astrolabe, saw in a desk drawer (and the handwriting made me tremble) obscene, incredible, detailed letters that Beatriz had sent Carlos Argentino, saw a beloved monument in Chacarita,* saw the horrendous remains of what had once, deliciously, been Beatriz Viterbo, saw the circulation of my dark blood, saw the coils and springs of love and the alterations of death, saw the Aleph from everywhere at once, saw the earth in the Aleph, and the Aleph once more in the earth and the earth in the Aleph, saw my face and my viscera, saw your face, and I felt dizzy, and I wept, because my eyes had seen that secret, hypothetical object whose name has been usurped by men but which no man has ever truly looked upon: the inconceivable universe.

I had a sense of infinite veneration, infinite pity.

"Serves you right, having your mind boggled, for sticking your nose in where you weren't wanted," said a jovial, bored voice. "And you may rack your brains, but you'll never repay me for this revelation—not in a hundred years. What a magnificent observatory, eh, Borges!"

Carlos Argentino's shoes occupied the highest step. In the sudden half-light, I managed to get to my feet.

"Magnificent . . . Yes, quite . . . magnificent," I stammered.

The indifference in my voice surprised me.

"You did see it?" Carlos Argentino insisted anxiously. "See it clearly? In color and everything?"

Instantly, I conceived my revenge. In the most kindly sort of way—manifestly pitying, nervous, evasive—I thanked Carlos Argentino Daneri for the hospitality of his cellar and urged him to take advantage of the demolition of his house to remove himself from the pernicious influences of the metropolis, which no one—believe me, no one!—can be immune to. I refused, with gentle firmness, to discuss the Aleph; I clasped him by both shoulders as I took my leave and told him again that the country—peace and quiet, you know—was the very best medicine one could take.

Out in the street, on the steps of the Constitución Station, in the subway, all the faces seemed familiar. I feared there was nothing that had the power to surprise or astonish me anymore, I feared that I would never again be without a sense of *déjà vu*. Fortunately, after a few unsleeping nights, forgetfulness began to work in me again.

Postscript (March 1, 1943): Six months after the demolition of the building on Calle Garay, Procrustes Publishers, undaunted by the length of Carlos Argentino Daneri's substantial poem, published the first in its series of "Argentine pieces." It goes without saying what happened: Carlos Argentino won second place in the National Prize for Literature.[2] The first prize went

[2] "I received your mournful congratulations," he wrote me. "You scoff, my lamentable friend, in envy, but you shall confess—though the words stick in your throat!—that this time I have crowned my cap with the most scarlet of plumes; my turban, with the most caliphal of rubies."

to Dr. Aita; third, to Dr. Mario Bonfanti; incredibly, my own work *The Sharper's Cards* did not earn a single vote. Once more, incomprehension and envy triumphed! I have not managed to see Daneri for quite a long time; the newspapers say he'll soon be giving us another volume. His happy pen (belabored no longer by the Aleph) has been consecrated to setting the compendia of Dr. Acevedo Díaz to verse.*

There are two observations that I wish to add: one, with regard to the nature of the Aleph; the other, with respect to its name. Let me begin with the latter: "aleph," as well all know, is the name of the first letter of the alphabet of the sacred language. Its application to the disk of my tale would not appear to be accidental. In the Kabbala, that letter signifies the En Soph, the pure and unlimited godhead; it has also been said that its shape is that of a man pointing to the sky and the earth, to indicate that the lower world is the map and mirror of the higher. For the *Mengenlehre,* the aleph is the symbol of the transfinite numbers, in which the whole is not greater than any of its parts. I would like to know: Did Carlos Argentino choose that name, or did he read it, *applied to another point at which all points converge,* in one of the innumerable texts revealed to him by the Aleph in his house? Incredible as it may seem, I believe that there is (or was) another Aleph; I believe that the Aleph of Calle Garay was a *false* Aleph.

Let me state my reasons. In 1867, Captain Burton was the British consul in Brazil; in July of 1942, Pedro Henríquez Ureña* discovered a manuscript by Burton in a library in Santos, and in this manuscript Burton discussed the mirror attributed in the East to Iskandar dhu-al-Qarnayn, or Alexander the Great of Macedonia. In this glass, Burton said, the entire universe was reflected. Burton mentions other similar artifices—the sevenfold goblet of Kai Khosru; the mirror that Ṭāriq ibn-Ziyād found in a tower (*1001 Nights,* 272); the mirror that Lucian of Samosata examined on the moon (*True History,* I:26); the specular spear attributed by the first book of Capella's *Satyricon* to Jupiter; Merlin's universal mirror, "round and hollow and ... [that] seem'd a world of glas" (*Faerie Queene,* III:2, 19)—and then adds these curious words: "But all the foregoing (besides sharing the defect of not existing) are mere optical instruments. The faithful who come to the Amr mosque in Cairo, know very well that the universe lies inside one of the stone columns that surround the central courtyard.... No one, of course, can see it, but those who put their ear to the surface claim to hear, within a short time, the bustling rumour of it.... The mosque dates to the seventh century; the columns were taken from other, pre-Islamic, temples, for as ibn-Khaldūn has written: *In the* *republics founded by nomads, the attendance of foreigners is essential for all those things that bear upon masonry.*"

Does that Aleph exist, within the heart of a stone? Did I see it when I saw all things, and then forget it? Our minds are permeable to forgetfulness; I myself am distorting and losing, through the tragic erosion of the years, the features of Beatriz.

For Estela Canto

Afterword

Aside from "Emma Zunz" (whose wonderful plot—much superior to its timid execution—was given me by Cecilia Ingenieros) and "Story of the Warrior and the Captive Maiden" (which attempts to interpret two supposedly real occurrences), the stories in this book belong to the genre of fantasy. Of them, the first is the most fully realized; its subject is the effect that immortality would have on humankind. That outline for an ethics of immortality is followed by "The Dead Man"; in that story, Azevedo Bandeira is a man from Rivera or Cerro Largo and also an uncouth sort of deity—a mulatto, renegade version of Chesterton's incomparable Sunday. (Chapter XXIX of *The Decline and Fall of the Roman Empire* tells of a fate much like Otálora's, though considerably grander and more incredible.) About "The Theologians," suffice it to say that they are a dream—a somewhat melancholy dream—of personal identity; about the "Biography of Tadeo Isidoro Cruz," that it is a gloss on the *Martín Fierro*. I owe to a canvas painted by Watts in 1896 the story called "The House of Asterion" and the character of its poor protagonist. "The Other Death" is a fantasy about time, which I wove under the suggestion of some of Pier Damiani's arguments. During the last war, no one could have wished more earnestly than I for Germany's defeat; no one could have felt more strongly than I the tragedy of Germany's fate; "*Deutsches Requiem*" is an attempt to understand that fate, which our own "Germanophiles" (who know nothing of Germany) neither wept over nor even suspected. "The Writing of the God" has been judged generously; the jaguar obliged me to put into the mouth of a "priest of the Pyramid of Qaholom" the arguments of a Kabbalist or a theologian. In "The Zahir" and "The Aleph," I think I can detect some influence of Wells' story "The Cristal Egg" (1899).

J.L.B.

Buenos Aires, May 3, 1949

Postscript (1952): I have added four stories to this new edition. "Ibn-Ḥakam al-Bokhari, Murdered in His Labyrinth" is not (I have been assured) memorable, in spite of its bloodcurdling title. We might think of it as a variation on the story of "The Two Kings in Their Two Labyrinths," interpolated into the *1001 Nights* by the copyists yet passed over by the prudent Galland. About "The Wait" I shall say only that it was suggested by a true police story that Alfredo Doblas read me, some ten years ago, while we were classifying books—following the manual of the Bibliographic Institute of Brussels, I might add, a code I have entirely forgotten save for the detail that God can be found under the number 231. The subject of the story was a Turk; I made him an Italian so that I could more easily get inside his skin. The momentary yet repeated sight of a long, narrow rooming house that sits around the corner of Calle Paraná, in Buenos Aires, provided me with the story titled "The Man on the Threshold"; I set it in India so that its improbability might be bearable.

J.L.B.

The Maker

(1960)

Foreword

*For Leopoldo Lugones**

The sounds of the plaza fall behind, and I enter the Library. Almost physically, I can feel the gravitation of the books, the serene atmosphere of orderliness, time magically mounted and preserved. To left and right, absorbed in their waking dream, rows of readers' momentary profiles in the light of the "scholarly lamps," as a Miltonian displacement of adjectives would have it. I recall having recalled that trope here in the Library once before, and then that other adjective of setting—the Lunario*'s "arid camel," and then that hexameter from the* Æneid *that employs, and surpasses, the same artifice:*

Ibant obscuri sola sub nocte per umbram.

These reflections bring me to the door of your office. I go inside. We exchange a few conventional, cordial words, and I give you this book. Unless I am mistaken, you didn't dislike me, Lugones, and you'd have liked to like some work of mine. That never happened, but this time you turn the pages and read a line or two approvingly, perhaps because you've recognized your own voice in it, perhaps because the halting poetry itself is less important than the clean-limbed theory.

At this point, my dream begins to fade and melt away, like water in water. The vast library surrounding me is on Calle México, not Rodríguez Peña, and you, Lugones, killed yourself in early '38. My vanity and my nostalgia have confected a scene that is impossible. Maybe so, I tell myself, but tomorrow I too will be dead and our times will run together and chronology will melt into an orb of symbols, and somehow it will be true to say that I have brought you this book and that you have accepted it.

J.L.B.

Buenos Aires, August 9, 1960

The Maker*

He had never lingered among the pleasures of memory. Impressions, momentary and vivid, would wash over him: a potter's vermilion glaze; the sky-vault filled with stars that were also gods; the moon, from which a lion had fallen; the smoothness of marble under his sensitive, slow fingertips; the taste of wild boar meat, which he liked to tear at with brusque, white bites; a Phoenician word; the black shadow cast by a spear on the yellow sand; the nearness of the sea or women; heavy wine, its harsh edge tempered by honey—these things could flood the entire circuit of his soul. He had known terror, but he had known wrath and courage as well, and once he had been the first to scale an enemy wall. Keen, curious, inadvertent, with no law but satisfaction and immediate indifference, he had wandered the various world and on now this, now that seashore, he had gazed upon the cities of men and their palaces. In teeming marketplaces or at the foot of a mountain upon whose uncertain peak there might be satyrs, he had listened to complex stories, which he took in as he took in reality—without asking whether they were true or false.

Gradually, the splendid universe began drawing away from him; a stubborn fog blurred the lines of his hand; the night lost its peopling stars, the earth became uncertain under his feet. Everything grew distant, and indistinct. When he learned that he was going blind, he cried out. ("Stoicism" had not yet been invented, and Hector could flee without self-diminution.) *Now* (he felt) *I will not be able to see the sky filled with mythological dread or this face that the years will transfigure.* Days and nights passed over this despair of his flesh, but one morning he awoke, looked (with calm now) at the blurred things that lay about him, and felt, inexplicably, the way one might feel upon recognizing a melody or a voice, that all this had happened to him before and that he had faced it with fear but also with joy and hopefulness and curiosity. Then he descended into his memory, which seemed to him endless, and managed to draw up from that vertigo the lost remembrance that gleamed like a coin in the rain—perhaps because he had never really looked at it except (perhaps) in a dream.

The memory was this: Another boy had insulted him, and he had run to his father and told him the story. As though he weren't paying attention, or didn't understand, his father let him talk, but then he took a bronze knife down from the wall—a beautiful knife, charged with power, that the boy had furtively coveted. Now he held it in his hands, and the surprise of possession wiped away the insult that he had suffered, but his father's voice was speaking: *Let it be known that you are a man,* and there was a command in the voice. Night's blindness was upon the paths; clutching to himself the knife in which he sensed a magical power, the boy descended the steep rough hillside that his house stood on and ran to the seashore, dreaming that he was Ajax and Perseus and peopling the dark salt air with wounds and battles. It was the precise flavor of that moment that he sought for now; the rest didn't matter—the insulting words of his challenge, the clumsy combat, the return with the bloodied blade.

Another memory, in which there was also a night and the foretaste of adventure, sprouted from that first one. A woman, the first woman the gods had given him, had awaited him in the darkness of a subterranean crypt, and he searched for her through galleries that were like labyrinths of stone and down slopes that descended into darkness. Why had those memories come to him, and why did they come without bitterness, like some mere foreshadowing of the present?

With grave wonder, he understood. In this night of his mortal eyes into which he was descending, love and adventure were also awaiting him. Ares and Aphrodite—because now he began to sense (because now he began to be surrounded by) a rumor of glory and hexameters, a rumor of men who defend a temple that the gods will not save, a rumor of black ships that set sail in search of a belovèd isle, the rumor of the *Odysseys* and *Iliads* that it was his fate to sing and to leave echoing in the cupped hands of human memory. These things we know, but not those that he felt as he descended into his last darkness.

*Dreamtigers**

In my childhood I was a fervent worshiper of the tiger—not the jaguar, that spotted "tiger"* that inhabits the floating islands of water hyacinths along the Paraná and the tangled wilderness of the Amazon, but the true tiger, the striped Asian breed that can be faced only by men of war, in a castle atop an elephant. I would stand for hours on end before one of the cages at the zoo; I would rank vast encyclopedias and natural history books by the splendor of their tigers. (I still remember those pictures, I who cannot recall without error a woman's brow or smile.) My childhood outgrown, the tigers and my passion for them faded, but they are still in my dreams. In that underground sea or chaos, they still endure. As I sleep I am drawn into some dream or other, and suddenly I realize that it's a dream. At those moments, I often think: *This is a dream, a pure diversion of my will, and since I have unlimited power, I am going to bring forth a tiger.*

Oh, incompetence! My dreams never seen to engender the creature I so hunger for. The tiger does appear, but it is all dried up, or it's flimsy-looking, or it has impure vagaries of shape or an unacceptable size, or it's altogether too ephemeral, or it looks more like a dog or bird than like a tiger.

A Dialog About a Dialog

A: Absorbed in our discussion of immortality, we had let night fall without lighting the lamp, and we couldn't see each other's faces. With an offhandedness or gentleness more convincing than passion would have been, Macedonio Fernández' voice said once more that the soul is immortal. He assured me that the death of the body is altogether insignificant, and that dying has to be the most unimportant thing that can happen to a man. I was playing with Macedonio's pocketknife, opening and closing it. A nearby accordion was infinitely dispatching *La Comparsita*, that dismaying trifle that so many people like because it's been misrepresented to them as being old. . . . I suggested to Macedonio that we kill ourselves, so we might have our discussion without all that racket.

Z: (mockingly) But I suspect that at the last moment you reconsidered.

A: (now deep in mysticism) Quite frankly, I don't remember whether we committed suicide that night or not.

Toenails

Gentle socks pamper them by day, and shoes cobbled of leather fortify them, but my toes hardly notice. All they're interested in is turning out toenails—semitransparent, flexible sheets of a hornlike material, as defense against—*whom*? Brutish, distrustful as only they can be, my toes labor ceaselessly at manufacturing that frail armament. They turn their backs on the universe and its ecstasies in order to spin out, endlessly, those ten pointless projectile heads, which are cut away time and again by the sudden snips of a Solingen. By the ninetieth twilit day of their prenatal confinement, my toes had cranked up that extraordinary factory. And when I am tucked away in Recoleta,* in an ash-colored house bedecked with dry flowers and amulets, they will still be at their stubborn work, until corruption at last slows them—them and the beard upon my cheeks.

Covered Mirrors

Islam tells us that on the unappealable Day of Judgment, all who have perpetrated images of living things will reawaken with their works, and will be ordered to blow life into them, and they will fail, and they and their works will be cast into the fires of punishment. As a child, I knew that horror of the spectral duplication or multiplication of reality, but mine would come as I stood before large mirrors. As soon as it began to grow dark outside, the constant, infallible functioning of mirrors, the way they followed my every movement, their cosmic pantomime, would seem eerie to me. One of my insistent pleas to God and my guardian angel was that I not dream of mirrors; I recall clearly that I would keep one eye on them uneasily. I feared sometimes that they would begin to veer off from reality; other times, that I would see my face in them disfigured by strange misfortunes. I have learned that this horror is monstrously abroad in the world again. The story is quite simple, and terribly unpleasant.

In 1927, I met a grave young woman, first by telephone (because Julia began as a voice without a name or face) and then on a corner at nightfall. Her eyes were alarmingly large, her hair jet black and straight, her figure severe. She was the granddaughter and great-granddaughter of Federalists, as I was the grandson and great-grandson of Unitarians,* but that ancient discord between our lineages was, for us, a bond, a fuller possession of our homeland. She lived with her family in a big run-down high-ceiling'd house, in the resentment and savorlessness of genteel poverty. In the afternoons—only very rarely at night—we would go out walking through her neighborhood, which was Balvanera.* We would stroll along beside the high blank wall of the railway yard; once we walked down Sarmiento all the way to the cleared grounds of the Parque Centenario.* Between us there was neither love itself nor the fiction of love; I sensed in her an intensity that was utterly unlike the intensity of eroticism, and I feared it. In order to forge an intimacy with women, one often tells them about true or apocryphal things that happened in one's youth; I must have told her at some point about my horror of mirrors, and so in 1928 I must have planted the hallucination that was to flower in 1931. Now I have just learned that she has gone insane, and that in her room all the mirrors are covered, because she sees my reflection in them—usurping her own—and she trembles and cannot speak, and says that I am magically following her, watching her, stalking her.

What dreadful bondage, the bondage of my face—or one of my former faces. Its odious fate makes *me* odious as well, but I don't care anymore.

Argumentum Ornithologicum

I close my eyes and see a flock of birds. The vision lasts a second, or perhaps less; I am not sure how many birds I saw. Was the number of birds definite or indefinite? The problem involves the existence of God. If God exists, the number is definite, because God knows how many birds I saw. If God does not exist, the number is indefinite, because no one can have counted. In this case I saw fewer than ten birds (let us say) and more than one, but did not see nine, eight, seven, six, five, four, three, or two birds. I saw a number between ten and one, which was not nine, eight, seven, six, five, etc. That integer—not-nine, not-eight, not-seven, not-six, not-five, etc.—is inconceivable. *Ergo,* God exists.

The Captive

In Junín or Tapalquén, they tell the story. A young boy disappeared in an Indian raid; people said the Indians had kidnapped him. His parents searched for him without success. Many years went by, and a soldier coming into town from the interior told them about an Indian with sky blue eyes who might well be their son. They finally managed to find this Indian (the story has lost many of its details, and I don't want to invent what I don't know) and thought they recognized him. Shaped by the wilderness and his barbaric life, the man could no longer understand the words of his mother tongue, but he allowed himself to be led—indifferently, docilely—back to the house. There, he stopped (perhaps because the others stopped). He looked at the door, almost uncomprehendingly. Then suddenly he bowed his head, gave an odd cry, rushed down the entryway and through the two long patios, and ran into the kitchen. He thrust his arm unhesitatingly up into the blackened chimney of the stove and took out the little horn-handled knife he had hidden there when he was a boy. His eyes gleamed with happiness and his parents wept, because they had found their son.

That memory may have been followed by others, but the Indian could not live a life that was hemmed about by walls, and one day he went off in search of his wilderness. I would like to know what he felt in that moment of vertigo when past and present intermingled; I would like to know whether the lost son was reborn and died in that ecstatic moment, and whether he ever managed to recognize, even as little as a baby or a dog might, his parents and the house.

The Mountebank

One day in July, 1952, the man dressed in mourning weeds appeared in that little village on the Chaco River.* He was a tall, thin man with vaguely Indian features and the inexpressive face of a half-wit or a mask. The townsfolk treated him with some deference, not because of who he was but because of the personage he was portraying or had by now become. He chose a house near the river; with the help of some neighbor women he laid a board across two sawhorses, and on it he set a pasteboard coffin with a blond-haired mannequin inside. In addition, they lighted four candles in tall candleholders and put flowers all around. The townsfolk soon began to gather. Old ladies bereft of hope, dumbstruck wide-eyed boys, peons who respectfully took off their pith hats—they filed past the coffin and said: *My condolences, General.* The man in mourning sat sorrowfully at the head of the coffin, his hands crossed over his belly like a pregnant woman. He would extend his right hand to shake the hand extended to him and answer with courage and resignation: *It was fate. Everything humanly possible was done.* A tin collection box received the two-peso price of admission, and many could not content themselves with a single visit.

What kind of man, I ask myself, thought up and then acted out that funereal farce—a fanatic? a grief-stricken mourner? a madman? a cynical impostor? Did he, in acting out his mournful role as the macabre widower, believe himself to be Perón? It is an incredible story, but it actually happened—and perhaps not once but many times, with different actors and local variants. In it, one can see the perfect symbol of an unreal time, and it is like the reflection of a dream or like that play within a play in *Hamlet.* The man in mourning was not Perón and the blond-haired mannequin was not the woman Eva Duarte, but then Perón was not Perón, either, nor was Eva, Eva—they were unknown or anonymous persons (whose secret name and true face we shall never know) who acted out, for the credulous love of the working class, a crass and ignoble mythology.

Delia Elena San Marco

We said good-bye on one of the corners of the Plaza del Once.*

From the sidewalk on the other side of the street I turned and looked back; you had turned, and you waved good-bye.

A river of vehicles and people ran between us; it was five o'clock on no particular afternoon. How was I to know that that river was the sad Acheron, which no one may cross twice?

Then we lost sight of each other, and a year later you were dead.

And now I search out that memory and gaze at it and think that it was false, that under the trivial farewell there lay an infinite separation.

Last night I did not go out after dinner. To try to understand these things, I reread the last lesson that Plato put in his teacher's mouth. I read that the soul can flee when the flesh dies.

And now I am not sure whether the truth lies in the ominous later interpretation or in the innocent farewell.

Because if the soul doesn't die, we are right to lay no stress on our good-byes.

To say good-bye is to deny separation; it is to say *Today we play at going our own ways, but we'll see each other tomorrow.* Men invented farewells because they somehow knew themselves to be immortal, even while seeing themselves as contingent and ephemeral.

One day we will pick up this uncertain conversation again, Delia—on the bank of what river?—and we will ask ourselves whether we were once, in a city that vanished into the plains, Borges and Delia.

A Dialog Between Dead Men

The man arrived from the south of England early one winter morning in 1877. As he was a ruddy, athletic, overweight man, it was inevitable that almost everyone should think that he was English, and indeed he looked remarkably like the archetypical John Bull. He wore a bowler hat and a curious wool cape with an opening in the center. A group of men, women, and babes were waiting for him anxiously; many of them had a red line scored across their throats, others were headless and walked with hesitant, fearful steps, as though groping through the dark. Little by little, they encircled the stranger, and from the back of the crowd someone shouted out a curse, but an ancient terror stopped them, and they dared go no further. From out of their midst stepped a sallow-skinned soldier with eyes like glowing coals; his long tangled hair and lugubrious beard seemed to consume his face; ten or twelve mortal wounds furrowed his body, like the stripes on a tiger's skin. When the newcomer saw him, he paled, but then he stepped forward and put out his hand.

"How grievous it is to see such a distinguished soldier brought low by the instruments of perfidy!" he said, grandiloquently. "And yet what deep satisfaction to have ordered that the torturers and assassins atone for their crimes on the scaffold in the Plaza de la Victoria!"

"If it's Santos Pérez and the Reinafé brothers you're referring to, be assured that I have already thanked them,"' the bloody man said with slow solemnity.

The other man looked at him as though smelling a gibe or a threat, but Quiroga* went on:

"You never understood me, Rosas.* But how could you understand me, if our lives were so utterly different? Your fate was to govern in a city that looks out toward Europe and that one day will be one of the most famous cities in the world; mine was to wage war across the solitudes of the Americas, in an impoverished land inhabited by impoverished gauchos. My empire was one of spears and shouts and sandy wastelands and virtually secret victories in godforsaken places. What sort of claim to fame is that? I live in people's memory—and will go on living there for many years—because I was murdered in a stagecoach in a place called Barranca Yaco by a gang of men with swords and horses. I owe to you that gift of a valiant death, which I cannot say I was grateful for at the time but which subsequent generations have been loath to forget. You are surely familiar with certain primitive lithographs and that interesting literary work penned by a worthy from San Juan?"

Rosas, who had recovered his composure, looked at the other man contemptuously.

"You are a romantic," he said with a sneer. "The flattery of posterity is worth very little more than the flattery of one's contemporaries, which is not worth anything, and can be bought with a pocketful of loose change."

"I know how you think," replied Quiroga. "In 1852, fate, which is generous, or which wanted to plumb you to the very depths, offered you a man's death, in battle. You showed yourself unworthy of that gift, because fighting, bloodshed, frightened you."

"Frightened me?" Rosas repeated. "Me, who've tamed horses in the South and then tamed an entire country?"

For the first time, Quiroga smiled.

"I know," he slowly said, "from the impartial testimony of your peons and seconds-in-command, that you did more than one pretty turn on horseback, but back in those days, across the Americas—and on horseback, too—other pretty turns were done in places named Chacabuco and Junín and Palma Redondo and Caseros."

Rosas listened expressionlessly, and then replied.

"'I had no need to be brave. One of those pretty turns of mine, as you put it, was to manage to convince braver men than I to fight and die for me. Santos Pérez, for example, who was more than a match for *you*. Bravery is a matter of bearing up; some men bear up better than others, but sooner or later, every man caves in."

"That may be," Quiroga said, "but I have lived and I have died, and to this day I don't know what fear is. And now I am going to the place where I will be given a new face and a new destiny, because history is tired of violent men. I don't know who the next man may be, what will be done with me, but I know I won't be afraid."

"I'm content to be who I am," said Rosas, "and I have no wish to be anybody else."

"Stones want to go on being stones, too, forever and ever," Quiroga replied. "And for centuries they are stones—until they crumble into dust. When I first entered into death, I thought the way you do, but I've learned many things here since. If you notice, we're both already changing."

But Rosas paid him no attention; he merely went on, as though thinking out loud:

"Maybe I'm not cut out to be dead, but this place and this conversation seem like a dream to me, and not a dream that *I* am dreaming, either. More like a dream dreamed by somebody else, somebody that's not born yet."

Then their conversation ended, because just then Someone called them.

The Plot

To make his horror perfect, Cæsar, hemmed about at the foot of a statue by his friends' impatient knives, discovers among the faces and the blades the face of Marcus Junius Brutus, his ward, perhaps his very son—and so Cæsar stops defending himself, and cries out *Et tu, Brute?* Shakespeare and Quevedo record that pathetic cry.

Fate is partial to repetitions, variations, symmetries. Nineteen centuries later, in the southern part of the province of Buenos Aires, a gaucho is set upon by other gauchos, and as he falls he recognizes a godson of his, and says to him in gentle remonstrance and slow surprise (these words must be heard, not read): *Pero, ¡ché!* He dies, but he does not know that he has died so that a scene can be played out again.

A Problem

Let us imagine that a piece of paper with a text in Arabic on it is discovered in Toledo, and that paleographers declare the text to have been written by that same Cide Hamete Benengeli from whom Cervantes derived *Don Quixote.* In it, we read that the hero (who, as everyone knows, wandered the roads of Spain armed with a lance and sword, challenging anyone for any reason) discovers, after one of his many combats, that he has killed a man. At that point the fragment breaks off; the problem is to guess, or hypothesize, how don Quixote reacts.

So far as I can see, there are three possibilities. The first is a negative one: Nothing in particular happens, because in the hallucinatory world of don Quixote, death is no more uncommon than magic, and there is no reason that killing a mere man should disturb one who does battle, or thinks he does battle, with fabled beasts and sorcerers. The second is pathetic: Don Quixote never truly managed to forget that he was a creation, a projection, of Alonso Quijano, reader of fabulous tales. The sight of death, the realization that a delusion has led him to commit the sin of Cain, awakens him from his willful madness, perhaps forever. The third is perhaps the most plausible: Having killed the man, don Quixote cannot allow himself to think that the terrible act is the work of a delirium; the reality of the effect makes him assume a like reality of cause, and don Quixote never emerges from his madness.

But there is yet another hypothesis, which is alien to the Spanish mind (even to the Western mind) and which requires a more ancient, more complex, and more timeworn setting. Don Quixote—who is no longer don Quixote but a king of the cycles of Hindustan—senses, as he stands before the body of his enemy, that killing and engendering are acts of God or of magic, which everyone knows transcend the human condition. He knows that death is illusory, as are the bloody sword that lies heavy in his hand, he himself and his entire past life, and the vast gods and the universe.

The Yellow Rose

It was neither that afternoon nor the next that Giambattista Marino died—that illustrious man proclaimed by the unanimous mouths of Fame (to use an image that was dear to him) as the new Homer or the new Dante—and yet the motionless and silent act that took place that afternoon was, in fact, the last thing that happened in his life. His brow laureled with years and glory, the man died in a vast Spanish bed with carven pillars. It costs us nothing to picture a serene balcony a few steps away, looking out toward the west, and, below, marbles and laurels and a garden whose terraced steps are mirrored in a rectangular pool. In a goblet, a woman has set a yellow rose; the man murmurs the inevitable lines of poetry that even he, to tell the truth, is a bit tired of by now:

> *Porpora de' giardin, pompa de' prato,*
> *Gemma di primavera, occhio d'aprile . . .*[*]

Then the revelation occurred. Marino *saw* the rose, as Adam had seen it in Paradise, and he realized that it lay within its own eternity, not within his words, and that we might speak about the rose, allude to it, but never truly express it, and that the tall, haughty volumes that made a golden dimness in the corner of his room were not (as his vanity had dreamed them) a mirror of the world, but just another thing added to the world's contents.

Marino achieved that epiphany on the eve of his death, and Homer and Dante may have achieved it as well.

The Witness

In a stable that stands almost in the shadow of the new stone church, a man with gray eyes and gray beard, lying amid the odor of the animals, humbly tries to will himself into death, much as a man might will himself to sleep. The day, obedient to vast and secret laws, slowly shifts about and mingles the shadows in the lowly place; outside lie plowed fields, a ditch clogged with dead leaves, and the faint track of a wolf in the black clay where the line of woods begins. The man sleeps and dreams, forgotten. The bells for orisons awaken him. Bells are now one of evening's customs in the kingdoms of England, but as a boy the man has seen the face of Woden, the sacred horror and the exultation, the clumsy wooden idol laden with Roman coins and ponderous vestments, the sacrifice of horses, dogs, and prisoners. Before dawn he will be dead, and with him, the last eyewitness images of pagan rites will perish, never to be seen again. The world will be a little poorer when this Saxon man is dead.

Things, events, that occupy space yet come to an end when someone dies may make us stop in wonder—and yet one thing, or an infinite number of things, dies with every man's or woman's death, unless the universe itself has a memory, as theosophists have suggested. In the course of time there was one day that closed the last eyes that had looked on Christ; the Battle of Junín and the love of Helen died with the death of one man. What will die with me the day I die? What pathetic or frail image will be lost to the world? The voice of Macedonio Fernández, the image of a bay horse in a vacant lot on the corner of Sarrano and Charcas, a bar of sulfur in the drawer of a mahogany desk?

Martín Fierro

Out of this city marched armies that seemed grand, and that in later days *were* grand, thanks to the magnifying effects of glory. After many years, one of the soldiers returned, and in a foreign accent told stories of what had happened to him in places called Ituzaingó or Ayacucho.* These things are now as though they had never been.

There have been two tyrannies in this land. During the first, a wagon pulled out of La Plata market; as the wagon passed through the streets, some men on the driver's seat cried out their wares, hawking white and yellow peaches; a young boy lifted the corner of the canvas that covered them and saw the heads of Unitarians, their beards bloody.* The second meant, for many, prison and death; for all, it meant discomfort, endless humiliation, a taste of shamefulness in the actions of every day. These things are now as though they had never been.

A man who knew all the words looked with painstaking love at the plants and birds of this land and defined them, perhaps forever, and in metaphors of metal wrote the vast chronicle of its tumultuous sunsets and the shapes of its moon.* These things are now as though they had never been.

Also in this land have generations known those common yet somehow eternal vicissitudes that are the stuff of art. These things are now as though they had never been, but in a hotel room in eighteen-hundred sixty-something a man dreamed of a knife fight. A gaucho lifts a black man off the ground with the thrust of his knife, drops him like a bag of bones, watches him writhe in pain and die, squats down to wipe off his knife, unties his horse's bridle and swings up into the saddle slowly, so no one will think he's running away from what he's done. This thing that was once, returns again, infinitely; the visible armies have gone and what is left is a common sort of knife fight; one man's dream is part of all men's memory.

Mutations

In a hallway I saw a sign with an arrow pointing the way, and I was struck by the thought that that inoffensive symbol had once been a thing of iron, an inexorable, mortal projectile that had penetrated the flesh of men and lions and clouded the sun of Thermopylæ and bequeathed to Harald Sigurdson, for all time, six feet of English earth.

Several days later, someone showed me a photograph of a Magyar horseman; a coil of rope hung about his mount's chest. I learned that the rope, which had once flown through the air and lassoed bulls in the pasture, was now just an insolent decoration on a rider's Sunday riding gear.

In the cemetery on the Westside I saw a runic cross carved out of red marble; its arms splayed and widened toward the ends and it was bounded by a circle. That circumscribed and limited cross was a figure of the cross with unbound arms that is in turn the symbol of the gallows on which a god was tortured—that "vile machine" decried by Lucian of Samosata.

Cross, rope, and arrow: ancient implements of mankind, today reduced, or elevated, to symbols. I do not know why I marvel at them so, when there is nothing on earth that forgetfulness does not fade, memory alter, and when no one knows what sort of image the future may translate it into.

Parable of Cervantes and the *Quixote*

Weary of his land of Spain, an old soldier of the king's army sought solace in the vast geographies of Ariosto, in that valley of the moon in which one finds the time that is squandered by dreams, and in the golden idol of Muhammad stolen by Montalbán.

In gentle self-mockery, this old soldier conceived a credulous man—his mind unsettled by the reading of all those wonders—who took it into his head to ride out in search of adventures and enchantments in prosaic places with names such as El Toboso and Montiel.

Defeated by reality, by Spain, don Quixote died in 1614 in the town of his birth. He was survived only a short time by Miguel de Cervantes.

For both the dreamer and the dreamed, that entire adventure had been the clash of two worlds; the unreal world of romances and the common everyday world of the seventeenth century.

They never suspected that the years would at last smooth away the discord, never suspected that in the eyes of the future, La Mancha and Montiel and the lean figure of the Knight of Mournful Countenance would be no less poetic than the adventures of Sindbad or the vast geographies of Ariosto.

For in the beginning of literature there is myth, as there is also in the end of it.

Devoto Clinic
January 1955

Paradiso, XXXI, 108

Diodorus Siculus tells the story of a god that is cut into pieces and scattered over the earth. Which of us, walking through the twilight or retracing some day in our past, has never felt that we have lost some infinite thing?

Mankind has lost a face, an irrecoverable face, and all men wish they could be that pilgrim (dreamed in the empyrean, under the Rose) who goes to Rome and looks upon the veil of St. Veronica and murmurs in belief: *My Lord Jesus Christ, very God, is this, indeed, Thy likeness in such fashion wrought?**

There is a face in stone beside a path, and an inscription that reads *The True Portrait of the Holy Face of the Christ of Jaén.* If we really knew what that face looked like, we would possess the key to the parables, and know whether the son of the carpenter was also the Son of God.

Paul saw the face as a light that struck him to the ground; John, as the sun when it shines forth in all its strength; Teresa de Jesús, many times, bathed in serene light, although she could never say with certainty what the color of its eyes was.

Those features are lost to us, as a magical number created from our customary digits can be lost, as the image in a kaleidoscope is lost forever. We can see them and yet not *grasp* them. A Jew's profile in the subway might be the profile of Christ; the hands that give us back change at a ticket booth may mirror those that soldiers nailed one day to the cross.

Some feature of the crucified face may lurk in every mirror; perhaps the face died, faded away, so that God might be all faces.

Who knows but that tonight we may see it in the labyrinths of dream, and not know tomorrow that we saw it.

Parable of the Palace

That day the Yellow Emperor showed his palace to the poet. Little by little, step by step, they left behind, in long procession, the first westward-facing terraces which, like the jagged hemicycles of an almost unbounded amphitheater, stepped down into a paradise, a garden whose metal mirrors and intertwined hedges of juniper were a prefiguration of the labyrinth. Cheerfully they lost themselves in it—at first as though condescending to a game, but then not without some uneasiness, because its straight *allées* suffered from a very gentle but continuous curvature, so that secretly the avenues were circles. Around midnight, observation of the planets and the opportune sacrifice of a tortoise allowed them to escape the bonds of that region that seemed enchanted, though not to free themselves from that sense of being lost that accompanied them to the end. They wandered next through antechambers and courtyards and libraries, and then through a hexagonal room with a water clock, and one morning, from a tower, they made out a man of stone, whom later they lost sight of forever. In canoes hewn from sandalwood, they crossed many gleaming rivers—or perhaps a single river many times. The imperial entourage would pass and people would fall to their knees and bow their heads to the ground, but one day the courtiers came to an island where one man did not do this, for he had never seen the Celestial Son before, and the executioner had to decapitate him. The eyes of the emperor and poet looked with indifference on black tresses and black dances and golden masks; the real merged and mingled with the dreamed—or the real, rather, was one of the shapes the dream took. It seemed impossible that the earth should be anything but gardens, fountains, architectures, and forms of splendor. Every hundred steps a tower cut the air; to the eye, their color was identical, but the first of them was yellow and the last was scarlet; that was how delicate the gradations were and how long the series.

It was at the foot of the penultimate tower that the poet (who had appeared untouched by the spectacles which all the others had so greatly marveled at) recited the brief composition that we link indissolubly to his name today, the words which, as the most elegant historians never cease repeating, garnered the poet immortality and death. The text has been lost; there are those who believe that it consisted of but a single line; others, of a single word.

What we do know—however incredible it may be—is that within the poem lay the entire enormous palace, whole and to the least detail, with every venerable porcelain it contained and every scene on every porcelain, all the lights and shadows of its twilights, and every forlorn or happy moment of the glorious dynasties of mortals, gods, and dragons that had lived within it through all its endless past. Everyone fell silent; then the emperor spoke. "You have stolen my palace!" he cried, and the executioner's iron scythe mowed down the poet's life.

Others tell the story differently. The world cannot contain two things that are identical; no sooner, they say, had the poet uttered his poem than the palace disappeared, as though in a puff of smoke, wiped from the face of the earth by the final syllable.

Such legends, of course, are simply literary fictions. The poet was the emperor's slave and died a slave; his composition fell into oblivion because it merited oblivion, and his descendants still seek, though they shall never find, the word for the universe.

*Everything and Nothing**

There was no one inside him; behind his face (which even in the bad paintings of the time resembles no other) and his words (which were multitudinous, and of a fantastical and agitated turn) there was no more than a slight chill, a dream someone had failed to dream. At first he thought that everyone was like him, but the surprise and bewilderment of an acquaintance to whom he began to describe that hollowness showed him his error, and also let him know, forever after, that an individual ought not to differ from its species. He thought at one point that books might hold some remedy for his condition, and so he learned the "little Latin and less Greek" that a contemporary would later mention. Then he reflected that what he was looking for might be found in the performance of an elemental ritual of humanity, and so he allowed himself to be initiated by Anne Hathaway one long evening in June.

At twenty-something he went off to London. Instinctively, he had already trained himself to the habit of feigning that he was somebody, so that his "nobodiness" might not be discovered. In London he found the calling he had been predestined to; he became an actor, that person who stands upon a stage and plays at being another person, for an audience of people who play at taking him for that person. The work of a thespian held out a remarkable happiness to him—the first, perhaps, he had ever known; but when the last line was delivered and the last dead man applauded off the stage, the hated taste of unreality would assail him. He would cease being Ferrex or Tamerlane and return to being nobody. Haunted, hounded, he began imagining other heroes, other tragic fables. Thus while his body, in whorehouses and taverns around London, lived its life as body, the soul that lived inside it would be Cæsar, who ignores the admonition of the sibyl, and

Juliet, who hates the lark, and Macbeth, who speaks on the moor with the witches who are also the Fates, the Three Weird Sisters. No one was as many men as that man—that man whose repertoire, like that of the Egyptian Proteus, was all the appearances of being. From time to time he would leave a confession in one corner or another of the work, certain that it would not be deciphered; Richard says that inside himself, he plays the part of many, and Iago says, with curious words, *I am not what I am.* The fundamental identity of living, dreaming, and performing inspired him to famous passages.

For twenty years he inhabited that guided and directed hallucination, but one morning he was overwhelmed with the surfeit and horror of being so many kings that die by the sword and so many unrequited lovers who come together, separate, and melodiously expire. That very day, he decided to sell his theater. Within a week he had returned to his birthplace, where he recovered the trees and the river of his childhood and did not associate them with those others, fabled with mythological allusion and Latin words, that his muse had celebrated. He had to be somebody; he became a retired businessman who'd made a fortune and had an interest in loans, lawsuits, and petty usury. It was in that role that he dictated the arid last will and testament that we know today, from which he deliberately banished every trace of sentiment or literature. Friends from London would visit his retreat, and he would once again play the role of poet for them.

History adds that before or after he died, he discovered himself standing before God, and said to Him: *I, who have been so many men in vain, wish to be* one, *to be myself.* God's voice answered him out of a whirlwind: *I, too, am not I; I dreamed the world as you, Shakespeare, dreamed your own work, and among the forms of my dream are you, who like me are many, yet no one.*

Ragnarök

The images in dreams, wrote Coleridge, figure forth the impressions that our intellect would call causes; we do not feel horror because we are haunted by a sphinx, we dream a sphinx in order to explain the horror that we feel. If that is true, how might a mere chronicling of its forms transmit the stupor, the exultation, the alarms, the dread, and the joy that wove together that night's dream? I shall attempt that chronicle, nonetheless; perhaps the fact that the dream consisted of but a single scene may erase or soften the essential difficulty.

The place was the College of Philosophy and Letters; the hour, nightfall. Everything (as is often the case in dreams) was slightly different; a slight magnification altered things. We chose authorities; I would speak with Pedro Henríquez Ureña,* who in waking life had died many years before. Suddenly, we were dumbfounded by a great noise of demonstrators or street musicians. From the Underworld, we heard the cries of humans and animals. A voice cried: *Here they come!* and then: *The gods! the gods!* Four or five individuals emerged from out of the mob and occupied the dais of the auditorium. Everyone applauded, weeping; it was the gods, returning after a banishment of many centuries. Looming larger than life as they stood upon the dais, their heads thrown back and their chests thrust forward, they haughtily received our homage. One of them was holding a branch (which belonged, no doubt, to the simple botany of dreams); another, with a sweeping gesture, held out a hand that was a claw; one of Janus' faces looked mistrustfully at Thoth's curved beak. Perhaps excited by our applause, one of them, I no longer remember which, burst out in a triumphant, incredibly bitter clucking that was half gargle and half whistle. From that point on, things changed.

It all began with the suspicion (perhaps exaggerated) that the gods were unable to talk. Centuries of a feral life of flight had atrophied that part of them that was human; the moon of Islam and the cross of Rome had been implacable with these fugitives. Beetling brows, yellowed teeth, the sparse beard of a mulatto or a Chinaman, and beastlike dewlaps were testaments to the degeneration of the Olympian line. The clothes they wore were not those of a decorous and honest poverty, but rather of the criminal luxury of the Underworld's gambling dens and houses of ill repute. A carnation bled from a buttonhole; under a tight suitcoat one could discern the outline of a knife. Suddenly, we felt that they were playing their last trump, that they were cunning, ignorant, and cruel, like agèd predators, and that if we allowed ourselves to be swayed by fear or pity, they would wind up destroying us.

We drew our heavy revolvers (suddenly in the dream there were revolvers) and exultantly killed the gods.

Inferno, I, 32

From the half-light of dawn to the half-light of evening, the eyes of a leopard, in the last years of the twelfth century, looked upon a few wooden boards, some vertical iron bars, some varying men and women, a blank wall, and perhaps a stone gutter littered with dry leaves. The leopard did not know, could not know, that it yearned for love and cruelty and the hot pleasure of tearing flesh and a breeze with the scent of deer, but something inside it was suffocating and howling in rebellion, and God spoke to it in a dream: *You shall live and die in this prison, so that a man that I have knowledge of may see you a certain number of times and never forget you and put your figure and your symbol into a poem, which has its exact place in the weft of the universe. You suffer captivity, but you shall have given a word to the poem.* In the dream, God illuminated the animal's rude understanding and the animal grasped the reasons and accepted its fate, but when it awoke there was only an obscure resignation in it, a powerful ignorance, because the machine of the world is exceedingly complex for the simplicity of a savage beast.

Years later, Dante was to die in Ravenna, as unjustified and alone as any other man. In a dream, God told him the secret purpose of his life and work; Dante, astonished, learned at last who he was and what he was, and he blessed the bitternesses of his life. Legend has it that when he awoke, he sensed that he had received and lost an infinite thing, something he would never be able to recover, or even to descry from afar, because the machine of the world is exceedingly complex for the simplicity of men.

Borges and I

It's Borges, the other one, that things happen to. I walk through Buenos Aires and I pause—mechanically now, perhaps—to gaze at the arch of an entryway and its inner door; news of Borges reaches me by mail, or I see his name on a list of academics or in some biographical dictionary. My taste runs to hourglasses, maps, eighteenth-century typefaces, etymologies, the taste of coffee, and the prose of Robert Louis Stevenson; Borges shares those preferences, but in a vain sort of way that turns them into the accoutrements of an actor. It would be an exaggeration to say that our relationship is hostile—I live, I allow myself to live, so that Borges can spin out his literature, and that literature is my justification. I willingly admit that he has written a number of sound pages, but those pages will not save *me,* perhaps because the good in them no longer belongs to any individual, not even to that other man, but rather to language itself, or to tradition. Beyond that, I am doomed—utterly and inevitably—to oblivion, and fleeting moments will be all of me that survives in that other man. Little by little, I have been turning everything over to him, though I know the perverse way he has of distorting and magnifying everything. Spinoza believed that all things wish to go on being what they are—stone wishes eternally to be stone, and tiger, to be tiger. I shall endure in Borges, not in myself (if, indeed, I am anybody at all), but I recognize myself less in his books than in many others', or in the tedious strumming of a guitar. Years ago I tried to free myself from him, and I moved on from the mythologies of the slums and outskirts of the city to games with time and infinity, but those games belong to Borges now, and I shall have to think up other things. So my life is a point-counterpoint, a kind of fugue, and a falling away—and everything winds up being lost to me, and everything falls into oblivion, or into the hands of the other man.

I am not sure which of us it is that's writing this page.

MUSEUM

On Exactitude in Science

. . . In that Empire, the Art of Cartography attained such Perfection that the map of a single Province occupied the entirety of a City, and the map of the Empire, the entirety of a Province. In time, those Unconscionable Maps no longer satisfied, and the Cartographers Guilds struck a Map of the Empire whose size was that of the Empire, and which coincided point for point with it. The following Generations, who were not so fond of the Study of Cartography as their Forebears had been, saw that that vast Map was Useless, and not without some Pitilessness was it, that they delivered it up to the Inclemencies of Sun and Winters. In the Deserts of the West, still today, there are Tattered Ruins of that Map, inhabited by Animals and Beggars; in all the Land there is no other Relic of the Disciplines of Geography.

Suárez Miranda, *Viajes de varones prudentes,* Libro IV, Cap. XLV, Lérida, 1658

In Memoriam, J.F.K.

This bullet is an old one.

In 1897, it was fired at the president of Uruguay by a young man from Montevideo, Avelino Arredondo,* who had spent long weeks without seeing anyone so that the world might know that he acted alone. Thirty years earlier, Lincoln had been murdered by that same ball, by the criminal or magical hand of an actor transformed by the words of Shakespeare into Marcus Brutus, Cæsar's murderer. In the mid-seventeenth century, vengeance had employed it for the assassination of Sweden's Gustavus Adolphus, in the midst of the public hecatomb of a battle.

In earlier times, the bullet had been other things, because Pythagorean metempsychosis is not reserved for humankind alone. It was the silken cord given to viziers in the East, the rifles and bayonets that cut down the defenders of the Alamo, the triangular blade that slit a queen's throat, the wood of the Cross and the dark nails that pierced the flesh of the Redeemer, the poison kept by the Carthaginian chief in an iron ring on his finger, the serene goblet that Socrates drank down one evening.

In the dawn of time it was the stone that Cain hurled at Abel, and in the future it shall be many things that we cannot even imagine today, but that will be able to put an end to men and their wondrous, fragile life.

Afterword

God grant that the essential monotony of this miscellany (which time has compiled, not I, and into which have been bundled long-ago pieces that I've not had the courage to revise, for I wrote them out of a different concept of literature) be less obvious than the geographical and historical diversity of its subjects. Of all the books I have sent to press, none, I think, is as personal as this motley, disorganized anthology, precisely because it abounds in reflections and interpolations. Few things have happened to me, though many things I have read. Or rather, few things have happened to me more worthy of remembering than the philosophy of Schopenhauer or England's verbal music.

A man sets out to draw the world. As the years go by, he peoples a space with images of provinces, kingdoms, mountains, bays, ships, islands, fishes, rooms, instruments, stars, horses, and individuals. A short time before he dies, he discovers that that patient labyrinth of lines traces the lineaments of his own face.

J.L.B.
Buenos Aires, October 31, 1960

In Praise of Darkness

(1969)

Foreword

Without realizing at first that I was doing so, I have devoted my long life to literature, teaching, idleness, the quiet adventures of conversation, philology (which I know very little about), the mysterious habit of Buenos Aires, and the perplexities which not without some arrogance are called metaphysics. Nor has my life been without its friendships, which are what really matter. I don't believe I have a single enemy—if I do, nobody ever told me. The truth is that no one can hurt us except the people we love. Now, at my seventy years of age (the phrase is Whitman's), I send to the press this fifth book of verse.

Carlos Frías has suggested that I take advantage of the foreword to this book to declare my æsthetics. My poverty, my will, resist that suggestion. I do not *have* an æsthetics. Time has taught me a few tricks—avoiding synonyms, the drawback to which is that they suggest imaginary differences; avoiding Hispanicisms, Argentinisms, archaisms, and neologisms; using everyday words rather than shocking ones; inserting circumstantial details, which are now demanded by readers, into my stories; feigning a slight uncertainty, since even though reality is precise, memory isn't; narrating events (this I learned from Kipling and the Icelandic sagas) as though I didn't fully understand them; remembering that tradition, conventions, "the rules," are not an obligation, and that time will surely repeal them—but such tricks (or habits) are most certainly not an æsthetics. Anyway, I don't believe in those formulations that people call "an æsthetics." As a general rule, they are no more than useless abstractions; they vary from author to author and even from text to text, and can never be more than occasional stimuli or tools.

This, as I said, is my fifth book of poetry. It is reasonable to assume that it will be no better or worse than the others. To the mirrors, labyrinths, and swords that my resigned reader will already have been prepared for have been added two new subjects: old age and ethics. Ethics, as we all know, was a constant preoccupation of a certain dear friend that literature brought me, Robert Louis Stevenson. One of the virtues that make me prefer Protestant nations to Catholic ones is their concern for ethics. Milton tried to educate the children in his academy in the knowledge of physics, mathematics, astronomy, and natural sciences; in the mid-seventeenth century Dr. Johnson was to observe that "Prudence and justice are preeminences and virtues which belong to all times and all places; we are perpetually moralists and only sometimes geometers."

In these pages the forms of prose and verse coexist, I believe, without discord. I might cite illustrious antecedents—Boethius' *Consolation of Philosophy*, Chaucer's *Tales*, the *Book of the Thousand Nights and a Night*; I prefer to say that those divergences look to me to be accidental—I hope this book will be read as a book of verse. A volume, *per se*, is not an æsthetic moment, it is one physical object among many; the æsthetic moment can only occur when the volume is written or read. One often hears that free verse is simply a typographical sham; I think there's a basic error in that statement. Beyond the rhythm of a line of verse, its typographical arrangement serves to tell the reader that it's poetic emotion, not information or rationality, that he or she should expect. I once yearned after the long breath line of the Psalms[1] or Walt Whitman; after all these years I now see, a bit melancholically, that I have done no more than alternate between one and another classical meter: the alexandrine, the hendecasyllable, the heptasyllable.

In a certain *milonga* I have attempted, respectfully, to imitate the florid valor of Ascasubi* and the *coplas* of the barrios.

Poetry is no less mysterious than the other elements of the orb. A lucky line here and there should not make us think any higher of ourselves, for such lines are the gift of Chance or the Spirit; only the errors are our own. I

[1]In the Spanish version of this Foreword, I deliberately spelled the word with its initial *p*, which is reprobated by most Peninsular grammarians. The members of the Spanish Royal Academy want to impose their own phonetic inabilities on the New World; they suggest such provincial forms as *neuma* for *pneuma, sicología* for *psicología*, and *síquico* for *psíquico*. They've even taken to prescribing *vikingo* for *viking*. I have a feeling we'll soon be hearing talk of the works of *Kiplingo*.

hope the reader may find in my pages something that merits being remembered; in this world, beauty is so common.

J.L.B.

Buenos Aires, June 24, 1969

The Ethnographer

I was told about the case in Texas, but it had happened in another state. It has a single protagonist (though in every story there are thousands of protagonists, visible and invisible, alive and dead). The man's name, I believe, was Fred Murdock. He was tall, as Americans are; his hair was neither blond nor dark, his features were sharp, and he spoke very little. There was nothing singular about him, not even that feigned singularity that young men affect. He was naturally respectful, and he distrusted neither books nor the men and women who write them. He was at that age when a man doesn't yet know who he is, and so is ready to throw himself into whatever chance puts in his way—Persian mysticism or the unknown origins of Hungarian, algebra or the hazards of war, Puritanism or orgy. At the university, an adviser had interested him in Amerindian languages. Certain esoteric rites still survived in certain tribes out West; one of his professors, an older man, suggested that he go live on a reservation, observe the rites, and discover the secret revealed by the medicine men to the initiates. When he came back, he would have his dissertation, and the university authorities would see that it was published.

Murdock leaped at the suggestion. One of his ancestors had died in the frontier wars; that bygone conflict of his race was now a link. He must have foreseen the difficulties that lay ahead for him; he would have to convince the red men to accept him as one of their own. He set out upon the long adventure. He lived for more than two years on the prairie, sometimes sheltered by adobe walls and sometimes in the open. He rose before dawn, went to bed at sundown, and came to dream in a language that was not that of his fathers. He conditioned his palate to harsh flavors, he covered himself with strange clothing, he forgot his friends and the city, he came to think in a fashion that the logic of his mind rejected. During the first few months of his new education he secretly took notes; later, he tore the notes up—perhaps to avoid drawing suspicion upon himself, perhaps because he no longer needed them. After a period of time (determined upon in advance by certain practices, both spiritual and physical), the priest instructed Murdock to start remembering his dreams, and to recount them to him at daybreak each morning. The young man found that on nights of the full moon he dreamed of buffalo. He reported these recurrent dreams to his teacher; the teacher at last revealed to him the tribe's secret doctrine. One morning, without saying a word to anyone, Murdock left.

In the city, he was homesick for those first evenings on the prairie when, long ago, he had been homesick for the city. He made his way to his professor's office and told him that he knew the secret, but had resolved not to reveal it.

"Are you bound by your oath?" the professor asked.

"That's not the reason," Murdock replied. "I learned something out there that I can't express."

"The English language may not be able to communicate it," the professor suggested.

"That's not it, sir. Now that I possess the secret, I could tell it in a hundred different and even contradictory ways. I don't know how to tell you this, but the secret is beautiful, and science, *our* science, seems mere frivolity to me now."

After a pause he added:

"And anyway, the secret is not as important as the paths that led me to it. Each person has to walk those paths himself."

The professor spoke coldly:

"I will inform the committee of your decision. Are you planning to live among the Indians?"

"No," Murdock answered. "I may not even go back to the prairie. What the men of the prairie taught me is good anywhere and for any circumstances."

That was the essence of their conversation.

Fred married, divorced, and is now one of the librarians at Yale.

Pedro Salvadores

For Juan Murchison

I want to put in writing, perhaps for the first time, one of the strangest and saddest events in the history of my country. The best way to go about it, I believe, is to keep my own part in the telling of the story small, and to suppress all picturesque additions and speculative conjectures.

A man, a woman, and the vast shadow of a dictator* are the story's three protagonists. The man's name was Pedro Salvadores; my grandfather Acevedo was a witness to his existence, a few days or weeks after the Battle of Monte Caseros.* There may have been no real difference between Pedro Salvadores and the common run of mankind, but his fate, the years of it, made him unique. He was a gentleman much like the other gentlemen of his day, with a place in the city and some land (we may imagine) in the country; he was a member of the Unitarian party.* His wife's maiden name was Planes; they lived together on Calle Suipacha, not far from the corner of Temple.* The house in which the events took place was much like the others on the street: the front door, the vestibule, the inner door, the rooms, the shadowy depth of the patios. One night in 1842, Pedro Salvadores and his wife heard the dull sound of hoofbeats coming closer and closer up the dusty street, and the wild huzzahs and imprecations of the horses' riders. But this time the horsemen of the tyrant's posse* did not pass them by. The whooping and shouting became insistent banging on the door. Then, as the men were breaking down the door, Salvadores managed to push the dining table to one side, lift the rug, and hide himself in the cellar. His wife moved the table back into place. The posse burst into the house; they had come to get Salvadores. His wife told them he'd fled—to Montevideo, she told them. They didn't believe her; they lashed her with their whips, smashed all the sky blue china,* and searched the house, but it never occurred to them to lift the rug. They left at midnight, vowing to return.

It is at this point that the story of Pedro Salvadores truly begins. He lived in that cellar for nine years. No matter how often we tell ourselves that years are made of days, and days of hours, and that nine years is an abstraction, an impossible sum, the story still horrifies and appalls. I suspect that in the darkness that his eyes learned to fathom, he came not to think of anything—not even his hatred or his danger. He was simply there, in the cellar. Now and again, echoes of that world he could not enter would reach him from above: his wife's footsteps as she went about her routine, the thump of the water pump and the pail, the pelting of rain in the patio. Every day, too, might be his last.

His wife gradually got rid of all the servants; they were capable of informing on them. She told her family that her husband was in Uruguay. She earned a living for the two of them by sewing for the army. In the course of time she had two children; her family, attributing the children to a lover, repudiated her. After the fall of the tyrant they got down on their knees to her and begged forgiveness.

What, who, was Pedro Salvadores? Was he imprisoned by terror, love, the invisible presence of Buenos Aires, or, in the final analysis, habit? To keep him from leaving her, his wife would give him vague news of conspiracies and victories. Perhaps he was a coward, and his wife faithfully hid from him that she knew that. I picture him in his cellar, perhaps without even an oil lamp, or a book. The darkness would draw him under, into sleep. He would dream, at first, of the dreadful night when the knife would seek the throat, or dream of open streets, or of the plains. Within a few years, he would be incapable of fleeing, and he would dream of the cellar. At first he was a hunted man, a man in danger; later . . . we will never know—a quiet animal in its burrows, or some sort of obscure deity?

All this, until that summer day in 1852 when the dictator Rosas fled the country. It was then that the secret man emerged into the light of day; my grandfather actually spoke with him. Puffy, slack-muscled, and obese, Pedro Salvadores was the color of wax, and he spoke in a faint whisper. The government had confiscated his land; it was never returned to him. I believe he died in poverty.

We see the fate of Pedro Salvadores, like all things, as a symbol of something that we are just on the verge of understanding. . . .

Legend

Cain and Abel came upon each other after Abel's death. They were walking through the desert, and they recognized each other from afar, since both men were very tall. The two brothers sat on the ground, made a fire, and ate. They sat silently, as weary people do when dusk begins to fall. In the sky, a star glimmered, though it had not yet been given a name. In the light of the fire, Cain saw that Abel's forehead bore the mark of the stone, and he dropped the bread he was about to carry to his mouth and asked his brother to forgive him.

"Was it you that killed me, or did I kill you?" Abel answered. "I don't remember anymore; here we are, together, like before."

"Now I know that you have truly forgiven me," Cain said, "because forgetting is forgiving. I, too, will try to forget."

"Yes," said Abel slowly. "So long as remorse lasts, guilt lasts."

A Prayer

Thousands of times, and in both of the languages that are a part of me, my lips have pronounced, and shall go on pronouncing, the Paternoster, yet I only partly understand it. This morning—July 1, 1969—I want to attempt a prayer that is personal, not inherited. I know that such an undertaking demands a sincerity that is more than human. First of all, obviously I am barred from asking for anything. Asking that my eyes not be filled with night would be madness; I know of thousands of people who can see, yet who are not particularly happy, just, or wise. Time's march is a web of causes and effects, and asking for any gift of mercy, however tiny it might be, is to ask that a link be broken in that web of iron, ask that it be *already* broken. No one deserves such a miracle. Nor can I plead that my trespasses be forgiven; forgiveness is the act of another, and only I myself can save me. Forgiveness purifies the offended party, not the offender, who is virtually untouched by it. The freeness of my "free will" is perhaps illusory, but I am able to give, or to dream that I give. I can give courage, which I do not possess; I can give hope, which does not lie within me; I can teach a willingness to learn that which I hardly know myself, or merely glimpse. I want to be remembered less as poet than as friend; I want someone to repeat a cadence from Dunbar or Frost or that man who, at midnight, looked upon that tree that bleeds, the Cross, and to reflect that he heard those words for the first time from my lips. None of the rest matters to me; I hope that oblivion will not long delay. The designs of the universe are unknown to us, but we do know that to think with lucidity and to act with fairness is to aid those designs (which shall never be revealed to us).

I want to die completely; I want to die with this body, my companion.

His End and His Beginning

The death throes done, he lay now alone—alone and broken and rejected—and then he sank into sleep. When he awoke, there awaited him his commonplace habits and the places of his everyday existence. He told himself that he shouldn't think too much about the night before, and, cheered by that resolve, he unhurriedly dressed for work. At the office, he got through his duties passably well, though with that uneasy sense (caused by weariness) of repeating things he'd already done. He seemed to notice that the others turned their eyes away; perhaps they already knew that he was dead. That night the nightmares began; he was left without the slightest memory of them—just the fear that they'd return. In time, that fear prevailed; it came between him and the page he was supposed to write, the books he tried to read. Letters would crawl about on the page like ants; faces, familiar faces, gradually blurred and faded, objects and people slowly abandoned him. His mind seized upon those changing shapes in a frenzy of tenacity.

However odd it may seem, he never suspected the truth; it burst upon him suddenly. He realized that he was unable to remember the shapes, sounds, and colors of his dreams; there were no shapes, colors, or sounds, nor were the dreams dreams. They were his reality, a reality beyond silence and sight, and therefore beyond memory. This realization threw him into even greater consternation than the fact that from the hour of his death he had been struggling in a whirlwind of senseless images. The voices he'd heard had been echoes; the faces he'd seen had been masks; the fingers of his hands had been shadows—vague and insubstantial, true, yet also dear to him, and familiar.

Somehow he sensed that it was his duty to leave all these things behind; now he belonged to this new world, removed from past, present, and future. Little by little this new world surrounded him. He suffered many agonies, journeyed through realms of desperation and loneliness—appalling peregrinations, for they transcended all his previous perceptions, memories, and hopes. All horror lay in their newness and their splendor. He had deserved grace—he had earned it; every second since the moment of his death, he had been in heaven.

Brodie's Report

(1970)

Foreword

Kipling's last stories were no less tortured and labyrinthine than Franz Kafka's or Henry James's, which they unquestionably surpass; in 1885, though, in Lahore, early in his career, Kipling began writing a series of brief tales composed in a plain style, and he published those stories in 1890. Not a few of them—"In the House of Suddhoo,"* "Beyond the Pale," "The Gate of the Hundred Sorrows"—are laconic masterpieces; it has occurred to me from time to time that that which a young man of genius is capable of conceiving and bringing to fruition, a man beginning to get along in years and who knows his craft might, without immodesty, himself attempt. The issue of that reflection is contained in this volume; my readers may judge it for themselves.

I have tried (I am not sure how successfully) to write plain tales. I dare not say they are simple; there is not a simple page, a simple word, on earth—for all pages, all words, predicate the universe, whose most notorious attribute is its complexity. But I do wish to make clear that I am not, nor have I ever been, what used to be called a fabulist or spinner of parables, what these days is called an *auteur engagé*. I do not aspire to be Æsop. My tales, like those of the *Thousand and One Nights*, are intended not to persuade readers, but to entertain and touch them. This intention does not mean that I shut myself, as Solomon's image would have it, into an ivory tower. My convictions with respect to political matters are well known; I have joined the Conservative Party (which act is a form of skepticism), and no one has ever called me a Communist, a nationalist, an anti-Semite, or a supporter of Hormiga Negra* or of Rosas.* I believe that in time we will have reached the point where we will deserve to be free of government. I have never hidden my opinions, even through the difficult years, but I have never allowed them to intrude upon my literary production, either, save that one time when I praised the Six-Day War. The craft is mysterious; our opinions are ephemeral, and I prefer* Plato's theory of the Muse to that of Poe, who argued, or pretended to argue, that the writing of a poem is an operation of the intelligence. (I never cease to be amazed that the Classics professed a Romantic theory while a Romantic poet espoused a Classical one.)

Aside from the text that gives its name to this book (and whose paternity, obviously, can be traced to Lemuel Gulliver's last voyage), my stories are "realistic," to use a term that is fashionable these days. They observe, I believe, all the conventions of the genre (a genre no less convention-ridden than all the others, and one we will soon enough grow tired of, if we are not already). They abound in the circumstantial details that writers are required to invent—details that we can find such splendid examples of in the tenth-century Anglo-Saxon ballad of the Battle of Maldon and the Icelandic sagas that came later. Two of the stories (I will not say which ones) can be opened with the same fantastic key. The curious reader will perceive certain secret affinities among the tales. A mere handful of arguments have haunted me all these years; I am decidedly monotonous.

For the general outline of the story called "The Gospel According to Mark," the best story of the volume, I am indebted to a dream that Hugo Ramírez Moroni* had one night; I fear I may have spoiled the dream with the changes that my imagination (or my reason) deemed it needed. But then literature is naught but guided dreaming, anyway.

I have renounced the shocks of a baroque style as well as those afforded by unforeseen or unexpected endings. I have, in short, preferred to prepare my readers for my endings, rather than to astound them. For many years I believed that it would be my fortune to achieve literature through variations and novelties; now that I am seventy years old I think I have found my own voice. A word changed here or there will neither spoil nor improve what I dictate, except when those alterations succeed in leavening a heavy sentence or softening an emphasis. Each language is a tradition, each word a shared symbol; the changes that an innovator may make are trifling—we should remember the dazzling but often unreadable work of a Mallarmé or a Joyce. These reasonable, rational arguments are quite likely the result of weariness; advanced age has taught me to resign myself to being Borges.

I care little about the Diccionario de la Real Academia (*"dont chaque édition fait regretter la précédente,"* as Paul Grossac glumly remarked), and equally little about these tiresome dictionaries of Argentinisms. All of them—on both this side of the Atlantic and the other—tend to stress the differences between our Spanish and theirs, and thereby to disintegrate the language. I recall that when somebody or other scolded Roberto Arlt because he knew so little about Lunfardo, the putative language of the Buenos Aires underworld, he answered his critic in this way: "I was raised in Villa Luro, among thugs and bullies and poor people, and I really had very little time to study the way they talked." Lunfardo is, in fact, a literary put-on, a language invented by composers of tangos and writers of comedies for the stage and screen; the lowlifes and thugs themselves, those who lived in the tough, ragged outskirts of the city and who are supposed to have created it and used it in their daily lives, actually know nothing about it, except what phonograph records may have taught them.

I have set my stories at some distance in both time and space. Imagination has more freedom to work, that way. Today, in 1970, who can recall exactly what those outskirts of Palermo or Lomas were like at the end of the nineteenth century? Incredible as it may seem, there are certain punctilious men and women who act as a sort of "trivia police." They will note, for example, that Martín Fierro would have talked about a *bag* of bones, not a *sack*, and they will criticize (perhaps unfairly, perhaps not) the golden-pink coat of a certain horse famous in our literature.*

God save you, reader, from long forewords.—The quotation is from Quevedo, who (not to commit an anachronism that would have been caught sooner or later) never read the prefaces of Shaw.

J.L.B.
Buenos Aires, April 19, 1970

The Interloper

2 Reyes 1:26*

They say (though it seems unlikely) that Eduardo, the younger of the Nelson brothers, told the story in eighteen-ninety-something at the wake for Cristián, the elder, who had died of natural causes in the district of Morón. What is unquestionably true is that as the cups of *mate* went their rounds in the course of that long night when there was nothing else to do, somebody heard it from *someone* and later repeated it to Santiago Dabove, from whom I first heard it. I was told the story again, years later, in Turdera, where it had actually occurred. This second, somewhat less succinct version corroborated the essential details of Santiago's, with the small divergences and variations one always expects. I commit it to writing now because I believe it affords us (though I may of course be mistaken) a brief and tragic window on the sort of men that once fought their knife fights and lived their harsh lives in the tough neighborhoods on the outskirts of Buenos Aires. I will tell the story conscientiously, though I can foresee myself yielding to the literary temptation to heighten or insert the occasional small detail.

· · ·

In Turdera they were known as the Nilsens. I was told by the parish priest that his predecessor recalled having seen, not without some surprise, a worn black-letter Bible in the house; on its last pages he had glimpsed handwritten names and dates. That black-bound volume was the only book they owned—its troubled chronicle of the Nilsens is now lost, as everything will one day be lost. The big ramshackle house (which is no longer standing) was of unplastered brick; from the entryway one could see a first interior patio of red tiles and another, farther back, of packed earth. Few people, however, entered that entryway; the Nilsens defended their solitude. They slept on cots in dilapidated and unfurnished bedrooms; their luxuries were horses, saddles, short-bladed daggers, flashy Saturday night clothes, and the alcohol that made them belligerent. I know that they were tall, with reddish hair—the blood of Denmark or Ireland (countries whose names they probably never heard) flowed in the veins of those two criollos.* The neighborhood was afraid of the Redheads, as they were called; it is not impossible that one or another killing had been their work. Once they had stood shoulder to shoulder and fought it out with the police. People say the younger brother had once traded words with Juan Iberra and not gone away with the worst of it—which according to those who knew about such things was saying a great deal. They were cattle drivers, teamsters, horse thieves, and sometime cardsharps. They had a reputation for tightfistedness, except when drinking and gambling made them generous. About their kinspeople, nothing is known even of where they came from. They owned an oxcart and a yoke of oxen.

Physically, they were unlike the toughs that gave Costa Brava* its reputation for lawlessness. That, and things we have no certain knowledge of, may help us understand how close they were. Having a falling-out with one of them was earning yourself two enemies.

The Nilsens were men who sought the pleasures of the flesh, but their romantic episodes had so far been on porches or in entryways or houses of ill repute. There was a good deal of talk, therefore, when Cristián carried Juliana Burgos home to live with him. The truth was, in doing so he had gained a servant, but it was also true that he lavished ghastly trinkets upon her and showed her off at parties—those shabby little tenement house parties where certain tango steps (the *quebrada* and the *corte,* for example) were considered indecent and weren't allowed, and where couples still danced "with a good bit of daylight between them," as the saying went. Juliana had almond eyes and dark skin; whenever someone looked at her she smiled. In a humble neighborhood, where work and neglect make women old before their time, she was not bad-looking.

At first, Eduardo lived with them. Then he went off to Arrecifes on some business, and on his return he brought a girl home with him, too; he had picked her up on the road. Within a few days he threw her out. He grew ever more sullen and bad-tempered; he would get drunk by himself in the corner general-store-and-bar and would not answer when someone spoke to him. He was in love with Cristián's woman. The neighborhood (which probably knew that before he himself did) sensed with secret and perfidious delight the latent rivalry that throbbed between the brothers.

One night, coming home late from a bout of drinking, Eduardo saw Cristián's black horse tied to the post at the front of the house. Cristián was sitting waiting for him in the patio; he was wearing his best clothes. The woman was walking about the house with her *mate* in her hand.

"I'm going off to that bust over at Farías' place. There's Juliana—if you want her, use her."

His tone was half-peremptory, half-cordial. Eduardo stood for a moment looking at him; he didn't know what to do. Cristián stood up, said good-bye to Eduardo—not to Juliana, who was a mere thing—mounted his horse, and rode off at an unhurried trot.

From that night onward, they shared her. No one will ever know the details of that sordid *ménage,* which outraged the neighborhood's sense of decency. The arrangement went well for a few weeks, but it couldn't last. Never, when the three of them were in the house, did the brothers speak Juliana's name, even to call her, but they looked for—and found—reasons to disagree. They bickered over the sale price of a load of skins, but it was something else they were really arguing about. Cristián's tendency was to raise his voice; Eduardo's, to fall silent. Without knowing it, they were jealous of each other. In those hard-bitten outskirts of the city, a man didn't say, nor was it said about him, that a woman mattered to him (beyond desire and ownership), but the two brothers were in fact in love. They felt humiliated by that, somehow.

One afternoon in the Lomas town plaza, Eduardo ran into Juan Iberra, who congratulated him on that beauty he'd found himself. It was then, I think, that Eduardo gave him a tongue-lashing. Nobody, in Eduardo's presence, was going to make Cristián the butt of such jokes.

The woman saw to the needs of both brothers with beastlike submissiveness, although she couldn't hide some preference for the younger, who had not refused to take part in the arrangement but hadn't initiated it, either.

One day, the brothers ordered Juliana to take two chairs out into the first patio and then make herself scarce; the two of them needed to talk. She was expecting a long talk, so she lay down for her siesta, but soon they called her back. They had her put everything she owned, even the rosary of glass beads and the little crucifix her mother had left her, in a sack. Without a word of explanation, they loaded her onto the oxcart and set off on a tedious and silent journey. It had rained; the roads were heavy, and it was sometime around five in the morning when they finally reached Morón. There, they woke up the madam of a whorehouse and offered to sell her Juliana. The deal was struck; Cristián took the money, and divided it later with Eduardo.

Back in Turdera, the Nilsens, who had been entangled in the thicket (which was also the routine) of that monstrous love, tried to take up their old life as men among men. They returned to their games of *truco,* their cockfights, their casual binges. They thought, once in a while, perhaps, that they were saved, but then, separately, they began to take unexplained (or overexplained) absences. Shortly before the end of the year, Eduardo announced that he had business in the capital, and he rode away. When he had gone, Cristián took the road to Morón; there, tied to the hitching post of the house which the story would lead us to expect, was Eduardo's pinto. Cristián went in; Eduardo was inside, waiting his turn.

Cristían, it seems, said to him. "If we keep on this way much longer, we're going to wear out the horses. Maybe we ought to have her where we can get at her."

He spoke to the madam, pulled some coins out of his purse, and they took Juliana away with them. She rode with Cristián; Eduardo put spurs to his palomino so he wouldn't have to see them.

They went back to the old arrangement. Their abominable solution had failed; both of them had given in to the temptation to cheat. Cain lurked about, but the love between the Nilsens was great (who can say what hardships and dangers they had shared!) and they chose to take their exasperation out on others: a stranger—the dogs—Juliana, who had introduced the seed of discord.

The month of March was nearing its close but the heat dragged on relentlessly. One Sunday (on Sunday people tended to call it a day early), Eduardo, who was coming home from the bar, saw that Cristián was yoking up the oxen.

"Come on," Cristián said, "we've got to take some skins over to the Nigger's place. I've already loaded them up—we can go in the cool of the evening."

The Nigger's store lay a little south of the Nilsens' place, I believe: they took the Troop Road, then turned off onto a road that was not so heavily traveled. The countryside grew larger and larger as the night came on.

They were driving along beside a field covered in dried-out straw; Cristián threw out the cigar he had lighted and stopped the oxcart.

"Let's go to work, brother. The buzzards'll come in to clean up after us. I killed 'er today. We'll leave 'er here, her and her fancy clothes. She won't cause any more hurt."

Almost weeping, they embraced. Now they were linked by yet another bond: the woman grievously sacrificed, and the obligation to forget her.

Unworthy

The picture of the city that we carry in our mind is always slightly out of date. The café has degenerated into a bar; the vestibule that allowed us a glimpse of patio and grapevine is now a blurred hallway with an elevator down at the far end. Thus, for years I thought that a certain bookstore, the Librería Buenos Aires, would be awaiting me at a certain point along Calle Talcahuano, but then one morning I discovered that an antiques shop had taken the bookstore's place, and I was told that don Santiago Fischbein, the owner of the bookstore, had died. Fischbein had tended toward the obese; his features are not as clear in my memory as our long conversations are. Firmly yet coolly he would condemn Zionism—it would make the Jew an ordinary man, he said, tied like all other men to a single tradition and a single country, and bereft of the complexities and discords that now enrich him. I recall that he once told me that a new edition of the works of Baruch Spinoza was being prepared, which would banish all that Euclidean apparatus that makes Spinoza's work so difficult to read yet at the same time imparts an illusory sense of rigor to the fantastic theory. Fischbein showed me (though he refused to sell me) a curious copy of Rosenroth's *Kabbala Denudata,* but my library does contain some books by Ginsburg and Waite that bear Fischbein's seal.

One afternoon when the two of us were alone, he confided to me an episode of his life, and today I can tell it. I will change the occasional detail—as is only to be expected.

· · ·

I am going to tell you about something (Fischbein began) that I have never told anyone before. My wife Ana doesn't know about this, nor do my closest friends. It happened so many years ago that it no longer feels like my own experience. Maybe you can use it for a story—no doubt you'll endow it with a knife fight or two. I don't know whether I've ever mentioned that I'm from Entre Ríos. I won't tell you that we were Jewish gauchos—there were never any Jewish gauchos. We were merchants and small farmers. I was born in Urdinarrain, which I only barely remember; when my parents came to Buenos Aires, to open a shop, I was just a little boy. The Maldonado* was a few blocks from us, and then came the empty lots.

Carlyle wrote that men need heroes. Grosso's *History* suggested that San Martín might be a fit object of worship, but all I ever saw in San Martín was a soldier who'd waged war in Chile and who'd now become a bronze statue and given his name to a plaza. Chance dealt me a very different hero, to the misfortune of us both: Francisco Ferrari. This is probably the first time you've ever heard of him.

Our neighborhood was not a bad one, the way Los Corrales and El Bajo were said to be, but every corner grocery-store-and-bar had its gang of toughs. Ferrari hung out in the one at Triunvirato and Thames. That was where the incident happened that led me to be one of his followers. I'd gone in to buy some yerba for the *mate.* A stranger with long hair and a mustache came in and ordered a gin.

"Say"—Ferrari's voice was as smooth as silk—"didn't I see you last night at the dance at Juliana's? Where're you from?"

"San Cristóbal," the other man replied.

"Well, I'll tell you for your own good," Ferrari said to him, "you ought to stay up there. There are people in this neighborhood that are liable to give you a hard time."

The man from San Cristóbal left, mustache and all. He may have been no less a man than Ferrari, but he knew he was up against the whole gang.

From that afternoon on, Francisco Ferrari was the hero that my fifteen-year-old heart yearned for. He had black hair and was rather tall, good-looking—handsome in the style of those days. He always wore black. It was a second episode that actually brought us together. I was walking along with my mother and my aunt when we came upon some street toughs, and one of them said loudly to the others:

"Let the old hens through. Meat's too gristly to eat."

I didn't know what to do. But Ferrari, who was just coming out of his house, stepped in. He stood face to face with one who'd spoken, and he said:

"If you boys feel like picking a fight with somebody, why don't you pick a fight with me?"

He walked down the line, slowly, one by one, but nobody said a word.

They knew him. He shrugged his shoulders, waved at us, and walked away. But before he left, he said to me:

"If you're not doing anything later on, stop by the joint."

I stood there unnerved and shaken. Sarah, my aunt, issued her verdict: "A gentleman that demands respect for ladies."

To save me from the spot that put me in, my mother corrected her:

"I would say, rather, a ruffian who won't allow competition."

I don't know how to explain it to you. Today I've carved out a place for myself. I have this bookstore that I enjoy and whose books I read; I have friendships, like ours; I have my wife and children; I've joined the Socialist Party—I'm a good Argentine and a good Jew. I am respected and respectable. The man you see now is almost bald; at that time I was a poor Jewish kid with red hair in a tough neighborhood on the outskirts of the city. People looked askance at me. I tried, as all young fellows do, to be like everyone else. I had started calling myself Santiago* to make the Jacob go away, but there was nothing I could do about the Fischbein. We all come to resemble the image others have of us; I sensed people's contempt for me, and I felt contempt for myself as well. At that time, and especially in that setting, it was important to be brave; I knew myself to be a coward. Women intimidated me; deep down, I was ashamed of my fainthearted chastity. I had no friends my own age.

I didn't go to the corner bar that night. I wish I'd never gone. But little by little I became convinced that the invitation was an order. One Saturday after dinner, I went in.

Ferrari was presiding over one of the tables. I knew the others' faces; there were probably seven, all told. Ferrari was the oldest one there, except for one old man of few words, and weary ones, whose name is the only one that from my memory has not faded: don Eliseo Amaro. A knife scar crossed his face, which was very broad and slack. I learned sometime later that he'd once been in prison for something. . . .

Ferrari had me sit at his left; don Eliseo had to change seats. I was nervous. I was afraid Ferrari would make some allusion to the unfortunate incident of a few days before, you see. But nothing of the sort happened; they talked about women, cards, elections, an itinerant singer that was supposed to come but never did—the things going on in the neighborhood. At first it was hard for them to swallow the little red-haired Jewish kid; they finally did, though, because Ferrari wanted it that way. In spite of their names, which were mostly Italian, they all felt themselves (and were felt to be) native Argentines, even gauchos. Some were teamsters or cart drivers, and there may even have been a butcher; their work with animals gave them a bond with the countrypeople. I suspect that they wished more than anything that they had been born Juan Moreira.* They wound up calling me Little Sheeny,* but there was no contempt in the nickname. I learned from those men how to smoke, and other things.

One night in one of the houses on Calle Junín,* someone asked me if I wasn't a friend of Francisco Ferrari's. I shook my head—I felt I would be almost bragging if I said yes.

The police came into the bar one night and frisked everyone. Several of us were taken to the police station—but they didn't mess with Ferrari. Two weeks later the scene was repeated; this second time, they arrested Ferrari too. He had a dagger in his belt. He may have fallen out of favor with the ward boss.

Today I see Ferrari as a poor kid misguided and betrayed; at the time, in my eyes, a god he was.

Friendship, you know, is as mysterious as love or any other state of this confusion we call life. In fact, I have sometimes suspected that the only thing that holds no mystery is happiness, because it is its own justification. However that may be, the fact was that Francisco Ferrari, the daring, strong Ferrari, felt a sense of friendship for me, contemptible me. I felt he was mistaken, that I was not worthy of that friendship. I tried to avoid him, but he wouldn't let me. My anxiety was made worse by my mother's disapproval; she could not resign herself to my associating with what she called "the riffraff," nor to the fact that I'd begun to ape them. The essential element in the story I am telling you, though, is my relationship with Ferrari, not the sordid events themselves, which I do not now regret. "So long as regret lasts, guilt lasts."

One night I came into the bar to find the old man, don Eliseo, who had taken his place again beside Ferrari, in whispered conversation with him. They were plotting something. From the other end of the table, I thought I heard the name Weidemann—Weidemann's weaving mill stood on the outskirts of the neighborhood. In a few minutes Ferrari and don Eliseo sent me off to have a look around the factory. I was given no explanation, but I was told to pay special attention to the doors. Night was falling when I crossed the Maldonado and the railroad tracks. I recall a few scattered houses, a stand of willow trees, and vacant lots. The factory was new, but it had a solitary, seedy look about it; in my memory now, its reddish color mingles with the sunset. There was a fence around it. Besides the main door, there were two doors in back, facing south, that opened directly into the workshops.

I confess it took me some time to grasp what I imagine you've already grasped. I made my report, which one of the other kids corroborated—his sister worked in the factory. If the gang had missed a Saturday night at the bar, everyone would have remembered, so Ferrari decided the robbery would take place the next Friday. I was to be the lookout. Meanwhile, it was best that no one see us together.

When we were alone together in the street outside, I asked Ferrari whether he really trusted me with this mission.

"Yes," he said. "I know you'll comport yourself like a man."

I slept well that night, and the nights that followed as well. On Wednesday I told my mother I was going downtown to see a new cowboy movie. I put on the best clothes I owned and set off for Calle Moreno. The trip on the streetcar was a long one. At the police station they made me wait, but finally one of the clerks, a man named Eald or Alt, would see me. I told him I had come to discuss a confidential matter. He told me I could speak freely. I told him what Ferrari was planning to do. I was astounded that the name was unknown to him; it was another thing when I mentioned don Eliseo.

"Ah!" he said, "he was one of the Uruguayan's gang."

Eald or Alt sent for another officer, one assigned to my precinct, and the two of them consulted. One of them asked me, not with sarcasm:

"Are you making this accusation because you think you're a good citizen? Is that it?"

I didn't feel he'd understand, so I answered.

"Yes, sir. I am a good Argentine."

They told me to carry out the orders the leader of my gang had given me, all except the part about whistling when I saw the police coming. As I was leaving, one of them warned me:

"Be careful. You know what happens to squealers."

Police officers love to show off their Lunfardo,* like fourth graders.

"I hope they kill me," I answered. "It's the best thing that could happen to me."

Beginning early Friday morning and all throughout that day, I was filled with a sense of relief that the day had come at last, and of remorse at feeling no remorse whatever. The hours seemed endless. I barely touched my food. At ten that night we began gathering, less than a block from the factory. There was one of us that didn't come; don Eliseo said there was always one washout. It occurred to me that the blame for what was to happen would fall on the absent man. It was about to rain. I was afraid that one of the others might stay behind with me, but I was left by myself at one of the back doors. Pretty soon the police came, an officer and several patrolmen. They came on foot, for stealth; they had left their horses in a field. Ferrari had forced the factory door, so the police were able to slip inside without a sound. Then I was stunned to hear four shots. There inside, in the darkness, I thought, they were killing each other. Then I saw the police come out with the men in handcuffs. Then two more policemen emerged, dragging the bodies of Francisco Ferrari and don Eliseo Amaro, who'd been shot at point-blank range. In their report the police said the robbers had failed to halt when they were ordered, and that Ferrari and don Eliseo had fired the first shots. I knew that was a lie, because I had never seen either of them with a revolver. The police had taken advantage of the occasion to settle an old score. Days later, I was told that Ferrari tried to get away, but one shot was all it took. The newspapers, of course, made him the hero that perhaps he never was, but that I had dreamed of.

I was arrested with the others, but a short while later they let me go.

The Story from Rosendo Juárez

It was about eleven o'clock one night; I had gone into the old-fashioned general-store-and-bar, which is now simply a bar, on the corner of Bolívar and Venezuela.* As I went in, I noticed that over in a corner, sitting at one of the little tables, was a man I had never seen before. He hissed to catch my eye and motioned me to come over. He must have looked like a man that one didn't want to cross, because I went at once toward his table. I felt, inexplicably, that he had been sitting there for some time, in that chair, before that empty glass. He was neither tall nor short; he looked like an honest craftsman, or perhaps an old-fashioned country fellow. His sparse mustache was grizzled. A bit stiff, as Porteños tend to be, he had not taken off his neck scarf.* He offered to buy me a drink; I sat down and we chatted. All this happened in nineteen-thirty-something.

"You've heard of me, sir, though we've never met," the man began, "but I know you. My name is Rosendo Juárez. It was Nicolás Paredes, no doubt, God rest his soul, that told you about me. That old man was something. I'll tell you—the stories he'd tell. . . . Not so as to fool anyone, of course—just to be entertaining. But since you and I are here with nothing else on our hands just now, I'd like to tell you what really happened that night . . . the night the Yardmaster was murdered. You've put the story in a novel,* sir—and I'm hardly qualified to judge that novel—but I want you to know the truth behind the lies you wrote."

He paused, as though to put his recollections in order, and then he began. . . .

. . .

Things happen to a man, you see, and a man only understands them as the years go by. What happened to me that night had been waiting to happen for a long time. I was brought up in the neighborhood of the Maldonado,* out beyond Floresta. It was one big open sewage ditch back then, if you know what I mean, but fortunately they've run sewer lines in there now. I've always been of the opinion that nobody has the right to stand in the way of progress. You just do the best you can with the hand you're dealt. . . .

It never occurred to me to find out the name of the father that begot me. Clementina Juárez, my mother, was a good honest woman that earned her living with her iron. If you were to ask me, I'd say she was from Entre Ríos or the Banda Oriental, what people now call Uruguay; be that as it may, she would always talk about her relatives over in Uruguay, in Concepción. For myself, I grew up the best I could. I learned to knife fight with the other boys, using a charred piece of stick. That was before we were all taken over by soccer, which back at that time was still just something the English did.

Anyway, while I was sitting in the bar one night, this fellow named Garmendia started trying to pick a fight with me. I ignored him for a while—playing deaf, you might say—but this Garmendia, who was feeling his liquor, kept egging me on. We finally took it outside; out on the sidewalk, Garmendia turned back a second, pushed the door open again a little, and announced—"Not to worry, boys, I'll be right back."

I had borrowed a knife. We walked down toward the Maldonado, slow, watching each other. He was a few years older than I was; he and I had practiced knife fighting together lots of times, and I had a feeling I was going to get positively gutted. I was walking down the right-hand side of the alley, and him down the left. Suddenly, he tripped over some big chunks of cement that were lying there. The second he tripped, I jumped him, almost without thinking about it. I cut his cheek open with one slash, then we locked together—there was a second when anything could've happened—and then I stabbed him once, which was all it took. . . . It was only sometime later that I realized he'd left his mark on me, too—scratches, though, that was about it. I learned that night that it isn't hard to kill a man, or get killed yourself. The creek was down; to keep the body from being found too soon, I half-hid it behind a brick kiln. I was so stunned I suppose I just stopped thinking, because I slipped off the ring Garmendia always wore and put it on. Then I straightened my hat and went back to the bar. I walked in as easy as you please.

"Looks like it's me that's come back," I said.

I ordered a shot of brandy, and the truth is, I needed it. That was when somebody pointed out the bloodstain.

That night I tossed and turned on my bunk all night; I didn't fall asleep till nearly dawn. About the time of early mass, two cops came looking for me. You should have seen the way my mother carried on, may she rest in peace, poor thing. I was dragged off like a criminal. Two days and two nights I sat in that stinking cell. Nobody came to visit me—except for Luis Irala, a true friend if ever there was one. But they wouldn't let him see me. Then one morning the captain sent for me. He was sitting there in his chair; he didn't even look at me at first, but he did speak.

"So you put Garmendia out of his misery?" he said.

"If you say so," I answered.

"It's 'sir' to you. And we'll have no ducking or dodging, now. Here are the statements from the witnesses, and here's the ring that was found in your house. Just sign the confession and get this over with."

He dipped the pen in the inkwell and handed it to me.

"Let me think about this, captain. —Sir," I added.

"I'll give you twenty-four hours to think about it real good, in your very own cell. I won't rush you. But if you decide not to see things in a reasonable way, you'd best start getting used to the idea of a vacation down on Calle Las Heras."

As you might imagine, I didn't understand that right away.

"If you decide to come around, you'll just be in for a few days. I'll let you go—don Nicolás Paredes has promised me he'll fix it for you."

But it was *ten* days. I'd almost given up hope when they finally remembered me. I signed what they put in front of me to sign and one of the cops took me over to Calle Cabrera. . . .*

There were horses tied to the hitching post, and standing out on the porch and all inside the place there were more people than a Saturday night at the whorehouse. It looked like a party committee headquarters. Don Nicolás, who was sipping at a *mate,* finally called me over. As calm as you please, he told me he was going to send me out to Morón, where they were setting up for the elections. He told me to look up a certain Sr. Laferrer; he'd try me out, he said. The letter I was to take was written by a kid in black that wrote poems* about tenement houses and riffraff—or anyway, that's what I was told. I can't imagine that educated people would be much interested in that sort of thing, much less if it's told in poetry. Anyway, I thanked Paredes for the favor, and I left. The cop didn't stay so infernally glued to me on the way back.

So it all turned out for the best. Providence knows what it's doing. Garmendia's killing, which at first had got me in such hot water, was now starting to open doors for me. Of course the cops had me over a barrel—if I didn't work out, if I didn't toe the line for the party, I'd be hauled in again. But I'd got some heart back, and I had faith in myself.

Laferrer warned me right off that I was going to have to walk the straight and narrow with him, but if I did, he said, he might make me his bodyguard. The work I did for 'em was all anyone could ask. In Morón, and later on in the neighborhood too, I gradually won my bosses' trust. The police and the party gradually spread the word that I was a man to be reckoned with; I was an important cog in the wheels of the elections in Buenos Aires, and out in the province too. Elections were fierce back then; I won't bore you, señor, with stories about the blood that would be shed. I did all I could to make life hard on the radicals, though to this day they're still riding on Alem's coattails. But as I say, there was no man that didn't show me respect. I got myself a woman, La Lujanera we called her, and a handsome copper sorrel. For years I pretended to be some kind of Moreira*—who in his day was probably imitating some other stage show gaucho. I played a lot of cards and drank a lot of absinthe. . . .

We old folks talk and talk and talk, I know, but I'm coming to what I wanted to tell you. I don't know if I mentioned Luis Irala. A true friend, the likes of which you'll not often find. . . . He was getting on in years when I knew him, and he'd never been afraid of hard work; for some reason he took a liking to me. He'd never set foot in a committee room—he earned his living carpentering. He didn't stick his nose in anybody else's business, and he didn't let anybody stick their nose in his. One morning he came to see me.

"I guess you've heard Casilda left me," he said. "Rufino Aguilera is the man that took her away from me."

I'd had dealings with that particular individual in Morón.

"I know Rufino," I told him. "I'd have to say that of all the Aguileras, he's the least disgusting."

"Disgusting or not, I've got a bone to pick with him."

I thought for a minute.

"Listen," I finally told him, "nobody takes anything away from anybody. If Casilda left you, it's because it's Rufino she wants, and she's not interested in you."

"But what'll people say? That I'm yellow? That I don't stand up to a man that wrongs me?"

"My advice to you is not to go looking for trouble because of what people might say, let alone because of a woman that doesn't love you anymore."

"I couldn't care less about her," he said. "A man that thinks longer than five minutes running about a woman is no man, he's a pansy. And Casilda's heartless, anyway. The last night we spent together she told me I was getting old."

"She was telling you the truth."

"And it hurts, but it's beside the point—Rufino's the one I'm after now."

"You want to be careful there," I told him. "I've seen Rufino in action, in the Merlo elections. He's like greased lightning."

"You think I'm afraid of Rufino Aguilera?"

"I know you're not afraid of him, but think about it—one of two things will happen: either you kill him and you get sent off to stir, or he kills you and you get sent off to Chacarita."*

"One of two things. So tell me, what would you do in my place?"

"I don't know, but then I'm not exactly the best example to follow. I'm a guy that to get his backside out of jail has turned into a gorilla for the party."

"I'm not planning to turn into a gorilla for the party, I'm planning to collect a debt a man owes me."

"You mean you're going to stake your peace of mind on a stranger you've never met and a woman you don't even love anymore?"

But Luis Irala wasn't interested in hearing what I had to say, so he left. The next day we heard that he'd picked a fight with Rufino in some bar over in Morón and that Rufino had killed him.

He went off to get killed, and he got himself killed right honorably, too—man to man. I'd done the best I could, I'd given him a friend's advice, but I still felt guilty.

A few days after the wake, I went to the cockfights. I'd never been all that keen on cockfights, but that Sunday, I'll tell you the truth, they made me sick. What in the world's wrong with those animals, I thought, that they tear each other to pieces this way, for no good reason?

The night of this story I'm telling you, the night of the end of the story, the boys and I had all gone to a dance over at the place that a black woman we called La Parda ran. Funny—all these years, and I still remember the flowered dress La Lujanera was wearing that night. . . . The party was out in the patio. There was the usual drunk trying to pick a fight, but I made sure things went the way they were supposed to go. It was early, couldn't have been midnight yet, when the strangers showed up. One of them—they called him the Yardmaster, and he was stabbed in the back and killed that very night, just the way you wrote it, sir—anyway, this one fellow bought a round of drinks for the house. By coincidence this Yardmaster and I were dead ringers for each other. He had something up his sleeve that night: he came up to me and started laying it on pretty thick—he was from up north, he said, and he'd been hearing about me. He couldn't say enough about my reputation. I let him talk, but I was beginning to suspect what was coming. He was hitting the gin hard, too, and I figured it was to get his courage up—and sure enough, pretty soon he challenged me to a fight. That was when it happened—what nobody wants to understand. I looked at that swaggering drunk just spoiling for a fight, and it was like I was looking at myself in a mirror, and all of a sudden I was ashamed of myself. I wasn't afraid of him; if I had been, I might've gone outside and fought him. I just stood there. This other guy, this Yardmaster, who by now had his face about this far from mine, raised his voice so everybody could hear him:

"You know what's wrong with you? You're yellow, that's what's wrong with you!"

"That may be," I said. "I can live with being called yellow. You can tell people you called me a son of a whore, too, and say I let you spit in my face. Now then, does that make you feel better?"

La Lujanera slipped her hand up my sleeve and pulled out the knife I always carried there and slipped it into my hand. And to make sure I got the message, she also said, "Rosendo, I think you're needing this." Her eyes were blazing.

I dropped the knife and walked out—taking my time about it. People stepped back to make way for me. They couldn't believe their eyes. What did I care what they thought.

To get out of that life, I moved over to Uruguay and became an oxcart driver. Since I came back, I've made my place here. San Telmo* has always been a peaceful place to live.

The Encounter

For Susana Bombal

Those who read the news each morning do so simply to forget it again, or for the sake of the evening's conversation, and so it should surprise no one that people no longer remember, or remember as though in a dream, the once-famous and much-discussed case of Maneco Uriarte and a man named Duncan. Of course the event took place in 1910, the year of the comet and the Centennial, and we have had and lost so many things since then. . . . The protagonists are dead now; those who were witness to the event swore an oath of solemn silence. I too raised my hand to swear, and I felt, with all the romantic seriousness of my nine or ten years, the gravity of that rite. I can't say whether the others noticed that I gave my word; I can't say whether they kept their own. However that may be, this is the story—with the inevitable changes that time, and good (or bad) literature, occasion.

. . .

That evening, my cousin Lafinur had taken me to an *asado,* one of those gatherings of men with the roasting of the fatted calf (or lamb, as it turned out to be), at a country place called Los Laureles. I cannot describe the topography; we should picture a town in the north of the country—peaceful and shady, and sloping down gently toward the river—rather than some flat, sprawling city. The journey by train lasted long enough for me to find it boring, but childhood's time, as we all know, flows slowly. Dusk had begun to settle when we drove through the gate to the large country house. There, I sensed, were the ancient elemental things: the smell of the meat as it turned golden on the spit, the trees, the dogs, the dry branches, the fire that brings men together.

There were no more than a dozen guests, all adults. (The oldest, I discovered later, was not yet thirty.) They were learnèd, I soon realized, in subjects that to this day I am unworthy of: racehorses, tailoring, automobiles, notoriously expensive women. No one disturbed my shyness, no one paid any mind to me. The lamb, prepared with slow skillfulness by one of the peons that worked on the estate, held us long in the dining room. The dates of the wines were discussed. There was a guitar; my cousin, I think I recall, sang Elías Regules' *La tapera* and *El gaucho* and a few *décimas* in Lunfardo,* which was *de rigueur* back then—verses about a knife fight in one of those houses on Calle Junín.* Coffee was brought in, and cigars. Not a word about heading back home. I felt, as Lugones once put it, "the fear of the lateness of the hour." I couldn't bring myself to look at the clock. To hide the loneliness I felt at being a boy among men, I drank down, without much pleasure, a glass or two of wine. Suddenly, Uriarte loudly challenged Duncan to a game of poker, just the two of them, *mano a mano.* Someone objected that two-handed poker usually was a sorry sort of game, and suggested a table of four. Duncan was in favor of that, but Uriarte, with an obstinacy that I didn't understand (and didn't try to), insisted that it be just the two of them. Outside of *truco* (whose essential purpose is to fill time with verses and good-natured mischief) and the modest labyrinths of solitaire, I have never cared much for cards. I slipped out of the room without anyone's noticing.

A big house that one has never been in before, its rooms in darkness (there was light only in the dining room), means more to a boy than an unexplored country to a traveler. Step by step I explored the house; I recall a billiard room, a conservatory with glass panes of rectangles and lozenges, a pair of rocking chairs, and a window from which there was a glimpse of a gazebo. In the dimness, I became lost; the owner of the house—whose name, after all these years, might have been Acevedo or Acébal—finally found me. Out of kindness, or, being a collector, out of vanity, he led me to a sort of museum case. When he turned on the light, I saw that it contained knives of every shape and kind, knives made famous by the circumstances of their use. He told me he had a little place near Pergamino, and that he had gathered his collection over years of traveling back and forth through the province. He opened the case and without looking at the little show cards for each piece he recounted the knives' histories, which were always more or less the same, with differences of place and date. I asked if among his knives he had the dagger that had been carried by Moreira* (at that time the very archetype of the gaucho, as Martín Fierro and Don Segundo Sombra* would later be). He had to admit he didn't, but he said he could show me one like it, with the same U-shaped cross guard. Angry voices interrupted him. He closed the case immediately; I followed him.

Uriarte was shouting that Duncan had been cheating. The others were standing around them. Duncan, I recall, was taller than the others; he was a sturdy-looking, inexpressive man a bit heavy in the shoulders, and his hair was so blond that it was almost white. Maneco Uriarte was a man of many nervous gestures and quick movements; he was dark, with features that revealed, perhaps, some trace of Indian blood, and a sparse, petulant mustache. Clearly, they were all drunk; I cannot say for certain whether there were two or three bottles scattered about on the floor or whether the cinematographer's abuses have planted that false memory in my mind. Uriarte's cutting (and now obscene) insults never ceased. Duncan seemed not to hear him; finally he stood up, as though weary, and hit Uriarte, once, in the face. Uriarte screamed—from the floor where he now lay sprawling—that he was not going to tolerate such an affront, and he challenged Duncan to fight.

Duncan shook his head.

"To tell the truth, I'm afraid of you," he added, by way of explanation.

A general burst of laughter greeted this.

"You're going to fight me, and now," Uriarte replied, once more on his feet.

Someone, God forgive him, remarked that there was no lack of weapons.

I am not certain who opened the vitrine. Maneco Uriarte selected the longest and showiest knife, the one with the U-shaped cross guard; Duncan, almost as though any one of them would serve as well as any other, chose a wood-handled knife with the figure of a little tree on the blade. Someone said it was like Maneco to choose a sword. No one was surprised that Maneco's hand should be shaking at such a moment; everyone was surprised to see that Duncan's was.

Tradition demands that when men fight a duel, they not sully the house they are in, but go outside for their encounter. Half in sport, half serious, we went out into the humid night. I was not drunk from wine, but I was drunk from the adventure; I yearned for someone to be killed, so that I could tell about it later, and remember it. Perhaps just then the others were no more adult than I. I also felt that a whirlpool we seemed incapable of resisting was pulling us down, and that we were about to be lost. No one really took Maneco's accusation seriously; everyone interpreted it as stemming from some old rivalry, tonight exacerbated by the wine.

We walked through the woods that lay out beyond the gazebo. Uriarte and Duncan were ahead of us; I thought it odd that they should watch each other the way they did, as though each feared a surprise move by the other. We came to a grassy patch.

"This place looks all right," Duncan said with soft authority.

The two men stood in the center indecisively.

"Throw down that hardware—it just gets in the way. Wrestle each other down for real!" a voice shouted.

But by then the men were fighting. At first they fought clumsily, as though afraid of being wounded; at first they watched their opponent's blade, but then they watched his eyes. Uriarte had forgotten about his anger; Duncan, his indifference or disdain. Danger had transfigured them; it was now two men, not two boys, that were fighting. I had imagined a knife fight as a chaos of steel, but I was able to follow it, or almost follow it, as though it were a game of chess. Time, of course, has not failed both to exalt and to obscure what I saw. I am not sure how long it lasted; there are events that cannot be held to ordinary measures of time.

As their forearms (with no ponchos wrapped around them for protection) blocked the thrusts, their sleeves, soon cut to ribbons, grew darker and darker with their blood. It struck me that we'd been mistaken in assuming they were unfamiliar with the knife. I began to see that the two men handled their weapons differently. The weapons were unequal; to overcome that disadvantage, Duncan tried to stay close to the other man, while Uriarte drew away in order to make long, low thrusts.

"They're killing each other! Stop them!" cried the same voice that had mentioned the showcase.

No one summoned the courage to intervene. Uriarte had lost ground; Duncan then charged him. Their bodies were almost touching now. Uriarte's blade sought Duncan's face. Abruptly it looked shorter; it had plunged into his chest. Duncan lay on the grass. It was then that he spoke, his voice barely audible:

"How strange. All this is like a dream."

He did not close his eyes, he did not move, and I had seen one man kill another.

Maneco Uriarte leaned down to the dead man and begged him to forgive him. He was undisguisedly sobbing. The act he had just committed overwhelmed and terrified him. I now know that he regretted less having committed a crime than having committed an act of senselessness.

I couldn't watch anymore. What I had longed to see happen had happened, and I was devastated. Lafinur later told me that they had to wrestle with the body to pull the knife out. A council was held among them, and they decided to lie as little as possible; the knife fight would be elevated to a duel with swords. Four of the men would claim to have been the seconds, among them Acébal. Everything would be taken care of in Buenos Aires; somebody always has a friend. . . .

On the mahogany table lay a confusion of playing cards and bills that no one could bring himself to look at or touch.

In the years that followed, I thought more than once about confiding the story to a friend, but I always suspected that I derived more pleasure from keeping the secret than I would from telling it. In 1929, a casual conversation suddenly moved me to break the long silence. José Olave, the retired chief of police, had been telling me stories of the knife fighters that hung out in the tough neighborhoods of Retiro, down near the docks—El Bajo and that area. He said men such as that were capable of anything—ambush, betrayal, trickery, the lowest and most infamous kind of villainy—in order to get the better of their opponents, and he remarked that before the Podestás and the Gutiérrezes,* there'd been very little knife fighting, the hand-to-hand sort of thing. I told him that I'd once actually witnessed such a fight, and then I told the story of that night so many years before.

He listened to me with professional attention, and then he asked me a question:

"Are you sure Uriarte and the other man had never used a knife in a fight before? That a stretch in the country at one time or another hadn't taught them something?"

"No," I replied. "Everyone there that night knew everyone else, and none of them could believe their eyes."

Olave went on unhurriedly, as though thinking out loud.

"You say one of those daggers had a U-shaped cross guard. . . . There were two famous daggers like that—the one that Moreira used and the one that belonged to Juan Almada, out around Tapalquén."

Something stirred in my memory.

"You also mentioned a wood-handled knife," Olave went on, "with the mark of a little tree on the blade. There are thousands of knives like that; that was the mark of the company that made them. But there was one . . ."

He stopped a moment, then went on:

"There was an Acevedo that had a country place near Pergamino. And there was another brawler of some repute that made his headquarters in that area at the turn of the century—Juan Almanza. From the first man he killed, at the age of fourteen, he always used one of those short knives, because he said it brought him luck. There was bad blood between Juan Almanza and Juan Almada, because people got them mixed up—their names, you see. . . . They kept their eyes open for each other a long time, but somehow their paths never crossed. Juan Almanza was killed by a stray bullet in some election or other. The other one, I think, finally died of old age in the hospital at Las Flores."

Nothing more was said that afternoon; we both sat thinking.

Nine or ten men, all of them now dead, saw what my eyes saw—the long thrust at the body and the body sprawled beneath the sky—but what they saw was the end of another, older story. Maneco Uriarte did not kill Duncan; it was the weapons, not the men, that fought. They had lain sleeping, side by side, in a cabinet, until hands awoke them. Perhaps they stirred when they awoke; perhaps that was why Uriarte's hand shook, and Duncan's as well. The two knew how to fight—the knives, I mean, not the men, who were merely their instruments—and they fought well that night. They had sought each other for a long time, down the long roads of the province, and at last they had found each other; by that time their gauchos were dust. In the blades of those knives there slept, and lurked, a human grudge.

Things last longer than men. Who can say whether the story ends here; who can say that they will never meet again.

Juan Muraña

For years I said I was brought up in Palermo.* It was, I know now, mere literary braggadocio, because the fact is, I grew up within the precincts of a long fence made of spear-tipped iron lances, in a house with a garden and my father's and grandfather's library. The Palermo of knife fights and guitars was to be found (I have been given to understand) on the street corners and in the bars and tenement houses.

In 1930, I devoted an essay to Evaristo Carriego, our neighbor, a poet whose songs glorified those neighborhoods on the outskirts of the city. A short time after that, chance threw Emilio Trápani in my way. I was taking the train to Morón; Trápani, who was sitting beside the window, spoke to me by name. It took me a moment to recognize him; so many years had gone by since we shared a bench in that school on Calle Thames. (Roberto Godel will recall that.) Trápani and I had never particularly liked each other; time, and reciprocal indifference, had put even greater distance between us. It was he, I now remember, who had taught me the rudiments of Lunfardo—the thieves' jargon of the day. There on the train we fell into one of those trivial conversations that are bent upon dredging up pointless information and that sooner or later yield the news of the death of a schoolmate who's nothing but a name to us anymore. Then suddenly Trápani changed the subject.

"Somebody lent me your book on Carriego," he said. "It's full of knife fighters and thugs and underworld types. Tell me, Borges," he said, looking at me as though stricken with holy terror, "what can *you* know about knife fighters and thugs and underworld types?"

"I've read up on the subject," I replied.

" 'Read up on it' is right," he said, not letting me go on. "But I don't need to 'read up'—I know those people."

After a silence, he added, as though sharing a secret with me:

"I am a nephew of Juan Muraña."*

Of all the knife fighters in Palermo in the nineties, Muraña was the one that people talked about most.

"Florentina, my mother's sister," he went on, "was Muraña's wife. You might be interested in the story."

Certain rhetorical flourishes and one or another overlong sentence in Trápani's narration made me suspect that this was not the first time he had told it.

. . .

It was always a source of chagrin to my mother that her sister would marry Juan Muraña, whom my mother considered a cold-blooded rogue, though Florentina saw him as a "man of action." There were many versions of the fate that befell my uncle. There were those who claimed that one night when he'd been drinking he fell off the seat of his wagon as he turned the corner of Coronel and cracked his skull on the cobblestones. Some said the law was after him and he ran off to Uruguay. My mother, who could never bear her brother-in-law, never explained it to me. I was just a tyke, and I don't really even remember him.

Around the time of the Centennial,* we were living on Russell Alley. It was a long, narrow house we lived in, so while the front door was on Russell, the back door, which was always locked, was on San Salvador. My aunt, who was getting on in years and had become a little odd, lived in a bedroom in the attic. A skinny, bony woman she was, or so she seemed to me—tall, and miserly with her words. She was afraid of fresh air, never went outside, and she wouldn't let us come in her room; more than once I caught her stealing food and hiding it. Around the neighborhood, people would sometimes say that Muraña's death, or disappearance, had driven her insane. I always picture her dressed in black. She'd taken to talking to herself.

The owner of our house was a man named Luchessi* who had a barbershop in Barracas.* My mother, who worked at home as a seamstress, was having a hard time making ends meet. Though I didn't really understand it all, I would overhear certain whispered words: *justice of the peace, dispossession, eviction for nonpayment.* My mother suffered terribly; my aunt would stubbornly say that Juan would never let that wop* throw us out. She would recall the case—which she'd told us about dozens of times—of a scurrilous thug from the Southside who'd had the audacity to cast aspersions on her husband's courage. When Juan Muraña found out, he'd gone all the way to the other side of the city, found the man, settled the dispute with one thrust of his knife, and thrown the body in the Riachuelo. I can't say whether the story was true; the important thing at the time was that it had been told and believed.

I pictured myself sleeping in the archways on Calle Serrano, or begging, or standing on a corner with a basket of peaches. I half liked the idea of selling peaches—it would get me out of going to school.

I'm not certain how long all the worrying and anguish lasted. Your father, rest his soul, told us once that time can't be measured in days the way money is measured in pesos and centavos, because all pesos are equal, while every day, perhaps every hour, is different. I didn't fully understand what he meant then, but the phrase stayed in my mind.

One night during this time, I had a dream that turned into a nightmare. It was a dream about my uncle Juan. I'd never known him, but in my dream he was a strong, muscular man with Indian features and a sparse mustache and long flowing hair. We were riding toward the south, through big quarries and stands of underbrush, but those quarries and stands of underbrush were also Calle Thames.* In my dream, the sun was high in the sky. Uncle Juan was dressed all in black. He stopped in a narrow pass, near some sort of scaffolding. He had his hand under his coat, over his heart—not like a man who's about to draw his weapon, but like one who's trying to hide it. He said to me, in a voice filled with sadness, "I've changed a great deal." Then he slowly pulled out his hand, and what I saw was a vulture's claw. I woke up screaming in the dark.

The next day my mother told me she was taking me with her to see Luchessi. I knew she was going to ask for more time; she was taking me along, I'm sure, so the landlord could see how pathetic she was. She didn't say a word to her sister, who would never have allowed her to lower herself that way. I'd never been in Barracas; to my eyes there were more people, more traffic, and fewer vacant lots than where we lived. When we came to a certain corner, we saw policemen and a crowd in front of the number we were looking for. One man who lived there on the street was going from group to group, telling the story of how he'd been awakened at three in the morning by banging noises; he'd heard the door open and somebody step inside. Nobody had ever closed the door—at dawn Luchessi was found lying in the entryway, half dressed. He'd been stabbed repeatedly. He had lived alone; the police never found the culprit. Nothing had been stolen. Someone recalled that recently the deceased man had been losing his eyesight. "His time had come," another person said in a voice of authority. That verdict, and the tone with which it was delivered, impressed me; as the years have gone by I've noticed that whenever someone dies, there's always some sententious soul who has the same revelation.

At the wake, somebody brought around coffee and I drank a cup. There was a wax dummy in the coffin instead of the dead man. I mentioned this fact to my mother; one of the mourners laughed and assured me that the figure dressed in black was indeed Sr. Luchessi. I stood there fascinated, staring at him. My mother had to take me by the arm and pull me away.

For months people talked about nothing else. Crimes were rare then; think of how much talk there was about the Longhair and Squealer and Chairmaker affair. The only person in Buenos Aires utterly unconcerned by the scandal was my aunt Florentina. With the insistence of old age, all she would say when the subject was brought up was, "I told you people that Juan would never stand for that wop putting us out in the street."

One day there was a terrible storm; it seemed as though the sky had opened and the clouds had burst. Since I couldn't go to school, I started opening doors and drawers and cabinets, rummaging inside the way boys do, to see what secret treasures the house might hide. After a while I went up into the attic. There was my aunt, sitting with her hands folded in her lap; I sensed that she wasn't even thinking. Her room smelled musty. In one corner stood the iron bed, with a rosary hanging on one of the bedposts; in another, the wooden wardrobe for her clothes. On one of the whitewashed walls there was a lithograph of the Virgen del Carmen. A candlestick sat on the nightstand.

"I know what brings you up here," my aunt said, without raising her eyes. "Your mother sent you. She can't get it through her head that it was Juan that saved us."

"Juan?" I managed to say. "Juan died over ten years ago."

"Juan is here," she said. "You want to see him?"

She opened the drawer of the nightstand and took out a dagger.

"Here he is," she said softly. "I knew he'd never leave me. There's never been a man like him on earth. The wop never had a chance."

It was only then that I understood. That poor foolish, misdirected woman had murdered Luchessi. Driven by hatred, madness—perhaps, who knows, even love—she had slipped out the back door, made her way through one street after another in the night, and come at last to the house. Then, with those big bony hands, she had plunged the dagger into his chest. The dagger was Muraña, it was the dead man that she went on loving.

I'll never know whether she told my mother. She died a short time before we were evicted.

. . .

That was the end of the story that Trápani told me. I've never seen him again since. In the tale of that woman left all alone in the world, the woman who confuses her man, her tiger, with that cruel object he has bequeathed to her, the weapon of his bloody deeds, I believe one can make out a symbol, or many symbols. Juan Muraña was a man who walked my own familiar streets, who knew and did the things that men know and do, who one day tasted death, and who then became a knife. Now he is the memory of a knife. Tomorrow—oblivion, the common oblivion, forgotten.

The Elderly Lady

On January 14, 1941, María Justina Rubio de Jáuregui would celebrate her hundredth birthday. She was the only living child of the soldiers who had fought the wars of independence.*

Colonel Mariano Rubio, her father, was what might without irony or disrespect be called a minor national hero. Born the son of provincial landowners in the parish of La Merced, Rubio was promoted to second lieutenant in the Army of the Andes and served at Chacabuco, at the defeat at Cancha Rayada, at Maipú, and, two years later, at Arequipa.* The story is told that on the eve of that action, he and José de Olavarría exchanged swords.* In early April of '23 there took place the famous Battle of Cerro Alto, which, since it was fought in the valley, is also called the Battle of Cerro Bermejo.* Always envious of our Argentine glories, the Venezuelans have attributed that victory to General Simón Bolívar, but the impartial observer, the *Argentine* historian, is not so easily taken in; he knows very well that the laurels won there belong to Colonel Mariano Rubio. It was Rubio, at the head of a regiment of Colombian hussars, who turned the tide of the uncertain battle waged with saber and lance, the battle that in turn prepared the way for the no less famous action at Ayacucho,* in which Rubio also fought, and indeed was wounded. In '27 he acquitted himself with courage at Ituzaingó,* where he served under the immediate command of Carlos María Alvear.* In spite of his kinship with Rosas,* Rubio was a Lavalle man,* a supporter of the Unitarian party, and he dispersed the *montonero* insurgents* in an action that he always characterized as "taking a swipe at them with our sabers."

When the Unitarians were defeated, Rubio left Argentina for Uruguay. There, he married. During the course of the Great War he died in

Montevideo, which was under siege by Oribe's White* army. He was just short of his forty-fourth birthday, which at that time was virtually old age. He was a friend of Florencio Varela's. It is entirely likely that he would never have got past the professors at the Military College, for he had been in battles but never taken a single course in warfare. He left two daughters; only María Justina, the younger, concerns us here.

In late '53 the colonel's widow and her daughters took up residence in Buenos Aires. They did not recover the place in the country that the tyrant* had confiscated from them, but the memory of those lost leagues of land, which they had never seen, survived in the family for many years. At the age of seventeen María Justina married Dr. Bernardo Jáuregui, who, though a civilian, fought at Pavón and at Cepeda* and died in the exercise of his profession during the yellow fever epidemic.* He left one son and two daughters: Mariano, the firstborn, was a tax inspector whose desire to write the complete biography of the hero (a book he never completed, and perhaps never began to write) led him to frequent the National Library and the Archives. The elder daughter, María Elvira, married her cousin, one Saavedra, who was a clerk in the Ministry of Finance*; the second daughter, Julia, married a Sr. Molinari, who though having an Italian surname was a professor of Latin and a very well-educated man. I pass over grandchildren and great-grandchildren; let it suffice that the reader picture an honest and honorable family of somewhat fallen fortune, over which there presides an epic shade and the daughter who was born in exile.

They lived modestly in Palermo, not far from the Guadalupe Church; there, Mariano still recalls having seen, from a trolley car, a lake that was bordered by laborers' and farmers' houses built of unplastered brick rather than sheets of zinc; the poverty of yesterday was less squalid than the poverty we purchase with our industry today. Fortunes were smaller then, as well.

The Rubios' residence was above the neighborhood dry goods store. The stairway at the side of the building was narrow; the railing on the right-hand side continued on to become one side of the dark vestibule, where there were a hall tree and a few chairs. The vestibule opened into the little parlor with its upholstered furnishings, the parlor into the dining room with its mahogany table and chairs and its china cabinet. The iron shutters (never opened, for fear of the glare of the sun) admitted a wan half-light. I recall the odor of things locked away. At the rear lay the bedrooms, the bath, a small patio with a washtub, and the maid's room. In the entire house the only books were a volume of Andrade, a monograph by the hero (with handwritten additions), and Montaner y Simón's Hispano-American Dictionary, purchased because it could be paid for in installments and because of the little dictionary stand that came with it. The family lived on a small pension, which always arrived late, and also received rent from a piece of land (the sole remnant of the once-vast cattle ranch) in Lomas de Zamora.

At the date of my story the elderly lady was living with Julia, who had been widowed, and one of Julia's sons. She still abominated Artigas, Rosas, and Urquiza.* World War I, which made her detest Germans (about whom she knew very little), was less real to her than the 1890 Revolution and the charge on Cerro Alto. Since 1932 her mind had been gradually growing dimmer; the best metaphors are the common ones, for they are the only true ones. She was, of course, a Catholic, which did not mean that she believed in a God Who Is Three yet One, or even in the immortality of the soul. She murmured prayers she did not understand and her fingers told her beads. Instead of the Paschal and Three Kings' Day celebrations that were the custom in Argentina, she had come to adopt Christmas, and to drink tea rather than *mate*. The words *Protestant, Jew, Mason, heretic,* and *atheist* were all synonymous to her, and all meaningless. So long as she was able, she spoke not of Spaniards but of Goths, as her parents had. In 1910 she refused to believe that the Infanta, who after all was a princess, spoke, against all one's expectations, like a common Galician and not like an Argentine lady. It was at her son-in-law's wake that she was told this startling news by a rich relative (who had never set foot in the house though the family eagerly looked for mention of her in the social columns of the newspaper). The names the elderly lady called things by were always out of date: she spoke of the Calle de las Artes, the Calle del Temple, the Calle Buen Orden, the Calle de la Piedad, the Dos Calles Largas, the Plaza del Parque, and the Plaza de los Portones. What were affectations in other members of the family (who would say *Easterners* instead of *Uruguayans,** for instance) came naturally to the widow Jáuregui. She never left her house; she may never have suspected that with the years Buenos Aires had grown and changed. One's first memories are the most vivid ones; the city that the elderly lady saw in her mind's eye on the other side of the front door was no doubt a much earlier one than the city that existed at the time they'd had to move toward the outskirts; the oxen of the oxcarts must still have stood at rest in Plaza del Once,* and dead violets still have perfumed the country houses of Barracas.* *All I dream about now is dead men* was one of the last things she was heard to say. She was never stupid, but she had never, so far as I know, enjoyed the pleasures of the intellect; there remained to her the pleasures of memory, and then, forgetfulness. She was always generous. I recall her tranquil blue eyes and her smile. Who can say what tumult of passions (now lost but erstwhile burning brightly) there had been in that old woman who had once been so charming and well favored. Sensitive to plants, whose modest, silent life was so much like her own, she raised begonias in her room and touched the leaves she could not see. Until 1929, when she fell into her reverie, she would tell stories of historical events, but always with the same words and in the same order, as though they were the Paternoster, and I suspect that after a while they no longer corresponded to images in her mind. She had no marked preferences in food. She was, in a word, happy.

Sleeping, as we all know, is the most secret thing we do. We devote one third of our lives to sleep, yet we do not understand it. Some believe it is only an eclipse of wakefulness; others, a more complex state which embraces at once yesterday, the present, and tomorrow; still others see it as an uninterrupted series of dreams. To say that the elderly lady of my story spent ten years in a state of serene chaos is perhaps an error; every moment of those ten years may have been pure present, without past or future. If so, we should not marvel overmuch at that present (which in our own case we count in days and nights and hundreds of pages torn from many calendars, and in anxieties and events)—we voyage through it every morning before we are fully awake and every night before we fall asleep. Twice every day we are that elderly lady.

The Jáureguis lived, as we have seen, in a somewhat equivocal position. They saw themselves as members of the aristocracy, but those who made up that class knew nothing of them; they were the descendants of a national hero, but most textbooks omitted his name. It was true that a street commemorated Colonel Mariano Rubio, but that street, which very few people were familiar with, was lost behind the cemetery on the west side of the city.

The day of her centennial was drawing near. On the tenth, a uniformed soldier appeared with a letter signed by the minister himself, announcing his visit on the fourteenth. The Jáureguis showed the letter to the entire neighborhood, pointing out the engraved letterhead and the minister's personal signature. The journalists who would be writing the newspaper reports then began dropping by. They were given all the facts; it was obvious they'd never in their lives heard of Colonel Rubio. Virtual strangers called on the telephone, hoping the family would invite them to the celebration.

The household labored diligently in preparation for the great day. They waxed the floors, washed the windows, removed the muslin covers from the chandeliers, shined the mahogany, polished the silver in the china cabinet, rearranged the furniture, and opened the piano in the parlor in order to show off the velvet keyboard cover. There was much scurrying about. The only person not involved in the bustle of activity was the elderly lady herself, who appeared not to understand what was going on. She would smile; Julia, with the help of the maid, dressed her smartly and arranged her hair, as though she were already dead. The first thing visitors would see when they came in the door was the oil portrait of the hero, and then, a little lower and to the right, the sword of his many battles. Even in the most penurious times, the family had refused to sell it; they planned to donate it to the Museum of History. A neighbor very thoughtfully lent them a pot of geraniums for the occasion.

The party was to begin at seven. The invitations gave the hour as six-thirty because the family knew everyone would come a little late, so as not to be the first to arrive. At seven-ten not a soul had come; somewhat acrimoniously, the family discussed the advantages and disadvantages of tardiness: Elvira, who prided herself on her punctuality, declared it was an unforgivable discourtesy to leave people waiting; Julia, repeating the words of her late husband, replied that visitors who arrived late showed their consideration, since if everyone arrives a little late it's more comfortable all around, and no one has to feel rushed. By seven-fifteen not another soul could squeeze into the house. The entire neighborhood could see and envy Sra. Figueroa's car and driver* (or *chauffeur,* as she was heard to call him); she almost never invited the sisters to her house, but they greeted her effusively, so nobody would suspect that they saw each other only once in a blue moon. The president sent his aide-de-camp, a very charming gentleman who said it was an honor to shake the hand of the daughter of the hero of Cerro Alto. The minister, who had to leave early, read a most high-sounding speech filled with excellent epigrams, in which, however, he spoke more of San Martín than of Colonel Rubio. The elderly lady sat in her chair amid the cushions, and at times her head would nod or she would drop her fan. A group of distinguished females, the Ladies of the Nation, sang the national anthem to her, though she seemed not to hear. Photographers arranged the guests into artistic groupings, and their flashbulbs dazzled the celebrants' eyes. There were not enough little glasses of port and sherry to go around. Several bottles of champagne were uncorked. The elderly lady spoke not a single word; she may not have known who she was. From that night onward she was bedridden.

When the strangers had left, the family improvised a little cold supper. The smell of tobacco and coffee had already dissipated the light odor of benzoin.*

The morning and evening newspapers told loyal untruths; they exclaimed upon the almost miraculous memory of the hero's daughter, who was "an eloquent archive of one hundred years of Argentine history." Julia tried to show her those reports. In the dim light, the elderly lady lay unmoving, her eyes closed. She did not have a fever; the doctor examined her and said everything was all right. In a few days she died. The storming of her house by the mob, the unwonted stir, the flashbulbs, the speech, the uniforms, the repeated handshakes, and the popping of the champagne corks had hastened her end. Perhaps she thought it was one of Rosas' posses* that had come.

I think about the men killed at Cerro Alto, I think about the forgotten men of our continent and Spain who perished under the horses' hooves, and it occurs to me that the last victim of that chaos of lances in Peru was to be, more than a hundred years afterward, an elderly lady in Buenos Aires.

The Duel

For Juan Osvaldo Viviano

It is the sort of story that Henry James (whose writings were first revealed to me by Clara Glencairn de Figueroa,* one of the two protagonists of my story) might not have scorned to use. He would have consecrated more than a hundred tender and ironic pages to it, and would have embellished them with complex and scrupulously ambiguous dialogue; he might well have added a touch of melodrama. The essence of the story would not have been altered by its new setting in London or Boston. But the events in fact took place in Buenos Aires, and there I shall leave them. I shall give just a summary of the case, since the slowness of its pace and the worldliness of the circles in which it occurred are foreign to my own literary habits. Dictating this story is for me a modest, sideline sort of adventure. I should warn the reader that the episodes of the tale are less important than the situation that led to them, and less important, too, than the characters that figure in them.

Clara Glencairn was tall and proud and had fiery red hair. Less intellectual than understanding, she was not clever yet she was able to appreciate the cleverness of others—even of other women. In her soul, there was room for hospitality. She was delighted by differences; perhaps that is why she traveled so much. She knew that the locale in which chance set her was a sometimes arbitrary conjunction of rites and ceremonies, yet she found those rituals amusing, and she carried them out with grace and dignity. Her parents, the Glencairns, married her off when she was still quite young to a Dr. Isidro Figueroa—at that time the Argentine ambassador to Canada, though he eventually resigned his post, declaring that in an age of telegrams and telephones, embassies were an anachronism and an unnecessary expense to the nation. That decision earned him the resentment of all his colleagues; though Clara herself liked Ottawa's climate (she was, after all, of Scottish decent) and did not find the duties of an ambassador's wife distasteful, she never dreamed of protesting. Dr. Figueroa died a short time later; Clara, after a few years of indecision and quiet casting about, decided to become a painter. She was inspired to this, perhaps, by her friend Marta Pizarro.

It is typical of Marta Pizarro that whenever she was mentioned, she was defined as the sister of the brilliant (married and separated) Nélida Sara.

Before taking up her brushes, Marta had considered the alternative of literature. She could be witty in French, the language her readings generally were drawn from; Spanish for her was no more than a household utensil, much like Guaraní for the ladies of Corrientes province. Newspapers had put the pages of Argentina's own Lugones and the Spaniard Ortega y Gasset into her hands; the style of those masters confirmed her suspicions that the language to which she had been fated was suited less to the expression of thought (or passion) than to prattling vanity. Of music she knew only what any person might know who dutifully attended concerts. She was from the province of San Luis; she began her career with meticulous portraits of Juan Crisóstomo Lafinur* and Colonel Pascual Pringles,* and these were predictably acquired by the Provincial Museum. From the portraiture of local worthies she progressed to that of the old houses of Buenos Aires, whose modest patios she limned with modest colors rather than the stagy garishness that others gave them. Someone (most certainly not Clara Figueroa) remarked that Marta Pizarro's *oeuvre* took for its models the solid works of certain nineteenth-century Genoese bricklayers.* Between Clara Glencairn and Nélida Sara (who was said to have fancied Dr. Figueroa at one point) there was always a certain rivalry; perhaps the duel was between those two women, and Marta but an instrument.

Everything, as we all know, happens first in other countries and then after a time in Argentina. The sect of painters, today so unfairly forgotten, that was called "concrete" or "abstract" (as though to indicate its contempt for logic and for language) is one of many examples of this phenomenon. The movement argued, I believe, that just as music is allowed to create a world made entirely of sound, so painting, music's sister art, might essay colors and forms that do not reproduce the forms and colors of the objects our eyes see. Lee Kaplan wrote that his canvases, which outraged the *bourgeoisie,* obeyed the biblical stricture, shared with Islam, against human hands' creating images (Gr. *eidōlon*) of living creatures. The iconoclasts, then, he argued, as breakers of the idols, were returning to the true tradition of pictorial art, a tradition which had been perverted by such heretics as Dürer and Rembrandt; Kaplan's detractors accused him of invoking a tradition exemplified by rugs, kaleidoscopes, and neckties. Aesthetic revolutions hold out the temptation of the irresponsible and the easy; Clara Glencairn decided to become an abstract artist. She had always worshiped Turner; she set out to enrich abstract art with her own vague splendors. She labored without haste. She reworked or destroyed several compositions, and in the winter of 1954 she exhibited a series of temperas in a gallery on Calle Suipacha—a gallery whose specialty was art that might be called, as the military metaphor then in fashion had it, "avant-garde." The result was paradoxical: general opinion was kind, but the sect's official organ took a dim view of the paintings' anomalous forms—forms which, while not precisely figurative, nonetheless seemed not content to be austere lines and curves, but instead suggested the tumult of a sunset, a jungle, or the sea. The first to smile, perhaps, was Clara Glencairn. She had set out to be modern, and the moderns rejected her. But painting itself—the act of painting—was much more important to her than any success that might come of it, and so she continued to paint. Far removed from this episode, Painting followed its own course.

The secret duel had now begun. Marta Pizarro was not simply an artist; she was passionately interested in what might not unfairly be called the administrative aspect of art, and she was undersecretary of a group called the Giotto Circle. In mid-1955 she managed things so that Clara, already admitted as a member, was elected to the group's new board of directors. This apparently trivial fact deserves some comment. Marta had supported her friend, yet the unquestionable if mysterious truth is that the person who bestows a favor is somehow superior to the person who receives it.

Then, in 1960 or thereabout, two "world-renowned artists" (if we may be pardoned the cliché) were competing for a single first prize. One of the candidates, the older of the two, had filled solemn canvases with portraits of bloodcurdling gauchos as tall as Norsemen; his rival, the merest youngster, had earned applause and scandal through studied and unwavering incoherence. The jurors, all past the half century mark, feared being thought to be old-fashioned, and so they were inclined to vote for the younger man, whose work, in their heart of hearts, they disliked. After stubborn debate (carried on at first out of courtesy and toward the end out of tedium), they could not come to an agreement. In the course of the third discussion, someone ventured the following:

"I do not think B is a good painter; I honestly don't think he's as good as Mrs. Figueroa."*

"Would you vote for her?" another asked, with a touch of sarcasm.

"I would," replied the first, now irritated.

That same afternoon, the jury voted unanimously to give the prize to Clara Glencairn de Figueroa. She was distinguished, lovable, of impeccable morality, and she tended to give parties, photographed by the most costly magazines, at her country house in Pilar. The celebratory dinner was given (and its costs assumed) by Marta. Clara thanked her with a few well-chosen words; she observed that there was no conflict between the traditional and the new, between order and adventure. Tradition, she said, is itself a centuries-long chain of adventures. The show was attended by numerous luminaries of society, almost all the members of the jury, and one or two painters.

We all think that fate has dealt us a wretched sort of lot in life, and that others must be better. The cult of gauchos and the *Beatus ille* . . . are urban nostalgias; Clara Glencairn and Marta Pizarro, weary of the routines of idleness, yearned for the world of artists—men and women who devoted their lives to the creation of beautiful things. I presume that in the heaven of the Blessèd there are those who believe that the advantages of that locale are much exaggerated by theologists, who have never been there themselves. And perhaps in hell the damned are not always happy.

Two or three years later the First International Congress of Latin American Art took place in the city of Cartagena. Each Latin American republic sent one representative. The theme of the congress was (if we may be pardoned the cliché) of burning interest: Can the artist put aside, ignore, fail to include the autochthonous elements of culture—can the artist leave out the fauna and flora, be insensitive to social issues, not join his or her voice to those who are struggling against U.S. and British imperialism, et cetera, et cetera? Before being ambassador to Canada, Dr. Figueroa had held a diplomatic post in Cartagena; Clara, made more than a little vain by the award that had been granted her, would have liked to return to that city, now as a recognized artist in her own right. But that hope was dashed—the government appointed Marta Pizarro to be the country's representative. Her performance, according to the impartial testimony of the Buenos Aires correspondents, was often brilliant, though not always persuasive.

Life must have its consuming passion. The two women found that passion in painting—or rather, in the relationship that painting forced them into. Clara Glencairn painted against, and in some sense for, Marta Pizarro;

each was her rival's judge and solitary audience. In their canvases, which no one any longer looked at, I believe I see (as there inevitably had to be) a reciprocal influence. And we must not forget that the two women loved each other, that in the course of that private duel they acted with perfect loyalty to one another.

It was around this same time that Marta, now no longer so young as before, rejected an offer of marriage; only her battle interested her.

On February 2, 1964, Clara Figueroa suffered a stroke and died. The newspapers printed long obituaries of the sort that are still *de rigueur* in Argentina, wherein the woman is a representative of the species, not an individual. With the exception of an occasional brief mention of her enthusiasm for art and her refined taste, it was her faith, her goodness, her constant and virtually anonymous philanthropy, her patrician lineage (her father, General Glencairn, had fought in the Brazil campaign), and her distinguished place in the highest social circles that were praised. Marta realized that her own life now had no meaning. She had never felt so useless. She recalled the first tentative paintings she had done, now so long ago, and she exhibited in the National Gallery a somber portrait of Clara in the style of the English masters they had both so much admired. Someone said it was her best work. She never painted again.

In that delicate duel (perceived only by those few of us who were intimate friends) there were no defeats or victories, nor even so much as an open clash—no visible circumstances at all, save those I have attempted to record with my respectful pen. Only God (whose æsthetic preferences are unknown to us) can bestow the final palm. The story that moved in darkness ends in darkness.

The Other Duel

One summer evening in Adrogué* many years ago, this story was told to me by Carlos Reyles, the son of the Uruguayan novelist. In my memory this chronicle of a long-held hatred and its tragic end still calls up the medicinal fragrance of the eucalyptus trees and the singing of the birds.

We were talking, as we always did, about the interwoven history of our two countries. At one point he said I'd surely heard of Juan Patricio Nolan, who had earned a reputation as a brave man, a teller of tall tales, and a practical joker. Lying myself, I said I had. Nolan had died in '90 or thereabout, but people still thought of him as a friend. He had his detractors, too, of course, as we all do. Carlos told me one of the many little pranks that Nolan was said to have played. The incident had taken place a short while before the Battle of Manantiales*; its protagonists were Manuel Cardoso and Carmen Silveira, two gauchos from Cerro Largo.*

How and why had the hatred between those two men begun? How, a century or more later, can we recover the shadowy story of those two men whose only fame was earned in their final duel? There was a man named Laderecha—an overseer at Reyles' father's ranch, "with a mustache like a tiger's"—who had gleaned from "oral tradition" certain details that I shall recount; I set them down here for what they are worth and with no further assurances as to their veracity, since both forgetfulness and recollection are creative.

Manuel Cardoso's and Carmen Silveira's small ranches bordered one another. As with the origins of other passions, the origins of a hatred are always obscure, but there was talk of a dispute over some unmarked animals, or, alternately, of a bareback horse race during which Silveira, who was the stronger, had bumped Cardoso's horse off the track. Months later, in the town's general store, there had been a long game of two-handed *truco;* Silveira congratulated his opponent on his play to virtually every trick, but he left him at the end without a penny. As he was raking the money into his purse, he thanked Cardoso for the lesson he had given him. It was then, I think, that they almost came to blows. The game had been hard fought; the onlookers (there had been many) had to separate them. On that frontier and at that time, man stood up to man and blade to blade; an unusual feature of this story is, as we will see, that Manuel Cardoso and Carmen Silveira crossed paths up in the mountains twice a day, morning and evening, though they never actually fought until the end. Perhaps their only possession in their coarse primitive lives was their hatred, and therefore they saved it and stored it up. Without suspecting, each of the two became the other's slave.

I have no way of knowing whether the events I am about to narrate are effects or causes.

Cardoso, less out of love than for something to do, took a fancy to a girl who lived nearby, a girl everyone called La Serviliana, and he began to court her; no sooner had Silveira discovered this than he began to court the girl in his own way, and carried her off to his shack. After a few months he threw her out; she got on his nerves. Indignant, the woman sought refuge at Cardoso's place; Cardoso spent one night with her and sent her off at noon. He didn't want the other man's leftovers.

It was at about the same time—a little before or after La Serviliana—that the incident with the sheepdog took place. Silveira was very fond of the dog, and had named it Thirty-three.* It was found dead in a ditch; Silveira always thought he knew who'd poisoned the dog.

In the winter of '70, Aparicio's revolution* caught Cardoso and Silveira drinking in that same general-store-and-bar where they'd played their game of *truco.* A Brazilian soldier with mulatto features, heading up a small band of *montoneros,** came through the door. He gave the men gathered there a rousing speech; their country needed them, he said—the government's oppression was intolerable. He passed out white badges* to pin on, and at the end of that exordium which they had not understood, he and his platoon impressed them into service—they were not even allowed to say good-bye to their families. Manuel Cardoso and Carmen Silveira accepted their fate; a soldier's life was no harder than a gaucho's. They were used to sleeping in the open with a horse blanket as a mattress and a saddle as a pillow, and for the hand accustomed to killing animals, killing a man was not a great deal different. Their lack of imagination freed them from fear and pity alike, though fear did touch them sometimes, just as the cavalry charged them.

(The rattle of stirrups and weapons is one of the things you can always hear when the cavalry rides into the action.) But if a man isn't wounded right away, he thinks himself invulnerable. They did not miss the places they'd been born and raised in. The concept of patriotism was foreign to them; in spite of the insignia worn on the hats, one side was much the same as the other to them. They learned what can be done with the lance. In the course of advances and retreats, they at last came to feel that being comrades allowed them to go on being rivals. They fought shoulder to shoulder yet they never, so far as is known, exchanged a single word.

In the fall of '71, which was a hard time, the end came to the two men.

The engagement, which lasted less than an hour, occurred at a place whose name they never learned—historians assign the names later. On the eve of the battle, Cardoso crawled into the captain's tent and asked him, in a whisper, to save one of the Reds for him if they won the next day—he had never cut anybody's throat,* he said, and he wanted to know what it was like. The captain promised that if he conducted himself like a man, he'd grant him that favor.

The Whites outnumbered the Reds, but the Reds had better weaponry. From the top of a hill they commanded, they rained devastation on the Whites. After two charges that failed to reach the peak, the White captain, gravely wounded, surrendered. There on the field, at his request, his men ended his life.

Then they laid down their arms. Captain Juan Patricio Nolan, commander of the Reds, gave a long-winded and flowery order that all the captives' throats be cut. But he was from Cerro Largo, and not unfamiliar with Silveira and Cardoso's long-standing grudge, so he had them brought to him.

"I know you two can't bear the sight of each other," he said, "and that you've been waiting a long time for the chance to settle scores. So I've got good news for you. Before the sun goes down, you're going to get the chance to show which one of you is the toughest. I'm going to have your throats cut, and then you're going to run a race. Like they say—may the best man win."

The soldier who had brought them took them away.

The news spread quickly through the camp. Nolan had wanted the race to crown that evening's performance, but the prisoners sent a committee to ask him if they couldn't watch it, too, and make bets on the winner. Nolan, a reasonable man, let himself be convinced. The men bet money, riding gear, knives, and horses; their winnings would be turned over to their widows and next of kin when the time came. The day was hot; so everyone could have a siesta, the event was put off till four. (They had a hard time waking

Silveira up.) Nolan, typically, kept them all waiting for an hour. He had no doubt been reliving the victory with the other officers; the orderly made the rounds with the *mate.*

On each side of the dusty road, against the tents, the ranks of prisoners sat on the ground and waited, hands tied behind their backs so they'd give nobody any trouble. One would occasionally unburden himself with an oath, another murmur the beginning of the Lord's Prayer; almost all were in a state verging on stupefaction. Naturally, they couldn't smoke. They no longer cared about the race, but they all watched.

"When they slit my throat, they're going to grab me by the hair and pull my head back, too," said one man, as though to ally himself with the centers of attention.

"Yeah, but you'll be along with the herd," replied another.

"Along with you," the first man spit.

A sergeant drew the line across the road with a saber. Silveira's and Cardoso's hands had been untied so they wouldn't have to run off-balance. They stood more than five yards apart. They put their toes against the line; some of the officers called out for them not to let them down—they were counting on them. A great deal of money was riding on each man.

Silveira drew Nigger Nolan, whose grandparents had doubtlessly been slaves of the captain's family, and so bore his name; Cardoso drew the regular executioner, an older man from Corrientes who always patted the condemned man on the back and told him: "Buck up, friend; women suffer more than this when they have a baby."

Their torsos straining forward, the two anxious men did not look at each other.

Nolan gave the signal.

The part Nigger Nolan had been given to play went to his head, and he overacted—he slashed Silveira's throat from ear to ear. The man from Corrientes made do with a neat slice. The blood gushed, though, from both men's throats; they stumbled a few steps and then fell headlong. As he fell, Cardoso stretched out his arms. He had won, but he likely never knew that.

Guayaquil*

Now I shall never see the peak of Higuerota mirrored in the waters of the Golfo Plácido, never make my journey to the Western State, never visit that library (which I, here in Buenos Aires, picture in so many different ways, though it must have its own precise existence, contain its own lengthening shadows) where I was to unriddle the handwriting of Bolívar.

As I reread the foregoing paragraph in order to compose the next one, I am surprised by its tone at once melancholy and pompous. It may be that one cannot speak about that Caribbean republic without echoing, however remotely, the monumental style of its most famous historiographer, Capt. Józef Korzeniowski; but in my case there is another reason—that first paragraph was dictated by the intention, deep within me, to imbue a mildly painful and altogether trivial incident with a tone of pathos. But I will relate what happened with absolute honesty; that, perhaps, will help me understand it. After all, when one confesses to an act, one ceases to be an actor in it and becomes its witness, becomes a man that observes and narrates it and no longer the man that performed it.

The incident happened to me last Friday in this same room I am writing in now, at this same hour of the afternoon (though today is somewhat cooler). I know that we tend to forget unpleasant things; I want to record my conversation with Dr. Eduardo Zimmermann (of our sister university to the south) before it is blurred by forgetfulness. My memory of it now is still quite vivid.

The story can be better understood, perhaps, with a brief recounting of the curious drama surrounding certain letters written by Simón Bolívar, "the Liberator of the Americas." These letters were recently exhumed from the files of the distinguished historian don José Avellanos, whose *Historia* *de cincuenta años de desgobierno* ["A History of Fifty Years of Misrule"] was itself initially believed lost (under circumstances which no one can fail to be familiar with), then discovered and published in 1939 by his grandson, Dr. Ricardo Avellanos. To judge by references I have gathered from various publications, most of these letters are of no great interest, but there is one, dated from Cartagena on August 13, 1822, in which Bolívar is said to give the details of his famous meeting in Guayaquil with Gen. José de San Martín.* One cannot overstress the value of a document in which Bolívar reveals, even if only partially, what took place at that encounter. Ricardo Avellanos, a staunch opponent of his country's current government, refused to surrender the correspondence to the Academy of History; he offered it, instead, to several Latin American republics. Thanks to the admirable zeal of our ambassador, Dr. Melaza, the government of the Argentine was the first to accept Avellanos' disinterested offer. It was decided that a delegate would be sent to Sulaco, the capital of our neighbor country, to make copies of the letters and publish them here. The chancellor of our university, where I am professor of Latin American history, was so kind as to recommend my name to the minister of education as the person to carry out that mission; I also obtained the more or less unanimous support of the National Academy of History, of which I am a member. Just as the date was set for my interview with the minister, we learned that the University of the South (which I prefer to think was unaware of these decisions) had proposed the name of Dr. Zimmermann.

Dr. Eduardo Zimmermann, as the reader perhaps may know, is a foreign-born historian driven from his homeland by the Third Reich and now an Argentine citizen. Of his professional work (doubtlessly estimable), I know at first hand only an article in vindication of the Semitic republic of Carthage (which posterity has judged through the writings of Roman historians, its enemies) and an essay of sorts which contends that government should function neither visibly nor by appeal to emotion. This hypothesis was thought worthy of refutation by Martin Heidegger, who proved decisively (using photocopies of newspaper headlines) that the modern head of state, far from being anonymous, is in fact the *prōtagōnistēs,* the *khoragos,* the David whose dancing (assisted by the pageantry of the stage, and with unapologetic recourse to the hyperboles of the art of rhetoric) enacts the drama of his people. Heidegger likewise proved that Zimmermann was of Hebrew, not to say Jewish, descent. That article by the venerable existentialist was the immediate cause of our guest's exodus and subsequent nomadism.

Zimmermann had no doubt come to Buenos Aires in order to meet the minister; the minister's personal suggestion, made to me through the intermediary of a secretary, was that, in order to forestall the unpleasant spectacle of our country's two universities disputing for the one prize, it be myself who spoke to Zimmermann, to apprise him of where the matter stood. Naturally, I agreed. When I returned home, I was informed that Dr. Zimmermann had phoned to tell me he was coming that evening at six. I live, as most people know, on Calle Chile.* It was exactly six o'clock when the doorbell rang.

With republican simplicity, I opened the door to Dr. Zimmermann myself and led him toward my private study. He paused to look at the patio; the black and white tiles, the two magnolia trees, and the wellhead drew his admiration. He was, I think, a bit nervous. There was nothing particularly striking about him; he was a man in his forties with a rather large head. His eyes were hidden by dark glasses, which he would occasionally lay on the table and then put back on again. When we shook hands, I noted with some satisfaction that I was the taller, but I was immediately ashamed of my smugness, since this was not to be a physical or even spiritual duel, but simply a *mise au point,* a "getting down to brass tacks," as some might say, though perhaps a rather uncomfortable one. I am a poor observer, but I do recall what a certain poet once called, with ugliness befitting the thing described, his "inelegant sartorial arrangements." I can still see his bright blue suit, much encumbered with buttons and pockets. His necktie, I noticed, was one of those stage magician's bow ties attached with two plastic clips. He was carrying a leather briefcase that I assumed was full of documents. He wore a well-trimmed, military-style mustache; during the course of our conversation he lighted a cigar, and at that, I felt there were too many things on that face. *Trop meublé,* I said to myself.

The linear nature of language, wherein each word occupies its own place on the page and its own instant in the reader's mind, unduly distorts the things we would make reference to; in addition to the visual trivialities that I have listed, the man gave one the impression of a past dogged by adversity.

On the wall in my office hangs an oval portrait of my great-grandfather, who fought in the wars of independence, and there are one or two glass cases around the room, containing swords, medals, and flags. I showed Zimmermann those old *objets de la gloire* and explained where some of them had come from; he would look at them quickly, like a man performing his duty, and (not without some impertinence, though I believe it was an involuntary and mechanical tic) complete my information. He would say, for example:

"Correct. Battle of Junín. August 6, 1824. Cavalry charge under Juárez."

"Suárez," I corrected.

I suspect that the error was deliberate.

"My first error," he exclaimed, opening his arms in an Oriental gesture, "and assuredly not my last! I live upon texts, and I get hopelessly muddled; in you, however, the fascinating past quite literally lives."

He pronounced the *v* almost as if it were an *f*.

Such fawning did not endear the man to me.

Zimmermann found my books more interesting. His eyes wandered over the titles almost lovingly, and I recall that he said:

"Ah, Schopenhauer, who never believed in history. . . . In Prague I had that same edition, Grisebach's, and I believed that I would grow old in the company of those volumes that were so comfortable in one's hand—but it was History itself, embodied in one senseless man, that drove me from that house and that city. And here I am in the New World, in your lovely home, with you. . . ."

He spoke the language fluently, but not without error; a noticeable German accent coexisted with the lisping *s*'s of the Spanish peninsula.

We had taken a seat by now, and I seized upon those last words in order to get down to our business.

"Here, history is kinder," I said. "I expect to die in this house, where I was born. It was to this house that my great-grandfather, who had been all over the continent, returned when he brought home that sword; it is in this house that I have sat to contemplate the past and write my books. I might almost say that I have never left this library—but now, at last, I am to leave it, to journey across the landscape I have only traveled on maps."

I softened my possible rhetorical excess with a smile.

"Are you referring to a certain Caribbean republic?" Zimmermann asked.

"Quite right," I replied. "I believe that it is to that imminent journey that I owe the honor of your visit."

Trinidad brought in coffee.

"You are surely aware," I went on with slow assurance, "that the minister has entrusted me with the mission of transcribing and writing an introduction to the letters of Bolívar that chance has disinterred from the files of Dr. Avellanos. This mission, with a sort of fortunate fatality, crowns my life's labor, the labor that is somehow in my blood."

It was a relief to me to have said what I had to say. Zimmermann seemed not to have heard me; his eyes were on not my face but the books behind me. He nodded vaguely, and then more emphatically.

"In your blood. You are the true historian. Your family roamed the lands of the Americas and fought great battles, while mine, obscure, was barely emerging from the ghetto. History flows in your veins, as you yourself so eloquently say; all you have to do is listen, attentively, to that occult voice. I, on the other hand, must travel to Sulaco and attempt to decipher stacks and stacks of papers—papers which may finally turn out to be apocryphal. Believe me, professor, when I say I envy you."

I could sense no trace of mockery in those words; they were simply the expression of a will that made the future as irrevocable as the past. Zimmermann's arguments were the least of it, however; the power lay in the man, not in the dialectic. He continued with a pedagogue's deliberateness:

"In all things regarding Bolívar—San Martín, I mean, of course—your own position, my dear professor, is universally acknowledged. *Votre siège est fait.* I have not yet read the letter in question, but it is inevitable, or certainly reasonable, to hypothesize that Bolívar wrote it as self-justification. At any rate, the much-talked-about epistle will reveal to us only what we might call the Bolívar—not San Martín—side of the matter. Once it is published, it will have to be weighed, examined, passed through the critical sieve, as it were, and, if necessary, refuted. There is no one more qualified to hand down that ultimate verdict than yourself, with your magnifying glass. And scalpel! if scientific rigor so requires! Allow me furthermore to add that the name of the person who presents the letter to the world will always remain linked to the letter. There is no way, professor, that such a yoking can be in your interest. The common reader does not readily perceive nuances."

I now realize that our subsequent debate was essentially pointless. Perhaps I even sensed as much then; in order not to face that possibility, I grasped at one thing he had said and asked Zimmermann whether he really believed the letters were apocryphal.

"Even if they were written by Bolívar himself," he replied, "—that does not mean they contain the whole truth. Bolívar may have wished to delude his correspondent, or may simply have been deluding himself. You, a historian, a contemplative, know better than I that the mystery lies within ourselves, and not in words."

The man's grandiloquent generalities irritated me, so I curtly observed that within the Great Enigma that surrounds us, the meeting in Guayaquil, in which Gen. San Martín renounced mere ambition and left the fate of the continent in the hands of Bolívar, is also an enigma worth studying.

"There are so many explanations . . . ," Zimmermann replied. "There are those who speculate that San Martín fell into a trap. Others, such as

Sarmiento, contend that he was in essence a European soldier, lost on a continent he never understood; others still—Argentines, generally—maintain that he acted out of abnegation; yet others, out of weariness. There are even those who speak of a secret order from some Masonic lodge."

I remarked that be all that as it might, it would be interesting to recover the precise words spoken between the Protector of Peru and the Liberator of the Americas.

"It is possible," Zimmermann pontificated, "that the words they exchanged were trivial. Two men met in Guayaquil; if one prevailed, it was because he possessed the stronger will, not because of dialectical games. As you see, I have not forgotten my Schopenhauer."

Then, with a smile he added:

"*Words, words, words.* Shakespeare, the unparalleled master of words, held them in contempt. In Guayaquil or in Buenos Aires, or in Prague, they always count for less than people do."

At that moment I felt that something was happening—or rather, that something had already happened. Somehow, we were now different. Twilight was stealing upon the room and I had not lighted the lamps. A little aimlessly I asked:

"You are from Prague, professor?"

"I was from Prague," he answered.

In order to avoid the central subject, I remarked:

"It must be a strange city. I am not familiar with it, but the first book I ever read in German was *The Golem,* by Meyrink."

"That is the only book by Gustav Meyrink that deserves to be remembered," Zimmermann replied. "The others, which are concoctions of bad literature and worse theosophy, one is best not to like. Nevertheless, there *is* something of Prague's strangeness to be found in that book of dreams dissolving into further dreams. Everything is strange in Prague—or, if you prefer, nothing is strange. Anything can happen. In London one afternoon, I had the same sensation."

"You mentioned will," I replied. "In the *Mabinogion,* you may recall, two kings are playing chess on the summit of a hill, while on the plain below, their armies clash in battle. One of the kings wins the game; at that instant, a horseman rides up with the news that the other king's army has been defeated. The battle of men on the battlefield below was the reflection of the battle on the chessboard."

"Ah, a magical operation," Zimmermann said.

"Or the manifestation," I said, "of one will acting upon two distinct battlegrounds. Another Celtic legend tells of the duel of two famous bards. One, accompanying himself on the harp, sang from the coming of day to the coming of twilight. Then, when the stars or the moon came out, the first bard handed the harp to the second, who laid the instrument aside and rose to his feet. The first singer admitted defeat."

"What erudition! What power of synthesis!" exclaimed Zimmermann. Then, in a calmer voice, he added: "I must confess my ignorance, my lamentable ignorance, of *la matière de Bretaigne.* You, like the day, embrace both East and West, while I hold down my small Carthaginian corner, which I now expand a bit with a tentative step into New World history. But I am a mere plodder."

The servility of the Jew and the servility of the German were in his voice, though I sensed that it cost him nothing to defer to me, even flatter me, given that the victory was his.

He begged me not to concern myself about the arrangements for his trip. ("Negotiatives" was the horrendous word he used.) Then in one motion he extracted from his briefcase a letter addressed to the minister, in which I explained the reasons for my withdrawal and listed the acknowledged virtues of Dr. Zimmermann, and laid in my hand his fountain pen so that I might sign it. When he put the letter away, I could not help seeing in his briefcase his stamped ticket for the Ezeiza–Sulaco flight.

As he was leaving, he paused again before the shelf of Schopenhauer.

"Our teacher, our master—our common master—surmised that no act is unintentional. If you remain in this house, in this elegant patrician house, it is because deep inside, you wish to. I respect your wish, and am grateful."

I received these final alms from Zimmermann without a word.

I went with him to the door.

"Excellent coffee," he said, as we were saying our good-byes.

I reread these disordered pages, which I will soon be consigning to the fire. Our interview had been short.

I sense that now I will write no more. *Mon siège est fait.*

The Gospel According to Mark

The incident took place on the Los Alamos ranch, south of the small town of Junín, in late March of 1928. Its protagonist was a medical student named Baltasar Espinosa.* We might define him for the moment as a Buenos Aires youth much like many others, with no traits worthier of note than the gift for public speaking that had won him more than one prize at the English school in Ramos Mejía* and an almost unlimited goodness. He didn't like to argue; he preferred that his interlocutor rather than he himself be right. And though he found the chance twists and turns of gambling interesting, he was a poor gambler, because he didn't like to win. He was intelligent and open to learning, but he was lazy; at thirty-three he had not yet completed the last requirements for his degree. (The work he still owed, incidentally, was for his favorite class.) His father, like all the gentlemen of his day a freethinker, had instructed Espinosa in the doctrines of Herbert Spencer, but once, before he set off on a trip to Montevideo, his mother had asked him to say the Lord's Prayer every night and make the sign of the cross, and never in all the years that followed did he break that promise. He did not lack courage; one morning, with more indifference than wrath, he had traded two or three blows with some of his classmates that were trying to force him to join a strike at the university. He abounded in debatable habits and opinions, out of a spirit of acquiescence: his country mattered less to him than the danger that people in other countries might think the Argentines still wore feathers; he venerated France but had contempt for the French; he had little respect for Americans but took pride in the fact that there were skyscrapers in Buenos Aires; he thought that the gauchos of the plains were better horsemen than the gauchos of the mountains. When his cousin Daniel invited him to spend the summer at Los Alamos, he immediately accepted—not because he liked the country but out of a natural desire to please, and because he could find no good reason for saying no.

The main house at the ranch was large and a bit run-down; the quarters for the foreman, a man named Gutre, stood nearby. There were three members of the Gutre family: the father, the son (who was singularly rough and unpolished), and a girl of uncertain paternity. They were tall, strong, and bony, with reddish hair and Indian features. They rarely spoke. The foreman's wife had died years before.

In the country, Espinosa came to learn things he hadn't known, had never even suspected; for example, that when you're approaching a house there's no reason to gallop and that nobody goes out on a horse unless there's a job to be done. As the summer wore on, he learned to distinguish birds by their call.

Within a few days, Daniel had to go to Buenos Aires to close a deal on some livestock. At the most, he said, the trip would take a week. Espinosa, who was already a little tired of his cousin's *bonnes fortunes* and his indefatigable interest in the vagaries of men's tailoring, stayed behind on the ranch with his textbooks. The heat was oppressive, and not even nightfall brought relief. Then one morning toward dawn, he was awakened by thunder. Wind lashed the casuarina trees. Espinosa heard the first drops of rain and gave thanks to God. Suddenly the wind blew cold. That afternoon, the Salado overflowed.

The next morning, as he stood on the porch looking out over the flooded plains, Baltasar Espinosa realized that the metaphor equating the pampas with the sea was not, at least that morning, an altogether false one, though Hudson had noted that the sea seems the grander of the two because we view it not from horseback or our own height, but from the deck of a ship. The rain did not let up; the Gutres, helped (or hindered) by the city dweller, saved a good part of the livestock, though many animals were drowned. There were four roads leading to the ranch; all were under water. On the third day, when a leaking roof threatened the foreman's house, Espinosa gave the Gutres a room at the back of the main house, alongside the toolshed. The move brought Espinosa and the Gutres closer, and they began to eat together in the large dining room. Conversation was not easy; the Gutres, who knew so much about things in the country, did not know how to explain them. One night Espinosa asked them if people still remembered anything about the Indian raids, back when the military command for the frontier had been in Junín. They told him they did, but they would have given the same answer if he had asked them about the day Charles I had been beheaded. Espinosa recalled that his father used to say that all the cases of longevity that occur in the country are the result of either poor memory or a vague notion of dates—gauchos quite often know neither the year they were born in nor the name of the man that fathered them.

In the entire house, the only reading material to be found were several copies of a farming magazine, a manual of veterinary medicine, a deluxe edition of the romantic verse drama *Tabaré*, a copy of *The History of the Shorthorn in Argentina*, several erotic and detective stories, and a recent novel that Espinosa had not read—*Don Segundo Sombra*, by Ricardo Güiraldes. In order to put some life into the inevitable after-dinner attempt at conversation, Espinosa read a couple of chapters of the novel* to the Gutres, who did not know how to read or write. Unfortunately, the foreman had been a cattle drover himself, and he could not be interested in the adventures of another such a one. It was easy work, he said; they always carried along a pack mule with everything they might need. If he had not been a cattle drover, he announced, he'd never have seen Lake Gómez, or the Bragado River, or even the Núñez ranch, in Chacabuco. . . .

In the kitchen there was a guitar; before the incident I am narrating, the laborers would sit in a circle and someone would pick up the guitar and strum it, though never managing actually to play it. That was called "giving it a strum."

Espinosa, who was letting his beard grow out, would stop before the mirror to look at his changed face; he smiled to think that he'd soon be boring the fellows in Buenos Aires with his stories about the Salado overrunning its banks. Curiously, he missed places in the city he never went, and would never go: a street corner on Cabrera where a mailbox stood; two cement lions on a porch on Calle Jujuy a few blocks from the Plaza del Once; a tile-floored corner grocery-store-and-bar (whose location he couldn't quite remember). As for his father and his brothers, by now Daniel would have told them that he had been isolated—the word was etymologically precise—by the floodwaters.

Exploring the house still cut off by the high water, he came upon a Bible printed in English. On its last pages the Guthries (for that was their real name) had kept their family history. They had come originally from Inverness and had arrived in the New World—doubtlessly as peasant laborers—in the early nineteenth century; they had intermarried with Indians. The chronicle came to an end in the eighteen-seventies; they no longer knew how to write. Within a few generations they had forgotten their English; by the time Espinosa met them, even Spanish gave them some difficulty. They had no faith, though in their veins, alongside the superstitions of the pampas, there still ran a dim current of the Calvinist's harsh fanaticism. Espinosa mentioned his find to them, but they hardly seemed to hear him.

He leafed through the book, and his fingers opened it to the first verses of the Gospel According to St. Mark. To try his hand at translating, and perhaps to see if they might understand a little of it, he decided that that would be the text he read the Gutres after dinner. He was surprised that they listened first attentively and then with mute fascination. The presence of gold letters on the binding may have given it increased authority. "It's in their blood," he thought. It also occurred to him that throughout history, humankind has told two stories: the story of a lost ship sailing the Mediterranean seas in quest of a beloved isle, and the story of a god who allows himself to be crucified on Golgotha. He recalled his elocution classes in Ramos Mejía, and he rose to his feet to preach the parables.

In the following days, the Gutres would wolf down the spitted beef and canned sardines in order to arrive sooner at the Gospel.

The girl had a little lamb; it was her pet, and she prettied it with a sky blue ribbon. One day it cut itself on a piece of barbed wire; to stanch the blood, the Gutres were about to put spiderwebs on the wound, but Espinosa treated it with pills. The gratitude awakened by that cure amazed him. At first, he had not trusted the Gutres and had hidden away in one of his books the two hundred forty pesos he'd brought; now, with Daniel gone, he had taken the master's place and begun to give timid orders, which were immediately followed. The Gutres would trail him through the rooms and along the hallway, as though they were lost. As he read, he noticed that they would sweep away the crumbs he had left on the table. One afternoon, he surprised them as they were discussing him in brief, respectful words. When he came to the end of the Gospel According to St. Mark, he started to read another of the three remaining gospels, but the father asked him to reread the one he'd just finished, so they could understand it better. Espinosa felt they were like children, who prefer repetition to variety or novelty. One night he dreamed of the Flood (which is not surprising) and was awakened by the hammering of the building of the Ark, but he told himself it was thunder. And in fact the rain, which had let up for a while, had begun again; it was very cold. The Gutres told him the rain had broken through the roof of the toolshed; when they got the beams repaired, they said, they'd show him where. He was no longer a stranger, a foreigner, and they all treated him with respect; he was almost spoiled. None of them liked coffee, but there was always a little cup for him, with spoonfuls of sugar stirred in.

That second storm took place on a Tuesday. Thursday night there was a soft knock on his door; because of his doubts about the Gutres he always locked it. He got up and opened the door; it was the girl. In the darkness he couldn't see her, but he could tell by her footsteps that she was barefoot, and afterward, in the bed, that she was naked—that in fact she had come from the back of the house that way. She did not embrace him, or speak a word; she lay down beside him and she was shivering. It was the first time she had lain with a man. When she left, she did not kiss him; Espinosa realized that he didn't even know her name. Impelled by some sentiment he did not attempt to understand, he swore that when he returned to Buenos Aires, he'd tell no one of the incident.

The next day began like all the others, except that the father spoke to Espinosa to ask whether Christ had allowed himself to be killed in order to save all mankind. Espinosa, who was a freethinker like his father but felt obliged to defend what he had read them, paused.

"Yes," he finally replied. "To save all mankind from hell."

"What *is* hell?" Gutre then asked him.

"A place underground where souls will burn in fire forever."

"And those that drove the nails will also be saved?"

"Yes," replied Espinosa, whose theology was a bit shaky. (He had worried that the foreman wanted to have a word with him about what had happened last night with his daughter.)

After lunch they asked him to read the last chapters again.

Espinosa had a long siesta that afternoon, although it was a light sleep, interrupted by persistent hammering and vague premonitions. Toward evening he got up and went out into the hall.

"The water's going down," he said, as though thinking out loud. "It won't be long now."

"Not long now," repeated Gutre, like an echo.

The three of them had followed him. Kneeling on the floor, they asked his blessing. Then they cursed him, spat on him, and drove him to the back of the house. The girl was weeping. Espinosa realized what awaited him on the other side of the door. When they opened it, he saw the sky. A bird screamed; *it's a goldfinch,* Espinosa thought. There was no roof on the shed; they had torn down the roof beams to build the Cross.

Brodie's Report

Tucked inside a copy, bought for me by my dear friend Paulino Keins, of the first volume of Lane's translation of the *Thousand and One Nights* (*An Arabian Night's Entertainment*, London, 1840), we discovered the manuscript that I now make known to the world. The meticulous penmanship—an art which typewriters are teaching us to forget—suggests that the note was written around that same date. Lane, as we all know, lavished long explanatory notes upon the tales; the margins of this volume had been filled with additions, question marks, and sometimes corrections, all in the same hand as that of the manuscript. From those marginalia, one might almost conclude that the reader of the volume was less interested in Scheherazade's wondrous tales than in the customs of Islam. About David Brodie, whose signature (with its fine artistic flourish) is affixed to the end of the manuscript, I have been able to discover nothing save that he was a Scottish missionary, born in Aberdeen, who preached Christianity throughout central Africa and later in certain parts of the jungles of Brazil, a country to which he was led by his knowledge of Portuguese. I do not know when or where he died. The manuscript has never, so far as I know, been published.

I will reproduce the manuscript and its colorless language verbatim, with no omissions save the occasional verse from the Bible and a curious passage treating the sexual practices of the Yahoo, which Brodie, a good Presbyterian, discreetly entrusted to Latin. The first page of the manuscript is missing.

· · ·

. . . of the region infested by the Ape-men is the area wherein one finds the *Mlch.*[1] Lest my readers should forget the bestial nature of this people (and

[1]The *ch* here has the sound of the *ch* in the word *loch.* [Author's note.]

also because, given the absence of vowels in their harsh language, it is impossible to transliterate their name exactly), I will call them Yahoos. The tribe consists, I believe, of no more than seven hundred individuals; this tally includes the *Nr*, who live farther south, in the dense undergrowth of the jungle. The figure I give here is conjectural, since with the exception of the king, queen, and various witch doctors, the Yahoos sleep wherever they may find themselves when night falls, in no fixed place. Marsh fever and the constant incursions of the Apemen have reduced their number. Only a very few have names. To call one another, they fling mud at each other. I have also seen Yahoos fall to the ground and throw themselves about in the dirt in order to call a friend. Physically they are no different from the Kroo, except for their lower forehead and a certain coppery cast that mitigates the blackness of their skin. Their food is fruits, tubers, and reptiles; they drink cat's and bat's milk and they fish with their hands. They hide themselves when they eat, or they close their eyes; all else, they do in plain sight of all, like the Cynic school of philosophers. They devour the raw flesh of their witch doctors and kings in order to assimilate their virtue to themselves. I upbraided them for that custom; they touched their bellies and their mouths, perhaps to indicate that dead men are food as well, or perhaps—but this is no doubt too subtle—to try to make me see that everything we eat becomes, in time, human flesh.

In their wars they use rocks, gathered and kept at hand for that purpose, and magical imprecations. They walk about naked; the arts of clothing and tattooing are unknown to them.

I find it worthy of note that while they have at their disposal a broad expanse of grassy tableland, with springs of fresh water and shady trees, they have chosen to huddle together in the swamps that surround the base of the plateau, as though delighting in the rigors of squalor and equatorial sun. Furthermore, the sides of the plateau are rugged, and would serve as a wall against the Apemen. In the Scottish Highlands, clans build their castles on the summit of a hill; I told the witch doctors of this custom, suggesting it as a model that they might follow, but it was to no avail. They did, however, allow me to erect a cabin for myself up on the tableland, where the night breeze is cooler.

The tribe is ruled over by a king whose power is absolute, but I suspect that it is the four witch doctors who assist the king and who in fact elected him that actually rule. Each male child born is subjected to careful examination; if certain stigmata (which have not been revealed to me) are seen, the boy becomes king of the Yahoos. Immediately upon his elevation he is gelded, blinded with a fiery stick, and his hands and feet are cut off, so that the world will not distract him from wisdom. He is confined within a cavern, whose name is Citadel (*Qzr*)*; the only persons who may enter are the four witch doctors and a pair of female slaves who serve the king and smear his body with dung. If there is a war, the witch doctors take him from the cavern, exhibit him to the tribe to spur the warriors' courage, sling him over their shoulders, and carry him as though a banner or a talisman into the fiercest part of the battle. When this occurs, the king generally dies within seconds under the stones hurled at him by the Apemen.

In another such citadel lives the queen, who is not permitted to see her king. The queen of the Yahoos was kind enough to receive me; she was young, of a cheerful disposition, and, insofar as her race allows, well favored. Bracelets made of metal and ivory and necklaces strung with teeth adorned her nakedness. She looked at me, smelled me, and touched me, and then—in full sight of her attendants—she offered herself to me. My cloth and my habits caused me to decline that honor, which is one granted generally to the witch doctors and to the slave hunters (usually Muslims) whose caravans pass through the kingdom. She pricked me two or three times with a long golden needle; these pricks are the royal marks of favor, and not a few Yahoos inflict them upon themselves in order to make it appear that they have been recipients of the queen's attentions. The ornaments which I have mentioned come from other regions: the Yahoos believe them to be objects that occur in nature, as they themselves are incapable of manufacturing even the simplest item. In the eyes of the tribe, my cabin was a tree, even though many of them watched me build it, and even aided me. Among other items, I had with me a watch, a pith helmet, a compass, and a Bible; the Yahoos would look at these objects and heft them and ask where I had found them. They would often grasp my hunting knife by the blade; one supposes they saw it differently than I. It is difficult to imagine what they would make of a chair. A house of several rooms would be for them a labyrinth, though they well might not get lost inside it, much as a cat is able to find its way about a house though it cannot conceive it. They all found my beard, which was at that time flaming red, a thing of wonder; they would stroke and caress it for long periods at a time.

The Yahoos are insensitive to pain and pleasure, with the exception of the pleasure they derive from raw and rancid meat and noxious-smelling things. Their lack of imagination makes them cruel.

I have spoken of the king and queen; I will now say something about the witch doctors. I have mentioned that there are four of them; this number is the largest that the Yahoos' arithmetic comprehends. They count on their fingers thus: *one, two, three, four, many;* infinity begins at the thumb. The same phenomenon may be seen, I am told, among the tribes that harass the region of Buenos-Ayres with their raids and pillaging. In spite of the fact that four is the largest number they possess, the Yahoos are not cheated by the Arabs who traffic with them, for in their exchanges all the goods are divided into lots of one, two, three, or four items, which each person keeps beside himself. The operation is slow, yet it allows no room for error or trickery. Of all the nation of the Yahoos, the witch doctors are the only persons who have truly aroused my interest. The common people say they have the power to transform anyone they please into an ant or a tortoise; one individual who noted my incredulity at this report showed me an anthill, as though that were proof. The Yahoos have no memory, or virtually none; they talk about the damage caused by an invasion of leopards, but they are unsure whether they themselves saw the leopards or whether it was their parents, or whether they might be recounting a dream. The witch doctors do possess some memory, though to only a very small degree; in the afternoon they can recall things that happened that morning or even on the previous evening. They also possess the ability to see the future; they quite calmly and assuredly predict what will happen in ten or fifteen minutes. They may say, for example: *A fly will light on the back of my neck,* or *It won't be long before we hear a bird start singing.* I have witnessed this curious gift hundreds of times, and I have thought about it a great deal. We know that past, present, and future are already, in every smallest detail, in the prophetic memory of God, in His eternity; it is curious, then, that men may look indefinitely into the past but not an instant into the future. If I am able to recall as though it were yesterday that schooner that sailed into port from Norway when I was four years old, why should I be surprised that someone is able to foresee an event that is about to occur? Philosophically speaking, memory is no less marvelous than prophesying the future; tomorrow is closer to us than the crossing of the Red Sea by the Jews, which, nonetheless, we remember.

The tribesmen are forbidden to look at the stars, a privilege reserved for the witch doctors. Each witch doctor has a disciple whom he instructs from childhood in the secret knowledge of the tribe and who succeeds him at his death. Thus there are always four—a number with magical qualities, since it is the highest number the mind of humankind may attain. In their own way, they profess the doctrine of heaven and hell. Both are subterranean. To hell, which is bright and dry, shall go the sick, the old, the mistreated,

Apemen, Arabs, and leopards; to heaven, which the Yahoos imagine to be dark and marshlike, shall go the king, the queen, the witch doctors, those who have been happy, hardhearted, and bloodthirsty on earth. They worship a god whose name is Dung; this god they may possibly have conceived in the image of their king, for the god is mutilated, blind, frail, and possesses unlimited power. It often assumes the body of an ant or a serpent.

No one should be surprised, after reading thus far in my account, that I succeeded in converting not a single Yahoo during the entire period of my residence among them. The phrase *Our Father* disturbed them, since they lack any concept of paternity. They do not understand that an act performed nine months ago may somehow be related to the birth of a child; they cannot conceive a cause so distant and so unlikely. And then again, all women engage in carnal commerce, though not all are mothers.

Their language is complex, and resembles none other that I know. One cannot speak of "parts of speech," as there are no sentences. Each monosyllabic word corresponds to a general idea, which is defined by its context or by facial expressions. The word *nrz,* for example, suggests a dispersion or spots of one kind or another: it may mean the starry sky, a leopard, a flock of birds, smallpox, something splattered with water or mud, the act of scattering, or the flight that follows a defeat. *Hrl,* on the other hand, indicates that which is compact, dense, or tightly squeezed together; it may mean the tribe, the trunk of a tree, a stone, a pile of rocks, the act of piling them up, a meeting of the four witch doctors, sexual congress, or a forest. Pronounced in another way, or with other facial expressions, it may mean the opposite. We should not be overly surprised at this: in our own tongue, the verb *to cleave* means to rend and to adhere. Of course, there are no sentences, even incomplete ones.

The intellectual power of abstraction demanded by such a language suggests to me that the Yahoos, in spite of their barbarity, are not a primitive people but a degenerate one. This conjecture is confirmed by inscriptions which I have discovered up on the tableland. The characters employed in these inscriptions, resembling the runes that our own forebears carved, can no longer be deciphered by the tribe; it is as though the tribe had forgotten the written language and retained only the spoken one.

The tribe's diversions are cat fights (between animals trained for that purpose) and executions. Someone is accused of offending the modesty of the queen or of having eaten within sight of another; there is no testimony from witnesses, no confession, and the king hands down the sentence of guilty. The condemned man is put to torments which I strive not to recall, and then is stoned. The queen has the right to throw the first stone and the last one, which is ordinarily unnecessary. The people applaud her in frenzy, lauding her skill and the beauty of her person and flinging roses and fetid things at her. The queen wordlessly smiles.

Another of the tribe's customs is its poets. It occurs to a man to string together six or seven words, generally enigmatic. He cannot contain himself, and so he shrieks them out as he stands in the center of a circle formed by the witch doctors and the tribesmen lying on the ground. If the poem does not excite the tribe, nothing happens, but if the words of the poet surprise or astound the listeners, everyone moves back from him, in silence, under a holy dread. They feel that he has been touched by the spirit; no one will speak to him or look at him, not even his mother. He is no longer a man, but a god, and anyone may kill him. The new poet, if he is able, seeks refuge in the deserts to the north.

I have already related how I came to the land of the Yahoos. The reader will recall that they surrounded me, that I fired a rifle shot in the air, and that they took the report for some sort of magical thunder. In order to keep that error alive, I made it a point never to walk about armed. But one spring morning just at daybreak, we were suddenly invaded by the Apemen; I ran down from my plateau, weapon in hand, and killed two of those beasts. The rest fled in terror. Bullets, of course, work invisibly. For the first time in my life, I heard myself applauded. It was then, I believe, that the queen received me. The Yahoos' memory is not to be depended upon; that same afternoon I left. My adventures in the jungle are of no concern; I came at last upon a village of black men, who were acquainted with plowing, sowing, and praying, and with whom I could make myself understood in Portuguese. A Romish missionary, Padre Fernandes, took me most hospitably into his cabin and cared for me until I was able to continue my painful journey. At first it caused me some revulsion to see him undisguisedly open his mouth and put food in. I would cover my eyes with my hands, or avert them; in a few days I regained my old custom. I recall with pleasure our debates on theological questions. I could not persuade him to return to the true faith of Jesus.

I am writing this now in Glasgow. I have told of my stay among the Yahoos, but not of its essential horror, which never entirely leaves me, and which visits me in dreams. In the street, I sometimes think I am still among them. The Yahoos, I know, are a barbarous people, perhaps the most barbarous of the earth, but it would be an injustice to overlook certain redeeming traits which they possess. They have institutions, and a king; they speak a language based on abstract concepts; they believe, like the Jews and the Greeks, in the divine origins of poetry; and they sense that the soul survives the death of the body. They affirm the efficacy of punishment and reward. They represent, in a word, culture, just as we do, in spite of our many sins. I do not regret having fought in their ranks against the Apemen. We have the obligation to save them. I hope Her Majesty's government will not turn a deaf ear to the remedy this report has the temerity to suggest.

The Book of Sand

(1975)

The Other

The incident occurred in February, 1969, in Cambridge, north of Boston. I didn't write about it then because my foremost objective at the time was to put it out of my mind, so as not to go insane. Now, in 1972, it strikes me that if I do write about what happened, people will read it as a story and in time I, too, may be able to see it as one.

I know that it was almost horrific while it lasted—and it grew worse yet through the sleepless nights that followed. That does not mean that anyone else will be stirred by my telling of it.

It was about ten o'clock in the morning. I was sitting comfortably on a bench beside the Charles River. Some five hundred yards to my right there was a tall building whose name I never learned. Large chunks of ice were floating down the gray current. Inevitably, the river made me think of time . . . Heraclitus' ancient image. I had slept well; the class I'd given the previous evening had, I think, managed to interest my students. There was not a soul in sight.

Suddenly, I had the sense (which psychologists tell us is associated with states of fatigue) that I had lived this moment before. Someone had sat down on the other end of my bench. I'd have preferred to be alone, but I didn't want to get up immediately for fear of seeming rude. The other man had started whistling. At that moment there occurred the first of the many shocks that morning was to bring me. What the man was whistling—or *trying* to whistle (I have never been able to carry a tune)—was the popular Argentine milonga *La tapera,* by Elías Regules. The tune carried me back to a patio that no longer exists and to the memory of Alvaro Melián Lafinur, who died so many years ago. Then there came the words. They were the words of the *décima* that begins the song. The voice was not Alvaro's but it tried to imitate Alvaro's. I recognized it with horror.

I turned to the man and spoke.

"Are you Uruguayan or Argentine?"

"Argentine, but I've been living in Geneva since '14," came the reply.

There was a long silence. Then I asked a second question.

"At number seventeen Malagnou, across the street from the Russian Orthodox Church?"

He nodded.

"In that case," I resolutely said to him, "your name is Jorge Luis Borges. I too am Jorge Luis Borges. We are in 1969, in the city of Cambridge."

"No," he answered in my own, slightly distant, voice, "I am here in Geneva, on a bench, a few steps from the Rhône."

Then, after a moment, he went on:

"It *is* odd that we look so much alike, but you are much older than I, and you have gray hair."

"I can prove to you that I speak the truth," I answered. "I'll tell you things that a stranger couldn't know. In our house there's a silver *mate* cup with a base of serpents that our great-grandfather brought from Peru. There's also a silver washbasin that was hung from the saddle. In the wardrobe closet in your room, there are two rows of books: the three volumes of Lane's translation of the *Thousand and One Nights*—which Lane called *The Arabian Nights Entertainment*—with steel engravings and notes in fine print between the chapters, Quicherat's Latin dictionary, Tacitus' *Germania* in Latin and in Gordon's English version, a *Quixote* in the Garnier edition, a copy of Rivera Indarte's *Tablas de sangre* signed by the author, Carlyle's *Sartor Resartus,* a biography of Amiel, and, hidden behind the others, a paperbound volume detailing the sexual customs of the Balkans. Nor have I forgotten a certain afternoon in a second-floor apartment on the Plaza Dubourg."

"Dufour," he corrected me.

"All right, Dufour," I said. "Is that enough for you?"

"No," he replied. "Those 'proofs' of yours prove nothing. If I'm dreaming you, it's only natural that you would know what I know. That long-winded catalog of yours is perfectly unavailing."

His objection was a fair one.

"If this morning and this encounter are dreams," I replied, "then each of us does have to think that he alone is the dreamer. Perhaps our dream will end, perhaps it won't. Meanwhile, our clear obligation is to accept the dream, as we have accepted the universe and our having been brought into it and the fact that we see with our eyes and that we breathe."

"But what if the dream should last?" he asked anxiously.

In order to calm him—and calm myself, as well—I feigned a self-assurance I was far from truly feeling.

"My dream," I told him, "has already lasted for seventy years. And besides—when one wakes up, the person one meets is always oneself. That is what's happening to us now, except that we are two. Wouldn't you like to know something about my past, which is now the future that awaits you?"

He nodded wordlessly. I went on, a bit hesitatingly:

"Mother is well, living happily in her house in Buenos Aires, on the corner of Charcas and Maipú, but Father died some thirty years ago. It was his heart. He had had a stroke—that was what finally killed him. When he laid his left hand over his right, it was like a child's hand resting atop a giant's. He died impatient for death, but without a word of complaint. Our grandmother had died in the same house. Several days before the end, she called us all in and told us, 'I am an old, old woman, dying very slowly. I won't have anyone making a fuss over such a common, ordinary thing as that.' Norah, your sister, is married and has two children. By the way—at home, how is everyone?"

"Fine. Father still always making his jokes against religion. Last night he said Jesus was like the gauchos, who'll never commit themselves, which is why He spoke in parables."

He thought for a moment, and then asked: "What about you?"

"I'm not sure exactly how many books you'll write, but I know there are too many. You'll write poetry that will give you a pleasure that others will not fully share, and stories of a fantastic turn. You will be a teacher—like your father, and like so many others of our blood."

I was glad he didn't ask me about the success or failure of the books. I then changed my tack.

"As for history . . . There was another war, with virtually the same antagonists. France soon capitulated; England and America battled a German dictator named Hitler—the cyclical Battle of Waterloo. Buenos Aires engendered another Rosas in 1946, much like our kinsman, the first one.* In '55, the province of Córdoba saved us, as Entre Ríos had before. Things are bad now. Russia is taking over the planet; America, hobbled by the superstition of democracy, can't make up its mind to be an empire. Our own country is more provincial with every passing day—more provincial and more self-important, as though it had shut its eyes. I shouldn't be surprised if the teaching of Latin were replaced by the teaching of Guaraní."

I realized that he was barely listening. The elemental fear of the impossible yet true had come over him, and he was daunted. I, who have never been a father, felt a wave of love for that poor young man who was dearer to me than a child of my own flesh and blood. I saw that his hands were clutching a book. I asked what he was reading.

"*The Possessed*—or, as I think would be better, *The Devils,* by Fyodor Dostoievsky," he answered without vanity.

"It's a bit hazy to me now. Is it any good?"

The words were hardly out of my mouth when I sensed that the question was blasphemous.

"The great Russian writer," he affirmed sententiously, "has penetrated more deeply than any other man into the labyrinths of the Slavic soul."

I took that rhetorical pronouncement as evidence that he had grown calmer.

I asked him what other works by Dostoievsky he had read.

He ticked off two or three, among them *The Double.*

I asked him whether he could tell the difference between the characters when he read, as one could with Joseph Conrad, and whether he planned to read on through Dostoievsky's entire corpus.

"The truth is, I don't," he answered with a slight note of surprise.

I asked him what he himself was writing, and he told me he was working on a book of poetry to be called *Red Anthems.* He'd also thought about calling it *Red Rhythms* or *Red Songs.*

"Why not?" I said. "You can cite good authority for it—Rubén Darío's blue poetry and Verlaine's gray song."

Ignoring this, he clarified what he'd meant—his book would be a hymn to the brotherhood of all mankind. The modern poet cannot turn his back on his age.

I thought about this for a while, and then asked if he really felt that he was brother to every living person—every undertaker, for example? every letter carrier? every undersea diver, everybody that lives on the even-numbered side of the street, all the people with laryngitis? (The list could go on.) He said his book would address the great oppressed and outcast masses.

"Your oppressed and outcast masses," I replied, "are nothing but an abstraction. Only individuals exist—if, in fact, anyone does. *Yesterday's man is not today's,* as some Greek said. We two, here on this bench in Geneva or in Cambridge, are perhaps the proof of that."

Except in the austere pages of history, memorable events go unaccompanied by memorable phrases. A man about to die tries to recall a print that he glimpsed in his childhood; soldiers about to go into battle talk about the mud or their sergeant. Our situation was unique and, frankly, we were unprepared. We talked, inevitably, about literature; I fear I said no more than I customarily say to journalists. My *alter ego* believed in the imagination, in creation—in the discovery of new metaphors; I myself believed in those that correspond to close and widely acknowledged likenesses, those our imagination has already accepted: old age and death, dreams and life, the flow of time and water. I informed the young man of this opinion, which he himself was to express in a book, years later.

But he was barely listening. Then suddenly he spoke.

"If you have been me, how can you explain the fact that you've forgotten that you once encountered an elderly gentleman who in 1918 told you that he, too was Borges?"

I hadn't thought of that difficulty. I answered with conviction.

"Perhaps the incident was so odd that I made an effort to forget it."

He ventured a timid question.

"How's your memory?"

I realized that for a mere boy not yet twenty, a man of seventy some-odd years was practically a corpse.

"It's often much like forgetfulness," I answered, "but it can still find what it's sent to find. I'm studying Anglo-Saxon, and I'm not at the foot of the class."

By this time our conversation had lasted too long to be a conversation in a dream.

I was struck by a sudden idea.

"I can prove to you this minute," I said, "that you aren't dreaming me. Listen to this line of poetry. So far as I can recall, you've never heard it before."

I slowly intoned the famous line: *"L'hydre-univers tordant son corps écaillé d'astres."*

I could sense his almost fear-stricken bafflement. He repeated the line softly, savoring each glowing word.

"It's true," he stammered, "I could never write a line like that."

Hugo had brought us together.

I now recall that shortly before this, he had fervently recited that short poem in which Whitman recalls a night shared beside the sea—a night when Whitman had been truly happy.

"If Whitman sang of that night," I observed, "it's because he desired it but it never happened. The poem gains in greatness if we sense that it is the expression of a desire, a longing, rather than the narration of an event."

He stared at me.

"You don't know him," he exclaimed. "Whitman is incapable of falsehood."*

A half century does not pass without leaving its mark. Beneath our conversation, the conversation of two men of miscellaneous readings and diverse tastes, I realized that we would not find common ground. We were too different, yet too alike. We could not deceive one another, and that makes conversation hard. Each of us was almost a caricature of the other. The situation was too unnatural to last much longer. There was no point in giving advice, no point in arguing, because the young man's inevitable fate was to be the man that I am now.

Suddenly I recalled a fantasy by Coleridge. A man dreams that he is in paradise, and he is given a flower as proof. When he wakes up, there is the flower.

I hit upon an analogous stratagem.

"Listen," I said, "do you have any money?"

"Yes," he replied. "About twenty francs. I invited Simón Jichlinski to have dinner with me at the Crocodile tonight."

"Tell Simón that he'll practice medicine in Carouge, and that he will do a great deal of good . . . now, give me one of your coins."

He took three silver pieces and several smaller coins out of his pocket. He held out one of the silver pieces to me; he didn't understand.

I handed him one of those ill-advised American bills that are all of the same size though of very different denominations. He examined it avidly.

"Impossible!" he cried. "It's dated 1964."

(Months later someone told me that banknotes are not dated.)

"This, all this, is a miracle," he managed to say. "And the miraculous inspires fear. Those who witnessed the resurrection of Lazarus must have been terrified."

We haven't changed a bit, I thought. Always referring back to books.

He tore the bill to shreds and put the coin back in his pocket.

I had wanted to throw the coin he gave me in the river. The arc of the silver coin disappearing into the silver river would have lent my story a vivid image, but fate would not have it.

I replied that the supernatural, if it happens twice, is no longer terrifying; I suggested that we meet again the next day, on that same bench that existed in two times and two places.

He immediately agreed, then said, without looking at his watch, that it was getting late, he had to be going. Both of us were lying, and each of us knew that the other one was lying. I told him that someone was coming to fetch me.

"Fetch you?" he queried.

"Yes. When you reach my age, you'll have almost totally lost your eyesight. You'll be able to see the color yellow, and light and shadow. But don't worry. Gradual blindness is not tragic. It's like the slowly growing darkness of a summer evening."

We parted without having touched one another. The next day, I did not go to the bench. The other man probably didn't, either.

I have thought a great deal about this encounter, which I've never told anyone about. I believe I have discovered the key to it. The encounter was real, but the other man spoke to me in a dream, which was why he could forget me; I spoke to him while I was awake, and so I am still tormented by the memory.

The other man dreamed me, but did not dream me *rigorously*—he dreamed, I now realize, the impossible date on that dollar bill.

Ulrikke

Hann tekr sverthit Gram ok leggr i methal theira bert
Völsunga Saga, 27

My story will be faithful to reality, or at least to my personal recollection of reality, which is the same thing. The events took place only a short while ago, but I know that the habit of literature is also the habit of interpolating circumstantial details and accentuating certain emphases. I wish to tell the story of my encounter with Ulrikke (I never learned her last name, and perhaps never will) in the city of York. The tale will span one night and one morning.

It would be easy for me to say that I saw her for the first time beside the Five Sisters at York Minster, those stained glass panes devoid of figural representation that Cromwell's iconoclasts left untouched, but the fact is that we met in the dayroom of the Northern Inn, which lies outside the walls. There were but a few of us in the room, and she had her back to me. Someone offered her a glass of sherry and she refused it.

"I am a feminist," she said. "I have no desire to imitate men. I find their tobacco and their alcohol repulsive."

The pronouncement was an attempt at wit, and I sensed this wasn't the first time she'd voiced it. I later learned that it was not like her—but what we say is not always like us.

She said she'd arrived at the museum late, but that they'd let her in when they learned she was Norwegian.

"Not the first time the Norwegians storm York," someone remarked.

"Quite right," she said. "England was ours and we lost her—if, that is, anyone can possess anything or anything can really be lost."

It was at that point that I looked at her. A line somewhere in William Blake talks about girls of soft silver or furious gold, but in Ulrikke there was both gold and softness. She was light and tall, with sharp features and gray eyes. Less than by her face, I was impressed by her air of calm mystery. She smiled easily, and her smile seemed to take her somewhere far away. She was dressed in black—unusual in the lands of the north, which try to cheer the dullness of the surroundings with bright colors. She spoke a neat, precise English, slightly stressing the *r*'s. I am no great observer; I discovered these things gradually.

We were introduced. I told her I was a professor at the University of the Andes, in Bogotá. I clarified that I myself was Colombian.

"What is 'being Colombian'?"

"I'm not sure," I replied. "It's an act of faith."

"Like being Norwegian," she said, nodding.

I can recall nothing further of what was said that night. The next day I came down to the dining room early. I saw through the windows that it had snowed; the moors ran on seamlessly into the morning. There was no one else in the dining room. Ulrikke invited me to share her table. She told me she liked to go out walking alone.

I remembered an old quip of Schopenhauer's.

"I do too. We can go out alone together," I said.

We walked off away from the house through the newly fallen snow. There was not a soul abroad in the fields. I suggested we go downriver a few miles, to Thorgate. I know I was in love with Ulrikke; there was no other person on earth I'd have wanted beside me.

Suddenly I heard the far-off howl of a wolf. I have never heard a wolf howl, but I know that it was a wolf. Ulrikke's expression did not change.

After a while she said, as though thinking out loud:

"The few shabby swords I saw yesterday in York Minster were more moving to me than the great ships in the museum at Oslo."

Our two paths were briefly crossing: that evening Ulrikke was to continue her journey toward London; I, toward Edinburgh.

"On Oxford Street," she said, "I will retrace the steps of de Quincey, who went seeking his lost Anna among the crowds of London."

"De Quincey," I replied, "stopped looking. My search for her, on the other hand, continues, through all time."

"Perhaps," Ulrikke said softly, "you have found her."

I realized that an unforeseen event was not to be forbidden me, and I kissed her lips and her eyes. She pushed me away with gentle firmness, but then said:

"I shall be yours in the inn at Thorgate. I ask you, meanwhile, not to touch me. It's best that way."

For a celibate, middle-aged man, proffered love is a gift that one no longer hopes for; a miracle has the right to impose conditions. I recalled my salad days in Popayán and a girl from Texas, as bright and slender as Ulrikke, who had denied me her love.

I did not make the mistake of asking her whether she loved me. I realized that I was not the first, and would not be the last. That adventure, perhaps the last for me, would be one of many for that glowing, determined disciple of Ibsen.

We walked on, hand in hand.

"All this is like a dream," I said, "and I never dream."

"Like that king," Ulrikke replied, "who never dreamed until a sorcerer put him to sleep in a pigsty."

Then she added:

"Ssh! A bird is about to sing."

In a moment we heard the birdsong.

"In these lands," I said, "people think that a person who's soon to die can see the future."

"And I'm about to die," she said.

I looked at her, stunned.

"Let's cut through the woods," I urged her. "We'll get to Thorgate sooner."

"The woods are dangerous," she replied.

We continued across the moors.

"I wish this moment would last forever," I murmured.

"*Forever* is a word mankind is forbidden to speak," Ulrikke declared emphatically, and then, to soften her words, she asked me to tell her my name again, which she hadn't heard very well.

"Javier Otárola," I said.

She tried to repeat it, but couldn't. I failed, likewise, with *Ulrikke.*

"I will call you Sigurd," she said with a smile.

"And if I'm to be Sigurd," I replied, "then you shall be Brunhild."

Her steps had slowed.

"Do you know the saga?" I asked.

"Of course," she said. "The tragic story that the Germans spoiled with their parvenu Nibelungen."

I didn't want to argue, so I answered:

"Brunhild, you are walking as though you wanted a sword to lie between us in our bed."

We were suddenly before the inn. I was not surprised to find that it, like the one we had departed from, was called the Northern Inn.

From the top of the staircase, Ulrikke called down to me:

"Did you hear the wolf? There are no wolves in England anymore. Hurry up."

As I climbed the stairs, I noticed that the walls were papered a deep crimson, in the style of William Morris, with intertwined birds and fruit. Ulrikke entered the room first. The dark chamber had a low, peaked ceiling. The expected bed was duplicated in a vague glass, and its burnished mahogany reminded me of the mirror of the Scriptures. Ulrikke had already undressed. She called me by my true name, Javier. I sensed that the snow was coming down harder. Now there was no more furniture, no more mirrors. There was no sword between us. Like sand, time sifted away. Ancient in the dimness flowed love, and for the first and last time, I possessed the image of Ulrikke.

The Congress

Ils s'acheminèrent vers un château immense, au frontispice duquel on lisait: "Je n'appartiens à personne et j'appartiens à tout le monde. Vous y étiez avant que d'y entrer, et vous y serez encore quand vous en sortirez."

Diderot: *Jacques Le Fataliste et son Maître* (1769)

My name is Alexander Ferri. There are martial echoes in the name, but neither the trumpets of glory nor the great shadow of the Macedonian (the phrase is borrowed from the author of *Los mármoles*, whose friendship I am honored to claim) accord very well with the gray, modest man who weaves these lines on the top floor of a hotel on Calle Santiago del Estero in a Southside that's no longer the Southside it once was. Any day now will mark the anniversary of my birth more than seventy years ago; I am still giving English lessons to very small classes of students. Indecisiveness or oversight, or perhaps other reasons, led to my never marrying, and now I am alone. I do not mind solitude; after all, it is hard enough to live with oneself and one's own peculiarities. I can tell that I am growing old; one unequivocal sign is the fact that I find novelty neither interesting nor surprising, perhaps because I see nothing essentially new in it—it's little more than timid variations on what's already been. When I was young, I was drawn to sunsets, slums, and misfortune; now it is to mornings in the heart of the city and tranquility. I no longer play at being Hamlet. I have joined the Conservative Party and a chess club, which I attend as a spectator—sometimes an absentminded one. The curious reader may exhume, from some obscure shelf in the National Library on Calle México, a copy of my book *A Brief Examination of the Analytical Language of John Wilkins*, a work which ought to be republished if only to correct or mitigate its many errors. The new director of the library, I am told, is a literary gentleman who has devoted himself to the study of antique languages, as though the languages of today were not sufficiently primitive, and to the demagogical glorification of an imaginary Buenos Aires of knife fighters. I have never wished to meet him. I arrived in this city in 1899, and fate has brought me face to face with a knife fighter, or an individual with a reputation as one, exactly once. Later, if the occasion presents itself, I will relate that incident.

I have said that I am alone; a few days ago, a fellow resident here in the hotel, having heard me talk about Fermín Eguren, told me that he had recently died, in Punta del Este.

I find my sadness over the death of that man (who most emphatically was never my friend) to be curiously stubborn. I know that I am alone; I am the world's only custodian of the memory of that *geste* that was the Congress, a memory I shall never share again. I am now its only delegate. It is true that all mankind are delegates, that there is not a soul on the planet who is not a delegate, yet I am a member of the Congress in another way—I *know* I am; that is what makes me different from all my innumerable colleagues, present and future. It is true that on February 7, 1904, we swore by all that's sacred—is there anything on earth that is sacred, or anything that's not?—that we would never reveal the story of the Congress, but it is no less true that the fact that I am now a perjurer is also part of the Congress. That statement is unclear, but it may serve to pique my eventual readers' curiosity.

At any rate, the task I have set myself is not an easy one. I have never attempted to produce narrative prose, even in its epistolary form; to make matters worse, no doubt, the story I am about to tell is not believable. It was the pen of José Fernández Irala, the undeservedly forgotten poet of *Los mármoles,* that fate had destined for this enterprise, but now it is too late. I will not deliberately misrepresent the facts, but I can foresee that sloth and clumsiness will more than once lead me into error.

The exact dates are of no importance. I would remind the reader that I came here from Santa Fe, the province of my birth, in 1899. I have never gone back; I have grown accustomed to Buenos Aires (a city I am not, however, particularly fond of) like a person grown accustomed to his own body, or an old ache. I sense, though I find little interest in the fact, that my death is near; I should, therefore, hold in check my tendency to digress, and get on with telling the story.

Years do not change our essence, if in fact we have an essence; the impulse that led me one night to the Congress of the World was that same impulse that had initially betaken me to the city room of the newspaper *Ultima Hora.** For a poor young man from the provinces, being a newspaperman can be a romantic life, much as a poor young man from the big city might conceive a gaucho's life to be romantic, or the life of a peon on his little piece of land. I am not embarrassed to have wanted to be a journalist, a profession which now strikes me as trivial. I recall having heard my colleague Fernández Irala say that the journalist writes to be forgotten, while he himself wanted to write to be remembered, and to last. By then he had already sculpted (the word was in common use) some of the perfect sonnets that were to appear sometime later, with the occasional slight retouching, in the pages of *Los mármoles.*

I cannot put my finger on the first time I heard someone mention the Congress. It may have been that evening when the paymaster paid me my monthly salary and to celebrate that proof that I was now a part of Buenos Aires I invited Irala to have dinner with me. Irala said he was sorry, he couldn't that night, he couldn't miss the Congress. I immediately realized that he was not referring to that pompous, dome-capped building at the far end of an avenue on which so many Spaniards chose to live, but rather to something more secret, and more important. People talked about the Congress—some with open contempt, others with lowered voices, still others with alarm or curiosity; all, I believe, in ignorance. A few Saturdays later, Irala invited me to go with him. He had seen, he said, to all the necessary arrangements.

It was somewhere between nine and ten at night. On the trolley, Irala told me that the preliminary meetings took place on Saturday and that don Alejandro Glencoe, perhaps inspired by my name, had already given leave for me to attend. We went into the Confitería del Gas.* The delegates, some fifteen or twenty I would say, were sitting around a long table; I am not certain whether there was a raised dais or whether memory has added it. I recognized the chairman immediately, though I had never seen him before. Don Alejandro was a gentleman of dignified air, well past middle age, with a wide, frank forehead, gray eyes, and a red beard flecked generously with white. I never saw him in anything but a dark frock coat; he tended to sit with his crossed hands resting on his walking stick. He was tall, and robust-looking. To his left sat a much younger man, likewise with red hair; the violent color of this latter fellow's hair suggested fire, however, while the color of Glencoe's beard was more like autumn leaves. To Glencoe's right sat a young man with a long face and a singularly low forehead, and quite the dandy. Everyone had ordered coffee; one and another had also ordered absinthe. The first thing that caught my attention was the presence of a woman, the only one among so many men. At the other end of the table there was a boy about ten years old, dressed in a sailor suit; he soon fell asleep. There were also a Protestant minister, two unequivocal Jews, and a Negro with a silk kerchief and very tight clothing in the style street corner toughs affected in those days. Before the Negro and the boy there sat cups of chocolate. I cannot recall the others, except for one Sr. Marcelo del Mazo, a man of exquisite manners and cultured conversation, whom I never saw again. I still have a blurred and unsatisfactory photograph of one of the meetings, though I shan't publish it because the clothing of the period, the hair and mustaches, would leave a comical and even seedy impression that would misrepresent the scene. All organizations tend to create their own dialects and their own rituals; the Congress, which was always slightly dreamlike to me, apparently wanted its delegates to discover gradually, and without haste, the goal that the Congress sought, and even the Christian names and patronymics of their colleagues. I soon realized that I was under an obligation not to ask questions, and so I abstained from questioning Fernández Irala, who for his own part volunteered nothing. I missed not a single Saturday, but a month or two passed before I understood. From the second meeting on, the person who sat next to me was Donald Wren, an engineer for the Southern Railway, who would later give me English lessons.

Don Alejandro spoke very little; the others did not address him directly, but I sensed that they were speaking for his benefit and sought his approval. A wave of his slow hand sufficed to change the subject of discussion. Little by little I discovered that the red-haired man to his left bore the odd name Twirl. I recall the impression of frailty he gave—the characteristic of certain very tall men, as though their height gave them vertigo and made them stoop. His hands, I recall, often toyed with a copper compass, which from time to time he would set on the table. He died in late 1914, an infantryman in an Irish regiment. The man who always sat at don Alejandro's right was the beetle-browed young man, Fermín Eguren, the chairman's nephew. I am not a believer in the methods of realism, an artificial genre if ever there was one; I prefer to reveal from the very beginning, and once and for all, what I only gradually came to know. But before that, I want to remind the reader of my situation at that time: I was a poor young man from Casilda, the son of farmers; I had made my way to Buenos Aires and suddenly found myself, or so I felt, at the very center of that great city—perhaps, who can say, at the center of the world. A half century has passed, yet I still feel that first sense of dazzled bewilderment—which would by no means be the last.

These, then, are the facts; I will relate them very briefly:

Don Alejandro Glencoe, the chairman, was a rancher from the eastern province,* the owner of a country estate on the border with Brazil. His father, originally from Aberdeen, had settled in South America in the middle of the last century. He had brought with him some hundred or so books—the only books, I daresay, that don Alejandro had ever read in his life. (I mention these heterogeneous books, which I have held in my own hands, because one of them contained the seed from which my tale springs.) When the elder Glencoe died, he left a daughter and a son; the son would grow up to be our chairman. The daughter, who married a man named Eguren, was Fermín's mother. Don Alejandro ran once for the House of Deputies, but political bosses barred his way to the Uruguayan Congress. This rebuff rankled him, and he resolved to found *another* Congress—a Congress of enormously grander scope. He recalled having read in one of Carlyle's volcanic pages of the fate of that Anacharsis Cloots, worshiper of the goddess Reason, who stood at the head of thirty-six foreigners and spoke, as the "spokesman for the human race," before an assembly in Paris. Inspired by Cloots' example, don Alejandro conceived the idea of establishing a Congress of the World, which would represent all people of all nations. The headquarters for the organizational meetings was the Confitería del Gas; the opening ceremonies, set for four years thence, would take place at don Alejandro's ranch. He, like so many Uruguayans, was no follower of Artigas,* and he loved Buenos Aires, but he was determined that the Congress should meet in his homeland. Curiously, the original date for that first meeting would be met with almost magical exactness.

At first we received a not inconsiderable honorarium for the meetings we attended, but the zeal that inflamed us all caused Fernández Irala, who was as poor as I was, to renounce his, and we others all followed suit. That gesture turned out to be quite salutary, as it separated the wheat from the chaff; the number of delegates dropped, and only the faithful remained. The only salaried position was that of the secretary, Nora Erfjord, who had no other means of subsistence and whose work was overwhelming. Keeping tabs on an entity which embraced the entire planet was no trivial occupation. Letters flew back and forth, as did telegrams. Messages of support came in from Peru, Denmark, and Hindustan. A Bolivian gentleman pointed out that his country was totally landlocked, with no access to the sea whatsoever, and suggested that that deplorable condition should be the topic of one of our first debates.

Twirl, a man of lucid intelligence, remarked that the Congress presented a problem of a philosophical nature. Designing a body of men and women which would represent all humanity was akin to fixing the exact number of Platonic archetypes, an enigma that has engaged the perplexity of philosophers for centuries. He suggested, therefore, that (to take but one example) don Alejandro Glencoe might represent ranchers, but also Uruguayans, as well as founding fathers and red-bearded men and men sitting in armchairs. Nora Erfjord was Norwegian. Would she represent secretaries, Norwegians, or simply all beautiful women? Was one engineer sufficient to represent all engineers, even engineers from New Zealand?

It was at that point, I believe, that Fermín interrupted.

"Ferri can represent wops,"* he said with a snort of laughter.

Don Alejandro looked at him sternly.

"Sr. Ferri," don Alejandro said serenely, "represents immigrants, whose labors are even now helping to build the nation."

Fermín Eguren could never stand me. He thought highly of himself on several counts: for being a Uruguayan, for coming of native stock, for having the ability to attract women, for having discovered an expensive tailor, and, though I shall never know why, for being descended from the Basques—a people who, living always on the margins of history, have never done anything but milk cows.

One particularly trivial incident sealed our mutual enmity. After one of our sessions, Eguren suggested that we go off to Calle Junín.* The idea held little interest for me, but I agreed, so as not to expose myself to his railery. Fernández Irala went with us. As we were leaving the house we had been to, we bumped into a big, burly brute of a man. Eguren, who'd no doubt been drinking a little too much, gave him a shove. The other man blocked our way angrily.

"The man that wants to leave here is going to have to get past this knife," he said.

I remember the gleam of the blade in the dimness of the vestibule. Eguren stepped back, terrified. I was scared, too, but my anger got the better of my fear. I put my hand inside my jacket, as though to pull out a knife.

"Let's settle this in the street," I said in a steady voice.

The stranger answered back, his voice changed.

"That's a man to my own heart! I just wanted to test you fellows, friend."

Now he was chuckling.

"*You* used the word 'friend,' I didn't," I rejoined, and we walked out.

The man with the knife went on into the whorehouse. I was told later that his name was Tapia or Paredes or something of the sort, and that he was a famous troublemaker. Out on the sidewalk, Irala, who'd been calm up to that point, slapped me on the back.

"At least there was one musketeer among the three of us!" he exclaimed. "*Salve, d'Artagnan!*"

Fermín Eguren never forgave me for having witnessed him back down.

I feel that it is at this point, and only at this point, that the story begins. The pages that have gone before have recorded only the conditions required by chance or fate in order for the incredible event (perhaps the only event of my entire life) to occur. Don Alejandro Glencoe was always at the center of the web of plans, but we gradually began to feel, not without some astonishment and alarm, that the real chairman was Twirl. This singular individual with his flaming mustache fawned upon Glencoe and even Fermín Eguren, but with such exaggeration that the fawning might be taken for mockery, and therefore not compromise his dignity. Glencoe prided himself upon his vast fortune, and Twirl figured out that all it took to saddle Glencoe with some new project was to suggest that the undertaking might be too costly. At first, I suspect, the Congress had been little more than a vague name; Twirl was constantly proposing ways to expand it, and don Alejandro always went along. It was like being at the center of an ever-widening, endlessly expanding circle that seemed to be moving farther and farther beyond one's reach. Twirl declared, for example, that the Congress could not do without a library of reference books; Nierenstein, who worked in a bookstore, began bringing us the atlases of Justus Perthes and sundry encyclopedias, from Pliny's *Historia Naturalis* and Beauvais' *Speculum* to the pleasant labyrinths (I reread these pages with the voice of Fernández Irala) of the illustrious French *encyclopédistes*, of the *Britannica*, of Pierre Larousse, Brockhaus, Larsen, and Montaner y Simón. I recall having reverently caressed the silky volumes of a certain Chinese encyclopedia, the beautiful brushstrokes of its characters seeming more mysterious to me than the spots on a leopard's skin. I will not reveal at this point the fate those silken pages met, a fate I do not lament.

Don Alejandro had conceived a liking for Fernández Irala and me, perhaps because we were the only delegates that did not try to flatter him. He invited us to spend a few days with him on his ranch, La Caledonia, where the carpenters, chosen from among the laborers on the estate, were already hard at work.

After a long journey upriver and a final crossing on a raft, we stepped one morning onto the eastern shore. Even after all that, we had to pass several nights in poverty-stricken general stores and open and close many a gate in many a stock fence across the Cuchilla Negra. We were riding in a gig; the landscape seemed much larger and more lonely to me than that of the little plot where I was born.

I still retain my two distinct images of the ranch: the one I'd pictured to myself before we arrived and the one my eyes actually took in. Absurdly, I had imagined, as though in a dream, an impossible combination of the flatlands around Santa Fe and the Palace of Running Waters*: La Caledonia was in fact a long adobe house with a peaked roof of thatched straw and a brick gallery. To my eyes, it looked built to last: the rough walls were almost a yard thick, and the doors were narrow. No one had thought of planting a tree; the place was battered by the first sun of morning and the last sun of evening. The corrals were of stone; the herd was large, the cows skinny and behorned; the swirling tails of the horses reached the ground. I tasted for the first time the meat of a just-slaughtered animal. The men brought out sacks of hardtack; a few days later, the foreman told me he'd never tasted bread in his life. Irala asked where the bathroom was; don Alejandro swept his arm through the air expansively, as much as to say "the entire continent." It was a moonlit night; I went out for a walk and came upon him, watched over by a rhea.

The heat, which nightfall had not softened, was unbearable, but everyone exclaimed over the evening's coolness. The rooms were low-ceiling'd and numerous, and they seemed run-down to me; Irala and I were given one that faced south. It had two cots and a washstand, whose pitcher and basin were of silver. The floor was of packed earth.

The next day I came upon the library and its volumes of Carlyle, and I looked up the pages devoted to that spokesman for the human race, Anacharsis Cloots, who had brought me to that morning and that solitude. After breakfast (identical to dinner) don Alejandro showed us the site of the Congress' new headquarters. We rode out a league on horseback, across the open plains. Irala, who sat his horse more than a bit nervously, had a spill.

"That city boy really knows how to get off a horse," the foreman said with a straight face.

We saw the building from a distance. A score or so of men had raised a sort of amphitheater, still in bits and pieces. I recall scaffolding, and tiers of seats through which one could glimpse stretches of sky.

More than once I tried to converse with the gauchos, but every attempt failed. Somehow they knew they were different. But they were sparing with their words even among themselves, speaking their nasal, Brazilianized sort of Spanish. No doubt their veins carried Indian and Negro blood. They were strong, short men; in La Caledonia I was tall, which I had never been before. Almost all of them wore the *chiripá,* and some wore the wide-legged *bombacha.** They had little or nothing in common with the mournful characters in Hernández or Rafael Obligado.* Under the spur of their Saturday alcohol, they could be casually violent. There were no women, and I never heard a guitar.

But the men that lived on that frontier did not make as great an impression on me as the complete change that had taken place in don Alejandro. In Buenos Aires he was an affable, moderate man; in La Caledonia, he was the stern patriarch of a clan, as his forebears had been. Sunday mornings he would read the Scripture to the laborers on his ranch; they understood not a word. One night, the foreman, a youngish man who had inherited the position from his father, came to tell us that a sharecropper and one of the laborers were about to have a knife fight. Don Alejandro stood up unhurriedly. He went out to the ring of men, took off the weapon he always wore, gave it to the foreman (who seemed to have turned fainthearted at all this), and stepped between the two blades. Immediately I heard his order:

"Put those knives down, boys."

Then in the same calm voice he added:

"Now shake hands and behave yourselves. I'll have no squawks of this sort here."

The two men obeyed. The next day I learned that don Alejandro had dismissed the foreman.

I felt I was being imprisoned by the solitude. I feared I would never make it back to Buenos Aires. I can't say whether Fernández Irala shared that fear, but we talked a great deal about Argentina and what we would do when we got back. I missed not the places one ordinarily might miss but rather the lions at the entrance to a house on Calle Jujuy near the Plaza del Once,* or the light from a certain store of inexact location. I was always a good rider; I soon fell into the habit of mounting a horse and riding for great distances. I still remember that big piebald I would saddle up—surely he's dead by now. I might even have ridden into Brazil one afternoon or evening, because the frontier was nothing but a line traced out by boundary stones.

I had finally taught myself not to count the days when, after a day much like all the others, don Alejandro surprised us.

"We're turning in now," he informed us. "Tomorrow morning we'll be leaving at first light."

Once I was downriver I began to feel so happy that I could actually think about La Caledonia with some affection.

We began to hold our Saturday sessions again. At the first meeting, Twirl asked for the floor. He said (with his usual flowery turn of phrase) that the library of the Congress of the World must not be limited to reference books alone—the classics of every land and language were a treasure we overlooked, he declared, only at our peril. His motion was passed immediately; Fernández Irala and Dr. Cruz, a professor of Latin, undertook to choose the necessary texts. Twirl had already spoken with Nierenstein about the matter.

At that time there was not an Argentine alive whose Utopia was not Paris. Of us all, the man who champed at the bit the most was perhaps Fermín Eguren; next was Fernández Irala, for quite different reasons. For the poet of *Los mármoles,* Paris was Verlaine and Leconte de Lisle; for Eguren, an improved extension of Calle Junín. He had come to an understanding, I presume, with Twirl. At another meeting, Twirl brought up the language that would be used by the delegates to the Congress, and he suggested that two delegates be sent immediately to London and Paris to do research. Feigning impartiality, he first proposed my name; then, after a slight pause, the name of his friend Eguren. Don Alejandro, as always, went along.

I believe I mentioned that Wren, in exchange for a few lessons in Italian, had initiated me into the study of that infinite language English. He passed over grammar and those manufactured "classroom" sentences (insofar as possible) and we plunged straight into poetry, whose forms demand brevity. My first contact with the language that would fill my life was Stevenson's courageous "Requiem"; after that came the ballads that Percy unveiled to the decorous eighteenth century. A short while before my departure for London, I was introduced to the dazzling verse of Swinburne, which led me (though it felt like sin) to doubt the preeminence of Irala's alexandrines.

I arrived in London in early January of 1902. I recall the caress of the snow, which I had never seen before, and which I must say I liked. Happily, I had not had to travel with Eguren. I stayed at a modest inn behind the British Museum, to whose library I would repair morning and afternoon, in search of a language worthy of the Congress of the World. I did not neglect the universal languages; I looked into Esperanto (which Lugones' *Lunario sentimental** calls "reasonable, simple, and economical") and Volapük, which attempts to explore all the possibilities of language, declining verbs and conjugating nouns. I weighed the arguments for and against reviving Latin (for which one still finds some nostalgia, even after so many centuries). I also devoted some time to a study of the analytical language of John Wilkins, in which the definition of each word is contained in the letters that constitute it. It was under the high dome of the reading room that I met Beatrice.

This is the general history of the Congress of the World, not the history of Alexander Ferri—emphatically not my own—and yet the first includes the second, as it includes all others. Beatrice was tall and slender, her features pure and her hair bright red; it might have reminded me of the devious Twirl's, but it never did. She was not yet twenty. She had left one of the northern counties to come and study literature at the university. Her origins, like mine, were humble. In the Buenos Aires of that time, being of Italian extraction was a questionable social recommendation; in London I discovered that for many people it was romantic. It took us but a few afternoons to become lovers; I asked her to marry me, but Beatrice Frost, like Nora Erfjord, was a votary of the religion of Ibsen and would not join herself to any man. From her lips came the word I dared not speak. Oh nights, oh shared warm darkness, oh love that flows in shadow like a secret river, oh that moment of joy in which two are one, oh innocence and openness of delight, oh the union into which we entered, only to lose ourselves afterward in sleep, oh the first soft lights of day, and myself contemplating her.

On that harsh border with Brazil I had been prey to homesickness; not so in the red maze of London, which gave me so many things. But in spite of the pretexts I invented to put off my departure, at the end of the year I had to return; we would celebrate Christmas together. I promised her that don Alejandro would ask her to join the Congress; she replied, vaguely, that she'd like to visit the Southern Hemisphere—a cousin of hers, she said, a dentist, had settled in Tasmania. Beatrice had no wish to see the boat off; farewells, in her view, were an emphasis, a senseless celebration of misfortune, and she hated emphases. We parted at the library where we had met the previous winter. I am a coward; to avoid the anguish of waiting for her letters, I did not give her my address.

I have noticed that return voyages are shorter than voyages out, but that particular crossing of the Atlantic, wallowing in memories and heavy seas, seemed inordinately long to me. Nothing pained me so much as thinking that Beatrice's life, parallel with my own, was continuing onward, minute by minute and night by night. I wrote a letter many pages long, and tore it up when we anchored in Montevideo. I arrived in my own country on a Thursday; Irala was at the dock to greet me. I returned to my old lodgings in Calle Chile. That day and the next we spent talking and walking; I wanted to recapture Buenos Aires. It was a relief to know that Fermín Eguren was still in Paris; the fact that I'd returned before him might somehow mitigate my long absence.

Irala was discouraged. Fermín was spending vast sums of money in Europe and more than once had disobeyed instructions to return immediately. That was all predictable enough. It was other news that I found more disturbing: despite the objections of Irala and Cruz, Twirl had invoked Pliny the Younger—who had affirmed that there was no book so bad that it didn't contain some good—to suggest that the Congress indiscriminately purchase collections of *La Prensa,* thirty-four hundred copies (in various formats) of *Don Quijote,* Balmes' *Letters,* and random collections of university dissertations, short stories, bulletins, and theater programs. "All things are testaments," he had said. Nierenstein had seconded him; don Alejandro, "after three thunderous Saturdays," had agreed to the motion. Nora Erfjord had resigned her post as secretary; she was replaced by a new member, Karlinski, who was a tool of Twirl's. The enormous packages now began piling up, uncataloged and without card files, in the back rooms and wine cellar of don Alejandro's mansion. In early July, Irala had spent a week in La Caledonia. The carpenters were not working. The foreman, questioned about this, explained that don Alejandro had ordered the work halted, and the workers were feeling the time on their hands.

In London I had drafted a report (which need not concern us here); on Friday, I went to pay my respects to don Alejandro and deliver the manuscript to him. Fernández Irala went with me. It was that hour of the evening when the pampas wind begins to blow; the house was filled with breezes. Before the iron gate on Calle Alsina there stood a wagon with three horses. I recall men, bent under the weight of their loads, carrying large bundles into the rear patio; Twirl was imperiously ordering them about. There too, as though they'd had a foreboding, were Nora Erfjord and Nierenstein and Cruz and Donald Wren and one or two others. Nora put her arms around me and kissed me, and that embrace, that kiss, reminded me of others. The Negro, high-spirited and gay, kissed my hand.

In one of the bedrooms the square trap-door to the cellar was lying open; crude cement steps led down into the dimness.

Suddenly we heard footsteps. Even before I saw him, I knew it was don Alejandro arriving home. He was almost running when he came into the room.

His voice was changed. It was not the voice of the thoughtful, deliberate gentleman who presided over our Saturday meetings, nor was it the voice of the feudal seigneur who stopped a knife fight and read the word of God to his gauchos, though it did resemble this latter one. He did not look at anyone when he spoke.

"Start bringing up everything that's piled down there," he commanded. "I don't want a book left in that cellar."

The job took almost an hour. In the earthen-floored patio we made a pile of books taller than the tallest among us. We all worked, going back and forth until every book had been brought up; the only person that did not move was don Alejandro.

Then came the next order:

"Now set that mound afire."

Twirl was pallid. Nierenstein managed to murmur:

"The Congress of the World cannot do without these precious aids that I have chosen with such love."

"The Congress of the World?" said don Alejandro, laughing scornfully—and I had never heard him laugh.

There is a mysterious pleasure in destruction; the flames crackled brightly while we cowered against the walls or huddled into the bedrooms. Night, ashes, and the smell of burning lingered in the patio. I recall a few lost pages that were saved, lying white upon the packed earth. Nora Erfjord, who professed for don Alejandro that sort of love that young women sometimes harbor for old men, finally, uncomprehending, spoke:

"Don Alejandro knows what he's doing."

Irala, one of literature's faithful, essayed a phrase:

"Every few centuries the Library at Alexandria must be burned."

It was then that we were given the explanation for all this.

"It has taken me four years to grasp what I am about to tell you. The task we have undertaken is so vast that it embraces—as I now recognize—the entire world. It is not a handful of prattling men and women muddying issues in the barracks of some remote cattle ranch. The Congress of the World began the instant the world itself began, and it will go on when we are dust. There is no place it is not. The Congress is the books we have burned. It is the Caledonians who defeated the Cæsars' legions. It is Job on the dunghill and Christ on the Cross. The Congress is even that worthless young man who is squandering my fortune on whores."

I could not restrain myself, and I interrupted.

"Don Alejandro, I am guilty too. I had finished my report, which I have here with me, but I stayed on in England, squandering your money, for the love of a woman."

"I supposed as much, Ferri," he said, and then continued: "The Congress is my bulls. It is the bulls I have sold and the leagues of countryside that do not belong to me."

An anguished voice was raised; it was Twirl's.

"You're not telling us you've sold La Caledonia?"

Don Alejandro answered serenely:

"I have. Not an inch of land remains of what was mine, but my ruin cannot be said to pain me because now I understand. We may never see each other again, because we no longer need the Congress, but this last night we shall all go out to contemplate the Congress."

He was drunk with victory; his firmness and his faith washed over us. No one thought, even for a second, that he had gone insane.

In the square we took an open carriage. I climbed into the coachman's seat, beside the coachman.

"Maestro," ordered don Alejandro, "we wish to tour the city. Take us where you will."

The Negro, standing on a footboard and clinging to the coach, never ceased smiling. I will never know whether he understood anything of what was happening.

Words are symbols that posit a shared memory. The memory I wish to set down for posterity now is mine alone; those who shared it have all died. Mystics invoke a rose, a kiss, a bird that is all birds, a sun that is the sun and yet all stars, a goatskin filled with wine, a garden, or the sexual act. None of these metaphors will serve for that long night of celebration that took us, exhausted but happy, to the very verge of day. We hardly spoke, while the wheels and horseshoes clattered over the paving stones. Just before dawn, near a dark and humble stream—perhaps the Maldonado, or perhaps the Riachuelo—Nora Erfjord's high soprano sang out the ballad of Sir Patrick Spens, and don Alejandro's bass joined in for a verse or two—out of tune. The English words did not bring back to me the image of Beatrice. Twirl, behind me, murmured:

"I have tried to do evil yet I have done good."

Something of what we glimpsed that night remains—the reddish wall of the Recoleta, the yellow wall of the prison, two men on a street corner dancing the tango the way the tango was danced in the old days, a checkerboard entryway and a wrought-iron fence, the railings of the railroad station, my house, a market, the damp and unfathomable night—but none of these fleeting things (which may well have been others) matters. What matters is having felt that that institution of ours, which more than once we had made jests about, truly and secretly existed, and that it was the universe and ourselves. With no great hope, through all these years I have sought the savor of that night; once in a great while I have thought I caught a snatch of it in a song, in lovemaking, in uncertain memory, but it has never fully come back to me save once, one early morning, in a dream. By the time we'd sworn we would tell none of this to anyone, it was Saturday morning.

I never saw any of those people again, with the exception of Irala, and he and I never spoke about our adventure; any word would have been a profanation. In 1914, don Alejandro Glencoe died and was buried in Montevideo. Irala had died the year before.

I bumped into Nierenstein once on Calle Lima, but we pretended we didn't see each other.

There Are More Things

To the memory of H. P. Lovecraft

Just as I was about to take my last examination at the University of Texas, in Austin, I learned that my uncle Edwin Arnett had died of an aneurysm on the remote frontier of South America. I felt what we always feel when someone dies—the sad awareness, now futile, of how little it would have cost us to have been more loving. One forgets that one is a dead man conversing with dead men. The subject I was studying was philosophy; I recalled that there in the Red House near Lomas, my uncle, without employing a single proper noun, had revealed to me the lovely perplexities of the discipline. One of the dessert oranges was the tool he employed for initiating me into Berkeleyan idealism; he used the chessboard to explain the Eleatic paradoxes. Years later, he lent me Hinton's treatises, which attempt to prove the reality of a fourth dimension in space, a dimension the reader is encouraged to intuit by means of complicated exercises with colored cubes. I shall never forget the prisms and pyramids we erected on the floor of his study.

My uncle was an engineer. Before retiring from his job at the railway, he made the decision to move to Turdera,* which offered him the combined advantages of a virtual wilderness of solitude and the proximity of Buenos Aires. There was nothing more natural than that the architect of his home there should be his close friend Alexander Muir. This strict man professed the strict doctrine of Knox; my uncle, in the manner of almost all the gentlemen of his time, was a freethinker—or an agnostic, rather—yet at the same time he was interested in theology, the way he was interested in Hinton's fallacious cubes and the well-thought-out nightmares of the young Wells. He liked dogs; he had a big sheepdog he called Samuel Johnson, in memory of Lichfield, the distant town he had been born in.

The Red House stood on a hill, hemmed in to the west by swampy land.

The Norfolk pines along the outside of the fence could not temper its air of oppressiveness. Instead of flat roofs where one might take the air on a sultry night, the house had a peaked roof of slate tiles and a square tower with a clock; these structures seemed to weigh down the walls and stingy windows of the house. As a boy, I accepted those facts of ugliness as one accepts all those incompatible things that only by reason of their coexistence are called "the universe."

I returned to my native country in 1921. To stave off lawsuits, the house had been auctioned off; it had been bought by a foreigner, a man named Max Preetorius, who paid double the amount bid by the next highest bidder. After the bill of sale was signed, he arrived one evening with two assistants and they threw all the furniture, all the books, and all the household goods in the house into a dump not far from the Military Highway. (I recall with sadness the diagrams in the volumes of Hinton and the great terraqueous globe.) The next day, he went to Muir and suggested certain changes to the house, which Muir indignantly refused to carry out. Subsequently, a firm from Buenos Aires undertook the work. The carpenters from the village refused to refurnish the house; a certain Mariani, from Glew,* at last accepted the conditions that Preetorius laid down. For a fortnight, he was to work at night, behind closed doors. And it was by night that the new resident of Red House took up his habitation. The windows were never opened anymore, but through the darkness one could make out cracks of light. One morning the milkman came upon the body of the sheepdog, decapitated and mutilated, on the walk. That winter the Norfolk pines were cut down. No one ever saw Preetorius again; he apparently left the country soon after.

Such reports, as the reader may imagine, disturbed me. I know that I am notorious for my curiosity, which has, variously, led me into marriage with a woman utterly unlike myself (solely so that I might discover who she was and what she was really like), into trying laudanum (with no appreciable result), into an exploration of transfinite numbers, and into the terrifying adventure whose story I am about to tell. Inevitably, I decided to look into this matter.

My first step was to go and see Alexander Muir. I remembered him as a ramrod-straight, dark man whose leanness did not rule out strength; now he was stooped with years and his jet black beard was gray. He greeted me at the door of his house in Temperley—which predictably enough resembled my uncle's, as both houses conformed to the solid rules of the good poet and bad builder William Morris.

Our conversation was flinty; not for nothing is the thistle the symbol of

Scotland. I sensed, however, that the strong Ceylon tea and the judicious plate of scones (which my host broke and buttered as though I were still a child) were, in fact, a frugal Calvinistic feast laid out to welcome his old friend's nephew. His theological debates with my uncle had been a long game of chess, which demanded of each player the collaborative spirit of an opponent.

Time passed and I could not bring myself to broach my subject. There was an uncomfortable silence, and then Muir himself spoke.

"Young man," he said, "you have not taken such trouble to come here to talk to me about Edwin or the United States, a country that holds little interest for me. What keeps you from sleeping at night is the sale of the Red House, and that curious individual that's bought it. Well, it keeps me from sleeping, too. Frankly, I find the whole affair most disagreeable, but I'll tell you what I can. It shan't be much."

In a moment, he went on, without haste.

"Before Edwin died, the mayor called me into his office. The parish priest was there. They wanted me to draw up the plans for a Catholic chapel. They would pay me well. I gave them my answer on the spot. No, I told them, I am a servant of the Lord, and I cannot commit the abomination of erecting altars for the worship of idols."

Here he stopped.

"That's all?" I hazarded.

"No. That Jewish whelp Preetorius wanted me to destroy my work, the house I'd built, and put up a monstrosity in its place. Abomination takes many forms."

He pronounced these words with great gravity, then he stood up.

As I turned the corner, Daniel Iberra approached me. We knew each other the way people in small towns do. He suggested we walk back together. I've never held any brief for hellions and that lot, and I could foresee a sordid string of more or less violent and more or less apocryphal bar stories, but I resigned myself and said I'd walk with him. It was almost dark. When he saw the Red House up on its hill a few blocks away, Iberra turned down another street. I asked him why. His answer was not what I'd expected.

"I'm don Felipe's right arm. Nobody's ever been able to say I backed down from anything. You probably remember that fellow Urgoiti that came all the way here from Merlo looking for me, and what happened to him when he found me. Well, listen—a few nights ago I was coming back from a big whoop-de-doo. About a hundred yards from the house, I saw something. My pinto spooked, and if I hadn't talked her down and turned down along that alleyway there, I might not be telling the story. What I saw was . . ." He shook his head. Then, angrily, he cursed.

That night I couldn't sleep. Toward sunrise I dreamed of an engraving in the style of Piranesi, one I'd never seen before or perhaps had seen and forgotten—an engraving of a kind of labyrinth. It was a stone amphitheater with a border of cypresses, but its walls stood taller than the tops of the trees. There were no doors or windows, but it was pierced by an infinite series of narrow vertical slits. I was using a magnifying glass to try to find the Minotaur. At last I saw it. It was the monster of a monster; it looked less like a bull than like a buffalo, and its human body was lying on the ground. It seemed to be asleep, and dreaming—but dreaming of what, or of whom?

That evening I passed by the Red House. The gate in the fence was locked, and some iron bars had been twisted around it. What had been the garden was now weeds. Off to the right there was a shallow ditch, and its banks were trampled.

I had one card still up my sleeve, but I put off playing it for several days, not only because I sensed how utterly useless it would be but also because it would drag me to the inevitable, the ultimate.

Finally, with no great hopes, I went to Glew. Mariani, the carpenter, now getting on in years, was a fat, rosy Italian—a very friendly, unpretentious fellow. The minute I saw him I discarded the stratagems that had seemed so promising the day before. I gave him my card, which he spelled out to himself aloud with some ceremony, and with a slight reverential hitch when he came to the *Ph.D.* I told him I was interested in the furnishings he had made for the house that had belonged to my uncle, in Turdera. The man talked on and on. I will not attempt to transcribe his many (and expressively gesticulated) words, but he assured me that his motto was "meet the client's demands, no matter how outrageous," and told me he'd lived up to it. After rummaging around in several boxes, he showed me some papers I couldn't read, signed by the elusive Preetorius. (No doubt he took me for a lawyer.) When we were saying our good-byes, he confided that all the money in the world couldn't persuade him to set foot again in Turdera, much less in that house. He added that the customer is always right, but that in his humble opinion, Sr. Preetorius was "not *quite* right," if I knew what he meant—he tapped his forehead with his finger. Then, regretting he'd gone so far, he would say no more. I could get not another word out of him.

I had foreseen this failure, but it is one thing to foresee something, and another thing when it comes to pass.

Over and over I told myself that time—that infinite web of yesterday, today, the future, forever, never—is the only true enigma. Such profound thoughts availed me nothing; after dedicating my evening to the study of Schopenhauer or Royce I would still wander, night after night, along the dirt roads bordering the Red House. At times I would make out a very white light up on the hill; at others I would think I could hear moaning. This went on until the nineteenth of January.

It was one of those days in Buenos Aires when one feels not only insulted and abused by the summer, but actually degraded. It was about eleven that night when the storm clouds burst. First came the south wind, and then sheets, waves, torrents of water. I scurried about in the darkness, trying to find a tree to take shelter under. In the sudden sharp light from a bolt of lightning, I found that I was but steps from the fence. I am not certain whether it was with fear or hopefulness that I tried the gate. Unexpectedly, it opened. Buffeted by the storm, I made my way in; sky and earth alike impelled me. The front door of the house was also ajar. A gust of rain lashed my face, and I went in.

Inside, the floor tiles had been taken up; my feet trod grass in clumps and patches. A sweetish, nauseating odor filled the house. To the left or right, I am not sure which, I stumbled onto a stone ramp. I scrambled up it. Almost unthinkingly my hand sought the light switch.

The dining room and library of my recollections were now (the dividing wall having been torn out) one large ruinous room, with pieces of furniture scattered here and there. I will not attempt to describe them, because in spite of the pitiless white light I am not certain I actually saw them. Let me explain: In order truly to see a thing, one must first understand it. An armchair implies the human body, its joints and members; scissors, the act of cutting. What can be told from a lamp, or an automobile? The savage cannot really perceive the missionary's Bible; the passenger does not see the same ship's rigging as the crew. If we truly saw the universe, perhaps we would understand it.

None of the insensate forms I saw that night corresponded to the human figure or any conceivable use. They inspired horror and revulsion. In one corner I discovered a vertical ladder that rose to the floor above. The wide iron rungs, no more than ten in all, were spaced irregularly; that ladder, which implied hands and feet, was comprehensible, and somehow it relieved me. I turned off the light and waited for a while in the darkness. I could hear not the slightest sound, but the presence of so many incomprehensible things unnerved me. At last, I made my decision.

Upstairs, my trembling hand once again reached out for the light switch. The nightmare prefigured by the downstairs rooms stirred and flowered in the upper story. There were many objects, or several interwoven ones. I now recall a long, U-shaped piece of furniture like an operating table, very high, with circular openings at the extremes. It occurred to me that this might be the bed used by the resident of the house, whose monstrous anatomy was revealed obliquely by this object in much the way the anatomy of an animal, or a god, may be known by the shadow it casts. From some page of Lucan, read years ago and then forgotten, there came to my lips the word *amphisbæna,* which suggested (though by no means fully captured) what my eyes would later see. I also recall a V of mirrors that faded into shadows above.

What must the inhabitant of this house be like? What must it be seeking here, on this planet, which must have been no less horrible to it than it to us? From what secret regions of astronomy or time, from what ancient and now incalculable twilight, had it reached this South American suburb and this precise night?

I felt that I had intruded, uninvited, into chaos. Outside, the rain had stopped. I looked at my watch and saw with astonishment that it was almost two A.M. I left the light on and began cautiously to climb back down the ladder. Climbing down what I had once climbed up was not impossible—climbing down before the inhabitant came back. I conjectured that it hadn't locked the front door and the gate because it hadn't known how.

My feet were just touching the next to last rung when I heard something coming up the ramp—something heavy and slow and plural. Curiosity got the better of fear, and I did not close my eyes.

The Sect of the Thirty

The original manuscript may be consulted in the library at the University of Leyden; it is in Latin, but its occasional Hellenism justifies the conjecture that it may be a translation from the Greek. According to Leisegang, it dates from the fourth century of the Christian era; Gibbon mentions it, in passing, in one of his notes to the fifteenth chapter of *The Decline and Fall.* These are the words of its anonymous author:

. . . The Sect was never large, but now its followers are few indeed. Their number decimated by sword and fire, they sleep by the side of the road or in the ruins spared them by war, as they are forbidden to build dwellings. They often go about naked. The events my pen describes are known to all men; my purpose here is to leave a record of that which has been given me to discover about their doctrine and their habits. I have engaged in long counsel with their masters, but I have not been able to convert them to Faith in Our Lord.

The first thing which drew my attention was the diversity of their opinion with respect to the dead. The most unschooled among them believe that they shall be buried by the spirits of those who have left this life; others, who do not cleave so tight to the letter, say that Jesus' admonition *Let the dead bury the dead* condemns the showy vanity of our funerary rites.

The counsel to sell all that one owns and give it to the poor is strictly observed by all; the first recipients give what they receive to others, and these to yet others. This is sufficient explanation for their poverty and their nakedness, which likewise brings them closer to the paradisal state. Fervently they cite the words *Consider the ravens: for they neither sow nor reap: which neither have storehouse nor barn: and God feedeth them: how much more are ye better than the fowls?* The text forbids saving, for *If God so clothe the grass, which is today in the field, and tomorrow is cast into the oven: how much more will he clothe you, O ye of little faith? And seek not what ye shall eat, or what ye shall drink, neither be ye of doubtful mind.*

The prescription *Whosoever looketh on a woman to lust after her hath committed adultery with her already in his heart* is an unmistakable exhortation to purity. Still, many are the members of the Sect who teach that because there is no man under heaven who has not looked upon a woman to desire her, then we have all committed adultery. And since the desire is no less sinful than the act, the just may deliver themselves up without risk of hellfire to the exercise of the most unbridled lustfulness.

The Sect shuns churches; its teachers preach in the open, from a mountaintop or the top of a wall, or sometimes from a boat upturned upon the shore.

There has been persistent speculation as to the origins of the Sect's name. One such conjecture would have it that the name gives us the number to which the body of the faithful has been reduced; this is ludicrous but prophetic, as the perverse doctrine of the Sect does indeed predestine it to extinction. Another conjecture derives the name from the height of the Ark, which was thirty cubits; another, misrepresenting astronomy, claims that the name is taken from the number of nights within the lunar month; yet another, from the baptism of the Savior; another, from the age of Adam when he rose from the red dust. All are equally false. No less untruthful is the catalog of thirty divinities or *thrones,* of which, one is Abraxxas, pictured with the head of a cock, the arms and torso of a man, and the coiled tail of a serpent.

I know the Truth but I cannot plead the Truth. To me the priceless gift of giving word to it has not been granted. Let others, happier men than I, save the members of the Sect by the word. By word or by fire. It is better to be killed than to kill oneself. I shall, therefore, limit myself to an account of the abominable heresy.

The Word was made flesh so that He might be a man among men, so that men might bind Him to the Cross, and be redeemed by Him. He was born from the womb of a woman of the chosen people not simply that He might teach the gospel of Love but also that He might undergo that martyrdom.

It was needful that all be unforgettable. The death of a man by sword or hemlock was not sufficient to leave a wound on the imagination of mankind until the end of days. The Lord disposed that the events should inspire pathos. That is the explanation for the Last Supper, for Jesus' words foretelling His deliverance up to the Romans, for the repeated sign to one of His disciples, for the blessing of the bread and wine, for Peter's oaths, for the solitary vigil on Gethsemane, for the twelve men's sleep, for the Son's human plea, for the sweat that was like blood, for the swords, the betraying kiss, the Pilate who washed his hands of it, the flagellation, the jeers and derision, the thorns, the purple and the staff of cane, the vinegar with honey, the Tree upon the summit of the Hill, the promise to the good thief, the earth that shook, and the darkness that fell upon the land.

Divine mercy, to which I myself owe so many blessings, has allowed me to discover the true and secret reason for the Sect's name. In Kerioth, where it is plausibly reputed to have arisen, there has survived a conventicle known as the Thirty Pieces of Silver. That was the Sect's original name, and it provides us with the key. In the tragedy of the Cross (and I write this with all the reverence which is its due) there were those who acted knowingly and those who acted unknowingly; all were essential, all inevitable. Unknowing were the priests who delivered the pieces of silver; unknowing, too, was the mob that chose Barabbas; unknowing the Judean judge, the Romans who erected the Cross on which He was martyred and who drove the nails and cast the lots. Of knowing actors, there were but two: Judas and the Redeemer. Judas cast away the thirty coins that were the price of our souls' salvation and immediately hanged himself. At that moment he was thirty-three years old, the age of the Son of Man. The Sect venerates the two equally, and absolves the others.

There is not one lone guilty man; there is no man that does not carry out, wittingly or not, the plan traced by the All-Wise. All mankind now shares in Glory.

My hand fails when I will it to write a further abomination. The initiates of the Sect, upon reaching a certain age, are mocked and crucified on the peak of a mountain, to follow the example of their masters. This criminal violation of the Fifth Commandment should be met with the severity that human and divine laws have ever demanded. May the curses of the Firmament, may the hatred of angels . . .

The end of the manuscript has not been discovered.

The Night of the Gifts

It was in the old Café Aguila, on Calle Florida near the intersection of Piedad,* that we heard the story.

We were debating the problem of knowledge. Someone invoked the Platonic idea that we have already seen all things in some former world, so that "knowing" is in fact "recognizing"; my father, I think it was, said that Bacon had written that if learning was remembering, then not knowing a thing was in fact having forgotten it. Another member of the group, an elderly gentleman, who was no doubt a bit lost in all that metaphysics, decided to put in his two cents' worth. He spoke with slow assurance.

· · ·

I've never been able to understand that business about Platonic archetypes. Nobody remembers the first time they saw yellow or black, or the first time they tasted some fruit—most likely because they were little and had no way of knowing they were at the beginning of a long, long series. There are other first times, of course, that nobody forgets. I could tell you fellows the memory of a certain night I often cast my mind back to—April 30, of '74.

Summers were longer in the old days, but I don't know why we'd stayed till such a late date at the place that some cousins of ours owned a few leagues from Lobos—Dorna, their name was. That was the summer that one of the laborers, a fellow named Rufino, initiated me into the customs of the country life. I was about to turn thirteen; he was a good bit older, and he had a reputation for being hot-tempered. He was quite a hand with a knife; when they practiced with burned sticks, the one that invariably wound up with a black smear across his face was the other fellow. One Friday he suggested that he and I might go to town on Saturday night for some fun. I jumped at the chance, of course, though I had no very clear idea of what fun he might be referring to. I warned him I didn't know how to dance; he said dancing was easy to learn. After dinner, must have been about seven-thirty, we headed out. Rufino had spruced himself up like a fellow on his way to a party, and he was sporting a knife with a silver handle; I left my little hatpin of a knife at home, for fear of being joshed some about it. It didn't take us long to come in sight of the first houses. Have any of you fellows ever been to Lobos? Just as well; there's not a town in the provinces that's not just like all the others—even to the point of thinking it's different. The same dirt streets with the same holes in them, the same squat houses—as though to make a man on horseback feel all the taller. We pulled up at this one corner in front of a house painted light blue or pink, with the name La Estrella painted on it. There were horses tied to the hitching post, with nice saddles, all of them. The front door was open a bit, and I could see a crack of light. Off the back of the vestibule there was a long room with plank benches all along the walls and between one bench and another all these dark doorways that led who knew where. An ugly little yellow dog scurried out yapping to make us feel welcome. There were quite a few people; half a dozen women wearing flowered housecoats were wandering around. A respectable-looking woman, dressed in black from head to toe, looked to me to be the owner of the house. Rufino walked up and said hello to her, then gestured toward me.

"I've brought you a new friend," he said, "but he's not much of a rider yet."

"He'll learn, don't worry your head about it," the lady replied.

That abashed me, of course. To cover my embarrassment, or maybe to make them see I was just a boy, I sat down on the end of a bench and started playing with the dog. On the kitchen table they had lit some tallow candles stuck in bottles, and I also remember the little wood stove in one corner of the room, at the back. On the whitewashed wall in front of me was a figure of the Virgen de la Merced.

There was a good bit of joking, and somebody was strumming at a guitar—not that it did him much good. Out of sheer timidity, I didn't say no to the gin somebody offered me, which burned my mouth like red-hot coals. Among the women there was one that seemed different to me from the others. They called her the Captive. There was something kind of Indian-featured about her, but she was as pretty as a picture—that sad-eyed look, you know. Her hair was in a braid that reached all the way to her waist. Rufino saw that I was looking at her.

"Tell us that story about the Indian raid again, to freshen up our memories some," he said to her.

The way the girl talked, there mightn't have been another soul in the room, and somehow I got the feeling there was nothing else she could think about, that this was the only thing that had happened to her in her whole life. She told the story this way—

"When they brought me from Catamarca I was just a little girl. What could I know about Indian raids? On the ranch they were so afraid of them they wouldn't even mention them. Gradually I learned about the raids, almost like they were a secret that nobody was supposed to tell—how Indians might swarm down like a thundercloud and kill people and steal the animals. Women, they carried off to the interior, and did terrible things to them. I tried as hard as I could not to believe it. Lucas, my brother, who later got speared, swore it was all lies, but when something's true, you know it the first time you hear it. The government sends them things—tobacco, *mate*, liquor, *hierba*—to keep them quiet, but they have crafty leaders—spirit men—that warn them off it. If a chief of theirs orders it, they think nothing of storming down on a fort. The forts are scattered. . . . From thinking about it so much, I almost wished they'd come, and I would sit and look out in the direction where the sun goes down. I never learned about keeping track of time, but I do know there came frosts and summers and branding seasons and the death of the foreman's son, and then they did come. It was like the very wind off the pampas brought them. I saw a thistle flower in a ravine and I dreamed of the Indians. The next morning it happened. Like in an earthquake, the animals knew it before we did. The whole herd was skittish, and birds were flying through the air every which way. We ran to look out in the direction I always looked in . . ."

"Who brought you the warning?" somebody asked.

The girl still seemed far away. She just repeated her last words.

"We ran to look out in the direction I always looked in. It was like the whole desert had up and started moving. Through those thick rods of the wrought-iron fence we saw the dust clouds before we saw the Indians. They were on a raid. They were slapping their mouths with their hands and yelping. There were rifles in Santa Irene, but all they were good for was stunning them and making them all the madder."

The Captive's way of speaking was like a person saying a prayer, from memory; but out in the street I could hear the Indians coming across the plain, and their yelping. Then a door banged open, and they were in the room—you'd have thought they'd ridden their horses inside, into the rooms of a dream. It was a bunch of drunken brawlers from the docks. Now, in my memory's eye, they look very tall. The one in the lead gave Rufino, who was by the door, an elbow for his trouble. Rufino turned pale, said not a word, and stepped off to one side. The lady, who'd not moved from her place, stood up.

"It's Juan Moreira,*" she announced.

Here, tonight, after so many years, I'm not sure anymore whether I remember the man that was actually there that night or whether it's the man I was to see so many times afterward around the slaughterhouses. I think about Podestá's long hair and black beard,* but there's also a blondish sort of face there somewhere, with smallpox scars. Anyway, that ugly dog skittered out yapping to greet the newcomers. With one crack of his bullwhip, Moreira laid it out dead on the floor. It fell over on its back and died waving its paws in the air. . . .

Now then, this is where the story really starts—

Without making a sound I crept over to one of the doors, which opened into a narrow hallway and a flight of stairs. Upstairs, I hid in a dark bedroom. Except for the bed, which was a low, squat affair, I couldn't say what sort of furniture there might have been. I was shaking all over. Downstairs there was yelling and shrieking, and then the sound of breaking glass. I heard a woman's footsteps coming up the stairs, and then I saw a slice of light. Then the voice of the Captive called me, almost in a whisper.

"I'm here to be of service, but only to peaceable folk. Come over here, I won't hurt you."

She had taken off her housecoat. I lay down beside her and took her face in my hands. I don't know how much time passed. There was not a word or a kiss between us. I undid her braid and played with her hair, which was long and straight, and then with her. We never saw each other again, and I never learned her name.

A gunshot stunned us.

"You can get out by the other staircase," the Captive told me.

Which is what I did, and I found myself out in the dirt street. There was a big moon that night. A police sergeant, carrying a rifle with fixed bayonet, was watching that side of the house. He laughed when he saw me.

"From all appearances," he said to me, "you like to get an early start in the morning."

I must have said something in return, but he paid me no further mind. A man was letting himself down the wall. In one movement, the sergeant ran him through with the bayonet. The man fell to the ground, where he lay on his back, whimpering and bleeding. That dog came to my mind. The sergeant stabbed the man good with the bayonet again, to finish him off once and for all.

With a happy kind of grin he said to the man, "Moreira, this time you might as well have saved your powder."

The uniformed men who'd been surrounding the house appeared from everywhere, and then came the neighbors. Andrés Chirino had to wrestle the gun out of his hand. Everybody wanted to congratulate him.

Laughing, Rufino said, "I guess that'll be this hoodlum's last dance!"

I went from group to group, telling people what I had seen. Suddenly I was very tired; it may be I had a fever. I slipped away, found Rufino, and we started back home. From the horse we could see the white light of the dawn. More than tired, I felt dazed—as though I'd been caught up in a rapids.

. . .

"In the river of the events of that night," mused my father.

The other man nodded.

"That's it exactly. Within the space of a few hours I'd learned how to make love and I'd seen death at first hand. To all men all things are revealed—or at least all those things that a man's fated to know; but from sundown of one day to sunup of the next, those two central things were revealed to me. The years go by, and I've told the story so many times that I'm not sure anymore whether I actually remember it or whether I just remember the words I tell it with. Maybe that's how it was with the Captive, with her Indian raid. At this point what difference does it make whether it was me or some other man that saw Moreira killed."

The Mirror and the Mask

When the armies clashed at the Battle of Clontarf, in which the Norwegian was brought low, the king spoke to his poet and said:

"The brightest deeds lose their luster if they are not minted in words. I desire you to sing my victory and my praises. I shall be Æneas; you shall be my Virgil. Do you believe you have the gifts worthy of this task I ask of you, which shall make us both immortal?"

"Yes, great king, I do," answered the poet. "I am Olan. For twelve winters I have honed my skills at meter. I know by heart the three hundred sixty fables which are the foundation of all true poetry. The Ulster cycle and the Munster cycle lie within my harp strings. I am licensed by law to employ the most archaic words of the language, and its most complex metaphors. I have mastered the secret script which guards our art from the prying eyes of the common folk. I can sing of love, of cattle theft, of sailing ships, of war. I know the mythological lineage of all the royal houses of Ireland. I possess the secret knowledge of herbs, astrology, mathematics, and canon law. I have defeated my rivals in public contest. I have trained myself in satire, which causes diseases of the skin, including leprosy. And I also wield the sword, as I have proven in your battle. There is but one thing that I do not know: how to express my thanks for this gift you make me."

The high king, who was easily wearied by other men's long speeches, said to the poet with relief:

"All these things I know full well. I have just been told that the nightingale has now sung in England. When the rains and snow have passed, when the nightingale has returned from its journey to the lands of the south, you shall recite your verses before the court and the Guild of Poets assembled. I give you one full year. Every letter and every word, you shall burnish to a fine gleam. The recompense, as you know, shall not be unworthy of my royal wont, nor of the hours you spend in sleepless inspiration."

"My lord, my greatest recompense is the sight of your face," said the poet, who was something of a courtier as well.

He bowed and retired, a verse or two already beginning to creep into his head.

When the allotted period had passed, a time filled with plague and rebellion, the panegyric was sung. The poet declaimed his verses with slow assurance, and without a glance at his manuscript. In the course of it, the king often nodded approvingly. Everyone imitated his gesture, even those who, crowding in at the doors, could not make out a word of it.

At last the king spoke.

"I accept this labor. It is another victory. You have given to each word its true meaning, to each noun the epithet bestowed upon it by the first poets. In all the work there is not an image which the classics did not employ. War is 'the fair cloth wov'n of men' and blood is 'sword-drink.' The sea has its god and the clouds foretell the future. You have marshaled rhyme, alliteration, assonance, scansion, the artifices of erudite rhetoric, the wise alternation of meters, and all with greatest skillfulness. If the whole of the literature of Ireland should—*omen absit*—be lost, well might it all be reconstructed, without loss, from your classic ode. Thirty scribes shall transcribe it, twelve times each."

There was a silence. Then the king went on:

"All that is well, and yet nothing has happened. In our veins the blood has beat no faster. Our hands have not gone for our bows. No one's cheeks have paled. No one has bellowed out a battle cry, no one has stood to meet the Viking attack. In one year, poet, we shall gather to applaud another poem. As a sign of our thanks, take this mirror, which is of silver."

"I thank you," said the poet, "and I understand and obey."

The stars of the sky once more journeyed their bright course. Once more sang the nightingale in the Saxon forests, and the poet returned with his scroll—shorter this time than before. He did not recite it from memory; he read it, visibly unsure, omitting certain passages, as though he himself did not entirely understand them, or did not wish to profane them. The verses were strange. They were not a description of the battle, they were the battle. In the warlike chaos of the lines there stirred the God Who Is Three Yet One, the pagan noumena of Ireland, and those who would war, centuries after, at the beginning of the Elder Edda. The poem's form was no less strange. A singular noun might govern a plural verb. The prepositions were foreign to common usage. Harshness vied with sweetness. The metaphors were arbitrary, or so they seemed.

The king exchanged a few words with the men of letters assembled about him, and he spoke in this way:

"Of your first hymn I was able to say that it was a happy summation of all that has been written in Ireland. *This* poem surpasses all that has gone before, and obliterates it. It holds one in thrall, it thrills, it dazzles. It will pass over the heads of the ignorant, and their praises will not be yours, but the praises of the few, the learned—ah! An ivory chest shall hold the only copy. From the pen that has penned such a lofty work, we may expect one that is more elevated yet. . . ."

Then he added, smiling:

"We are figures in a fable, and it is only right that we recall that in fables, the number three is first above all others."

"The three gifts of the wizard, the triads, and the indubitable Trinity," was all that the poet dared allow himself to murmur.

The king went on:

"As a token of our thanks, take this mask. It is of gold."

"I thank you, and I understand and obey," the poet said.

The anniversary returned. The palace sentinels noticed that this time the poet did not bring a manuscript. Not without dismay did the king look upon the poet: he was greatly changed. Something, which was not simply time, had furrowed and transformed his features. His eyes seemed to stare far into the distance, or to have been rendered blind. The poet begged to be allowed to speak to the king. The slaves cleared the hall.

"Have you not composed the ode?" asked the king.

"I have," said the poet sadly. "Would that Christ our Lord had forbade it."

"Can you recite it?"

"I dare not."

"I charge you with the courage that you need," the king declared.

The poet spoke the poem. It was a single line.

Unable to summon the courage to speak it again aloud, the poet and his king mouthed the poem, as though it were a secret supplication, or a blasphemy. The king was no less astounded and cowed than the poet. The two men, very pale, looked at each other.

"In the years of my youth," said the king, "I sailed toward the setting sun. On an island there, I saw silver greyhounds that hunted golden boars to their death. On another we were feted with the fragrance of magic apples.

On yet another I saw walls of fire. On the most remote of all, there was a vaulted river that hung from the sky, and in its waters swam fish and sailing ships. Those were marvels, but they do not compare with your poem, which somehow contains them all. What sorcery has given you this?"

"At dawn," said this poet, "I awoke speaking words that at first I did not understand. Those words are the poem. I felt I had committed some sin, perhaps that sin which the Holy Spirit cannot pardon."

"The sin the two of us now share," mused the king. "The sin of having known Beauty, which is a gift forbidden mankind. Now we must atone for it. I gave you a mirror and a golden mask; here is the third gift, which shall be the last."

He laid in the poet's right hand a dagger.

Of the poet, we know that he killed himself when he left the palace; of the king, that he is a beggar who wanders the roads of Ireland, which once was his kingdom, and that he has never spoken the poem again.

"Undr"

I must inform the reader that the pages I translate and publish here will be sought in vain in the *Libellus* (1615) of Adam of Bremen, who, as we all know, was born and died in the eleventh century. Lappenberg found the text within a manuscript in the Bodleian, at Oxford; given its wealth of circumstantial detail, he judged it to be a late interpolation, but he did publish it as a curiosity in his *Analecta Germanica* (Leipzig, 1894). The opinion of a mere Argentine *amateur* is worth very little; readers may judge these pages as they will. My translation is not literal, but it is faithful.

Thus writes Adam of Bremen:

. . . Of the several nations that border the wide desert which lies on the far shore of the Gulf, beyond the lands where the wild horse mates, that one most worthy of mention is the nation of the Urns. The imprecise or fabulous reports of merchants, the difficulty of the road, and the depredations of nomads prevented me from ever reaching its borders. I know, however, that its precarious and remote villages lie within the lowlands of the Wisla River. Unlike the Swedes, the Urns profess the true faith in Christ, unsullied by the Arianism and bloody worship of devils from which the royal houses of England and the other nations of the North draw their lineage. They are shepherds, ferrymen, sorcerers, swordsmiths, and ropemakers. The severity of their wars almost entirely prevents them from tilling their lands. The plains and the tribes that roam them have made the Urns skillful with horse and bow. In time, one inevitably comes to resemble one's enemies. Their lances are longer than ours, for theirs are made for horsemen, not for infantry.

As one might imagine, the use of pen, inkhorn, and parchment is unknown to them. They carve their characters in stone, as our forebears carved the runes revealed to them by Odin, after having hung from the ash tree—Odin sacrificed to Odin—for nine long nights.

To these general bits of knowledge I will add the story of my conversation with the Icelander Ulf Sigurdarson, a man of grave and measured speech. We had met in Uppsala, near the temple. The wood fire had died; the cold and the dawn light were seeping in through the uneven chinks in the walls. Outside, the gray wolves that devour the flesh of pagans sacrificed to the three gods were leaving their cautious spoor upon the snow. Our talk had begun in Latin, as is the habit between members of the clergy, but soon we had passed into the language of the North, known from Ultima Thule to the markets of Asia. This is what the man told me:

"I am of the line of *skalds;* the moment I learned that the poetry of the Urns is a poetry of a single word, I went in quest of them, in quest of the route that would lead me to their land. Not without weariness and labor did I reach it, one year later. It was night; I noticed that the men I met along my way regarded me curiously, and I could not fail to note that I was struck by an occasional stone. I saw the glow of a smith's forge, and I entered.

"The smith offered me shelter for the night. His name, he said, was Orm, and his language was more or less our own. We exchanged a few words. It was from his lips that I first heard the name of the king who then ruled over them—Gunnlaug. I learned that he had fought in their last war, that he looked with suspicion upon foreigners, and that it was his custom to crucify them. In order to avoid that fate, which was more fitting for a God than for a man, I undertook to write a *drāpa,* a laudatory composition—a sort of eulogy praising the king's victories, his fame, and his mercy. No sooner had I committed the poem to memory than two men came for me. I refused to relinquish my sword, but I allowed myself to be led away.

"The stars were still in the sky. We traveled through a stretch of land with huts scattered here and there along the way. I had heard tales of pyramids; what I saw in the first square we came to was a stake of yellow wood. On its sharp point I could make out the black figure of a fish. Orm, who had accompanied us, told me that the fish was the Word. In the next square I saw a red stake, with a disk. Orm said once more that this was the Word. I asked him to tell me what word it was; he replied that he was but a simple artisan, and did not know.

"In the third square, which was the last, I saw a stake painted black, bearing a design I no longer remember. On the far side of the square there was a long straight wall, whose ends I could not see. I later found that it was circular, roofed with clay, without interior doors, and that it girded the entire city. The horses tied to a wooden post were compact and thick-maned.

"The smith was not allowed to enter. There were armed men inside, all standing. Gunnlaug, the king, who was suffering under some great affliction, was lying with half-closed eyes upon a kind of dais; his pallet was of camel skins. He was a worn, yellow man, a sacred and almost forgotten object; long, time-blurred scars made a tracery across his chest. One of the soldiers made way for me. Someone had brought a harp. I knelt and softly intoned the *drāpa.* It was adorned with the tropes, alliterations, and accents required by the genre. I am not certain that the king understood it, but he gave me a silver ring, which I still possess. Under his pillow I glimpsed the blade of a dagger. To his right there was a chessboard of a hundred or more squares and several scattered pieces.

"The king's guards pushed me back. A man took my place, but he stood as he offered his own poem. He plucked at the harp's strings as though tuning them, and then very softly repeated the word that I wish I might have caught, but did not. Someone reverently said *Now, meaningless.*

"I saw tears here and there. The man would raise his voice or it would grow distant; the nearly identical chords were monotonous, or, more precisely, infinite. I wished the chant could go on forever, I wished it were my life. Suddenly, it ended. I heard the sound of the harp when the singer, no doubt exhausted, cast it to the floor. We made our way in disorder from the room. I was one of the last. I saw with astonishment that the light was fading.

"I walked a few steps. A hand upon my shoulder detained me. A voice said to me:

" 'The king's ring was a talisman bestowed upon you, yet soon your death shall come, for you have heard the Word. I, Bjarni Thorkelsson, will save you. I am of the lineage of the *skalds.* In your dithyramb you called blood "sword-drink" and battle "man-battle." I remember hearing those tropes from my father's father. You and I are poets; I shall save you. Now we do not name every thing or event that fires our song; we encode it in a single word, which is the Word.'

" 'I could not hear it,' I replied to him. 'I beg you to tell me what word it is.'

"He hesitated for a moment, and then said:

" 'I am sworn not to reveal it. And besides, no one can teach another anything. You must seek it on your own. We must hurry, for your life is in danger. I will hide you in my house, where they will not dare come to look for you. If the wind is with you, you shall sail tomorrow to the South.'

"Thus began the adventure that was to last for so many winters. I shall not tell its hazards, nor shall I attempt to recall the true order of its vicissitudes. I was oarsman, slave merchant, slave, woodcutter, robber of caravans, cantor, assayer of deep water and of metals. I suffered a year's captivity in the mercury mines, which loosens the teeth. I fought with men from Sweden in the militia of Mikligarthr—Constantinople. On the banks of the Azov I was loved by a woman I shall never forget; I left her, or she left me, which is the same. I betrayed and was betrayed. More than once fate made me kill. A Greek soldier challenged me to fight him, and offered me the choice of two swords. One was a handspan longer than the other. I realized that he was trying to intimidate me, so I chose the shorter. He asked me why. I told him that the distance from my hand to his heart did not vary. On the shore of the Black Sea sits the runic epitaph I carved for my comrade Leif Arnarson. I have fought with the Blue Men of Serkland, the Saracens. In the course of time I have been many men, but that whirlwind of events was one long dream. The essential thing always was the Word. There were times when I did not believe in it. I would tell myself that renouncing the lovely game of combining lovely words was foolish, that there was no reason to seek the single, perhaps illusory, One. That argument failed. A missionary suggested the word *God,* which I rejected. One sunrise, on the banks of a river that widened into the sea, I believed that the revelation had been vouchsafed me.

"I returned to the land of the Urns, and with difficulty found the poet's house.

"I entered and said my name. Night had fallen. Thorkelsson, from his place upon the ground, told me to light the candle in the bronze candelabrum. His face had aged so greatly that I could not help thinking that I myself was now old. As was the custom, I asked after the health of the king.

" 'His name is no longer Gunnlaug,' he replied. 'Now his name is other. Tell me of your travels.'

"I did so in the best order I could, and in verbose detail, which I shall here omit. Before I came to the end, the poet interrupted me.

" 'Did you often sing in those lands?' he asked.

"The question took me by surprise.

" 'At first,' I said, 'I sang to earn my bread. Then, from a fear that I do not understand, I grew distant from the singing and the harp.'

" 'Hmm.' He nodded. 'Now, go on with your story.'

"I complied. Then there fell a long silence.

" 'What were you given by the first woman you slept with?' he asked.

" 'Everything,' I answered.

" 'I, too, have been given everything, by life. Life gives all men everything, but most men do not know this. My voice is tired and my fingers weak, but listen to me. . . .'

"He spoke the word *Undr,* which means *wonder.*

"I was overwhelmed by the song of the man who lay dying, but in his song, and in his chord, I saw my own labors, the slave girl who had given me her first love, the men I had killed, the cold dawns, the northern lights over the water, the oars. I took up the harp and sang—a different word.

" 'Hmm,' said the poet, and I had to draw close to hear him. 'You have understood me.' "

A Weary Man's Utopia

He called it "Utopia," a Greek word which means "there is no such place."

Quevedo

No two mountain peaks are alike, but anywhere on earth the plains are one and the same. I was riding down a road across the plains. I asked myself without much curiosity whether I was in Oklahoma or Texas or the region that literary men call "the pampas." There was not a fence to left or right. As on other occasions, I slowly murmured these lines, more or less from Emilio Oribe:

> Riding through the ongoing, ongoing and interminable
> Terrifying plains, near the frontier of Brazil . . .

The road was rutted and uneven. Rain began to fall. Some two or three hundred yards down the road, I saw the light of a house. It was squat and rectangular and surrounded by trees. The door was opened by a man so tall it almost frightened me. He was dressed in gray. I sensed that he was waiting for someone. There was no latch or lock on the door.

We went inside, into a long room with walls of exposed wood. From the ceiling hung a lamp that gave a yellowish light. The table seemed odd, somehow. There was a water clock on the table, the first I'd ever seen, save for the occasional steel engraving in dictionaries and encyclopedias. The man motioned me to one of the chairs.

I tried several languages, but we couldn't make ourselves understood to each other. When he spoke, it was in Latin. I gathered my recollections of my distant student days and girded myself for conversation.

"By your clothing," he said, "I can see that you have come from another time. The diversity of languages encouraged the diversity of nations, and even encouraged war; the earth has returned to Latin. There are those who fear that it will degenerate into French, Limousine, or Papiamento, but the danger is not imminent. And in any case, neither that which has been nor that which is to be holds any interest for me."

I said nothing; the man went on.

"If it does not repulse you to see another person eat, would you like to join me?"

I realized that he had seen that I was at an utter loss, so I said I would.

We went down a corridor with several doors leading off it and came into a small kitchen in which everything was made of metal. We returned to the first room with our dinner on a tray: bowls of cornflakes, a bunch of grapes, a fruit that was unknown to me but whose taste was something like a fig, and a large pitcher of water. I don't believe there was any bread. My host's features were sharp, and there was something peculiar about his eyes. I shall never forget that stern, pale face that I shall never see again. He did not gesture with his hands when he talked.

I was a bit tongue-tied by having to speak Latin, but at last I said:

"You are not astounded by my sudden appearance here?"

"No," he replied, "every century or so we receive these visits. They do not last long; you will be back home by tomorrow, at the latest."

The certainty in his voice relieved me. I thought it proper to introduce myself:

"I am Eudoro Acevedo. I was born in 1897 in the city of Buenos Aires. I am now seventy years old, a professor of English and American literature and a writer of tales of fantasy."

"I remember having read without displeasure," he said, "two tales of fantasy—the Travels of Captain Lemuel Gulliver, which many people believe to have really taken place, and the *Summa Theologica.* But let us not talk of facts. No one cares about facts anymore. They are mere points of departure for speculation and exercises in creativity. In school we are taught Doubt, and the Art of Forgetting—especially forgetting all that is personal and local. We live in time, which is successive, but we try to live *sub specie æternitatis.* There are a few names from the past that are still with us, though the language tends to forget them. We avoid pointless precision. There is no chronology or history; no statistics, either. You told me your name is Eudoro; I cannot tell you mine, because everyone calls me 'somebody' or 'you.' "

"But what was your father's name?"

"He had none."

On one of the walls I noticed a bookshelf. I opened a volume at random; the letters were clear and indecipherable and written by hand. Their angular lines reminded me of the runic alphabet, though it had been used only for inscriptions. It occurred to me that the people of the future were not only taller, they were more skilled as well. I instinctively looked at the man's long elegant fingers.

"Now," he said to me, "you are going to see something you have never seen before."

He carefully handed me a copy of More's *Utopia,* the volume printed in Basel in 1518; some pages and illustrations were missing.

It was not without some smugness that I replied:

"It is a printed book. I have more than two thousand at home, though they are not as old or as valuable."

I read the title aloud.

The man laughed.

"No one can read two thousand books. In the four hundred years I have lived, I've not read more than half a dozen. And in any case, it is not the reading that matters, but the rereading. Printing, which is now forbidden, was one of the worst evils of mankind, for it tended to multiply unnecessary texts to a dizzying degree."

"In that strange yesterday from which I have come," I replied, "there prevailed the superstition that between one evening and the next morning, events occur that it would be shameful to have no knowledge of. The planet was peopled by spectral collectives—Canada, Brazil, the Swiss Congo, the Common Market. Almost no one knew the prior history of those Platonic entities, yet everyone was informed of the most trivial details of the latest conference of pedagogues or the imminent breaking off of relations between one of these entities and another and the messages that their presidents sent back and forth—composed by a secretary to the secretary, and in the prudent vagueness that the form requires.

"All this was no sooner read than forgotten, for within a few hours it would be blotted out by new trivialities. Of all functions, that of the politician was without doubt the most public. An ambassador or a minister was a sort of cripple who had to be transported in long, noisy vehicles surrounded by motorcyclists and grenadiers and stalked by eager photographers. One would have thought their feet had been cut off, my mother used to say. Images and the printed word were more real than things. People believed only what they could read on the printed page. The principle, means, and end of our singular conception of the world was *esse est percipi*—'to be is to be portrayed.' In the past I lived in, people were credulous; they believed that a piece of merchandise was good because the manufacturer of that piece of merchandise said it was. Robbery was also a frequent occurrence, though everyone knew that the possession of money brings with it neither greater happiness nor greater peace of mind."

"Money?" my host repeated. "No one any longer suffers poverty, which must have been unbearable—nor suffers wealth, for that matter, which must have been the most uncomfortable form of vulgarity. Every person now has a job to perform."

"Like rabbis," I said.

He seemed not to understand; he continued on.

"There are no cities, either. To judge by the ruins of Bahía Blanca,* which curiosity once led me to explore, it's no great loss. Since there are no possessions, there is no inheritance. When a man reaches a hundred years of age, he is ready to confront himself and his solitude. He will have engendered one child."

"One child?" I asked.

"Yes. One. It is not advisable that the human race be too much encouraged. There are those who think that awareness of the universe is a faculty that comes from the deity, yet no one knows for a certainty whether this deity exists. I believe that what is being discussed now is the advantages and disadvantages of the gradual or simultaneous suicide of every person on earth. But let us return to the matter at hand."

I nodded.

"When the individual has reached a hundred years of age, he is able to do without love and friendship. Illness and inadvertent death are not things to be feared. He practices one of the arts, or philosophy or mathematics, or plays a game of one-handed chess. When he wishes, he kills himself. When a man is the master of own life, he is also the master of his death."

"Is that a quotation?" I asked.

"Of course. There is nothing but quotations left for us. Our language is a system of quotations."

"What about the great adventure of my times—space travel?" I asked.

"It's been hundreds of years since we have done any of that traveling about—though it was undoubtedly admirable. We found we could never escape the here and now."

Then, with a smile he added:

"And besides, every journey is a journey through space. Going from one planet to another is much like going to the farm across the way. When you stepped into this room, you were engaging in space travel."

"That's true," I replied. "There was also much talk of 'chemical substances' and 'zoological animals.' "

The man now turned his back to me and looked out the windows. Outside, the plains were white with silent snow and moonlight.

I emboldened myself to ask:

"Are there still museums and libraries?"

"No. We want to forget the past, save for the composition of elegies. There are no commemorations or anniversaries or portraits of dead men. Each person must produce on his own the arts and sciences that he has need for."

"In that case, every man must be his own Bernard Shaw, his own Jesus Christ, and his own Archimedes."

He nodded wordlessly.

"What happened to the governments?" I inquired.

"It is said that they gradually fell into disuse. Elections were called, wars were declared, taxes were levied, fortunes were confiscated, arrests were ordered, and attempts were made at imposing censorship—but no one on the planet paid any attention. The press stopped publishing pieces by those it called its 'contributors,' and also publishing their obituaries. Politicians had to find honest work; some became comedians, some witch doctors—some excelled at those occupations. The reality was no doubt more complex than this summary."

Then his tone changed, and he said:

"I have built this house, which is like all other houses. I have built these furnishings and made these household goods. I have worked in the fields, though other men, whose faces I have not seen, may well have worked them better. I can show you some things."

I followed him into an adjoining room. He lighted a lamp, which also hung from the ceiling. In one corner I saw a harp; it had very few strings. On the walls hung rectangular paintings in which the color yellow predominated. They did not look as if the same hand had painted them all.

"This is my work," he said.

I examined the paintings, and I stopped before the smallest of them, which portrayed, or suggested, a sunset, though there was something of the infinite about it.

"If you like it, you may take it back with you, as a souvenir of a future friend," he said serenely.

I thanked him, but the other canvases disturbed me. I will not say that they were blank, but they were almost blank.

"They are painted with colors that your ancient eyes cannot see."

His delicate hands plucked the strings of the harp and I could hear faint occasional notes.

It was then that the banging began.

A tall woman and three or four men came into the house. One would have said they were brothers and sister, or that time had made them resemble one another. My host spoke first to the woman:

"I knew you would not fail to come tonight. Have you seen Nils?"

"Every few evenings. He is still mad about painting."

"Let us hope he has better luck at it than his father had."

Manuscripts, paintings, furniture, household goods—we left nothing in the house.

The woman worked as hard as the men. I felt embarrassed at my own weakness, which kept me from being much help to them. No one closed the door as, loaded down with our burden, we left. I noticed that the house had a peaked roof.

After about fifteen minutes of walking, we turned toward the left. In the distance I saw a kind of tower, crowned with a dome.

"It is the crematory," someone said. "The death chamber is inside. They say it was invented by a philanthropist whose name, I believe, was Adolf Hitler."

The caretaker, whose height did not take me aback, opened the gate to us.

My host whispered a few words. Before going in, he waved good-bye.

"There'll be more snow," the woman announced.

In my study on Calle México still hangs the canvas that someone will paint, thousands of years from now, with substances that are now scattered across the planet.

The Bribe

The story I shall tell is about two men, or rather about an incident in which two men played a part. The event, which is not at all singular or fantastic, is less important than the character of the two men involved. Both were vain, though in very different ways and with very different results. The anecdote (for it's really very little more than that) took place a short time ago in one of the states of the United States. In my opinion, it couldn't have happened anywhere else.

In late 1961, at the University of Texas in Austin, I was fortunate enough to have a long conversation with one of the two men, Dr. Ezra Winthrop. Dr. Winthrop was a professor of Old English (he did not approve of calling it Anglo-Saxon, which suggests an artifact cobbled together out of two separate pieces). I recall that without ever actually contradicting me he corrected my many errors and presumptuous temerities. I was told that on oral examinations he never put questions to the candidate—instead he invited the candidate to chat about this or that subject, leaving to the person being examined the choice of the topic to be discussed. Of old Puritan stock, a native of Boston, he'd found it hard to adapt to the customs and prejudices of the south. He missed the snow, but I've noticed that northerners are taught to take measures against the cold the way we are against the heat. The hazy image that remains to me is that of a man on the tall side, with gray hair, less spry than strong. My recollection of his colleague Herbert Locke is clearer; Locke gave me a copy of his book *Toward a History of the Kenning*, which declares that the Saxons soon put aside those somewhat mechanical metaphors they used (the sea as "whale-road," the eagle as "battle-falcon"), while the Scandinavian poets were combining and intermingling them almost to the point of inextricability. I mention Herbert Locke because he is an integral part of my story.

I come now to the Icelander Eric Einarsson, perhaps the true protagonist. I never saw him. He had come to Texas in 1969, when I was in Cambridge, but letters from a mutual friend, Ramón Martínez López, have left me with the conviction that I knew him intimately. I know that he is impetuous, energetic, and cold; in a land of tall men he is tall. Given his red hair, it was inevitable that students should start calling him Eric the Red. It was his view that the use of an inevitably error-ridden slang makes the foreigner an interloper, and so he never condescended to use the ubiquitous "O.K." A fine scholar of English, Latin, the Scandinavian languages, and (though he wouldn't admit it) German, he easily made a way for himself in American universities. His first article was a monograph on the four articles de Quincey had written on the influence of the Danes on the lake region of Westmoreland. This was followed by a second, on the dialect of the Yorkshire peasant. Both studies were well received, but Einarsson thought his career needed something a bit more "astonishing." In 1970, Yale published his copiously annotated critical edition of the ballad of the Battle of Maldon. The scholarship of the notes was undeniable, but certain hypotheses in the introduction aroused some controversy in the virtually hermetic spheres of academe. Einarsson claimed, for example, that the style of the ballad is similar, though admittedly in a distant sort of way, to the epic fragment *Finnsburh,* rather than to the measured rhetoric of *Beowulf,* and that the poem's employment of moving circumstantial details oddly prefigures the methods that we admire, not without good reason, in the Icelandic sagas. He also proposed emendations for several readings in Elphinston's edition. In 1969 he had been given an appointment at the University of Texas. As we all know, American universities are forever sponsoring conferences of Germanists. Dr. Winthrop had chaired the previous conference, in East Lansing. The head of his department, who was preparing to go abroad on his sabbatical, asked Winthrop to suggest a person to chair the next one, in Wisconsin. There were really only two candidates to choose between—Herbert Locke and Eric Einarsson.

Winthrop, like Carlyle, had renounced the Puritan faith of his forebears, but not their sense of right and wrong. He did not decline to offer his opinion; his duty was clear. Since 1954 Herbert Locke had been of inestimable help in the preparation of a certain annotated edition of *Beowulf* which, at certain institutions of higher learning, had replaced that of Klaeber; he was now compiling a work that would be of great usefulness to Germanists: an English/Anglo-Saxon dictionary that was certain to save readers hours of often fruitless searching through etymological dictionaries. Einarsson was much the younger. His sharpness and impertinence had won him general dislike, including Winthrop's, but his critical edition of *Finnsburh* had contributed not a little to building a reputation. And he was disputatious; at the conference he would be a better moderator than the shy and taciturn Locke. That was the state of Winthrop's deliberations when the incident occurred.

From the Yale press there appeared a long article on the teaching of Anglo-Saxon language and literature in universities. At the end of the last page appeared the transparent initials *E.E.* and, to dispel any doubt as to the authorship, the words *"University of Texas."* The article, written in the correct English of a nonnative speaker, never stooped to incivility, yet it did have a certain belligerence about it. It argued that beginning the study of Anglo-Saxon with *Beowulf*, a work of ancient date but a rhetorical, pseudo-Virgilian style, was no less arbitrary than beginning the study of English with the intricate verses of Milton. It advised that chronological order be inverted: begin with the eleventh-century poem "The Grave," through which something of the modern-day language might be glimpsed, and then work backward to the beginnings. As for *Beowulf*, some fragment excerpted from the tedious 3000-line amalgam would suffice—the funerary rites of the Scyld, for example, who returned to the sea as they had come from the sea. Not once was Winthrop's name mentioned, but Winthrop felt persistently attacked. The attack, if there was one, mattered less to him than the fact that his pedagogical methods were being impugned.

There were but a few days left. Winthrop wanted to be fair, and he could not allow Einarsson's article (already being reread and talked about by many people) to influence his decision. But the decision was not easy. One morning Winthrop spoke with his director; that same afternoon, Einarsson received official word that he would be going to Wisconsin to chair the conference.

On the day before the nineteenth of March, the day of his departure, Einarsson appeared in Ezra Winthrop's office. He had come to say good-bye and to thank him. One of the windows overlooked a diagonal, tree-lined walk, and the office was lined with books. Einarsson immediately recognized the parchment-bound first edition of the *Edda Islandorum*. Winthrop replied that he knew Einarsson would carry out his mission well, and that he had nothing to thank him for. The conversation was, unless I am mistaken, a long one.

"Let's speak frankly," Einarsson said. "There's not a soul in this university that doesn't know that it is on your recommendation that Dr. Lee Rosenthal, our director, has honored me with the mission of representing our university. I will try not to disappoint him. I am a good Germanist; the language of the sagas is the language of my childhood, and I speak Anglo-Saxon better than my British colleagues. My students say *cyning,* not *cunning.* They also know that they are absolutely forbidden to smoke in class and that they cannot come in dressed like hippies. As for my frustrated rival, it would be the worst of bad taste for me to criticize him; the *Kenning* book clearly shows that he has looked into not only the primary sources but the pertinent articles by Meissner and Marquardt as well. But let us not pursue those trivialities.

"I owe you an explanation, Dr. Winthrop. I left my homeland in late 1967. When a man decides to leave his country and go to a distant land, he inevitably assumes the burden of 'getting ahead' in that new place. My first two little articles, which were strictly philological, were written for reasons other than to prove my ability. That, clearly, would not be enough. I had always been interested in 'Maldon,' which except for an occasional stumble I can recite from memory. I managed to persuade Yale to publish my critical edition. The ballad, as you know, records a Scandinavian victory, but as to my claim that it influenced the later Icelandic sagas, I believe that to be an absurd and even unthinkable idea. I included it in order to flatter English readers.

"I come now to the essential point—my controversial note in the *Yale Monthly.* As you must surely be aware, it presents, or attempts to present, the case for my approach to the subject, but it deliberately exaggerates the shortcomings in yours, which, in exchange for subjecting students to the tedium of three thousand consecutive complex verses that narrate a confused story, provides them with a large vocabulary that will allow them to enjoy—if by then they have not abandoned it—the entire corpus of Anglo-Saxon literature. Going to Wisconsin was my real goal. You and I, my dear friend, know that conferences are silly, that they require pointless expenditures, but that they are invaluable to one's *curriculum vitæ.*"

Winthrop looked at him quizzically. He was intelligent, but he tended to take things seriously, including conferences and the universe, which could well be a cosmic joke.

"Perhaps you recall our first conversation," Einarsson went on. "I had just arrived from New York. It was a Sunday; the university dining hall was closed so we went over to the Nighthawk to have lunch. I learned many things that day. Like all good Europeans, I had always assumed that the Civil War was a crusade against slavery; you argued that the South had had a right to secede from the Union and maintain its own institutions. To make your arguments all the more forceful, you told me that you yourself were from the North and that one of your forebears had fought in the ranks with Henry Halleck. But you also praised the bravery of the Confederate troops. Unlike most men, I can grasp almost immediately what sort of person the other person is. That lunch was all I needed. I realized, my dear Winthrop, that you are ruled by that curious American passion for impartiality. You wish above all else to be 'fair-minded.' Precisely because you are from the North, you tried to understand and defend the South's cause. The moment I discovered that my trip to Wisconsin depended upon your recommendation to Rosenthal, I decided to take advantage of my little discovery. I realized that calling into question the methodology that you always use in your classes was the most effective way of winning your support. I wrote my article that very day. The submissions criteria for the journal specify that articles may be signed only with initials, but I did everything within my power to remove any doubt as to the author's identity. I even told many colleagues that I had written it."

There was a long silence. Winthrop was the first to break it.

"Now I see," he said. "I'm an old friend of Herbert's, whose work I admire; you attacked me, directly or indirectly. Refusing to recommend you would have been a kind of reprisal. I compared the merits of the two of you and the result was . . . well, we both know what the result was, don't we?"

He then added, as though thinking out loud:

"I may have given in to the vanity of not being vengeful. As you see, your stratagem worked."

" 'Stratagem' is the proper word for it," replied Einarsson, "but I do not apologize for what I did. I acted in the best interests of our institution. I had decided to go to Wisconsin come what might."

"My first Viking," said Winthrop, looking him in the eye.

"Another romantic superstition. It isn't Scandinavian blood that makes a man a Viking. My forebears were good ministers of the evangelical church; at the beginning of the tenth century, my ancestors were perhaps good solid priests of Thor. In my family, so far as I know, there has never been a man of the sea."

"In mine there have been many," Winthrop replied. "Yet perhaps we aren't so different, you and I. We share one sin, at least—vanity. You've come to my office to throw in my face your ingenious stratagem; I gave you my support so I could boast of my integrity."

"But there is something else," Einarsson responded. "Our nationality. I am an American citizen. My destiny lies here, not in Ultima Thule. You will no doubt contend that a passport does not change a man's nature."

They shook hands and said good-bye.

Avelino Arredondo

The incident occurred in Montevideo in 1897.

Every Saturday the friends took the same table, off to one side, in the Café del Globo, like the poor honest men they were, knowing they cannot invite their friends home, or perhaps escaping it. They were all from Montevideo; at first it had been hard to make friends with Arredondo, a man from the interior who didn't allow confidences or ask questions. He was hardly more than twenty, a lean, dark-skinned young man, a bit on the short side, and perhaps a little clumsy. His face would have been anonymous had it not been rescued by his eyes, which were both sleepy and full of energy. He was a clerk in a dry goods store on Calle Buenos Aires, and he studied law in his spare time. When the others condemned the war that was ravaging the country* and that the president (so general opinion believed) was waging for reprehensible reasons, Arredondo remained silent. He also remained silent when the others laughed at him and called him a tightwad.

A short time after the Battle of Cerros Blancos,* Arredondo told his friends that they wouldn't be seeing him for a while; he had to go to Mercedes. The news disturbed no one. Someone told him to watch out for Aparicio Saravia's gang of gauchos*; Arredondo smiled and said he wasn't afraid of the Whites. His interlocutor, who had joined the party, said nothing.

It was harder to say good-bye to Clara, his sweetheart. He did it with almost the same words. He told her not to expect a letter, since he was going to be very, very busy. Clara, who was not in the habit of writing, accepted the condition without protest. The two young people loved each other very much.

Arredondo lived on the outskirts. He had a black servant woman with the same last name as his; her forebears had been slaves of the family back in the time of the Great War. She was a woman of absolute trustworthiness; Arredondo instructed her to tell anyone asking for him that he was away in the country. He had picked up his last wages at the dry goods store.

He moved into a room at the back of the house, the room that opened onto the patio of packed earth. The step was pointless, but it helped him begin that reclusion that his will imposed on him.

From the narrow iron bed in which he gradually recovered his habit of taking an afternoon siesta, he looked with some sadness upon an empty bookcase. He had sold all his books, even the volumes of the Introduction to Law. All he had kept was a Bible, which he had never read and never managed to finish.

He went through it page by page, sometimes with interest and sometimes with boredom, and he set himself the task of memorizing an occasional chapter of Exodus and the last of Ecclesiastes. He did not try to understand what he was reading. He was a freethinker, but he let not a night go by without repeating the Lord's Prayer, as he'd promised his mother when he came to Montevideo—breaking that filial promise might bring bad luck.

He knew that his goal was the morning of August 25. He knew exactly how many days he had to get through. Once he'd reached his goal, time would cease, or rather nothing that happened afterward would matter. He awaited the day like a man waiting for his joy and his liberation. He had stopped his watch so he wouldn't always be looking at it, but every night, when he heard the dark, far-off sound of the twelve chimes, he would pull a page off the calendar and think *One day less.*

At first he tried to construct a routine. Drink some *mate,* smoke the black cigarettes he rolled, read and review a certain number of pages, try to chat a bit with Clementina when she brought his dinner on a tray, repeat and embellish a certain speech before he blew out the lamp. Talking with Clementina, a woman along in years, was not easy, because her memory had halted far from the city, back in the mundane life of the country.

Arredondo also had a chessboard on which he would play chaotic games that never managed to come to any end. A rook was missing; he would use a bullet or a coin in its place.

To pass the time, every morning Arredondo would clean his room with a rag and a big broom, even chasing down spiderwebs. The black woman didn't like him to lower himself to such chores—not only because they fell within her purview but also because Arredondo didn't really do them very well.

He would have liked to wake up when the sun was high, but the habit of getting up with the dawn was stronger than his mere will. He missed his friends terribly, though he knew without bitterness that they didn't miss him, given his impregnable reserve. One afternoon, one of them came around to ask after him but was met in the vestibule and turned away. The black woman didn't know him; Arredondo never learned who it had been. An avid reader of the news, Arredondo found it hard to renounce those museums of ephemera. He was not a thinking man, or one much given to meditation.

His days and his nights were the same, but Sundays weighed on him.

In mid-July he surmised he'd been mistaken in parceling out his time, which bears us along one way or another anyway. At that point he allowed his imagination to wander through the wide countryside of his homeland, now bloody, through the rough fields of Santa Irene where he had once flown kites, to a certain stocky little piebald horse, surely dead by now, through the dust raised by the cattle when the drovers herded them in, to the exhausted stagecoach that arrived every month with its load of trinkets from Fray Bentos, through the bay of La Agraciada where the Thirty-three came ashore, to the Hervidero, through ragged mountains, wildernesses, and rivers, through the Cerro he had scaled to the lighthouse, thinking that on the two banks of the River Plate there was not another like it. From the Cerro on the bay he traveled once to the peak on the Uruguayan coat of arms,* and he fell asleep.

Each night the sea breeze was cool, and good for sleeping. He never spent a sleepless night.

He loved his sweetheart with all his soul, but he'd been told that a man shouldn't think about women, especially when there were none to be had. Being in the country had accustomed him to chastity. As for the other matter . . . he tried to think as little as possible of the man he hated.

The sound of the rain on the roof was company for him.

For the man in prison, or the blind man, time flows downstream as though down a slight decline. As he reached the midpoint of his reclusion, Arredondo more than once achieved that virtually timeless time. In the first patio there was a wellhead, and at the bottom, a cistern where a toad lived; it never occurred to Arredondo that it was the toad's time, bordering on eternity, that he sought.

As the day grew near he began to be impatient again. One night he couldn't bear it anymore, and he went out for a walk. Everything seemed different, bigger. As he turned a corner, he saw a light and went into the general store, where there was a bar. In order to justify being there, he called for a shot of cane brandy. Sitting and talking, their elbows on the wooden bar, were some soldiers. One of them said:

"All of you know that it's strictly outlawed to give out any news about battles—formal orders against it. Well, yesterday afternoon something happened to us that you boys are going to like. Some barracks-mates of mine and I were walking along in front of the newspaper over there, *La Razón*. And we heard a voice inside that was breaking that order. We didn't waste a second going in there, either. The city room was as dark as pitch, but we gunned down that loose-lipped traitor that was talking. When he finally shut up, we hunted around for him to drag him out by the heels, but we saw it was a machine!—a *phonograph* they call it, and it talks all by itself!"

Everyone laughed.

Arredondo had been listening intently.

"What do you think—pretty disappointing, eh, buddy?"

Arredondo said nothing. The uniformed man put his face very near Arredondo's.

"I want to hear how loud you can yell *Viva the President of our Country, Juan Idiarte Borda!*"*

Arredondo did not disobey. Amid jeers and clapping he gained the door; in the street, he was hit by one last insult:

"Nobody ever said cowards were stupid—or had much temper, either!"

He had behaved like a coward, but he knew he wasn't one. He returned slowly and deliberately to his house.

On August 25, Avelino Arredondo woke up at a little past nine. He thought first of Clara, and only later of what day it was. *Good-bye to all this work of waiting—I've made it,* he said to himself in relief.

He shaved slowly, taking his time, and in the mirror he met the same face as always. He picked out a red tie and his best clothes. He had a late lunch. The gray sky threatened drizzle; he'd always pictured this day as radiant. He felt a touch of bitterness at leaving his damp room forever. In the vestibule he met the black woman, and he gave her the last pesos that were left. On the sign at the hardware store he saw some colored diamond shapes, and he realized it had been more than two months since he'd thought of them. He headed toward Calle Sarandi. It was a holiday, and very few people were about.

It was not yet three o'clock when he reached the Plaza Matriz. The *Te Deum* had been sung; a group of well-dressed men, military officers, and prelates was coming down the slow steps of the church. At first glance, the top hats (some still in their hands), the uniforms, the gold braid, the weapons, and the tunics might create the illusion that there were many of them; the truth was, there were no more than about thirty. Though Arredondo felt no fear, he did feel a kind of respect. He asked which of the men was the president.

"The one there walking beside the archbishop with the miter and staff," he was told.

He took out his pistol and fired.

Idiarte Borda took a few steps, fell forward to the ground, and said very clearly, "I've been killed."

Arredondo gave himself up to the authorities.

"I am a Red and I'm proud to say so. I have killed the president, who betrayed and sullied our party. I left my friends and my sweetheart so they would not be dragged into this; I didn't read the newspapers so that no one could say the newspapers incited me to do this. I alone am responsible for this act of justice. Now try me."

This is how the events* might have taken place, though perhaps in a more complex way; this is how I can dream they happened.

The Disk

I am a woodcutter. My name doesn't matter. The hut I was born in, and where I'm soon to die, sits at the edge of the woods. They say these woods go on and on, right to the ocean that surrounds the entire world; they say that wooden houses like mine travel on that ocean. I wouldn't know; I've never seen it. I've not seen the *other* side of the woods, either. My older brother, when we were boys he made me swear that between the two of us we'd hack away at this woods till there wasn't a tree left standing. My brother is dead now, and now it's something else I'm after, and always will be. Over in the direction where the sun goes down there's a creek I fish in with my hands. There are wolves in the woods, but the wolves don't scare me, and my ax has never failed me. I've not kept track of how old I am, but I know I'm old—my eyes don't see anymore. Down in the village, which I don't venture into anymore because I'd lose my way, everyone says I'm a miser, but how much could a woodcutter have saved up?

I keep the door of my house shut with a rock so the snow won't get in. One evening I heard heavy, dragging footsteps and then a knock. I opened the door and a stranger came in. He was a tall, elderly man all wrapped up in a worn-out old blanket. A scar sliced across his face. The years looked to have given him more authority than frailty, but even so I saw it was hard for him to walk without leaning on his stick. We exchanged a few words I don't recall now. Then finally the man said:

"I am without a home, and I sleep wherever I can. I have wandered all across Saxony."

His words befitted his age. My father always talked about "Saxony"; now people call it England.

There was bread and some fish in the house. While we ate, we didn't talk. It started raining. I took some skins and made him a pallet on the dirt floor where my brother had died. When night came we slept.

It was toward dawn when we left the house. The rain had stopped and the ground was covered with new snow. The man dropped his stick and he ordered me to pick it up.

"Why should I do what you tell me to?" I said to him.

"Because I am a king," he answered.

I thought he was mad. I picked up the stick and gave it to him.

With his next words, his voice was changed.

"I am the king of the Secgens. Many times did I lead them to victory in hard combat, but at the hour that fate decreed, I lost my kingdom. My name is Isern and I am of the line of Odin."

"I do not worship Odin," I answered. "I worship Christ."

He went on as though he'd not heard me.

"I wander the paths of exile, but still I am king, for I have the disk. Do you want to see it?"

He opened his hand and showed me his bony palm. There was nothing in it. His hand was empty. It was only then that I realized he'd always kept it shut tight.

He looked me in the eye.

"You may touch it."

I had my doubts, but I reached out and with my fingertips I touched his palm. I felt something cold, and I saw a quick gleam. His hand snapped shut. I said nothing.

"It is the disk of Odin," the old man said in a patient voice, as though he were speaking to a child. "It has but one side. There is not another thing on earth that has but one side. So long as I hold it in my hand I shall be king."

"Is it gold?" I said.

"I know not. It is the disk of Odin and it has but one side."

It was then I felt a gnawing to own the disk myself. If it were mine, I could sell it for a bar of gold and then *I* would be a king.

"In my hut I've got a chest full of money hidden away. Gold coins, and they shine like my ax," I told the wanderer, whom I hate to this day. "If you give the disk of Odin to me, I will give you the chest."

"I will not," he said gruffly.

"Then you can continue on your way," I said.

He turned away. One ax blow to the back of his head was all it took; he wavered and fell, but as he fell he opened his hand, and I saw the gleam of the disk in the air. I marked the place with my ax and I dragged the body down to the creek bed, where I knew the creek was swollen. There I dumped his body.

When I got back to my house I looked for the disk. But I couldn't find it. I have been looking for it for years.

The Book of Sand

. . . thy rope of sands . . .
George Herbert (1593–1623)

The line consists of an infinite number of points; the plane, of an infinite number of lines; the volume, of an infinite number of planes; the hypervolume, of an infinite number of volumes . . . No—this, *more geometrico,* is decidedly not the best way to begin my tale. To say that the story is true is by now a convention of every fantastic tale; mine, nevertheless, *is* true.

I live alone, in a fifth-floor apartment on Calle Belgrano. One evening a few months ago, I heard a knock at my door. I opened it, and a stranger stepped in. He was a tall man, with blurred, vague features, or perhaps my nearsightedness made me see him that way. Everything about him spoke of honest poverty: he was dressed in gray, and carried a gray valise. I immediately sensed that he was a foreigner. At first I thought he was old; then I noticed that I had been misled by his sparse hair, which was blond, almost white, like the Scandinavians'. In the course of our conversation, which I doubt lasted more than an hour, I learned that he hailed from the Orkneys.

I pointed the man to a chair. He took some time to begin talking. He gave off an air of melancholy, as I myself do now.

"I sell Bibles," he said at last.

"In this house," I replied, not without a somewhat stiff, pedantic note, "there are several English Bibles, including the first one, Wyclif's. I also have Cipriano de Valera's, Luther's (which is, in literary terms, the worst of the lot), and a Latin copy of the Vulgate. As you see, it isn't exactly Bibles I might be needing."

After a brief silence he replied.

"It's not only Bibles I sell. I can show you a sacred book that might interest a man such as yourself. I came by it in northern India, in Bikaner."

He opened his valise and brought out the book. He laid it on the table.

It was a clothbound octavo volume that had clearly passed through many hands. I examined it; the unusual heft of it surprised me. On the spine was printed *Holy Writ,* and then *Bombay.*

"Nineteenth century, I'd say," I observed.

"I don't know," was the reply. "Never did know."

I opened it at random. The characters were unfamiliar to me. The pages, which seemed worn and badly set, were printed in double columns, like a Bible. The text was cramped, and composed into versicles. At the upper corner of each page were Arabic numerals. I was struck by an odd fact: the even-numbered page would carry the number 40,514, let us say, while the odd-numbered page that followed it would be 999. I turned the page; the next page bore an eight-digit number. It also bore a small illustration, like those one sees in dictionaries: an anchor drawn in pen and ink, as though by the unskilled hand of a child.

It was at that point that the stranger spoke again.

"Look at it well. You will never see it again."

There was a threat in the words, but not in the voice.

I took note of the page, and then closed the book. Immediately I opened it again. In vain I searched for the figure of the anchor, page after page. To hide my discomfiture, I tried another tack.

"This is a version of Scripture in some Hindu language, isn't that right?"

"No," he replied.

Then he lowered his voice, as though entrusting me with a secret.

"I came across this book in a village on the plain, and I traded a few rupees and a Bible for it. The man who owned it didn't know how to read. I suspect he saw the Book of Books as an amulet. He was of the lowest caste; people could not so much as step on his shadow without being defiled. He told me his book was called the Book of Sand because neither sand nor this book has a beginning or an end."

He suggested I try to find the first page.

I took the cover in my left hand and opened the book, my thumb and forefinger almost touching. It was impossible: several pages always lay between the cover and my hand. It was as though they grew from the very book.

"Now try to find the end."

I failed there as well.

"This can't be," I stammered, my voice hardly recognizable as my own.

"It can't be, yet it *is,*" the Bible peddler said, his voice little more than a whisper. "The number of pages in this book is literally infinite. No page is the first page; no page is the last. I don't know why they're numbered in this arbitrary way, but perhaps it's to give one to understand that the terms of an infinite series can be numbered any way whatever."

Then, as though thinking out loud, he went on.

"If space is infinite, we are anywhere, at any point in space. If time is infinite, we are at any point in time."

His musings irritated me.

"You," I said, "are a religious man, are you not?"

"Yes, I'm Presbyterian. My conscience is clear. I am certain I didn't cheat that native when I gave him the Lord's Word in exchange for his diabolic book."

I assured him he had nothing to reproach himself for, and asked whether he was just passing through the country. He replied that he planned to return to his own country within a few days. It was then that I learned he was a Scot, and that his home was in the Orkneys. I told him I had great personal fondness for Scotland because of my love for Stevenson and Hume.

"And Robbie Burns," he corrected.

As we talked I continued to explore the infinite book.

"Had you intended to offer this curious specimen to the British Museum, then?" I asked with feigned indifference.

"No," he replied, "I am offering it to you," and he mentioned a great sum of money.

I told him, with perfect honesty, that such an amount of money was not within my ability to pay. But my mind was working; in a few moments I had devised my plan.

"I propose a trade," I said. "You purchased the volume with a few rupees and the Holy Scripture; I will offer you the full sum of my pension, which I have just received, and Wyclif's black-letter Bible. It was left to me by my parents."

"A black-letter Wyclif!" he murmured.

I went to my bedroom and brought back the money and the book. With a bibliophile's zeal he turned the pages and studied the binding.

"Done," he said.

I was astonished that he did not haggle. Only later was I to realize that he had entered my house already determined to sell the book. He did not count the money, but merely put the bills into his pocket.

We chatted about India, the Orkneys, and the Norwegian jarls that had once ruled those islands. Night was falling when the man left. I have never seen him since, nor do I know his name.

I thought of putting the Book of Sand in the space left by the Wyclif, but I chose at last to hide it behind some imperfect volumes of the *Thousand and One Nights.*

I went to bed but could not sleep. At three or four in the morning I turned on the light. I took out the impossible book and turned its pages. On one, I saw an engraving of a mask. There was a number in the corner of the page—I don't remember now what it was—raised to the ninth power.

I showed no one my treasure. To the joy of possession was added the fear that it would be stolen from me, and to that, the suspicion that it might not be truly infinite. Those two points of anxiety aggravated my already habitual misanthropy. I had but few friends left, and those, I stopped seeing. A prisoner of the Book, I hardly left my house. I examined the worn binding and the covers with a magnifying glass, and rejected the possibility of some artifice. I found that the small illustrations were spaced at two-thousand-page intervals. I began noting them down in an alphabetized notebook, which was very soon filled. They never repeated themselves. At night, during the rare intervals spared me by insomnia, I dreamed of the book.

Summer was drawing to a close, and I realized that the book was monstrous. It was cold consolation to think that I, who looked upon it with my eyes and fondled it with my ten flesh-and-bone fingers, was no less monstrous than the book. I felt it was a nightmare thing, an obscene thing, and that it defiled and corrupted reality.

I considered fire, but I feared that the burning of an infinite book might be similarly infinite, and suffocate the planet in smoke.

I remembered reading once that the best place to hide a leaf is in the forest. Before my retirement I had worked in the National Library, which contained nine hundred thousand books; I knew that to the right of the lobby a curving staircase descended into the shadows of the basement, where the maps and periodicals are kept. I took advantage of the librarians' distraction to hide the Book of Sand on one of the library's damp shelves; I tried not to notice how high up, or how far from the door.

I now feel a little better, but I refuse even to walk down the street the library's on.*

Afterword

Writing a foreword to stories the reader has not yet read is an almost impossible task, for it requires that one talk about plots that really ought not to be revealed beforehand. I have chosen, therefore, to write an afterword instead.

The first story once more takes up the old theme of the double, which so often inspired Stevenson's ever-happy pen. In England the double is called the fetch *or, more literarily,* the wraith of the living; *in Germany it is known as the* Doppelgänger. *I suspect that one of its first aliases was the* alter ego. *This spectral apparition no doubt emerged from mirrors of metal or water, or simply from the memory, which makes each person both spectator and actor. My duty was to ensure that the interlocutors were different enough from each other to be two, yet similar enough to each other to be one. Do you suppose it's worth saying that I conceived the story on the banks of the Charles River, in New England, and that its cold stream reminded me of the distant waters of the Rhône?*

The subject of love is quite common in my poetry; not so in my prose, where the only example is "Ulrikke." Readers will perceive its formal affinity with "The Other."

"The Congress" is perhaps the most ambitious of this book's fables; its subject is a company so vast that it merges at last into the cosmos itself and into the sum of days. The story's murky beginning attempts to imitate the way Kafka's stories begin; its ending attempts, no doubt unsuccessfully, to ascend to the ecstasy of Chesterton or John Bunyan. I have never merited such a revelation, but I have tried to dream of it. In the course of the story I have interwoven, as is my wont, certain autobiographical features.

Fate, which is widely known to be inscrutable, would not leave me in peace until I had perpetrated a posthumous story by Lovecraft, a writer I have always considered an unwitting parodist of Poe. At last I gave in; the lamentable result is titled "There Are More Things."

"The Sect of the Thirty" saves from oblivion (without the slightest documentary support) the history of a possible heresy.

"The Night of the Gifts" is perhaps the most innocent, violent, and overwrought of these tales.

"The Library of Babel," written in 1941, envisions an infinite number of books; " 'Undr' " and "The Mirror and the Mask" envision age-old literatures consisting of but a single word.

"A Weary Man's Utopia" is, in my view, the most honest, and most melancholy, piece in the book.

I have always been surprised by the Americans' obsession with ethics; "The Bribe" is an attempt to portray that trait.

In spite of John Felton, Charlotte Corday, and the well-known words of Rivera Indarte ("It is a holy deed to kill Rosas") and the Uruguayan national anthem ("For tyrants, Brutus' blade"), I do not approve of political assassination. Be that as it may, readers of the story of Arredondo's solitary crime will want to know its dénouement. *Luis Melián Lafinur asked that he be pardoned, but Carlos Fein and Cristóbal Salvañac, the judges, sentenced him to one month in solitary confinement and five years in prison. A street in Montevideo now bears his name.*

Two unlucky and inconceivable objects are the subject of the last two stories. "The Disk" is the Euclidean circle, which has but one face; "The Book of Sand," a volume of innumerable pages.

I doubt that the hurried notes I have just dictated will exhaust this book, but hope, rather, that the dreams herein will continue to ramify within the hospitable imaginations of the readers who now close it.

J.L.B.
Buenos Aires, February 3, 1975

Shakespeare's Memory

(1983)

August 25, 1983

I saw by the clock at the little station that it was past eleven. I began walking through the night toward the hotel. I experienced, as I had at other times in the past, the resignation and relief we are made to feel by those places most familiar to us. The wide gate was open; the large country house itself, in darkness. I went into the vestibule, whose pale mirrors echoed back the plants of the salon. Strangely, the owner did not recognize me; he turned the guest register around for me to sign. I picked up the pen chained to the register stand, dipped it in the brass inkwell, and then, as I leaned over the open book, there occurred the first of the many surprises the night would have in store for me—my name, Jorge Luis Borges, had already been written there, and the ink was not yet dry.

"I thought you'd already gone upstairs," the owner said to me. Then he looked at me more closely and corrected himself: "Oh, I beg your pardon, sir. You look so much like the other gentleman, but you are younger."

"What room is he in?" I asked.

"He asked for Room 19," came the reply.

It was as I had feared.

I dropped the pen and hurried up the stairs. Room 19 was on the third floor; it opened onto a sad, run-down sort of terrace with a park bench and, as I recall, a railing running around it. It was the hotel's most secluded room. I tried the door; it opened at my touch. The overhead light still burned. In the pitiless light, I came face to face with myself. There, in the narrow iron bed—older, withered, and very pale—lay I, on my back, my eyes turned up vacantly toward the high plaster moldings of the ceiling. Then I heard the voice. It was not exactly my own; it was the one I often hear in my recordings, unpleasant and without modulation.

"How odd," it was saying, "we are two yet we are one. But then nothing is odd in dreams."

"Then . . ." I asked fearfully, "all this is a dream?"

"It is, I am sure, my last dream." He gestured toward the empty bottle on the marble nightstand. "You, however, shall have much to dream, before you come to this night. What date is it for you?"

"I'm not sure," I said, rattled. "But yesterday was my sixty-first birthday."

"When in your waking state you reach this night again, yesterday will have been your eighty-fourth. Today is August 25, 1983."

"So long to wait," I murmured.

"Not for me," he said shortly. "For me, there's almost no time left. At any moment I may die, at any moment I may fade into that which is unknown to me, and still I dream these dreams of my double . . . that tiresome subject I got from Stevenson and mirrors."

I sensed that the evocation of Stevenson's name was a farewell, not some empty stroke of pedantry. I was he, and I understood. It takes more than life's most dramatic moments to make a Shakespeare, hitting upon memorable phrases. To distract him, I said:

"I knew this was going to happen to you. Right here in this hotel, years ago, in one of the rooms below, we began the draft of the story of this suicide."

"Yes," he replied slowly, as though piecing together the memories, "but I don't see the connection. In that draft I bought a one-way ticket for Adrogué,* and when I got to the Hotel Las Delicias I went up to Room 19, the room farthest from all the rest. It was there that I committed suicide."

"That's why I'm here," I said.

"*Here?* We've always been *here.* It's here in this house on Calle Maipú that I am dreaming you. It is here, in this room that belonged to Mother, that I am taking my departure."

". . . that belonged to Mother," I repeated, not wanting to understand. "I am dreaming you in Room 19, on the top floor, next to the rooftop terrace."

"Who is dreaming whom? I know I am dreaming you—I do not know whether you are dreaming me. That hotel in Adrogué was torn down years and years ago—twenty, maybe thirty. Who knows?"

"I am the dreamer," I replied, with a touch of defiance.

"Don't you realize that the first thing to find out is whether there is only one man dreaming, or two men dreaming each other?"

"I am Borges. I saw your name in the register and I came upstairs."

"But I am Borges, and I am dying in a house on Calle Maipú."

There was a silence, and then he said to me:

"Let's try a test. What was the most terrible moment of our life?"

I leaned over him and the two of us spoke at once. I know that neither of us spoke the truth.

A faint smile lit up the aged face. I felt that that smile somehow reflected my own.

"We've lied to each other," he said, "because we feel that we are two, not one. The truth is that we are two yet we are one."

I was beginning to be irritated by this conversation, and I told him so. Then I added: "And you, there in 1983—are you not going to tell me anything about the years I have left?"

"What can I tell you, poor Borges? The misfortunes you are already accustomed to will repeat themselves. You will be left alone in this house. You will touch the books that have no letters and the Swedenborg medallion and the wooden tray with the Federal Cross. Blindness is not darkness; it is a form of solitude. You will return to Iceland."

"Iceland! Sea-girt Iceland!"

"In Rome, you will once more recite the poetry of Keats, whose name, like all men's names, was writ in water."

"I've never been in Rome."

"There are other things. You will write our best poem—an elegy."

"On the death of . . ." I began. I could not bring myself to say the name.

"No. She will outlive *you*."

We grew silent. Then he went on:

"You will write the book we've dreamed of for so long. In 1979 you will see that your supposed career has been nothing but a series of drafts, miscellaneous drafts, and you will give in to the vain and superstitious temptation to write your great book—the superstition that inflicted upon us Goethe's *Faust*, and *Salammbô*, and *Ulysses*. I filled, incredible to tell, many, many pages."

"And in the end you realized that you had failed."

"Worse. I realized that it was a masterpiece in the most overwhelming sense of the word. My good intentions hadn't lasted beyond the first pages; those that followed held the labyrinths, the knives, the man who thinks he's an image, the reflection that thinks it's real, the tiger that stalks in the night, the battles that are in one's blood, the blind and fatal Juan Muraña, the voice of Macedonio Fernández, the ship made with the fingernails of the dead, Old English repeated in the evening."

"That museum rings a bell," I remarked sarcastically.

"Not to mention false recollections, the doubleness of symbols, the long catalogs, the skilled handling of prosaic reality, the imperfect symmetries that critics so jubilantly discover, the not always apocryphal quotations."

"Did you publish it?"

"I toyed, without conviction, with the melodramatic possibility of destroying the book, perhaps by fire. But I wound up publishing it in Madrid, under a pseudonym. I was taken for a clumsy imitator of Borges—a person who had the defect of not actually being Borges yet of mirroring all the outward appearances of the original."

"I'm not surprised," I said. "Every writer sooner or later becomes his own least intelligent disciple."

"That book was one of the roads that led me to this night. The others . . . The humiliation of old age, the conviction of having already lived each day . . ."

"I will not write that book," I said.

"You will, though. My words, which are now your present, will one day be but the vaguest memory of a dream."

I found myself annoyed by his dogmatic tone, the tone that I myself no doubt use in my classes. I was annoyed by the fact that we resembled each other so much and that he was taking advantage of the impunity lent him by the nearness of death.

"Are you so sure," I said, to get back at him a bit, "that you're going to die?"

"Yes," he replied. "I feel a sort of sweetness and relief I've never felt before. I can't describe it; all words require a shared experience. Why do you seem so annoyed at what I'm saying?"

"Because we're too much like each other. I loathe your face, which is a caricature of mine, I loathe your voice, which is a mockery of mine, I loathe your pathetic syntax, which is my own."

"So do I," he smiled. "Which is why I decided to kill myself."

A bird sang from the garden.

"It's the last one," the other man said.

He motioned me toward him. His hand sought mine. I stepped back; I was afraid the two hands would merge.

"The Stoics teach," he said to me, "that we should not complain of life—the door of the prison is open. I have always understood that; I myself saw life that way, but laziness and cowardice held me back. About twelve days ago, I was giving a lecture in La Plata on Book VI of the *Æneid*. Suddenly, as I was scanning a hexameter, I discovered what my path was to be. I made this decision—and since that moment, I have felt myself invulnerable. You shall one day meet that fate—you shall receive that sudden revelation, in the midst of Latin and Virgil, yet you will have utterly forgotten this curious prophetic dialogue that is taking place in two times and two places. When you next dream it, you shall be who I am, and you shall be my dream."

"I won't forget it—I'm going to write it down tomorrow."

"It will lie in the depths of your memory, beneath the tides of your dreams. When you write it, you will think that you're weaving a tale of fantasy. And it won't be tomorrow, either—it will be many years from now."

He stopped talking; I realized that he had died. In a way, I died with him—in grief I leaned over his pillow, but there was no one there anymore.

I fled the room. Outside, there was no patio, no marble staircase, no great silent house, no eucalyptus trees, no statues, no gazebo in a garden, no fountains, no gate in the fence surrounding the hotel in the town of Adrogué.

Outside awaited other dreams.

Blue Tigers

A famous poem by Blake paints the tiger as a fire burning bright and an eternal archetype of Evil; I prefer the Chesterton maxim that casts the tiger as a symbol of terrible elegance. Apart from these, there are no words that can rune the tiger, that shape which for centuries has lived in the imagination of mankind. I have always been drawn to the tiger. I know that as a boy I would linger before one particular cage at the zoo; the others held no interest for me. I would judge encyclopedias and natural histories by their engravings of the tiger. When the *Jungle Books* were revealed to me I was upset that the tiger, Shere Khan, was the hero's enemy. As the years passed, this strange fascination never left me; it survived my paradoxical desire to become a hunter as it did all common human vicissitudes. Until not long ago (the date feels distant but it really is not), it coexisted peacefully with my day-to-day labors at the University of Lahore. I am a professor of Eastern and Western logic, and I consecrate my Sundays to a seminar on the philosophy of Spinoza. I should add that I am a Scotsman; it may have been my love of tigers that brought me from Aberdeen to Punjab. The outward course of my life has been the common one, but in my dreams I always saw tigers. Now it is other forms that fill them.

I have recounted all these facts more than once, until now they seem almost to belong to someone else. I let them stand, however, since they are required by my statement.

Toward the end of 1904, I read that in the region of the Ganges delta a blue variety of the species had been discovered. The news was confirmed by subsequent telegrams, with the contradictions and incongruities that one expects in such cases. My old love stirred once more. Nevertheless, I suspected some error, since the names of colors are notoriously imprecise. I remembered having once read that in Icelandic, Ethiopia was "Blaland," Blue Land *or* the Land of Black Men. The blue tiger might well be a black panther. Nothing was mentioned of stripes; the picture published by the London press, showing a blue tiger with silver stripes, was patently apocryphal. Similarly, the blue of the illustration looked more like that of heraldry than reality. In a dream, I saw tigers of a blue I had never seen before, and for which I could find no word. I know it was almost black, but that description of course does scant justice to the shade I saw.

Some months later, a colleague of mine told me that in a certain village miles from the Ganges he had heard talk of blue tigers. I was astonished by that piece of news, because tigers are rare in that area. Once again I dreamed of the blue tiger, throwing its long shadow as it made its way over the sandy ground. I took advantage of the end of term to make a journey to that village, whose name (for reasons that will soon be clear) I do not wish to recall.

I arrived toward the end of the rainy season. The village squatted at the foot of a hill (which looked to me wider than it was high) and was surrounded and menaced by the jungle, which was a dark brown color. Surely one of the pages of Kipling contains that village of my adventure, since all of India, all the world somehow, can be found there. Suffice it to report that a ditch, and swaying cane-stalk bridges, constituted the huts' fragile defense. Toward the south there were swamps and rice fields and a ravine with a muddy river whose name I never learned, and beyond that, again, the jungle.

The people who lived in the village were Hindus. I did not like this, though I had foreseen it. I have always gotten along better with Muslims, though Islam, I know, is the poorest of the religions that spring from Judaism.

We feel ordinarily that India teems with humanity; in the village I felt that India teemed with *jungle*. It crept virtually into the huts. The days were oppressive, and the nights brought no relief.

I was greeted upon my arrival by the elders, with whom I sustained a tentative conversation constructed of vague courtesies. I have mentioned the poverty of the place, but I know that it is an axiom of every man's belief that the land he lives in and owes his allegiance to possesses some unique distinction, and so I praised in glowing terms the dubious habitations and the no less dubious delicacies served me, and I declared that the fame of that region had reached Lahore. The expressions on the men's faces changed; I immediately sensed that I had committed a *faux pas* I might come to regret. I sensed that these people possessed a secret they would not share with a stranger. Perhaps they worshiped the blue tiger, perhaps they were devotees of a cult that my rash words had profaned.

I waited until the next morning. When the rice had been consumed and the tea drunk down, I broached my subject. Despite the previous night's experience, I did not understand—was incapable of understanding—what took place then. The entire village looked at me with stupefaction, almost with terror, but when I told them that my purpose was to capture the beast with the curious skin, they seemed almost relieved at my words. One of them said he had seen the animal at the edge of the jungle.

In the middle of the night, they woke me. A boy told me that a goat had escaped from the corral and that as he'd gone to look for it, he'd seen the blue tiger on the far bank of the river. I reflected that the scant light of the new moon would hardly have allowed him to make out the color, but everyone confirmed the tale; one of them, who had been silent up until that moment, said he had seen it, too. We went out with the rifles and I saw, or thought I saw, a feline shadow slink into the shadows of the jungle. They did not find the goat, but the creature that had taken it might or might not have been my blue tiger. They emphatically pointed out to me other traces—which of course proved nothing.

After a few nights I realized that these false alarms were a sort of routine. Like Daniel Defoe, the men of the village were skilled at inventing circumstantial details. The tiger might be glimpsed at any hour, out toward the rice fields to the south or up toward the jungle to the north, but it did not take me long to realize that there was a suspicious regularity in the way the villagers seemed to take turns spotting it. My arrival upon the scene of the sighting invariably coincided with the precise instant that the tiger had just run off. I was always shown a trail, a paw mark, some broken twig, but a man's fist can counterfeit a tiger's prints. Once or twice I witnessed a dead dog. One moonlit night we staked out a goat as a lure, but we watched fruitlessly until dawn. I thought at first that these daily fables were meant to encourage me to prolong my stay, for it did benefit the village—the people sold me food and did domestic chores for me. To verify this conjecture, I told them that I was thinking of moving on to another region, downstream, in quest of the tiger. I was surprised to find that they welcomed my decision. I continued to sense, however, that there was a secret, and that everyone was keeping a wary eye on me.

I mentioned earlier that the wooded hill at whose foot the village sprawled was not really very high; it was flat on top, a sort of plateau. On the other side of the mountain, toward the west and north, the jungle began again. Since the slope was not a rugged one, one afternoon I suggested that we climb it. My simple words threw the villagers into consternation. One exclaimed that the mountainside was too steep. The eldest of them said gravely that my goal was impossible to attain, the summit of the hill was sacred, magical obstacles blocked the ascent to man. He who trod the peak with mortal foot was in danger of seeing the godhead, and of going blind or mad.

I did not argue, but that night, when everyone was asleep, I stole soundlessly from my hut and began to climb the easy hillside.

There was no path, and the undergrowth held me back. The moon was just at the horizon. I took note of everything with singular attentiveness, as though I sensed that this was to be an important day, perhaps the most important day of all my days. I still recall the dark, almost black, shadings of the leaves and bushes. It was close to dawn, and the sky was beginning to turn pale, but in all the jungle around, not one bird sang.

Twenty or thirty minutes' climb brought me to the summit. It took me very little effort to imagine that it was cooler there than in the village, which sweltered down below. I had been right that this was not a peak, but rather a plateau, a sort of terrace, not very broad, and that the jungle crept up to it all around, on the flanks of the hill. I felt free, as though my residence in the village had been a prison. I didn't care that the villagers had tried to fool me; I felt they were somehow children.

As for the tiger . . . Constant frustration had exhausted my curiosity and my faith, but almost mechanically I looked for tracks.

The ground was cracked and sandy. In one of the cracks—which by the way were not deep, and which branched into others—I caught a glimpse of a color. Incredibly, it was the same color as the tiger of my dreams. I wish I had never laid eyes on it. I looked closely. The crevice was full of little stones, all alike, circular, just a few centimeters in diameter and very smooth. Their regularity lent them an air almost of artificiality, as though they were coins, or buttons, or counters in some game.

I bent down, put my hand into the crevice, and picked out some of the stones. I felt a faint quivering. I put the handful of little stones in the right pocket of my jacket, where there were a small pair of scissors and a letter from Allahabad. Those two chance objects have their place in my story.

Back in my hut, I took off my jacket. I lay down and dreamed once more of the tiger. In my dream I took special note of its color; it was the color of the tiger I had dreamed of, and also of the little stones from the plateau. The late-morning sun in my face woke me. I got up. The scissors and the letter made it hard to take the disks out of the pocket; they kept getting in the way. I pulled out a handful, but felt that there were still two or three I had missed. A tickling sensation, the slightest sort of quivering, imparted a soft warmth to my palm. When I opened my hand, I saw that it held thirty or forty disks; I'd have sworn I'd picked up no more than ten. I left them on the table and turned back to get the rest out of the pocket. I didn't need to count them to see that they had multiplied. I pushed them together into a single pile, and tried to count them out one by one.

That simple operation turned out to be impossible. I would look fixedly at any one of them, pick it up with my thumb and index finger, yet when I had done that, when that one disk was separated from the rest, it would have become many. I checked to see that I didn't have a fever (which I did not), and then I performed the same experiment, over and over again. The obscene miracle kept happening. I felt my feet go clammy and my bowels turn to ice; my knees began to shake. I do not know how much time passed.

Without looking at the disks, I scooped them into a pile and threw them out the window. With a strange feeling of relief, I sensed that their number had dwindled. I firmly closed the door and lay down on my bed. I tried to find the exact position I had been lying in before, hoping to persuade myself that all this had been a dream. So as not to think about the disks yet somehow fill the time, I repeated, with slow precision, aloud, the eight definitions and seven axioms of Ethics. I am not sure they helped.

In the midst of these exorcistic exercises, a knock came at my door. Instinctively fearing that I had been overheard talking to myself, I went to the door and opened it.

It was the headman of the village, Bhagwan Dass. For a second his presence seemed to restore me to everyday reality. We stepped outside. I harbored some hope that the disks might have disappeared, but there they were, on the ground. I no longer can be sure how many there were.

The elder looked down at them and then looked at me.

"These stones are not from here. They are stones from up there," he said, in a voice that was not his own.

"That's true," I replied. I added, not without some defiance, that I had found them up on the plateau, but I was immediately ashamed of myself for feeling that I owed anyone an explanation. Bhagwan Dass ignored me; he continued to stare in fascination at the stones. I ordered him to pick them up. He did not move.

I am grieved to admit that I took out my revolver and repeated the order, this time in a somewhat more forceful tone of voice.

"A bullet in the breast is preferable to a blue stone in the hand," stammered Bhagwan Dass.

"You are a coward," said I.

I was, I believe, no less terrified than he, but I closed my eyes and picked up a handful of stones with my left hand. I tucked the pistol in my belt and dropped the stones one by one into the open palm of my right hand. Their number had grown considerably.

I had unwittingly become accustomed to those transformations. They now surprised me less than Bhagwan Dass' cries.

"These are the stones that spawn!" he exclaimed. "There are many of them now, but they can change. Their shape is that of the moon when it is full, and their color is the blue that we are permitted to see only in our dreams. My father's father spoke the truth when he told men of their power."

The entire village crowded around us.

I felt myself to be the magical possessor of those wondrous objects. To the astonishment of all, I picked up the disks, raised them high, dropped them, scattered them, watched them grow and multiply or mysteriously dwindle.

The villagers huddled together, seized with astonishment and horror. Men forced their wives to look upon the wonder. One woman covered her face with her forearm, another squeezed her eyes shut tight. No one had the courage to touch the disks—save one happy boy-child that played with them. Just at that moment I sensed that all this confusion was profaning the miracle. I gathered the disks, all of them I could, and returned to my hut.

It may be that I have tried to forget the rest of that day, which was the first of a misfortunate series that continues even until now. Whether I tried to forget the day or not, I do not remember it. Toward evening, I began to think back on the night before, which had not been a particularly happy one, with a sort of nostalgia; at least it, like so many others, had been filled with my obsession with the tiger. I tried to find solace in that image once charged with power, now trivial. The blue tiger seemed no less innocuous than the Roman's black swan, which was discovered subsequently in Australia.

Rereading what I have written, I see that I have committed a fundamental error. Led astray by the habit of that good or bad literature wrongly called psychology, I have attempted to recover—I don't know why—the linear chronology of my find. Instead, I should have stressed the monstrousness of the disks.

If someone were to tell me that there are unicorns on the moon, I could accept or reject the report, or suspend judgment, but it is something I could imagine. If, on the other hand, I were told that six or seven unicorns on the moon could be three, I would declare *a priori* that such a thing was impossible. The man who has learned that three plus one are four doesn't have to go through a proof of that assertion with coins, or dice, or chess pieces, or pencils. He knows it, and that's that. He cannot conceive a different sum. There are mathematicians who say that three plus one is a *tautology* for four, a *different way of saying* "four" . . . But I, Alexander Craigie, of all men on earth, was fated to discover the only objects that contradict that essential law of the human mind.

At first I was in a sort of agony, fearing that I'd gone mad; since then, I have come to believe that it would have been better had I been merely insane, for my personal hallucinations would be less disturbing than the discovery that the universe can tolerate disorder. If three plus one can be two, or fourteen, then reason is madness.

During that time, I often dreamed about the stones. The fact that the dream did not recur every night left me a sliver of hope, though a hope that soon turned to terror. The dream was always more or less the same; the beginning heralded the feared end. A spiral staircase—an iron railing and a few iron treads—and then a cellar, or system of cellars, leading through the depths to other stairways that might abruptly end, or suddenly lead into ironworks, locksmith's forges, dungeons, or swamps. At the bottom, in their expected crevice in the earth, the stones, which were also Behemoth, or Leviathan—the creatures of the Scriptures that signify that God is irrational. I would awaken trembling, and there the stones would be, in their box, ready to transform themselves.

The villagers' attitude toward me began to change. I had been touched by something of the divinity that inhered in the stones the villagers had named "blue tigers," but I was also known to have profaned the summit. At any moment of the night, at any moment of the day, the gods might punish me. The villagers dared not attack me or condemn what I had done, but I noticed that everyone was now dangerously servile. I never again laid eyes on the child who had played with the stones. I feared poison, or a knife in the back. One morning before dawn I slipped out of the village. I sensed that its entire population had been keeping an eye on me, and that my escape would be a relief to them. Since that first morning, no one had ever asked to see the stones.

I returned to Lahore, the handful of disks in my pocket. The familiar environment of my books did not bring the relief I sought. That abominable village, and the jungle, and the jungle's thorny slope rising to the plateau, and on the plateau the little crevices, and within the crevices, the stones—all that, I felt, continued to exist on the planet. My dreams confused and multiplied those dissimilar things. The village was the stones, the jungle was the swamp, the swamp was the jungle.

I shunned the company of my friends. I feared that I would yield to the temptation of showing them that dreadful miracle that undermined humanity's science.

I performed several experiments. I made a cross-shaped incision in one of the disks, put that disk with the others, and shuffled them around; within one or two conversions, I had lost it, though the number of disks had increased. I performed an analogous test with a disk from which I filed a semicircular notch. That disk also disappeared. I punched a hole in the center of one disk with an awl and tried the test again. That disk disappeared forever. The next day the disk with the cross cut in it reappeared from its journey into the void. What mysterious sort of space was this, which in obedience to inscrutable laws or some inhuman will absorbed the stones and then in time threw an occasional one back again?

The same yearning for order that had created mathematics in the first place made me seek some order in that aberration of mathematics, the insensate stones that propagate themselves. I attempted to find a law within their unpredictable variations. I devoted days and nights alike to establishing statistics on the changes. From that stage of my investigations I still have several notebooks, vainly filled with ciphers. My procedure was this: I would count the stones by eye and write down the figure. Then I would divide them into two handfuls that I would scatter separately on the table. I would count the two totals, note them down, and repeat the operation. This search for order, for a secret design within the rotations, led nowhere. The largest number of stones I counted was 419; the smallest, three. There was a moment when I hoped, or feared, that they would disappear altogether. It took little experimenting to show that one of the disks, isolated from the others, could not multiply or disappear.

Naturally, the four mathematical operations—adding, subtracting, multiplying, and dividing—were impossible. The stones resisted arithmetic as they did the calculation of probability. Forty disks, divided, might become nine; those nine in turn divided might yield three hundred. I do not know how much they weighed. I did not have recourse to a scale, but I am sure that their weight was constant, and light. Their color was always that same blue.

These operations helped save me from madness. As I manipulated the stones that destroyed the science of mathematics, more than once I thought of those Greek stones that were the first ciphers and that had been passed down to so many languages as the word "calculus." Mathematics, I told myself, had its origin, and now has its end, in stones. If Pythagoras had worked with these . . .

After about a month I realized that there was no way out of the chaos. There lay the unruly disks, there lay the constant temptation to touch them, to feel that tickling sensation once more, to scatter them, to watch them increase or decrease, and to note whether they came out odd or even. I came to fear that they would contaminate other things—particularly the fingers that insisted upon handling them.

For several days I imposed upon myself the private obligation to think continually about the stones, because I knew that forgetting them was possible only for a moment, and that rediscovering my torment would be unbearable.

I did not sleep the night of February 10. After a walk that led me far into the dawn, I passed through the gates of the mosque of Wazil Khan. It was the hour at which light has not yet revealed the colors of things. There was not a soul in the courtyard. Not knowing why, I plunged my hands into the water of the fountain of ablutions. Inside the mosque, it occurred to me that God and Allah are two names for a single, inconceivable Being, and I prayed aloud that I be freed from my burden. Unmoving, I awaited some reply.

I heard no steps, but a voice, quite close, spoke to me:

"I am here."

A beggar was standing beside me. In the soft light I could make out his turban, his sightless eyes, his sallow skin, his gray beard. He was not very tall.

He put out a hand to me, and said, still softly:

"Alms, oh Protector of the Poor . . ."

I put my hands in my pocket.

"I have not a single coin," I replied.

"You have many," was the beggar's answer.

The stones were in my right pocket. I took out one and dropped it into his cupped palm. There was not the slightest sound.

"You must give me all of them," he said. "He who gives not all has given nothing."

I understood, and I said:

"I want you to know that my alms may be a curse."

"Perhaps that gift is the only gift I am permitted to receive. I have sinned."

I dropped all the stones into the concave hand. They fell as though into the bottom of the sea, without the slightest whisper.

Then the man spoke again:

"I do not yet know what your gift to me is, but mine to you is an awesome one. You may keep your days and nights, and keep wisdom, habits, the world."

I did not hear the blind beggar's steps, or see him disappear into the dawn.

The Rose of Paracelsus

De Quincey: *Writings*, XIII, 345*

Down in his laboratory, to which the two rooms of the cellar had been given over, Paracelsus prayed to his God, his indeterminate God—any God—to send him a disciple.

Night was coming on. The guttering fire in the hearth threw irregular shadows into the room. Getting up to light the iron lamp was too much trouble. Paracelsus, weary from the day, grew absent, and the prayer was forgotten. Night had expunged the dusty retorts and the furnace when there came a knock at his door. Sleepily he got up, climbed the short spiral staircase, and opened one side of the double door. A stranger stepped inside. He too was very tired. Paracelsus gestured toward a bench; the other man sat down and waited. For a while, neither spoke.

The master was the first to speak.

"I recall faces from the West and faces from the East," he said, not without a certain formality, "yet yours I do not recall. Who are you, and what do you wish of me?"

"My name is of small concern," the other man replied. "I have journeyed three days and three nights to come into your house. I wish to become your disciple. I bring you all my possessions."

He brought forth a pouch and emptied its contents on the table. The coins were many, and they were of gold. He did this with his right hand. Paracelsus turned his back to light the lamp; when he turned around again, he saw that the man's left hand held a rose. The rose troubled him.

He leaned back, put the tips of his fingers together, and said:

"You think that I am capable of extracting the stone that turns all elements to gold, and yet you bring me gold. But it is not gold I seek, and if it is gold that interests you, you shall never be my disciple."

"Gold is of no interest to me," the other man replied. "These coins merely symbolize my desire to join you in your work. I want you to teach me the Art. I want to walk beside you on that path that leads to the Stone."

"The path *is* the Stone. The point of departure is the Stone. If these words are unclear to you, you have not yet begun to understand. Every step you take is the goal you seek." Paracelsus spoke the words slowly.

The other man looked at him with misgiving.

"But," he said, his voice changed, "is there, then, no goal?"

Paracelsus laughed.

"My detractors, who are no less numerous than imbecilic, say that there is not, and they call me an impostor. I believe they are mistaken, though it is possible that I am deluded. I know that there *is* a Path."

There was silence, and then the other man spoke.

"I am ready to walk that Path with you, even if we must walk for many years. Allow me to cross the desert. Allow me to glimpse, even from afar, the promised land, though the stars prevent me from setting foot upon it. All I ask is a proof before we begin the journey."

"When?" said Paracelsus uneasily.

"Now," said the disciple with brusque decisiveness.

They had begun their discourse in Latin; they now were speaking German.

The young man raised the rose into the air.

"You are famed," he said, "for being able to burn a rose to ashes and make it emerge again, by the magic of your art. Let me witness that prodigy. I ask that of you, and in return I will offer up my entire life."

"You are credulous," the master said. "I have no need of credulity; I demand belief."

The other man persisted.

"It is precisely because I am *not* credulous that I wish to see with my own eyes the annihilation and resurrection of the rose."

"You are credulous," he repeated. "You say that I can destroy it?"

"Any man has the power to destroy it," said the disciple.

"You are wrong," the master responded. "Do you truly believe that something may be turned to nothing? Do you believe that the first Adam in paradise was able to destroy a single flower, a single blade of grass?"

"We are not in paradise," the young man stubbornly replied. "Here, in the sublunary world, all things are mortal."

Paracelsus had risen to his feet.

"Where are we, then, if not in paradise?" he asked. "Do you believe that the deity is able to create a place that is not paradise? Do you believe that the Fall is something other than not realizing that we are in paradise?"

"A rose can be burned," the disciple said defiantly.

"There is still some fire there," said Paracelsus, pointing toward the hearth. "If you cast this rose into the embers, you would believe that it has been consumed, and that its ashes are real. I tell you that the rose is eternal, and that only its appearances may change. At a word from me, you would see it again."

"A word?" the disciple asked, puzzled. "The furnace is cold, and the retorts are covered with dust. What is it you would do to bring it back again?"

Paracelsus looked at him with sadness in his eyes.

"The furnace is cold," he nodded, "and the retorts are covered with dust. On this leg of my long journey I use other instruments."

"I dare not ask what they are," said the other man humbly, or astutely.

"I am speaking of that instrument used by the deity to create the heavens and the earth and the invisible paradise in which we exist, but which original sin hides from us. I am speaking of the Word, which is taught to us by the science of the Kabbalah."

"I ask you," the disciple coldly said, "if you might be so kind as to show me the disappearance and appearance of the rose. It matters not the slightest to me whether you work with alembics or with the Word."

Paracelsus studied for a moment; then he spoke:

"If I did what you ask, you would say that it was an appearance cast by magic upon your eyes. The miracle would not bring you the belief you seek. Put aside, then, the rose."

The young man looked at him, still suspicious. Then Paracelsus raised his voice.

"And besides, who are you to come into the house of a master and demand a miracle of him? What have you done to deserve such a gift?"

The other man, trembling, replied:

"I know I have done nothing. It is for the sake of the many years I will study in your shadow that I ask it of you—allow me to see the ashes and then the rose. I will ask nothing more. I will believe the witness of my eyes."

He snatched up the incarnate and incarnadine rose that Paracelsus had left lying on the table, and he threw it into the flames. Its color vanished, and all that remained was a pinch of ash. For one infinite moment, he awaited the words, and the miracle.

Paracelsus sat unmoving. He said with strange simplicity:

"All the physicians and all the pharmacists in Basel say I am a fraud.

Perhaps they are right. There are the ashes that were the rose, and that shall be the rose no more."

The young man was ashamed. Paracelsus was a charlatan, or a mere visionary, and he, an intruder, had come through his door and forced him now to confess that his famed magic arts were false.

He knelt before the master and said:

"What I have done is unpardonable. I have lacked belief, which the Lord demands of all the faithful. Let me, then, continue to see ashes. I will come back again when I am stronger, and I will be your disciple, and at the end of the Path I will see the rose."

He spoke with genuine passion, but that passion was the pity he felt for the agèd master—so venerated, so inveighed against, so renowned, and therefore so hollow. Who was he, Johannes Grisebach, to discover with sacrilegious hand that behind the mask was no one?

Leaving the gold coins would be an act of almsgiving to the poor. He picked them up again as he went out. Paracelsus accompanied him to the foot of the staircase and told him he would always be welcome in that house. Both men knew they would never see each other again.

Paracelsus was then alone. Before putting out the lamp and returning to his weary chair, he poured the delicate fistful of ashes from one hand into the concave other, and he whispered a single word. The rose appeared again.

Shakespeare's Memory

There are devotees of Goethe, of the Eddas, of the late song of the Nibelungen; my fate has been Shakespeare. As it still is, though in a way that no one could have foreseen—no one save one man, Daniel Thorpe, who has just recently died in Pretoria. There is another man, too, whose face I have never seen.

My name is Hermann Sörgel. The curious reader may have chanced to leaf through my *Shakespeare Chronology,* which I once considered essential to a proper understanding of the text: it was translated into several languages, including Spanish. Nor is it beyond the realm of possibility that the reader will recall a protracted diatribe against an emendation inserted by Theobald into his critical edition of 1734—an emendation which became from that moment on an unquestioned part of the canon. Today I am taken a bit aback by the uncivil tone of those pages, which I might almost say were written by another man. In 1914 I drafted, but did not publish, an article on the compound words that the Hellenist and dramatist George Chapman coined for his versions of Homer; in forging these terms, Chapman did not realize that he had carried English back to its Anglo-Saxon origins, the *Ursprung* of the language. It never occurred to me that Chapman's voice, which I have now forgotten, might one day be so familiar to me. . . . A scattering of critical and philological "notes," as they are called, signed with my initials, complete, I believe, my literary biography. Although perhaps I might also be permitted to include an unpublished translation of *Macbeth,* which I began in order to distract my mind from the thought of the death of my brother, Otto Julius, who fell on the western front in 1917. I never finished translating the play; I came to realize that English has (to its credit) two registers—the Germanic and the Latinate—while our own German, in spite of its greater musicality, must content itself with one.

I mentioned Daniel Thorpe. I was introduced to Thorpe by Major Barclay at a Shakespeare conference. I will not say where or when; I know all too well that such specifics are in fact vaguenesses.

More important than Daniel Thorpe's face, which my partial blindness helps me to forget, was his notorious lucklessness. When a man reaches a certain age, there are many things he can feign; happiness is not one of them. Daniel Thorpe gave off an almost physical air of melancholy.

After a long session, night found us in a pub—an undistinguished place that might have been any pub in London. To make ourselves feel that we were in England (which of course we were), we drained many a ritual pewter mug of dark warm beer.

"In Punjab," said the major in the course of our conversation, "a fellow once pointed out a beggar to me. Islamic legend apparently has it, you know, that King Solomon owned a ring that allowed him to understand the language of the birds. And this beggar, so everyone believed, had somehow come into possession of that ring. The value of the thing was so beyond all reckoning that the poor bugger could never sell it, and he died in one of the courtyards of the mosque of Wazil Khan, in Lahore."

It occurred to me that Chaucer must have been familiar with the tale of that miraculous ring, but mentioning it would have spoiled Barclay's anecdote.

"And what became of the ring?" I asked.

"Lost now, of course, as that sort of magical thingamajig always is. Probably in some secret hiding place in the mosque, or on the finger of some chap who's off living somewhere where there're no birds."

"Or where there are so many," I noted, "that one can't make out what they're saying for the racket. Your story has something of the parable about it, Barclay."

It was at that point that Daniel Thorpe spoke up. He spoke, somehow, impersonally, without looking at us. His English had a peculiar accent, which I attributed to a long stay in the East.

"It is not a parable," he said. "Or if it is, it is nonetheless a true story. There are things that have a price so high they can never be sold."

The words I am attempting to reconstruct impressed me less than the conviction with which Daniel Thorpe spoke them. We thought he was going to say something further, but suddenly he fell mute, as though he regretted having spoken at all. Barclay said good night. Thorpe and I returned together to the hotel. It was quite late by now, but Thorpe suggested we continue our conversation in his room. After a short exchange of trivialities, he said to me:

"Would you like to own King Solomon's ring? I offer it to you. That's a metaphor, of course, but the thing the metaphor stands for is every bit as wondrous as that ring. Shakespeare's memory, from his youngest boyhood days to early April, 1616—I offer it to you."

I could not get a single word out. It was as though I had been offered the ocean.

Thorpe went on:

"I am not an impostor. I am not insane. I beg you to suspend judgment until you hear me out. Major Barclay no doubt told you that I am, or was, a military physician. The story can be told very briefly. It begins in the East, in a field hospital, at dawn. The exact date is not important. An enlisted man named Adam Clay, who had been shot twice, offered me the precious memory almost literally with his last breath. Pain and fever, as you know, make us creative; I accepted his offer without crediting it—and besides, after a battle, nothing seems so very strange. He barely had time to explain the singular conditions of the gift: The one who possesses it must offer it aloud, and the one who is to receive it must accept it the same way. The man who gives it loses it forever."

The name of the soldier and the pathetic scene of the bestowal struck me as "literary" in the worst sense of the word. It all made me a bit leery.

"And you, now, possess Shakespeare's memory?"

"What I possess," Thorpe answered, "are still *two* memories—my own personal memory and the memory of that Shakespeare that I partially am. Or rather, two memories possess *me.* There is a place where they merge, somehow. There is a woman's face . . . I am not sure what century it belongs to."

"And the one that was Shakespeare's—" I asked. "What have you done with it?"

There was silence.

"I have written a fictionalized biography," he then said at last, "which garnered the contempt of critics but won some small commercial success in the United States and the colonies. I believe that's all. . . . I have warned you that my gift is not a sinecure. I am still waiting for your answer."

I sat thinking. Had I not spent a lifetime, colorless yet strange, in pursuit of Shakespeare? Was it not fair that at the end of my labors I find him?

I said, carefully pronouncing each word:

"I accept Shakespeare's memory."

Something happened; there is no doubt of that. But I did not feel it happen.

Perhaps just a slight sense of fatigue, perhaps imaginary.

I clearly recall that Thorpe did tell me:

"The memory has entered your mind, but it must be 'discovered.' It will emerge in dreams or when you are awake, when you turn the pages of a book or turn a corner. Don't be impatient; don't *invent* recollections. Chance in its mysterious workings may help it along, or it may hold it back. As I gradually forget, you will remember. I can't tell you how long the process will take."

We dedicated what remained of the night to a discussion of the character of Shylock. I refrained from trying to discover whether Shakespeare had had personal dealings with Jews. I did not want Thorpe to imagine that I was putting him to some sort of test. I did discover (whether with relief or uneasiness, I cannot say) that his opinions were as academic and conventional as my own.

In spite of that long night without sleep, I hardly slept at all the following night. I found, as I had so many times before, that I was a coward. Out of fear of disappointment, I could not deliver myself up to openhanded hope. I preferred to think that Thorpe's gift was illusory. But hope did, irresistibly, come to prevail. I would possess Shakespeare, and possess him as no one had ever possessed anyone before—not in love, or friendship, or even hatred. I, in some way, would *be* Shakespeare. Not that I would write the tragedies or the intricate sonnets—but I would recall the instant at which the witches (who are also the Fates) had been revealed to me, the other instant at which I had been given the vast lines:

> And shake the yoke of inauspicious stars
> From this world-weary flesh.

I would remember Anne Hathaway as I remembered that mature woman who taught me the ways of love in an apartment in Lübeck so many years ago. (I tried to recall that woman, but I could only recover the wallpaper, which was yellow, and the light that streamed in through the window. This first failure might have foreshadowed those to come.)

I had hypothesized that the images of that wondrous memory would be primarily visual. Such was not the case. Days later, as I was shaving, I spoke into the mirror a string of words that puzzled me; a colleague informed me that they were from Chaucer's "A. B. C." One afternoon, as I was leaving the British Museum, I began whistling a very simple melody that I had never heard before.

The reader will surely have noted the common thread that links these first revelations of the memory: it was, in spite of the splendor of some metaphors, a good deal more auditory than visual.

De Quincey says that our brain is a palimpsest. Every new text covers the previous one, and is in turn covered by the text that follows—but all-powerful Memory is able to exhume any impression, no matter how momentary it might have been, if given sufficient stimulus. To judge by the will he left, there had been not a single book in Shakespeare's house, not even the Bible, and yet everyone is familiar with the books he so often repaired to: Chaucer, Gower, Spenser, Christopher Marlowe, Holinshed's *Chronicle,* Florio's Montaigne, North's Plutarch. I possessed, at least potentially, the memory that had been Shakespeare's; the reading (which is to say the rereading) of those old volumes would, then, be the stimulus I sought. I also reread the sonnets, which are his work of greatest immediacy. Once in a while I came up with the explication, or with many explications. Good lines demand to be read aloud; after a few days I effortlessly recovered the harsh *r*'s and open vowels of the sixteenth century.

In an article I published in the *Zeitschrift für germanische Philologie,* I wrote that Sonnet 127 referred to the memorable defeat of the Spanish Armada. I had forgotten that Samuel Butler had advanced that same thesis in 1899.

A visit to Stratford-on-Avon was, predictably enough, sterile.

Then came the gradual transformation of my dreams. I was to be granted neither splendid nightmares *à la* de Quincey nor pious allegorical visions in the manner of his master Jean Paul*; it was unknown rooms and faces that entered my nights. The first face I identified was Chapman's; later there was Ben Jonson's, and the face of one of the poet's neighbors, a person who does not figure in the biographies but whom Shakespeare often saw.

The man who acquires an encyclopedia does not thereby acquire every line, every paragraph, every page, and every illustration; he acquires the *possibility* of becoming familiar with one and another of those things. If that is the case with a concrete, and relatively simple, entity (given, I mean, the alphabetical order of its parts, etc.), then what must happen with a thing which is abstract and variable—*ondoyant et divers?* A dead man's magical memory, for example?

No one may capture in a single instant the fullness of his entire past.

That gift was never granted even to Shakespeare, so far as I know, much less to me, who was but his partial heir. A man's memory is not a summation; it is a chaos of vague possibilities. St. Augustine speaks, if I am not mistaken, of the palaces and the caverns of memory. That second metaphor is the more fitting one. It was into those caverns that I descended.

Like our own, Shakespeare's memory included regions, broad regions, of shadow—regions that he willfully rejected. It was not without shock that I remembered how Ben Jonson had made him recite Latin and Greek hexameters, and how his ear—the incomparable ear of Shakespeare—would go astray in many of them, to the hilarity of his fellows.

I knew states of happiness and darkness that transcend common human experience.

Without my realizing it, long and studious solitude had prepared me for the docile reception of the miracle. After some thirty days, the dead man's memory had come to animate me fully. For one curiously happy week, I almost believed myself Shakespeare. His work renewed itself for me. I know that for Shakespeare the moon was less the moon than it was Diana, and less Diana than that dark drawn-out word *moon.* I noted another discovery: Shakespeare's apparent instances of inadvertence—those *absences dans l'infini* of which Hugo apologetically speaks—were deliberate. Shakespeare tolerated them—or actually interpolated them—so that his discourse, destined for the stage, might appear to be spontaneous, and not overly polished and artificial (*nicht allzu glatt und gekünstelt*). That same goal inspired him to mix his metaphors:

my way of life
Is fall'n into the sear, the yellow leaf.

One morning I perceived a sense of guilt deep within his memory. I did not try to define it; Shakespeare himself has done so for all time. Suffice it to say that the offense had nothing in common with perversion.

I realized that the three faculties of the human soul—memory, understanding, and will—are not some mere Scholastic fiction. Shakespeare's memory was able to reveal to me only the circumstances of *the man* Shakespeare. Clearly, these circumstances do not constitute the uniqueness of *the poet;* what matters is the literature the poet produced with that frail material.

I was naive enough to have contemplated a biography, just as Thorpe had. I soon discovered, however, that that literary genre requires a talent for writing that I do not possess. I do not know how to tell a story. I do not know how to tell *my own* story, which is a great deal more extraordinary than Shakespeare's. Besides, such a book would be pointless. Chance, or fate, dealt Shakespeare those trivial terrible things that all men know; it was his gift to be able to transmute them into fables, into characters that were much more alive than the gray man who dreamed them, into verses which will never be abandoned, into verbal music. What purpose would it serve to unravel that wondrous fabric, besiege and mine the tower, reduce to the modest proportions of a documentary biography or a realistic novel the sound and fury of *Macbeth*?

Goethe, as we all know, is Germany's official religion; the worship of Shakespeare, which we profess not without nostalgia, is more private. (In England, the official religion is Shakespeare, who is so unlike the English; England's sacred book, however, is the Bible.)

Throughout the first stage of this adventure I felt the joy of being Shakespeare; throughout the last, terror and oppression. At first the waters of the two memories did not mix; in time, the great torrent of Shakespeare threatened to flood my own modest stream—and very nearly did so. I noted with some nervousness that I was gradually forgetting the language of my parents. Since personal identity is based on memory, I feared for my sanity.

My friends would visit me; I was astonished that they could not see that I was in hell.

I began not to understand the everyday world around me (*die alltägliche Umwelt*). One morning I became lost in a welter of great shapes forged in iron, wood, and glass. Shrieks and deafening noises assailed and confused me. It took me some time (it seemed an infinity) to recognize the engines and cars of the Bremen railway station.

As the years pass, every man is forced to bear the growing burden of his memory. I staggered beneath two (which sometimes mingled)—my own and the incommunicable other's.

The wish of all things, Spinoza says, is to continue to be what they are. The stone wishes to be stone, the tiger, tiger—and I wanted to be Hermann Sörgel again.

I have forgotten the date on which I decided to free myself. I hit upon the easiest way: I dialed telephone numbers at random. The voice of a child or a woman would answer; I believed it was my duty to respect their vulnerable estates. At last a man's refined voice answered.

"Do you," I asked, "want Shakespeare's memory? Consider well: it is a solemn thing I offer, as I can attest."

An incredulous voice replied:

"I will take that risk. I accept Shakespeare's memory."

I explained the conditions of the gift. Paradoxically, I felt both a *nostalgie* for the book I should have written, and now never would, and a fear that the guest, the specter, would never abandon me.

I hung up the receiver and repeated, like a wish, these resigned words:

Simply the thing I am shall make me live.

I had invented exercises to awaken the antique memory; I had now to seek others to erase it. One of many was the study of the mythology of William Blake, that rebellious disciple of Swedenborg. I found it to be less complex than merely complicated.

That and other paths were futile; all led me to Shakespeare.

I hit at last upon the only solution that gave hope courage: strict, vast music—Bach.

P.S. (1924)—I am now a man among men. In my waking hours I am Professor Emeritus Hermann Sörgel; I putter about the card catalog and compose erudite trivialities, but at dawn I sometimes know that the person dreaming is that other man. Every so often in the evening I am unsettled by small, fleeting memories that are perhaps authentic.

A Note on the Translation

The first known English translation of a work of fiction by the Argentine Jorge Luis Borges appeared in the August 1948 issue of *Ellery Queen's Mystery Magazine*, but although seven or eight more translations appeared in "little magazines" and anthologies during the fifties, and although Borges clearly had his champions in the literary establishment, it was not until 1962, fourteen years after that first appearance, that a book-length collection of fiction appeared in English.

The two volumes of stories that appeared in that *annus mirabilis*—one from Grove Press, edited by Anthony Kerrigan, and the other from New Directions, edited by Donald A. Yates and James E. Irby—caused an impact that was immediate and overwhelming. John Updike, John Barth, Anthony Burgess, and countless other writers and critics have eloquently and emphatically attested to the unsettling yet liberating effect that Jorge Luis Borges' work had on their vision of the way literature was thenceforth to be done. Reading those stories, writers and critics encountered a disturbingly *other* writer (Borges seemed, sometimes, to come from a place even more distant than Argentina, another literary planet), transported into their ken by translations, who took the detective story and turned it into metaphysics, who took fantasy writing and made it, with its questioning and reinventing of everyday reality, central to the craft of fiction. Even as early as 1933, Pierre Drieu La Rochelle, editor of the influential *Nouvelle Revue Française*, returning to France after visiting Argentina, is famously reported to have said, "*Borges vaut le voyage*"; now, thirty years later, readers didn't have to make the long, hard (though deliciously exotic) journey into Spanish—Borges had been brought to them, and indeed he soon was being paraded through England and the United States like one of those New World indigenes taken back, captives, by Columbus or Sir Walter Raleigh, to captivate the Old World's imagination.

But while for many readers of these translations Borges was a new writer appearing as though out of nowhere, the truth was that by the time we were reading Borges for the first time in English, he had been writing for forty years or more, long enough to have become a self-conscious, self-possessed, and self-*critical* master of the craft.

The reader of the forewords to the fictions will note that Borges is forever commenting on the style of the stories or the entire volume, preparing the reader for what is to come stylistically as well as thematically. More than once he draws our attention to the "plain style" of the pieces, in contrast to his earlier "baroque." And he is right: Borges' prose style is characterized by a determined economy of resources in which every word is weighted, every word (every mark of punctuation) "tells." It is a quiet style, whose effects are achieved not with bombast or pomp, but rather with a single exploding word or phrase, dropped almost as though offhandedly into a quiet sentence: "He examined his wounds and saw, without astonishment, that they had healed." This laconic detail ("without astonishment"), coming at the very beginning of "The Circular Ruins," will probably only at the end of the story be recalled by the reader, who will, retrospectively and somewhat abashedly, see that it changes *everything* in the story; it is quintessential Borges.

Quietness, subtlety, a laconic terseness—these are the marks of Borges' style. It is a style that has often been called intellectual, and indeed it is dense with allusion—to literature, to philosophy, to religion or theology, to myth, to the culture and history of Buenos Aires and Argentina and the Southern Cone of South America, to the other contexts in which his words may have appeared. But it is also a simple style: Borges' sentences are almost invariably classical in their symmetry, in their balance. Borges likes parallelism, chiasmus, subtle repetitions-with-variations; his only indulgence in "shocking" the reader (an effect he repudiated) may be the "Miltonian displacement of adjectives" to which he alludes in his foreword to *The Maker.*

Another clear mark of Borges' prose is its employment of certain words with, or for, their etymological value. Again, this is an adjectival device, and it is perhaps the technique that is most unsettling to the reader. One of the most famous opening lines in Spanish literature is this: *Nadie lo vio desembarcar en la unánime noche:* "No one saw him slip from the boat in the unanimous night." What an odd adjective, "unanimous." It is so odd, in fact, that other translations have not allowed it. But it is just as odd in Spanish, and it clearly responds to Borges' intention, explicitly expressed in such fictions as "The Immortal," to let the Latin root govern the Spanish (and, by extension, English) usage. There is, for instance, a "splendid" woman: Her red hair glows. If the translator strives for similarity of effect in the translation (as I have), then he or she cannot, I think, avoid using this technique—which is a technique that Borges' beloved Emerson and de Quincey and Sir Thomas Browne also used with great virtuosity.

Borges himself was a translator of some note, and in addition to the translations per se that he left to Spanish culture—a number of German lyrics, Faulkner, Woolf, Whitman, Melville, Carlyle, Swedenborg, and others—he left at least three essays on the act of translation itself. Two of these, I have found, are extraordinarily liberating to the translator. In "Versions of Homer" ("Las versiones homéricas," 1932), Borges makes it unmistakably clear that every translation is a "version"—not *the* translation of Homer (or any other author) but *a* translation, one in a never-ending series, at least an infinite *possible* series. The very idea of *the* (definitive) translation is misguided, Borges tells us; there are only drafts, approximations—*versions,* as he insists on calling them. He chides us: "The concept of 'definitive text' is appealed to only by religion, or by weariness." Borges makes the point even more emphatically in his later essay "The Translators of the 1001 Nights" ("Los traductores de las *1001 Noches,*" 1935).

If my count is correct, at least seventeen translators have preceded me in translating one or more of the fictions of Jorge Luis Borges. In most translator's notes, the translator would feel obliged to justify his or her new translation of a classic, to tell the potential reader of this new *version* that the shortcomings and errors of those seventeen or so prior translations have been met and conquered, as though they were enemies. Borges has tried in his essays to teach us, however, that we should not translate "against" our predecessors; a new translation is always justified by the new voice given the old work, by the new life in a new land that the translation confers on it, by the "shock of the new" that both old and new readers will experience from this inevitably new (or renewed) work. What Borges teaches is that we should simply commend the translation to the reader, with the hope that the reader will find in it a literary experience that is rich and moving. I have listened to Borges' advice as I have listened to Borges' fictions, and I—like the translators who have preceded me—have rendered Borges in the style that I hear when I listen to him. I think that the reader of my version will hear something of the genius of his storytelling and his style. For those who wish to read Borges as Borges wrote Borges, there is always *le voyage à l'espagnol.*

The text that the Borges estate specified to be used for this new translation is the three-volume *Obras completas,* published by Emecé Editores in 1989.

In producing this translation, it has not been our intention to produce an annotated or scholarly edition of Borges, but rather a "reader's edition." Thus, bibliographical information (which is often confused or terribly complex even in the most reliable of cases) has not been included except in a couple of clear instances, nor have we taken variants into account in any way; the Borges Foundation is reported to be working on a fully annotated, bibliographically reasoned variorum, and scholars of course can go to the several bibliographies and many other references that now exist. I have, however, tried to provide the Anglophone reader with at least a modicum of the general knowledge of the history, literature, and culture of Argentina and the Southern Cone of South America that a Hispanophone reader of the fictions, growing up in that culture, would inevitably have. To that end, asterisks have been inserted into the text of the fictions, tied to corresponding notes at the back of the book. (The notes often cite sources where interested readers can find further information.)

One particularly thorny translation decision that had to be made involved *A Universal History of Iniquity.* This volume is purportedly a series of biographies of reprehensible evildoers, and as biography, the book might be expected to rely greatly upon "sources" of one sort or another—as indeed Borges' "Index of Sources" seems to imply. In his preface to the 1954 reprinting of the volume, however, Borges acknowledges the "fictive" nature of his stories: This is a case, he says, of "changing and distorting (sometimes without æsthetic justification) the stories of other men" to produce a work singularly his own. This sui generis use of sources, most of which were in English, presents the translator with something of a challenge: to translate Borges even while Borges is cribbing from, translating, and "changing and distorting" other writers' stories. The method I have chosen to employ is to go to the sources Borges names, to see the ground upon which those changes and distortions were wrought; where Borges is clearly translating phrases, sentences, or even larger pieces of text, I have used the English of the original source. Thus, the New York gangsters in "Monk Eastman" speak as Asbury quotes them, not as I might have translated Borges' Spanish into English had I been translating in the usual sense of the word; back-translating Borges' translation did not seem to make much sense. But even while returning to the sources, I have made no attempt, either in the text or in my notes, to "correct" Borges; he has changed names (or their spellings), dates, numbers, locations, etc., as his literary vision led him to, but the tracing of those "deviations" is a matter which the editors and I have decided should be left to critics and scholarly publications.

More often than one would imagine, Borges' characters are murderers, knife fighters, throat slitters, liars, evil or casually violent men and women—

and of course many of them "live" in a time different from our own. They sometimes use language that is strong, and that today may well be offensive—words denoting membership in ethnic and racial groups, for example. In the Hispanic culture, however, some of these expressions can be, and often are, used as terms of endearment—*negro/negra* and *chino/china* come at once to mind. (I am not claiming that Argentina is free of bigotry; Borges chronicles that, too.) All this is to explain a decision as to my translation of certain terms—specifically *rusito* (literally "little Russian," but with the force of "Jew," "sheeny"), *pardo/parda* (literally "dark mulatto," "black-skinned"), and *gringo* (meaning Italian immigrants: "wops," etc.)—that Borges uses in his fictions. I have chosen to use the word "sheeny" for *rusito* and the word "wop" for *gringo* because in the stories in which these words appear, there is an intention to be offensive—a *character's* intention, not Borges'. I have also chosen to use the word "nigger" for *pardo/parda.* This decision is taken not without considerable soul-searching, but I feel there is historical justification for it. In the May 20, 1996, edition of *The New Yorker* magazine, p. 63, the respected historian and cultural critic Jonathan Raban noted the existence of a nineteenth-century "Nigger Bob's saloon," where, out on the Western frontier, husbands would await the arrival of the train bringing their wives from the East. Thus, when a character in one of Borges' stories says, "I knew I could count on you, old nigger," one can almost hear the slight tenderness, or respect, in the voice, even if, at the same time, one winces. In my view, it is not the translator's place to (as Borges put it) "soften or mitigate" these words. Therefore, I have translated the epithets with the words I believe would have been used in English—in the United States, say—at the time the stories take place.

The footnotes that appear throughout the text of the stories in the *Collected Fictions* are Borges' own, even when they say "Ed."

This translation commemorates the centenary of Borges' birth in 1899; I wish it also to mark the fiftieth anniversary of the first appearance of Borges in English, in 1948. It is to all translators, then, Borges included, that this translation is—unanimously—dedicated.

Andrew Hurley
San Juan, Puerto Rico
June 1998

Acknowledgments

I am indebted to the University of Puerto Rico at Río Piedras for a sabbatical leave that enabled me to begin this project. My thanks to the administration, and to the College of Humanities and the Department of English, for their constant support of my work not only on this project but throughout my twenty-odd years at UPR.

The University of Texas at Austin, Department of Spanish and Portuguese, and its director, Madeline Sutherland-Maier, were most gracious in welcoming the stranger among them. The department sponsored me as a Visiting Scholar with access to all the libraries at UT during my three years in Austin, where most of this translation was produced. My sincerest gratitude is also owed those libraries and their staffs, especially the Perry-Castañeda, the Benson Latin American Collection, and the Humanities Research Center (HRC). Most of the staff, I must abashedly confess, were nameless to me, but one person, Cathy Henderson, has been especially important, as the manuscripts for this project have been incorporated into the Translator Archives in the HRC.

For many reasons this project has been more than usually complex. At Viking Penguin, my editors, Kathryn Court and Michael Millman, have been steadfast, stalwart, and (probably more often than they would have liked) inspired in seeing it through. One could not possibly have had more supportive colleagues, or co-conspirators who stuck by one with any greater solidarity.

Many, many people have given me advice, answered questions, and offered support of all kinds—they know who they are, and will forgive me, I know, for not mentioning them all personally; I have been asked to keep these acknowledgments brief. But two people, Carter Wheelock and Margaret Sayers Peden, have contributed in an especially important and intimate way, and my gratitude to them cannot go unexpressed here. Carter Wheelock read word by word through an "early-final" draft of the translation, comparing it against the Spanish for omissions, misperceptions and mistranslations, and errors of fact. This translation is the cleaner and more honest for his efforts. Margaret Sayers Peden (a.k.a. Petch), one of the finest translators from Spanish working in the world today, was engaged by the publisher to be an outside editor for this volume. Petch read through the late stages of the translation, comparing it with the Spanish, suggesting changes that ranged from punctuation to "readings." Translators want to translate, *love* to translate; for a translator at the height of her powers to read a translation in this painstaking way and yet, while suggesting changes and improvements, to respect the other translator's work, his approach, his thought processes and creativity—even to applaud the other translator's (very) occasional strokes of brilliance—is to engage in an act of selflessness that is almost superhuman. She made the usual somewhat tedious editing process a joy.

I would never invoke Carter Wheelock's and Petch Peden's readings of the manuscripts of this translation—or those of Michael Millman and the other readers at Viking Penguin—as giving it any authority or credentials or infallibility beyond its fair deserts, but I must say that those readings have given me a security in this translation that I almost surely would not have felt so strongly without them. I am deeply and humbly indebted.

First, last, always, and in number of words inversely proportional to my gratitude—I thank my wife, Isabel Garayta.

Andrew Hurley
San Juan, Puerto Rico
June 1998

Notes to the Fictions

These notes are intended only to supply information that a Latin American (and especially Argentine or Uruguayan) reader would have and that would color or determine his or her reading of the stories. Generally, therefore, the notes cover only Argentine history and culture; I have presumed the reader to possess more or less the range of general or world history or culture that JLB makes constant reference to, or to have access to such reference books and other sources as would supply any need there. There is no intention here to produce an "annotated Borges," but rather only to illuminate certain passages that might remain obscure, or even be misunderstood, without that information.

For these notes, I am deeply indebted to *A Dictionary of Borges* by Evelyn Fishburn and Psiche Hughes (London: Duckworth, 1990). Other dictionaries, encyclopedias, reference books, biographies, and works of criticism have been consulted, but none has been as thorough and immediately useful as the *Dictionary of Borges.* In many places, and especially where I quote Fishburn and Hughes directly, I cite their contribution, but I have often paraphrased them without direct attribution; I would not want anyone to think, however, that I am unaware or unappreciative of the use I have made of them. Any errors are my own responsibility, of course, and should not be taken to reflect on them or their work in any way. Another book that has been invaluable is Emir Rodríguez Monegal's *Jorge Luis Borges: A Literary Biography* (New York: Paragon Press, [paper] 1988), now out of print. In the notes, I have cited this work as "Rodríguez Monegal, p. x."

The names of Arab and Persian figures that appear in the stories are taken, in the case of historical persons, from the English transliterations of Philip K. Hitti in his work *History of the Arabs from the Earliest Times to the Present* (New York: Macmillan, 1951). (JLB himself cites Hitti as an authority in this field.) In the case of fictional characters, the translator has used the system of transliteration implicit in Hitti's historical names in comparison with the same names in Spanish transliteration.—*Translator.*

Notes to *A Universal History of Iniquity,* pp. 1–64

For the peculiarities of the text of the fictions in this volume, the reader is referred to A Note on the Translation.

Preface to the First Edition

p. 3: Evaristo Carriego: Carriego (1883–1912) was in fact a popular poet and playwright, and the "particular biography" was the one Borges himself wrote of him (published 1930). Carriego was only a mediocre poet, perhaps, and he left but a single volume (*Misas herejes,* "Heretical Masses") upon his early death by tuberculosis, but his ties to "old Buenos Aires," and especially to the lower-class (and mostly Italian) suburb of Palermo, made him an important figure for Borges. While it is probably exaggerated to say that much of JLB's fascination with the *compadre* (see the note to the title of "Man on Pink Corner" below) and the knife fights and tangos that are associated with that "type" can be traced to Carriego, there is no doubt that as an example of the literary possibilities to which such subject matter can be put, Carriego was very important to JLB and JLB's imagination. Carriego was also the first *professional* writer Borges had ever run across, a man who made his living at writing, and not some "mere" amateur; he held out therefore the possibilities of a true literary career to match Borges's clear literary calling.

Preface to the 1954 Edition

p. 4: Baltasar Gracián: Gracián (1601–1658) was a Jesuit priest and a writer (and sometime æsthetician) of the baroque. His name is associated with a treatise called *Agudeza y arte de ingenio* ("Keenness of Mind and the Art of Wit"), and with the Spanish baroque poets Francisco Quevedo and Luis de Góngora.

The Cruel Redeemer Lazarus Morell

p. 6: Pedro Figari: Figari (1861–1938) was a Uruguayan painter "who used fauvist techniques [Rodríguez Monegal, p. 194]" (this perhaps explains his success in Paris, where he lived from 1925 to 1933) and who spent an important part of his life in Buenos Aires (1921–1925). Borges knew the painter rather well and wrote an introduction to a book on him; Figari was also feted by the literary group associated with the review *Martín Fierro,* of which Borges was an important member. His work "was inspired by the life of Negroes and gauchos" (*Oeuvres complètes,* vol. I, ed. Jean Pierre Bernès [Paris: Gallimard, p. 1489].

p. 6: Vicente Rossi: Rossi (1871–1945) was the author of a volume titled *Cosas de negros* ("Negro Matters" [1926]), to which this mention surely points, but he also produced the first reference book on the birth and development of Argentine theater and an important book on the gaucho. He was, then, something of a folklorist and literary historian. In *Evaristo Carriego*, Borges calls Rossi "our best writer of combat prose."

p. 6: Antonio ("Falucho") Ruiz: "Falucho" (d. 1824) was a black Argentine soldier who fought in the wars of independence. His statue once stood near that of General San Martín near the center of Buenos Aires.

p. 6: The stout bayonet charge of the regiment of "Blacks and Tans" . . . against that famous hill near Montevideo: On the last day of 1812 a troop of soldiers made up of Negroes and mulattoes (the reference to the English military group organized to fight the Irish independence uprising is the translator's, but it is almost inevitable, and the irony of the situation would not be lost on Borges; see the story "Theme of the Hero and Traitor" in *Fictions*), under the leadership of the Argentine general Miguel Estanislao Soler, defeated the Spanish troops at the Cerrito, a prominent hill overlooking Montevideo.

p. 6: Lazarus Morell: This particular rogue's true name seems to have been John A. Murrell (Bernard De Voto, *Mark Twain's America* [Boston: Little, Brown, 1932], pp. 16–17 et seq.) or Murell (Mark Twain, *Life on the Mississippi*, intro. James M. Cox [New York: Penguin, 1984 (orig. publ. in United States by James R. Osgood in 1883)].) Interestingly, Twain never gives the rogue's first name; it is possible, then, that JLB, needing a name, took "Lazarus" to fit the ironic notion that Morell gave a second life to the slaves he freed.

p. 12: "I walked four days . . . my course for Natchez": Here Borges is quoting/translating fairly directly from Twain's *Life on the Mississippi*, pp. 214–215 (Penguin ed. cited in the note just above). Throughout this story, JLB inserts a phrase here, a sentence there from Twain, but then, when he says he is quoting, as in the case of the preaching and horse thieving, he is in reality inventing the quotation and imagining a scene that Twain only suggests.

The Widow Ching—Pirate

p. 19: Aixa's rebuke to Boabdil: Boabdil is Abu 'Abd Allah (Muhammad XII), the last Moorish king of Granada (r. 1482–1492); Aixa was his mother. The reproof that supposedly was given Boabdil by Aixa upon the Moors' defeat and expulsion from what had been Islamic Spain is substantially as Borges reports it here, and the words here given Anne Bonney are substantially those given in Gosse's *History of Piracy*, p. 203. (See the "Index of Sources" p. 64.)

p. 21: Rules for pirates: These may actually be found, as quoted, but in a different order, in Gosse's *History of Piracy*, p. 272. (See "Index of Sources," p. 64, for bibliographical information.)

p. 24: Quotation on peace in the waters of China: Gosse, p. 278. Note also that the widow's new name, while indeed given in Gosse, is attributed to another personage who learned a lesson from the emperor. This is but one of countless examples of the way JLB changes things, even dates, to fit his purposes, purposes that one must confess sometimes are enigmatic. Why change the date of Tom Castro's being found guilty from February 26 to February 27? Monk Eastman's death from December 26 to December 25? The spelling of Morell/Murrell/Murell's name? Here the theory of translation must needs be a theory of artistic creativity.

Monk Eastman, Purveyor of Iniquities

p. 25: Resigned: Borges uses this curious word, which I have not wanted to "interpret," apparently to indicate the fatedness, or ritual aspect, of this duel. It is as though the word indicated "resigned to fate." This aspect of violence, of duels, can be seen throughout Borges; I would especially refer the reader to the story titled "The Encounter," in the volume *Brodie's Report,* p. 364.

p. 28: Junín: Site of a famous battle in the wars of independence. The Battle of Junín took place in the then department of Peru; on August 6, 1824, a cavalry engagement was fought between Simón Bolívar's nationalist forces and the royalist forces under José de Canterac. The tide was turning against the independence forces until the royalist rear was attacked by a force of Peruvian hussars under the command of Isidoro Suárez—one of JLB's forebears and a man who in varying degrees and under varying permutations lends his name to JLB's fictions. The royalists were routed.

p. 30: The Death of Monk Eastman: This story is taken, as JLB indicates, from Asbury's *The Gangs of New York,* generally pp. 274–298, but also, for the quotation about "nicks in his stick," p. xviii. Where JLB has clearly borrowed directly from Asbury and it has been possible to use Asbury's words, I have done so; in other cases, I have just borrowed the appropriate terminology, such as the "Mikado tuck-ups" and the "stuss" games.

The Disinterested Killer Bill Harrigan

p. 32: Always coiled and ready to strike: One of the sources that JLB gives for this story is Frederick Watson's *A Century of Gunmen,* though the truth is, there is not much there that JLB seems actually to have used. With, that is, the possible exception of this phrase, *siempre aculebrado* in the Spanish, which I have rendered conjecturally in this way. *"Aculebrado,"* from the Spanish *culebra,* "snake," calls to mind in the native Spanish speaker the notion of "coiled, like a snake" and also of "snakelike, slithering." On page 77 of his book, Watson quotes an old western novel, which says this: "It's not the custom to war without fresh offence, openly given. You must not smile and shoot. You must not shoot an unarmed man, and you must not shoot an unwarned man. . . . The rattlesnake's code, to warn before he strikes, no better, [i.e., there's no better extant code for a man of the West]: a queer, lop-sided, topsy-turvy, jumbled and senseless code—but a code for all that." Thus it seems that JLB may have wanted to paint Billy the Kid as an even worse "varmint" than the rattlesnake, since the rattlesnake at least gives fair warning, unlike Billy, who, as we see in a moment, shoots the Mexican Villagrán before Villagrán knows what's happening. Perhaps, in fact, that was what made Billy the Kid so dangerous—so dangerous that his *friend* Pat Garrison shot him in cold blood. But whatever JLB's motivation for this word, it is a very mysterious one to use here, however related to all the other animal imagery used throughout this volume.

The Uncivil Teacher of Court Etiquette Kôtsuké no Suké

p. 36: Rônins: In A. B. Mitford's *Tales of Old Japan,* which is the source of much of this story, Mitford inevitably uses this word for the "loyal retainers" of the dead nobleman. The word "Rônin" means literally a "wave-man," one who is tossed about hither and thither, as a wave of the sea. It is used "to designate persons of gentle blood, entitled to bear arms, who, having become separated from their feudal lords [or in this case, of course, vice versa], wander about the country in the capacity of knights-errant. Some went into trade, and became simple wardsmen" (Mitford). While Borges himself does not use this word, the word is inevitably used in English reports of the phenomenon, and so I have thought it appropriate to translate what the Spanish has as "retainers," "captains," etc., by the technical word.

It is possible, of course, that JLB is doing with the Chinese system of loyalties what he did to the world's architecture: remaking it in the likeness of Argentina's. One notes that virtually all the houses that JLB uses in his fictions have long, narrow entrances and interior patios, the very floor plan of the Buenos Aires house of the end of the nineteenth century. Likewise, one senses that JLB may have used the word "captains" in the story to indicate the sort of relationship between the lord and his retainers that was common in the Argentina of caudillos and *their* captains. Thus I recognize that if JLB was trying, consciously or not, to produce this effect, it may be somewhat risky to go all the way to the source, to "Rônin," for the "translation." The reader is notified. Likewise, "Chushingura" is the name by which the dramas, poems, and films are inevitably known in English, so I have incorporated that inevitable cultural reference. From its absence in the Spanish text, one supposes that in Spanish the word "Chushingura" was not used.

p. 39: The source for this story: Much of this story is indeed taken from Mitford's *Tales of Old Japan*, pp. 3–19. I have taken the spelling of the characters' names and several quotations, such as the "Satsumi man's," from there.

Man on Pink Corner

p. 45: Title: The title of this story in Spanish is "Hombre de la esquina rosada"; it presents many intriguing possibilities, and therefore many problems, to the translator, not so much for the words as for the cultural assumptions underlying them. This story is in a way a portrait of the *compadrito* (the tough guy of the slums) or the *cuchillero* (knife fighter) and his life; as such, many items of that "local color" that Borges deplored in, for example, stories of the "exotic" Orient are found, though casually and unemphatically presented. The first thing that must be dealt with is perhaps that "pink corner." *Esquina* ("corner") is both the actual street corner (as other translations of this story have given it, without the colorful adjective) and the neighborhood general-store-and-bar, generally located on corners, which was the hangout for the lowlife of the barrio. The reader can see this establishment clearly in "Unworthy" (in the volume titled *Brodie's Report*) and more fleetingly in many other stories. What of the adjective "pink" (*rosada*) then? The Buenos Aires of JLB's memory and imagination still had high, thick stucco or plastered brick walls lining the streets, such as the reader may see in the colonial cities of the Caribbean and Central and South America even today: Havana, San Juan, Santo Domingo in the Dominican Republic, etc. Those walls in Buenos Aires were painted generally bright pastel colors; Borges refers to "sky blue" walls more even than to pink ones. Thus Borges was able to evoke in two words (*esquina rosada*) an old neighborhood of Buenos Aires, populated by toughs and knife fighters, and characterized by bars and bordellos in which that "scandalous" dance the tango was danced. (In its beginnings, the tango was so scandalous that no respectable woman would dance it, and one would see two men—*compadritos*—dancing together on street corners; nor would the tenement houses, which had moved into the large old houses vacated by the higher classes, allow such goings-on, even though these *conventillos,* as they were called, might be none too "respectable"—certainly none too "genteel"—themselves.) In evoking that old Buenos Aires, Borges also evoked "the man"—here, the Yardmaster, Rosendo Juárez, and the nameless narrator of the story, all of whom participate in the coldly violent *ethos* of the *orillero,* the (to us, today) exaggeratedly macho slum dweller (especially along the banks of the Maldonado [see note below]) who defended his honor against even the most imagined slight. However, certain aspects of this "man" will probably strike the non-Argentine reader as curious—for example, those "boots with high-stacked heels" (in the original Spanish, "women's shoes") and that "red carnation" in the first paragraph of the story "Monk Eastman, Purveyor of Iniquities," the same sort of carnation that appears in this story. There is also the shawl worn by the gaucholike Yardmaster. These elements, however, were authentic "touches"; the *compadrito* affected these appearances. Previous translations have apparently tried to give all this "information" by calling the story "Streetcorner Man," emphasizing the "tough guy hanging out on the corner" aspect of the story, and one can be sympathetic to that solution. Another intriguing possibility, however, is suggested by Bernès in the first volume of the Gallimard edition of JLB's *Oeuvres complètes.* I translate the relevant paragraph: "The title of the original publication, which omits the definite article, reminds the reader of the title of a painting given in the catalog of an art exhibit. It stresses the graphic aspect of the scene, which Borges, in the preface to the 1935 edition, called the 'pictorial intention' of his work. One should think of some title of a piece by Pedro Figari. . . . [p. 1497]" This "impressionist" title, then, should perhaps be retained; what one loses in "information" one gains in suggestion.

p. 45: Maldonado: The Maldonado was a creek that at the time of this story (and many of JLB's other stories) marked the northern boundary of the city of Buenos Aires. The neighborhood around this area was called Palermo, or also Maldonado. This story evokes its atmosphere at one period (perhaps partly legendary); the Maldonado (barrio) was a rough place, and the creek was terribly polluted by the tanneries along its banks.

p. 45: Don Nicolás Paredes . . . Morel: Paredes was a famous knife fighter and ward boss for the conservative party in Palermo; Morel was another famed political boss, or caudillo.

p. 52: I couldn't say whether they gutted him: Here and elsewhere in Borges (one thinks, of course, especially of the story titled "The Story from Rosendo Juárez" in the volume *Brodie's Report* and the story in this volume titled "The Cruel Redeemer Lazarus Morell"), a corpse is gutted, or somebody thinks about gutting it. This, according to folk wisdom, is to keep the body from floating up and revealing the murder before the culprit has had good time to get away. Apparently a gutted body did not produce as much gas, or the gas (obviously) would not be contained in an inner cavity. Thus there is an unacknowledged "piece of information" here that the ruffians of the Maldonado and other such neighborhoods tacitly shared—tacitly because it was so obvious that no one needed to spell it out.

Et cetera

A THEOLOGIAN IN DEATH

p. 54: Attribution: The Swedenborg Concordance: A Complete Work of Reference to the Theological Writings of Emanuel Swedenborg, based on the original Latin writings of the author, compiled, edited, and translated by the Rev. John Faulkner Potts, B.A., 4 vols. (London: Swedenborg Society, 1888). The text quoted here appears in the index (p. 622 of the appropriate volume) under "Melancthon" and is a mixture of the entries indicating two different Swedenborg texts: *A Continuation of the Last Judgment* and *The True Christian Religion.* The reader may find the text under "C.J. 47" and "T.797, 1–4." The full entry on Melancthon in the Concordance runs to p. 624.

THE CHAMBER OF STATUES

p. 56: Attribution: Freely taken from Sir Richard Burton's *Book of the Thousand Nights and a Night* (New York: Heritage Press, 1934 [1962]), pp. 1319–1321. The reader is referred to A Note on the Translation for more detailed comment on JLB's and the translator's uses of translations.

THE STORY OF THE TWO DREAMERS

p. 57: Attribution: This is freely adapted from a different version of the *1001 Nights*, Edward William Lane's *The Arabian Nights Entertainments*—or *The Thousand and One Nights* (New York: Tudor Publ., 1927), p. 1156. There are several other editions of this work, so the reader may find the tale in another place; Lane does not divide his book quite in the way JLB indicates.

THE MIRROR OF INK

p. 62: Attribution: One would not want to spoil JLB's little joke, if joke it is, but others before me have pointed out the discrepancy between this attribution and the fact. This story appears nowhere in Burton's *Lake Regions* and only sketchily in the volume that di Giovanni and many others give as the source: Edward William Lane's *Manners and Customs of the Modern Egyptians* (1837). Nonetheless, where Borges does seem to be translating (or calquing) the words of the last-named book, I have incorporated Lane's wording and word choices.

MAHOMED'S DOUBLE

p. 63: Attribution: Emanuel Swedenborg, *The True Christian Religion, containing the Universal Theology of the New Church, foretold by the Lord in Daniel VII, 13, 14, and in the Apocalypse XXI, 1, 2,* translated from the Latin of ES (New York: American Swedenborg Printing and Publishing Society, 1886), ¶¶. 829–830.

Index of Sources

p. 64: Source for "The Improbable Impostor Tom Castro": The source given by Borges here is the Philip Gosse book *The History of Piracy*; as one can clearly see, it is the same source cited for "The Widow Ching—Pirate," just below it. In my view, this attribution is the result of an initial error seized upon by Borges for another of his "plays with sources"; as he subsequently admitted freely, and as many critics have noted, much of this story comes from the *Encyclopædia Britannica*, Eleventh Edition, in the article titled "Tichborne Claimant." Here again, where JLB is clearly translating or calquing that source, I have followed it without slavish "transliteration" of JLB's Spanish.

p. 64: Source for "The Disinterested Killer Bill Harrigan": Neither the Walter Noble Burns book nor the Frederick Watson book contains anything remotely approaching the story given by Borges here. Some details are "correct" (if that is the word), such as Billy's long and blasphemous dying, spewing Spanish curses, but little in the larger pattern of the "biography" seems to conform to "life." While Borges claimed in the "Autobiographical Essay" (written with Norman Thomas di Giovanni and published in *The Aleph and Other Stories* [1970]) that he was "in flagrant contradiction" of his "chosen authorit[ies]," the truth is that he followed the authorities fairly closely for all the characters herein portrayed *except* that of Billy the Kid. He did, of course, "change and distort" the stories to suit his own purposes, but none is so cut from whole cloth as that of this gunfighter of the Wild West. The lesson in the "Autobiographical Essay" is perhaps that JLB's predilection for the red herring was lifelong.

Notes to *Fictions* ("The Garden of Forking Paths" and "Artifices"), pp. 65–128; 129–180.

p. 65: Title: First published as *Ficciones* (1935–1944) by Editorial Sur in 1944, this book was made up of two volumes: *El jardín de senderos que se bifurcan* ("The Garden of Forking Paths"), which had originally been published in 1941–1942, and *Artificios* ("Artifices"), dated 1944 and never before published as a book. Each volume in the 1944 edition had its own title page and its own preface. (In that edition, and in all successive editions, *The Garden of Forking Paths* included the story "El acercamiento a Almotasím" (The Approach to Al-Mu'tasim"), collected first in *Historia de la eternidad* ("History of Eternity"), 1936, and reprinted in each successive edition of that volume until 1953; this story now appears in the *Obras Completas* in *Historia de la eternidad*, but it is included here as a "fiction" rather than an "essay.") In 1956 Emecé published a volume titled *Ficciones*, which was identical to the 1944 Editorial Sur edition except for the inclusion in *Artificios* of three new stories ("The End," "The Cult of the Phoenix," and "The South") and a "Postscript" to the 1944 preface to *Artificios*. It is this 1956 edition of *Fictions*, plus "The Approach to Al-Mu'tasim," that is translated for this book.

THE GARDEN OF FORKING PATHS

Foreword

p. 67: The eight stories: The eighth story, here printed as the second, "The Approach to Al-Mu'tasim," was included in all editions subsequent to the 1941–1942 original edition. It had originally been published (1936) in *Historia de la eternidad* ("A History of Eternity"). Ordinals and cardinals used in the Foreword have been adjusted to reflect the presence of this story.

p. 67: Sur: "[T]he most influential literary publication in Latin America" (Rodríguez Monegal, p. 233), it was started by Victoria Ocampo, with the aid of the

Argentine novelist Eduardo Mallea and the American novelist Waldo Frank. Borges was one of the journal's first contributors, certainly one of its most notable (though *Sur* published or discussed virtually every major poet, writer, and essayist of the New or Old World) and he acted for three decades as one of its "guardian angels." Many of JLB's fictions, some of his poetry, and many critical essays and reviews appeared for the first time in the pages of *Sur*.

Tlön, Uqbar, Orbis Tertius

p. 68: Ramos Mejía: "A part of Buenos Aires in which the rich had weekend houses containing an English colony. It is now an industrial suburb" (Hughes and Fishburn).

p. 68: Bioy Casares: Adolfo Bioy Casares (1914–): Argentine novelist, JLB's closest friend and collaborator with JLB on numerous projects, including some signed with joint pseudonyms. In their joint productions, the two men were interested in detective stories, innovative narrative techniques (as the text here hints), and tales of a somewhat "fantastic" nature. Unfortunately rather eclipsed by Borges, especially in the English-speaking world, Bioy Casares is a major literary figure with a distinguished body of work; a description of the reciprocal influence of the two writers would require (at least) its own book-length study.

p. 69: Volume XLVI: The *Obras completas*, on which this translation is based, has "Volume XXVI," which the translator takes to be a typographical error, the second *X* slipped in for the correct *L*.

p. 70: Johannes Valentinus Andreä in the writings of Thomas de Quincey: It is perhaps significant that de Quincey credits Andreä (1586–1654) with "inventing" the Rosicrucian order by writing satirical works (and one especially: *Fama Fraternitatis of the meritorious Order of the Rosy Cross, addressed to the learned in general and the Governors of Europe*) describing an absurd mystico-Christian secret society engaged not only in general beneficence and the improvement of humanity but also in alchemy and gold making. The public did not perceive Andreä's satirical intent, and many rushed to "join" this society, though they could never find anyone to admit them. At last, according to de Quincey, a group of "Paracelsists" decided that if nobody else would admit to being a Rosicrucian, *they* would take over the name and "be" the society.

p. 70: Carlos Mastronardi: Mastronardi (1901–1976) was "a poet, essayist, and journalist [in Buenos Aires], a member of the group of writers identified with the avant-garde literary magazine *Martín Fierro*" (Fishburn and Hughes). Balderston (*The Literary Universe of JLB*: An Index . . . [New York: Greenwood Press], 1986) gives some of his titles: *Luz de Provincia, Tierra amanecida, Conocimiento de la noche*. Mastronardi was one of JLB's closest friends throughout the thirties and forties (Borges too was closely associated with *Martín Fierro*), and Rodríguez Monegal reported in his biography of JLB that Borges was still seeing Mastronardi as the biography (publ. 1978) was written; it seems safe to say, therefore, that Borges and Mastronardi were friends until Mastronardi's death.

p. 71: Capangas: Overseers or foremen of gangs of workers, usually either slaves or indentured semislaves, in rural areas, for cutting timber, etc., though not on ranches, where the foreman is known as a *capataz*. This word is of Guaraní or perhaps African origin and came into Spanish, as JLB indicates, from the area of Brazil.

p. 72: Néstor Ibarra: (b. 1908) "Born in France of an Argentine father who was the son of a French Basque émigré, *NI* went to the University of Buenos Aires around 1925 to complete his graduate education. While [there] he discovered Borges' poems and . . . tried to persuade his teachers to let him write a thesis on Borges' ultraist poetry" (Rodríguez Monegal, p. 239). Ibarra's groundbreaking and very important study of JLB, *Borges et Borges*, and his translations of JLB (along with those of Roger Caillois) into French in the 1950s were instrumental in the worldwide recognition of JLB's greatness. Among the other telling associations with this and other stories is the fact that Ibarra and Borges invented a new language ("with surrealist or ultraist touches"), a new French school of literature, Identism, "in which objects were always compared to themselves," and a new review, titled *Papers for the Suppression of Reality* (see "Pierre Menard," in this volume; this information, Rodríguez Monegal, pp. 240–241). The *N.R.F.* is the *Nouvelle Revue Française*, an extremely important French literary magazine that published virtually every important modern writer in the first three decades of this century.

p. 72: Ezequiel Martínez Estrada: Martínez Estrada (1895–1964) was an influential Argentine writer whose work *Radiografía de la pampa* (*X-ray of the Pampa*) JLB reviewed very favorably in 1933 in the literary supplement (*Revista Multicolor de los Sábados* ["Saturday Motley Review"]) to the Buenos Aires newspaper *Crítica*.

p. 72: Drieu La Rochelle: Pierre-Eugene Drieu La Rochelle (1893–1945) was for a time the editor of the *Nouvelle Revue Française*; he visited Argentina in 1933, recognized JLB's genius, and is reported to have said on his return to France that "*Borges vaut le voyage*" (Fishburn and Hughes).

p. 72: Alfonso Reyes: Reyes (1889–1959) was a Mexican poet and essayist, ambassador to Buenos Aires (1927–1930 and again 1936–1937), and friend of JLB's (Fishburn and Hughes). Reyes is recognized as one of the great humanists of the Americas in the twentieth century, an immensely cultured man who was a master of the Spanish language and its style ("direct and succinct without being thin or prosaic" [Rodríquez Monegal]).

p. 73: Xul Solar: Xul Solar is the nom de plume–turned–name of Alejandro Schultz (1887–1963), a lifelong friend of JLB; JLB compared Xul favorably with William Blake. Xul was a painter and something of a "creative linguist," having invented a language he called creol: a "language . . . made up of Spanish enriched by neologisms and by monosyllabic English words . . . used as adverbs" (Roberto Alifano, interviewer and editor, *Twenty-Four Conversations with Borges*, trans. Nicomedes Suárez Araúz, Willis Barnstone, and Noemí Escandell [Housatonic, Mass.: Lascaux Publishers, 1984], p. 119). In another place, JLB also notes another language invented by Xul Solar: "a philosophical language after the manner of John Wilkins" ("Autobiographical Essay," p. 237: *The Aleph and Other Stories: 1933–1969* [New York: Dutton, 1970], pp. 203–260). JLB goes on to note that "Xul was his version of Schultz and Solar of Solari." Xul Solar's painting has often been compared with that of Paul Klee; "strange" and "mysterious" are adjectives often applied to it. Xul illustrated three of JLB's books: *El tamaño de mi esperanza* (1926), *El idioma de los argentinos* (1928), and *Un modelo para la muerte*, the collaboration between JLB and Adolfo Bioy Casares that was signed "B. Suárez Lynch." In his biography of Borges, Emir Rodríguez Monegal devotes several pages to Xul's influence on JLB's writing; Borges himself also talks at length about Xul in the anthology of interviews noted above. Xul was, above all, a "character" in the Buenos Aires of the twenties and thirties and beyond.

p. 80: Amorim: Enrique Amorim (1900–1960) was a Uruguayan novelist, related to Borges by marriage. He wrote about the pampas, the gaucho, and gaucho life; Borges thought his *El Paisano Aguilar* "a closer description of gaucho life than Güiraldes' more famous *Don Segundo Sombra*" (Fishburn and Hughes).

Pierre Menard, Author of the *Quixote*

p. 93: Local color in Maurice Barrès or Rodríguez Larreta: Barrès (1862–1923) was a "French writer whose works include a text on bull-fighting entitled *Du sang, de la volupté et de la mort*" (Fishburn and Hughes); one can see what the narrator is getting at in terms of romanticizing the foreign. Enrique Rodríguez Larreta (1875–1961) wrote historical novels; one, set in Avila and Toledo in the time of Philip II (hence the reference to that name in the text) and titled *La gloria de Don Ramiro*, used an archaic Spanish for the dialogue; clearly this suggests the archaism of Menard's *Quixote*. (Here I paraphrase Fishburn and Hughes.)

A Survey of the Works of Herbert Quain

p. 108: The Siamese Twin Mystery: A novel by Ellery Queen, published in 1933. Here the literary critic–narrator is lamenting the fact that Quain's novel was overshadowed by the much more popular Queen's.

ARTIFICES

Funes, His Memory

p. 131: Title: This story has generally appeared under the title "Funes the Memorious," and it must be the brave (or foolhardy) translator who dares change such an odd and memorable title. Nor would the translator note (and attempt to justify) his choice of a translation except in unusual circumstances. Here, however, the title in the original Spanish calls for some explanation. The title is "Funes el memorioso"; the word *memorioso* is not an odd Spanish word; it is in fact perfectly common, if somewhat colloquial. It simply means "having a wonderful or powerful memory," what in English one might render by the expression "having a memory like an elephant." The beauty of the Spanish is that the entire long phrase is compressed into a single word, a single adjective, used in the original title as an epithet: Funes the Elephant-Memoried. (The reader can see that that translation won't do.) The word "memorist" is perhaps the closest thing that common English yields up without inventing a new word such as "memorious," which strikes the current translator as vaguely Lewis Carroll–esque, yet "memorist" has something vaguely show business about it, as though Funes worked vaudeville or the carnival sideshows. The French title of this story is the lovely eighteenth-century-sounding "*Funes ou La Mémoire*"; with a nod to JLB's great admirer John Barth, I have chosen "Funes, His Memory."

p. 131: The Banda Oriental: The "eastern bank" of the River Plate, the old name of Uruguay before it became a country, and a name used for many years afterward by the "old-timers" or as a sort of nickname.

p. 131: Pedro Leandro Ipuche: The Uruguayan Ipuche was a friend of the young ultraist-period Borges (ca. 1925), with whom (along with Ricardo Güiraldes, author of the important novel *Don Segundo Sombra*) he worked on the literary magazine *Proa* (Fishburn and Hughes). *Proa* was an influential little magazine, and Borges and friends took it seriously; they were engaged, as Rodríguez Monegal quotes the "Autobiographical Essay" as saying, in "renewing both prose and poetry."

p. 131: Fray Bentos: "A small town on the banks of the Uruguay River, famous for its meat-canning industry. In his youth Borges was a regular visitor to his cousins' ranch near Fray Bentos" (Fishburn and Hughes). Haedo was in fact the family name of these cousins.

p. 135: The thirty-three Uruguayan patriots: The "Thirty-three," as they were called, were a band of determined patriots under the leadership of Juan Antonio Lavalleja who crossed the River Plate from Buenos Aires to Montevideo in order to "liberate" the Banda Oriental (Uruguay) from the Spaniards. Their feat of bravery, under impossible odds, immortalized them in the mythology of the Southern Cone. For fuller detail, see the note to p. 474, for the story "Avelino Arredondo" in the volume *The Book of Sand.*

Three Versions of Judas

p. 165 (note): *Euclides da Cunha:* Cunha (1866–1909) was a very well-known Brazilian writer whose most famous novel is a fictional retelling of an uprising in the state of Bahia. He was moved by the spiritualism (Fishburn and Hughes note its mystical qualities) of the rebels.

p. 165 (note): *Antonio Conselheiro:* (1828–1897). Conselheiro was "a Brazilian religious dissident who led a rebellion in Canudos, in the northern state of Bahía. The rebels were peasants . . . who lived in a system of communes, working out their own salvation. They rose against the changes introduced by the new Republican government, which they regarded as the Antichrist. . . . Conselheiro's head was cut off and put on public display" (Fishburn and Hughes). His real name was Antonio Maciel; *conselheiro* means "counselor," and so his messianic, ministerial role is here emphasized.

p. 165 (note): *Almafuerte:* The pseudonym of Pedro Bonifacio Palacio (1854–1917), one of Argentina's most beloved poets. A kind of role model and hero to young writers, akin to the phenomenon of Dylan Thomas in Britain and the United States a few years ago, Almafuerte was one of JLB's most admired contemporaries.

The End

p. 169: "It'd been longer than seven years that I'd gone without seeing my children. I found them that day, and I wouldn't have it so's I looked to them like a man on his way to a knife fight": It is not these words that need noting, but an "intertextual event." It is about here that the Argentine reader will probably realize what this story is about: It is a retelling of the end of José Hernández' famous tale *Martín Fierro.* As Fierro is a knife fighter, and as a black man figures in the poem, and as there is a famous song contest, the reader will put two and two together, no doubt, even before Martín Fierro's name is mentioned a few lines farther on. This is the way Fishburn and Hughes state the situation: "The episode alluded to in 'The End' is the *payada,* or song contest, between Martín Fierro and *el moreno* ["the black man"] who was the brother of the murdered negro. In the contest the gauchos discuss metaphysical themes, but towards the end *el moreno* reveals his identity, and his desire for revenge is made clear.

In keeping with the more conciliatory tone of pt. 2 [of Hernández' original poem] a fight is prevented between the two contestants, each going his own way. 'The End' is a gloss on this episode, the fight that might have taken place." By this late in the volume, JLB's Preface to the stories, hinting at the coexistence of a "famous book" in this story, may have dimmed in the reader's memory, but for the Latin American reader, the creeping familiarity of the events, like the echoes of Shakespeare in the assassination of Kilpatrick in "Theme of the Traitor and the Hero," should come into the foreground in this section of the story, and the reader, like Ryan in that other story, make the "connection."

The South

p. 174: Buenos Aires: Here the province, not the city. The reference is to the northern border, near Entre Ríos and Santa Fe provinces, on the Paraná River.

p. 174: Catriel: Cipriano Catriel (d. 1874). Catriel was an Indian chieftain who fought against the Argentines in the Indian wars. Later, however, he fought on the side of the revolutionary forces (Fishburn and Hughes).

p. 178: His gaucho trousers: This is the *chiripá,* a triangular worsted shawl tied about the waist with the third point pulled up between the legs and looped into a knot to form a rudimentary pant, or a sort of diaper. It is worn over a pair of pantaloons (ordinarily white) that "stick out" underneath. Sometimes, incredible as it strikes Anglo-Saxons that the extraordinarily *machista* gauchos would wear such clothing (but think of the Scots' kilts), the pantaloons had lace bottoms.

Notes to *The Aleph,* pp. 181–288

The Dead Man

p. 196: Rio Grande do Sul: The southernmost state of Brazil, bordering both Argentina and Uruguay on the north. Later in this story, a certain wildness is attributed to this region; JLB often employed the implicit contrast between the more "civilized" city and province of Buenos Aires (and all of Argentina) and the less "developed" city of Montevideo and nation of Uruguay and its "wilderness of horse country," the "plains," "the interior," here represented by Rio Grande do Sul.

p. 196: Paso del Molino: "A lower-to-middle-class district outside Montevideo" (Fishburn and Hughes).

Story of the Warrior and the Captive Maiden

p. 210: The Auracan or Pampas tongue: The Pampas Indians were a nomadic people who inhabited the plains of the Southern Cone at the time of the Conquest; they were overrun by the Araucans, and the languages and cultures merged; today the two names are essentially synonymous (Fishburn and Hughes). English seems not to have taken the name Pampas for anything but the plains of Argentina.

p. 211: Pulpería: A country store or general store, though not the same sort of corner grocery-store-and-bar, the *esquina* or *almacén,* that Borges uses as a setting in the stories that take place in the city. The *pulpería* would have been precisely the sort of frontier general store that one sees in American westerns.

A Biography of Tadeo Isidoro Cruz (1829–1874)

p. 212: Montoneros: Montoneros were the men of guerrilla militias (generally gauchos) that fought in the civil wars following the wars of independence. They tended to rally under the banner of a leader rather than specifically under the banner of a cause; Fishburn and Hughes put it in the following way: "[T]heir allegiance to their leader was personal and direct, and they were largely indifferent to his political leanings."

p. 212: Lavalle: Juan Galo Lavalle (1797–1841) was an Argentine hero who fought on the side of the Unitarians, the centralizing Buenos Aires forces, against the Federalist *montoneros* of the outlying provinces and territories, whose most famous leader was Juan Manuel de Rosas, the fierce dictator who appears in several of JLB's stories. The mention here of Lavalle and López would indeed locate this story in 1829, a few months before Lavalle was defeated by the combined Rosas and López forces (Fishburn and Hughes). One would assume, then, that the man who fathered Tadeo Isidoro Cruz was fighting with Rosas' forces themselves.

p. 212: Suárez' cavalry: Probably Manuel Isidoro Suárez (1759–1843), JLB's mother's maternal grandfather, who fought on the side of the Unitarians in the period leading up to 1829 (Fishburn and Hughes). Borges may have picked up the protagonist's name, as well, in part from his forebear.

p. 213: Thirty Christian men . . . Sgt. Maj. Eusebio Laprida . . . two hundred Indians: Eusebio Laprida (1829–1898) led eighty, not thirty, men against a regular army unit of two hundred soldiers, not Indians, in a combat at the Cardoso Marshes on January 25, not 23, 1856 (data, Fishburn and Hughes). The defeat of the Indians took place during a raid in 1879. JLB here may be conflating the famous Thirty-three led by Lavalleja against Montevideo (see note to "Avelino Arredondo" in *The Book of Sand)*, Laprida's equally heroic exploit against a larger "official" army unit, and Laprida's exploit against the Indians two decades later.

p. 214: Manuel Mesa executed in the Plaza de la Victoria: Manuel Mesa (1788–1829) fought on the side of Rosas and the Federalists. In 1829 he organized a force of *montoneros* and friendly Indians and battled Lavalle, losing that engagement. In his retreat, he was met by Manuel Isidoro Suárez and captured. Suárez sent him to Buenos Aires, where he was executed in the Plaza Victoria.

p. 214: The deserter Martín Fierro: As JLB tells the reader in the Afterword to this volume, this story has been a retelling, from the "unexpected" point of view of a secondary character, of the famous gaucho epic poem *Martín Fierro*, by José Hernández. Since this work is a classic (or *the* classic) of nineteenth-century Argentine literature, every reader in the Southern Cone would recognize "what was coming": Martín Fierro, the put-upon gaucho hero, stands his ground against the authorities, and his friend abandons his uniform to stand and fight with him. This changing sides is a recurrent motif in Borges; see "Story of the Warrior and the Captive Maiden" in this volume, for instance. It seems to have been more interesting to JLB that one might change sides than that one would exhibit the usual traits of heroism. Borges is also fond of rewriting classics: See "The House of Asterion," also in this volume, and note that the narrator in "The Zahir" retells to himself, more or less as the outline of a story he is writing, the story of the gold of the Nibelungen. One could expand the list to great length.

Emma Zunz

p. 215: Bagé: A city in southern Rio Grande do Sul province, in Brazil.

p. 215: Gualeguay: "A rural town and department in the province of Entre Ríos" (Fishburn and Hughes).

p. 215: Lanús: "A town and middle-class district in Greater Buenos Aires, southwest of the city" (Fishburn and Hughes).

p. 217: Almagro: A lower-middle-class neighborhood near the center of Buenos Aires.

p. 217: Calle Liniers: As the story says, a street in the Almagro neighborhood.

p. 217: Paseo de Julio: Now the Avenida Alem. This street runs parallel with the waterfront; at the time of this story it was lined with tenement houses and houses of ill repute.

p. 218: A westbound Lacroze: The Lacroze Tramway Line served the northwestern area of Buenos Aires at the time; today the city has an extensive subway system.

p. 218: Warnes: A street in central Buenos Aires near the commercial district of Villa Crespo, where the mill is apparently located.

The Other Death

p. 223: Gualeguaychú: "A town on the river of the same name in the province of Entre Ríos, opposite the town of Fray Bentos, with which there is considerable interchange" (Fishburn and Hughes).

p. 223: Masoller: Masoller, in northern Uruguay, was the site of a decisive battle on September 1, 1904, between the rebel forces of Aparicio Saravia (see below) and the National Army; Saravia was defeated and mortally wounded (Fishburn and Hughes).

p. 223: The banners of Aparicio Saravia: Aparicio Saravia (1856–1904) was a Uruguayan landowner and caudillo who led the successful Blanco (White party) revolt against the dictatorship of Idiarte Borda (the Colorados, or Red party). Even in victory, however, Saravia had to continue to fight against the central government, since Borda's successor, Batlle, refused to allow Saravia's party to form part of the new government. It is the years of this latter revolt that are the time of "The Other Death." See also, for a longer explanation of the political situation of the time, the story "Avelino Arredondo" in *The Book of Sand.*

p. 223: Río Negro or Paysandú: Río Negro is the name of a department in western Uruguay on the river of the same name, just opposite the Argentine province of Entre Ríos. Paysandú is a department in Uruguay bordering Río Negro. Once again JLB is signaling the relative "wildness" of Uruguay in comparison with Argentina, which was not touched by these civil wars at the time.

p. 223: Gualeguay: See note to p. 215 above. Note the distinction between "Gualeguay" and "Gualeguaychú" (see note to p. 223 above).

p. 223: Ñancay: "A tributary of the Uruguay River that flows through the rich agricultural lands of southern Entre Ríos province" (Fishburn and Hughes).

p. 224: Men whose throats were slashed through to the spine: This is another instance in which JLB documents the (to us today) barbaric custom by the armies of the

South American wars of independence (and other, lesser combats as well) of slitting defeated troops' throats. In other places, he notes offhandedly that "no prisoners were taken," which does not mean that all the defeated troops were allowed to return to their bivouacs. In this case, a rare case, Borges actually "editorializes" a bit: "a civil war that struck me as more some outlaw's dream than the collision of two armies."

p. 224: Illescas, Tupambaé, Masoller: All these are the sites of battles in northern and central Uruguay fought in 1904 between Saravia's forces and the National Army of Uruguay.

p. 224: White ribbon: Because the troops were often irregulars, or recruited from the gauchos or farmhands of the Argentine, and therefore lacking standardized uniforms, the only way to tell friend from enemy was by these ribbons, white in the case of the Blancos, red in the case of the Colorados. Here the white ribbon worn by the character marks him as a follower of Saravia, the leader of the Whites. (See notes *passim* about the significance of these parties.)

p. 224: Zumacos: The name by which regulars in the Uruguayan National Army were known.

p. 225: Artiguismo: That is, in accord with the life and views of José Gervasio Artigas (1764–1850), a Uruguayan hero who fought against both the Spaniards and the nascent Argentines to forge a separate nation out of what had just been the Banda Oriental, or east bank of the Plate. The argument was that Uruguay had its own "spirit," its own "sense of place," which the effete Argentines of Buenos Aires, who only romanticized the gaucho but had none of their own, could never truly understand or live.

p. 225: Red infantry: The Reds, or Colorados, were the forces of the official national government of Uruguay, in contradistinction to the Blancos, or Whites, of Saravia's forces; the Reds therefore had generally better weapons and equipment, and better-trained military officers on the whole, than the irregular and largely gaucho Whites.

p. 225: ¡Viva Urquiza!: Justo José Urquiza (1801–1870) was president of the Argentinian Confederation between 1854 and 1860. Prior to that, he had fought with the Federalists under Rosas (the provincial forces) against the Unitarians (the Buenos Aires–based centralizing forces), but in 1845 he broke with Rosas (whom JLB always excoriates as a vicious dictator) and eventually saw Buenos Aires province and the other provinces of the Argentinian Confederation brought together into the modern nation of Argentina, though under the presidency of Bartolomé Mitre.

p. 225: Cagancha or India Muerta: The perplexity here derives from the fact that while the battle at Masoller, in which Damián took part, occurred in 1904, the cry *¡Viva Urquiza!* would have been heard at the Battle of Cagancha (1839) or India Muerta (1845), where Urquiza's rebel Federalist forces fought the Unitarians. At Cagancha, Urquiza was defeated by the Unitarians; at India Muerta he defeated them. This story may also, thus, have certain subterranean connections with "The Theologians," in its examination of the possibilities of repeating or circular, or at least nondiscrete, time.

p. 227: He "marked" no one: He left his mark on no man in a knife fight; in a fight, when the slight might, even by the standards of the day, be deemed too inconsequential to kill a man for, or if the other man refused to fight, the winner would leave his mark, a scar, that would settle the score.

Averroës' Search

p. 239: "The seven sleepers of Ephesus": This is a very peculiar story to put in the minds of these Islamic luminaries, for the story of the seven sleepers of Ephesus is a Christian story, told by Gregory of Tours. Clearly the breadth of culture of these gentlemen is great, but it is difficult (at least for this translator) to see the relationship of this particular tale (unlike the other "stories," such as the children playing or "representing" life and the "if it had been a snake it would have bitten him" story told by abu-al-Ḥasan) to Averroës' quest.

The Zahir

p. 243: Calle Aráoz: Fishburn and Hughes tell us that in the 1930s, Calle Aráoz was "a street of small houses inhabited by the impoverished middle class"; it is near the penitentiary Las Heras.

p. 244: On the corner of Chile and Tacuarí: A corner in the Barrio Sur, or southern part of Buenos Aires, as the story says; it is some ten blocks from the Plaza Constitución and its great station.

p. 244: Truco: A card game indigenous, apparently, to Argentina and played very often in these establishments. Borges was fascinated by this game and devoted an essay and two or three poems to it, along with references, such as this one, scattered throughout his œuvre. The phrase "to my misfortune" indicates the inexorability of the attraction that the game held for him; the narrator could apparently simply not avoid going into the bar. Truco's nature, for JLB, is that combination of fate and chance that seems to rule over human life as well as over games: an infinitude of possibilities within a limited number of cards, the limitations of the rules. See "Truco" in *Borges: A Reader.*

p. 244: La Concepción: A large church in the Barrio Sur, near the Plaza Constitución.

p. 244: The chamfered curb in darkness: Here JLB's reference is to an *ochava*—that is, a "corner with the corner cut off" to form a three-sided, almost round curb, and a somewhat wider eight-sided rather than four-sided intersection, as the four corners of the intersection would all be chamfered in that way. This reference adds to the "old-fashioned" atmosphere of the story, because chamfered corners were common on streets traveled by large horse-drawn wagons, which would need extra space to turn the corners so that their wheels would not ride up onto the sidewalks.

p. 245: I went neither to the Basílica del Pilar that morning nor to the cemetery: That is, the narrator did not go to Teodelina's funeral. The Basílica del Pilar is one of the most impressive churches in central Buenos Aires, near the Recoleta cemetery where Teodelina Vilar would surely have been buried.

p. 248: "She's been put into Bosch": Bosch was "a well-known private clinic frequented by the *porteño* elite" (Fishburn and Hughes).

The Writing of the God

p. 253: I saw the origins told by the Book of the People. I saw . . . the dogs that tore at their faces: Here the priest is remembering the story of the creation of the world told in the Popul Vuh, the Mayan sacred text. The standard modern translation is by Dennis Tedlock: *Popul Vuh: The Mayan Book of the Dawn of Life* (New York: Simon & Schuster Touchstone, 1985). For this part of the genesis story, cf. pp. 84–85.

The Wait

p. 267: Plaza del Once: Pronounced *óhn-say,* not *wunce.* This is actually "Plaza Once," but the homonymy of the English and Spanish words makes it advisable, I think, to modify the name slightly in order to alert the English reader to the Spanish ("eleven"), rather than the English ("onetime" or "past"), sense of the word. Plaza Once is one of Buenos Aires' oldest squares, "associated in Borges's memory with horse-drawn carts" (Fishburn and Hughes), though later simply a modern square.

The Aleph

p. 275: Quilmes: A district in southern Buenos Aires; "at one time favoured for weekend villas, particularly by the British, Quilmes has since become unfashionable, a heavily industrialised area, known mainly for Quilmes Beer, the largest brewing company in the world" (Fishburn and Hughes). Thus JLB is evoking a world of privilege and luxe.

p. 276: Juan Crisóstomo Lafinur Library: This library is named after JLB's great-uncle (1797–1824), who occupied the chair of philosophy at the Colegio de la Unión del Sud until, under attack for teaching materialism, he was forced into exile.

p. 278: "The most elevated heights of Flores": Here Daneri's absurdity reaches "new heights," for though the neighborhood of Flores had been very much in vogue among the affluent of Buenos Aires society during the nineteenth century, it was only about a hundred feet above sea level. Moreover, it had lost much of its exclusiveness, and therefore glamour, by the time of this story, since in the yellow fever epidemic of 1871 people fled "central" Buenos Aires for the "outlying" neighborhood.

p. 283: Chacarita: One of the two enormous cemeteries in Buenos Aires; the other is Recoleta. A modern guidebook* has this to say about the cemeteries of Buenos Aires:

> *Life and Death in Recoleta & Chacarita*
>
> Death is an equalizer, except in Buenos Aires. When the arteries harden after decades of dining at Au Bec Fin and finishing up with coffee and dessert at La Biela or Café de la Paix, the wealthy and powerful of Buenos Aires move ceremoniously across the street to Recoleta Cemetery, joining their forefathers in a place they have visited religiously all their lives. . . . According to Argentine novelist Tomás Eloy Martínez, Argentines are "cadaver cultists" who honor their most revered national figures not on the date of their birth but of their death. . . . Nowhere is this obsession with mortality and corruption more evident than in Recoleta, where generations of the elite repose in the grandeur of ostentatious mausoleums. It is a common saying and only a slight exaggeration that "it is cheaper to live extravagantly all your life than to be buried in Recoleta." Traditionally, money is not enough: you must have a surname like Anchorena, Alvear, Aramburu, Avellaneda, Mitre, Martínez de Hoz, or Sarmiento. . . .
>
> Although more democratic in conception, Chacarita has many tombs which match the finest in Recoleta. One of the most visited belongs to Carlos Gardel, the famous tango singer. (**Argentina, Uruguay & Paraguay,* Wayne Bernhardson

and María Massolo, Hawthorne, Vic, Australia; Berkeley, CA, USA; and London, UK: Lonely Planet Publications [Travel Survival Kit], 1992)

p. 285: Compendia of Dr. Acevedo Díaz: Eduardo Acevedo Díaz (1882–1959) won the Premio Nacional for his novel *Cancha Larga*; JLB's entry that year, *The Garden of Forking Paths,* won second prize.

p. 285: Pedro Henríquez Ureña: Henríquez Ureña (1884–1946), originally from the Dominican Republic, lived for years in Buenos Aires and was an early contributor to *Sur,* the magazine that Victoria Ocampo founded and that JLB assiduously worked on. It was through Henríquez Ureña, who had lived for a time in Mexico City, that JLB met another close friend, the Mexican humanist Alfonso Reyes. Henríquez Ureña and JLB collaborated on the *Antología de la literatura argentina* (1937).

Notes to *The Maker,* pp. 289–328

Foreword

p. 291: Leopoldo Lugones: Lugones (1874–1938) was probably Argentina's leading poet in the second to fourth decades of this century; he was influenced by Spanish *modernismo* and by the French Symbolists. To a degree he represented to the young Turks of Argentine poetry the *ancien régime*; therefore he was often attacked, and often tastelessly so. Early on, JLB joined in these gibes at Lugones, though clearly Borges also recognized Lugones' skills and talents as a poet. Rodríguez Monegal (pp. 197–198) speculates that JLB had mixed feelings about Lugones, especially in his person, but suggests that respect for Lugones as a poet no doubt prevailed, especially as JLB matured. Monegal quotes Borges (quoted by Fernández Moreno) as follows: Lugones was "a solitary and dogmatic man, a man who did not open up easily. . . . Conversation was difficult with him because he [would] bring everything to a close with a phrase which was literally a period. . . . Then you had to begin again, to find another subject. . . . And that subject was also dissolved with a period. . . . His kind of conversation was brilliant but tiresome. And many times his assertions had nothing to do with what he really believed; he just had to say something extraordinary. . . . What he wanted was to control the conversation. Everything he said was final. And . . . we had a great respect for him." (Fernández Moreno [1967], pp. 10–11, in Rodríguez Monegal, p. 197; ellipses in Rodríguez Monegal.) Another problem with Lugones was his partiality to military governments, his proto- and then unfeigned fascism; obviously this did not endear him to many, more liberal, thinkers. In this introduction JLB seems to recognize that while he and his friends were experimenting with a "new" poetics in the first decades of the century, Lugones kept on his amiable way, and to admit that later he, JLB, had put aside some of the more shocking and radical of his notions of poetry in favor of a cleaner, less "poetic" poetry, which Lugones would probably have recognized as much closer to his own. So the "son" comes to see that he has come to resemble the resented "father" (no Freudian implications intended; genetics only; no political implications intended, either; Borges hated military governments and hated fascism and Nazism).

p. 292: The Maker: The Spanish title of this "heterogeneous" volume of prose and poetry (only the prose is included in this volume) is *El hacedor,* and *hacedor* is a troublesome word for a translator into English. JLB seems to be thinking of the Greek word *poeta,* which means "maker," since a "true and literal" translation of *poeta* into Spanish would indeed be *hacedor.* Yet *hacedor* is in this translator's view, and in the view of all those native speakers he has consulted, a most uncommon word. It is not used in Spanish for "poet" but instead makes one think of someone who makes things with his hands, a kind of artisan, perhaps, or perhaps even a tinkerer. The English word *maker* is perhaps strange too, yet it exists; however, it is used in English (in such phrases as "he went to meet his Maker" and the brand name Maker's Mark) in a way that dissuades one from seizing upon it immediately as the "perfect" translation for *hacedor.* (The Spanish word *hacedor* would never be used for "God," for instance.) Eliot Weinberger has suggested to me, quite rightly, perhaps, that JLB had in mind the Scots word *makir,* which means "poet." But there are other cases: Eliot's dedication of *The Waste Land* to Ezra Pound, taken from Dante—*il miglior fabbro,* where *fabbro* has exactly the same range as *hacedor.* Several considerations seem to militate in favor of the translation "artificer": first, the sense of someone's making something with his hands, or perhaps "sculptor," for one of JLB's favorite metaphors for poetry was at one time sculpture; second, the fact that the second "volume" in the volume *Fictions* is clearly titled *Artifices;* third, the overlap between art and craft or artisanry that is implied in the word, as in the first story in this volume. But a translational decision of this kind is never easy and perhaps never "done"; one wishes one could call the volume *Il fabbro,* or *Poeta,* or leave it *El hacedor.* The previous English translation of this volume in fact opted for *Dreamtigers.* Yet sometimes a translator is spared this anguish (if he or she finds the key to the puzzle in time to forestall it); in this case there is an easy solution. I quote from Emir Rodríguez Monegal's *Jorge Luis Borges: A Literary Biography,* p. 438: "Borges was sixty when the ninth volume of his complete works came out. . . . For the new book he had thought up the title in English: *The Maker,* and had translated it into Spanish as *El hacedor;* but when the book came out in the United States the American translator preferred to avoid the theological implications and used instead the title of one of the pieces: *Dreamtigers.*" And so a translation problem becomes a problem *created* in the first place by a translation! (Thanks to Eliot Weinberger for coming across this reference *in time* and bringing it to my attention.)

Dreamtigers

p. 294: Title: The title of this story appears in italics because JLB used the English nonce word in the Spanish original.

p. 294: That spotted "tiger": While there are many indigenous words for the predatory cats of South America—puma, jaguar, etc.—that have been adopted into Spanish, Peninsular Spanish called these cats tigers. (One should recall that Columbus simply had no words for the myriad new things in this New World, so if an indigenous word did not "catch on" immediately, one was left with a European word for the thing: hence "Indians"!) Here, then, JLB is comparing the so-called tiger of the Southern Cone with its Asian counterpart, always a more intriguing animal for him. Cf., for instance, "Blue Tigers" in the volume titled *Shakespeare's Memory.*

Toenails

p. 296: Recoleta: The "necropolis" near the center of Buenos Aires, where the elite of Porteño society buries its dead. See also note to "The Aleph" in *The Aleph.*

Covered Mirrors

p. 297: Federalists/Unitarians: The Federalists were those nineteenth-century conservatives who favored a federal (i.e., decentralized) plan of government for Argentina, with the provinces having great autonomy and an equal say in the government; the Federalists were also "Argentine," as opposed to the internationalist, Europe-looking Unitarians, and their leaders tended to be populist caudillos, their fighters in the civil wars to be gauchos. The Unitarians, on the other hand, were a Buenos Aires–based party that was in favor of a centralizing, liberal government; they tended to be "freethinkers," rather than Catholics per se, intellectuals, internationalists, and Europophile in outlook. Unitarians deplored the barbarity of the gaucho ethos, and especially sentimentalizing that way of life; they were urban to a fault. This old "discord between their lineages," as Borges puts it in this story, is the discord of Argentina, never truly overcome in the Argentina that JLB lived in.

p. 297: Balvanera: One can assume that at the time "Borges" had this experience, Balvanera was a neighborhood of "genteel poverty" much as one might envision it from the description of "Julia," but in the story "The Dead Man," in *The Aleph,* Balvanera is the neighborhood that the "sad sort of hoodlum" Benjamín Otálora comes from, and it is described as a district on the outskirts of the Buenos Aires of 1891 (which does not, emphatically, mean that it would be on the outskirts of the Buenos Aires of 1927, the time of the beginning of "Covered Mirrors"), a neighborhood of "cart drivers and leather braiders." Thus Balvanera is associated not so much with gauchos and cattle (though the Federalist connection hints at such a connotation) as with the stockyards and their industries, the *secondary* (and romantically inferior) spin-offs of the pampas life. Balvanera here, like Julia's family itself, is the decayed shadow of itself and the life it once represented.

p. 297: Blank wall of the railway yard . . . Parque Centenario: The railway ran (and runs) through Balvanera from the Plaza del Once station westward, out toward the outskirts of Buenos Aires. Sarmiento runs westward, too, but slightly north of the railway line, and running slightly northwest. It meets the Parque Centenario about a mile and a half from the station.

The Mountebank

p. 301: Chaco River: In the Litoral region of northern Argentina, an area known for cattle raising and forestry.

Delia Elena San Marco

p. 303: Plaza del Once (pronounced *óhn-say,* not *wunce*). This is actually usually given as Plaza Once, but the homonymy of the English and Spanish words makes it advisable, I think, to modify the name slightly so as to alert the English reader to the Spanish ("eleven"), rather than English ("onetime" or "past"), sense of the word. JLB himself uses "Plaza del Once" from time to time, as in the *Obras completas,* vol. II, p.

428, in the story "La señora mayor," in *Informe de Brodie* ("The Elderly Lady," in *Brodie's Report*, p. 375). Plaza Once is one of Buenos Aires' oldest squares, "associated in Borges's memory with horse-drawn carts" (Fishburn and Hughes), though later simply a modern square, and now the site of Buenos Aires' main train station for westbound railways.

A Dialog Between Dead Men

p. 304: Quiroga: Like many of the pieces in this volume ("The Captive," "*Martín Fierro*," "*Everything and Nothing*"), "A Dialog Between Dead Men" sets up a "dialog" with others of Borges' writings, especially a famous poem called "General Quiroga Rides to His Death in a Carriage" ("El general Quiroga va en coche al muere [*sic*, for "*a su muerte, a la muerte*," etc.]"). There the reader will find the scene that is not described but only alluded to here, the murder of General Quiroga by a sword-wielding gang of horsemen under the leadership of the Reinafé brothers. Some biographical information is essential here: Juan Facundo Quiroga (1793–1835) was a Federalist caudillo (which means that he was on the side of Rosas [see below]), and was, like Rosas, a leader feared by all and hated by his opponents; he was known for his violence, cruelty, and ruthlessness and made sure that his name was feared by slitting the throats of the prisoners that his forces captured and of the wounded in the battles that he fought. So great was his charisma, and so ruthless his personality, that his supposed ally in the fight against the Unitarians, Juan Manuel de Rosas, began to resent (and perhaps mistrust) him. As Quiroga was leaving a meeting with Rosas in 1835, he was ambushed by the Reinafé gang, and he and his companions were brutally murdered, their bodies hacked to pieces; it was widely believed (though stubbornly denied by Rosas) that Rosas had ordered the assassination.

p. 304: Rosas: Juan Manuel de Rosas (1793–1877) was the dictator of Argentina for eighteen years, from 1835 to 1852. His dictatorship was marked by terror and persecution, and he is for JLB one of the most hated figures in Argentine history; JLB's forebears, Unitarians, suffered the outrages of Rosas and his followers. Early in his career Rosas was a Federalist (later the distinction became meaningless, as Rosas did more than anyone to unify Argentina, though most say he did so for all the wrong reasons), a caudillo whose followers were gangs of gauchos and his own private vigilante force, the so-called *mazorca* (see the story "Pedro Salvadores" in *In Praise of Darkness*). He methodically persecuted, tortured, and killed off his opponents both outside *and inside* his party, until he at last reigned supreme over the entire country. See the poem "Rosas" in JLB's early volume of poetry *Fervor de Buenos Aires.*

p. 305: "Chacabuco and Junín and Palma Redondo and Caseros": Battles in the wars of independence of the countries of the Southern Cone.

The Yellow Rose

p. 310: Porpora de' giardin, pompa de' prato, / Gemma di primavera, occhio d'aprile . . . : These lines are from a poem, *L'Adone*, written by Marino (1569–1625) himself (III:158, ll. 1–2).

Martín Fierro

p. 312: Ituzaingó or Ayacucho: Battles (1827 and 1824 respectively) in the wars of independence against Spain.

p. 312: Peaches . . . a young boy . . . the heads of Unitarians, their beards bloody: This terrible image captures the cruelty and horror of the civil war that racked Argentina in the early nineteenth century, and the brutality with which the Federalists, when they were in power under Rosas, persecuted and terrorized the Unitarians. In other stories I have noted that slitting throats was the preferred method of dispatching captured opponents and the wounded of battles; here the opponents are decapitated. Making this all the more horrific is the fact that it was JLB's maternal grandfather, Isidoro Acevedo, who as a child witnessed this scene. In *JLB: Selected Poems 1923–1967* (Harmondsworth: Penguin, 1985), p. 316, the editor quotes Borges (without further citation): "One day, at the age of nine or ten, he [Isidoro Acevedo] walked by the Plata Market. It was in the time of Rosas. Two gaucho teamsters were hawking peaches. He lifted the canvas covering the fruit, and there were the decapitated heads of Unitarians, with blood-stained beards and wide-open eyes. He ran home, climbed up into the grapevine growing in the back patio, and it was only later that night that he could bring himself to tell what he had seen in the morning. In time, he was to see many things during the civil wars, but none ever left so deep an impression on him."

p. 312: A man who knew all the words . . . metaphors of metal . . . the shapes of its moon: This is probably Leopoldo Lugones. See the note, above, to the foreword to *The Maker*, p. 291.

Paradiso, XXXI, 108

p. 316: "My Lord Jesus Christ, . . . is this, indeed, Thy likeness in such fashion wrought?": Borges is translating Dante, *Paradiso*, XXXI: 108–109; in English, the lines read as given. Quoted from *The Portable Dante*, ed. Paolo Milano, *Paradiso*, trans. Laurence Binyon (1869–1943) (New York: Penguin, 1975 [orig. copyright, 1947]), p. 532.

Everything and Nothing

p. 319: Title: In italics here because the story was titled originally in this way by JLB, in English.

Ragnarök

p. 321: Pedro Henríquez Ureña: Henríquez Ureña (1884–1946), originally from the Dominican Republic, lived for years in Buenos Aires and was an early contributor to *Sur*, the magazine that Victoria Ocampo founded and that JLB assiduously worked on. It was through Henríquez Ureña, who had lived for a time in Mexico City, that JLB met another friend, the Mexican humanist Alfonso Reyes. Henríquez Ureña and JLB collaborated on the *Antología de la literatura argentina* (1937), and they were very close friends.

In Memoriam, J.F.K.

p. 326: Avelino Arredondo: The assassin, as the story says, of the president of Uruguay, Juan Idiarte Borda (1844–1897). See the story "Avelino Arredondo" in the volume *The Book of Sand.*

Notes to *In Praise of Darkness,* pp. 329–342

Foreword

p. 332: Ascasubi: Hilario Ascasubi (1807–1875) was a prolific, if not always successful, writer of gaucho poetry and prose. (The *Diccionario Oxford de Literatura Española e Hispano-Americana* gives several titles of little magazines begun by Ascasubi that didn't last beyond the first number.) He was a fervid opponent of the Rosas regime and was jailed for his opposition, escaping in 1832 to Uruguay. There and in Paris he produced most of his work.

Pedro Salvadores

p. 336: A dictator: Juan Manuel de Rosas (1793–1877). In Borges, Rosas is variously called "the tyrant" and "the dictator"; as leader of the Federalist party he ruled Argentina under an iron hand for almost two decades, from 1835 to 1852. Thus the "vast shadow," which cast its pall especially over the mostly urban, mostly professional (and generally landowning) members of the Unitarian party, such as, here, Pedro Salvadores. Rosas confiscated lands and property belonging to the Unitarians in order to finance his campaigns and systematically harassed and even assassinated Unitarian party members.

p. 336: Battle of Monte Caseros: At this battle, in 1852, Rosas was defeated by forces commanded by Justo José Urquiza, and his tyranny ended.

p. 336: Unitarian party: The Unitarian party was a Buenos Aires–based party whose leaders tended to be European-educated liberals who wished to unite Argentina's several regions and economies (the Argentinian Confederation) into a single nation and wished also to unite that new Argentine economy with Europe's, through expanded exports: hence the party's name. The party's color was sky blue; thus the detail, later in the story, of the "sky blue china" in Pedro Salvadores' house.

p. 336: They lived . . . on Calle Suipacha, not far from the corner of Temple: Thus, in what was at this time a northern suburb of Buenos Aires about a mile north of the Plaza de Mayo. This area, later to become the Barrio Norte, was clearly respectable but not yet fashionable (as it was to become after the yellow fever outbreak of 1871 frightened the upper classes out of the area south of the Plaza de Mayo up into the more northern district).

p. 336: The tyrant's posse: The Mazorca (or "corn cob," so called to stress its agrarian rather than urban roots), Rosas' private army, or secret police. The Mazorca was beyond the control of the populace, the army, or any other institution, and it systematically terrorized Argentina during the Rosas years.

p. 337: Smashed all the sky blue china: The color of the china used in the house is the color symbolizing the Unitarian party (see above, note to p. 336) and denounces Salvadores as a follower.

Notes to *Brodie's Report*, pp. 343–408

Foreword

p. 345: "In the House of Suddhoo": Borges often drops hints as to where one might look to find clues not only to the story or essay in question but also to other stories or essays; he gives signposts to his own "intertextuality." In this case, the reader who looks at this Kipling story will find that there is a character in it named Bhagwan Dass; the name, and to a degree the character, reappear in "Blue Tigers," in the volume *Shakespeare's Memory.*

p. 345: Hormiga Negra: "The Black Ant," a gaucho bandit. Borges includes a note on Hormiga Negra in his essay on *Martín Fierro:* "During the last years of the nineteenth century, Guillermo Hoyo, better known as the 'Black Ant,' a bandit from the department of San Nicolás, fought (according to the testimony of Eduardo Gutiérrez) with bolos [stones tied to the ends of rope] and knife" (*Obras completas en colaboración* [Buenos Aires: Emecé, 1979], p. 546, trans. A.H.).

p. 345: Rosas: Juan Manuel de Rosas (1793–1877), tyrannical ruler of Argentina from 1835 to 1852, was in many ways a typical Latin American caudillo. He was the leader of the Federalist party and allied himself with the gauchos against the "city slickers" of Buenos Aires, whom he harassed and even murdered once he came to power. Other appearances of Rosas may be found in "Pedro Salvadores" (*In Praise of Darkness*) and "The Elderly Lady" (in this volume).

p. 346: And I prefer . . . Here the *Obras completas* seems to have a textual error; the text reads *apto* (adjective: "germane, apt, appropriate") when logic would dictate *opto* (verb: "I prefer, I choose, I opt.").

p. 346: Hugo Ramírez Moroni: JLB was fond of putting real people's names into his fictions; of course, he also put "just names" into his fictions. But into his forewords? Nevertheless, the translator has not been able to discover who this person, if person he be, was.

p. 347: The golden-pink coat of a certain horse famous in our literature: The reference is to the *gauchesco* poem "Fausto" by Estanislao del Campo, which was fiercely criticized by Paul Groussac, among others, though praised by Calixto Oyuela ("never charitable with *gauchesco* writers," in JLB's own words) and others. The color of the hero's horse (it was an *overo rosado*) came in for a great deal of attack; Rafael Hernández, for instance, said such a color had never been found in a fast horse; it would be, he said, "like finding a three-colored cat." Lugones also said this color would be found only on a horse suited for farm work or running chores. (This information from JLB, "La poesía gauchesca," *Discusión* [1932].)

The Interloper

p. 348: 2 Reyes 1:26: This citation corresponds to what in most English Bibles is the Second Book of Samuel (2 Samuel); the first chapter of the "Second Book of Kings" has only eighteen verses, as the reader will note. In the *New Catholic Bible,* however, 1 and 2 Samuel are indexed in the Table of Contents as 1 and 2 Kings, with the King James's 1 and 2 Kings bumped to 3 and 4 Kings. Though my own Spanish-language Bible uses the same divisions as the King James, one presumes that JLB was working from a "Catholic Bible" in Spanish. In a conversation with Norman Thomas di Giovanni, Borges insisted that this was a "prettier" name than "Samuel," so this text respects that sentiment. The text in question reads: "I am distressed for thee, my brother: very pleasant hast thou been unto me: thy love to me was wonderful, passing the love of women." (See Daniel Balderston, "The 'Fecal Dialectic': Homosexual Panic and the Origin of Writing in Borges," in *¿Entiendes?: Queer Readings, Hispanic Writings*, ed. Emilie L. Bergmann and Paul Julian Smith [Durham: Duke University Press, 1995], pp. 29–45, for an intriguing reading of this story and others.)

p. 349: Those two criollos: There is no good word or short phrase for the Spanish word *criollo.* It is a word that indicates race, and so class; it always indicates a white-skinned person (and therefore presumed to be "superior") born in the New World colonies, and generally, though not always, to parents of Spanish descent (another putative mark of superiority). Here, however, clearly that last characteristic does not apply. JLB is saying with this word that the genetic or cultural roots of these men lie in Europe, and that their family's blood has apparently not mixed with black or Indian blood, and that they are fully naturalized as New Worlders and Argentines. The implicit reference to class (which an Argentine would immediately understand) is openly ironic.

p. 349: Costa Brava: "A small town in the district of Ramallo, a province of Buenos Aires, not to be confused with the island of the same name in the Paraná River, scene of various battles, including a naval defeat of Garibaldi" (Fishburn and Hughes). *Bravo/a* means "tough, mean, angry," etc.; in Spanish, therefore, Borges can say the toughs gave Costa Brava its *name,* while in translation one can only say they gave the town its reputation.

Unworthy

p. 353: The Maldonado: The Maldonado was a stream that formed the northern boundary of the city of Buenos Aires at the turn of the century; the neighborhood around it, Palermo, was known as a rough part of town, and JLB makes reference to it repeatedly in his work. See the story "Juan Muraña," p. 370, for example. Thus, Fischbein and his family lived on the tough outskirts of the city. See also mention of this area on p. 359, below.

p. 354: I had started calling myself Santiago . . . but there was nothing I could do about the Fischbein: The terrible thing here, which most Spanish-language readers would immediately perceive, is that the little red-headed Jewish boy has given himself a saint's name: Santiago is "Saint James," and *as* St. James is the patron saint of Spain, Santiago Matamoros, St. James the Moor Slayer. The boy's perhaps unwitting self-hatred and clearly conscious attempt to "fit in" are implicitly but most efficiently communicated by JLB in these few words.

p. 355: Juan Moreira: A gaucho turned outlaw (1819–1874) who was famous during his lifetime and legendary after death. Like Jesse James and Billy the Kid in the United States, he was seen as a kind of folk hero, handy with (in Moreira's case) a knife, and hunted down and killed by a corrupt police. Like the U.S. outlaws, his fictionalized life, by Eduardo Gutiérrez, was published serially in a widely read magazine, *La Patria Argentina,* and then dramatized, most famously by José de Podestá (for Podestá, see below, in note to "The Encounter," p. 368).

p. 355: Little Sheeny: Fishburn and Hughes gloss this nickname (in Spanish *el rusito,* literally "Little Russian") as being a "slang term for Ashkenazi Jews . . . (as opposed to immigrants from the Middle East, who were known as *turcos,* 'Turks')." An earlier English translation gave this, therefore, as "sheeny," and I follow that solution. The slang used in Buenos Aires for ethnic groups was (and is) of course different from that of the English-speaking world, which leads to a barber of Italian extraction being called, strange to our ears, a gringo in the original Spanish version of the story "Juan Muraña" in this volume.

p. 355: Calle Junín: In Buenos Aires, running from the Plaza del Once to the prosperous northern district of the city; during the early years of the century, a stretch of Junín near the center of the city was the brothel district.

p. 356: Lunfardo: For an explanation of this supposed "thieves' jargon," see the Foreword to this volume, p. 347.

The Story from Rosendo Juárez

p. 358: The corner of Bolívar and Venezuela: Now in the center of the city, near the Plaza de Mayo, and about two blocks from the National Library, where Borges was the director. Thus the narrator ("Borges") is entering a place he would probably have been known to frequent (in "Guayaquil," the narrator says that "everyone knows" that he lives on Calle Chile, which also is but a block or so distant); the impression the man gives, of having been sitting at the table a good while, reinforces the impression that he'd been waiting for "Borges." But this area, some six blocks south of Rivadavia, the street "where the Southside began," also marks more or less the northern boundary of the neighborhood known as San Telmo, where Rosendo Juárez says he himself lives.

p. 358: His neck scarf: Here Rosendo Juárez is wearing the tough guy's equivalent of a tie, the *chalina,* a scarf worn much like an ascot, doubled over, the jacket buttoned up tight to make a large "bloom" under the chin. This garb marks a certain "type" of character.

p. 358: "You've put the story in a novel": Here "the man sitting at the table," Rosendo Juárez, is referring to what was once perhaps JLB's most famous story, "Man on Pink Corner," in *A Universal History of Iniquity,* q.v., though he calls it a novel rather than a story.

p. 359: Neighborhood of the Maldonado: The Maldonado was the creek marking the northern boundary of the city of Buenos Aires around the turn of the century; Rosendo Juárez' words about the creek are true and mark the story as being told many years after the fact. The neighborhood itself would have been Palermo.

p. 360: Calle Cabrera: In Palermo, a street in a rough neighborhood not far from the center of the city.

p. 360: A kid in black that wrote poems: Probably Evaristo Carriego, JLB's neighbor in Palermo who was the first to make poetry about the "riffraff"—the knife fighters and petty toughs—of the slums. JLB wrote a volume of essays dedicated to Carriego.

p. 361: Moreira: See note to "Unworthy," p. 355.

p. 362: Chacarita: one of the city's two large cemeteries; La Recoleta was where the elite buried their dead, so Chacarita was the graveyard of the "commoners."

p. 363: San Telmo: One of the city's oldest districts, it was a famously rough neighborhood by the time of the story's telling. Fishburn and Hughes associate it with a popular song that boasts of its "fighting spirit" and note that the song would have given "an ironic twist to the last sentence of the story."

The Encounter

p. 365: Lunfardo: For an explanation of this supposed "thieves' jargon," see the Foreword to this volume, p. 347.

p. 365: One of those houses on Calle Junín: See note to "Unworthy," p. 355.

p. 365: Moreira: See note to "Unworthy," p. 355.

p. 365: Martín Fierro and Don Segundo Sombra: Unlike the real-life Juan Moreira, Martín Fierro and Don Segundo Sombra were fictional gauchos. Martín Fierro is the hero of the famous poem of the same name by José Hernández; the poem is centrally important in Argentine literature and often figures in JLB's work, as a reference, as a subject of meditation in essays, or rewritten (in "The End," in the volume *Fictions*, q.v.); his headstrong bravery and antiauthoritarianism are perhaps the traits that were most approved by the "cult of the gaucho" to which JLB alludes here. Don Segundo Sombra is the protagonist of a novel by Ricardo Güiraldes; for this novel, see the note, below, to "The Gospel According to Mark," p. 399. It is interesting that JLB notes that the model for the gaucho shifts from a real-life person to fictional characters, perhaps to indicate that the true gaucho has faded from the Argentine scene and that (in a common Borges trope) all that's left is the memory of the gaucho.

p. 368: The Podestás and the Gutiérrezes: The Podestá family were circus actors; in 1884, some ten years after the outlaw gaucho Juan Moreira's death, Juan de Podestá put on a pantomime version of the life of Moreira. "Two years later," Fishburn and Hughes tell us, "he added extracts from the novel [by Eduardo Gutiérrez] to his performance." The plays were extraordinarily successful. Eduardo Gutiérrez was a prolific and relatively successful, if none too "literary," novelist whose potboilers were published serially in various Argentine magazines. His *Juan Moreira,* however, brought himself and Moreira great fame, and (in the words of the *Diccionario Oxford de Literatura Española e Hispano-Americana*) "created the stereotype of the heroic gaucho." The dictionary goes on to say that "Borges claims that Gutiérrez is much superior to Fenimore Cooper."

Juan Muraña

p. 370: Palermo: A district in Buenos Aires, populated originally by the Italians who immigrated to Argentina in the nineteenth century. Trápani's name marks him as a "native" of that quarter, while Borges and his family moved there probably in search of a less expensive place to live than the central district where they had been living; Borges always mentioned the "shabby genteel" people who lived in that "shabby genteel" neighborhood (Rodríguez Monegal, pp. 48–55).

p. 371: Juan Muraña: As noted in "The Encounter," at one point Juan *Moreira* was the very model of the gaucho and therefore of a certain kind of swaggering masculinity; Juan Muraña's name so closely resembles Moreira's that one suspects that JLB is trading on it to create the shade that so literarily haunts this story. In the dream, especially, Muraña has the look of the gaucho: dressed all in black, with long hair and mustache, etc. Nor, one suspects, is it pure coincidence that the story "Juan Muraña" immediately follows the story in which Juan Moreira's ghost plays such a large part.

p. 371: Around the time of the Centennial: The Centennial of the Argentine Declaration of Independence, signed 1810, so the story takes place around 1910.

p. 371: A man named Luchessi: Luchessi's name marks him too as a "native" of Palermo, though he has now moved into a district in southern Buenos Aires, near the bustling (if "somewhat dilapidated" [Fishburn and Hughes]) Plaza de la Constitución and its railway station.

p. 371: Barracas: Fishburn and Hughes gloss this as a "working-class district in southern Buenos Aires near La Boca and Constitución [see note just above] and bordering the Riachuelo."

p. 371: Wop: See note to "Little Sheeny," p. 355, above. In Spanish, *gringo* was the word used to refer to Italian immigrants; see A Note on the Translation.

p. 372: Calle Thames: In Palermo.

The Elderly Lady

p. 375: Wars of independence: For the independence not only of Argentina but of the entire continent. During this period there were many famous generals and leaders, many named in the first pages of this story. Thus Rubio is associated with the grand forces of continental self-determination that battled in the second and third decades of the nineteenth century.

p. 375: Chacabuco, Cancha Rayada, Maipú, Arequipa: Chacabuco (Chile, 1817): The Army of the Andes under General José San Martín fought the Spanish royalist forces under General Marcó del Pont and won. Cancha Rayada (Chile, March 1818): San Martín's army was defeated by the royalists and independence was now very uncertain. Maipú (Chile, April 1818): San Martín's army decisively defeated the royalist forces and secured the independence of Chile. Arequipa (Peru, 1825): General Antonio José de Sucre, leading Bolívar's army, accepted Spain's surrender of the city after a siege; this, after the Battle of Ayacucho (see below), meant the full independence of Peru.

p. 375: He and José de Olavarría exchanged swords: Olavarría (1801–1845) was an Argentine military leader who fought at the battles just mentioned and perhaps at the great Battle of Ayacucho, which determined the full independence of Peru. Exchanging swords was a "romantic custom among generals, and Borges recalls that his own grandfather had exchanged swords with Gen. Mansilla on the eve of a battle" (Fishburn and Hughes). Olavarría and Lavalle (see below) are probably the models for Rubio.

p. 375: The famous battle of Cerro Alto . . . Cerro Bermejo: However famous this battle may be, I confess I have not been able to locate it. I hope (for the good name of the humble research that has gone into these notes) that this is an example of Borges' famous put-ons (see A Note on the Translation). I feel that it may well be; this is the bird's-eye statement given in the *Penguin History of Latin America* (Edwin Williamson, New York/London: Penguin, 1992), p. 228, of the years 1823–1824 as they apply to Bolívar (who is mentioned as winning this battle): "Arriving in Peru in September 1823, Bolívar began to prepare for the final offensive against the royalists. By the middle of 1824 he launched his campaign, winning an important battle at Junín, which opened to him the road to Lima, the ultimate prize. In December, while Bolívar was in Lima, Marshal Sucre defeated Viceroy De la Serna's army at the battle of

Ayacucho. Spanish power in America had been decisively broken and the Indies were at last free." Thus, it appears that in April of 1823 Bolívar was planning battles, not fighting them. If it is a real battle, I ask a kind reader to inform me of the date and location so that future editions, should there be any, may profit from the knowledge.

p. 375: Ayacucho: In Peru between Lima and Cuzco (1824). Here Sucre's Peruvian forces decisively defeated the Spanish royalists.

p. 375: Ituzaingó: In the province of Corrientes (1827). Here the Argentine and Uruguayan forces defeated the Brazilians.

p. 375: Carlos María Alvear: Alvear (1789–1852) had led the Argentine revolutionary forces against the Spanish forces in Montevideo in 1814 and defeated them. When he conspired against the Unitarian government, however, he was forced into exile in Uruguay, but was recalled from exile to lead the republican army of Argentina against the Brazilians. He defeated the Brazilians at Ituzaingó, ending the war. He was a diplomat for the Rosas government.

p. 375: Rosas: Juan Manuel de Rosas (1793–1877), tyrannical ruler of Argentina from 1835 to 1852. See note to Foreword, p. 345.

p. 375: Rubio was a Lavalle man: Juan Galo Lavalle (1797–1841), chosen to lead the Unitarians against the Federalists under Rosas, whom Lavalle defeated in 1828. Lavalle was defeated in turn by Rosas in 1829; then "after ten years in Montevideo he returned to lead the Unitarians in another attempt to oust Rosas" (Fishburn and Hughes). Thus he spent his life defending the policies and the principles of the Buenos Aires political party against those of the gaucho party headed by Rosas.

p. 375: The montonero *insurgents:* These were gaucho guerrillas who fought under their local caudillo against the Buenos Aires–based Unitarian forces. While it is claimed that they would have had no particular political leanings, just a sense of resistance to the centralizing tendencies of the Unitarians, the effect would have been that they were in alliance with the Federalists, led by Rosas, etc.

p. 376: Oribe's White army: The White party, or Blancos, was "a Uruguayan political party founded by the followers of Oribe, . . . [consisting] of rich landowners who supported the Federalist policy of Rosas in Buenos Aires. . . . The Blancos are now known as the Nationalists and represent the conservative classes" (Fishburn and Hughes). Manuel Oribe (1792–1856) was a hero of the Wars of Independence and fought against the Brazilian invasion of Uruguay. He served as minister of war and the navy under Rivera; then, seeking the presidency for himself, he sought the support of Rosas. Together they attacked Montevideo in a siege that lasted eight days. (This information, Fishburn and Hughes). See also note to p. 386, "Battle of Manantiales," in the story "The Other Duel."

p. 376: The tyrant: Rosas (see various notes above).

p. 376: Pavón and Cepeda: Cepeda (Argentina, 1859) and Pavón (Argentina, 1861) were battles between the Confederation forces under Urquiza and the Buenos Aires–based Porteño forces (basically Unitarian) under Mitre, fought to determine whether Buenos Aires would join the Argentine Confederation or would retain its autonomy. Buenos Aires lost at Cepeda but won at Pavón, enabling Mitre to renegotiate the terms of association between the two entities, with more favorable conditions for Buenos Aires.

p. 376: Yellow fever epidemic: 1870–1871.

p. 376: Married . . . one Saavedra, who was a clerk in the Ministry of Finance:

Fishburn and Hughes tell us that "employment in the Ministry of Finance is considered prestigious, and consistent with the status of a member of an old and well-established family." They tie "Saavedra" to Cornelio de Saavedra, a leader in the first criollo government of Argentina, in 1810, having deposed the Spanish viceroy. This is a name, then, that would have had resonances among the Argentines similar to a Jefferson, Adams, or Marshall among the Americans, even if the person were not directly mentioned as being associated with one of the founding families. "Saavedra" will also invariably remind the Spanish-language reader of Miguel de Cervantes, whose second (maternal) surname was Saavedra.

p. 377: She still abominated Artigas, Rosas, and Urquiza: Rosas has appeared in these notes several times. Here he is the archenemy not only of the Buenos Aires Unitarians but of the family as well, because he has confiscated their property and condemned them to "shabby gentility," as Borges would have put it. José Gervasio Artigas (1764–1850) fought against the Spaniards for the liberation of the Americas but was allied with the gauchos and the Federalist party against the Unitarians; in 1815 he defeated the Buenos Aires forces but was later himself defeated by help from Brazil. Justo José Urquiza (1801–1870) was president of the Argentinian Confederation from 1854 to 1860, having long supported the Federalists (and Rosas) against the Unitarians. As a military leader he often fought against the Unitarians, and often defeated them. In addition, he was governor (and caudillo) of Entre Ríos province.

p. 377: Easterners *instead of* Uruguayans: Before Uruguay became a country in 1828, it was a Spanish colony which, because it lay east of the Uruguay River, was called the Banda Oriental ("eastern shore"). (The Uruguay meets the Paraná to create the huge estuary system called the Río de la Plata, or River Plate; Montevideo is on the eastern bank of this river, Buenos Aires on the west.) *La Banda Oriental* is an old-fashioned name for the country, then, and *orientales* ("Easterners") is the equally old-fashioned name for those who live or were born there. Only the truly "elderly" have a right to use this word.

p. 377: Plaza del Once: Pronounced *óhn-say,* not *wunce.* This is generally called Plaza Once, but the homonymy of the English and Spanish words make it advisable, I think, to modify the name slightly in order to alert the English reader to the Spanish ("eleven"), rather than English ("one time" or "past"), sense of the word. Plaza Once is one of Buenos Aires' oldest squares, "associated in Borges's memory with horse-drawn carts" (Fishburn and Hughes), though later simply a modern square.

p. 377: Barracas: Once a district virtually in the country, inhabited by the city's elite, now a "working-class district" in southern Buenos Aires, near the Plaza Constitución (Fishburn and Hughes).

p. 379: Sra. Figueroa's car and driver: Perhaps the Clara Glencairn de Figueroa of the next story in this volume, "The Duel"; certainly the social sphere in which these two Sras. Figueroa move is the same.

p. 380: Benzoin: Probably used, much as we use aromatic preparations today, to clear the nasal passages and give a certain air of health to the elderly. An aromatic preparation called *alcoholado* (alcohol and bay leaves, basically) is much used in Latin America as a kind of cureall for headaches and various aches and pains and for "refreshing" the head and skin; one presumes this "benzoin" was used similarly.

p. 380: One of Rosas' posses: The Mazorca ("corncob," so called [or so folk etymology has it] for the Federalist party's agrarian ties), a private secret police force–*cum*–army employed by Rosas to intimidate and terrorize the Unitarians after his rise to Federalist power. The Mazorcas beat and murdered many people, and so the elderly lady is right to have been shocked and frightened. (See also the story "Pedro Salvadores" in *In Praise of Darkness.*)

The Duel

p. 381: Clara Glencairn de Figueroa: Clara's name is given here as Christian name + patronymic or family (father's) name + *de* indicating "belonging to" or, less patriarchally, "married to" + the husband's last name. This indication of a character by full name, including married name, underscores Clara's equivocal position in life and in the world of art that she aspires to: a woman of some (limited) talent in her own right, with a "career" or at least a calling in which she is entitled to *personal* respect, versus the "wife of the ambassador." This tension is noted a couple of pages later, when "Mrs." Figueroa, having won a prize, now wants to return to Cartagena "in her own right," not as the ambassador's wife that she had been when she had lived there before. It is hard for the English reader, with our different system of naming, to perceive the subtleties of JLB's use of the conventions of naming in Hispanic cultures.

p. 382: Juan Crisóstomo Lafinur: Lafinur (1797–1824), a great-uncle of Borges', was the holder of the chair of philosophy "at the newly-formed Colegio de la Unión del Sud" (Fishburn and Hughes) and thus a "personage."

p. 382: Colonel Pascual Pringles: Pringles (1795–1831) was a distinguished Unitarian military leader from the province of San Luis. "[R]ather than surrender his sword to the enemy" in defeat, Fishburn and Hughes tell us, "he broke it and threw himself into the river."

p. 382: The solid works of certain nineteenth-century Genoese bricklayers: This snide comment refers to the Italian immigrant laborers and construction foremen who built those "old houses of Buenos Aires" that Marta paints; she is influenced, that is, not by an Italian school of painting (which would be acceptable, as "European" was good; see the first line of the next paragraph in the text) but by Italian immigrant (and therefore, in Buenos Aires society hierarchy, "undesirable" or "inferior") artisans. Note in "The Elderly Lady" the narrator's mild bigotry in the statement that one of the daughters married a "Sr. Molinari, who though of Italian surname was a professor of Latin and a very well-educated man." The social lines between the old criollo families (descendants of European, especially Spanish, colonists), the newer immigrant families, those with black or Indian blood, etc. were clear, especially in the nineteenth century and the early years of the twentieth.

p. 384: Mrs. Figueroa: Here, clear in the Spanish, though difficult to convey in the English, the judge slights Clara Glencairn de Figueroa by referring to her by her married name (Figueroa's *wife*) rather than by her "personal" and "professional" name, Clara Glencairn. She is looked down on, as the story subtly shows, for her social standing, which is in contrast to the *vie bohème* that she would like to think she had lived and the reputation as a painter she would like to think she had earned for herself. Note "Clara Glencairn" throughout the paragraph on p. 383, for the more "professional" or "personally respectful" mode of naming, and note the way the story swings between the two modes as one or another of Clara's "statuses" is being emphasized.

The Other Duel

p. 386: Adrogué: In the early years of the century, a town south of Buenos Aires (now simply a suburb or enclave of the city) where Borges and his family often spent vacations; a place of great nostalgia for Borges.

p. 386: Battle of Manantiales: In Uruguay. For many years (ca. 1837–ca. 1886) Uruguay was torn by rivalry and armed conflicts between the Blancos (the conservative White party) led by, among others, Manuel Oribe and Timoteo Aparicio (see below), and the Colorados (the more liberal Red party) led by Venancio Flores and Lorenzo Batlle. Manantiales (1871) marked the defeat of Aparicio's Blancos by the Colorados under Batlle. Once Cardoso and Silveira are seen joining up with Aparicio's forces, this understated sentence tells the Argentine or Uruguayan reader (or any other Latin American reader familiar, through little more than high school history classes, with the history of the Southern Cone—these dates and places are the very stuff of Latin American history) that their end was fated to be bloody.

p. 386: Cerro Largo: A frontier area in northeast Uruguay, near the Brazilian border. Aparicio had to recruit from all over the countryside, as he was faced by the Triple Alliance of Brazil, Argentina, and the Uruguayan Colorado government.

p. 387: Thirty-three: This in homage to the tiny band of thirty-three soldiers who in 1825 crossed the Uruguay River along with Juan Antonio Lavalleja and Manuel Oribe in order to galvanize the Uruguayans to rise up against the Brazilians who at that time governed them. The flag of the Uruguayan rebellion against Brazil carried the motto *Libertad o Muerte* ("Liberty or Death"). Thus Silveira asserts himself as a tough, independent, and yet "patriotic" gaucho.

p. 387: Aparicio's revolution: See the note to p. 386, above.

p. 387: Montoneros: The *montoneros* were gaucho (Blanco, or White, party) forces, something like quasi-independent armies, organized under local leaders to fight the Unitarians (the Colorados, or Red party) during the civil wars that followed the wars of independence.

p. 387: White badges: To identify them with the Blancos, as opposed to the Colorados (Red party). The armies would have been somewhat ragtag groups, so these badges (or sometimes hatbands) would have been virtually the only way to distinguish ally from enemy in the pitched battles of the civil war.

p. 388: Cut anybody's throat: Here and in many other places in Borges, the slashing of opponents' throats is presented in the most matter-of-fact way. It was a custom of armies on the move not to take prisoners; what would they do with them? So as a matter of course, and following the logic of this type of warfare (however "barbaric" it may seem to us today), losers of battles were summarily executed in this way.

Guayaquil

p. 390: Guayaquil: The name of this city in Ecuador would evoke for the Latin American reader one of the most momentous turns in the wars of independence, since it was here that Generals Simón Bolívar and José San Martín met to decide on a strategy for the final expulsion of the Spaniards from Peru. After this meeting, San Martín left his armies under the command of Bolívar, who went on to defeat the Spaniards, but there is no record of what occurred at the meeting or of the reasons that led San Martín to retire from the command of his own army and leave the glory of liberation to Bolívar. A long historical controversy has been waged over the possible reasons, which the story briefly recounts. Clearly, the "contest of wills" thought by some to have occurred between the two generals is reflected in the contest of wills between the two modern historians. For a fuller (and very comprehensible) summary of this event and the historiographic controversy surrounding it, see Daniel Balderston, *Out of Context: Historical Reference and the Representation of Reality in Borges* (Durham, N.C.: Duke University Press, 1993), pp. 115–131. In this chapter Balderston also discusses Borges' equating of history *with* fiction, providing us another important way of reading the story. See also, for a brief historical summary, *The Penguin History of Latin America* (Edwin Williamson, New York / London: Penguin, 1992), pp. 227–228 and *passim* in that chapter.

p. 391: Gen. José de San Martín: As the note just above indicates, San Martín (1778–1850), an Argentine, was one of the two most important generals of the wars of independence, the other being Simón Bolívar, a Venezuelan. This story is subtly written from the Argentine point of view, because it deals with the reasons—psychological, perhaps, or perhaps military, or, indeed, perhaps other—for which San Martín, after winning extraordinary battles in his own country and in Peru (where he came to be called Protector of Peru), turned his entire army over to Bolívar so that Bolívar could go on to win the independence of the continent from Spain. The enigma of San Martín is one that absorbed the Argentine historical mind for decades, and perhaps still does, so any letters that might have even the slightest, or the most self-serving (if Argentines will forgive me that possible slur on the general's psyche), explanation for his actions would be of supreme importance to Argentine history. This story, then, is filled with those pulls and tugs between one sort of (or nationality of) history and another, one sort of "rationale" and another.

Fishburn and Hughes note that the Masonic lodge mentioned in the story (p. 395) is the Logia Lautaro, of which San Martín was indeed a member. Masonic lodges were famed as centers of progressive, not to say revolutionary, thought in the seventeenth and eighteenth centuries. Modern Freemasonry was founded in the seventeenth century.

p. 392: Calle Chile: It is Fishburn and Hughes's contention that the physical, geographical location of this street is not really important here, though they give that location as "in the southern part of Buenos Aires, . . . some ten blocks from Plaza Constitución"; their interesting view of this street's mention here is, rather, that it is a symbolic name, linking JLB (that library he had inhabited [see "Juan Muraña" in this volume], the house, and perhaps some of the *objets de la gloire* that JLB had inherited from his grandfather and other members of his family) with the narrator of "Guayaquil": "The narrator lives in a street called Chile, Borges lived in a street called Maipú and both names are associated in the Argentine mind, since San Martín's great victory in Chile was the battle of Maipú."

The Gospel According to Mark

p. 397: Baltasar Espinosa: The Spanish reader will sooner or later associate the young man's surname, Espinosa ("thorny") with the Christian "crown of thorns" evoked at the end of this story.

p. 397: Ramos Mejía: "A part of Buenos Aires in which the rich had weekend houses containing an English colony; now an industrial suburb" (Fishburn and Hughes).

p. 399: A couple of chapters of [*Don Segundo Sombra*]*:* The next sentence is perhaps not altogether opaque, but both its sense and its humor are clearer if the reader knows the novel in question. *Don Segundo Sombra* deals with the life of a gaucho (considerably romanticized by nostalgia) and the customs of life on the pampas. Therefore, Gutre *père* sees nothing in it for him; indeed, the *gauchesco* novel was an urban form, a manifestation perhaps of what Marie Antoinette's critics were wont to call *nostalgie de la boue,* or so "The Gospel According to Mark" would seem to imply. JLB himself makes reference to this "urban nostalgia" in the story titled "The Duel," above, on p. 384.

Brodie's Report

p. 404: Qzr: The English reader will not, probably, be able to perceive the fine irony here. Brodie has said that these barbarous people do not have vowels, so he will call them Yahoos. He then gives a few words in their language. Here, the word for "citadel," *qzr,* is the Spanish word for citadel, *alcázar,* with the vowels removed. But the Spanish derives from the Arabic, which does not have vowels; the vowels are sometimes marked, sometimes not; thus, *qzr* is a transliteration of a word that any Spanish speaker would recognize as being fully and legitimately Arabic. Thus the Yahoos are, or might be, Arabs. Here Borges' "traveler's satire" is acute: one can find "barbarism" even in the most refined and advanced of societies; the intolerant eye can see barbarities in others that are invisible in ourselves; "otherness" may itself, to some, be "barbarity."

Notes to *The Book of Sand,* pp. 409–486

The Other

p. 413: Another Rosas in 1946, much like our kinsman, the first one: The second Rosas, of course, is Juan Domingo Perón, the Fascist military leader who in 1945 was asked to resign all his commissions and retire, and who did so, only (Napoleon-like) to return eight days later to address huge crowds of people and later, in 1946, to be elected president. All this information is from Rodríguez Monegal, who then adds: "he was Argentina's first king" (390–391). As for "our kinsman," the details are a bit blurry, but Borges seems to have been related, on his father's side, to Rosas. Fishburn and Hughes talk about a "relative of Borges's great-great-grandfather." Borges hated and despised both these men.

p. 416: "Whitman is incapable of falsehood": Daniel Balderston believes that he has identified this poem: "When I heard at the close of the day," in Walt Whitman, *Complete Poetry and Collected Prose,* ed. Justin Kaplan (New York: Library of America), 1982, pp. 276–277. The essay in which Balderston identifies the poem referred to by the older "Borges" is "The 'Fecal Dialectic': Homosexual Panic and the Origin of Writing in Borges," in *¿Entiendes?: Queer Readings, Hispanic Writing,* ed. Emilie L. Bergmann and Paul Julian Smith (Durham/London: Duke University Press), 1995, pp. 29–45. While these notes are not intended to add "scholarly" information to the text of

Borges, this remarkable identification, and the reading that accompanies it, in the translator's view warrants mention. The old man/young man motif, the public/private motif, the issue of "sex in the oeuvre of Borges," readings of a number of important stories, and, to a degree, the issue of violence in the fictions—all of these questions are impacted by Balderston's contentions in this essay.

The Congress

p. 423: The newspaper Ultima Hora: The title can be translated in two ways, *The Eleventh Hour* or *The Latest News*, depending on whether one wishes to give it an apocalyptic reading or a quotidian one.

p. 424: Confitería del Gas: This pastry shop (see also the note to p. 446, "Café Aguila," in the story "The Night of the Gifts" in this volume, for a further explanation of this sort of establishment) is located on Alsina between Bolívar and Defensa, about two blocks from the Casa de Gobierno (or as most Porteños know it, the Casa Rosada, or Pink House), at the River Plate end of the avenue that runs from the Casa de Gobierno to the Plaza del Congreso. I have not been able to learn where this café's curious name came from, perhaps a gas-company office in the neighborhood; the problem with translating it into something such as Café Gas is, as the English-language reader will immediately perceive, the hint of indigestion that it (the translation and the name) leaves. Nor is it a truck stop. Clearly, in locating the confitería in this neighborhood, JLB is attempting to associate one "congress" with that of the institutionalized government in whose neighborhood it takes up residence. Porteños know this particular confitería as more of a pastry shop than a café per se; we are told that the meringues with crème de Chantilly are the house specialty.

p. 426: Rancher from the eastern province: Before Uruguay became a country, in 1828, it was a Spanish colony which, because it lay east of the Uruguay River, was called the Banda Oriental, or "eastern shore." (The Uruguay meets the Paraná to create the huge estuary system called the Río de la Plata, or River Plate; Montevideo is on the eastern bank of this river, Buenos Aires on the west.) "La Banda Oriental" is an old-fashioned name for the country, then, and *"orientales,"* or "Easterners," is the equally old-fashioned name for those who live or were born there. Here, the narrator refers to "the eastern province" because for a very long time the shifting status of Uruguay—colony and protectorate of Spain, annex of Brazil and/or Argentina, etc.—led the nationalistic elements in Buenos Aires to consider it an "eastern province" of Argentina. Uruguay was founded on cattle raising.

p. 426: Artigas: José Gervasio Artigas (1764–1850), Uruguayan, a political and military leader who opposed first the Spaniards and then the Argentines who wished to keep the Banda Oriental (the east bank of the River Plate) in fealty to one or another of those powers. When Argentina, instead of supporting the Banda Oriental's independence from Spain, asserted Spain's authority over the area (in part to keep the Brazilians/Portuguese out), Artigas led a huge exodus of citizens out of Montevideo and "into the wilderness." Recognized as a hero in Uruguay, he might not have been so regarded by a cosmopolite such as Glencoe, especially because of his legendary (but perhaps exaggerated) bloodthirstiness and his association with "the provinces" rather than "the city."

p. 427: Wops: "*Gringo*" was the somewhat pejorative term used for immigrant Italians; the closest English equivalent is "wop." As with all such designations, the tone of voice with which it is spoken will determine the level of offense; it can even be affectionate if spoken appropriately.

p. 427: Calle Junín: At this time, a street lined with brothels, many of which were relatively tame and in which men might not only solicit the services of prostitutes but also have a drink, talk, and generally be "at their ease."

p. 429: Palace of Running Waters: El Palacio de Aguas Corrientes is a building in central Buenos Aires housing a pumping station and some offices for the water company; it is an extravagantly decorated edifice, its walls covered in elaborate mosaic murals—a building that one Porteño described to this translator as "hallucinatory" and "absurd." The official name of this building is the "Grand Gravitational Repository"; it is, according to *Buenos Aires, Ciudad Secreta* by Germinal Nogués (Buenos Aires: Editorial Ruiz Díaz, 2nd ed., pp. 244–245),

> located on the block bounded by Avenida Córdoba and calles Riobamba, Viamonte, and Ayacucho. It is set—or at least was—on one of the highest points of the city. The building of the Palace of Running Waters was begun in 1887, and it is a gigantic jigsaw puzzle designed by the Swedish engineer A. B. Nystromer.
>
> All this architectural effort was invested in a building destined to store 72,700,000 liters of water per day, which was the amount estimated to be needed for the daily consumption of the Porteños. . . .
>
> The four walls of this palace . . . were capable of withstanding this pressure without support except at the center of each side. Solid buttresses were also incorporated into the design; these were set at intervals between the corner towers and the central towers, both inside and outside. . . .
>
> Vicente Blasco Ibáñez said of this edifice: "This 'palace' is not a palace. It has arcades and grand doors and windows but it is all a fake. Inside, there are no rooms. Its four imposing façades mask the retaining walls of the reservoir inside. The builders tried to beautify it with all this superfluity, so that it would not offend the aesthetic of the [city's] central streets." [Trans., A.H.]

p. 430: The chiripá . . . *the wide-legged* bombacha: These are articles of the dress of the gaucho. The *chiripá* was a triangular worsted shawl tied about the waist with the third point pulled up between the legs and looped into the knot to form a rudimentary pant or a sort of diaper. It was worn over a pair of pantaloons (ordinarily white) that "stick out" underneath. The *bombacha* is a wide-legged pant that was worn gathered at the calf or ankle and tucked into the soft boots, sometimes made of the hide of a young horse, that the gaucho wore. The *bombacha* resembles the pant of the Zouave infantryman.

p. 430: Those mournful characters in Hernández or Rafael Obligado: José Hernández (1834–1886), author of *Martín Fierro*, a long semi-epic poem celebrating the gaucho and his life; Rafael Obligado (1851–1920), a *litterateur* who hosted a literary salon and founded the Academia Argentina. Obligado was the author of a very well-known poem dealing with the life of a *payador*, or traveling singer, named Santos Vega. While the characters in these poems were portrayed not without defects, their lives and they themselves were to a degree romanticized; as ways of life per se, the gaucho and the *payador* were part of the mythology of Argentina. Borges examines these ways of life (and the literature that chronicled them) in many of his essays.

p. 430: Calle Jujuy near the Plaza del Once: At its northern end Calle Jujuy runs directly into the Plaza del Once; on the other (north) side of the Plaza, it has become Puerreydon. Thus, in a sense, it begins at Rivadavia, where Borges (and apparently all older Porteños) said "the Southside began." The "Plaza del Once" (pronounced *óhnsay,* not *wunce*) is generally called "Plaza Once" in Buenos Aires, but the homonymy of the English and Spanish words make it advisable, the translator thinks, to slightly modify the name in order to alert the English reader to the Spanish ("eleven"), rather than English ("onetime" or "past"), sense of the word. Plaza Once is one of Buenos Aires' oldest squares, "associated in Borges's memory with horse-drawn carts" (Fishburn and Hughes), though later simply a modern square.

p. 431: Lugones' Lunario sentimental: Leopoldo Lugones (1874–1938) was one of Argentina's most famous and influential (and most talented) poets; the *Lunario sentimental* is a 1909 book of his poetry.

There Are More Things

p. 437: Turdera: A town south of Buenos Aires, rustic and apparently at this time somewhat uninviting (see the story "The Interloper," p. 348, set there).

p. 438: Glew: A town near Turdera.

The Night of the Gifts

p. 446: Café Aguila, on Calle Florida near the intersection of Piedad: Here two things need pointing out: First the Café Aguila, whose name in Spanish is the Confitería del Aguila, actually existed. The *confitería* was the equivalent of a coffeehouse or tearoom, a place for conversation and taking one's time over coffee or tea and pastry (or light food) in the late afternoon and early evening. (One might think of Paris.) The Aguila was a center for intellectuals and artists, as this sketch clearly suggests. Second is the location: Calle Florida (pronounced Flor-*ee*-da) was, and remains, at least near the Plaza de Mayo, one of the most exclusive streets in downtown Buenos Aires; this intersection is just one block from that square. Piedad's name was changed to Bartolomé Mitre in 1906; therefore, this story must take place before that date. If this "Borges," like Borges himself, was born in 1899, he must have been just a young boy overhearing this conversation, and the "we," in that case, must be something of a stretch!

p. 449: Juan Moreira: A gaucho turned outlaw (1819–1874) who was famous during his lifetime and legendary after death. Like Jesse James and Billy the Kid in the United States, he was seen as a kind of folk hero, handy with weapons (in Moreira's case a knife), and hunted down and killed (as this story shows) by a corrupt police. That does not mean he was not to be feared by all when he was "on a tear," as this story also shows.

p. 449: Podestá's long hair and black beard: The Podestá family were circus actors. In 1884, some ten years after the outlaw gaucho Juan Moreira's death, Juan de Podestá put on a pantomime version of the life of Moreira. Podestá and the performances were enormously famous, seen by everyone, and surely colored perceptions of the real-life story of Moreira, as movies have colored those of Jesse James and Billy the Kid.

A Weary Man's Utopia

p. 463: Bahía Blanca: A city in Buenos Aires province, south of the city of Buenos Aires; the bay of that name as well. Thus the "future man" has either traveled a bit south or the story itself takes place south of Buenos Aires.

Avelino Arredondo

p. 472: The war that was ravaging the country: This story takes place, as its first sentence reminds us, in 1897, but one must go back some four decades in order to understand the situation. Since the Battle of Monte Caseros in 1852, in which Rosas (whose troops had been occupying Uruguay) had been defeated and with his defeat Uruguay's titular independence had been won, Uruguay had undergone a series of revolts, uprisings, and power struggles that left the country reeling. Constitutional democracy was an experiment that seemed destined to fail. As in Argentina, it was the Whites (Blancos) against the Reds (Colorados), though the parties in Uruguay were conceived somewhat differently from those in Argentina; in some ways, and at the worst of times, they were simply banners under which generals vied for power, and alliances among the generals and among the Southern Cone nations were by nature shifting. Generally speaking, however, the Blancos were the traditional followers of Manuel Oribe; they were conservative, usually Catholic (as opposed to the "freethinkers" JLB sometimes mentions), and tended to favor the rural areas over the cities; thus the party often was led by provincial, landowning caudillos whose gaucho followers made up the largest number of its members. The Colorados were the liberal, urban party, whose roots went back to the nineteenth-century caudillo Fructuoso Rivera; this was the "ruling" party in Uruguay for many years, though one president resigned saying the Uruguayans were an ungovernable people, and though the Whites were constantly pressuring the Reds (sometimes by armed uprising) for greater representation in the government. Just prior to the time of this story, the Blancos and Colorados had come to an uneasy truce, and the Cabinet of Conciliation *(ministerio de conciliación)* was formed. In 1894 the unlikely (and compromise) Colorado candidate Juan Idiarte Borda was elected president on the forty-seventh ballot, but in 1897 the uneasy alliance broke down; Idiarte Borda was perceived as abusing his power, of engaging in cronyism and neglecting to respect the right of the factions that elected him to enjoy some of the fruits of power, and perhaps even of rigging the upcoming elections. Just at this time the Blancos began a revolt in the interior, led by the gaucho caudillo Aparicio Saravia (see below). Idiarte Borda apparently perceived this revolt as directed against himself, but a faction within the Red party perceived it as a power grab against the entire party, which Idiarte Borda could not really be said to represent; the prominent national figure José Batlle y Ordoñez gave a call to arms to this Colorado faction, and suddenly Idiarte Borda found himself besieged not only by the Blancos but by a large number of his own party as well. The armed conflicts fought in the interior were marked by what must seem to us today grisly and cold-blooded brutality on the part of all contending sides in the skirmishes and battles that were fought; one history of Uruguay says that by 1897 there was a general reaction and outcry against the wholesale slitting of the throats of "prisoners." See, for instance, the story "The Other Duel" in *Brodie's Report,* which, though not dealing specifically with this conflict, shows the "naturalness" of this practice to the conflicts of the time.

p. 472: Battle of Cerros Blancos: In the department of Rivera; white chalk hills, with a creek of the same name at their foot. In 1897 a body of government troops under General José Villar met insurrectionist Blanco forces led by Aparicio Saravia; the "battle" (called that, not "skirmish," because of the ferocity of the fighting rather than the number of troops) was indecisive, but the Colorados came out marginally ahead. No prisoners were taken.

p. 472: Aparicio Saravia's gang of gauchos: Saravia (1856–1904) was, as Fishburn and Hughes tell us, a "landowner and caudillo, uncultured and politically unsophisticated, whose magnetic personality secured him a following among the gauchos of the Interior." Saravia and his troops fought on the Blanco side against the government of Juan Idiarte Borda; Saravia had long battled for the Blanco cause against the entrenched Colorado governments.

p. 474: [Traveled] through the bay of La Agraciada where the Thirty-three came ashore, to the Hervidero, through ragged mountains, wildernesses, and rivers, through the Cerro he had scaled to the lighthouse, thinking that on the two banks of the River Plate there was not another like it. From the Cerro on the bay he traveled once to the peak on the Uruguayan coat of arms: La Agraciada is indeed a bay; the Thirty-three were a band of determined patriots under the leadership of Juan Antonio Lavelleja. Lavelleja, a Uruguayan, was the manager of a meat-salting plant in Buenos Aires when the victory at Ayacucho (1824, liberating Peru from the Spaniards) was announced; he was so inspired by patriotic zeal that he gathered his "thirty-three" and they crossed the River Plate to La Agraciada Bay, and several years (and many battles fought by thousands of volunteers) later liberated Uruguay (1829). Hervidero was the place of Artigas' encampment when he ruled the five provinces he had "conquered" and put under Uruguayan rule; this rustic headquarters was on a tableland in the northwest of Uruguay, far from the "capital" city of Montevideo; it showed his "humility" and symbolized his philosophy of government. The Cerro is the conical hill on a spit of land opposite Montevideo; there is a fortress on the top, and a lighthouse, and it is represented in the top right quadrant of the country's coat of arms. All these references are the touchstones of Uruguayan patriotism; Arredondo dreams of country in its most heroic manifestations.

p. 475: Juan Idiarte Borda: Borda (1844–1897) was the president of Uruguay, elected under the conditions explained in note to p. 472, above.

p. 476: The events: The people and events of this story are "true." The real Avelino Arredondo was in fact the assassin of the real Juan Idiarte Borda (1897). An Argentine reader would almost certainly not recognize the name Avelino Arredondo, and a Uruguayan might or might not; that is why there is no note appended to the first appearance of Arredondo's name, in the title, as there is, for example, to the immediately recognizable name of the city of Guayaquil in the story of that name in the volume *Brodie's Report*. But the year, the historical events, the tracing of the legendary "sites" of Uruguayan history, and various other hints at what is about to occur would certainly have given the reader who hailed from the Southern Cone a sense of familiarity; this story would ring a bell. Certainly Borges tried, subtly, though surely, to plant the seeds of that feeling. In his "statement," Arredondo shows that he is of the Batlle faction of the Colorado Party, not the "faction" (made up of cronies) of Idiarte Borda. (See note to p. 472, above.)

The Book of Sand

p. 483: The street the library's on: Calle México, the site of the National Library, where Borges was director. The street's name is given in the Spanish-language story as a kind of punch line, but that bang cannot be achieved for the non-Argentine reader by simply naming the street; thus the explicitation.

Notes to *Shakespeare's Memory,* pp. 487–515

August 25, 1983

p. 490: Adrogué: In the early years of the century, a town south of Buenos Aires (now simply a suburb or enclave of the city) where Borges and his family often spent vacations; a place of great nostalgia for Borges.

The Rose of Paracelsus

p. 504: De Quincey, Writings, *XIII, 345:* "Insolent vaunt of Paracelsus, that he would restore the original rose or violet out of the ashes settling from its combustion—*that* is now rivalled in this modern achievement" ("The Palimpsest of the Human Brain," *Suspiria de Profundis*). The introductory part of de Quincey's essay deals with the way modern chemistry had been able to recover the effaced writing *under* the latest writing on rolls of parchment or vellum, which were difficult to obtain and therefore reused: "The vellum, from having been the setting of the jewel, has risen at length to be the jewel itself; and the burden of thought, from having given the chief value to the vellum, has now become the chief obstacle to its value; nay, has totally extinguished its value." Though this is the thrust of the beginning of de Quincey's argument and seems to inspire "The Rose of Paracelsus," the latter part of the essay turns to memory. This Borges turns to his own uses in "Shakespeare's Memory," p. 508, perhaps with the idea of unifying the volume of stories thereby. It is perhaps the following lines from de Quincey's essay that inspired the idea in "Shakespeare's Memory": "Chemistry, a witch as potent as the Erictho of Lucan, has exorted by her torments, from the dust and ashes of forgotten centuries, the secrets of a life extinct for the general eye, but still glowing in the embers. . . . What else than a natural and mighty palimpsest is the human brain? . . . Everlasting layers of ideas, images, feelings have fallen upon your brain softly as light. Each succession has seemed to bury all that went before. And yet, in reality, not one has been extinguished." If only we could fan those embers into fire again . . .

Shakespeare's Memory

p. 512: [De Quincey's] master Jean Paul: Jean Paul Friedrich Richter (1763–1825, pen name Jean Paul) was early influenced by Sterne. While his writings on literary æsthetics influenced Carlyle (who translated him) and many others, it was his dream literature that influenced Novalis and de Quincey.

Don't miss the other two volumes in the acclaimed three-volume centenary edition of Jorge Luis Borges's collected works

SELECTED POEMS

Edited by Alexander Coleman

This new bilingual selection brings together some two hundred poems—the largest collection of Borges's poetry ever assembled in English, including scores of poems never previously translated. Edited by Alexander Coleman, the selection draws from a lifetime's work—from Borges's first published volume of verse, *Fervor de Buenos Aires* (1923), to his final work, *Los conjurados*, published just a year before his death in 1986. Throughout this unique collection the brilliance of the Spanish originals is matched by luminous English versions rendered be a remarkable cast of translators: Willis Barnstone, Alexander Coleman, Robert Fitzgerald, Stephen Kessler, Kenneth Krabbenhoft, Eric McHenry, W.S. Merwin, Alastair Reid, Hoyt Rogers, Mark Strand, Charles Tomlinson, Alan S. Trueblood, and John Updike.

"An unprecedented and invaluable collection . . . Poetry is at the heart of Borges's metaphysical, mythical, and cosmopolitan oeuvre." —*Bookist*

ISBN 0-670-84941-3

SELECTED NON-FICTIONS

Edited by Eliot Weinberger

Though best known in the United States for his short fictions and poems, Borges is just as revered in Latin America as an immensely prolific writer of nonfiction prose. Now, with Viking's *Selected Non-Fictions*, more than 150 of Borges's most brilliant writings come together for the first time in one volume—all in superb new translations. Even Borges aficionados are sure to be amazed to discover the extent of the Master's interests. Like the Aleph in his famous story—the magical point in a certain basement in Buenos Aires from which one can view everything in the world—Borges's unlimited curiosity and almost superhuman erudition become, in his nonfiction, a vortex for seemingly the entire universe. He was equally at home with Schopenhauer or Ellery Queen, King Kong or the Kabbalists, Lady Murasaki or Alfred Hitchcock, Flaubert, the Buddha or the Dionne Quints. The first comprehensive selection of this work in any language, the *Selected Non-Fictions* presents Borges at once as a deceptively self-effacing guide to the universe and the inventor of a universe that is an indispensable guide to Borges.

ISBN 0-670-84947-2